Selected
Stories

Selected
Stories

WILLIAM TREVOR

Viking

VIKING
Published by the Penguin Group
Penguin Group (USA) Inc., 375 Hudson Street,
New York, New York 10014, U.S.A.
Penguin Group (Canada), 90 Eglinton Avenue East, Suite 700,
Toronto, Ontario, Canada M4P 2Y3
(a division of Pearson Penguin Canada Inc.)
Penguin Books Ltd, 80 Strand, London WC2R 0RL, England
Penguin Ireland, 25 St. Stephen's Green, Dublin 2, Ireland
(a division of Penguin Books Ltd)
Penguin Books Australia Ltd, 250 Camberwell Road, Camberwell,
Victoria 3124, Australia
(a division of Pearson Australia Group Pty Ltd)
Penguin Books India Pvt Ltd, 11 Community Centre, Panchsheel Park,
New Delhi – 110 017, India
Penguin Group (NZ), 67 Apollo Drive, Rosedale, North Shore 0632,
New Zealand (a division of Pearson New Zealand Ltd)
Penguin Books (South Africa) (Pty) Ltd, 24 Sturdee Avenue,
Rosebank, Johannesburg 2196, South Africa

Penguin Books Ltd, Registered Offices:
80 Strand, London WC2R 0RL, England

First American edition
Published in 2010 by Viking Penguin,
a member of Penguin Group (USA) Inc.

1   3   5   7   9   10   8   6   4   2

The stories in this collection appeared in the following books by William Trevor, all published by Viking Penguin:
After Rain, copyright © William Trevor, 1992, 1993, 1994, 1995, 1996
The Hill Bachelors, copyright © William Trevor, 1997, 1998, 1999, 2000
A Bit on the Side, copyright © William Trevor, 1991, 1997, 2000, 2001, 2002, 2003, 2004
Cheating at Canasta, copyright © William Trevor, 2004, 2005, 2006, 2007

They were first published in the following publications: *Antaeus; Glimmer Train; Harper's; The Hudson Review; London Magazine; New Statesman; The New Yorker; The Oldie; The Sewanee Review; The Spectator; The Sunday Times* (London); and *The Tatler.* "Le Visiteur" (as "The Summer Visitor"), "Death of a Professor," and "The Telephone Game" were published in Great Britain in individual volumes by Travelman Publishing, Colophon Press, and Waterstone, respectively.

Publisher's Note

These selections are works of fiction. Names, characters, places, and incidents either are the product of the author's imagination or are used fictitiously, and any resemblance to actual persons, living or dead, business establishments, events, or locales is entirely coincidental.

LIBRARY OF CONGRESS CATALOGING IN PUBLICATION DATA

Trevor, William
Selected stories / William Trevor.
v. cm.
A new definitive collection of Trevor's short stories in two volumes, including earlier stories from his *Collected Stories*
(Viking, 1992).
ISBN 978-0-670-02206-9
I. Title.
PR6070.R4A6 2010
823'.914—dc22
2010019583
Printed in the United States of America

Contents

Selected Stories

The Piano Tuner's Wives

Violet married the piano tuner when he was a young man. Belle married him when he was old.

There was a little more to it than that, because in choosing Violet to be his wife the piano tuner had rejected Belle, which was something everyone remembered when the second wedding was announced. 'Well, she got the ruins of him anyway,' a farmer of the neighbourhood remarked, speaking without vindictiveness, stating a fact as he saw it. Others saw it similarly, though most of them would have put the matter differently.

The piano tuner's hair was white and one of his knees became more arthritic with each damp winter that passed. He had once been svelte but was no longer so, and he was blinder than on the day he married Violet – a Thursday in 1951, June 7th. The shadows he lived among now had less shape and less density than those of 1951.

'I will,' he responded in the small Protestant church of St Colman, standing almost exactly as he had stood on that other afternoon. And Belle, in her fifty-ninth year, repeated the words her one-time rival had spoken before this altar also. A decent interval had elapsed; no one in the church considered that the memory of Violet had not been honoured, that her passing had not been distressfully mourned. '. . . and with all my worldly goods I thee endow,' the piano tuner stated, while his new wife thought she would like to be standing beside him in white instead of suitable wine-red. She had not attended the first wedding, although she had been invited. She'd kept herself occupied that day, whitewashing the chicken shed, but even so she'd wept. And tears or not, she was more beautiful – and younger by almost five years – than the bride who so vividly occupied her thoughts as she battled with her jealousy. Yet he had preferred Violet – or the prospect of the house that would one day become hers, Belle told herself bitterly in the chicken shed, and the little bit of money there was, an easement in a blind man's existence. How understandable, she was reminded later on, whenever she saw Violet guiding him as they walked, whenever she thought of Violet making everything work for him, giving him a life. Well, so could she have.

As they left the church the music was by Bach, the organ played by someone else today, for usually it was his task. Groups formed in the small graveyard that was scattered around the small grey building, where the piano tuner's father and mother were buried, with ancestors on his father's side from previous generations. There would be tea and a few drinks for any of the wedding guests who cared to make the journey to the house, two miles away, but some said goodbye now, wishing the pair happiness. The piano tuner shook hands that were familiar to him, seeing in his mental eye faces that his first wife had described for him. It was the depth of summer, as in 1951, the sun warm on his forehead and his cheeks, and on his body through the heavy wedding clothes. All his life he had known this graveyard, had first felt the letters on the stones as a child, spelling out to his mother the names of his father's family. He and Violet had not had children themselves, though they'd have liked them. He was her child, it had been said, a statement that was an irritation for Belle whenever she heard it. She would have given him children, of that she felt certain.

'I'm due to visit you next month,' the old bridegroom reminded a woman whose hand still lay in his, the owner of a Steinway, the only one among all the pianos he tuned. She played it beautifully. He asked her to whenever he tuned it, assuring her that to hear was fee enough. But she always insisted on paying what was owing.

'Monday the third I think it is.'

'Yes, it is, Julia.'

She called him Mr Dromgould: he had a way about him that did not encourage familiarity in others. Often when people spoke of him he was referred to as the piano tuner, this reminder of his profession reflecting the respect accorded to the possessor of a gift. Owen Francis Dromgould his full name was.

'Well, we had a good day for it,' the new young clergyman of the parish remarked. 'They said maybe showers but sure they got it wrong.'

'The sky —?'

'Oh, cloudless, Mr Dromgould, cloudless.'

'Well, that's nice. And you'll come on over to the house, I hope?'

'He must, of course,' Belle pressed, then hurried through the gathering in the graveyard to reiterate the invitation, for she was determined to have a party.

Some time later, when the new marriage had settled into a routine, people wondered if the piano tuner would begin to think about retiring. With a bad knee, and being sightless in old age, he would readily have been forgiven in the houses and the convents and the school halls where he applied his skill. Leisure was his due, the good fortune of company as his years slipped by no more than he deserved. But when, occasionally, this was put to him by the loquacious or the inquisitive he denied that anything of the kind was in his thoughts, that he considered only the visitation of death as bringing any kind of end. The truth was, he would be lost without his work, without his travelling about, his arrival every six months or so in one of the small towns to which he had offered his services for so long. No, no, he promised, they'd still see the white Vauxhall turning in at a farm gate or parked for half an hour in a convent play-yard, or drawn up on a verge while he ate his lunchtime sandwiches, his tea poured out of a Thermos by his wife.

It was Violet who had brought most of this activity about. When they married he was still living with his mother in the gate-lodge of Barnagorm House. He had begun to tune pianos – the two in Barnagorm House, another in the town of Barnagorm, and one in a farmhouse he walked to four miles away. In those days he was a charity because he was blind, was now and again asked to repair the sea-grass seats of stools or chairs, which was an ability he had acquired, or to play at some function or other the violin his mother had bought him in his childhood. But when Violet married him she changed his life. She moved into the gate-lodge, she and his mother not always agreeing but managing to live together none the less. She possessed a car, which meant she could drive him to wherever she discovered a piano, usually long neglected. She drove to houses as far away as forty miles. She fixed his charges, taking the consumption of petrol and wear and tear to the car into account. Efficiently, she kept an address book and marked in a diary the date of each next tuning. She recorded a considerable improvement in earnings, and saw that there was more to be made from the playing of the violin than had hitherto been realized: Country-and-Western evenings in lonely public houses, the crossroads platform dances of summer – a practice that in 1951 had not entirely died out. Owen Dromgould delighted in his violin and would play it anywhere, for profit or not. But Violet was keen on the profit.

So the first marriage busily progressed, and when eventually Violet inherited her father's house she took her husband to live there. Once a farmhouse, it was no longer so, the possession of the land that gave it this title having long ago been lost through the fondness for strong drink that for generations had dogged the family but had not reached Violet herself.

'Now, tell me what's there,' her husband requested often in their early years, and Violet told him about the house she had brought him to, remotely situated on the edge of the mountains that were blue in certain lights, standing back a bit from a bend in a lane. She described the nooks in the rooms, the wooden window shutters he could hear her pulling over and latching when wind from the east caused a draught that disturbed the fire in the room once called the parlour. She described the pattern of the carpet on the single flight of stairs, the blue-and-white porcelain knobs of the kitchen cupboards, the front door that was never opened. He loved to listen. His mother, who had never entirely come to terms with his affliction, had been impatient. His father, a stableman at Barnagorm House who'd died after a fall, he had never known. 'Lean as a greyhound,' Violet described his father from a photograph that remained.

She conjured up the big, cold hall of Barnagorm House. 'What we walk around on the way to the stairs is a table with a peacock on it. An enormous silvery bird with bits of coloured glass set in the splay of its wings to represent the splendour of the feathers. Greens and blues,' she said when he asked the colour, and yes, she was certain it was only glass, not jewels, because once, when he was doing his best with the badly flawed grand in the drawing-room, she had been told that. The stairs were on a curve, he knew from going up and down them so often to the Chappell in the nursery. The first landing was dark as a tunnel, Violet said, with two sofas, one at each end, and rows of unsmiling portraits half lost in the shadows of the walls.

'We're passing Doocey's now,' Violet would say. 'Father Feely's getting petrol at the pumps.' Esso it was at Doocey's, and he knew how the word was written because he'd asked and had been told. Two different colours were employed; the shape of the design had been compared with shapes he could feel. He saw, through Violet's eyes, the gaunt façade of the McKirdys' house on the outskirts of Oghill. He saw the pallid face of the stationer in Kiliath. He saw his mother's eyes closed in death, her hands crossed on her breast. He saw the mountains, blue on some days, misted away to grey on others. 'A primrose isn't flamboyant,' Violet said. 'More like straw or country butter, with a spot of colour in the middle.' And he would nod, and know. Soft blue like smoke, she said about the mountains; the spot in the middle more orange than red. He knew no more about smoke than what she had told him also, but he could tell those sounds. He knew what red was, he insisted, because of the sound; orange because you could taste it. He could see red in the Esso sign and the orange spot in the primrose. 'Straw' and 'country butter' helped him, and when Violet called Mr Whitten gnarled it was enough. A certain Mother Superior was austere. Anna Craigie was fanciful about the eyes. Thomas in the sawmills was a streel. Bat Conlon had the forehead of the Merricks' retriever, which was stroked every time the Merricks' Broadwood was attended to.

*

Between one woman and the next, the piano tuner had managed without anyone, fetched by the possessors of pianos and driven to their houses, assisted in his shopping and his housekeeping. He felt he had become a nuisance to people, and knew that Violet would not have wanted that. Nor would she have wanted the business she built up for him to be neglected because she was no longer there. She was proud that he played the organ in St Colman's Church. 'Don't ever stop doing that,' she whispered some time before she whispered her last few words, and so he went alone to the church. It was on a Sunday, when two years almost had passed, that the romance with Belle began.

Since the time of her rejection Belle had been unable to shake off her jealousy, resentful because she had looks and Violet hadn't, bitter because it seemed to her that the punishment of blindness was a punishment for her too. For what else but a punishment could you call the dark the sightless lived in? And what else but a punishment was it that darkness should be thrown over her beauty? Yet there had been no sin to punish and they would have been a handsome couple, she and Owen Dromgould. An act of grace it would have been, her beauty given to a man who did not know that it was there.

It was because her misfortune did not cease to nag at her that Belle remained unmarried. She assisted her father first and then her brother in the family shop, making out tickets for the clocks and watches that were left in for repair, noting the details for the engraving of sports trophies. She served behind the single counter, the Christmas season her busy time, glassware and weather indicators the most popular wedding gifts, cigarette lighters and inexpensive jewellery for lesser occasions. In time, clocks and watches required only the fitting of a battery, and so the gift side of the business was expanded. But while that time passed there was no man in the town who lived up to the one who had been taken from her.

Belle had been born above the shop, and when house and shop became her brother's she continued to live there. Her brother's children were born, but there was still room for her, and her position in the shop itself was not usurped. It was she who kept the chickens at the back, who always had been in charge of them, given the responsibility on her tenth birthday: that, too, continued. That she lived with a disappointment had long ago become part of her, had made her what she was for her nieces and her nephew. It was in her eyes, some people noted, even lent her beauty a quality that enhanced it. When the romance began with the man who had once rejected her, her brother and his wife considered she was making a mistake, but did not say so, only laughingly asked if she intended taking the chickens with her.

That Sunday they stood talking in the graveyard when the handful of other parishioners had gone. 'Come and I'll show you the graves,' he said, and led the way, knowing exactly where he was going, stepping on to the grass and feeling the first gravestone with his fingers. His grandmother, he said, on his father's side, and for a moment Belle wanted to feel the incised letters herself instead of looking at them. They both knew, as they moved among the graves, that the parishioners who'd gone home were very much aware of the two who had been left behind. On Sundays, ever since Violet's death, he had walked to and from his house, unless it happened to be raining, in which case the man who drove old Mrs Purtill to church took him home also. 'Would you like a walk, Belle?' he asked when he had shown her his family graves. She said she would.

Belle didn't take the chickens with her when she became a wife. She said she'd had enough of chickens. Afterwards she regretted that, because every time she did anything in the house that had been Violet's she felt it had been done by Violet before her. When she cut up meat for a stew, standing with the light falling on the board that Violet had used, and on the knife, she felt herself a follower. She diced carrots, hoping that Violet had sliced them. She bought new wooden spoons because Violet's had shrivelled away so. She painted the upright rails of the banisters. She painted the inside of the front door that was never opened. She disposed of the stacks of women's magazines, years old, that she found in an upstairs cupboard. She threw away a frying-pan because she considered it unhygienic. She ordered new vinyl for the kitchen floor. But she kept the flowerbeds at the back weeded in case anyone coming to the house might say she was letting the place become run-down.

There was always this dichotomy: what to keep up, what to change. Was she giving in to Violet when she tended her flower-beds? Was she giving in to pettiness when she threw away a frying-pan and three wooden spoons? Whatever Belle did she afterwards doubted herself. The dumpy figure of Violet, grey-haired as she had been in the end, her eyes gone small in the plumpness of her face, seemed irritatingly to command. And the unseeing husband they shared, softly playing his violin in one room or another, did not know that his first wife had dressed badly, did not know she had thickened and become sloppy, did not know she had been an unclean cook. That Belle was the one who was alive, that she was offered all a man's affection, that she plundered his other woman's possessions and occupied her bedroom and drove her car, should have been enough. It should have been everything, but as time went on it seemed to Belle to be scarcely anything at all. He had become set in ways that had been allowed and hallowed in a marriage of nearly forty years: that was what was always there.

A year after the wedding, as the couple sat one lunchtime in the car which Belle had drawn into the gateway to a field, he said:

'You'd tell me if it was too much for you?'

'Too much, Owen?'

'Driving all over the county. Having to get me in and out. Having to sit there listening.'

'It's not too much.'

'You're good the way you've patience.'

'I don't think I'm good at all.'

'I knew you were in church that Sunday. I could smell the perfume you had on. Even at the organ I could smell it.'

'I'll never forget that Sunday.'

'I loved you when you let me show you the graves.'

'I loved you before that.'

'I don't want to tire you out, with all the traipsing about after pianos. I could let it go, you know.'

He would do that for her, her thought was as he spoke. He wasn't much for a woman, he had said another time: a blind man moving on towards the end of his days. He confessed that when first he wanted to marry her he hadn't put it to her for more than two months, knowing better than she what she'd be letting herself in for if she said yes. 'What's that Belle look like these days?' he had asked Violet a few years ago, and Violet hadn't answered at first. Then apparently she'd said: 'Belle still looks a girl.'

'I wouldn't want you to stop your work. Not ever, Owen.'

'You're all heart, my love. Don't say you're not good.'

'It gets me out and about too, you know. More than ever in my life. Down all those avenues to houses I didn't know were there. Towns I've never been to. People I never knew. It was restricted before.'

The word slipped out, but it didn't matter. He did not reply that he understood about restriction, for that was not his style. When they were getting to know one another, after that Sunday by the church, he said he'd often thought of her in her brother's jeweller's shop, wrapping up what was purchased there, as she had wrapped for him the watch he bought for one of Violet's birthdays. He'd thought of her putting up the grilles over the windows in the evenings and locking the shop door, and then going upstairs to sit with her brother's family. When they were married she told him more: how most of the days of her life had been spent, only her chickens her own. 'Smart in her clothes,' Violet had added when she said the woman he'd rejected still looked a girl.

There hadn't been any kind of honeymoon, but a few months after he had wondered if travelling about was too much for her he took Belle away to a seaside resort where he and Violet had many times spent a week. They stayed in the same boarding-house, the Sans Souci, and walked on the long, empty strand and in lanes where larks scuttered in and out of the fuchsia, and on the cliffs. They drank in Malley's public house. They lay in autumn sunshine on the dunes.

'You're good to have thought of it.' Belle smiled at him, pleased because he wanted her to be happy.

'Set us up for the winter, Belle.'

She knew it wasn't easy for him. They had come to this place because he knew no other; he was aware before they set out of the complication that might develop in his emotions when they arrived. She had seen that in his face, a stoicism that was there for her. Privately, he bore the guilt of betrayal, stirred up by the smell of the sea and seaweed. The voices in the boarding-house were the voices Violet had heard. For Violet, too, the scent of honeysuckle had lingered into October. It was Violet who first said a week in the autumn sun would set them up for the winter: that showed in him, also, a moment after he spoke the words.

'I'll tell you what we'll do,' he said. 'When we're back we'll get you the television, Belle.'

'Oh, but you –'

'You'd tell me.'

They were walking near the lighthouse on the cape when he said that. He would have offered the television to Violet, but Violet must have said she wouldn't be bothered with the thing. It would never be turned on, she had probably argued; you only got silliness on it anyway.

'You're good to me,' Belle said instead.

'Ah no, no.'

When they were close enough to the lighthouse he called out and a man called back from a window. 'Hold on a minute,' the man said, and by the time he opened the door he must have guessed that the wife he'd known had died. 'You'll take a drop?' he offered when they were inside, when the death and the remarriage had been mentioned. Whiskey was poured, and Belle felt that the three glasses lifted in salutation were an honouring of her, although this was not said. It rained on the way back to the boarding-house, the last evening of the holiday.

'Nice for the winter,' he said as she drove the next day through rain that didn't cease. 'The television.'

When it came, it was installed in the small room that once was called the parlour, next to the kitchen. This was where mostly they sat, where the radio was. A fortnight after the arrival of the television set Belle acquired a small black sheepdog that a farmer didn't want because it was afraid of sheep. This dog became hers and was always called hers. She fed it and looked after it. She got it used to travelling with them in the car. She gave it a new name, Maggie, which it answered to in time.

But even with the dog and the television, with additions and disposals in the house, with being so sincerely assured that she was loved, with being told she was good, nothing changed for Belle. The woman who for so long had taken her husband's arm, who had guided him into rooms of houses where he coaxed pianos back to life, still claimed existence. Not as a tiresome ghost, some unforgiving spectre uncertainly there, but as if some part of her had been left in the man she'd loved.

Sensitive in ways that other people weren't, Owen Dromgould continued to sense his second wife's unease. She knew he did. It was why he had offered to give up his work, why he'd taken her to Violet's seashore and borne there the guilt of his betrayal, why there was a television set now, and a sheepdog. He had guessed why she'd re-covered the kitchen floor. Proudly, he had raised his glass to her in the company of a man who had known Violet. Proudly, he had sat with her in the dining-room of the boarding-house and in Malley's public house.

Belle made herself remember all that. She made herself see the bottle of John Jameson taken from a cupboard in the lighthouse, and hear the boarding-house voices. He understood, he did his best to comfort her; his affection was in everything he did. But Violet would have told him which leaves were on the turn. Violet would have reported that the tide was going out or coming in. Too late Belle realized that. Violet had been his blind man's vision. Violet had left her no room to breathe.

One day, coming away from the house that was the most distant they visited, the first time Belle had been there, he said:

'Did you ever see a room as sombre as that one? Is it the holy pictures that do it?'

Belle backed the car and straightened it, then edged it through a gateway that, thirty years ago, hadn't been made wide enough.

'Sombre?' she said on a lane like a riverbed, steering around the potholes as best she could.

'We used wonder could it be they didn't want anything colourful in the way of a wallpaper in case it wasn't respectful to the pictures.'

Belle didn't comment on that. She eased the Vauxhall out on to the tarred road and drove in silence over a stretch of bogland. Vividly she saw the holy pictures in the room where Mrs Grenaghan's piano was: Virgin and Child, Sacred Heart, St Catherine with her lily, the Virgin on her own, Jesus in glory. They hung against non-descript brown; there were statues on the mantelpiece and on a corner shelf. Mrs Grenaghan had brought tea and biscuits to that small, melancholy room, speaking in a hushed tone as if the holiness demanded that.

'What pictures?' Belle asked, not turning her head, although she might have, for there was no other traffic and the bog road was straight.

'Aren't the pictures still in there? Holy pictures all over the place?'

'They must have taken them down.'

'What's there then?'

Belle went a little faster. She said a fox had come from nowhere, over to the left. It was standing still, she said, the way foxes do.

'You want to pull up and watch him, Belle?'

'No. No, he's moved on now. Was it Mrs Grenaghan's daughter who played that piano?'

'Oh, it was. And she hasn't seen that girl in years. We used say the holy pictures maybe drove her away. What's on the walls now?'

'A striped paper.' And Belle added: 'There's a photograph of the daughter on the mantelpiece.'

Some time later, on another day, when he referred to one of the sisters at the convent in Meena as having cheeks as flushed as an eating apple, Belle said that that nun was chalky white these days, her face pulled down and sunken. 'She has an illness so,' he said.

Suddenly more confident, not caring what people thought, Belle rooted out Violet's plants from the flowerbeds at the back, and grassed the flowerbeds over. She told her husband of a change at Doocey's garage: Texaco sold instead of Esso. She described the Texaco logo, the big red star and how the letters of the word were arranged. She avoided stopping at Doocey's in case a conversation took place there, in case Doocey were asked if Esso had let him down, or what. 'Well, no, I wouldn't call it silvery exactly,' Belle said about the peacock in the hall of Barnagorm house. 'If they cleaned it up I'd say it's brass underneath.' Upstairs, the sofas at each end of the landing had new loose covers, bunches of different-coloured chrysanthemums on them. 'Well no, not *lean*, I wouldn't call him that,' Belle said with the photograph of her husband's father in her hand. 'A sturdy face, I'd say.' A schoolteacher whose teeth were once described as gusty had false teeth now, less of a mouthful, her smile sedate. Time had apparently drenched the bright white of the McKirdys' façade, almost a grey you'd call it. 'Forget-me-not blue,' Belle said one day, speaking of the mountains that were blue when the weather brought that colour out. 'You'd hardly credit it.' And it was never again said in the piano tuner's house that the blue of the mountains was the subtle blue of smoke.

Owen Dromgould had run his fingers over the bark of trees. He could tell the difference in the outline of their leaves; he could tell the thorns of gorse and bramble. He knew birds from their song, dogs from their bark, cats from the touch of them on his legs. There were the letters on the gravestones, the stops of the organ, his violin. He could see red, berries on holly and cotoneaster. He could smell lavender and thyme.

All that could not be taken from him. And it didn't matter if, overnight, the colour had worn off the kitchen knobs. It didn't matter if the china light-shade in the kitchen had a crack he hadn't heard about before. What mattered was damage done to something as fragile as a dream.

The wife he had first chosen had dressed drably: from silence and inflexions – more than from words – he learned that now. Her grey hair straggled to her shoulders, her back was a little humped. He poked his way about, and they were two old people when they went out on their rounds, older than they were in their ageless happiness. She wouldn't have hurt a fly, she wasn't a person you could be jealous of, yet of course it was hard on a new wife to be haunted by happiness, to be challenged by the simplicities there had been. He had given himself to two women; he hadn't withdrawn himself from the first, he didn't from the second.

Each house that contained a piano brought forth its contradictions. The pearls old Mrs Purtill wore were opals, the pallid skin of the stationer in Kiliath was freckled, the two lines of oaks above Oghill were surely beeches? 'Of course, of course,' Owen Dromgould agreed, since it was fair that he should do so. Belle could not be blamed for making her claim, and claims could not be made without damage or destruction. Belle would win in the end because the living always do. And that seemed fair also, since Violet had won in the beginning and had had the better years.

A Friendship

Jason and Ben – fair-haired, ten and eight respectively – found that a bucketful of ready-mixed concrete was too heavy to carry, so they slopped half of it out again. Sharing the handle of the bucket, they found they could now manage to convey their load, even though Ben complained. They carried it from the backyard, through the kitchen and into the hall, to where their father's golf-bag stood in a corner. The bag, recently new, contained driver, putter and a selection of irons, as well as tees, balls and gloves in various side pockets. A chair stood in front of the bag, on to which both boys now clambered, still precariously grasping the bucket. They had practised; they knew what they were doing.

After five such journeys the golf-bag was half full of liquid concrete, the chair carried back to the kitchen, and small splashes wiped from the tiles of the hall. Then the workmen who were rebuilding the boiler-shed returned from the Red Lion, where they had spent their lunchtime.

'We know nothing about it,' Jason instructed his brother while they watched the workmen shovelling more sand and cement into the concrete-mixer.

'Nothing about it,' Ben obediently repeated.

'Let's go and watch *Quick Draw*.'

'OK.'

When their mother returned to the house half an hour later, with her friend Margy, it was Margy who noticed the alien smell in the hall. Being inquisitive by nature she poked about, and was delighted when she discovered the cause, since she considered that the victim of the joke would benefit from the inroads it must inevitably make on his pomposity. She propped the front door open for a while so that the smell of fresh concrete would drift away. The boys' mother, Francesca, didn't notice anything.

'Come on!' Francesca called, and the boys came chattering into the kitchen for fish fingers and peas, no yoghurt for Ben because someone had told him it was sour milk, Ribena instead of hot chocolate for Jason.

'You did your homework before you turned on that television?' Francesca asked.

'Yes,' Ben lied.

'I bet you didn't,' Margy said, not looking up from the magazine she was flipping through. Busy with their food, Francesca didn't hear that.

Francesca was tall, with pale, uncurled hair that glistened in the sunlight. Margy was small and dark, brown-eyed, with thin, fragile fingers. They had known one another more or less all their lives.

'Miss Martindale's mother died,' Ben divulged, breaking the monotony of a silence that had gathered. 'A man interfered with her.'

'My God!' Francesca exclaimed, and Margy closed the magazine, finding little of interest in it.

'Miss Martindale saw him,' Jason said. 'Miss Martindale was just arriving and she saw this figure. First she said a black man, then she said he could be any colour.'

'You mean, Miss Martindale came to school today after something like that?'

'Miss Martindale has a sense of duty,' Jason said.

'Actually she was extremely late,' Ben said.

'But how ghastly for the poor woman!'

Miss Martindale was a little thing with glasses, Francesca told her friend, not at all up to sustaining something like this. Ben said all the girls had cried, that Miss Martindale herself had cried, that her face was creased and funny because actually she'd been crying all night.

Margy watched Jason worrying in case his brother went too far. They could have said it was Miss Martindale who'd been murdered; they had probably intended to, but had changed it to her mother just in time. It wouldn't have worked if they'd said Miss Martindale because sooner or later Miss Martindale would be there at a parents' evening.

'*Neighbours* now,' Jason said.

'Started actually,' Ben pointed out.

Margy lit a cigarette when she was alone with Francesca, and suggested a drink. She poured gin and Cinzano Bianco for both of them, saying she didn't believe there was much wrong with Miss Martindale's mother, and Francesca, bewildered, looked up from the dishes she was washing. Then, without a word, she left the kitchen and Margy heard her noisily reprimanding her sons, declaring that it was cruel and unfeeling to say people were dead who weren't. Abruptly, the sound of the television ceased and there were footsteps on the stairs. Margy opened a packet of Mignons Morceaux.

Francesca and Margy could remember being together in a garden when they were two, meeting there for the first time, they afterwards presumed, Francesca smiling, Margy scowling. Later, during their schooldays, they had equally disliked a sarcastic teacher with gummy false teeth, and had considered the visiting mathematics man handsome, though neither of them cared for his subject. Later still Francesca became the confidante of Margy's many love affairs, herself confiding from the calmer territory of marriage. Margy brought mild adventure into Francesca's life, and Francesca recognized that Margy would never suffer the loneliness she feared herself, the vacuum she was certain there would be if her children had not been born. They telephoned one another almost every day, to chat inconsequentially or to break some news, it didn't matter which. Their common ground was the friendship itself: they shared some tastes and some opinions, but only some.

When Philip – father of Jason and Ben – arrived in the house an hour later Francesca and Margy had moved to the sitting-room, taking with them the gin, the Cinzano Bianco, what remained of the Mignons Morceaux, and their glasses.

'Hi, Philip,' Margy greeted him, and watched while he kissed Francesca. He nodded at Margy.

'Margy's going to make us her paella,' Francesca said, and Margy knew that when Philip turned away it was to hide a sigh. He didn't like her paella. He didn't like the herb salad she put together to go with it. He had never said so, being too polite for that, but Margy knew.

'Oh, good,' Philip said.

He hadn't liked the whiff of cigarettes that greeted him when he opened the hall-door, nor the sound of voices that had come from the sitting-room. He didn't like the crumpled-up Mignons Morceaux packet, the gin bottle and the vermouth bottle on his bureau, Margy's lipstained cigarette-ends, the way Margy was lolling on the floor with her shoes off. Margy didn't have to look to see if this small cluster of aversions registered in Philip's tight features. She knew it didn't; he didn't let things show.

'They've been outrageous,' Francesca said, and began about Miss Martindale's mother.

Margy looked at him then. Nothing moved in his lean face; he didn't blink before he turned away to stand by the open french windows. *Golf and gardening* he gave as his hobbies in *Who's Who*.

'Outrageous?' he repeated eventually, an inflection in his tone – unnoticed by Francesca – suggesting to Margy that he questioned the use of this word in whatever domestic sense it was being employed. He liked being in *Who's Who*: it was a landmark in his life. One day he would be a High Court judge: everyone said that. One day he would be honoured with a title, and Francesca would be also because she was his wife.

'I was really furious with them,' Francesca said.

He didn't know what all this was about, he couldn't remember who Miss Martindale was because Francesca hadn't said. Margy smiled at her friend's husband, as if to indicate her understanding of his bewilderment, as if in sympathy. It would be the weekend before he discovered that his golf-clubs had been set in concrete.

'Be cross with them,' Francesca begged, 'when you go up. Tell them it was a horrid thing to say about anyone.'

He nodded, his back half turned on her, still gazing into the garden.

'Have a drink, Philip,' Margy suggested because it was better usually when he had one, though not by much.

'Yes,' Philip said, but instead of going to pour himself something he walked out into the garden.

'I've depressed him,' Francesca commented almost at once. 'He's not in the house more than a couple of seconds and I'm nagging him about the boys.'

She followed her husband into the garden, and a few minutes later, when Margy was gathering together the ingredients for her paella in the kitchen, she saw them strolling among the shrubs he so assiduously tended as a form of relaxation after his week in the courts. The boys would be asleep by the time he went up to say goodnight to them and if they weren't they'd pretend; he wouldn't have to reprimand them about something he didn't understand. Of course all he had to do was to ask a few questions, but he wouldn't because anything domestic was boring for him. It was true that when Mrs Sleet's headscarf disappeared from the back-door pegs he asked questions – precise and needling, as if still in one of his court-rooms. And he had reached a conclusion: that the foolish woman must have left her headscarf on the bus. He rejected out of hand Francesca's belief that a passing thief had found the back door open and reached in for what immediately caught his eye. No one would want such an item of clothing, Philip had maintained, no thief in his senses. And of course he was right. Margy remembered the fingernails of the two boys engrained with earth, and guessed that the headscarf had been used to wrap up Mabel, Ben's guinea-pig, before confining her to the gerbil and guinea-pig graveyard beside the box hedge.

Smoking while she chopped her herb salad – which he would notice, and silently deplore, as he passed through the kitchen – Margy wondered why Philip's presence grated on her so. He was handsome in his way and strictly speaking he wasn't a bore, nor did he arrogantly impose his views. It was, she supposed, that he was simply a certain kind of man, inimical to those who were not of his ilk, unable to help himself even. Several times at gatherings in this house Margy had met Philip's legal colleagues and was left in no doubt that he was held in high regard, that he commanded both loyalty and respect. Meticulous, fair, precise as a blade, he was feared by his court-room opponents, and professionally he did not have a silly side: in his anticipated heights of success, he would surely not become one of those infamous elderly judges who flapped about from court to court, doling out eccentric sentences, lost outside the boundaries of the real world. On the other hand, among a circle of wives and other women of his acquaintance, he was known as 'Bad News', a reference to the misfortune of being placed next to him at a dinner party. On such occasions, when he ran out of his stock of conversational questions he tried no more, and displayed little interest in the small-talk that was, increasingly desperately, levelled at him. He had a way of saying, flatly, 'I see' when a humorous anecdote, related purely for his entertainment, came to an end. And through all this he was not ill at ease; others laboured, never he.

As Margy dwelt on this catalogue of Philip's favourable and less favourable characteristics, husband and wife passed by the kitchen window. Francesca smiled through the glass at her friend, a way of saying that all was well again after her small *faux pas* of nagging too soon after her husband's return. Then Margy heard the french windows of the sitting-room being closed and Philip's footsteps passed through the hall, on their way to the children's bedroom.

Francesca came in to help, and to open wine. Chatting about other matters, she laid out blue tweed mats on the Formica surface of the table, and forks and other cutlery and glasses. It wasn't so much Philip, Margy thought; had he been married to someone else, she was sure she wouldn't have minded him so. It was the marriage itself: her friend's marriage astonished her.

Every so often Margy and Francesca had lunch at a local bistro called La Trota. It was an elegant rendezvous, though inexpensive and limited in that it offered only fish and a few Italian cheeses. Small and bright and always bustling, its decorative tone was set by a prevalence of aluminium and glass, and matt white surfaces. Its walls were white also, its floor colourfully tiled – a crustacea pattern that was repeated on the surface of the bar. Two waitresses – one from Sicily, the other from Salerno – served at the tables. Usually, Francesca and Margy had Dover sole and salad, and a bottle of Gavi.

La Trota was in Barnes, not far from Bygone Antiques, where Margy was currently employed. In the mornings Francesca helped in the nearby Little Acorn Nursery School, which both Jason and Ben had attended in the past. Margy worked in Bygone Antiques because she was, 'for the time being' as she put it, involved with its proprietor, who was, as she put it also, 'wearily married'.

On the Tuesday after Philip's discovery of the concrete in his golf-bag they lunched outside, at one of La Trota's three pavement tables, the June day being warm and sunny. Two months ago, when Margy had begun her stint at Bygone Antiques, Francesca was delighted because it meant they would be able to see more of one another: Margy lived some distance away, over the river, in Pimlico.

'He was livid of course,' Francesca reported. 'I mean, they said it was a *joke*.'

Margy laughed.

'I mean, how could it be a joke? And how could it be a joke to say Miss Martindale's mother was dead?'

'Did Mrs Sleet's headscarf ever turn up?'

'You don't think they stole Mrs Sleet's headscarf?'

'What I think is you're lucky to have lively children. Imagine if they never left the straight and narrow.'

'How lovely it would be!'

Francesca told of the quarrel that had followed the discovery of the golf-bag, the worst quarrel of her marriage, she said. She had naturally been blamed because it was clear from what had occurred that the boys had been alone in the house when they shouldn't have been. Philip wanted to know how this had happened, his court-room manner sharpening his questioning and his argument. How long had his children been latchkey children, and for what reason were they so?

'I wish I'd had girls,' Francesca complained pettishly. 'I often think that now.'

Their Dover soles arrived. 'Isn't no help,' the Sicilian waitress muttered crossly as she placed the plates in front of them. 'Every day we say too many tables. Twice times, maybe hundred times. Every day they promise. Next day the same.'

'Ridiculous.' Margy smiled sympathetically at the plump Sicilian girl. 'Poor Francesca,' she sympathized with her friend, taking a piece of lettuce in her fingers.

But Francesca, still lost in the detail of the rumpus there had been, hardly heard. An hour at the very least, Philip was arguing all over again; possibly two hours they must have been on their own. It was absurd to spend all morning looking after children in a nursery school and all afternoon neglecting your own. That Jason and Ben had been sent back early that day, that she had been informed of this beforehand and had forgotten, that she would naturally have been there had she remembered: all this was mere verbiage apparently, not worth listening to, much less considering. Mrs Sleet left the house at one o'clock on the dot, and Francesca was almost always back by three, long before the boys returned. Jason and Ben were not latchkey children; she had made a mistake on a particular day; she had forgotten; she was sorry.

'If you're asked to do anything,' had been the final shaft, 'it's to see to the children, Francesca. You have all the help in the house you ask for. I don't believe you want for much.' The matter of Andy Konig's video had been brought up, and Jason's brazen insistence at the time that it was for Social Studies. Andy Konig's video wouldn't have been discovered if it hadn't become stuck in the video-player, repeating an endless sequence of a woman undressing in a doctor's surgery. 'You didn't even look to see what was on it,' had been the accusation, repeated now, which of course was true. It was over, all this was followed by; they would forget it; he'd drive to the Mortlake tip with the golf-bag, there'd be no television for thirty days, no sweets, cake or biscuits. 'I would ask you to honour that, Francesca.' As the rumpus subsided, she had sniffed back the last of her tears, not replying.

'Oh Lord!' she cried in frustration at La Trota. 'Oh Lord, the guilt!'

Cheering her friend up, Margy insisted that they change the subject. She recounted an episode that morning in the antique shop, a woman she knew quite well, titled actually, slipping a Crown Derby piece into a shopping bag. She touched upon her love affair with the shop's proprietor, which was not going well. One of these days they should look up Sebastian, she idly suggested. 'It's time I settled down,' she murmured over their cappuccinos.

'I'm not sure that Sebastian . . .' Francesca began, her concentration still lingering on the domestic upset.

'I often wonder about Sebastian,' Margy said.

Afterwards, in the antique shop, it was cool among the polished furniture, the sofa-tables and revolving libraries, the carved pew ends and sewing cabinets. The collection of early Victorian wall clocks – the speciality of the wearily married proprietor – ticked gracefully; occupying most of the window space, the figure of Christ on a donkey cast shadows that were distorted by the surfaces they reached. A couple in summer clothes, whom Margy had earlier noticed in La Trota, whispered among these offerings. A man with someone else's wife, a wife with someone else's husband: Margy could tell at once. 'Of course,' she'd said when they asked if they might look around, knowing that they wouldn't buy anything: people in such circumstances rarely did. 'Oh, isn't that pretty!' the girl whispered now, taken with a framed pot-lid – an 1868 rifle contest in Wimbledon, colourfully depicted.

'Forty-five pounds I think,' Margy replied when she was asked the price, and went away to consult the price book. One day, she believed, Francesca would pay cruelly for her passing error of judgement in marrying the man she had. Hearing about the fuss over the golf-bag, she had felt that instinct justified: the marriage would go from bad to worse, from fusses and quarrels over two little boys' obstreperousness to fusses and quarrels about everything else, a mound of pettiness accumulating, respect all gone and taking with it what once had seemed like love. Too often Margy had heard from married men the kind of bitter talk that was the evidence of this, and had known she would have heard still worse from the wives they spoke of. Yet just as often, she fairly admitted, people made a go of it. They rarely said so because of course that wasn't interesting, and sometimes what was making a go of it one day was later, in the divorce courts, called tedium.

'Look in again,' she invited the summery couple as they left without the pot-lid.

'Thanks a lot,' the man said, and the girl put her head on one side, a way of indicating, possibly, that she was grateful also.

Margy had mentioned Sebastian at lunch, not because she wished to look him up on her own account but because it occurred to her that Sebastian was just the person to jolly Francesca out of her gloom. Sebastian was given to easy humour and exuded an agreeableness that was pleasant to be exposed to. Since he had once, years ago, wanted to marry Francesca, Margy often imagined what her friend's household would have been like with Sebastian there instead.

'Hullo,' her employer said, entering the shop with a Regency commode and bringing with him the raw scent of the stuff he dabbed on his underarms, and a whiff of beer.

'Handsome,' Margy remarked, referring to the commode.

It was Francesca who telephoned Sebastian. 'A voice from the past,' she said and he knew immediately, answering her by name. He was pleased she'd rung, he said, and all the old telephone inflections, so familiar once, registered again as their conversation progressed. 'Margy?' he repeated when Francesca suggested lunch for three. He sounded disappointed, but Francesca hardly noticed that, caught up with so much else, wondering how in fact it would affect everything if, somehow or other, Sebastian and Margy hit it off now, as she and Sebastian had in the past. She knew Sebastian hadn't married. He had been at her wedding; she would have been at his, their relationship transformed on both sides then. Like Margy, Francesca imagined, Sebastian had free-wheeled through the time that had passed since. At her wedding she had guessed they would lose touch, and in turn he had probably guessed that that was, sensibly, what she wanted. Sebastian, who had never honoured much, honoured that. When marriage occurs, the past clams up, lines are drawn beneath a sub-total.

'Well, well, well,' he murmured at La Trota, embracing Margy first and then Francesca. There were flecks of grey in his fair hair; his complexion was a little ruddier. But his lazy eyes were touched with the humour that both women remembered, and his big hands seemed gentle on the table.

'You haven't changed a bit,' Sebastian said, choosing Francesca to say it to.

'Oh heavens, I've said the wrong thing!' a woman exclaimed in horror at a party, eyes briefly closed, a half-stifled breath drawn in.

'No, not at all,' Philip said.

'It's just that —'

'We see Sebastian quite often, actually.'

He wondered why he lied, and realized then that he was saving face. He had been smiling when the woman first mentioned Sebastian, when she'd asked how he was these days. Almost at once the woman had known she was saying the wrong thing, her expression adding more and more as she stumbled on, endeavouring to muddle with further words her original statement about trying unsuccessfully to catch Francesca's and Sebastian's attention in Wigmore Street.

'So very nice,' the woman floundered, hot-faced. 'Sebastian.'

A mass of odds and ends gathered in Philip's mind. 'The number of this taxi is 22003,' he had said after he'd kissed Francesca in it. Their first embrace, and he had read out the number from the enamel disc on the back of the driver's seat, and neither of them had since forgotten it. The first present Francesca gave him was a book about wine which to this day he wouldn't lend to people.

No one was as honest as Francesca, Philip reflected as the woman blundered on: it was impossible to accept that she had told lies, even through reticence. Yet now there were — as well — the odds and ends of the warm summer that had just passed, all suddenly transformed. Dates and the order of events glimmered in Philip's brain; he was good at speedy calculation and accurately recalling. Excuses, and explanations, seemed elaborate in the bare light of the hindsight that was forced upon him. A note falling to the floor had been too hastily retrieved. There were headaches and cancellations and apologies. There'd been a difference in Francesca that hadn't at the time seemed great but seemed great now.

'Yes, Sebastian's very nice,' Philip said.

*

'It's over,' Francesca said in their bedroom. 'It's been over for weeks, as a matter of fact.'

Still dressed, sitting on the edge of their bed, Francesca was gazing at the earrings she'd just taken off, two drops of amber in the palm of her hand. Very slowly she made a pattern of them, moving them on her palm with the forefinger of her other hand. In their bedroom the light was dim, coming only from a bedside lamp. Francesca was in the shadows.

'It doesn't make much difference that it's over,' Philip said. 'That's not the point.'

'I know.'

'You've never told lies before.'

'Yes, I know. I hated it.'

Even while it was happening, she had sometimes thought it wasn't. And for the last few lonely weeks it had felt like madness, as indeed it had been. Love was madness of a kind, Margy had said once, years ago, and Francesca at that time hadn't understood: being fond of Sebastian in the past, and loving Philip, had never been touched by anything like that. Her recent inexplicable aberration felt as if she had taken time off from being herself, and now was back again where she belonged, not understanding, as bouts of madness are never understood.

'That's hardly an explanation,' her husband said when she endeavoured to relate some of this.

'No, I know it isn't. I would have told you about it quite soon; I couldn't not tell you.'

'I didn't even notice I wasn't loved.'

'You are loved, Philip. I ended it. And besides, it wasn't much.'

A silence grew between them. 'I love you,' Sebastian had said no longer ago than last June, and in July and in August and September also. And she had loved him too. More than she loved anyone else, more than she loved her children: that thought had been there. Yet now she could say it wasn't much.

As though he guessed some part of this, Philip said: 'I'm dull compared to him. I'm grey and dull.'

'No.'

'I mooch about the garden, I mooch about on golf courses. You've watched me becoming greyer in middle age. You don't want to share our middle age.'

'I never think things like that. Never, Philip.'

'No one respects a cuckold.'

Francesca did not reply. She was asked if she wanted a divorce. She shook her head. Philip said:

'One day in the summer you and Margy were talking about a key when I came in, and you stopped and said, "Have a drink, darling?" I remember now. Odd, how stuff's dredged up. The key to Margy's flat, I think?'

Francesca stood up. She placed her amber earrings in the drawer of their bedside table and slowly began to undress. Philip, standing by the door, said he had always trusted her, which he had said already.

'I'm sorry I hurt you, Philip.' Tiredly, she dropped into a cliché, saying that Sebastian had been banished as a ghost may be, that at last she had got him out of her system. But what she said had little relevance, and mattered so slightly that it was hardly heard. What was there between them were the weekends Philip had been in charge of the children because Francesca needed a rest and had gone, with Margy, to some seaside place where Margy was looking after a house for people who were abroad. And the evenings she helped to paint Margy's flat. And the mornings that were free after she gave up helping in the Little Acorn Nursery School. Yes, that key had been Margy's, Francesca said. Left for her under a stone at the foot of a hydrangea bush in Pimlico, in a block of flats' communal garden: she didn't add that. Found there with a frisson of excitement: nor that, either.

'I'm ashamed because I hurt you,' she said instead. 'I'm ashamed because I was selfish and a fool.'

'You should have married him in the first place.'

'It was you I wanted to marry, Philip.'

Francesca put on her nightdress, folded her underclothes, and draped her tights over the back of a chair. She sat for a moment in front of her dressing-table looking-glass, rubbing cold cream into her face, stroking away the moisture of tears.

'You have every right to turn me out,' she said, calmly now.

'You have every right to have the children to yourself.'

'D'you want that?'

'No.'

He hated her, Francesca thought, but she sensed as well that this hatred was a visitation only, that time would take it away. And she guessed that Philip sensed this also, and resented it that something as ordinary as passing time could destroy the high emotions he was experiencing now. Yet it was the truth.

'It happened by chance,' Francesca said, and made it all sound worse. 'I thought that Margy and Sebastian – oh well, it doesn't matter.'

They quarrelled then. The tranquillity that had prevailed was shattered in a moment, and their children woke and heard the raised voices. Underhand, hole-in-corner, shabby, untrustworthy, dishonourable, grubby: these words had never described Francesca in the past, but before the light of morning they were used. And to add a garnish to all that was said, there was Margy's treachery too. She had smiled and connived even though there was nothing in it for her.

Francesca countered when her spirit returned, after she'd wept beneath this lash of accusation, and the condemnation of her friend. Philip had long ago withdrawn himself from the family they were: it was an irony that her misbehaviour had pulled him back, that occasionally he had had to cook beans and make the bacon crispy for their children, and see that their rooms were tidied, their homework finished. At least her lies had done that.

But there was no forgiveness when they dressed again. Nothing was over yet. Forgiveness came later.

There was a pause after Francesca made her bleak statement in La Trota. Margy frowned, beginning to lean across the table because the hubbub was considerable that day. No longer working at Bygone Antiques, she had come across London specially.

'Drop me?' Margy said, and Francesca nodded: that was her husband's request.

The restaurant was full of people: youngish, well-to-do, men together, women together, older women with older men, older men with girls, five businessmen at a table. The two waitresses hurried with their orders, too busy to mutter their complaints about the overcrowding.

'But why on earth?' Margy said. 'Why should you?'

Expertly the Sicilian waitress opened the Gavi and splashed some into their glasses. '*Buon appetito*,' she briskly wished them, returning in a moment with the sole. They hadn't spoken since Margy had asked her questions.

'He has a right to something, is that it?' Margy squeezed her chunk of lemon over the fish and then on to her salad. 'To punish?'

'He thinks you betrayed him.'

'*I* betrayed him? *I*?'

'It's how Philip feels. No, not a punishment,' Francesca said. 'Philip's not doing that.'

'What then?'

Francesca didn't reply, and Margy poked at the fish on her plate, not wanting to eat it now. Some vague insistence hovered in her consciousness: some truth, not known before and still not known, was foggily sensed.

'I don't understand this,' Margy said. 'Do you?'

A salvaging of pride was a wronged husband's due: she could see that and could understand it, but there was more to this than pride.

'It's how Philip feels,' Francesca said again. 'It's how all this has left him.'

She knew, Margy thought: whatever it was, it had been put to Francesca in Philip's court-room manner, pride not even mentioned. Then, about to ask and before she could, she knew herself: the forgiving of a wife was as much as there could be. How could a wronged husband, so hurt and so aggrieved, forgive a treacherous friend as well?

'Love allows forgiveness,' Francesca said, guessing what Margy's thoughts were, which was occasionally possible after years of intimacy.

But Margy's thoughts were already moving on. Every time she played with his children he would remember the role she had played that summer: she could hear him saying it, and Francesca's silence. Every present she brought to the house would seem to him to be a traitor's bribe. The summer would always be there, embalmed in the friendship that had made the deception possible – the key to the flat, the seaside house, the secret kept and then discovered. What the marriage sought to forget the friendship never would because the summer had become another part of it. The friendship could only be destructive now, the subject of argument and quarrels, the cause of jealousy and pettiness and distress: this, Philip presented as his case, his logic perfect in all its parts. And again Margy could hear his voice.

'It's unfair, Francesca.'

'It only seems so.' Francesca paused, then said: 'I love Philip, you know.'

'Yes, I do know.'

In the crowded bistro their talk went round in muddled circles, the immediacy of the blow that had been struck at them lost from time to time in the web of detail that was their friendship, lost in days and moments and occasions not now recalled but still remembered, in confidences, and conversation rattling on, in being different in so many ways and that not mattering. Philip, without much meaning to, was offering his wife's best friend a stature she had not possessed before in his estimation: she was being treated with respect. But that, of course, was neither here nor there.

'What was her name,' Margy asked, 'that woman with the gummy teeth?'

'Hyatt. Miss Hyatt.'

'Yes, of course it was.'

There was a day when Margy was cross and said Francesca was not her friend and never would be, when they were six. There was the time the French girl smoked when they were made to take her for a walk on the hills behind their boarding-school. Margy fell in love with the boy who brought the papers round. Francesca's father died and Margy read Tennyson to cheer her up. They ran out of money on their cycling tour and borrowed from a lorry driver who got the wrong idea. Years later Francesca was waiting afterwards when Margy had her abortion.

'You like more cappuccinos?' the Sicilian waitress offered, placing fresh cups of coffee before them because they always had two each.

'Thanks very much,' Francesca said.

In silence, in the end, they watched the bistro emptying. The two waitresses took the tablecloths off and lifted the chairs on to the tables in order to mop over the coloured patterns of shellfish on the tiled floor. Quite suddenly a wave of loneliness caused Margy to shiver inwardly, as the chill news of death does.

'Perhaps with a bit of time,' she began, but even as she spoke she knew that time would make no difference. Time would simply pass, and while it did so Francesca's guilt would still be there; she would always feel she owed this sacrifice. They would not cheat; Francesca would not do that a second time. She would say that friends meeting stealthily was ridiculous, a grimier deception than that of lovers.

'It's all my fault,' Francesca said.

Hardly perceptibly, Margy shook her head, knowing it wasn't. She had gone too far; she had been sillily angry because of a children's prank. She hadn't sought to knock a marriage about, only to give her friend a treat that seemed to be owing to her, only to rescue her for a few summer months from her exhausting children and her exhausting husband, from Mrs Sleet and the Little Acorn Nursery School, from her too-safe haven. But who was to blame, and what intentions there had been, didn't matter in the least now.

'In fairness,' Francesca said, 'Philip has a point of view. Please say you see it, Margy.'

'Oh yes, I see it.' She said it quickly, knowing she must do so before it became impossible to say, before all generosity was gone. She knew, too, that one day Francesca would pass on this admission to her husband because Francesca was Francesca, who told the truth and was no good at deception.

'See you soon,' the Sicilian waitress called out when eventually they stood up to go.

'Yes,' Margy agreed, lying for her friend as well. On the pavement outside La Trota they stood for a moment in a chill November wind, then moved away in their two different directions.

Timothy's Birthday

They made the usual preparations. Charlotte bought a small leg of lamb, picked purple broccoli and sprigs of mint. All were Timothy's favourites, purchased every year for April 23rd, which this year was a Thursday. Odo ensured that the gin had not gone too low: a gin and tonic, and then another one, was what Timothy liked. Odo did not object to that, did not in fact object to obtaining the gin specially, since it was not otherwise drunk in the house.

They were a couple in their sixties who had scarcely parted from each other in the forty-two years of their marriage. Odo was tall, thin as a straw, his bony features receding into a freckled dome on which little hair remained. Charlotte was small and still pretty, her grey hair drawn back and tidy, her eyes an arresting shade of blue. Timothy was their only child.

Deciding on a fire, Odo chopped up an old seed-box for kindling and filled a basket with logs and turf. The rooks were cawing and chattering in the high trees, their nests already in place – more of them this year, Odo noticed, than last. The cobbles of the yard were still damp from a shower. Grass, occasionally ragwort or a dock, greened them in patches. Later perhaps, when Timothy had gone, he'd go over them with weed-killer, as he did every year in April. The outhouses that bounded the yard required attention also, their wooden doors rotted away at the bottom, the whitewash of their stucco gone grey, brambles growing through their windows. Odo resolved that this year he would rectify matters, but knew, even as the thought occurred, that he would not.

'Cold?' Charlotte asked him as he passed through the kitchen, and he said yes, a little chilly outside. The kitchen was never cold because of the range. A long time ago they had been going to replace it with a second-hand Aga Charlotte had heard about, but when it came to the point Odo hadn't wanted to and anyway there hadn't been the funds.

In the drawing-room Odo set the fire, crumpling up the pages of old account books because no newspaper was delivered to the house and one was rarely bought: they had the wireless and the television, which kept them up with things. The account books were of no use to anyone, belonging entirely to the past, to the time of Odo's grandfather and generations earlier. Kept for the purpose in a wall-cupboard by the fireplace, their dry pages never failed to burn well. *Slating: £2. 15s.*, Odo read as he arranged the kindling over the slanted calligraphy. He struck a match and stacked on logs and turf. Rain spattered against the long-paned windows; a sudden gust of wind tumbled something over in the garden.

Charlotte pressed rosemary into the slits she'd incised in the lamb. She worked swiftly, from long experience knowing just what she was doing. She washed the grease from her fingertips under a running tap and set aside what remained of the rosemary, even though it was unlikely that she would have a use for it: she hated throwing things away.

The oven was slow; although it was still early, the meat would have to go in within half an hour, and potatoes to roast – another Timothy favourite – at eleven. The trifle, gooey with custard and raspberry jam and jelly – a nursery pudding – Charlotte had made the night before. When Timothy came he chopped the mint for the mint sauce, one of the first of his childhood tasks. He'd been a plump little boy then.

'I can't go,' Timothy said in the flat that had recently been left to him by Mr Kinnally.

Eddie didn't respond. He turned the pages of the *Irish Times*, wishing it were something livelier, the *Star* or the *Express*. With little interest he noticed that schools' entrance tests were to be abolished and that there was to be a canine clean-up, whatever that was, in Limerick.

'I'll drive you down,' he offered then. His own plans were being shattered by this change of heart on the part of Timothy, but he kept the annoyance out of his voice. He had intended to gather his belongings together and leave as soon as he had the house to himself: a bus out to the N4, the long hitch-hike, then start all over again. 'No problem to drive you down,' he said. 'No problem.'

The suggestion wasn't worth a reply, Timothy considered. It wasn't even worth acknowledgement. No longer plump at thirty-three, Timothy wore his smooth fair hair in a ponytail. When he smiled, a dimple appeared in his left cheek, a characteristic he cultivated. He was dressed, this morning, as he often was, in flannel trousers and a navy-blue blazer, with a plain blue tie in the buttoned-down collar of his plain blue shirt.

'I'd get out before we got there,' Eddie offered. 'I'd go for a walk while you was inside.'

'What I'm saying is I can't face it.'

There was another silence then, during which Eddie sighed without making a sound. He knew about the birthday tradition because as the day approached there had been a lot of talk about it. The house called

Coolattin had been described to him: four miles from the village of Baltinglass, a short avenue from which the entrance gates had been removed, a
faded green hall-door, the high grass in the garden, the abandoned con-
servatory. And Timothy's people – as Timothy always called them – had
been as graphically presented: Charlotte's smile and Odo's solemnity, their
fondness for one another evident in how they spoke and acted, their fondness for Coolattin. Charlotte cut what remained of Odo's hair, and Timothy said you could tell. And you could tell, even when they were not in
their own surroundings, that they weren't well-to-do: all they wore was
old. Hearing it described, Eddie had visualized in the drawing-room the
bagatelle table between the windows and Odo's ancestor in oils over the
fireplace, the buttoned green sofa, the rugs that someone had once brought
back from India or Egypt. Such shreds of grace and vigour from a family's
past took similar form in the dining-room that was these days used only
once a year, on April 23rd, and in the hall and on the staircase wall, where
further portraits hung. Except for the one occupied by Odo and Charlotte, the bedrooms were musty, with patches of grey damp on the ceilings,
and plaster fallen away. Timothy's, in which he had not slept for fifteen
years, was as he'd left it, but in one corner the wallpaper had billowed out
and now was curling away from the surface. The kitchen, where the television and the wireless were, where Odo and Charlotte ate all their meals
except for lunch on Timothy's birthday, was easily large enough for this
general purpose: a dresser crowded with crockery and a lifetime's odds
and ends, a long scrubbed table on the flagged floor, with upright kitchen
chairs around it. As well, there were the two armchairs Odo had brought
in from the drawing-room, a washing-machine Timothy had given his
mother, wooden draining-boards on either side of the sink, ham hooks in
the panelled ceiling, and a row of bells on springs above the door to the
scullery. A cheerful place, that kitchen, Eddie estimated, but Timothy said
it was part and parcel, whatever he meant by that.

'Would you go, Eddie? Would you go down and explain, say I'm feeling
unwell?'

Eddie hesitated. Then he said:

'Did Mr Kinnally ever go down there?'

'No, of course he didn't. It's not the same.'

Eddie walked away when he heard that reply. Mr Kinnally had been
far too grand to act as a messenger in that way. Mr Kinnally had given
Timothy birthday presents: the chain he wore on his wrist, shoes and
pullovers. 'Now, I don't want you spending your money on me,' Timothy
had said a day or two ago. Eddie, who hadn't been intending to, didn't
even buy a card.

In the kitchen he made coffee, real coffee from Bewley's, measured into the percolator, as Timothy had shown him. Instant gave you cancer, Timothy maintained. Eddie was a burly youth of nineteen, with curly black hair to which he daily applied gel. His eyes, set on a slant, gave him a furtive air, accurately reflecting his nature, which was a watchful one, the main chance being never far out of his sights. When he got away from the flat in Mountjoy Street he intended to go steady for a bit, maybe settle down with some decent girl, maybe have a kid. Being in the flat had suited him for the five months he'd been here, even if – privately – he didn't much care for certain aspects of the arrangement. Once, briefly, Eddie had been apprenticed to a plumber, but he hadn't much cared for that either.

He arranged cups and saucers on a tray and carried them to the sitting-room, with the coffee and milk, and a plate of croissants. Timothy had put a CD on, the kind of music Eddie didn't care for but never said so, sonorous and grandiose. The hi-fi was Bang and Olufsen, the property of Mr Kinnally in his lifetime, as everything in the flat had been.

'Why not?' Timothy asked, using the telecommander on the arm of his chair to turn the volume down. 'Why not, Eddie?'

'I couldn't do a thing like that. I'll drive you –'

'I'm not going down.'

Timothy reduced the volume further. As he took the cup of coffee Eddie offered him, his two long eye-teeth glistened the way they sometimes did, and the dimple formed in his cheek.

'All I'm asking you to do is pass a message on. I'd take it as a favour.'

'The phone –'

'There's no phone in that place. Just say I couldn't make it due to not feeling much today.'

Timothy broke in half a croissant that had specks of bacon in it, the kind he liked, that Eddie bought in Fitz's. A special favour, he softly repeated, and Eddie sensed more pressure in the words. Timothy paid, Timothy called the tune. Well, two can play at that game, Eddie said to himself, and calculated his gains over the past five months.

The faded green hall-door, green also on the inside, was sealed up because of draughts. You entered the house at the back, crossing the cobbled yard to the door that led to the scullery.

'He's here,' Charlotte called out when there was the sound of a car, and a few minutes later, as Odo arrived in the kitchen from the hall, there were footsteps in the scullery passage and then a hesitant knock on the kitchen door. Since Timothy never knocked, both thought this odd, and odder still when a youth they did not know appeared.

'Oh,' Charlotte said.

'He's off colour,' the youth said. 'A bit naff today. He asked me would I come down and tell you.' The youth paused, and added then: 'On account you don't have no phone.'

Colour crept into Charlotte's face, her cheeks becoming pink. Illness worried her.

'Thank you for letting us know,' Odo said stiffly, the dismissive note in his tone willing this youth to go away again.

'It's nothing much, is it?' Charlotte asked, and the youth said seedy, all morning in the toilet, the kind of thing you wouldn't trust yourself with on a car journey. His name was Eddie, he explained, a friend of Timothy's. Or more, he added, a servant really, depending how you looked at it.

Odo tried not to think about this youth. He didn't want Charlotte to think about him, just as for so long he hadn't wanted her to think about Mr Kinnally. 'Mr Kinnally died,' Timothy said on this day last year, standing not far from where the youth was standing now, his second gin and tonic on the go. 'He left me everything, the flat, the Rover, the lot.' Odo had experienced relief that this elderly man was no longer alive, but had been unable to prevent himself from considering the inheritance ill-gotten. The flat in Mountjoy Street, well placed in Dublin, had had its Georgian plasterwork meticulously restored, for Mr Kinnally had been that kind of person. They'd heard about the flat, its contents too, just as Eddie had heard about Coolattin. Timothy enjoyed describing things.

'His tummy played up a bit once,' Charlotte was saying with a mother's recall. 'We had a scare. We thought appendicitis. But it wasn't in the end.'

'He'll rest himself, he'll be all right.' The youth was mumbling, not meeting the eye of either of them. Shifty, Odo considered, and dirty-looking. The shoes he wore, once white, the kind of sports shoes you saw about these days, were filthy now. His black trousers hung shape-lessly; his neck was bare, no sign of a shirt beneath the red sweater that had some kind of animal depicted on it.

'Thank you,' Odo said again.

'A drink?' Charlotte offered. 'Cup of coffee? Tea?'

Odo had known that would come. No matter what the circumstances, Charlotte could never help being hospitable. She hated being thought otherwise.

'Well . . .' the youth began, and Charlotte said:

'Sit down for a minute.' Then she changed her mind and suggested the drawing-room because it was a pity to waste the fire.

Odo didn't feel angry. He rarely did with Charlotte. 'I'm afraid we haven't any beer,' he said as they passed through the hall, both coffee and tea having been rejected on the grounds that they would be troublesome to provide, although Charlotte had denied that. In the drawing-room what there was was the sherry that stood near the bagatelle, never touched by either of them, and Timothy's Cork gin, and two bottles of tonic.

'I'd fancy a drop of Cork,' the youth said. 'If that's OK.'

Would Timothy come down another day? Charlotte wanted to know. Had he said anything about that? It was the first time his birthday had been missed. It was the one occasion they spent together, she explained.

'Cheers!' the youth exclaimed, not answering the questions, appearing to Odo to be simulating denseness. 'Great,' he complimented when he'd sipped the gin.

'Poor Timothy!' Charlotte settled into the chair she always occupied in the drawing-room, to the left of the fire. The light from the long-paned windows fell on her neat grey hair and the side of her face. One of them would die first, Odo had thought again in the night, as he often did now. He wanted it to be her; he wanted to be the one to suffer the loneliness and the distress. It would be the same for either of them, and he wanted it to be him who had to bear the painful burden.

Sitting forward, on the edge of the sofa, Eddie felt better when the gin began to glow.

'Refreshing,' he said. 'A drop of Cork.'

The day Mr Kinnally died there were a number of them in the flat. Timothy put the word out and they came that night, with Mr Kinnally still stretched out on his bed. In those days Eddie used to come in the mornings to do the washing-up, after Mr Kinnally had taken a fancy to him in O'Connell Street. An hour or so in the mornings, last night's dishes, paid by the hour; nothing of the other, he didn't even know about it then. On the day of the death Timothy shaved the dead face himself and got Mr Kinnally into his tweeds. He sprayed a little Krizia Uomo, and changed the slippers for lace-ups. He made him as he had been, except of course for the closed eyes, you couldn't do anything about that. 'Come back in the evening, could you?' he had requested Eddie, the first time there'd been such a summons. 'There'll be a few here.' There were more than a few, paying their respects in the bedroom, and afterwards in the sitting-room Timothy put on the music and they just sat there. From the scraps of conversation that were exchanged Eddie learned that Timothy had inherited, that Timothy was in the dead man's shoes, the new Mr Kinnally. 'You'd never think of moving in, Eddie?' Timothy suggested a while later, and afterwards Eddie guessed that that was how Timothy himself had been invited to Mountjoy Street, when he was working in the newsagent's in Ballsbridge, on his uppers as he used to say.

'As a matter of fact,' Eddie said in the drawing-room, 'I never touch a beer.'

Timothy's father – so thin and bony in Eddie's view that when he sat down you'd imagine it would cause him pain – gave a nod that was hardly a nod at all. And the mother said she couldn't drink beer in any shape or form. Neither of them was drinking now.

'Nothing in the gassy line suits me,' Eddie confided. It wasn't easy to know what to say. Timothy had said they'd ask him to stop for a bite of grub when they realized he'd come down specially; before he knew where he was they'd have turned him into the birthday boy. Odo his father's name was, Timothy had passed on, extraordinary really.

'Nice home you got here,' Eddie said. 'Nice place.'

A kind of curiosity had brought him to the house. Once Timothy had handed him the keys of the Rover, he could as easily have driven straight to Galway, which was the city he had decided to make for, having heard a few times that it was lively. But instead he'd driven as directed, to Baltinglass, and then by minor roads to Coolattin. He'd head for Galway later: the N80 to Portlaoise was what the map in the car indicated, then on to Mountmellick and Tullamore, then Athlone. Eddie didn't know any of those towns. Dublin was his place.

'Excuse me,' he said, addressing Timothy's father, lowering his voice. 'D'you have a toilet?'

Charlotte had years ago accepted her son's way of life. She had never fussed about it, and saw no reason to. Yet she sympathized with Odo, and was a little infected by the disappointment he felt. 'This is how Timothy wishes to live,' she used, once, gently to argue, but Odo would look away, saying he didn't understand it, saying – to Timothy, too – that he didn't want to know. Odo was like that; nothing was going to change him. Coolattin had defeated him, and he had always hoped, during Timothy's childhood, that Timothy would somehow make a go of it where he himself had failed. In those days they had taken in overnight guests, but more recently too much went wrong in the house, and the upkeep was too burdensome, to allow that to continue without financial loss. Timothy, as a child, had been both imaginative and practical: Odo had seen a time in the future when there would be a family at Coolattin again, when in some clever way both house and gardens would be restored. Timothy had even talked about it, describing it, as he liked to: a flowery hotel, the kitchen filled with modern utensils and machines, the bedrooms fresh with paint, new wallpapers and fabrics. Odo could recall a time in his own childhood when visitors came and went, not paying for their sojourn, of course, but visitors who paid would at least be something.

'You'll have to ask him if he wants to stay to lunch,' Charlotte said when Timothy's friend had been shown where the downstairs lavatory was.

'Yes, I know.'

'I'd fix that toilet for you,' Eddie offered, explaining that the flow to the bowl was poor. Nothing complicated, corrosion in the pipe. He explained that he'd started out as a plumber once, which was why he knew a thing or two. 'No sweat,' he said.

When lunch was mentioned he said he wouldn't want to trouble any-one, but they said no trouble. He picked up a knife from the drinks table and set off with his gin and tonic to the downstairs lavatory to effect the repair.

'It's very kind of you, Eddie.' Timothy's mother thanked him and he said honestly, no sweat.

When he returned to the drawing-room, having poked about in the cistern with the knife, the room was empty. Rain was beating against the windows. The fire had burnt low. He poured another dollop of gin into his glass, not bothering with the tonic since that would have meant open-ing the second bottle. Then the old fellow appeared out of nowhere with a basket of logs, causing Eddie to jump.

'I done it best I could,' Eddie said, wondering if he'd been seen with the bottle actually in his hand and thinking he probably had. 'It's better than it was anyway.'

'Yes,' Timothy's father said, putting a couple of the logs on to the fire and a piece of turf at the back. 'Thanks very much.'

'Shocking rain,' Eddie said.

Yes, it was heavy now, the answer came, and nothing more was said until they moved into the dining-room. 'You sit there, Eddie,' Timothy's mother directed, and he sat as she indicated, between the two of them. A plate was passed to him with slices of meat on it, then vegetable dishes with potatoes and broccoli in them.

'It was a Thursday, too, the day Timothy was born,' Timothy's mother said. 'In the newspaper they brought me it said something about a royal audience with the Pope.'

1959, Eddie calculated, fourteen years before he saw the light of day himself. He thought of mentioning that, but decided they wouldn't want to know. The drop of Cork had settled in nicely, the only pity was they hadn't brought the bottle in to the table.

'Nice bit of meat,' he said instead, and she said it was Timothy's favourite, always had been. The old fellow was silent again. The old fellow hadn't believed him when he'd said Timothy was off colour. The old fellow knew exactly what was going on, you could tell that straight away.

'Pardon me a sec.' Eddie rose, prompted by the fact that he knew where both of them were. In the drawing-room he poured himself more gin, and grimaced as he swallowed it. He poured a smaller measure and didn't, this time, gulp it. In the hall he picked up a little ornament that might be silver: two entwined fish he had noticed earlier. In the lavatory he didn't close the door in the hope that they would hear the flush and assume he'd been there all the time.

'Great,' he said in the dining-room as he sat down again.

The mother asked about his family. He mentioned Tallaght, no reason not to since it was what she was after. He referred to the tinker encampment, and said it was a bloody disgrace, tinkers allowed like that. 'Pardon my French,' he apologized when the swearword slipped out.

'More, Eddie?' she was saying, glancing at the old fellow since it was he who was in charge of cutting the meat.

'Yeah, great.' He took his knife and fork off his plate, and after it was handed back to him there was a bit of a silence so he added:

'A new valve would be your only answer in the toilet department. No problem with your pressure.'

'We must get it done,' she said.

It was then – when another silence gathered and continued for a couple of minutes – that Eddie knew the mother had guessed also: suddenly it came into her face that Timothy was as fit as a fiddle. Eddie saw her glance once across the table, but the old fellow was intent on his food. On other birthday occasions Timothy would have talked about Mr Kinnally, about his 'circle', which was how the friends who came to the flat were always described. Blearily, through a fog of Cork gin, Eddie knew all that, even heard the echo of Timothy's rather high-pitched voice at this same table. But talk about Mr Kinnally had never been enough.

''Course it could go on the way it is for years,' Eddie said, the silence having now become dense. 'As long as there's a drop coming through at all you're in business with a toilet cistern.'

He continued about the faulty valve, stumbling over some of the words, his speech thickened by the gin. From time to time the old man nodded, but no sign came from the mother. Her features were bleak now, quite unlike they'd been a moment ago, when she'd kept the conversation going. The two had met when she walked up the avenue of Coolattin one day, looking for petrol for her car: Timothy had reported that too. The car was broken down a mile away; she came to the first house there was, which happened to be Coolattin. They walked back to the car together and they fell in love. A Morris 8, Timothy said; 1950 it was. 'A lifetime's celebration of love,' he'd said that morning, in the toneless voice he sometimes adopted. 'That's what you'll find down there.'

It wouldn't have been enough, either, to have had Kinnally here in person. Kinnally they could have taken; Kinnally would have oozed about the place, remarking on the furniture and the pictures on the walls. Judicious, as he would have said himself, a favourite word. Kinnally could be judicious. Rough trade was different.

'There's trifle,' Eddie heard the old woman say before she rose to get it.

The rain came in, heavier now, from the west. A signpost indicated Athlone ahead, and Eddie remembered being informed in a classroom that this town was more or less the centre of Ireland. He drove slowly. If for any reason a police car signalled him to stop he would be found to have more than the permitted quantity of alcohol in his bloodstream; if for any reason his clothing was searched he would be found to be in possession of stolen property; if he was questioned about the car he was driving he would not be believed when he said it had been earlier lent to him for a purpose.

The Rover's windscreen wipers softly swayed, the glass of the windscreen perfectly clear in their wake. Then a lorry went by, and threw up surface water from the road. On the radio Chris de Burgh sang.

The sooner he disposed of the bit of silver the better, Athlone maybe. In Galway he would dump the car in a car park somewhere. The single effect remaining after his intake of gin was the thirst he experienced, as dry as paper his mouth was.

He turned Chris de Burgh off, not trying another channel. It was one thing to scarper off, as Timothy had from that house: he'd scarpered himself from Tallaght. To turn the knife was different. Fifteen years later to make your point with rough trade and transparent lies, to lash out venomously: how had they cocked him up, how had they hurt him, to deserve it? All the time when there had been that silence they had gone on eating, as if leaving the food on their plates would be too dramatic a gesture. The old man nodded once or twice about the valve, but she had given no sign that she even heard. Very slightly, as he drove, Eddie's head began to ache.

'Pot of tea,' he ordered in Athlone, and said no, nothing else when the woman waited. The birthday presents had remained on the sideboard, not given to him to deliver, as Timothy had said they probably would be. The two figures stood, hardly moving, at the back door while he hurried across the puddles in the cobbled yard to the car. When he looked back they were no longer there.

'Great,' Eddie said when the woman brought the tea, in a metal pot, cup and saucer and a teaspoon. Milk and sugar were already on the pink patterned oilcloth that covered the table top. 'Thanks,' Eddie said, and when he had finished and had paid he walked through the rain, his headache clearing in the chilly air. In the first jeweller's shop the man said he didn't buy stuff. In the second Eddie was questioned so he said he came from Fardrum, a village he'd driven through. His mother had given him the thing to sell, he explained, the reason being she was sick in bed and needed a dose of medicine. But the jeweller frowned, and the trinket was handed back to him without a further exchange. In a shop that had ornaments and old books in the window Eddie was offered a pound and said he thought the entwined fish were worth more. 'One fifty,' came the offer then, and he accepted it.

It didn't cease to rain. As he drove on through it, Eddie felt better because he'd sold the fish. He felt like stopping in Ballinasloe for another pot of tea but changed his mind. In Galway he dropped the car off in the first car park he came to.

Together they cleared away the dishes. Odo found that the gin in the drawing-room had been mostly drunk. Charlotte washed up at the sink. Then Odo discovered that the little ornament was gone from the hall and slowly went to break this news, the first communication between them since their visitor had left.

'These things happen,' Charlotte said, after another silence.

The rain was easing when Eddie emerged from a public house in Galway, having been slaking his thirst with 7-Up and watching *Glenroe*. As he walked into the city, it dribbled away to nothing. Watery sunshine slipped through the unsettled clouds, brightening the façades in Eyre Square. He sat on a damp seat there, wondering about picking up a girl, but none passed by so he moved away. He didn't want to think. He wasn't meant to understand, being only what he was. Being able to read Timothy like a book was just a way of putting it, talking big when nobody could hear.

Yet the day still nagged, its images stumbling about, persisting in Eddie's bewilderment. Timothy smiled when he said all he was asking was that a message should be passed on. Eddie's own hand closed over the silver fish. In the dining-room the life drained out of her eyes. Rain splashed the puddles in the cobbled yard and they stood, not moving, in the doorway.

On the quays the breeze from the Atlantic dried the pale stone of the houses and cooled the skin of Eddie's face, freshening it also. People had come out to stroll, an old man with a smooth-haired terrier, a couple speaking a foreign language. Seagulls screeched, swooping and bickering in the air. It had been the natural thing to lift the ornament in the hall since it was there and no one was around: in fairness you could call it payment for scraping the rust off the ballcock valve, easily ten quid that would have cost them. 'A lifetime's celebration,' Timothy said again.

'It has actually cleared up,' Odo said at the window, and Charlotte rose from the armchair by the fire and stood there with him, looking out at the drenched garden. They walked in it together when the last drops had fallen.

'Fairly battered the delphiniums,' Odo said.

'Hasn't it just.'

She smiled a little. You had to accept what there was; no point in brooding. They had been hurt, as was intended, punished because one of them continued to be disappointed and repelled. There never is fairness when vengeance is evoked: that had occurred to Charlotte when she was washing up the lunchtime dishes, and to Odo when he tidied the dining-room. 'I'm sorry,' he had said, returning to the kitchen with forks and spoons that had not been used. Not turning round, Charlotte had shaken her head.

They were not bewildered, as their birthday visitor was: they easily understood. Their own way of life was so much debris all around them, but since they were no longer in their prime that hardly mattered. Once it would have, Odo reflected now; Charlotte had known that years ago. Their love of each other had survived the vicissitudes and the struggle there had been; not even the bleakness of the day that had passed could affect it.

They didn't mention their son as they made their rounds of the garden that was now too much for them and was derelict in places. They didn't mention the jealousy their love of each other had bred in him, that had flourished into deviousness and cruelty. The pain the day had brought would not easily pass, both were aware of that. And yet it had to be, since it was part of what there was.

Child's Play

Gerard and Rebecca became brother and sister after a turmoil of distress. Each had witnessed it from a different point of view, Gerard in one house, Rebecca in another. Two years of passionate quarrelling, arguing and agreeing, of beginning again, of failure and reconciliation, of final insults and rejection, constituted the peepshow they viewed.

There were no other children of the two wrecked marriages, and when the final period of acrimonious wrangling came to an end there was an unexpected accord as to the division of the families. This, it was decided, would be more satisfactorily decreed by the principals involved than by the divorce courts. Gerard's father, innocent in what had occurred, agreed that Gerard should live with his mother since that was convenient. Rebecca's mother, innocent also, declared herself unfit to raise the child of a marriage she had come to loathe, and declared as well that she could not bring herself to go on living in the house of the marriage. She claimed that suicidal tendencies had developed in her, aggravated by the familiar surroundings: she would suffer the loss of her child for her child's sake. 'She's trying all this on,' the other woman insisted, but in the end it appeared she wasn't, and so the arrangement was made.

On a warm Wednesday afternoon, the day Quest for Fame won the Derby, Gerard's mother married Rebecca's father. Afterwards all four of them stood, eyes tightened against strong sunlight, while someone took a photograph. The two children were of an age, Gerard ten, Rebecca nine. Gerard was dark-haired, quite noticeably thin, with glasses. Rebecca's reddish hair curved roundly about her rounded cheeks. Her eyes were bright, a deep shade of blue. Gerard's, brown, were solemn.

They were neutrally disposed to one another, with neither fondness nor distaste on either side: they did not know one another well. Gerard was an intruder in the house that had been Rebecca's, but this was far less to bear than the departure from it of her mother.

'They'll settle,' Rebecca's father murmured in a teashop after the wedding.

Watching the two children, silent beside one another, his new wife said she hoped so.

*

They did settle. Thrown together as helpless parties in the stipulations of the peace, they became companions. They missed the past; resentment and deprivation drew them close. They talked about the two people whom they visited on Sundays, and how those two, once at the centre of things, were now defeated and displaced.

At the top of the house, attic space had been reclaimed to form a single, low-roofed room with windows to the ground and a new parquet floor that seemed to stretch for ever. The walls were a shade of washed-out primrose, and shafts of sunlight made the pale ash of the parquet seem almost white. There was no furniture. Two bare electric light-bulbs hung from the long, slanted ceiling. This no-man's-land was where Gerard and Rebecca played their game of marriage and divorce. It became a secret game, words fading on their lips if someone entered, politeness disguising their deceit.

Rebecca recalled her mother weeping at lunch, a sudden collapse into ugly distress while she was spooning peas on to Rebecca's plate. 'Whatever's up?' Rebecca asked, watching as her mother hurried from the table. Her father did not answer, but instead left the dining-room himself, and a few moments later there were the sounds of a quarrel. 'You've made me hate you,' Rebecca's mother kept screaming so shrilly that Rebecca thought the people in the house next door would hear. 'How could you have made me hate you?'

Gerard entered a room and found his mother nursing the side of her face. His father stood at the window, looking out. Behind his back one hand gripped the other as if in restraint. Gerard was frightened and went away, his brief presence unnoticed.

'Think of that child,' Rebecca's mother pleaded in another mood. 'Stay with us if only for that child.'

'You vicious bitch!' This furious accusation stuttered out of Gerard's father, his voice peculiar, his lips trembling in a grimace he could not control.

Such scenes, seeming like the end of everything that mattered, were later surveyed from the unemotional safety of the new companionship. Regret was exorcized, sore places healed; harshness was the saviour. From information supplied by television a world of sin and romance was put together in the empty attic room. 'Think of that child!' Rebecca mimicked, and Gerard adopted his father's grimace the time he called his mother a vicious bitch. It was fun because the erring couple were so virtuous now.

'I can't think how it happened.' Gerard's version of the guilty husband's voice was not convincing, but it passed whatever muster was required. 'I can't think how I could have been such a fool as to marry her in the first place.'

'Poor thing, it's not her fault.'

'It's that that makes it such an awful guilt.' This came from an old black-and-white film and was used a lot because they liked the sound of it.

When romance was to the fore they spoke in whispers, making a murmuring sound when they didn't know what to say. They tried out dance steps in the attic, pretending they were in a dance-hall they called the Ruby Ballroom or a night-club they called the Nitelite, a title they'd seen in neon somewhere. They called a bar the Bee's Knees, which Rebecca said was a name suitable for a bar, although the original was a stocking shop. They called a hotel the Grand Splendide.

'Some sleazy hotel?' Gerard's father had scornfully put it. 'Some sleazy pay-at-the-door hotel for his sleazy one-night stands?'

'No, actually,' the reply had been. 'It was rather grand.'

Downstairs they watched a television serial in which the wronged ones made the kind of fuss that both Gerard and Rebecca had witnessed. The erring ones met in car parks, or on waste land in the early morning.

'Gosh!' Rebecca exclaimed, softly astonished at what was occurring on the screen. 'He took his tongue out of her mouth. Definitely.'

'She's chewing his lips actually.'

'But his tongue —'

'I know.'

'Horrid great thing, it looked.'

'Look, you be Mrs Edwina, Rebecca.'

They turned the television off and climbed to the top of the house, not saying anything on the way. They closed the door behind them.

'OK,' Rebecca said. 'I'm Mrs Edwina.'

Gerard made his bell-ringing sound.

'Oh, go away!' Staring intently into space, Rebecca went on doing so until the sound occurred again. She sighed, and rose from where she'd been sitting on the floor. Grumbling wordlessly, she ran on the spot, descending stairs.

'Yes, what is it, please?'

'Mrs Edwina?'

'Sure I'm Mrs Edwina.'

'I saw your card in the window of that newsagent's. What's it called? The Good News, is it?'

'What d'you want, please?'

'It says you have a room to let.'

'What of it? I was watching *Dallas*.'

'I'm sorry, Mrs Edwina.'

'D'you want to rent a room?'

'I have a use for a room, yes.'

'You'd best come in.'

'Cold evening, Mrs Edwina.'

'I hope you're not planning a love nest. I don't want no filth in my house.'

'Oh, what a lovely little room!'

'If it's for a love nest it'll be ten pounds more per week. Another ten on top of that if you're into call-girls.'

'I can assure you, Mrs Edwina –'

'You read some terrible tales in the papers these days. *Beauty Queen a Call-girl!* it said the other day. Are you fixing to bring in beauty queens?'

'No, no, nothing like that. A friend and myself have been going to the Grand Splendide but it's not the same.'

'You'd be a married man?'

'Yes.'

'I get the picture.'

Rebecca's mother had demanded to know where the sinning had taken place. Gerard's mother, questioned similarly, had revealed that the forbidden meetings had taken place in different locations – once or twice in her lover's office, after hours; over lunch or five-thirty drinks. A hotel was mentioned, and finally a hired room. 'How sordid!' Rebecca's mother cried, then weeping overcame her and Rebecca crept away. But, elsewhere, Gerard remained. He reported that extraordinary exchanges had followed, that great importance was attached to the room that had been specially acquired, great offence taken.

'I'm tired of this ghastly hole.' Rebecca was good at introducing a whine into her tone, a bad-tempered, spoilt-child sound that years ago she'd once or twice tried on in reality before being sharply told to cease immediately.

'Oh, it's not too bad, darling!'

'It's most unpleasant. It's dirty for a start. Look at the sheets, I've never seen sheets as soiled as that. Then Mrs Edwina is dirty. You can see it on her neck. Filthy dirty that woman is.'

'Oh, she's not too bad.'

'There's a smell of meat in the hall. She never opens a window.'

'Darling –'

'I want to live in a house. I want us to be divorced and married again.'

'I know. I know. But there're the children. And there's the awful guilt I feel.'

'What *I* feel is sick in my bowels. Every time I walk in that door I feel it. Every time I look at that filthy wallpaper I get vomit in my throat.'

'We could paint the place out.'

'Let's go to the Bee's Knees for a cocktail. Let's never come back here.'

'But, angel –'

'Our love's not like it used to be. It's not like it was when we went dancing in the Ruby Ballroom. We haven't been to the Nitelite for a year. Nor the Grand Splendide –'

'You wanted a home-from-home.'

'I don't think you love me any more.'

'Of course I do.'

'Then tell Mrs Edwina what she can do with her horrid old room and let's live in a house.'

'But, dear, the children.'

'Drown the brats in a bucket. Make a present of them to Mrs Edwina for all I care. Cement them into a wall.'

'We'll just get into bed for five minutes –'

'I don't want to get into bed today. Not the way those sheets are.'

'OK. We'll go and have a Babycham.'

'I'd love a Babycham.'

When the house was empty except for themselves it was best. It often was empty in the early afternoon, after the woman who came to clean had gone, when Gerard's mother was out, doing the voluntary work she had recently taken up. They wandered from room to room then, poking into everything. Among other items of interest they found letters, some written by Gerard's mother to Rebecca's father, some by him to her. They were in a dressing-table drawer, in a slim cardboard box, with a rubber band around them. Twice the love affair had broken up. Twice there were farewells, twice the admission that one could not live without the other. They could not help themselves. They had to meet again.

'My, my,' Rebecca enthused. 'Hot stuff, this.'

After their weekend visits to the two who had been wronged Gerard and Rebecca exchanged reports on Sunday evenings. Gerard's father cooked and used the washing-machine, vacuum-cleaned the house, ironed his own shirts, made his bed and weeded the flowerbeds. Rebecca's mother was in a bedsitting-room, a sorry sight. She ate nuts and chocolate while watching the television, saying it wasn't worth cooking for one, not that she minded in the least. She was keeping her end up, Rebecca's mother insisted. 'You can see,' she confided, 'why I didn't think I should look after you, dear? It wasn't because I didn't want you. You're all that's left to me. You're what I live for, darling.'

Rebecca saw perfectly. The bedsitting-room was uncomfortable.

In one corner the bedclothes of a divan, pulled roughly up in daytime, were lumpy beneath a stained pink bedspread. Possessions Rebecca remembered, though had not known were particularly her mother's – ornaments and a tea set, two pictures of medieval people on horses, a table-lamp, chairs and floor rugs and, inappropriately, a gong – cluttered the limited space. Her mother's lipstick was carelessly applied. The same clothes she'd worn in the past, smart then, seemed like cast-offs now. She refused to take a penny of alimony, insisting that part of keeping her end up was to stand on her own two feet. She'd found a job in a theatre café and talked a lot about the actors and actresses who bought cups of coffee or tea from her. All this theatrical talk was boring, Rebecca reported on Sunday evenings: her mother had never been boring before.

Gerard's father, hurrying through his household chores so that he could devote himself to entertaining Gerard, was not the same either. He was more serious. He didn't spread himself about in the sitting-room the way he used to, his legs stretched awkwardly out so that people fell over them. Another boy had once shown Gerard how to untie his father's shoe-laces and tie them together while his attention was diverted. His father had never minded being laughed at; Gerard wasn't so sure about that now.

'She said she had three miscarriages,' Rebecca reported. 'I never knew that.'

Gerard wasn't certain what a miscarriage was, and Rebecca, who had been uncertain also, explained that the baby came out too soon, a lot of mush apparently.

'I wonder if I'm adopted,' Gerard mused.

The next weekend he asked his father, and was assured he wasn't. His father said his mother hadn't wanted more than a single child, but from his tone Gerard decided that she hadn't wanted any children at all. 'I'm a mistake,' he said when he and Rebecca were again alone.

Rebecca agreed that this was probably so. She supposed she should be glad she wasn't just a lot of mush. 'You be the detective,' she said.

Gerard rapped with his knuckles on the parquet floor and Rebecca opened and closed the door.

'What do you want?'

'Hotel detective, lady.'

'So what?'

'I'll tell you so what. So what is I have grounds for believing you and your companion are not Mr and Mrs Smith, as per the entry in the register.'

'Of course we're Mr and Mrs Smith.'

'I would appreciate a word with Mr Smith, ma'am.'

'Mr Smith's in the lavatory.'

'Do you categorically state that you are named Mrs Smith, ma'am? Do you categorically state that you and the party in the lavatory are man and wife?'

'Definitely.'

'Do you categorically state you are not in the prostitution business?'

'The very idea!'

'Then what we have here is a case of mistaken identity. Accept my apologies, ma'am. We get all sorts in the Grand Splendide these days.'

'No offence taken, officer. The public has a right to be protected.'

'Time was when only royalty stayed at the Grand Splendide. I knew the King of Greece, you know.'

'Fancy that.'

'Generous to a fault he was. Oh, thank you very much, lady.'

'Fancy a cocktail, officer? Babycham on the rocks OK?'

'Certainly is. Oh, and, ma'am?'

'How can I help you, officer?'

'Feel free to ply your trade, ma'am.'

'A little brother,' Gerard's mother informed them. 'Or perhaps a sister.'

Gerard didn't ask if this was another mistake because he could tell from the delight in his mother's eyes that it wasn't. There might even be further babies, Rebecca speculated when they were alone. She didn't care for the idea of other children in the house. 'They'll be the real thing,' she said.

Something else happened: Gerard returned after a weekend to say there had been a black-haired Frenchwoman in his father's house. She strolled about the kitchen in stockinged feet, and did the cooking. One result of this person's advent was to cause Gerard to feel less sympathetically disposed towards his father. He felt his father would be all right now, as his mother and Rebecca's father were all right.

'That'll be nice for you,' Rebecca's mother remarked sourly when Rebecca passed on the information about the expected baby. 'Nice for you and Gerard.'

When Rebecca told her about the Frenchwoman she said that that was nice too. These were the only comments she made, Rebecca told Gerard afterwards. Keeping her end up, her mother engaged in a tedious rigmarole about some famous actor or other, whom Rebecca had never heard of. She also kept saying the rigmarole was funny, a view Rebecca didn't share.

'Let's do the time she caught them,' Rebecca suggested when she'd gone through the rigmarole for Gerard.

'OK.'

Gerard lay down on the parquet and Rebecca went out of the room. Gerard worked his lips in an imaginary embrace. His tongue lolled out.

'This is disgusting!' Rebecca cried, bursting into the room again.

Gerard sat up. He asked her what she was doing here.

'A cleaner let me in. She said I'd find you on the office floor.'

'You'd better go,' Gerard muttered quietly to his pretend companion, pushing himself to his feet.

'I've known for ages.' Real tears spread on Rebecca's rounded cheeks. Quite a gush she managed. She'd always been good at real tears.

'I'm sorry.'

'Sorry, my God!'

'I know.'

'She forgot her panties. She left her panties by the wastepaper basket when she scurried out.'

'Look –'

'She's on the street without her panties. Some man on the tube –'

'Look, don't be bitter.'

'Why not? Why shouldn't I be whatever I want to be? Isn't anything my due? You were down there on the floor with a second-class tart and you expect me to be like the Virgin Mary.'

'I do not expect you to be like anyone.'

'You want me to share you with her, is that it? What a jolliness!'

'Look –'

'Oh, don't keep saying look.'

Rebecca's real tears came in a torrent now, dribbling on to a grey cardigan, reddening her eyes.

'I'd better go after her,' Gerard said, picking up, in pantomime, a garment from the floor.

The baby was born, a girl. The black-haired Frenchwoman moved in with Gerard's father. One Sunday evening Rebecca said:

'She wants me back.'

That day had been spent trailing round flats that were to rent. Each time they entered one Rebecca's mother told whoever was showing them around that she worked in the theatre, and mentioned actresses and actors by name. Afterwards, in the bedsitting-room, she said her new life in the theatre had helped her to pull herself together. She said she felt a

strength returning. She intended to take the alimony. She saw it differently now: the alimony was her due.

'So are you, dear,' she said. If there was difficulty, a court of law would
put the matter right, no doubt about that: a child goes to the mother if
the mother's fit and well.

'What did you say?' Gerard asked.

'Nothing.'

'Not that you'd rather be here?'

'No.'

'*Would* you rather be here, Rebecca?'

'Yes.'

Gerard was silent. He looked away.

'I couldn't say it,' Rebecca said.

'I see you couldn't.'

'She's my mother,' Rebecca said.

'Yes, I know.'

A week ago they had been angry together because unhappiness had
made her mother foolish. A week ago Gerard said his father had reverted
to something like his old self, his legs stuck out while he read the newspaper. But it was far from being the same as it had been. His father reading
the newspaper like that was only a reminder.

Rebecca's real tears began, and when the sound of sobbing ceased
there was silence in the room they had made their own. Gerard wanted
to comfort her, as once his father had comforted his mother, saying he
forgave her, saying they would try again. But their game wouldn't stretch
to that.

They sat on the virgin floor, some distance away from one another,
while the white shafts of sunlight faded and the washed-out yellow of the
walls dimmed to nothing. Their thoughts were similar and they knew
they were. The house that had been Rebecca's would be Gerard's because
that was laid down now. Rebecca would come to it at weekends because
her father was there, but she would not bring with her her mother's sad
tales of the theatre, nor would Gerard relate the latest from his father's
new relationship. The easy companionship that had allowed them to sip
cocktails and sign the register of the Hotel Grand Splendide had been
theirs by chance, a gift thrown out from other people's circumstances.
Helplessness was their natural state.

A Bit of Business

On a warm Saturday morning the city was deserted. Its suburbs dozed, its streets had acquired a tranquillity that did not belong to the hour. Shops and cafés were unexpectedly closed. Where there were people, they sat in front of television sets, or listened to transistors.

In Westmoreland Street two youths hurried, their progress marked by a businesslike air. They did not speak until they reached St Stephen's Green. 'No. On ahead,' one said when his companion paused. 'Off to the left in Harcourt Street.' His companion did not argue.

They had been friends since childhood; and today, their purpose being what it was, they knew better than to argue. Argument wasted time, and would distract them. The one who'd given the instruction, the older and taller of the two, was Mangan. The other was a pock-marked, sallow youth known as Lout Gallagher, the sobriquet an expression of scorn on the part of a Christian Brother ten or so years ago. Mangan had gelled short hair, nondescript as to colour, and small eyes that squinted slightly, and a flat, broad nose. 'Here,' he commanded at the end of Harcourt Street, and the two veered off in the direction he indicated.

A marmalade cat sauntered across the street they were in now; no one was about. 'The blue Ford,' Mangan said. Gallagher, within seconds, forced open the driver's door. As swiftly, the bonnet of the car was raised. Work was done with wire; the engine started easily.

In the suburb of Rathgar, in Cavendish Road, Mr Livingston watched the red helicopter touch down behind the vesting tents in Phoenix Park. Earlier, at the airport, the Pope's right hand had been raised in blessing, lowered, and then raised again and again, a benign smile accompanying each gesture. In Phoenix Park the crowds knelt in their corrals, and sang 'Holy God, We Praise Thy Name'. Now and again the cameras caught the black dress of clergymen and nuns, but for the most part the crowds were composed of the kind of people Mr Livingston met every day on the streets or noticed going to Mass on a Sunday. The crowds were orderly, awed by the occasion. The yellow and white papal flags fluttered everywhere; occasionally a degree of shoving developed in an effort to gain a better view. Four times already the cameras had shown women fainting

– from marvelling, so Mr Livingston was given to understand, rather than heat or congestion. Somewhere in Phoenix Park were the Herlihys, but so far Mr Livingston had failed to identify them. 'I'll wave,' the Herlihy twins had promised, speaking in unison as they always did. Mr Livingston knew they'd forget; in all the excitement they wouldn't even know that a camera had skimmed over them. It was Herlihy himself who would be noticeable, being so big and his red hair easy to pick out. Monica, of course, you could miss.

Mr Livingston, attired now in a dark-blue suit, was a thin man in his sixties, only just beginning to go grey. His lean features, handsome in youth, were affected by wrinkles, his cheeks a little flushed. He had been a widower for a year.

Preceded by Cardinal Ó Fiaich and Archbishop Ryan, the Pope emerged from the papal vesting chamber under the podium. Cheering began in the corrals. Twice the Pope stopped and extended his arms. There was cheering then such as Mr Livingston had never in his life heard before. The Pope approached the altar.

Mangan and Gallagher worked quickly, though with no great skill. They pulled open drawers and scattered their contents. They rooted among clothes, and wrenched at the locks of cupboards. Jewellery was not examined, since its worth could not be even roughly estimated. All they found they pocketed, with loose change and notes. A transistor radio was secreted beneath Gallagher's jacket.

'Nothing else,' Mangan said. 'Useless damn place.'

They left the house that they had entered, through a kitchen window. They strolled towards the parked blue Ford, Mangan shaking his head as though, having arrived at the house on legitimate business, they disappointedly failed to find anyone at home. Gallagher drove, slowly in the road where the house was, and then more rapidly. 'Off to the left,' Mangan said, and when the opportunity came Gallagher did as he was bidden. The car drew up again; the two remained seated, both their glances fixed on the driving mirror. 'OK,' Mangan said.

Mr Livingston heard a noise and paid it no attention. Although his presence in the Herlihys' house was, officially, to keep an eye on it, he believed that the Herlihys had invited him because he had no television himself. It was their way to invent a reason; their way to want to thank him whenever it was possible for all the baby-sitting he did – not that there wasn't full and adequate payment at the time, the 'going rate' as Monica called it. Earlier that morning, as he'd risen and dressed himself, it had not occurred to him that Herlihy might have been serious when he said it was nice to have someone about the place on a day like this, when the Guards were all out at Phoenix Park. The sound of the television, Herlihy suggested, was as good as a dog.

'A new kind of confrontation,' stated the Pope, 'with values and trends which, up to now, have been unknown and alien to Irish society.'

Mr Livingston nodded in agreement. It would have been nice for Rosie, he thought; she'd have appreciated all this, the way she'd appreciated the royal weddings. When his wife was alive Mr Livingston had hired a television set like everyone else, but later he'd ceased to do so because he found he never watched it on his own. It made him miss her more, sitting there with the same programmes coming on, her voice not commenting any more. They would certainly have watched the whole of the ceremony today, but naturally they wouldn't have attended it in person, being Protestants.

'The sacredness of life,' urged the Pope, 'the indissolubility of marriage, the true sense of human sexuality, the right attitude towards the material goods that progress has to offer.' He advocated the Sacraments, especially the Sacrament of Penance.

Applause broke out, and again Mr Livingston nodded his agreement.

Gallagher had wanted to stop, but Mangan said one more house. So they went for the one at the end of the avenue, having noticed that no dog was kept. 'They've left that on,' Mangan whispered in the kitchen when they heard the sound of the television. 'Check it, though, while I'm up there.'

In the Herlihys' main bedroom he slipped the drawers out softly, and eased open anything that was locked. They'd been right to come. This place was the best yet.

Suddenly the sound of the television was louder, and Mangan knew that Gallagher had opened the door of the room it came from. He glanced towards the windows in case he should have to hurry away, but no sound of protest came from downstairs. They'd drive the car to Milltown and get on to the first bus going out of the city. Later on they'd pick up a bus to Bray. It was always worth making the journey to Bray because Cohen gave you better prices.

'Hey,' Gallagher called, not loudly, not panicking in any way whatsoever. At once Mangan knew there was a bit of trouble. He knew, by the sound of the television, that the door Gallagher had opened hadn't been closed again. Once, in a house at night, a young girl had walked across a landing with nothing on her except a sanitary thing. He and Gallagher had been in the shadows, alerted by the flush of a lavatory. She hadn't seen them.

He stuffed a couple of ties into his pockets and closed the bedroom
door behind him. On the way downstairs he heard Gallagher's voice
before he saw him.

'There's an old fellow here,' Gallagher said, making no effort to speak
privately, 'watching His Holiness.'

Gallagher was as cool as a cucumber. You had to admire that in him.
The time Mangan had gone with Ossie Power it had been nerves that
landed them in it. You couldn't do a job with shaking hands, he'd told
Power before they began, but it hadn't been any use. He should have
known, of course.

'He's staying quiet,' Gallagher said in a low voice. 'Like I told him, he's
keeping his trap tight.'

The youth in the doorway was wearing a crushed imitation suede jacket
and dark trousers. His white T-shirt was dirty; his chin and cheeks were
pitted with the remains of acne. For an instant Mr Livingston received
an impression of a second face: a flat, wide nose between two bead-like
eyes. Then both intruders stepped back into the hall. Whispering took
place but Mr Livingston couldn't hear what was said. On the screen the
Popemobile moved slowly through the vast crowd. Hands reached out to
touch it.

'Keep your eyes on your man,' a voice commanded, and Mr Livingston
knew it belonged to the one he had seen less of because it was gruffer
than the other voice. 'Keep company with His Holiness.'

Mr Livingston did not attempt to disobey. Something was placed over
his eyes and knotted at the back of his head. The material was rough, like
tweed. With something similar his wrists were tied in his lap. Each ankle
was tied to a leg of the chair he occupied. His wallet was slipped out of
the inside pocket of his jacket.

He had failed the Herlihys; even though it was a pretence, he had agreed
to perform a small and simple task; the family would return to disappointment. Mr Livingston had been angry as soon as he realized what was happening, as soon as the first youth appeared. He'd wanted to get up, to look
around for something to use as a weapon, but only just in time he'd realized it would be foolish to do that. Helpless in his chair, he felt ashamed.

On the television the cheering continued, and voices described what
was happening. 'Ave! Ave!' people sang.

'Pull up,' Mangan said in the car. 'Go down that road and pull up at the
bottom.'

Lout Gallagher did so, halting the car at the opening to a half-built estate. They had driven further than they'd intended, anxious to move swiftly from the neighbourhood of their morning's work. 'If there's ever a squawk out of you,' Mangan had threatened before they parted from Mr Livingston, 'you'll rue the bloody day, mister.' Taking the third of the ties he'd picked up in the bedroom, he had placed it round the old man's neck. He had crossed the two ends and pulled them tight, watching while Mr Livingston's face and neck became flushed. He released them in good time in case anything went wrong.

'You never know with a geezer like that,' he said now. He turned his head and glanced out of the back window of the car. They were both still edgy. It was the worst thing that could happen, being seen.

'Wouldn't we dump the wagon?' Gallagher said.

'Drive it in on the site.'

They left the car behind the back wall of one of the new houses, and since the place was secluded they counted the money they'd trawled. 'Forty-two pound fifty-four,' Mangan said. As well, there were various pieces of jewellery and the transistor radio. 'You could be caught with that,' Mangan advised, and the transistor was thrown into a cement-mixer.

'He'll issue descriptions,' Mangan said before they turned away from the car. 'He'll squawk his bloody guts out.'

They both knew that. In spite of the ugliness Mangan had injected into his voice, in spite of the old man's face going purple, he would recall the details of the occasion. In the glimpse Mangan had caught of him there was anger in his eyes and his forehead was puckered in a frown.

'I'm going back there,' Mangan said.

'The car's hot.'

Mangan didn't answer, but swore instead, repeatedly and furiously; then they lit cigarettes and both felt calmer. Mangan led the way from the car, through the half-built site and out on to a lane. Within five minutes they reached a main road and came eventually to a public house. High up on the wall above the bar a large television set continued to record the Pope's presence in Ireland. No one took any notice of the two youths who ordered glasses of Smithwick's, and crisps.

The people who had been robbed returned to their houses and counted the cost of the Pope's personal blessing. The Herlihys returned and found Mr Livingston tied up with neck-ties, and the television still on. A doctor was summoned, though against Mr Livingston's wishes. The police came later.

That afternoon in Bray, after they'd been to see Cohen, Mangan and Gallagher picked up two girls. 'Jaysus, I could do with a mott,' Lout

Gallagher had said the night before, which was how the whole thing began, Mangan realizing he could do with one too. 'Thirty,' Cohen had offered that afternoon, and they'd pushed him up to thirty-five.

They felt better after the few drinks. Today of all days a bit of fecking wouldn't interest the police, with the headaches they'd have when the crowds headed back to the city. 'Why'd they be bothered with an old geezer like that?' Mangan said, and they felt better still.

In the Esplanade Ice-cream Parlour the girls requested a Peach Melba and a sundae. One was called Carmel, the other Marie. They said they were nurses, but in fact they worked in a paper mill.

'Bray's quiet,' Mangan said.

The girls agreed it was. They'd been intending to go to see the Pope themselves, but they'd slept it out. A quarter past twelve it was before Carmel opened her eyes, and Marie was even worse. She wouldn't like to tell you, she said.

'We seen it on the television,' Mangan said. 'Your man's in great form.'

'What line are you in?' Carmel asked.

'Gangsters,' said Mangan, and everyone laughed.

Gallagher wagged his head in admiration. Mangan always gave the same response when asked that question by girls. You might have thought he'd restrain himself today, but that was Mangan all over. Gallagher lit a cigarette, thinking he should have hit the old fellow before he had a chance to turn round. He should have rushed into the room and struck him a blow on the back of the skull with whatever there was to hand, hell take the consequences.

'What's it mean, gangsters?' Marie asked, still giggling, glancing at Carmel and giggling even more.

'Banks,' Mangan said, 'is our business.'

The girls thought of Butch Cassidy and the Sundance Kid and the adventures of Bonnie and Clyde, and laughed again. They knew that if they pressed their question it wouldn't be any good. They knew it was a kind of flirtation, their asking and Mangan teasing with his replies. Mangan was a wag. Both girls were drawn to him.

'Are the ices to our ladyships' satisfaction?' he enquired; causing a further outbreak of giggling.

Gallagher had ordered a banana split. Years ago he used to think that if you filled a room with banana splits he could eat them all. He'd been about five then. He used to think the same thing about fruitcake.

'Are the flicks on today?' Mangan asked, and the girls said on account of the Pope they mightn't be. It might be like Christmas Day, they didn't know.

'We seen what's showing in Bray,' Marie said. 'In any case.'

'We'll go dancing later on,' Mangan promised. He winked at Gallagher, and Gallagher thought the day they made a killing you wouldn't see him for dust. The mail boat and Spain, posh Cockney girls who called you Mr Big. Never lift a finger again.

'Will we sport ourselves on the prom?' Mangan suggested, and the girls laughed again. They said they didn't mind. Each wanted to be Mangan's. He sensed it, so he walked between them on the promenade, linking their arms. Gallagher walked on the outside, linking Carmel.

'Spot of the ozone,' Mangan said. He pressed his forearm against Marie's breast. She was the one, he thought.

'D'you like the nursing?' Gallagher asked, and Carmel said it was all right. A sharp breeze was darting in from the sea, stinging their faces, blowing the girls' hair about. Gallagher saw himself stretched out by a blue swimming-pool, smoking and sipping at a drink. There was a cherry in the drink, and a little stick with an umbrella on the end of it. A girl with one whole side of her bikini open was sharing it with him.

'Bray's a great place,' Mangan said.

'The pits,' Carmel corrected.

You could always tell by the feel of a girl on your arm, Mangan said to himself. Full of sauce the fat one was, no more a nurse than he was. Gallagher wondered if they had a flat, if there'd be anywhere to go when the moment came.

'We could go into the bar of the hotel,' the other one was saying, the way girls did when they wanted to extract their due.

'What hotel's this?' he asked.

'The International.'

'Oh, listen to Miss Ritzy!'

They turned and walked back along the promenade, guided by the girls to the bar in question. Gin and tonic the girls had. Gallagher and Mangan had Smithwick's.

'We could go into town later,' Carmel casually suggested. 'There'll be celebrations on.'

'We'll give the matter thought,' Mangan said.

Another couple of pulls of the tie, Mangan said to himself, and who'd have been the wiser? You get to that age, you'd had your life anyway. As it was, the old geezer had probably conked it on his own, tied up like that. Most likely he was stiffening already.

'Isn't there a disco on in Bray?' he suggested. 'What's wrong with a slap-up meal and then the light fantastic?'

The girls were again amused at his way of putting it. Gallagher was glad to hear the proposal that they should stay where they were. If they went into town the whole opportunity could fall asunder. If you didn't end up near a mott's accommodation you were back where you started.

'You'd die of the pace of it in Bray,' Marie said, and Mangan thought a couple more gins and a dollop of barley wine with their grill and chips. He edged his knee against Marie's. She didn't take hers away.

'Have you a flat or rooms or something?' Gallagher asked, and the girls said they hadn't. They lived at home, they said. They'd give anything for a flat.

A few minutes later, engaged at the urinals in the lavatory, the two youths discussed the implications of that. Mangan had stood up immediately on hearing the news. He'd given a jerk of his head when the girls weren't looking.

'No bloody go,' Gallagher said.

'The fat one's on for it.'

'Where though, man?'

Mangan reminded his companion of other occasions, in car parks and derelict buildings, of the time they propped up the bar of the emergency exit of the Adelphi cinema and went back in afterwards, of the time in the garden shed in Drumcondra.

Gallagher laughed, feeling more optimistic when he remembered all that. He winked to himself, the way he did when he was beginning to feel drunk. He spat into the urinal, another habit at this particular juncture. The seashore was the place; he'd forgotten about the seashore.

'Game ball,' Mangan said.

The memory of the day that had passed seemed rosy now – the empty streets they had hurried through, the quiet houses where their business had been, the red blotchiness in the old man's face and neck, the processions on the television screen. Get a couple more gins into them, Mangan thought again, and then the barley wine. Stretch the fat one out on the soft bloody sand.

'Oh, lovely,' the fat one said when more drinks were offered.

Gallagher imagined the wife of a businessman pleading down a telephone, reporting that her captors intended to slice off the tips of her little fingers unless the money was forthcoming. The money was a package in a telephone booth, stashed under the seat. The pictures of Spain began again.

'Hi,' Carmel said.

She'd been to put her lipstick on, but she didn't look any different.

'What d'you do really?' she asked on the promenade.

'Unemployed.'

'You're loaded for an unemployed.' Her tone was suspicious. He watched her trying to focus her eyes. Vaguely, he wondered if she liked him.

'A man's car needed an overhaul,' he said.

Ahead of them, Mangan and Marie were laughing, the sound drifting lightly back above the swish of the sea.

'He's great sport, isn't he?' Carmel said.

'Oh, great all right.'

Mangan turned round before they went down the steps to the shingle. Gallagher imagined his fancy talk and the fat one giggling at it. He wished he was good at talk like that.

'We had plans made to go into town,' Carmel said. 'There'll be great gas in town tonight.'

When they began to cross the shingle she said it hurt her feet, so Gallagher led her back to the concrete wall of the promenade and they sat down with their backs to it. It wasn't quite dark. Cigarette packets and chocolate wrappings were scattered on the sand and pebbles. Gallagher put his arm round Carmel's shoulders. She let him kiss her. She didn't mind when he twisted her sideways so that she no longer had her back to the wall. She felt limp in his arms, and for a moment Gallagher thought she'd passed out, but then she kissed him back. She murmured something and her arms pulled him down on top of her. He realized it didn't matter about the fancy talk.

'When then?' Marie whispered, pulling down her clothes. Five minutes ago Mangan had promised they would meet again; he'd sworn there was nothing he wanted more; the sooner the better, he'd said.

'Monday night,' he added now. 'Outside the railway station. Six.' It was where they'd picked the two girls up. Mangan could think of nowhere else and it didn't matter anyway since he had no intention of being anywhere near Bray on Monday night.

'Geez, you're great,' Marie said.

On the bus to Dublin they did not say much. Carmel had spewed up a couple of mouthfuls, and in Gallagher's nostrils the sour odour persisted. Marie in the end had been a nag, going on about Monday evening, making sure Mangan wouldn't forget. What both of them were thinking was that Cohen, as usual, had done best out of the bit of business there'd been.

Then the lean features of Mr Livingston were recalled by Mangan, the angry eyes, the frown. They'd made a mess of it, letting him see them, they'd bollocksed the whole thing. That moment in the doorway when the old man's glance had lighted on his face he had hardly been able to control his bowels. 'I'm going back there,' his own voice echoed from a later moment, but he'd known, even as he spoke, that if he returned he would do no more than he had done already.

Beside him, on the inside seat, Gallagher experienced similar recollections. He stared out into the summery night, thinking that if he'd hit the old man on the back of the skull he could have finished him. The thought of that had pleased him when they were with the girls. It made him shiver now.

'God, she was great,' Mangan said, dragging out of himself a single snigger.

His bravado obscured a longing to be still with the girls, ordering gins at the bar and talking fancy. He would have paid what remained in his pocket still to taste her lipstick on the seashore, or to hear her gasp as he touched her for the first time.

Gallagher tried for his dream of Mr Big, but it would not come to him. 'Yeah,' he said, replying to his friend's observation.

The day was over; there was nowhere left to hide from the error that had been made. As they had at the time, they sensed the old man's shame and the hurt to his pride, as animals sense fear or resolution. Privately, each calculated how long it would be before the danger they'd left behind in the house caught up with them.

They stepped off the bus on the quays. The crowds that had celebrated in the city during their absence had dwindled, but people who were on the streets spoke with a continuing excitement about the Pope's presence in Ireland and the great Mass there had been in the sunshine. The two youths walked the way they'd come that morning, both of them wondering if the nerve to kill was something you acquired.

After Rain

In the dining-room of the Pensione Cesarina solitary diners are fitted in around the walls, where space does not permit a table large enough for two. These tables for one are in three of the room's four corners, by the door of the pantry where the jugs of water keep cool, between one family table and another, on either side of the tall casement windows that rattle when they're closed or opened. The dining-room is large, its ceiling high, its plain cream-coloured walls undecorated. It is noisy when the pensione's guests are there, the tables for two that take up all the central space packed close together, edges touching. The solitary diners are well separated from this mass by the passage left for the waitresses, and have a better view of the dining-room's activity and of the food before it's placed in front of them – whether tonight it is *brodo* or pasta, beef or chicken, and what the *dolce* is.

'*Dieci*,' Harriet says, giving the number of her room when she is asked. The table she has occupied for the last eleven evenings has been joined to one that is too small for a party of five: she doesn't know where to go. She stands a few more moments by the door, serving dishes busily going by her, wine bottles grabbed from the marble-topped sideboard by the rust-haired waitress, or the one with a wild look, or the one who is plump and pretty. It is the rust-haired waitress who eventually leads Harriet to the table by the door of the pantry where the water jugs keep cool. '*Da here?*' she asks and Harriet, still feeling shy although no one glanced in her direction when she stood alone by the door, orders the wine she has ordered on other nights, Santa Cristina.

Wearing a blue dress unadorned except for the shiny blue buckle of its belt, she has earrings that hardly show and a necklace of opaque white beads that isn't valuable. Angular and thin, her dark hair cut short, her long face strikingly like the sharply chiselled faces of Modigliani, a month ago she passed out of her twenties. She is alone in the Pensione Cesarina because a love affair is over.

A holiday was cancelled, there was an empty fortnight. She wanted to be somewhere else then, not in England with time on her hands. '*Io sola*,' she said on the telephone, hoping she had got that right, choosing the Cesarina because she'd known it in childhood, because she thought that being alone would be easier in familiar surroundings.

'*Va bene?*' the rust-haired waitress enquires, proffering the Santa Cristina.

'*Sì, sì.*'

The couples who mostly fill the dining-room are German, the guttural sound of their language drifting to Harriet from the tables that are closest to her. Middle-aged, the women more stylishly dressed than the men, they are enjoying the heat of August and the low-season tariff: demi-pensione at a hundred and ten thousand lire. The heat may be too much of a good thing for some, although it's cooler by dinnertime, when the windows of the dining-room are all open, and the Cesarina is cooler anyway, being in the hills. 'If there's a breeze about,' Harriet's mother used to say, 'it finds the Cesarina.'

Twenty years ago Harriet first came here with her parents, when she was ten and her brother twelve. Before that she had heard about the pensione, how the terracotta floors were oiled every morning before the guests were up, and how the clean smell of oil lingered all day, how breakfast was a roll or two, with tea or coffee on the terrace, how dogs sometimes barked at night, from a farm across the hills. There were photographs of the parched garden and of the stately, ochre-washed exterior, and of the pensione's vineyard, steeply sloping down to two enormous wells. And then she saw for herself, summer after summer in the low season: the vast dining-room at the bottom of a flight of stone steps from the hall, and the three salons where there is Stock or grappa after dinner, with tiny cups of harsh black coffee. In the one with the bookcases there are Giotto reproductions in a volume on the table lectern, and *My Brother Jonathan* and *Rebecca* among the detective novels by George Goodchild on the shelves. The guests spoke in murmurs when Harriet first knew these rooms, English mostly, for it was mostly English who came then. To this day, the Pensione Cesarina does not accept credit cards, but instead will take a Eurocheque for more than the guaranteed amount.

'*Ecco, signora.*' A waitress with glasses, whom Harriet has seen only once or twice before, places a plate of tagliatelle in front of her.

'*Grazie.*'

'*Prego, signora. Buon appetito.*'

If the love affair hadn't ended – and Harriet has always believed that love affairs are going to last – she would now be on the island of Skyros. If the love affair hadn't ended she might one day have come to the Cesarina as her parents had before their children were born, and later might have occupied a family table in the dining-room. There is an American family tonight, and an Italian one, and other couples besides the Germans. A couple, just arrived, spoke what sounded like Dutch upstairs.

Another Harriet knows to be Swiss, another she guesses to be Dutch also. A nervous English pair are too far away to allow eavesdropping.

'*Va bene?*' the rust-haired waitress enquires again, lifting away her empty plate.

'*Molto bene. Grazie.*'

Among the other solitary diners is a grey-haired dumpy woman who has several times spoken to Harriet upstairs, an American. A man is noticeable every evening because of his garish shirts, and there's a man who keeps looking about him in a jerky, nervous way, and a woman – stylish in black – who could be French. The man who looks about – small, with delicate, well-tended good features – often glances in this woman's direction, and sometimes in Harriet's. An elderly man whose white linen suit observes the formalities of the past wears a differently striped silk tie each dinnertime.

On the first night of her stay Harriet had *The Small House at Allington* in her handbag, intending to prop it up in front of her in the dining-room, but when the moment came that seemed all wrong. Already, then, she regretted her impulse to come here on her own and wondered why she had. On the journey out the rawness of her pain had in no way softened, if anything had intensified, for the journey on that day should have been different, and not made alone: she had forgotten there would be that.

With the chicken pieces she's offered there are roast potatoes, tomatoes and zucchini, and salad. Then Harriet chooses cheese: pecorino, a little Gorgonzola. Half of the Santa Cristina is left for tomorrow, her room number scribbled on the label. On the envelope provided for her napkin this is more elegantly inscribed, in a sloping hand: *Camera Dieci*. She folds her napkin and tucks it away, and for a moment as she does so the man she has come here to forget pushes through another crowded room, coming towards her in the King of Poland, her name on his lips. 'I love you, Harriet,' he whispers beneath the noise around them. Her eyes close when their caress is shared. 'My darling Harriet,' he says.

Upstairs, in the room where the bookcases are, Harriet wonders if this solitude is how her life will be. Has she returned to this childhood place to seek whatever comfort a happy past can offer? Is that a truer reason than what she told herself at the time? Her thoughts are always a muddle when a love affair ends, the truth befogged; the truth not there at all, it often seems. Love failed her was what she felt when another relationship crumbled into nothing; love has a way of doing that. And since wondering is company for the companionless, she wonders why it should be so. This is the first time that a holiday has been cancelled, that she has come away alone.

'*Mi dispiace*,' a boy in a white jacket apologizes, having spilt some of a liqueur on a German woman's arm. The woman laughs and says in English that it doesn't matter. '*Non importa*,' her husband adds when the boy looks vacant, and the German woman laughs again.

'*Mais oui*, I study the law,' a long-legged girl is saying. 'And Eloise is a stylist.'

These girls are Belgian: the questions of two Englishmen are answered. The Englishmen are young, both of them heavily built, casually turned out, one of them moustached.

'Is stylist right? Is that what you say?'

'Oh, yes.' And both young men nod. When one suggests a liqueur on the terrace Eloise and her friend ask for cherry brandy. The boy in the white jacket goes to pour it in a cupboard off the hall, where the espresso machine is.

'And you?' Eloise enquires as the four pass through the room, through the french windows to the terrace.

'Nev's in business. I go down after wrecks.' The voice that drifts back is slack, accented, confident. English or German or Dutch, these are the people who have made the Pensione Cesarina move with the times, different from the people of Harriet's childhood.

A bearded man is surreptitiously sketching a couple on one of the sofas. The couple, both reading, are unaware. In the hall the American family is much in evidence, the mother with a baby in her arms pacing up and down, the father quietening two other children, a girl and a boy.

'Good evening,' someone interrupts Harriet's observations, and the man in the linen suit asks if the chair next to hers is taken by anyone else. His tie tonight is brown and green, and Harriet notices that his craggy features are freckled with an old man's blotches, that his hair is so scanty that whether it's grey or white doesn't register. What is subtle in his face is the washed-out blue of his eyes.

'You travel alone, too,' he remarks, openly seeking the companionship of the moment when Harriet has indicated that the chair beside her is not taken.

'Yes, I do.'

'I can always pick out the English.'

He offers the theory that this is perhaps something the traveller acquires with age and with the experience of many journeys. 'You'll probably see,' he adds.

The companion of the bearded man who is sketching the couple on the sofa leans forward and smiles over what she sees. In the hall the American father has persuaded his older children to go to bed. The mother still

soothes her baby, still pacing up and down. The small man who so agitatedly glanced about the dining-room passes rapidly through the hall, carrying two cups of coffee.

'They certainly feed you,' Harriet's companion remarks, 'these days at
the Cesarina.'

'Yes.'

'Quite scanty, the food was once.'

'Yes, I remember.'

'I mean, a longish time ago.'

'The first summer I came here I was ten.'

He calculates, glancing at her face to guess her age. Before his own first
time, he says, which was the spring of 1987. He has been coming since, he
says, and asks if she has.

'My parents separated.'

'I'm sorry.'

'They'd been coming here all their married lives. They were fond of
this place.'

'Some people fall for it. Others not at all.'

'My brother found it boring.'

'A child might easily.'

'I never did.'

'Interesting, those two chaps picking up the girls. I wonder if they'll
ever cope with coach tours at the Cesarina.'

He talks. Harriet doesn't listen. This love affair had once, like the other
affairs before it, felt like the exorcism of the disappointment that so
drearily coloured her life when her parents went their separate ways.
There were no quarrels when her parents separated, no bitterness, no
drama. They told their children gently, neither blamed the other. Both –
for years apparently – had been involved with other people. Both said the
separation was a happier outcome than staying together for the sake of
the family. They used those words, and Harriet has never forgotten them.
Her brother shrugged the disappointment off, but for Harriet it did not
begin to go away until the first of her love affairs. And always, when a love
affair ended, there had been no exorcism after all.

'I'm off tomorrow,' the old man says.

She nods. In the hall the baby in the American mother's arms is sleeping at last. The mother smiles at someone Harriet can't see and then
moves towards the wide stone staircase. The couple on the sofa, still unaware that they've been sketched, stand up and go away. The agitated
little man bustles through the hall again.

'Sorry to go,' Harriet's companion finishes something he has been saying, then tells her about his journey: by train because he doesn't care for flying. Lunch in Milan, dinner in Zurich, on neither occasion leaving the railway station. The eleven-o'clock sleeper from Zurich.

'We used to drive out when I came with my parents.'

'I haven't ever done that. And of course won't ever now.'

'I liked it.'

At the time it didn't seem unreal or artificial. Their smiling faces didn't, nor the pleasure they seemed to take in poky French hotels where only the food was good, nor their chattering to one another in the front of the car, their badinage and arguments. Yet retrospect insisted that reality was elsewhere; that reality was surreptitious lunches with two other people, and afternoon rooms, and guile; that reality was a web of lies until one of them found out, it didn't matter which; that reality was when there had to be something better than what the family offered.

'So this time you have come alone?'

He may have said it twice, she isn't sure. Something about his expression suggests he has.

'Yes.'

He speaks of solitude. It offers a quality that is hard to define; much more than the cliché of getting to know yourself. He himself has been on his own for many years and has discovered consolation in that very circumstance, which is an irony of a kind, he supposes.

'I was to go somewhere else.' She doesn't know why she makes this revelation. Politeness, perhaps. On other evenings, after dinner, she has seen this man in conversation with whomever he has chosen to sit beside. He is polite himself. He sounds more interested than inquisitive.

'You changed your mind?'

'A friendship fell apart.'

'Ah.'

'I should be on an island in the sun.'

'And where is that, if I may ask?'

'Skyros it's called. Renowned for its therapies.'

'Therapies?'

'They're a fashion.'

'For the ill, is this? If I may say so, you don't look ill.'

'No, I'm not ill.' Unable to keep the men she loves in love with her. But of course not ill.

'In fact, you look supremely healthy.' He smiles. His teeth are still his own. 'If I may say so.'

'I'm not so sure that I like islands in the sun. But even so I wanted to go there.'

'For the therapies?'

'No, I would have avoided that. Sand therapy, water therapy, sex therapy, image therapy, holistic counselling. I would have steered clear, I think.'

'Being on your own's a therapy too, of course. Although it's nice to have a chat.'

She doesn't listen; he goes on talking. On the island of Skyros tourists beat drums at sunset and welcome the dawn with song. Or they may simply swim and play, or discover the undiscovered self. The Pensione Cesarina – even the pensione transformed by the Germans and the Dutch – offers nothing like it. Nor would it offer enough to her parents any more. Her divided parents travel grandly now.

'I see *The Spanish Farm* is still on the shelves.' The old man has risen and hovers for a moment. 'I doubt that anyone's read it since I did in 1987.'

'No, probably not.'

He says goodnight and changes it to goodbye because he has to make an early start. For a moment, it seems to Harriet, he hesitates, something about his stance suggesting that he'd like to be invited to stay, to be offered a cup of coffee or a drink. Then he goes, without saying anything else. Lonely in old age, she suddenly realizes, wondering why she didn't notice that when he was talking to her. Lonely in spite of all he claims for solitude.

'Goodbye,' she calls after him, but he doesn't hear. They were to come back here the summer of the separation; instead there were cancellations then too, and an empty fortnight.

'*Buona notte.*' The boy in the white jacket smiles tentatively from his cupboard as she passes through the hall. He's new tonight; it was another boy before. She hasn't realized that either.

She walks through the heat of the morning on the narrow road to the town, by the graveyard and the abandoned petrol pumps. A few cars pass her, coming from the pensione, for the road leads hardly anywhere else, petering out eventually. It would have been hotter on the island of Skyros.

Clouds have gathered in one part of the sky, behind her as she walks. The shade of clouds might make it cooler, she tells herself, but so far they are not close enough to the sun for that. The road widens and gradually the incline becomes less steep as she approaches the town. There's a park with concrete seats and the first of the churches, its chosen saint Agnese of this town.

There's no one in the park until Harriet sits there beneath the chestnut trees in a corner. Far below her, as the town tails off again, a main road begins to wind through clumps of needle pines and umbrella pines to join, far out of sight, a motorway. 'But weren't we happy?' she hears herself exclaim, a little shrill because she couldn't help it. Yes, they were happy, he agreed at once, anxious to make that clear. Not happy enough was what he meant, and you could tell; something not quite right. She asked him and he didn't know, genuine in his bewilderment.

When she feels cooler she walks on, down shaded, narrow streets to the central piazza of the town, where she rests again, with a cappuccino at a pavement table.

Italians and tourists move slowly in the unevenly paved square, women with shopping bags and dogs, men leaving the barber's, the tourists in their summery clothes. The church of Santa Fabiola dominates the square, grey steps in front, a brick and stone façade. There is another café, across from the one Harriet has chosen, and a line of market stalls beside it. The town's banks are in the square but not its shops. There's a trattoria and a gelateria, their similar decoration connecting them, side by side. 'Yes, they're all one,' her father said.

In this square her father lifted her high above his head and she looked down and saw his laughing, upturned face and she laughed too, because he joked so. Her mother stuttered out her schoolgirl French in the little hotels where they stayed on the journey out, and blushed with shame when no one understood. 'Oh, this is pleasant!' her mother murmured, a table away from where Harriet is now.

A priest comes down the steps of the church, looks about him, does not see whom he thought he might. A skinny dog goes limping by. The bell of Santa Fabiola chimes twelve o'clock and when it ceases another bell, farther away, begins. Clouds have covered the sun, but the air is as hot as ever. There's still no breeze.

It was in the foyer of the Rembrandt Cinema that he said he didn't think their love affair was working. It was then that she exclaimed, 'But weren't we happy?' They didn't quarrel. Not even afterwards, when she asked him why he had told her in a cinema foyer. He didn't know, he said; it just seemed right in that moment, some fragment of a mood they shared. If it hadn't been for their holiday's being quite soon their relationship might have dragged on for a while. Much better that it shouldn't, he said.

The fourteenth of February in London was quite as black, and cold, and as wintersome as it was at Allington, and was, perhaps, somewhat more melancholy in its coldness. She has read that bit before and couldn't settle to it, and cannot now. She takes her dark glasses off: the clouds are not the pretty bundles she noticed before, white cottonwool as decoration is by Raphael or Perugino. The clouds that have come up so quickly are grey as lead, a sombre panoply pegged out against a blue that's almost lost. The first drops fall when Harriet tries the doors of Santa Fabiola and finds them locked. They will remain so, a notice tersely states, until half-past two.

It had been finally arranged that the marriage should take place in London, she reads in the trattoria. *There were certainly many reasons which would have made a marriage from Courcy Castle more convenient. The De Courcy family were all assembled at their country family residence, and could therefore have been present at the ceremony without cost or trouble.* She isn't hungry; she has ordered risotto, hoping it will be small, and mineral water without gas.

'*C'è del pane o della farina nel piatto? Non devo mangiare della farina,*' a woman is saying, and the gaunt-faced waiter carefully listens, not understanding at first and then excitedly nodding. '*Non c'è farina,*' he replies, pointing at items on the menu. The woman is from the pensione. She's with a lanky young man who might be her son, and Harriet can't identify the language they speak to one another.

'Is fine?' the same waiter asks Harriet as he passes, noticing that she has begun to eat her risotto. She nods and smiles and reads again. The rain outside is heavy now.

The Annunciation in the church of Santa Fabiola is by an unknown artist, perhaps of the school of Filippo Lippi, no one is certain. The angel kneels, grey wings protruding, his lily half hidden by a pillar. The floor is marble, white and green and ochre. The Virgin looks alarmed, right hand arresting her visitor's advance. Beyond – background to the encounter – there are gracious arches, a balustrade and then the sky and hills. There is a soundlessness about the picture, the silence of a mystery: no words are spoken in this captured moment, what's said between the two has been said already.

Harriet's eye records the details: the green folds of the angel's dress, the red beneath it, the mark in the sky that is a dove, the Virgin's book, the stately pillars and the empty vase, the Virgin's slipper, the bare feet of the angel. The distant landscape is soft, as if no heat has ever touched it. It isn't alarm in the Virgin's eyes, it's wonderment. In another moment there'll be serenity. A few tourists glide about the church, whispering now and again. A man in a black overall is mopping the floor of the central aisle and has roped it off at either end. An elderly woman prays before a statue of the Virgin, each bead of her rosary fingered, lips silently murmuring. Incense is cloying on the air.

Harriet walks slowly past flaring candles and the tomb of a local family, past the relics of the altar, and the story of Santa Fabiola flaking in a side chapel. She has not been in this church before, neither during her present visit nor in the past. Her parents didn't bother much with churches; she might have come here on her own yesterday or on any day of her stay but she didn't bother either. Her parents liked the sun in the garden of the pensione, the walk down to the cafés and drives into the hills or to other little towns, to the swimming-pool at Ponte Nicolo.

The woman who has been praying hobbles to light another candle, then prays again, and hobbles off. Returning to the Annunciation, Harriet sits down in the pew that's nearest it. There is blue as well as grey in the wings of the angel, little flecks of blue you don't notice when you look at first. The Virgin's slipper is a shade of brown, the empty vase is bulb-shaped with a slender stem, the Virgin's book had gold on it but only traces remain.

The rain has stopped when Harriet leaves the church, the air is fresher. Too slick and glib, to use her love affairs to restore her faith in love: that thought is there mysteriously. She has cheated in her love affairs: that comes from nowhere too.

Harriet stands a moment longer, alone on the steps of the church, bewildered by this personal revelation, aware instinctively of its truth. The dust of the piazza paving has been washed into the crevices that separate the stones. At the café where she had her cappuccino the waiter is wiping dry the plastic of the chairs.

The sun is still reluctant in the watery sky. On her walk back to the Pensione Cesarina it seems to Harriet that in this respite from the brash smother of heat a different life has crept out of the foliage and stone. A coolness emanates from the road she walks on. Unseen, among the wild geraniums, one bird sings.

Tomorrow, when the sun is again in charge at its time of year, a few midday minutes will wipe away what lingers of this softness. New dust will settle, marble will be warm to touch. Weeks it may be, months perhaps, before rain coaxes out these fragrances that are tender now.

The sun is always pitiless when it returns, harsh in its punishment. In the dried-out garden of the Pensione Cesarina they made her wear a hat she didn't like but they could take the sun themselves, both of them skulking behind dark glasses and high-factor cream. Skyros's sun is its attraction. 'What I need is sun,' he said, and Harriet wonders if he went there after all, if he's there today, not left behind in London, if he even found someone to go with. She sees him in Skyros, windsurfing in Atsitsa Bay, which he has talked about. She sees him with a companion who is uncomplicated and happy in Atsitsa Bay, who tries out a therapy just to see what it's like.

The deck-chairs are sodden at the Pensione Cesarina, rose petals glisten. A glass left on a terrace table has gathered an inch of water. The umbrellas in the outer hall have all been used. Windows, closed for a while, are opened; on the vineyard slopes the sprinklers are turned on again.

Not wanting to be inside, Harriet walks in the garden and among the vines, her shoes drenched. From the town comes the chiming of bells: six o'clock at Santa Fabiola, six o'clock a minute later somewhere else. While she stands alone among the dripping vines she cannot make a connection that she knows is there. There is a blankness in her thoughts, a density that feels like muddle also, until she realizes: the Annunciation was painted after rain. Its distant landscape, glimpsed through arches, has the temporary look that she is seeing now. It was after rain that the angel came: those first cool moments were a chosen time.

In the dining-room the table where the man with the garish shirts sat has been joined to a family table to allow for a party of seven. There is a different woman where the smart Frenchwoman sat, and no one at the table of the old man. The woman who was explaining in the trattoria that she must not eat food containing flour is given consommé instead of ravioli. New faces are dotted everywhere.

'*Buona sera,*' the rust-haired waitress greets Harriet, and the waitress with glasses brings her salad.

'*Grazie,*' Harriet murmurs.

'*Prego, signora.*'

She pours her wine, breaks off a crust of bread. It's noisy in the dining-room now, dishes clattering, the babble of voices. It felt like noise in the foyer of the Rembrandt Cinema when he told her: the uproar of shock, although in fact it was quite silent there. Bright, harsh colours flashed through her consciousness, as if some rush of blood exploded in a kaleidoscope of distress. For a moment in the foyer of the cinema she closed her eyes, as she had when they told her they weren't to be a family any more.

She might have sent them postcards, but she hasn't. She might have reported that breakfast at the pensione is more than coffee and rolls since the Germans and the Dutch and the Swiss have begun to come: cheese and cold meats, fruit and cereals, fresh sponge cake, a buffet on the terrace. Each morning she has sat there reading *The Small House at Allington*, wondering if they would like to know of the breakfast-time improvement. She wondered today if it would interest them to learn that the abandoned petrol pumps are still there on the road to the town, or that she sat in the deserted park beneath the chestnut trees. She thought of sending him a postcard too, but in the end she didn't. His predecessor it was who encouraged her to bring long novels on holiday, *The Tenant of Wildfell Hall, The Mill on the Floss.*

It's beef tonight, with spinach. And afterwards Harriet has *dolce,* remembering this sodden yellow raisin cake from the past. She won't taste that again; as mysteriously as she knows she has cheated without meaning to in her love affairs, she knows she won't come back, alone or with someone else. Coming back has been done, a private journey that chance suggested. Tomorrow she'll be gone.

In the room with the bookcases and the Giotto reproductions she watches while people drink their grappa or their Stock, or ask the white-jacketed boy for more coffee, or pick up conversations with one another. The Belgian girls have got to know the young Englishman who goes down after wrecks and Nev who's in the business world. All four pass through the room on their way to the terrace, the girls with white cardigans draped on their shoulders because it isn't as warm as it was last night. 'That man drew us!' a voice cries, and the couple who were sketched last night gaze down at their hardly recognizable selves in the pensione's comment book.

He backed away, as others have, when she asked too much of love, when she tried to change the circumstances that are the past by imposing a brighter present, and constancy in the future above all else. She has been the victim of herself: with vivid clarity she knows that now and wonders why she does and why she didn't before. Nothing tells her when she ponders the solitude of her stay in the Pensione Cesarina, and she senses that nothing ever will.

She sees again the brown-and-green striped tie of the old man who talked about being on your own, and the freckles that are blotches on his forehead. She sees herself walking in the morning heat past the graveyard and the rusted petrol pumps. She sees herself seeking the shade of the chestnut trees in the park, and crossing the piazza to the trattoria when the first raindrops fell. She hears the swish of the cleaner's mop in the church of Santa Fabiola, she hears the tourists' whisper. The fingers of the praying woman flutter on her beads, the candles flare. The story of Santa Fabiola is lost in the shadows that were once the people of her life, the family tomb reeks odourlessly of death. Rain has sweetened the breathless air, the angel comes mysteriously also.

Widows

Waking on a warm, bright morning in early October, Catherine found herself a widow. In some moment during the night Matthew had gone peacefully: had there been pain or distress she would have known it. Yet what lay beside her in the bed was less than a photograph now, the fallen jaw harshly distorting a face she'd loved.

Tears ran on Catherine's cheeks and dripped on to her nightdress. She knelt by the bedside, then drew the sheet over the still features. Quiet, gently spoken, given to thought before offering an opinion, her husband had been regarded by Catherine as cleverer and wiser than she was herself, and more charitable in his view of other people. In his business life – the sale of agricultural machinery – he had been known as a man of his word. For miles around – far beyond the town and its immediate neighbourhood – the farm people who had been his customers repaid his honesty and straight dealing with respect. At Christmas there had been gifts of fowls and fish, jars of cream, sacks of potatoes. The funeral would be well attended. 'There'll be a comfort in the memories, Catherine,' Matthew had said more than once, attempting to anticipate the melancholy of their separation: they had known that it was soon to be.

He would have held the memories to him if he'd been the one remaining. 'Whichever is left,' he reminded Catherine as they grew old, 'it's only for the time being.' And in that time-being one of them would manage in what had previously been the other's domain: he ironing his sheets and trousers, working the washing-machine, cooking as he had watched her cook, using the Electrolux; she arranging for someone to undertake the small repairs he had attended to in the house if she or her sister couldn't manage them, paying the household bills and keeping an eye on the bank balance. Matthew had never minded talking about their separation, and had taught her not to mind either.

On her knees by the bedside Catherine prayed, then her tears came again. She reached out for his hand and grasped the cold, stiff fingers beneath the bedclothes. 'Oh, love,' she whispered. 'Oh, love.'

The three sons of the marriage came for the funeral, remaining briefly, with their families, in the town where they had spent their childhood.

Father Cahill intoned the last words in the cemetery, and soon after that
Catherine and her sister Alicia were alone in the house again. Alicia had
lived there since her own husband's death, nine years ago; she was the
older of the two sisters – fifty-seven, almost fifty-eight.

The house that for Catherine was still haunted by her husband's recent
presence was comfortable, with a narrow hall and a kitchen at the back,
and bedrooms on two floors. Outside, it was colour-washed blue, with
white window-frames and hall-door, the last house of the town, the first
on the Dublin road. Opposite was the convent school, behind silver-
painted railings, three sides enclosed by the drab concrete of its classrooms and the nuns' house, its play-yard often bustling into noisy
excitement. Once upon a time Catherine and Alicia had played there
themselves, hardly noticing the house across the road, blue then also.

'You're all right?' Alicia said on the evening of the funeral, when
together they cleared up the glasses sherry had been drunk from, and
cups and saucers. On the sideboard in the dining-room the stoppers of
the decanters had not yet been replaced, crumbs not yet brushed from the
dining-table cloth. 'Yes, I'm all right,' Catherine said. In her girlhood she
had been pretty – slender and dark, and shyly smiling, dimples in both
cheeks. Alicia, taller, dark also, had been considered the beauty of the
town. Now, Catherine was greying, and plump about the face, the joints
of her fingers a little swollen. Alicia was straight-backed, her beauty still
recalled in features that were classically proportioned, her hair greyer
than her sister's.

'Good of them all to come,' Catherine said.

'People liked Matthew.'

'Yes.'

For a moment Catherine felt the rising of her tears, the first time since
the morning of the death, but stoically she held them in. Their marriage
had not gone. Their marriage was still there in children and in grandchildren, in the voices that had spoken well of it, in the bed they had shared,
and in remembering. The time-being would not be endless: he had said
that too. 'You're managing, Catherine?' people asked, the same words
often used, and she tried to convey that strength still came from all there
had been.

The day after the funeral Fagan from the solicitors' office explained to
Catherine the contents of the few papers he brought to the house. It took
ten minutes.

'Well, that's that,' he said, and for a moment the finality with which he
spoke reminded Catherine of the coffin slipping down, filling the hole

that had been dug for it. The papers lay neatly on the well-polished surface of the dining-room table, cleared now of the debris of the day before,
and of the cloth that had protected it. Fagan drank a cup of instant coffee
and said she had only to pick up the phone if ever there was anything.

'I'll help you,' Alicia said later that same morning when Catherine
mentioned Matthew's personal belongings. Clothes and shoes would be
accepted gratefully by one of the charities with which Alicia was connected. The signet ring, the watch, the tie-pin, the matching fountain-pen
and propelling pencil were earmarked for the family, to be shared among
Catherine's sons. Shaving things were thrown away.

Recalling the same sorting out of possessions at the time of her own
loss, Alicia was in no way distressed. She had experienced little emotion
when her husband's death occurred: for the last nineteen years of her
marriage she had not loved him.

'You've been a strength,' Catherine said, for her sister had been that
and more, looking after her as she used to, years ago, when they were
children.

'Oh no, no,' came Alicia's deprecation.

Thomas Pius John Leary was by trade a painter and decorator. He had,
for this work, no special qualifications beyond experience; he brought to
it no special skill. As a result, he was often accused of poor workman-
ship, which in turn led to disputes about payment. But he charged less
than his competitors and so ensured a reasonably steady demand for his
services. When for one reason or another the demand wasn't there he
took on any kind of odd job he was offered.

Leary was middle-aged now, married, the father of six children. He
was a small, wiry man with tight features and bloodshot eyes, his spare-
ness occasionally reminding people of a hedgerow animal they could not
readily name. Sparse grey hair was brushed straight back from the narrow dome of his forehead. Two forefingers, thumbs, middle fingers, upper
lip and teeth, were stained brown from cigarettes he manufactured with
the aid of a small machine. Leary did not wear overalls when at work and
was rarely encountered in clothes that did not bear splashes of paint.

It was in this condition, the damp end of a cigarette emerging from a
cupped palm, that he presented himself to Catherine and Alicia one afternoon in November, six weeks after the death. He stood on the doorstep,
declaring his regrets and his sympathy in a low voice, not meeting Catherine's eye. In the time that had passed, other people had come to the
door and said much the same thing, not many, only those who found it
difficult to write a letter and considered the use of the telephone to be

inappropriate in such circumstances. They'd made a brief statement and then had hurried off. Leary appeared inclined to linger.

'That's very good of you, Mr Leary,' Catherine said.

A few months ago he had repainted the front of the house, the same pale blue. He had renewed the white gloss of the window-frames. 'Poor Leary's desperate for work,' Matthew had said. 'Will we give the rogue a go?' Alicia had been against it, Leary not being a man she'd cared for when he'd done other jobs for them. Catherine, although she didn't much care for Leary either, felt sorry for anyone who was up against it.

'Could I step in for a minute?'

Across the street the convent children were running about in the play-yard before their afternoon classes began. Still watching them, Catherine was aware of checking a frown that had begun to gather. He was looking for more work, she supposed, but there was no question of that. Alicia's misgivings had been justified: there'd been skimping on the amount and quality of the paint used, and inadequate preparation. 'We'll know not to do that again,' Matthew had said. Besides, there wasn't anything else at present.

'Of course.' Catherine stood aside while Leary passed into the long, narrow hall. She led the way down it, to the kitchen because it was warm there. Alicia was polishing the cutlery at the table, a task she undertook once a month.

'Sit down, Mr Leary,' Catherine invited, pulling a chair out for him.

'I was saying I was sorry,' he said to Alicia. 'If there's any way I can assist at all, any little job, I'm always there.'

'It's kind of you, Mr Leary,' Catherine said swiftly, in case her sister responded more tartly.

'I knew him since we were lads. He used be at the Christian Brothers'.'

'Yes.'

'Great old days.'

He seemed embarrassed. He wanted to say something but was having difficulty. One hand went into a pocket of his jacket. Catherine watched it playing with the little contrivance he used for rolling his cigarettes. But the hand came out empty. Nervously, it was rubbed against its partner.

'It's awkward,' Leary said.

'What's awkward, Mr Leary?'

'It isn't easy, how to put it to you. I didn't come before because of your trouble.'

Alicia laid down the cloth with which she had been applying God-dard's Silver Polish to the cutlery and Catherine watched her sister's slow, deliberate movements as she shined the last of the forks and then drew off her pink rubber gloves and placed them one on top of the other beside her. Alicia could sense something; she often had a way of knowing what was coming next.

'I don't know are you aware,' Leary enquired, addressing only Catherine, 'it wasn't paid for?'

'What wasn't?'

'The job I done for you.'

'You don't mean painting the front?'

'I do, ma'am.'

'But of course it was paid for.'

He sighed softly. An outstanding bill was an embarrassment, he said. Because of the death it was an embarrassment.

'My husband paid for the work that was done.'

'Ah no, no.'

The frown Catherine had checked a few moments ago wrinkled her forehead. She knew the bill had been paid. She knew because Matthew had said Leary would want cash, and she had taken the money out of her own Irish Nationwide account since she had easy access to it. 'I'll see you right at the end of the month,' Matthew had promised. It was an arrangement they often had; the building-society account in her name existed for this kind of thing.

'Two hundred and twenty-six pounds is the extent of the damage.' Leary smiled shiftily. 'With the discount for cash.'

She didn't tell him she'd withdrawn the money herself. That wasn't his business. She watched the extreme tip of his tongue licking his upper lip. He wiped his mouth with the back of a paint-stained hand. Softly, Alicia was replacing forks and spoons in the cutlery container.

'It was September the account was sent out. The wife does all that type of thing.'

'The bill was paid promptly. My husband always paid bills promptly.'

She remembered the occasion perfectly. 'I'll bring it down to him now,' Matthew had said, glancing across the kitchen at the clock. Every evening he walked to McKenny's bar and remained there for three-quarters of an hour or so, depending on the company. That evening he'd have gone the long way round, by French Street, in order to call in at the Learys' house in Brady's Lane. Before he left he had taken the notes from the brown Nationwide envelope and counted them, slowly, just as she'd done herself earlier. She'd seen the bill in his hand. 'Chancing his arm with the taxman,' she remembered his remarking lightly, a reference to Leary's preference for cash.

On his return he would have hung his cap on its hook in the scullery passage and settled down at the kitchen table with the *Evening Press*, which he bought in Healy's sweetshop on his way back from McKenny's. He went to the public house for conversation as much as anything, and afterwards passed on to Alicia and herself any news he had gleaned. Bottled Smithwick's was his drink.

'D'you remember it?' Catherine appealed to her sister because although she could herself so clearly recall Matthew's departure from the house on that particular September evening, his return eluded her. It lay smothered somewhere beneath the evening routine, nothing making it special, as the banknotes in the envelope had marked the other.

'I remember talk about money,' Alicia recalled, 'earlier that day. If I've got it right, I was out at the Legion of Mary in the evening.'

'A while back the wife noticed the way the bill was unpaid,' Leary went on, having paused politely to hear these recollections. '"It's the death that's in it," the wife said. She'd have eaten the face off me if I'd bothered you in your trouble.'

'Excuse me,' Catherine said.

She left the kitchen and went to look on the spike in the side-cupboard in the passage, where all receipts were kept. This one should have been close to the top, but it wasn't. It wasn't further down either. It wasn't in the cupboard drawers. She went through the contents of three box-files in case it had been bundled into one in error. Again she didn't find it.

She returned to the kitchen with the next best thing: the Nationwide Building Society account book. She opened it and placed it in front of Leary. She pointed at the entry that recorded the withdrawal of two hundred and twenty-six pounds. She could tell that there had been no conversation in her absence. Leary would have tried to get some kind of talk going, but Alicia wouldn't have responded.

'September the eighth,' Catherine said, emphasizing the printed date with a forefinger. 'A Wednesday it was.'

In silence Leary perused the entry. He shook his head. The tight features of his face tightened even more, bunching together into a knot of bewilderment. Catherine glanced at her sister. He was putting it on, Alicia's expression indicated.

'The money was taken out all right,' Leary said eventually. 'Did he put it to another use in that case?'

'Another use?'

'Did you locate a receipt, missus?'

He spoke softly, not in the cagey, underhand tone of someone attempting to get something for nothing. Catherine was still standing. He turned his head to one side in order to squint up at her. He sounded apologetic, but all that could be put on also.

'I brought the receipt book over with me,' he said.

He handed it to her, a fat greasy notebook with a grey marbled cover that had *The Challenge Receipt Book* printed on it. Blue carbon paper protruded from the dog-eared pages.

'Any receipt that's issued would have a copy left behind here,' he said, speaking now to Alicia, across the table. 'The top copy for the customer, the carbon for ourselves. You couldn't do business without you keep a record of receipts.'

He stood up then. He opened the book and displayed its unused pages, each with the same printed heading: *In account with T. P. Leary.* He showed Catherine how the details of a bill were recorded on the flimsy page beneath the carbon sheet and how, when a bill was paid, acknowledgement was recorded also: *Paid with thanks*, with the date and the careful scrawl of Mrs Leary's signature. He passed the receipt book to Alicia, pointing out these details to her also.

'Anything could have happened to that receipt,' Alicia said. 'In the circumstances.'

'If a receipt was issued, missus, there'd be a record of it here.'

Alicia placed the receipt book beside the much slimmer building-society book on the pale surface of the table. Leary's attention remained with the former, his scrutiny an emphasis of the facts it contained. The evidence offered otherwise was not for him to comment upon: so the steadiness of his gaze insisted.

'My husband counted those notes at this very table,' Catherine said. 'He took them out of the brown envelope that they were put into at the Nationwide.'

'It's a mystery so.'

It wasn't any such thing; there was no mystery whatsoever. The bill had been paid. Both sisters knew that; in their different ways they guessed that Leary – and presumably his wife as well – had planned this dishonesty as soon as they realized death gave them the opportunity. Matthew had obliged them by paying cash so that they could defraud the taxation authorities. He had further obliged them by dying. Catherine said:

'My husband walked out of this house with that envelope in his pocket. Are you telling me he didn't reach you?'

'Was he robbed? Would it be that? You hear terrible things these days.'

'Oh, for heaven's sake!'

Leary wagged his head in his meditative way. It was unlikely certainly, he agreed. Anyone robbed would have gone to the Guards. Anyone robbed would have mentioned it when he came back to the house again.

'The bill was paid, Mr Leary.'

'All the same, we have to go by the receipt. At the heel of the hunt there's the matter of a receipt.'

Alicia shook her head. Either a receipt wasn't issued in the first place, she said, or else it had been mislaid. 'There's a confusion when a person dies,' she said.

If Catherine had been able to produce the receipt Leary would have blamed his wife. He'd have blandly stated that she'd got her wires crossed. He'd have said the first thing that came into his head and then have gone away.

'The only thing is,' he said instead, 'a sum like that is sizeable. I couldn't afford let it go.'

Both Catherine and Alicia had seen Mrs Leary in the shops, red-haired, like a tinker, a bigger woman than her husband, probably the brains of the two. The Learys were liars and worse than liars; the chance had come and the temptation had been too much for them. 'Ah sure, those two have plenty,' the woman would have said. The sisters wondered if the Learys had tricked the bereaved before, and imagined they had. Leary said:

'It's hard on a man that's done work for you.'

Catherine moved towards the kitchen door. Leary ambled after her down the hall. She remembered the evening more clearly even than a while ago: a Wednesday it definitely had been, the day of the Sweetman girl's wedding; and it came back to her, also, Alicia hurrying out on her Legion of Mary business. There'd been talk in McKenny's about the wedding, the unusual choice of mid-week, which apparently had something to do with visitors coming from America. She opened the hall-door in silence. Across the street, beyond the silver-coloured railings, the children were still running about in the convent yard. Watery sunlight lightened the unadorned concrete of the classrooms and the nuns' house.

'What'll I do?' Leary asked, wide-eyed, bloodshot, squinting at her.

Catherine said nothing.

They talked about it. It could be, Alicia said, that the receipt had remained in one of Matthew's pockets, that a jacket she had disposed of to one of her charities had later found itself in the Learys' hands, having passed through a jumble sale. She could imagine Mrs Leary coming across it, and the temptation being too much. Leary was as weak as water, she said, adding that the tinker wife was a woman who never looked you in the eye. Foxy-faced and furtive, Mrs Leary pushed a ramshackle pram about the streets, her ragged children cowering in her presence. It was she who would have removed the flimsy carbon copy from the soiled receipt book. Leary would have been putty in her hands.

In the kitchen they sat down at the table from which Alicia had cleared away the polished cutlery. Matthew had died as tidily as he'd lived, Alicia said: all his life he'd been meticulous. The Learys had failed to take that into account in any way whatsoever. If it came to a court of law the Learys wouldn't have a leg to stand on, with the written evidence that the precise amount taken out of the building society matched the amount of the bill, and further evidence in Matthew's reputation for promptness about settling debts.

'What I'm wondering is,' Alicia said, 'should we go to the Guards?'

'The Guards?'

'He shouldn't have come here like that.'

That evening there arrived a bill for the amount quoted by Leary, marked *Account rendered*. It was dropped through the letter-box and was discovered the next morning beneath the *Irish Independent* on the hall doormat.

'The little twister!' Alicia furiously exclaimed.

From the road outside the house came the morning commands of the convent girl in charge of the crossing to the school. 'Get ready!' 'Prepare to cross!' 'Cross now!' Impertinence had been added to dishonesty, Alicia declared in outraged tones. It was as though it had never been pointed out to Leary that Matthew had left the house on the evening in question with two hundred and twenty-six pounds in an envelope, that Leary's attention had never been drawn to the clear evidence of the building-society entry.

'It beats me,' Catherine said, and in the hall Alicia turned sharply and said it was as clear as day. Again she mentioned going to the Guards. A single visit from Sergeant McBride, she maintained, and the Learys would abandon their cheek. From the play-yard the yells of the girls increased as more girls arrived there, and then the hand-bell sounded; a moment later there was silence.

'I'm only wondering,' Catherine said, 'if there's some kind of a mistake.'

'There's no mistake, Catherine.'

Alicia didn't comment further. She led the way to the kitchen and half filled a saucepan with water for their two boiled eggs. Catherine cut bread for toast. When she and Alicia had been girls in that same play-yard she hadn't known of Matthew's existence. Years passed before she even noticed him, at Mass one Saturday night. And it was ages before he first invited her to go out with him, for a walk the first time, and then for a drive.

'What d'you think happened then?' Alicia asked. 'That Matthew bet the money on a dog? That he owed it for drink consumed? Have sense, Catherine.'

Had it been Alicia's own husband whom Leary had charged with neg-ligence, there would have been no necessary suspension of disbelief: feck-less and a nuisance, involved during his marriage with at least one other woman in the town, frequenter of race-courses and dog-tracks and bars, he had ended in an early grave. This shared thought – that behaviour which was ludicrous when attached to Matthew had been as natural in Alicia's husband as breathing – was there between the sisters, but was not mentioned.

'If Father Cahill got Leary on his own,' Alicia began, but Catherine interrupted. She didn't want that, she said; she didn't want other people brought into this, not even Father Cahill. She didn't want a fuss about whether or not her husband had paid a bill.

'You'll get more of these,' Alicia warned, laying a finger on the enve-lope that had been put through the letter-box. 'They'll keep on coming.'

'Yes.'

In the night Catherine had lain awake, wondering if Matthew had maybe lost the money on his walk to the Learys' house that evening, if he'd put his hand in his pocket and found it wasn't there and then been too ashamed to say. It wasn't like him; it didn't make much more sense than thinking he had been a secretive man, with private shortcomings all the years she'd been married to him. When Alicia's husband died Mat-thew had said it was hard to feel sorry, and she'd agreed. Three times Alicia had been left on her own, for periods that varied in length, and on each occasion they'd thought the man was gone for good; but he returned and Alicia always took him back. Of course Matthew hadn't lost the money; it was as silly to think that as to wonder if he'd been a gambler.

'In case they'd try it on anyone else,' Alicia was saying, 'isn't it better they should be shown up? Is a man who'd get up to that kind of game safe to be left in people's houses the way a workman is?'

That morning they didn't mention the matter again. They washed up the breakfast dishes and then Catherine went out to the shops, which was always her chore, while Alicia cleaned the stairs and the hall, the day being a Thursday. As Catherine made her way through the familiar streets, and then while Mr Deegan sliced bacon for her and Gilligan greeted her in the hardware, she thought about the journey her husband had made that Wednesday evening in September. Involuntarily, she glanced into Healy's, where he had bought the *Evening Press*, and into McKenny's bar. Every evening except Sunday he had brought back the news, bits of gos-sip, anything he'd heard. It was at this time, too, that he went to Confes-sion, on such occasions leaving the house half an hour earlier.

In French Street a countrywoman opened her car door without looking and knocked a cyclist over. 'Ah, no harm done,' the youth on the bicycle said, the delivery boy for Lawless the West Street butcher, the last delivery boy in the town. 'Sure, I never saw him at all,' the countrywoman protested to Catherine as she went by. The car door was dinged, but the woman said what did it matter if the lad was all right?

Culliney, the traveller from Limerick Shirts, was in town that day. Matthew had always bought his shirts direct from Culliney, the same striped pattern, the stripe blue or brown. Culliney had his measurements, the way he had the measurements of men all over Munster and Connacht, which was his area. Catherine could tell when she saw Culliney coming towards her that he didn't know about the death, and she braced herself to tell him. When she did so he put a hand on her arm and spoke in a whisper, saying that Matthew had been a good man. If there was anything he could ever do, he said, if there was any way he could help. More people said that than didn't.

It was then that Catherine saw Mrs Leary. The house-painter's wife was pushing her pram, a child holding on to it as she advanced. Catherine crossed the street, wondering if the woman had seen her and suspecting she had. In Jerety's she selected a pan loaf from the yesterday's rack, since neither she nor Alicia liked fresh bread and yesterday's was always reduced. When she emerged, Mrs Leary was not to be seen.

'Nothing only a woman knocked young Nallen off his bike,' she reported to Alicia when she returned to the house. '*Is* he a Nallen, that boy of Lawless's?'

'Or a Keane, is he? Big head on him?'

'I don't think he's a Keane. Someone told me a Nallen. Whoever he is, there's no harm done.' She didn't say she'd seen Mrs Leary because she didn't want to raise the subject of what had occurred again. She knew that Alicia was right: the bill would keep coming unless she did something about it. Once they'd set out on the course they'd chosen, why should the Learys give up? Alicia didn't refer to the Learys either but that evening, when they had switched off the television and were preparing to go to bed, Catherine said:

'I think I'll pay them. Simplest, that would be.'

With her right hand on the newel of the banister, about to ascend the stairs, Alicia stared in disbelief at her sister. When Catherine nodded and continued on her way to the kitchen she followed her.

'But you can't.' Alicia stood in the doorway while Catherine washed and rinsed the cups they'd drunk their bedtime tea from. 'You can't just pay them what isn't owing.'

Catherine turned the tap off at the sink and set the cups to drain, slipping the accompanying saucers between the plastic bars of the drainer. Tomorrow she would withdraw the same sum from the building-society account and take it herself to the Learys in Brady's Lane. She would stand there while a receipt was issued.

'Catherine, you can't hand out more than two hundred pounds.'

'I'd rather.'

As she spoke, she changed her mind about the detail of the payment. Matthew had been obliging Leary by paying cash, but there was no need to oblige him any more. She would arrange for the Irish Nationwide to draw a cheque payable to T. P. Leary. She would bring it round to the Learys instead of a wad of notes.

'They've taken you for a fool,' Alicia said.

'I know they have.'

'Leary should go behind bars. You're aiding and abetting him. Have sense, woman.'

A disappointment rose in Alicia, bewildering and muddled. The death of her own husband had brought an end, and her expectation had been that widowhood for her sister would be the same. Her expectation had been that in their shared state they would be as once they were, now that marriage was over, packed away with their similar mourning clothes. Yet almost palpable in the kitchen was Catherine's resolve that what still remained for her should not be damaged by a fuss of protest over a confidence trick. The Guards investigating clothes sold at a jumble sale, strangers asked if a house-painter's wife had bought this garment or that, private intimacies made public: Catherine was paying money in case, somehow, the memory of her husband should be accidentally tarnished. And knowing her sister well, Alicia knew that this resolve would become more stubborn as more time passed. It would mark and influence her sister; it would breed new eccentricities in her. If Leary had not come that day there would have been something else.

'You'd have the man back, I suppose?' Alicia said, trying to hurt and knowing she succeeded. 'You'd have him back in to paint again, to lift the bits and pieces from your dressing-table?'

'It's not to do with Leary.'

'What's it to do with then?'

'Let's leave it.'

Hanging up a tea-towel, Catherine noticed that her fingers were trembling. They never quarrelled; even in childhood they hadn't. In all the years Alicia had lived in the house she had never spoken in this unpleasant way, her voice rudely raised.

'They're walking all over you, Catherine.'

'Yes.'

They did not speak again, not even to say goodnight. Alicia closed her bedroom door, telling herself crossly that her expectation had not been a greedy one. She had been unhappy in her foolish marriage, and after it she had been beholden in this house. Although it ran against her nature to do so, she had borne her lot without complaint; why should she not fairly have hoped that in widowhood they would again be sisters first of all?

In her bedroom Catherine undressed and for a moment caught a glimpse of her nakedness in her dressing-table looking-glass. She missed his warmth in bed, a hand holding hers before they slept, that last embrace, and sometimes in the night his voice saying he loved her. She pulled her nightdress on, then knelt to pray before she turned the light out.

Some instinct, vague and imprecise, drew her in the darkness on to the territory of Alicia's disappointment. In the family photographs – some clearly defined, some drained of detail, affected by the sun – they were the sisters they had been: Alicia beautiful, confidently smiling; Catherine in her care. Catherine's first memory was of a yellow flower, and sunlight, and a white cloth hat put on her head. That flower was a cowslip, Alicia told her afterwards, and told her that they'd gone with their mother to the ruins by the river that day, that it was she who found the cowslip. 'Look, Catherine,' she'd said. 'A lovely flower.' Catherine had watched in admiration when Alicia paraded in her First Communion dress, and later when boys paid her attention. Alicia was the important one, responsible, reliable, right about things, offered the deference that was an older sister's due. She'd been a strength, Catherine said after the funeral, and Alicia was pleased, even though she shook her head.

Catherine dropped into sleep after half an hour of wakefulness. She woke up a few times in the night, on each occasion to find her thoughts full of the decision she had made and of her sister's outraged face, the two tiny patches of red that had come into it, high up on her cheeks, the snap of disdain in her eyes. 'A laughing-stock,' Alicia said in a dream. 'No more than a laughing-stock, Catherine.'

As Catherine lay there she imagined the silent breakfast there would be, and saw herself walking to Brady's Lane, and Leary fiddling with his cigarette-making gadget, and Mrs Leary in fluffy pink slippers, her stockingless legs mottled from being too close to the fire. Tea would be offered, but Catherine would refuse it. 'A decenter man never stood in a pair of shoes,' Leary could be counted upon to state.

She did not sleep again. She watched the darkness lighten, heard the first cars of the day pass on the road outside the house. By chance, a petty dishonesty had made death a potency for her sister, as it had not been when she was widowed herself. Alicia had cheated it of its due; it took from her now, as it had not then.

Catherine knew this intuition was no trick of her tired mind. While they were widows in her house Alicia's jealousy would be the truth they shared, tonight's few moments of its presence lingering insistently. Widows were widows first. Catherine would mourn, and feel in solitude the warmth of love. For Alicia there was the memory of her beauty.

Gilbert's Mother

On November 20th 1989, a Monday, in an area of South London not previously notable for acts of violence, Carol Dickson, a nineteen-year-old shop assistant, was bludgeoned to death between the hours of ten-fifteen and midnight. At approximately nine-fifty she had said goodnight to her friend Lindsayanne Trotter, with whom she had been watching *Coronation Street*, *Brookside* and *Boon*. She set out to walk the seven hundred yards to her parents' house on the Ralelands estate, but did not arrive. Her parents, imagining that she and Lindsayanne had gone to a disco – notwithstanding that the night was Monday – went to bed at eleven o'clock, their normal practice whether their daughter had returned to the house or not. Carol Dickson's body was discovered by a window-cleaner the following morning, lying on fallen leaves and woody straggles of cotoneaster, more than a mile and a half away, in Old Engine Way. Not wishing to become involved in what he described as 'obviously something tacky', the window-cleaner remounted his bicycle and rode on; an hour later schoolchildren reported a dead body in the bushes in Old Engine Way. Since the window-cleaner – Ronald Craig Thomas – was known to take this route along Old Engine Way every weekday morning, he was later interrupted in his work and questioned by the police. At midday on that same day, in broadcasting news of the tragedy, a radio announcer drew attention to this fact, stating that a man was helping the police with their enquiries. He also stated that Carol Dickson had been raped before her death, which was either a misinterpretation of information passed on to him or speculation on his part. It was not true.

Rosalie Mannion, fifty a month ago, peeled potatoes at the sink in her kitchen, listening to *The Archers*. Middle age suited her features; her round, pretty face had taken charge of what wrinkles had come, by chance distributing them favourably. Still a slight figure, she had in no way run to fat; the grey in her hair lent it a distinction that had not been there before. Her brown eyes had lost only a little of the luminosity that had been distinctive in Rosalie's childhood.

'Hullo,' she called out, hearing her son's footsteps on the stairs. She didn't catch Gilbert's reply because of the chatter of voices on the radio, but she knew he would have made one because he always did. *The Arch-ers'* music came on, and then there was talk about irradiated food.

At the time of her divorce it was decided that Rosalie should have the house. That was sixteen years ago, in 1973. There hadn't been a quarrel about the house, nor even an argument. It was Gilbert's home; it was only fair that Gilbert's life should be disrupted as slightly as possible. So 21 Blenheim Avenue, SW15, was made over to her, while the man she'd been married to joined another woman in a Tudor-style property near Virginia Water. Rosalie returned to the botanical research she'd been engaged in before her marriage but after three years she found herself so affected by tiredness that she gave it up. She worked part-time now, in a shop that sold furniture fabrics.

At the back of Rosalie's mind was the comforting feeling that 21 Blen-heim Avenue would one day become Gilbert's livelihood. She planned to convert the attics and the first floor, making them into self-contained flats. She and Gilbert would easily find room to spread themselves on the ground floor, which would of course retain the garden, and after her death that pattern would continue, and there would be an income from what Gilbert's father had invested on his behalf. Gilbert, she knew, would never marry. At present he worked in an architect's office – filing draw-ings, having photocopies made, taking the correspondence to be franked at the post office, delivering packages or collecting them, making tea and coffee, tidying. In the evenings Rosalie heard about the inspirations Gil-bert had had about rearranging the contents of the drawings' cabinets or heard that Kall Kwik were cheaper than Instant Action by twopence a sheet. 'Oh, great,' was all anyone at the office ever said apparently; but his mother listened to the details.

'Was everything all right today?' she asked when he came downstairs again on the evening of November 21st. He rooted in the kitchen drawers for knives and forks and table-mats.

'Mega,' he said, telling her about his day while he made the mustard.

He assembled the cutlery and the table-mats with the galleons on them, and took a tray into the dining-room, where he set the table and turned the television on. They always ate watching the television, but not with plates on their knees, which both of them disliked. They sat side by side at the table and when they'd finished Gilbert helped to wash up and then usually went out, walking to the Arab Boy or the Devonshire Arms, sometimes driving over to the Bull or the Market Gardener. Rosalie had often listened while he explained that he liked to relax in this way after his day's work; that he liked having people around him, while being alone himself; that he liked the sound of voices, and music if someone played the juke-box. He didn't drink much; cider because he didn't care for beer, a couple of half pints in the course of an evening. He often told her that also. He told her everything, Gilbert said, looking at her steadily, his tone of voice indicating that this was not true.

The window-cleaner, Ron, had been reprimanded by the police inspector in charge of the case, and later by a sergeant and by a woman constable. The body in the cotoneaster could have been still alive, he was told; it hadn't been, but it easily could have. It was the duty of any citizen to report something of that nature, instead of which he'd callously ridden off.

Ron, who happened to be the same age as Gilbert Mannion – twenty-five – replied that he had a contract: the shop windows in Disraeli Street and Lower Street had to be washed by nine o'clock; if he delayed, either in the work itself or on his journey to it, that deadline would not be met. As well as which, he had been unnerved by the sight of a half-dressed girl lying all twisted up like that, her two eyes staring at him; no one like that could be alive, he maintained.

For five hours the police had worried about Ron Thomas. He had previous convictions, for petty larceny and damage to property. But there was still nothing to connect him with the crime that had been committed, beyond the fact that he'd failed to report it. In reprimanding him on that count, the inspector, the sergeant and the woman constable managed to assuage their impatience and frustration. The night before, between the hours of ten-fifteen and midnight, Ron Thomas's whereabouts were firmly accounted for. 'You appear to be a brute, Thomas,' the inspector pronounced in a take-it-or-leave-it voice, and turned his attention to a silver-coloured Vauxhall that had been noticed in the vicinity.

A woman called Mathers had seen it, as had a couple who'd been kissing in a doorway. The car drove down Old Engine Way earlier in the evening, nine or so it would have been, then turned into a cul-de-sac – Stables Lane – where it remained parked for half an hour, although no one had emerged. Mrs Mathers, who lived in Stables Lane, heard the engine of a car and went to the window to look. The headlights had been switched off; Mrs Mathers had the feeling that whoever was in the vehicle was up to no good and remarked as much to her sister. The couple in the doorway said that when the headlights came on again the car turned very slowly in the cul-de-sac; as it emerged into Old Engine Way, they were dazzled by its lights for a moment; they couldn't see its occupant.

'Occupants more like,' the inspector wearily corrected when the couple had left. 'Some slag on the game.'

Even so, a description of the Vauxhall was put together, its bodywork scraped and rusty, its radio aerial twisted into a knot: within minutes, calls came in from all over London, of silver-coloured Vauxhalls with such distinguishing features. Some of the calls were malicious – the opportunity seized to settle old scores against the owners of such vehicles; others led nowhere. But a woman, phoning from a call-box, said that a friend of hers had been driven to Stables Lane the night before, at the time in question. The woman gave neither her name nor her profession, only adding that her friend had been driven to Stables Lane because there was a family matter to be discussed in the car and Stables Lane was quiet. It was assumed that this was the prostitute or part-time prostitute suggested by the inspector; as with Ron Thomas, interest in the silver-coloured Vauxhall was abandoned.

Gilbert was dark-haired, five foot eight tall, sparely made. His features were neat, a neat mouth and nose, brown eyes very like his mother's, high cheekbones. Everything about Gilbert went together; even his voice – soft and unemphatic – belonged to a whole. The most distinctive thing about him was that – for no apparent reason, and even when he was not being loquacious – his presence in a room could not be overlooked; and often his presence lingered after he had left.

When Gilbert was two there had been an intensity in his gaze that Rosalie considered strange. Staring at the leg of a chair or at his own foot, he managed not to blink for minutes on end. He made no sound, and it was this she found unnerving. He took to examining, very closely, the palms of his hands. He splayed his fingers the way an old man might, and still in silence appeared to search the skin for flaws. Then, as abruptly as it all began, the staring ceased. But when he was five certain small objects from the kitchen disappeared – teaspoons, egg-cups, a potato-peeler. They were never found.

When he was nine Gilbert underwent psychiatric attention. The immediate reason for this was because one day he did not return from school. He should have returned on the bus, travelling with a handful of other children who lived in the same neighbourhood. Later that afternoon the police were informed, but Gilbert wasn't found and there were no reports of his having been seen anywhere. At half-past seven the next morning he rang the bell of 21 Blenheim Avenue, having spent the night in the basement of a block of flats. He gave his mother no explanation. Silence replaced his normal eagerness to communicate, as it had when he had first begun to examine his hands and when the kitchen objects disappeared.

Soon after that Gilbert refused to do the homework he was set and took to sitting, silent and still, in the classroom, refusing to open his books or even to take them out of his satchel. When asked, he again offered no explanation. The doggedness that was to characterize Gilbert in adult life began then: a psychiatrist declared that the child believed he was being deprived of certain rights, and a psychoanalyst – some time later – read the trouble similarly, while presenting it with his own professional variation and an adjustment of jargon. Gilbert, fourteen in 1978, spent that year in a centre devoted to the observation of erratic behavioural tendencies. 'Gilbert'll be encouraged to share his difficulties with us,' a man with a beard told Rosalie, adding vaguely: 'And of course there'll be regular counselling.' But when Gilbert returned to 21 Blenheim Avenue he was the same as he'd been before except that he'd grown almost two inches and possessed a noticeable fuzz of down on his upper lip and chin. Since the time he'd refused to co-operate in school he had successfully taught himself mathematics, Latin, geography, French and rudimentary German. He read voraciously, mainly history and historical biographies; in correctly spelt, grammatical prose he wrote long essays and talked to Rosalie about Cavour and Charlemagne and various treaties and land settlements. In 1984, when he was twenty, he disappeared for a week. At the end of the following year he disappeared for longer, but sent Rosalie picture postcards from a number of South Coast seaside resorts, saying he was OK, working in hotels. Later he didn't elaborate on that, and the next time he disappeared there were cards from the same area; when he returned he had acquired a Skoda. His mother never discovered when and where he had learnt to drive, or in what manner he had obtained the licence she discovered in one of his dressing-table drawers. He worked for a while in the potting department of a jam factory before moving to the architect's office, which he said was a more interesting place to be. A social worker – a conscientious woman who had known Gilbert during his time in the behavioural centre – still occasionally visited him, coming to the house on Saturday mornings, when he didn't have to go to work. *Talks excessively about photocopying*, she noted once, and felt it was too harsh to add that Gilbert's loquaciousness was very boring to listen to. In the end, remarking to Rosalie that her son did not appear to be benefiting from her counselling and had settled well into his employment, she ceased her Saturday-morning visits. *Seems satisfactory*, she noted. *Gives no trouble*.

Rosalie did not share that sanguine view. She did not believe her son was satisfactory. She had not believed it for a long time, and was aware that the afternoon he had failed to return from school was a single bead in the chain of unease that was beginning to form. When he had been taken into the behavioural centre her hope was that he would remain there indefinitely. 'Now, let's try to discover why you wish that, Mrs Mannion,' one of the staff had pressed her, his manner loftily clinical. But when she said it was simply something she felt, she was brought up sharply. It was pointed out to her that the centre was for observation and study, and the accumulation of case histories: in that respect it was doing well by Gilbert, but it stood to reason he could not remain there. Her son was fortunate to have her, she was informed. She had a role, that same lofty manner insisted, without words. She was, after all, the mother.

On the evening of Tuesday, November 21st Gilbert helped with the washing-up as usual, and then said he intended to drive over to the Bull public house. He reminded his mother where it was, as he often did: at the corner of Upper Richmond Road and Sheen Lane.

'I'll not stay long,' he said.

On the nine o'clock television News a picture was shown of the straggling cotoneaster and the dead leaves where Carol Dickson's body had lain. Carol's mother, appealing for witnesses to come forward, broke down in the middle of what she was saying; the camera lingered on her distress.

Rosalie turned the television off, not moving from where she sat, using the remote control. For the moment she couldn't even remember if Gilbert had gone out last night, then she remembered that he had and had come back earlier than usual. It was always the News, on the radio or the television, that prompted her dread. When a fire was said to have been started deliberately, or a child enticed, or broken glass discovered in baby-food jars in a supermarket, the dread began at once – the hasty calculations, the relief if time and geography ruled out involvement. More than once, before she became used to it, she had gone to lie trembling on her bed, struggling to control the frenzy that threatened. The second time he sent his picture postcards, her mocking little screen had shown a burnt-out dance hall, fourteen fatalities obscured by blankets in a Brighton car park. There had been a fire – deliberately started also, so the News suspected – on a cross-channel ferry four days after Gilbert had announced, 'I'll just take the Skoda here and there.' He had been away when a branch of the Halifax Building Society was held up by a gunman who left his weapon on the counter, a water-pistol as it was afterwards discovered. He had been away when an old woman was tied to a chair in her council flat and only an alarm clock stolen from her, which reminded Rosalie of the teaspoons and egg-cups and the potato-peeler. She was certain a kind of daring came into it, even if the chances he took were loaded in his favour:

he did not place himself in danger, he had a right to survive his chosen acts of recklessness, he had a right to silence. He would not be caught.

Last night he had come back earlier than usual: again, unable to help herself, she established that. But the recollection hardly made a difference. As soon as she'd seen the place where the body had been and noted the tired bewilderment in the police inspector's eyes, she knew there was a mystery; that weeks, or months, would pass without progress, that the chances were the crime would remain unsolved. She knew, as well, that if she went to Gilbert's room she'd find not a single leaf of cotoneaster, no titbit taken from the girl's clothing. There wouldn't be a scratch anywhere on Gilbert, nor a tear in his clothes, nor a speck of blood in his Skoda.

It had never been said that Rosalie's marriage failed because of Gilbert, but often during the sixteen years that had passed since the divorce she wondered if somehow this could be so. Had she, even then – when Gilbert was only nine – been half destroyed by the nagging of her fears, made unattractive, made limp, wrung out by an obsession that spread insidiously? None of that was said: the other woman was the reason and the cause. An irresistible love was what was spoken of.

Rosalie had often since considered that the irresistible love had picked up the fragments that were already there. Hidden at the time – like something beneath a familiar stone, something that had arrived without being noticed as a danger – was the reason and the cause. This view was strengthened by subsequent events. Since the divorce there had been kindness from men who liked her, theatre visits and tête-à-tête dinners, hints of romance. But there had always been a fizzling-out, caution creeping in. She tried on all such occasions not to talk about her son, but she knew that he was somehow there anyway, and dread is hard to hide. It intensified her solitude, spread nerviness and was exhausting. In the fabrics shop, when voices all around her were saying what a terrible thing, it wasn't easy to keep her hands from shaking.

'I've brought you back the *Evening Standard*,' Gilbert said, smiling at her. It was a habit of his to pick up newspapers in public houses. He played a game sometimes, watching the people who were reading them, trying to guess which one would be left behind. He never bought a newspaper himself.

'Thank you, dear,' she said, returning his smile. *I believe Gilbert has stolen a car*, she had written to his father, who phoned as soon as he received the letter, listening without interrupting to everything she said. But he'd pointed out, quite gently, that she was merely guessing, that it was suspicion, nothing more.

'Cake?' Gilbert said. 'A Mr Kipling's, have we?'

She said there was a cake in the kitchen, in the Quality Street tin.

'Tea?' he offered.

She shook her head. 'No, not tonight, dear.'

He didn't leave the room, telling her instead about his visit to the public house. He had drunk half a pint of cider and watched the other drinkers. Two girls were crawling all over a man with a moustache, a man who was much older than they were. The girls were drunk, shrill when they laughed or spoke. The red, white-spotted skirt of one of them had ridden up so far that Gilbert could see her panties. Blue the panties were.

'Funny, that,' Gilbert said. 'The way she didn't mind.'

On the front of the *Evening Standard* she could see a half-page photograph of Carol Dickson, not a particularly pretty girl, her mouth clenched tight in a grin, bright blonde hair. She might have guessed he'd bring in the *Evening Standard*; she would have if she'd thought about it. 'You're an imaginative woman,' one of the experts she'd pleaded with had stated, fingering papers on his desk. 'Better, really, to be down to earth in a case like this.'

In the public house an old man had bothered him, he said. 'Busy tonight,' the old man had remarked.

Gilbert had agreed, moving slightly so that he could watch the girls, but the old man was still in his way.

'Fag, dear?' the old man offered, holding out a packet of Benson & Hedges.

She could always guess, Rosalie sometimes thought: what would happen next, how he wouldn't refer to the girl on the front of the *Evening Standard*, how the panic would softly gather inside her and harden without warning into a knot, how the dryness in her mouth would make speech difficult.

'Afterwards I flagged down a police car,' Gilbert said. '"That old poufta's out again tonight," I told them. Well, I had to.'

He'd noticed the police car crawling along, he said, so he drew in in front of it and made a hand signal. 'I told them he'd still be there if they went along immediately. They wrote down what he'd said to me, tone of voice and everything. When I put it to them they agreed an obscene way of talking is against the law. Quite nice they were. I thought I'd better report it, I explained to them, in case the next time it was some young boy. They said quite right. They'll have him on their books now. Even if they decide not to take him in tonight they'll have him on their books. They can give a man like that a warning or they can take him in if there are charges preferred. I'd always be ready to prefer charges because of the harm that could be done to an innocent boy. I said that. I said this was the

eighth or ninth time he'd addressed me in that tone of voice. They quite
agreed that people should be allowed to have a drink in peace.'

'You didn't go out again last night, did you, dear?'

'*Last* night? It was tonight the poufta —'

'No, I meant last night. You were back quite early, weren't you?'

Headachy for no particular reason, she'd gone to bed after supper. But
she'd heard him coming in, no later than a quarter-past nine, certainly no
later than half-past. She'd fallen asleep about ten; she thought she remembered the sound of the television just before she dropped off.

'*The Big Sleep* last night,' he said. 'But you can't re-set a thing like that
in England. It doesn't make sense. A girl in the Kall Kwik was saying it
was great, but I said I thought it was pathetic. I said it didn't make any
sense, interfering with an original like that. Silly of them to go interfering, I said.'

'Yes.'

'West Indian the girl was.'

Rosalie smiled and nodded.

'Funny, saying it was great. Funny kind of view.'

'Perhaps she didn't know there'd been an original.'

'I said. I explained about it. But she just kept saying it was great.
They're like that, the West Indian girls.'

Sometimes, when he went on talking, she felt like the shadow of a person who was not there. Ordinary-sounding statements he made exhausted
her. Was it a deliberate act, that tonight he'd had a conversation with the
police? Was it all part of being daring, of challenging the world that
would take his rights from him? Often it seemed to her that his purposeless life was full of purpose.

'I'll make us tea,' he said. 'Really cold it is tonight.'

'Not tea for me, dear.'

'Chap in the Kall Kwik was saying the anti-freeze on his wind-screen
froze. If you can believe him, of course. Whopper Toms they call him.
Says he likes the taste of paper. Eats paper bags, cardboard, anything like
that. *If* you can believe him. Means no harm, though.'

'No, I'm sure he doesn't.'

'Congenital. Pity, really. I mean, I've seen him chewing, always chewing
he is. It's just that it could be gum. Could be a toffee, come to that.'

Impassive she sat, staring at the grey empty screen of the television set
when he went to make his tea. His father had found it impossible to love
him, long before the marriage had collapsed. That had not been said
either, but she knew it was true. For some reason he did not inspire love,
even in a father. Yet it had broken her heart to say he should be retained

in the centre where they'd studied him. It had broken her heart each time she'd begged that he should be put somewhere else, when they'd said the centre wasn't suitable. Vigilance was his due, a vigilance she was herself unable, adequately, to supply. All she could do was listen to his rigmaroles, and care that he couldn't bear wool next to his skin. The policemen he'd flagged down would have said he had a screw loose. In the Kall Kwik they would say the same.

'You saw it to the end?' she asked when he returned with a tray. 'You saw that film to the end even though it was so silly?'

'What film's that?'

'*The Big Sleep.*'

'Really grotty it was.'

He turned the television on. Politicians discussed Romania. His features, coloured by the highlights from the screen, displayed no emotion, neither elation nor melancholy. He was meticulous about taking the drugs prescribed. 'There is nothing to fear,' she had been assured, 'if the medication is taken. Nothing whatsoever.'

The time of the dance-hall fire she'd thought she'd never see him again. She'd thought he wouldn't come back and that eventually there'd be questions, two and two put together. She had imagined waiting, and nothing happening, day after day; and then, in some unexpected place, his apprehension. Instead he returned.

'Mr Kipling's Fancies,' he said, offering her the iced cakes, still in their cardboard carton. When she shook her head he poured his tea.

'Bet you it's gum he chews,' he said. 'Bet you.'

If he'd gone out again last night she'd have heard the car starting. The car would have woken her. She'd have sat up, worrying. She'd have turned her bedside light on and waited to hear the car returning. Even if he'd left the house again almost as soon as he'd entered it he would have to have driven very fast to reach that part of London by five to ten, which was the time they gave; five to ten at the latest, since the girl had said goodnight to her friend at nine-fifty and only had seven hundred yards to walk. There was nothing unusual about his bringing back the *Evening Standard*. He'd mentioned the old homosexual who bothered him before: it just happened that tonight there was a police car prowling.

'This is lousy stuff,' he said, and changed the television channel. His hands were thin – delicate hands, not much larger than her own. He was not given to violence. 'No! No!' he used to cry, still sometimes did, when she swatted a fly. In all his acts of bravado there had never been violence – when he refused to open his schoolbooks, when he spent a night in a basement, when he acquired a motor-car without money. No one would deny his cleverness, cunningly concealed beneath his tedious chatter. No one would deny being baffled by him, but there was never violence.

'Hey, look at that,' he suddenly exclaimed, drawing her attention to overweight people at a holiday camp for the obese. He laughed, and she remembered his infant's face when first they showed it to her. People didn't want him. His father and a whole army of medical people, the social worker, people he tried to make friends with: all of them deserted him too soon. He was on sufferance in the architect's office; wherever he went he was on sufferance.

'Awful,' he said, 'as fat as that.'

Then the News was on again, on Channel 3, and he sat silent – that awful silence that closed him down. On the screen the face of Carol Dickson was just as it was in the newspaper. Her mother broke down, the police inspector gave out his facts: all of it was repetition.

She watched him staring at the screen intently, as if mesmerized. He listened carefully. When the News was over he crossed the room and picked up the *Evening Standard*. He read it, his tea and cakes forgotten. She turned the television off.

'Goodnight, Gilbert,' she said when he rose to go to bed. He did not answer.

The newspaper was on the floor beside his chair, the face of Carol Dickson spread out for her, the right way up. She remembered how he'd stood when he'd come back after his first disappearance, how he leaned against the kitchen door-frame, following her with his eyes, silent. When he'd come back with the Skoda she'd thought of going to the police. She'd thought of trying to explain to some kindly older man in a uniform, asking for help. But of course she hadn't.

She might dial 999 now. Or she might go tomorrow to a police station, apologizing even before she began, hoping for reassurance. But even as these thoughts occurred she knew they were pretence. Before his birth she had possessed him. She had felt the tug of his lips on her breasts, a helpless creature then, growing into the one who controlled her now, who made her isolation total. Her fear made him a person, enriching him with power. He had sensed it when he had first idly examined the palms of his hands, and felt her mother's instinct disturbed. He had sensed it when he had hidden the kitchen objects where they could not be found, when he had not come back from school, when he had talked to the social worker about photocopying. He knew about the jaded thoughts recurring, the worry coursing round and round at its slow, familiar pace. The Skoda had been stolen; parked outside the house, it was always a reminder.

All night, she knew, she would sit there, the muzzy image of Carol

Dickson where he had left it, a yard away. She did not want to sleep because sleeping meant waking up and there would be the moment when reality began to haunt again. Her role was only to accept: he had a screw loose, she had willed him to be born. No one would ever understand the mystery of his existence, or the unshed tears they shared.

The Potato Dealer

Mulreavy would marry her if they paid him, Ellie's uncle said: she couldn't bring a fatherless child into the world. He didn't care what was done nowadays; he didn't care what the fashion was; he wouldn't tolerate the talk there'd be. 'Mulreavy,' her uncle repeated. 'D'you know who I mean by Mulreavy?'

She hardly did. An image came into her mind of a big face that had a squareness about it, and black hair, and a cigarette butt adhering to the lower lip while a slow voice agreed or disagreed, and eyes that were small, and sharp as splinters. Mulreavy was a potato dealer. Once a year he came to the farm, his old lorry rattling into the yard, then backed up to where the sacks stood ready for him. Sometimes he shook his head when he examined the potatoes, saying they were too small. He tried that on, Ellie's uncle maintained. Cagey, her uncle said.

'I'll tell you one thing, girl,' her uncle said when she found the strength to protest at what was being proposed. 'I'll tell you this: you can't stay here without there's something along lines like I'm saying. Nowadays is nothing, girl. There's still the talk.'

He was known locally as Mr Larrissey, rarely by his Christian name, which was Joseph. Ellie didn't call him 'Uncle Joseph', never had; 'uncle' sometimes, though not often, for even in that there seemed to be an intimacy that did not belong in their relationship. She thought of him as Mr Larrissey.

'It's one thing or the other, girl.'

Her mother – her uncle's sister – didn't say anything. Her mother hadn't opened her mouth on the subject of Mulreavy, but Ellie knew that she shared the sentiments that were being expressed, and would accept, in time, the solution that had been offered. She had let her mother down; she had embittered her; why should her mother care what happened now? All of it was a mess. In the kitchen of the farmhouse her mother and her uncle were thinking the same thing.

Her uncle – a worn, tired man, not used to trouble like this – didn't forgive her and never would: so he had said, and Ellie knew it was true. Since the death of her father she and her mother had lived with him on the farm on sufferance: that was always in his eyes, even though her

mother did all the cooking and the cleaning of the house, even though
Ellie, since she was eleven, had helped in summer in the fields, had collected and washed the eggs and nourished the pigs. Her uncle had never
married; if she and her mother hadn't moved on to the farm in 1978,
when Ellie was five, he'd still be on his own, managing as best he could.

'You have the choice, girl,' he said now, the repetition heavy in the
farmhouse kitchen. He was set in his ways, Ellie's mother often said; lifelong bachelors sometimes were.

He'd said at first − a fortnight ago − that his niece should get herself
seen to, even though it was against religion. Her mother said no, but later
wondered if it wasn't the only way out, the trip across the water that
other girls had gone on, what else was there? They could go away and
have it quietly done, they could be visiting the Galway cousins, no one
would be the wiser. But Ellie, with what spirit was left in her, though she
was in disgrace and crying, would not agree. In the fortnight that passed
she many times, tearfully, repeated her resolve to let the child be born.

Loving the father, Ellie already loved the child. If they turned her out,
if she had to walk the roads, or find work in Moyleglass or some other
town, she would. But Ellie didn't want to do that; she didn't want to find
herself penniless because it would endanger the birth. She would never
do that was the decision she had privately reached the moment she was
certain she was to have a child.

'Mulreavy,' her uncle said again.

'I know who he is.'

Her mother sat staring down at the lines of grain that years of scrub-
bing had raised on the surface of the kitchen table. Her mother had said
everything she intended to say: disgrace, shame, a dirtiness occurring
when people's backs were turned, all the thanks you get for what you give,
for sacrifices made. 'Who'd want you now?' her mother had asked her,
more than once.

'Mind you, I'm not saying Mulreavy'll bite,' Ellie's uncle said. 'I'm not
saying he'd take the thing on.'

Ellie didn't say anything. She left the kitchen and walked out into the
yard, where the turkeys screeched and ran towards her, imagining she carried meal to scatter, as often she did. She passed them by, and let herself
through the black iron gate that led to the sloping three-cornered field
beyond the outbuildings, the worst two acres of her uncle's property. Rag-
weed and gorse grew in profusion, speckled rock-surfaces erupted. It was
her favourite field, perhaps because she had always heard it cursed and as
a child had felt sorry for it. 'Oh, now, that's nice!' the father of her unborn
baby said when she told him she felt sorry for the three-cornered field. It

was then that he'd said he wished he'd known her as a child, and made her describe herself as she had been.

When it was put to Mulreavy he pretended offence. He didn't expostulate, for that was not his way. But as if in melancholy consideration of a personal affront he let the two ends of his mouth droop, as he sometimes did when he held a potato in his palm, shaking his head over its unsatisfactory size or shape. Ash from his cigarette dribbled down his shirt-front, the buttons of a fawn cardigan open because the day was warm, his shirt-collar open also and revealing a line of grime where it had been most closely in contact with the skin of his neck.

'Well, that's a quare one,' Mulreavy said, his simulated distaste slipping easily from him, replaced by an attempt at outraged humour.

'There's a fairish sum,' Mr Larrissey said, but didn't say what he had in mind and Mulreavy didn't ask. Nor did he ask who the father was. He said in a by-the-way voice that he was going out with a woman from Ballina who'd come to live in Moyleglass, a dressmaker's assistant; but the information was ignored.

'I only thought it was something would interest you,' Mr Larrissey said.

Their two vehicles were drawn up on the road, a rusting Ford Cortina and Mulreavy's lorry, the driving-side windows of both wound down. Mulreavy offered a cigarette. Mr Larrissey took it. As if about to drive away, he had put his hand on the gear when he said he'd only thought the proposition might be of interest.

'What's the sum?' Mulreavy asked when the cigarettes were lit, and a horn hooted because the vehicles were blocking the road. Neither man took any notice: they were of the neighbourhood, local people, the road was more theirs than strangers'.

When the extent of the money offered was revealed Mulreavy knew better than to react, favourably or otherwise. It would be necessary to give the matter thought, he said, and further considerations were put to him, so that at leisure he could dwell on those also.

Ellie's mother knew how it was, and how it would be: her brother would profit from the episode. The payment would be made by her: the accumulated pension, the compensation from the time of the accident in 1978. Her brother saw something for himself in the arrangement he hoped for with the potato dealer; the moment he had mentioned Mulreavy's name he'd been aware of a profit to be made. Recognizing at first, as she had herself, only shame and folly in the fact that his niece was pregnant, he had none the less explored the situation meticulously: that was his way. She had long been aware of her brother's hope that one day Ellie would marry some suitable young fellow who would join them in the farmhouse and could be put to work, easing the burden in the fields: that was how the debt of taking in a sister and a niece might at last be paid. But with a disaster such as there had been, there would be no young fellow now. Instead there was the prospect of Mulreavy, and what her brother had established in his mind was that Mulreavy could ease the burden too. A middle-aged potato dealer wasn't ideal for the purpose, but he was better than nothing.

Ellie's mother, resembling her brother in appearance, lean-faced and with his tired look, often recalled the childhood he and she had shared in this same house. More so than their neighbours, they were known to be a religious family, never missing Mass, going all together in the trap on Sundays and later by car, complimented for the faith they kept by Father Hanlon and his successor. The Larrisseys were respected people, known for the family virtues of hard work and disdain for ostentation, never seeming to be above themselves. She and her brother had all their lives been part of that, had never rebelled against these laid-down *mores* during the years of their upbringing.

Now, out of the cruel blue, there was this; and as far as brother and sister could remember, in the farmhouse there had never been anything as dispiriting. The struggle in bad seasons to keep two ends together, to make something of the rock-studded land even in the best of times, had never been lowering. Adversity of that kind was expected, the lot the family had been born into.

It had been expected also, when the accident occurred to the man she'd married, that Ellie's mother would return to the house that had become her brother's. She was forty-one then; her brother forty-four, left alone two years before when their parents had died within the same six months. He hadn't invited her to return, and though it seemed, in the circumstances, a natural consequence to both of them, she knew her brother had always since considered her beholden. As a child, he'd been like that about the few toys they shared, insisting that some were more his than hers.

'I saw Mulreavy,' he said on the day of the meeting on the road, his unsmiling, serious features already claiming a successful outcome.

Mulreavy's lorry had reached the end of its days and still was not fully paid for: within six months or so he would find himself unable to continue trading. This was the consideration that had crept into his mind when the proposition was put to him, and it remained there afterwards. There was a lorry he'd seen in McHugh Bros. with thirty-one thousand on the clock and at an asking price that would be reduced, the times being what they were. Mulreavy hadn't entirely invented the dressmaker from Ballina in whom he had claimed an interest: she was a wall-eyed woman he had recently seen about the place, who had arrived in Moyleglass to assist Mrs Toomey in her cutting and stitching. Mulreavy had wondered if she had money, if she'd bought her way into Mrs Toomey's business, as he'd heard it said. He'd never spoken to her or addressed her in any way, but after his conversation with Mr Larrissey he made further enquiries, only to discover that rumour now suggested the woman was employed by Mrs Toomey at a small wage. So Mulreavy examined in finer detail the pros and cons of marrying into the Larrisseys.

'There'd be space for you in the house,' was how it had been put to him. 'Maybe better than if you took her out of it. And storage enough for the potatoes in the big barn.'

A considerable saving of day-to-day expenses would result, Mulreavy had reflected, closing his eyes against the smoke from his cigarette when those words were spoken. He made no comment, waiting for further enticements, which came in time. Mr Larrissey said:

'Another thing is, the day will come when the land'll be too much for me. Then again, the day will come when there'll be an end to me altogether.'

Mr Larrissey had crossed himself. He had said no more, allowing the references to land and his own demise to dangle in the silence. Soon after that he jerked his head in a farewell gesture and drove away.

He'd marry the girl, Mulreavy's thoughts were later, after he'd heard the news about the dressmaker; he'd vacate his property, holding on to it until the price looked right and then disposing of it, no hurry whatsoever since he'd already be in the Larrisseys' farmhouse, with storage facilities and a good lorry. If he attended a bit to the land, the understanding was that he'd inherit it when the day came. It could be done in writing; it could be drawn up by Blaney in Moyleglass.

Eight days after their conversation on the road the two men shook hands, as they did when potatoes were bought and sold. Three weeks went by and then there was the wedding.

The private view of Ellie's mother – shared with neither her daughter nor her brother – was that the presence of Mulreavy in the farmhouse was a punishment for the brazen sin that had occurred. When the accident that had made a widow of her occurred, when she'd looked down at the broken body lying there, knowing it was lifeless, she had not felt that there was punishment in that, either directed at her or at the man she'd married. He had done little wrong in his life; indeed, had often sought to do good. Neither had she transgressed, herself, except in little ways. But what had led to the marriage of her daughter and the potato dealer was deserving of this harsh reprimand, which was something that must now be lived with.

Mulreavy was given a bedroom that was furnished with a bed and a cupboard. He was not offered, and did not demand, his conjugal rights. He didn't mind; that side of things didn't interest him; it hadn't been mentioned; it wasn't part of the arrangement. Instead, daily, he surveyed the land that was to be his inheritance. He walked it, lovingly, at first when no one was looking, and later to identify the weed that had to be sprayed and to trace the drains. He visualized a time when he no longer travelled about as a middle-man, buying potatoes cheaply and selling at a profit, when the lorry he had acquired with the dowry would no longer be necessary. On these same poor acres sufficient potatoes could be grown to allow him to trade without buying in. Mulreavy wasn't afraid of work when there was money to be made.

The midwife called down the farmhouse stairs a few moments after Mulreavy heard the first cry. Mr Larrissey poured out a little of the whiskey that was kept in the wall-cupboard in case there was toothache in the house. His sister was at the upstairs bedside. The midwife said a girl had been born.

A year ago, it was Mr Larrissey, not his sister, who had first known about the summer priest who was the father of this child. On his way back from burning stubble he had seen his niece in the company of the man and had known from the way they walked that there was some kind of intimacy between them. When his niece's condition was revealed he had not, beneath the anger he displayed, been much surprised.

Mulreavy, clenching his whiskey glass, his lips touched with a smile, had not known he would experience a moment of happiness when the birth occurred; nor had he guessed that the dourness of Mr Larrissey would be affected, that whiskey would be offered. The thing would happen, he had thought, maybe when he was out in the fields. He would walk into the kitchen and they would tell him. Yet in the kitchen, now, there was almost an air of celebration, a satisfaction that the arrangement lived up to its promise.

Above where the two men sat, Ellie's mother did as the midwife directed in the matter of the afterbirth's disposal. She watched the baby being taken from its mother's arms and placed, sleeping now, in the cradle by the bedside. She watched her daughter struggling for a moment against the exhaustion that possessed her, before her eyes closed too.

The child was christened Mary Josephine – these family names chosen by Ellie's mother, and Ellie had not demurred. Mulreavy played his part, cradling the infant in his big arms for a moment at the font, a suit bought specially for the occasion. It wasn't doubted that he was the father, although the assumption also was that the conception had come first, the marriage later, as sometimes happened. There'd been some surprise at the marriage, not much.

Ellie accepted with equanimity what there was. She lived a little in the past, in the summer of her love affair, expecting of the future only what she knew of the present. The summer curate who had loved her, and whom she loved still, would not miraculously return. He did not even know that she had given life to his child. 'It can't be,' he'd said when they lay in the meadow that was now a potato field. 'It can't ever be, Ellie.' She knew it couldn't be: a priest was a priest. There would never, he promised, as if in compensation, be another love like this in all his life. 'Nor for me,' she swore as eagerly, although he did not ask for that, in fact said no, that she must live her normal life. 'No, not for me,' she repeated. 'I feel it too.' It was like a gift when she knew her child was to be born, a fulfilment, a forgiveness almost for their summer sin.

As months and then years went by, the child walked and spoke and suffered childhood ills, developed preferences, acquired characteristics that slipped away again or stubbornly remained. Ellie watched her mother and her uncle ageing, while they in turn were reminded by the child's presence of their own uneasy companionship in the farmhouse when they were as young as the child was now. Mulreavy, who did not go in for nostalgia or observing changes in other people, increased his potato yield. Like Mr Larrissey, he would have preferred the child who had been born to be a boy since a boy, later on, would be more useful, but he did not ever complain on this count. Mr Larrissey himself worked less, in winter often spending days sitting in the kitchen, warm by the Esse stove. For Ellie's mother, passing time did not alter her belief that the bought husband was her daughter's reprimand on earth.

All that was how things were on the farm and in the farmhouse. A net of compromise and acceptance and making the best of things held the household together. Only the child was aware of nothing, neither that a man had been bought to be her father nor that her great-uncle had benefited by the

circumstances, nor that her grandmother had come to terms with a punishment, nor that her mother still kept faith with an improper summer
love. The child's world when she was ten had more to do with reading
whole pages more swiftly than she had a year ago, and knowing where
Heligoland was, and reciting by heart *The Wreck of the Hesperus.*

But, without warning, the household was disturbed. Ellie was aware
only of some inner restlessness, its source not identified, which she
assumed would pass. But it did not pass, and instead acquired the intensity of unease: what had been satisfactory for the first ten years of her
child's life was strangely not so now. In search of illumination, she pondered all that had occurred. She had been right not to wish to walk the
roads with her fatherless infant, she had been right to agree to the proposal put to her: looking back, she could not see that she should, in any
way whatsoever, have done otherwise. A secret had been kept; there were
no regrets. It was an emotion quite unlike regret that assailed her. Her
child smiled back at her from a child's innocence, and she remembered
those same features, less sure and less defined, when they were newly in
the farmhouse, and wondered how they would be when another ten years
had passed. Not knowing now, her child would never know. She would
never know that her birth had been accompanied by money changing
hands. She would never know that, somewhere else, her father forgave the
sins of other people, and offered Our Saviour's blood and flesh in solemn
expiation.

'Can you manage them?' Ellie's husband asked when she was loading
sacks on to the weighing scales, for she had paused in the work as if to
rest.

'I'm all right.'

'Take care you don't strain yourself.'

He was often kind in practical ways. She was strong, but the work was
not a woman's work and, although it was never said, he was aware of
this. In the years of their marriage they had never quarrelled or even disagreed, not being close enough for that, and in this way their relationship
reflected that of the brother and sister they shared the house with.

'They're a good size, the Kerrs,' he said, referring to the produce they
worked with. 'We hit it right this year.'

'They're nice all right.'

She had loved her child's father for every day of their child's life and
before it. She had falsified her confessions and a holy baptism. Black,
ugly lies were there when their child smiled from her innocence, nails in
another cross. It hadn't mattered at first, when their child wouldn't have
understood.

'I'll stop now,' Ellie said, recording in the scales book the number of sacks that were ready to be sealed. 'I have the tea to get.'

Her mother was unwell, confined to her bedroom. It was usually her mother who attended to the meals.

'Go on so, Ellie,' he said. He still smoked forty cigarettes a day, his life's indulgence, a way to spend a fraction of the money he accumulated. He had bought no clothes since his purchase of the christening suit except for a couple of shirts, and he questioned the necessity of the clothes Ellie acquired herself or for her child. Meanness was a quality he was known for; commercially, it had assisted him.

'Oh, I got up,' Ellie's mother said in the kitchen, the table laid and the meal in the process of preparation. 'I couldn't lie there.'

'You're better?'

'I'd say I was getting that way.'

Mr Larrissey was washing traces of fertilizer from his hands at the sink, roughly rubbing in soap. From the yard came the cries of the child, addressing the man she took to be her father as she returned from her evening task of ensuring that the bullocks still had grass to eat.

All the love there had been, all the love there still was – love that might have nourished Ellie's child, that might have warmed her – was the deprivation the child suffered. Ellie remembered the gentle, pale hands of the lover who had given her the gift of her child, and heard again the whisper of his voice, and his lips lingered softly on hers. She saw him as she always now imagined him, in his cassock and his surplice, the embroidered cross that marked his calling repeated again in the gestures of his blessing. His eyes were still a shade of slate, his features retained their delicacy. Why should a child not have some vision of him too? Why should there be falsity?

'You've spoken to them, have you?' her husband asked when she said what she intended.

'No, only you.'

'I wouldn't want the girl told.'

He turned away in the potato shed, to heft a sack on to the lorry. She felt uneasy in herself, she said, the way things were, and felt that more and more. That feeling wasn't there without a reason. It was a feeling she was aware of most at Mass and when she prayed at night.

Mulreavy didn't reply. He had never known the identity of the father. Some runaway fellow, he had been told at the time by Mr Larrissey, who had always considered the shame greater because a priest was involved. 'No need Mulreavy should know that,' Ellie had been instructed by her mother, and had abided by this wish.

'It was never agreed,' Mulreavy maintained, not pausing in his loading. 'It wasn't agreed the girl would know.'

Ellie spoke of a priest then; her husband said nothing. He finished with the potato sacks and lit a cigarette. That was a shocking thing, he eventually remarked, and lumbered out of the barn.

'Are you mad, girl?' Her mother rounded on her in the kitchen, turning from the draining-board, where she was shredding cabbage. Mr Larrissey, who was present also, told her not to be a fool. What good in the world would it do to tell a child the like of that?

'Have sense, for God's sake,' he crossly urged, his voice thick with the bluster that obscured his confusion.

'You've done enough damage, Ellie,' her mother said, all the colour gone from her thin face. 'You've brought enough on us.'

When Mulreavy came into the kitchen an hour later he guessed at what had been said, but he did not add anything himself. He sat down to wait for his food to be placed in front of him. It was the first time since the arrangement had been agreed upon that any reference to it had been made in the household.

'That's the end of it,' Ellie's mother laid down, the statement made as much for Mulreavy's benefit as for Ellie's. 'We'll hear no more of this.'

Ellie did not reply. That evening she told her child.

People knew, and talked about it now. What had occurred ten years ago suddenly had an excitement about it that did not fail to please. Minds were cast back, memories ransacked in a search for the name and appearance of the summer priest who had been and gone. Father Mooney, who had succeeded old Father Hanlon, spoke privately to Ellie, deploring the exposure she had 'so lightly' been responsible for.

With God's grace, he pointed out, a rough and ready solution had been found and disgrace averted ten years ago. There should have been gratitude for that, not what had happened now. Ellie explained that every time she looked at her child she felt a stab of guilt because a deception of such magnitude had been perpetrated. 'Her life was no more than a lie,' Ellie said, but Father Mooney snappishly replied that that was not for her to say.

'You flew in the face of things once,' he fulminated, 'and now you've done it again.' When he glared at her, it showed in his expression that he considered her an unfit person to be in his parish. He ordered Hail Marys to be repeated, and penitence practised, with humility and further prayer.

But Ellie felt that a weight had been lifted from her, and she explained to her child that even if nothing was easy now, a time would come when the difficulties of the moment would all be gone.

Mulreavy suffered. His small possession of pride was bruised; he hardly had to think to know what people said. He went about his work in the fields, planting and harvesting, spreading muck and fertilizer, folding away cheques until he had a stack ready for lodgement in Moyleglass. The sour atmosphere in the farmhouse affected him, and he wondered if people knew, on top of everything else, that he occupied a bedroom on his own and always had, that he had never so much as embraced his wayward young bride. Grown heavier over the years, he became even heavier after her divulgence, eating more in his despondency.

He liked the child; he always had. The knowledge that a summer priest had fathered her caused him to like her no less, for the affection was rooted in him. And the child did not change in her attitude to him, but still ran to him at once when she returned from school, with tales of how the nuns had been that day, which one bad-tempered, which one sweet. He listened as he always had, always pausing in his work to throw in a word or two. He continued to tell brief stories of his past experiences on the road: he had traded in potatoes since he was hardly more than a child himself, fifteen when he first assisted his father.

But in the farmhouse Mulreavy became silent. In his morose mood he blamed not just the wife he'd married but her elders too. They had deceived him. And knowing more than he did about these things, they should have foreseen more than they had. The child bore his name. 'Mrs Mulreavy' they called his wife. He was a laughing-stock.

'I don't remember that man,' he said when almost a year had passed, a September morning. He had crossed the furrows to where she was picking potatoes from the clay he'd turned, the plough drawn by the tractor. 'I don't know did I ever see him.'

Ellie looked up at the dark-jowelled features, above the rough, thick neck. She knew which man he meant. She knew, as well, that it had required an effort to step down from his tractor and cross to where she was, to stand unloved in front of her. She said at once:

'He was here only a summer.'

'That would be it so. I was always travelling then.'

She gave the curate's name and he nodded slowly over it, then shook his head. He'd never heard that name, he said.

The sun was hot on her shoulders and her arms. She might have pointed across the ploughed clay to the field that was next to the one they were in.

It was there, below the slope, that the conception had taken place. She wanted to say so, but she didn't. She said:

'I had to tell her.'

He turned to go away, then changed his mind, and again looked down at her.

'Yes,' he said.

She watched him slowly returning to where he'd left the tractor. His movements were always slow, his gait suggesting an economy of energy, his arms loose at his sides. She mended his clothes, she kept them clean. She assisted him in the fields, she made his bed. In all the time she'd known him she had never wondered about him.

The tractor started. He looked behind to see that the plough was as he wanted it. He lit another cigarette before he set off on his next brief journey.

Lost Ground

On the afternoon of September 14th 1989, a Thursday, Milton Leeson was addressed by a woman in his father's upper orchard. He was surprised. If the woman had been stealing the apples she could easily have dodged out of sight around the slope of the hill when she heard his footfall. Instead, she came forward to greet him, a lean-faced woman with straight black hair that seemed too young for her wasted features. Milton had never seen her before.

Afterwards he remembered that her coat, which did not seem entirely clean, was a shade of dark blue, even black. At her throat there was a scarf of some kind. She wasn't carrying anything. If she'd been stealing the apples she might have left whatever contained her takings behind the upper orchard's single growth of brambles, only yards from where she stood.

The woman came close to Milton, smiling at him with her eyes and parted lips. He asked her what she wanted; he asked her what she was doing in the orchard, but she didn't reply. In spite of her benign expression he thought for a moment she was mad and intended to attack him. Instead, the smile on her lips increased and she raised her arms as if inviting him to step into her embrace. When Milton did not do so the woman came closer still. Her hands were slender, her fingers as frail as twigs. She kissed him and then turned and walked away.

Afterwards Milton recalled very thin calves beneath the hem of her dark coat, and narrow shoulders, and the luxuriant black hair that seemed more than ever not to belong. When she'd kissed him her lips hadn't been moist like his mother's. They'd been dry as a bone, the touch of them so light he had scarcely felt it.

'Well?' Mr Leeson enquired that evening in the farmhouse kitchen.

Milton shook his head. In the upper orchard the Cox's were always the first to ripen. Nobody expected them to be ready as soon as this, but just occasionally, after a sunny summer, the first of the crop could catch you out. Due to his encounter with the stranger, he had forgotten to see if an apple came off easily when he twisted it on the branch. But he had noticed that not many had fallen, and guessed he was safe in intimating that the

crop was better left for a while yet. Shyness prevented him from reporting
that there'd been a woman in the orchard; if she hadn't come close to him,
if she hadn't touched his lips with hers, it would have been different.

Milton was not yet sixteen. He was chunky, like his father and his brothers, one of them much older, the other still a child. The good looks of the
family had gone into the two girls, which Mrs Leeson privately gave thanks
for, believing that otherwise neither would have married well.

'They look laden from the lane,' Mr Leeson said, smearing butter on
half a slice of bread cut from the loaf. Mr Leeson had small eyes and a
square face that gave an impression of determination. Sparse grey hair
relieved the tanned dome of his head, more abundant in a closely cropped
growth around his ears and the back of his neck.

'They're laden all right,' Milton said.

The Leesons' kitchen was low-ceilinged, with a flagged floor and pale
blue walls. It was a rambling, rectangular room, an illusion of greater
spaciousness created by the removal of the doors from two wall-
cupboards on either side of a recess that for almost fifty years had held
the same badly stained Esse cooker. Sink and draining-boards, with further cupboards, lined the wall opposite, beneath narrow windows. An
oak table, matching the proportions of the room, dominated its centre.
There was a television set on a corner shelf, to the right of the Esse. Beside
the door that led to the yard a wooden settee with cushions on it, and a
high-backed chair, were placed to take advantage of the heat from the
Esse while viewing the television screen. Five unpainted chairs were
arranged around the table, four of them now occupied by the Leesons.

Generations of the family had sat in this kitchen, ever since 1809, when
a Leeson had married into a household without sons. The house, four-
square and slated, with a porch that added little to its appeal, had been
rebuilt in 1931, when its walls were discovered to be defective. The services of a reputable local builder being considered adequate for the modi-
fications, no architect had been employed. Nearly sixty years later, with a
ragged front garden separating it from a lane that was used mainly by the
Leesons, the house still stood white and slated, no tendrils of creeper
softening its spare usefulness. At the back, farm buildings with red corrugated roofs and breeze-block walls were clustered around a concrete
yard; fields and orchards were on either side of the lane. For three-quarters of a mile in any direction this was Leeson territory, a tiny fraction of
County Armagh. The yard was well kept, the land well tended, both
reflecting the hard-working Protestant family the Leesons were.

'There's more, Milton.'

His mother offered him salad and another slice of cold bacon. She had

fried the remains of the champ they'd had in the middle of the day: potatoes mashed with butter and spring onions now had a crispy brown crust.
She dolloped a spoonful on to Milton's plate beside the bacon and passed
the plate back to him.

'Thanks,' Milton said, for gratitude was always expressed around this
table. He watched his mother cutting up a slice of bacon for his younger
brother, Stewart, who was the only other child of the family still at home.
Milton's sister Addy had married the Reverend Herbert Cutcheon a year
ago; his other sister was in Leicester, married also. His brother Garfield
was a butcher's assistant in Belfast.

'Finish it up.' Mrs Leeson scooped the remains of the champ and
spooned it on to her husband's plate. She was a small, delicately made
woman with sharp blue eyes and naturally wavy hair that retained in
places the reddish-brown of her girlhood. The good looks of her daughters had once been hers also and were not yet entirely dispelled.

Having paused while the others were served – that, too, being a tradition in the family – Milton began to eat again. He liked the champ best
when it was fried. You could warm it in the oven or in a saucepan, but it
wasn't the same. He liked crispness in his food – fingers of a soda farl
fried, the spicy skin of a milk pudding, fried champ. His mother always
remembered that. Milton sometimes thought his mother knew everything
about him, and he didn't mind: it made him fond of her that she bothered. He felt affection for her when she sat by the Esse on winter's evenings or by the open back door in summer, sewing and darning. She never
read the paper and only glanced up at the television occasionally. His
father read the paper from cover to cover and never missed the television
News. When Milton was younger he'd been afraid of his father, although
he'd since realized that you knew where you were with him, which came
from the experience of working with him in the fields and the orchards.
'He's fair,' Mrs Leeson used to repeat when Milton was younger. 'Always
remember that.'

Milton was the family's hope, now that Garfield had gone to Belfast.
Questioned by his father three years ago, Garfield had revealed that if he
inherited the farm and the orchards he would sell them. Garfield was
urban by inclination; his ambition during his growing-up was to find his
feet in Belfast and to remain there. Stewart was a mongol.

'We'll fix a day for the upper orchard,' his father said. 'I'll fix with
Gladdy about the boxes.'

That night Milton dreamed it was Esme Dunshea who had come to the
upper orchard. Slowly she took off her dark coat, and then a green dress.

She stood beneath an apple tree, skimpy underclothes revealing skin as white as flour. Once he and Billie Carew had followed his sisters and Esme Dunshea when they went to bathe in the stream that ran along the bottom of the orchards. In his dream Esme Dunshea turned and walked away, but to Milton's disappointment she was fully dressed again.

The next morning that dream quickly faded to nothing, but the encounter with the stranger remained with Milton, and was as vivid as the reality had been. Every detail of the woman's appearance clung tightly to some part of his consciousness – the black hair, the frail fingers outstretched, her coat and her scarf.

On the evening of that day, during the meal at the kitchen table, Milton's father asked him to cut the bramble patch in the upper orchard. He meant the next morning, but Milton went at once. He stood among the trees in the twilight, knowing he was not there at his father's behest but because he knew the woman would arrive. She entered the upper orchard by the gate that led to the lane and called down to where he was. He could hear her perfectly, although her voice was no more than a whisper.

'I am St Rosa,' the woman said.

She walked down the slope toward him, and he saw that she was dressed in the same clothes. She came close to him and placed her lips on his.

'That is holy,' she whispered.

She moved away. She turned to face him again before she left the orchard, pausing by the gate to the lane.

'Don't be afraid,' she said, 'when the moment comes. There is too much fear.'

Milton had the distinct impression that the woman wasn't alive.

Milton's sister Hazel wrote every December, folding the pages of the year's news inside her Christmas card. Two children whom their grandparents had never seen had been born to her in Leicester. Not once since her wedding had Hazel been back to County Armagh.

We drove to Avignon the first day even though it meant being up half the night. The children couldn't have been better, I think the excitement exhausted them.

On the third Sunday in December the letter was on the mantelpiece of what the household had always called the back room, a room used only on Sundays in winter, when the rest of the year's stuffiness was disguised by the smoke from a coal fire. Milton's sister Addy and Herbert Cutcheon were present on the third Sunday in December, and Garfield was visiting for the weekend. Stewart sat on his own Sunday chair, grimacing to himself. Four o'clock tea with sandwiches, apple-pie and cakes, was taken on winter Sundays, a meal otherwise dispensed with.

'They went travelling to France,' Mr Leeson stated flatly, his tone betraying the disappointment he felt concerning his older daughter's annual holiday.

'*France?*' Narrow-jawed and beaky, head cocked out inquisitively, the Reverend Herbert Cutcheon dutifully imbued his repetition of the word with a note of surprised disdain. It was he who had conducted Hazel's wedding, who had delivered a private homily to the bride and bridegroom three days before the ceremony, who had said that at any time they could turn to him.

'See for yourself.' Mr Leeson inclined his tanned pate toward the mantelpiece. 'Have you read Hazel's letter, Addy?'

Addy said she had, not adding that she'd been envious of the journey to Avignon. Once a year she and Herbert and the children went for a week to Portrush, to a boarding-house with reduced rates for clergy.

'France,' her husband repeated. 'You'd wonder at that.'

'Aye, you would,' her father agreed.

Milton's eyes moved from face to face as each person spoke. There was fatigue in Addy's prettiness now, a tiredness in the skin even, although she was only twenty-seven. His father's features were impassive, nothing reflecting the shadow of resentment in his voice. A thought glittered in Herbert Cutcheon's pale brown eyes and was accompanied by a private nod: Milton guessed he was saying to himself it was his duty to write to Hazel on this matter. The clergyman had written to Hazel before: Milton had heard Addy saying so in the kitchen.

'I think Hazel explained in the letter,' Mrs Leeson put in. 'They'll come one of these years,' she added, although she, more than anyone, knew they wouldn't. Hazel had washed her hands of the place.

'Sure, they will,' Garfield said.

Garfield was drunk. Milton watched him risking his observation, his lips drawn loosely back in a thick smile. Specks of foam lingered on the top of the beer can he held, around the triangular opening. He'd been drinking Heineken all afternoon. Mr Leeson drank only once a year, on the occasion of the July celebration; Herbert Cutcheon was teetotal. But neither disapproved of Garfield's tippling when he came back for the weekend, because that was Garfield's way and if you raised an objection you wouldn't see him for dust.

Catching Milton's eye on him, Garfield winked. He was not entirely the reason why Hazel would not return, but he contributed to it. For in Belfast Garfield was more than just a butcher's assistant. Garfield had a role among the Protestant paramilitaries, being what he himself called a 'hard-man volunteer' in an organization intent on avenging the atrocities of the other side. The tit-for-tat murders spawned by that same hard-man mentality, the endless celebration of a glorious past on one side and the picking over of ancient rights on the other, the reluctance to forgive: all this was what Hazel had run away from. 'Only talk,' Mrs Leeson confidently dismissed Garfield's reports of his activities as, recalling that he had always been a boaster. Mr Leeson did not comment.

'Hi!' Stewart suddenly exclaimed in the back room, the way he often did. 'Hi! Hi!' he shouted, his head bent sideways to his shoulder, his mouth flopping open, eyes beginning to roll.

'Behave yourself, Stewart,' Mrs Leeson sternly commanded. 'Stop it now.'

Stewart took no notice. He completed his effort at communication, his fat body becoming awkward on the chair. Then the tension left him and he was quiet. *Give Stewart a hug from all of us*, Hazel's letter said.

Addy collected her husband's cup and her father's. More tea was poured. Mrs Leeson cut more cake.

'Now, pet.' She broke a slice into portions for Stewart. 'Good boy now.'

Milton wondered what they'd say if he mentioned the woman in the orchard, if he casually said that on the fourteenth of September, and again on the fifteenth, a woman who called herself St Rosa had appeared to him among the apple trees of the upper orchard. It wouldn't have been necessary to say he'd dreamed about her also; the dream was just an ordinary thing, a dream he might have had about any woman or girl. 'Her hair was strange,' he might have said.

But Milton, who had kept the whole matter to himself, continued to do so. Later that evening, alone in the back room with Garfield, he listened while his brother hinted at his city exploits, which he always did when he'd been drinking. Milton watched the damp lips sloppily opening and closing, the thick smile flashing between statements about punishment meted out and premises raided, youths taken in for questioning, warnings issued. There was always a way to complete the picture, Garfield liked to repeat, and would tell about some Catholic going home in the rain and being given a lift he didn't want to accept. Disposal completed the picture, you could call it that: you could say he was in the disposal business. When the phone rang in the middle of the night he always knew at once. No different from dealing with the side of a cow, a professional activity. Garfield always stopped before he came to the end of his tales; even when he'd had a few he left things to the imagination.

*

Every summer Mr Leeson gave the six-acre field for the July celebration – a loyal honouring, yet again renewed, of King William's famous victory over Papist James in 1690. Bowler-hatted and sashed, the men assembled there on the twelfth of the month, their drums and flutes echoing over the Leeson lands. At midday there was the long march to the village, Mr Leeson himself prominent among the marchers. He kept a dark serge suit specially for Sundays and the July celebration, as his father and his grandfather had. Before Garfield had gone to Belfast he'd marched also, the best on the flute for miles around. Milton marched, but didn't play an instrument because he was tone-deaf.

Men who had not met each other since the celebration last year came to the six-acre field in July. Mr Leeson's elderly Uncle Willie came, and Leeson cousins and relatives by marriage. Milton and his friend Billie Carew were among the younger contingent. It pleased Mr Leeson and the other men of his age that boys made up the numbers, that there was no falling away, new faces every year. The Reverend Cutcheon gave an address before the celebration began.

With the drums booming and the flutes skilfully establishing the familiar tunes, the marchers swung off through the iron gate of the field, out on to the lane, later turning into the narrow main road. Their stride was jaunty, even that of Mr Leeson's Uncle Willie and that of Old Knipe, who was eighty-four. Chins were raised, umbrellas carried as rifles might be. Pride was everywhere on these faces; in the measured step and the music's beat, in the swing of the arms and the firm grip of the umbrellas. No shoe was unpolished, no dark suit unironed. The men of this neighbourhood, by long tradition, renewed their Protestant loyalty and belief through sartorial display.

Milton's salt-and-pepper jacket and trousers had been let down at the cuffs. This showed, but only on close scrutiny – a band of lighter cloth and a second band, less noticeable because it had faded, where the cuffs had been extended in the past. His mother had said, only this morning, that that was that, what material remained could not be further adjusted. But she doubted that Milton would grow any more, so the suit as it was should last for many years yet. While she spoke Milton felt guilty, as many times he had during the ten months that had passed since his experience in the upper orchard. It seemed wrong that his mother, who knew everything about him, even that he wouldn't grow any more, shouldn't have been confided in, yet he hadn't been able to do it. Some instinct assured him that the woman would not return. There was no need for her to return, Milton's feeling was, although he did not know where the feeling came from: he would have found it awkward, explaining all that to his mother. Each of the seasons that had passed since September had been suffused by the memory of the woman. That autumn had been warm, its shortening days mellow with sunshine until the rain came in November. She had been with him in the sunshine and the rain, and in the bitter cold that came with January. On a day when the frost remained, to be frozen again at nightfall, he had walked along the slope of the upper orchard and looked back at the long line of his footsteps on the whitened grass, for a moment surprised that hers weren't there, miraculously, also. When the first primroses decorated the dry, warm banks of the orchards he found himself thinking that these familiar flowers were different this year because he was different himself and saw them in some different way. When summer came the memory of the woman was more intense.

'They'll draw in,' a man near the head of the march predicted as two cars advanced upon the marchers. Obediently the cars pressed into a gateway to make room, their engines turned off, honouring the music. Women and children in the cars waved and saluted; a baby was held up, its small paw waggled in greeting. 'Does your heart good, that,' one of the men remarked.

The day was warm. White clouds were stationary, as if pasted on to the vast dome of blue. It was nearly always fine for the July celebration, a fact that did not pass unnoticed in the neighbourhood, taken to be a sign. Milton associated the day with sweat on his back and in his armpits and on his thighs, his shirt stuck to him in patches that later became damply cold. As he marched now the sun was hot on the back of his neck. 'I wonder will we see the Kissane girl?' Billie Carew speculated beside him.

The Kissane girl lived in one of the houses they passed. She and her two younger sisters usually came out to watch. Her father and her uncles and her brother George were on the march. She was the best-looking girl in the neighbourhood now that Milton's sisters were getting on a bit. She had glasses, which she took off when she went dancing at the Cuchulainn Inn. She had her hair done regularly and took pains to get her eyeshadow right; she matched the shade of her lipstick to her dress. There wasn't a better pair of legs in Ulster, Billie Carew claimed.

'Oh, God!' he muttered when the marchers rounded a bend and there she was with her two young sisters. She had taken her glasses off and was wearing a dress that was mainly pink, flowers like roses on it. When they drew nearer, her white sandals could be seen. 'Oh, God!' Billie Carew exclaimed again, and Milton guessed he was undressing the Kissane girl, the way they used to undress girls in church. One of the girl's sisters had a Union Jack, which she waved.

Milton experienced no excitement. Last year he, too, had undressed the Kissane girl, which hadn't been much different from undressing Esme Dunshea in church. The Kissane girl was older than Esme Dunshea, and older than himself and Billie Carew by five or six years. She worked in the chicken factory.

'D'you know who she looks like?' Billie Carew said. 'Ingrid Bergman.'

'Ingrid Bergman's dead.'

Busy with his thoughts, Billie Carew didn't reply. He had a thing about Ingrid Bergman. Whenever *Casablanca* was shown on the television nothing would get him out of the house. For the purpose he put her to it didn't matter that she was dead.

'God, man!' Billie Carew muttered, and Milton could tell from the urgency of his intonation that the last of the Kissane girl's garments had been removed.

At ten to one the marchers reached the green corrugated-iron sheds of McCourt's Hardware and Agricultural Supplies. They passed a roadside water pump and the first four cottages of the village. They were in Catholic country now: no one was about, no face appeared at a window. The village was a single wide street, at one end Vogan's stores and public house, at the other Tiernan's grocery and filling station, where newspapers could be obtained. Next door was O'Hanlon's public house and then the road widened, so that cars could turn in front of the Church of the Holy Rosary and the school. The houses of the village were colourwashed different colours, green and pink and blue. They were modest houses, none of more than two storeys.

As the marchers melodiously advanced upon the blank stare of so many windows, the stride of the men acquired an extra fervour. Arms were swung with fresh intent, jaws were more firmly set. The men passed the Church of the Holy Rosary, then halted abruptly. There was a moment of natural disarray as ranks were broken so that the march might be reversed. The Reverend Herbert Cutcheon's voice briefly intoned, a few glances were directed at, and over, the nearby church. Then the march returned the way it had come, the music different, as though a variation were the hidden villagers' due. At the corrugated sheds of McCourt's Hardware and Agricultural Supplies the men swung off to the left, marching back to Mr Leeson's field by another route.

The picnic was the reward for duty done, faith kept. Bottles appeared. There were sandwiches, chicken legs, sliced beef and ham, potato crisps and tomatoes. The men urinated in twos, against a hedge that never suffered from its annual acidic dousing – this, too, was said to be a sign. Jackets were thrown off, bowler hats thrown down, sashes temporarily laid aside. News was exchanged; the details of a funeral or a wedding passed on; prices for livestock deplored. The Reverend Herbert Cutcheon passed among the men who sat easily on the grass, greeting those from outside his parish whom he hadn't managed to greet already, enquiring after womenfolk. By five o'clock necks and faces were redder than they had earlier been, hair less tidy, beads of perspiration catching the slanting sunlight. There was euphoria in the field, some drunkenness, and an occasional awareness of the presence of God.

'Are you sick?' Billie Carew asked Milton. 'What's up with you?'

Milton didn't answer. He was maybe sick, he thought. He was sick or going round the bend. Since he had woken up this morning she had been there, but not as before, not as a tranquil presence. Since he'd woken she had been agitating and nagging at him.

'I'm OK,' he said.

He couldn't tell Billie Carew any more than he could tell his mother, or anyone in the family, yet all the time on the march he had felt himself being pressed to tell, all the time in the deadened village while the music played, when they turned and marched back again and the tune was different. Now, at the picnic, he felt himself being pressed more than ever.

'You're bloody not OK,' Billie Carew said.

Milton looked at him and found himself thinking that Billie Carew would be eating food in this field when he was as old as Old Knipe. Billie Carew with his acne and his teeth would be satisfied for life when he got the Kissane girl's knickers off. 'Here,' Billie Carew said, offering him his half-bottle of Bushmills.

'I want to tell you something,' Milton said, finding the Reverend Herbert Cutcheon at the hedge where the urinating took place.

'Tell away, Milton.' The clergyman's edgy face was warm with the pleasure the day had brought. He adjusted his trousers. Another day to remember, he said.

'I was out in the orchards a while back,' Milton said. 'September it was. I was seeing how the apples were doing when a woman came in the top gate.'

'A woman?'

'The next day she was there again. She said she was St Rosa.'

'What d'you mean, St Rosa, Milton?'

The Reverend Cutcheon had halted in his stroll back to the assembled men. He stood still, frowning at the grass by his feet. Then he lifted his head and Milton saw bewilderment, and astonishment, in his opaque brown eyes.

'What d'you mean, St Rosa?' he repeated.

Milton told him, and then confessed that the woman had kissed him twice on the lips, a holy kiss, as she'd called it.

'No kiss is holy, boy. Now, listen to me, Milton. Listen to this carefully, boy.'

A young fellow would have certain thoughts, the Reverend Cutcheon explained. It was the way of things that a young fellow could become confused, owing to the age he was and the changes that had taken place in his body. He reminded Milton that he'd left school, that he was on the way to manhood. The journey to manhood could have a stumble or two in it, he explained, and it wasn't without temptation. One day Milton would inherit the farm and the orchards, since Garfield had surrendered all claim to them. That was something he needed to prepare himself for. Milton's mother was goodness itself, his father would do anything for you. If a neighbour had a broken fence while he was laid up in bed, his father would be the first to see to it. His mother had brought up four fine children, and it was God's way that the fifth was afflicted. God's grace could turn affliction into a gift: poor Stewart, you might say, but you only had to look at him to realize you were glad Stewart had been given life.

'We had a great day today, Milton, we had an enjoyable day. We stood up for the people we are. That's what you have to think of.'

In a companionable way the clergyman's arm was placed around Milton's shoulders. He'd put the thing neatly, the gesture suggested. He'd been taken aback but had risen to the occasion.

'She won't leave me alone,' Milton said.

Just beginning to move forward, the Reverend Cutcheon halted again. His arm slipped from Milton's shoulders. In a low voice he said:

'She keeps bothering you in the orchards, does she?'

Milton explained. He said the woman had been agitating him all day, since the moment he awoke. It was because of that that he'd had to tell someone, because she was pressing him to.

'Don't tell anyone else, Milton. Don't tell a single soul. It's said now between the two of us and it's safe with myself. Not even Addy will hear the like of this.'

Milton nodded. The Reverend Cutcheon said:

'Don't distress your mother and your father, son, with talk of a woman who was on about holiness and the saints.' He paused, then spoke with emphasis, and quietly. 'Your mother and father wouldn't rest easy for the balance of their days.' He paused again. 'There are no better people than your mother and father, Milton.'

'Who was St Rosa?'

Again the Reverend Cutcheon checked his desire to rejoin the men who were picnicking on the grass. Again he lowered his voice.

'Did she ask you for money? After she touched you did she ask you for money?'

'Money?'

'There are women like that, boy.'

Milton knew what he meant. He and Billie Carew had many a time talked about them. You saw them on television, flamboyantly dressed on city streets. Billie Carew said they hung about railway stations, that your best bet was a railway station if you were after one. Milton's mother, once catching a glimpse of these street-traders on the television, designated them 'Catholic strumpets'. Billie Carew said you'd have to go careful with them in case you'd catch a disease. Milton had never heard of such women in the neighbourhood.

'She wasn't like that,' he said.

'You'd get a travelling woman going by and maybe she'd be thinking you had a coin or two on you. Do you understand what I'm saying to you, Milton?'

'Yes.'

'Get rid of the episode. Put it out of your mind.'

'I was only wondering about what she said in relation to a saint.'

'It's typical she'd say a thing like that.'

Milton hesitated. 'I thought she wasn't alive,' he said.

Mr Leeson's Uncle Willie used to preach. He had preached in the towns until he was too old for it, until he began to lose the thread of what he was saying. Milton had heard him. He and Garfield and his sisters had been brought to hear Uncle Willie in his heyday, a bible clenched in his right hand, gesturing with it and quoting from it. Sometimes he spoke of what happened in Rome, facts he knew to be true: how the Pope drank himself into a stupor and had to have the sheets of his bed changed twice in a night, how the Pope's own mother was among the women who came and went in the papal ante-rooms.

Men still preached in the towns, at street corners or anywhere that might attract a crowd, but the preachers were fewer than they had been in the heyday of Mr Leeson's Uncle Willie because the popularity of television kept people in at nights, and because people were in more of a hurry. But during the days that followed the July celebration Milton remembered his great-uncle's eloquence. He remembered the words he had used and the way he could bring in a quotation, and the way he was so certain. Often he had laid down that a form of cleansing was called for, that vileness could be exorcized by withering it out of existence.

The Reverend Cutcheon had been more temperate in his advice, even if what he'd said amounted to much the same thing: if you ignored what happened it wouldn't be there any more. But on the days that followed the July celebration Milton found it increasingly impossible to do so. With a certainty that reminded him of his great-uncle's he became convinced beyond all doubt that he was not meant to be silent. Somewhere in him there was the uncontrollable urge that he should not be. He asked his mother why the old man had begun to preach, and she replied that it was because he had to.

Father Mulhall didn't know what to say.

To begin with, he couldn't remember who St Rosa had been, even if he ever knew. Added to which, there was the fact that it wasn't always plain what the Protestant boy was trying to tell him. The boy stammered rapidly through his account, beginning sentences again because he realized his meaning had slipped away, speaking more slowly the second time but softening his voice to a pitch that made it almost inaudible. The whole thing didn't make sense.

'Wait now till we have a look,' Father Mulhall was obliged to offer in the end. He'd said at first that he would make some investigations about this saint, but the boy didn't seem satisfied with that. 'Sit down,' he invited in his living-room, and went to look for *Butler's Lives of the Saints*.

Father Mulhall was fifty-nine, a tall, wiry man, prematurely white-haired. Two sheepdogs accompanied him when he went to find the relevant volume. They settled down again, at his feet, when he returned. The room was cold, hardly furnished at all, the carpet so thin you could feel the boards.

'There's the Blessed Roseline of Villeneuve,' Father Mulhall said, turning over the pages. 'And the Blessed Rose Venerini. Or there's St Rose of Lima. Or St Rosalia. Or Rose of Viterbo.'

'I think it's that one. Only she definitely said Rosa.'

'Could you have fallen asleep? Was it a hot day?'

'It wasn't a dream I had.'

'Was it late in the day? Could you have been confused by the shadows?'

'It was late the second time. The first time it was the afternoon.'

'Why did you come to me?'

'Because you'd know about a saint.'

Father Mulhall heard how the woman who'd called herself St Rosa wouldn't let the boy alone, how she'd come on stronger and stronger as the day of the July celebration approached, and so strong on the day itself that he knew he wasn't meant to be silent, the boy said.

'About what though?'

'About her giving me the holy kiss.'

The explanation could be that the boy was touched. There was another boy in that family who wasn't the full shilling either.

'Wouldn't you try getting advice from your own clergyman? Isn't Mr Cutcheon your brother-in-law?'

'He told me to pretend it hadn't happened.'

The priest didn't say anything. He listened while he was told how the presence of the saint was something clinging to you, how neither her features nor the clothes she'd worn had faded in any way whatsoever. When the boy closed his eyes he could apparently see her more clearly than he could see any member of his family, or anyone he could think of.

'I only wanted to know who she was. Is that place in France?'

'Viterbo is in Italy actually.'

One of the sheepdogs had crept on to the priest's feet and settled down to sleep. The other was asleep already. Father Mulhall said:

'Do you feel all right in yourself otherwise?'

'She said not to be afraid. She was on about fear.' Milton paused. 'I can still feel her saying things.'

'I would talk to your own clergyman, son. Have a word with your brother-in-law.'

'She wasn't alive, that woman.'

Father Mulhall did not respond to that. He led Milton to the hall-door of his house. He had been affronted by the visit, but he didn't let it show. Why should a saint of his Church appear to a Protestant boy in a neighbourhood that was overwhelmingly Catholic, when there were so many Catholics to choose from? Was it not enough that that march should occur every twelfth of July, that farmers from miles away should bang their way through the village just to show what was what, strutting in their get-up? Was that not enough without claiming the saints as well? On the twelfth of July they closed the village down, they kept people inside. Their noisy presence was a reminder that beyond this small, immediate neighbourhood there was a strength from which they drew their own. This boy's father would give you the time of day if he met you on the road, he'd even lean on a gate and talk to you, but once your back was turned he'd come out with his statements. The son who'd gone to Belfast would salute you and maybe afterwards laugh because he'd saluted a priest. It was widely repeated that Garfield Leeson belonged in the ganglands of the Protestant back streets, that his butcher's skills came in handy when a job had to be done.

'I thought she might be foreign,' Milton said. 'I don't know how I'd know that.'

Two scarlet dots appeared in Father Mulhall's scrawny cheeks. His anger was more difficult to disguise now; he didn't trust himself to speak. In silence Milton was shown out of the house.

When he returned to his living-room Father Mulhall turned on the television and sat watching it with a glass of whiskey, his sheepdogs settling down to sleep again. 'Now, that's amazing!' a chat-show host exclaimed, leading the applause for a performer who balanced a woman on the end of his finger. Father Mulhall wondered how it was done, his absorption greater than it would have been had he not been visited by the Protestant boy.

Mr Leeson finished rubbing his plate clean with a fragment of loaf bread, soaking into it what remained of bacon fat and small pieces of black pudding. Milton said:

'She walked in off the lane.'

Not fully comprehending, Mr Leeson said the odd person came after the apples. Not often, but you knew what they were like. You couldn't put an orchard under lock and key.

'Don't worry about it, son.'

Mrs Leeson shook her head. It wasn't like that, she explained; that wasn't what Milton was saying. The colour had gone from Mrs Leeson's face. What Milton was saying was that a Papist saint had spoken to him in the orchards.

'An apparition,' she said.

Mr Leeson's small eyes regarded his son evenly. Stewart put his side plate on top of the plate he'd eaten his fry from, with his knife and fork on top of that, the way he had been taught. He made his belching noise and to his surprise was not reprimanded.

'I asked Father Mulhall who St Rosa was.'

Mrs Leeson's hand flew to her mouth. For a moment she thought she'd scream. Mr Leeson said:

'What are you on about, boy?'

'I have to tell people.'

Stewart tried to speak, gurgling out a request to carry his two plates and his knife and fork to the sink. He'd been taught that also, and was always obedient. But tonight no one heeded him.

'Are you saying you went to the priest?' Mr Leeson asked.

'You didn't go into his house, Milton?'

Mrs Leeson watched, incredulous, while Milton nodded. He said

Herbert Cutcheon had told him to keep silent, but in the end he couldn't. He explained that on the day of the march he had told his brother-in-law when they were both standing at the hedge, and later he had gone into Father Mulhall's house. He'd sat down while the priest looked the saint up in a book.

'Does anyone know you went into the priest's house, Milton?' Mrs Leeson leaned across the table, staring at him with widened eyes that didn't blink. 'Did anyone see you?'

'I don't know.'

Mr Leeson pointed to where Milton should stand, then rose from the table and struck him on the side of the face with his open palm. He did it again. Stewart whimpered, and became agitated.

'Put them in the sink, Stewart,' Mrs Leeson said.

The dishes clattered into the sink, and the tap was turned on as Stewart washed his hands. The side of Milton's face was inflamed, a trickle of blood came from his nose.

Herbert Cutcheon's assurance that what he'd heard in his father-in-law's field would not be passed on to his wife was duly honoured. But when he was approached on the same subject a second time he realized that continued suppression was pointless. After a Sunday-afternoon visit to his in-laws' farmhouse, when Mr Leeson had gone off to see to the milking and Addy and her mother were reaching down pots of last year's plum jam for Addy to take back to the rectory, Milton had followed him to the yard. As he drove the four miles back to the rectory, the clergyman repeated to Addy the conversation that had taken place.

'You mean he wants to *preach*?' Frowning in astonishment, Addy half shook her head, her disbelief undisguised.

He nodded. Milton had mentioned Mr Leeson's Uncle Willie. He'd said he wouldn't have texts or scriptures, nothing like that.

'It's not Milton,' Addy protested, this time shaking her head more firmly.

'I know it's not.'

He told her then about her brother's revelations on the day of the July celebration. He explained he hadn't done so before because he considered he had made her brother see sense, and these matters were better not referred to.

'Heavens above!' Addy cried, her lower jaw slackened in fresh amazement. The man she had married was not given to the kind of crack that involved lighthearted deception, or indeed any kind of crack at all. Herbert's virtues lay in other directions, well beyond the realm of jest. Even so, Addy emphasized her bewilderment by stirring doubt into her disbelief. 'You're not serious surely?'

He nodded without taking his eyes from the road. Neither of them knew of the visit to the priest or of the scene in the kitchen that had ended in a moment of violence. Addy's parents, in turn believing that Milton had been made to see sense by his father's spirited response, and sharing Herbert Cutcheon's view that such matters were best left unaired, had remained silent also.

'Is Milton away in the head?' Addy whispered.

'He's not himself certainly. No way he's himself.'

'He never showed an interest in preaching.'

'D'you know what he said to me just now in the yard?'

But Addy was still thinking about the woman her brother claimed to have conversed with. Her imagination had stuck there, on the slope of her father's upper orchard, a Catholic woman standing among the trees.

'Dudgeon McDavie,' Herbert Cutcheon went on. 'He mentioned that man.'

Nonplussed all over again, Addy frowned. Dudgeon McDavie was a man who'd been found shot dead by the roadside near Loughgall. Addy remembered her father coming into the kitchen and saying they'd shot poor Dudgeon. She'd been seven at the time; Garfield had been four, Hazel a year older; Milton and Stewart hadn't been born. 'Did he ever do a minute's harm?' she remembered her father saying. 'Did he ever so much as raise his voice?' Her father and Dudgeon McDavie had been schooled together; they'd marched together many a time. Then Dudgeon McDavie had moved out of the neighbourhood, to take up a position as a quantity surveyor. Addy couldn't remember ever having seen him, although from the conversation that had ensued between her mother and her father at the time of his death it was apparent that he had been to the farmhouse many a time. 'Blew half poor Dudgeon's skull off': her father's voice, leaden and grey, echoed as she remembered. 'Poor Dudgeon's brains all over the tarmac.' Her father had attended the funeral, full honours because Dudgeon McDavie had had a hand in keeping law and order, part-time in the UDR. A few weeks later two youths from Loughgall were set upon and punished, although they vehemently declared their innocence.

'Dudgeon McDavie's only hearsay for Milton,' Addy pointed out, and her husband said he realized that.

Drawing up in front of the rectory, a low brick building with metal-framed windows, he said he had wondered about going in search of Mr Leeson when Milton had come out with all that in the yard. But Milton had hung about by the car, making the whole thing even more difficult.

'Did the woman refer to Dudgeon McDavie?' Addy asked. 'Is that it?'

'I don't know if she did. To tell you the truth, Addy, you wouldn't know where you were once Milton gets on to this stuff. For one thing, he said to me the woman wasn't alive.'

In the rectory Addy telephoned. 'I'll ring you back,' her mother said and did so twenty minutes later, when Milton was not within earshot. In the ensuing conversation what information they possessed was shared: the revelations made on the day of the July celebration, what had later been said in the kitchen and an hour ago in the yard.

'Dudgeon McDavie,' Mrs Leeson reported quietly to her husband as soon as she replaced the receiver. 'The latest thing is he's on to Herbert about Dudgeon McDavie.'

Milton rode his bicycle one Saturday afternoon to the first of the towns in which he wished to preach. In a car park two small girls, sucking sweets, listened to him. He explained about St Rosa of Viterbo. He felt he was a listener too, that his voice came from somewhere outside himself – from St Rosa, he explained to the two small girls. He heard himself saying that his sister Hazel refused to return to the province. He heard himself describing the silent village, and the drums and the flutes that brought music to it, and the suit his father wore on the day of the celebration. St Rosa could mourn Dudgeon McDavie, he explained, a Protestant man from Loughgall who'd been murdered ages ago. St Rosa could forgive the brutish soldiers and their masked adversaries, one or other of them responsible for the shattered motor-cars and shrouded bodies that came and went on the television screen. Father Mulhall had been furious, Milton said in the car park, you could see it in his eyes: he'd been furious because a Protestant boy was sitting down in his house. St Rosa of Viterbo had given him her holy kiss, he said: you could tell that Father Mulhall considered that impossible.

The following Saturday Milton cycled to another town, a little further away, and on the subsequent Saturday he preached in a third town. He did not think of it as preaching, more just telling people about his experience. It was what he had to do, he explained, and he noticed that when people began to listen they usually didn't go away. Shoppers paused, old men out for a walk passed the time in his company, leaning against a shop window or the wall of a public lavatory. Once or twice in an afternoon someone was abusive.

On the fourth Saturday Mr Leeson and Herbert Cutcheon arrived in Mr Leeson's Ford Granada and hustled Milton into it. No one spoke a word on the journey back.

'Shame?' Milton said when his mother employed the word.

'On all of us, Milton.'

In church people regarded him suspiciously, and he noticed that Addy sometimes couldn't stop staring at him. When he smiled at Esme Dunshea she didn't smile back; Billie Carew avoided him. His father insisted that in no circumstances whatsoever should he ever again preach about a woman in the orchards. Milton began to explain that he must, that he had been given the task.

'No,' his father said.

'That's the end of it, Milton,' his mother said. She hated it even more than his father did, a woman kissing him on the lips.

The next Saturday afternoon they locked him into the bedroom he shared with Stewart, releasing him at six o'clock. But on Sunday morning he rode away again, and had again to be searched for on the streets of towns. After that, greater care was taken. Stewart was moved out of the bedroom and the following weekend Milton remained under duress there, the door unlocked so that he could go to the lavatory, his meals carried up to him by his mother, who said nothing when she placed the tray on a chest of drawers. Milton expected that on Monday morning everything would be normal again, that his punishment would then have run its course. But this was not so. He was released to work beside his father, clearing out a ditch, and all day there were never more than a couple of yards between them. In the evening he was returned to the bedroom. The door was again secured, and so it always was after that.

On winter Sundays when his sister Addy and the Reverend Cutcheon came to sit in the back room he remained upstairs. He no longer accompanied the family to church. When Garfield came from Belfast at a weekend he refused to carry food to the bedroom, although Milton often heard their mother requesting him to. For a long time now Garfield had not addressed him or sought his company.

When Milton did the milking his father didn't keep so close to him. He put a padlock on the yard gate and busied himself with some task or other in one of the sheds, or else kept an eye on the yard from the kitchen. On two Saturday afternoons Milton climbed out of the bedroom window and set off on his bicycle, later to be pursued. Then one day when he returned from the orchards with his father he found that Jimmy Logan had been to the farmhouse to put bars on his bedroom window. His bicycle was no longer in the turf shed; he caught a glimpse of it tied on to the boot of the Ford Granada and deduced that it was being taken to be sold. His mother unearthed an old folding card-table, since it was a better height for eating off than the chest of drawers. Milton knew that people had been told he had become affected in the head, but he could tell from his mother's demeanour that not even this could exorcize the shame he had brought on the family.

When the day of the July celebration came again Milton remained in his bedroom. Before he left the house his father led him to the lavatory and waited outside it in order to lead him back again. His father didn't say anything. He didn't say it was the day of the July celebration, but Milton could tell it was, because he was wearing his special suit. Milton watched the car drawing out of the yard and then heard his mother chatting to Stewart in the kitchen, saying something about sitting in the sun. He imagined the men gathering in the field, the clergyman's blessing, the drums strapped on, ranks formed. As usual, the day was fine; from his bedroom window he could see there wasn't a cloud in the sky.

It wasn't easy to pass the time. Milton had never been much of a one for reading, had never read a book from cover to cover. Sometimes when his mother brought his food she left him the weekly newspaper and he read about the towns it gave news of, and the different rural neighbourhoods, one of which was his own. He listened to his transistor. His mother collected all the jigsaw puzzles she could find, some of which had been in the farmhouse since Hazel and Garfield were children, others of a simple nature bought specially for Stewart. She left him a pack of cards, with only the three of diamonds missing, and a cardboard box containing scraps of wool and a spool with tacks in it that had been Addy's French-knitting outfit.

On the day of the celebration he couldn't face, yet again, completing the jigsaw of Windsor Castle or the Battle of Britain, or playing patience with the three of diamonds drawn on the back of an envelope, or listening all day to cheery disc-jockeys. He practised preaching, all the time seeing the woman in the orchard instead of the sallow features of Jesus or a cantankerous-looking God, white-haired and bearded, frowning through the clouds.

From time to time he looked at his watch and on each occasion established the point the march had reached. The Kissane girl and her sisters waved. Cars drew courteously in to allow the celebration to pass by. McCourt's Hardware and Agricultural Supplies was closed, the village street was empty. Beyond the school and the Church of the Holy Rosary the march halted, then returned the way it had come, only making a change when it reached McCourt's again, swinging off to the left.

Mrs Leeson unlocked the door and handed in a tray, and Milton imagined the chicken legs and the sandwiches in the field, bottles coming out, the men standing in a row by the hedge. 'No doubt about it,' his father said. 'Dr Gibney's seen cases like it before.' A nutcase, his father intimated without employing the term, but when he was out of hearing one of the men muttered that he knew for a fact Dr Gibney hadn't been asked for an opinion. In the field the shame that was spoken about spread from his father to the men themselves.

Milton tumbled out on the card-table the jigsaw pieces of a jungle scene and slowly turned them right side up. He didn't know any more what would happen if they opened the door and freed him. He didn't know if he would try to walk to the towns, if he'd feel again the pressure to do so or if everything was over, if he'd been cleansed, as his father's old uncle would have said. Slowly he found the shape of a chimpanzee among the branches of a tree. He wished he were in the field, taking the half-bottle from Billie Carew. He wished he could feel the sun on his face and feel the ache going out of his legs after the march.

He completed the top left-hand corner of the jungle scene, adding brightly coloured birds to the tree with the chimpanzees in it. The voices of his mother and Stewart floated up to him from the yard, the incoherent growling of his brother, his mother soothing. From where he sat he saw them when they moved into view, Stewart lumbering, his mother holding his hand. They passed out of the yard, through the gate that was padlocked when he did the milking. Often they walked down to the stream on a warm afternoon.

Again he practised preaching. He spoke of his father ashamed in the field, and the silent windows of the village. He explained that he had been called to go among people, bearing witness on a Saturday afternoon. He spoke of fear. It was that that was most important of all. Fear was the weapon of the gunmen and the soldiers, fear quietened the village. In fear his sister had abandoned the province that was her home. Fearful, his brother disposed of the unwanted dead.

Later Milton found the two back legs of an elephant and slipped the piece that contained them into place. He wondered if he would finish the jigsaw or if it would remain on the mildewed baize of the card-table with most of its middle part missing. He hadn't understood why the story of Dudgeon McDavie had occurred to him as a story he must tell. It had always been there; he'd heard it dozens of times; yet it seemed a different kind of story when he thought about the woman in the orchard, when over and over again he watched her coming towards him, and when she spoke about fear.

He found another piece of the elephant's grey bulk. In the distance he could hear the sound of a car. He paid it no attention, not even when the engine throbbed with a different tone, indicating that the car had drawn up by the yard gate. The gate rattled in a familiar way, and Milton went to his window then. A yellow Vauxhall moved into the yard.

He watched while a door opened and a man he had never seen before stepped out from the driver's seat. The engine was switched off. The man stretched himself. Then Garfield stepped out too.

'It took a death to get you back,' her father said.

On the drive from the airport Hazel did not reply. She was twenty-six, two years younger than Addy, small and dark-haired, as Addy was, too. Ever since the day she had married, since her exile had begun, the truth had not existed between her and these people she had left behind. The present occasion was not a time for prevarication, not a time for pretence, yet already she could feel both all around her. Another death in a procession of deaths had occurred; this time close to all of them. Each death that came was close to someone, within some family: she'd said that years ago, saying it only once, not arguing because none of them wanted to have a conversation like that.

Mr Leeson slowed as they approached the village of Glenavy, then halted to allow two elderly women to cross the street. They waved their thanks, and he waved back. Eventually he said:

'Herbert's been good.'

Again Hazel did not respond. 'God took him for a purpose,' she imagined Herbert Cutcheon comforting her mother. 'God has a job for him.'

'How's Addy?'

Her sister was naturally distressed also, she was told. The shock was still there, still raw in all of them.

'That stands to reason.'

They slid into a thin stream of traffic on the motorway, Mr Leeson not accelerating much. He said:

'I have to tell you what it was with Milton before we get home.'

'Was it the Provos? Was Milton involved in some way?'

'Don't call them the Provos, Hazel. Don't give them any kind of title. They're not worthy of a title.'

'You have to call them something.'

'It wasn't them. There was no reason why it should have been.'

Hazel, who had only been told that her brother had died violently – shot by intruders when he was alone in the house – heard how Milton had insisted he'd received a supernatural visitation from a woman. She heard how he had believed the woman was the ghost of a Catholic saint, how he had gone to the priest for information, how he had begun street-corner preaching.

'He said things people didn't like?' she suggested, ignoring the more incredible aspect of this information.

'We had to keep him in. I kept him by me when we worked, Garfield wouldn't address him.'

'You kept him in?'

'Poor Milton was away in the head, Hazel. He'd be all right for a while, maybe for weeks, longer even. Then suddenly he'd start about the woman in the orchard. He wanted to travel the six counties preaching about her. He told me that. He wanted to stand up in every town he came to and tell his tale. He brought poor Dudgeon McDavie into it.'

'What d'you mean, you kept him in?'

'We sometimes had to lock his bedroom door. Milton didn't know what he was doing, girl. We had to get rid of his bicycle, but even so he'd have walked. A couple of times on a Saturday he set off to walk, and myself and Herbert had to get him back.'

'My God!'

'You can't put stuff like that in a letter. You can't blame anyone for not writing that down for you. Your mother didn't want to. "What've you said to Hazel?" I asked her one time and she said, "Nothing," so we left it.'

'Milton went mad and no one told me?'

'Poor Milton did, Hazel.'

Hazel endeavoured to order the confusion of her thoughts. Pictures formed: of the key turned in the bedroom door; of the household as it had apparently become, her parents' two remaining children a double burden – Stewart's mongol blankness, Milton's gibberish. 'Milton's been shot,' she had said to her husband after the telephone call, shocked that Milton had apparently become involved, as Garfield was, drawn into it no doubt by Garfield. Ever since, that assumption had remained.

They left the motorway, bypassed Craigavon, then again made their way on smaller roads. This is home, Hazel found herself reflecting in that familiar landscape, the reminder seeming alien among thoughts that were less tranquil. Yet in spite of the reason for her visit, in spite of the upsetting muddle of facts she'd been presented with on this journey, she wanted to indulge the moment, to close her eyes and let herself believe that it was a pleasure of some kind to be back where she belonged. Soon they would come to Drumfin, then Anderson's Crossroads. They would pass the Cuchulainn Inn, and turn before reaching the village. Everything would be familiar then, every house and cottage, trees and gateways, her father's orchards.

'Take it easy with your mother,' he said. 'She cries a lot.'

'Who was it shot Milton?'

'There's no one has claimed who it was. The main concern's your mother.'

Hazel didn't say anything, but when her father began to speak again she interrupted him.

'What about the police?'

'Finmoth's keeping an open mind.'

The car passed the Kissanes' house, pink and respectable, delphiniums in its small front garden. Next came the ruined cowshed in the middle of Malone's field, three of its stone walls standing, the fourth tumbled down, its disintegrating roof mellow with rust. Then came the orchards, and the tarred gate through which you could see the stream, steeply below.

Her father turned the car into the yard of the farmhouse. One of the dogs barked, scampering back and forth, wagging his tail as he always did when the car returned.

'Well, there we are.' With an effort Mr Leeson endeavoured to extend a welcome. 'You'd recognize the old place still!'

In the kitchen her mother embraced her. Her mother had a shrunken look; a hollowness about her eyes, and shallow cheeks that exposed the shape of bones beneath the flesh. A hand grasped at one of Hazel's and clutched it tightly, as if in a plea for protection. Mr Leeson carried Hazel's suitcase upstairs.

'Sit down.' With her free hand Hazel pulled a chair out from the table and gently eased her mother toward it. Her brother grinned across the kitchen at her.

'Oh, Stewart!'

She kissed him, hugging his awkward body. Pimples disfigured his big forehead, his spiky short hair tore uncomfortably at her cheek.

'We should have seen,' Mrs Leeson whispered. 'We should have known.'

'You couldn't. Of course you couldn't.'

'He had a dream or something. That's all he was on about.'

Hazel remembered the dreams she'd had herself at Milton's age, half-dreams because sometimes she was awake – close your eyes and you could make Mick Jagger smile at you, or hear the music of U2 or The Damage. 'Paul Hogan had his arms round me,' Addy giggled once. Then you began going out with someone and everything was different.

'Yet how would he know about a saint?' her mother whispered. 'Where'd he get the name from?'

Hazel didn't know. It would have come into his head, she said to herself, but didn't repeat the observation aloud. In spite of what she said, her mother didn't want to think about it. Maybe it was easier for her mother, too, to believe her son had been away in the head, or maybe it made it worse. You wouldn't know that, you couldn't tell from her voice or from her face.

'Don't let it weigh on you,' she begged. 'Don't make it worse for yourself.'

Later Addy and Herbert Cutcheon were in the kitchen. Addy made tea and tumbled biscuits on to a plate. Herbert Cutcheon was solemn, Addy subdued. Like her father, Hazel sensed, both of them were worried about her mother. Being worried about her mother was the practical aspect of the grief that was shared, an avenue of escape from it, a distraction that was permitted. Oblivious to all emotion, Stewart reached out for a biscuit with pink marshmallow in it, his squat fingers and bitten nails ugly for an instant against the soft prettiness.

'He'll get the best funeral the Church can give him,' Herbert Cutcheon promised.

Garfield stood a little away from them, with a black tie in place and his shoes black also, not the trainers he normally wore. Looking at him across the open grave, Hazel suddenly knew. In ignorance she had greeted him an hour ago in the farmhouse; they had stood together in the church; she had watched while he stepped forward to bear the coffin. Now, in the bleak churchyard, those images were illuminated differently. The shame had been exorcized, silence silently agreed upon.

'*I will keep my mouth as it were with a bridle,*' Herbert Cutcheon proclaimed, his voice heavy with the churchiness that was discarded as soon as his professional duties ceased, never apparent on a Sunday afternoon in the back room of the farmhouse. 'Forasmuch as it hath pleased Almighty God.'

Earth was thrown on to the coffin. '*Our Father, who art in heaven,*' Herbert Cutcheon suitably declared, and Hazel watched Garfield's lips, in unison with Addy's and their parents'. Stewart was there too, now and again making a noise. Mrs Leeson held a handkerchief to her face, clinging on to her husband in sudden bright sunshine. '*And forgive us our trespasses.*' Garfield mouthed the words too.

With bitter calmness, Hazel allowed the facts to settle into place. Milton had been told not to. He had been told, even by Garfield himself, that you had fancies when you were fifteen. He had been told that talk about a Catholic saint was like the Catholics claiming one of their idolatrous statues had been seen to move. But in spite of all that was said to him Milton had disobeyed. 'Your bodies a living sacrifice,' Hazel's Great-Uncle Willie used to thunder, steadfast in his certainty. Prominent among the mourners, the old man's granite features displayed no emotion now.

'Amen,' Herbert Cutcheon prompted, and the mourners murmured and Mrs Leeson sobbed. Hazel moved closer to her, as Addy did, receiving her from their father's care. All of them knew, Hazel's thoughts ran on: her father knew, and her mother, and Addy, and Herbert Cutcheon. It was known in every house in the neighbourhood; it was known in certain Belfast bars and clubs, where Garfield's hard-man reputation had been threatened, and then enhanced.

'It's all right, Mother,' Addy whispered as the three women turned from the grave, but Hazel did not attempt to soothe her mother's distress because she knew she could not. Her mother would go to her own grave with the scalding agony of what had happened still alive within her; her father would be reminded of the day of the occurrence on all the July marches remaining to him. The family would not ever talk about the day, but through their pain they would tell themselves that Milton's death was the way things were, the way things had to be: that was their single consolation. Lost ground had been regained.

A Day

In the night Mrs Lethwes wakes from time to time, turns and murmurs in her blue-quilted twin bed, is aware of fleeting thoughts and fragments of memory that dissipate swiftly. Within her stomach, food recently consumed is uneasily digested. Briefly, she suffers a moment of cramp.

Mrs Lethwes dreams: a child again, she remains in the car while her brother, Charlie, visits the Indian family who run the supermarket. Kittens creep from beneath inverted flowerpots in the Bunches' back yard, and she is there, in the yard too, looking for Charlie because he is visiting the Bunches now. 'You mustn't go bothering the Bunches,' their mother upbraids him. 'People are busy.' There are rivers to cross, and the streets aren't there any more; there is a seashore, and tents.

In her garden, while Mrs Lethwes still sleeps, the scent of night-stock fades with the cool of night. Dew forms on roses and geraniums, on the petals of the cosmos and the yellow spikes of broom. Slugs creep towards lettuce plants, avoiding a line of virulent bait; a silent cat, far outside its own domain, waits for the emergence of the rockery mice.

It is July. Dawn comes early, casting a pale twilight on the brick of the house, on the Virginia creeper that covers half a wall, setting off white-painted window-frames and decorative wrought-iron. This house and garden, in a tranquil wooded neighbourhood, constitute one part of the achievement of Mrs Lethwes's husband, are a symbol of professional advancement conducted over twenty years, which happens also to be the length of this marriage.

Abruptly, Mrs Lethwes is fully awake and knows her night's sleep is over. Hunched beneath the bedclothes in the other bed, her husband does not stir when she rises and crosses the room they share to the window. Drawing aside the edge of a curtain, she glances down into the early-morning garden and almost at once drops the curtain back into place. In bed again, she lies on her side, facing her husband because, being fond of him, she likes to watch him sleeping. She feels blurred and headachy, as she always does at this time, the worst moment of her day, Mrs Lethwes considers.

Is Elspeth awake too? She wonders that. Does Elspeth, in her city precinct, share the same pale shade of dawn? Is there, as well, the orange glow of a street lamp and now, beginning in the distance somewhere, the soft swish of a milk dray, a car door banging, a church bell chiming five? Mrs Lethwes doesn't know where Elspeth lives precisely, or in any way what she looks like, but imagines short black hair and elfin features, a small, thin body, fragile fingers. An hour and three-quarters later – still conducting this morning ritual – she hears bath-water running; and later still there is music. Vivaldi, Mrs Lethwes thinks.

Her husband wakes. His eyes remember, becoming troubled, and then the trouble lifts from them when he notices, without surprise, that she's not asleep. In another of her dreams during the night that has passed he carried her, and his voice spoke softly, soothing her. Or was it quite a dream, or only something like one? She tries to smile; she says she's sorry, knowing now.

At ten, when the cleaning woman comes, Mrs Lethwes goes out to shop. She parks her small, white Peugeot in the Waitrose car park, and in a leisurely manner gathers vegetables and fruit, and tins and jars, pork chops for this evening, vermouth and Gordon's gin, Edam, and Normandy butter because she has noticed the butter is getting low, Comfort and the cereal her husband favours, the one called Common Sense. Afterwards, with everything in the boot, she makes her way to the Trompe-L'Oeil for coffee. Her make-up is in place, her hair drawn up, the way she has taken to wearing it lately. She smiles at people she knows by sight, the waitress and other women who are having coffee, at the cashier when she pays her bill. There is some conversation, about the weather.

In her garden, later, the sound of the Hoover reaches her from the open windows of the house as the cleaning woman, Marietta, moves from room to room. The day is warm, Mrs Lethwes's legs are bare, her blue dress light on her body, her Italian sandals comfortable yet elegant. Marietta claims to be Italian also, having had an Italian mother, but her voice and manner are Cockney and Mrs Lethwes doubts that she has ever been in Italy, even though she regularly gives the impression that she knows Venice well.

Mrs Lethwes likes to be occupied when Marietta comes. When it's fine she finds something to do in the garden, and when the weather doesn't permit that she lingers for longer in the Trompe-L'Oeil and there's the pretence of letter-writing or tidying drawers. She likes to keep a closed door between herself and Marietta, to avoid as best she can the latest about Marietta's daughter Ange, and Liam, whom Ange has been contemplating marriage with for almost five years, and the latest about the people in the house next door, who keep Alsatians.

In the garden Mrs Lethwes weeds a flowerbed, wishing that Marietta didn't have to come to the house three times a week, but knowing that of course she must. She hopes the little heart-leafed things she's clearing from among the delphiniums are not the germination of seeds that Mr Yatt has sown, a misfortune that occurred last year with his Welsh poppies. Unlike Marietta, Mr Yatt is dour and rarely speaks, but he has a way of slowly raising his head and staring, which Mrs Lethwes finds disconcerting. When he's in the garden – Mondays only, all day – she keeps out of it herself.

Not Vivaldi now, perhaps a Telemann minuet, run Mrs Lethwes's thoughts in her garden. Once, curious about the music a flautist plays, she read the information that accompanied half a dozen compact discs in a music shop. She didn't buy the discs but, curious again, she borrowed some from the music section of the library and played them all one morning. Thirty-six, or just a little younger, she sees Elspeth as, unmarried of course and longing to bear the child of the man she loves: Mrs Lethwes is certain of that, since she has experienced this same longing herself. In the flat she imagines, there's a smell of freshly made coffee. The fragile fingers cease their movement. The instrument is laid aside, the coffee poured.

It was in France, in the Hôtel St-Georges during their September holiday seven years ago, that Mrs Lethwes found out about her husband's other woman. There was a letter, round feminine handwriting on an airmail envelope, an English stamp: she knew at once. The letter had been placed in someone else's key-box by mistake, and was later handed to her with a palaver of apologies when her husband was swimming in the Mediterranean. 'Ah, *merci*,' she thanked the smooth-haired girl receptionist and said the error didn't matter in the very least. She knew at once: the instinct of a barren wife, she afterwards called it to herself. So this was why he made a point of being down before her every morning, why he had always done so during their September holiday in France; she'd never wondered about it before. On the terrace she examined the post-mark. It was indecipherable, but again the handwriting told a lot, and only a woman with whom a man had an association would write to him on holiday. From the letter itself, which she read and then destroyed, she learned all there was otherwise to know.

There are too many of the heart-leafed plants, and when she looks in other areas of the border and in other beds she finds they're not in evidence there. Clearly, it's the tragedy of the Welsh poppies all over again. Mrs Lethwes begins to put back what she has taken out, knowing as she does so that this isn't going to work.

'"Silly girl," I said, straight to her face. "Silly girl, Ange, no way you're not."'

Marietta has established herself at the kitchen table, her shapeless bulk straining the seams of a pink overall, her feet temporarily removed from the carpet slippers she brings with her because they're comfortable to work in.

'No, not for me, thanks,' Mrs Lethwes says, which is what she always says when she is offered instant coffee at midday. Real coffee doesn't agree with Marietta, never has. Toxic in Marietta's view.

'All she give's a giggle. That's Ange all over, that. Always has been.'

This woman has watched Ange's puppy-fat go, has seen her through childhood illnesses. And Bernardo, too. This woman could have had a dozen children, borne them and nursed them, loved them and been loved herself. 'Well, I drew a halt at two, dear. Drew the line, know what I mean? He said have another go, but I couldn't agree.'

Five goes, Mrs Lethwes has had herself: five failures, in bed for every day the third and fourth time, told she mustn't try again, but she did. The same age she was then as she imagines her husband's other woman to be: thirty-six when she finally accepted she was a childless wife.

'Decent a bloke as ever walked a street is little Liam, but Ange don't see it. One day she'll look up and he'll be gone and away. Talking to a wall you are.'

'Is Ange in love, though?'

'Call it how you like, dear. Mention it to Ange and all she give's a giggle. Well, Liam's small. A little fellow, but then where's the harm in small?'

Washing traces of soil from her hands at the sink, Mrs Lethwes says there is no harm in a person being small. Hardly five foot, she has many times heard Liam is. But strong as a horse.

'I said it to her straight, dear. Wait for some bruiser and you'll build your life on regrets. No good to no one, regrets.'

'No good at all.'

Of course was what she'd thought on the terrace of the Hôtel St-Georges: a childless marriage was a disappointment for any man. She'd failed him, although naturally it had never been said; he wasn't in the least like that. But she had failed and had compounded her failure by turning away from talk of adoption. She had no feeling for the idea; she wasn't the kind to take on other people's kids. Their own particular children were the children she wanted, an expression of their love, an expression of their marriage: more and more, she'd got that into her head. When the letter arrived at the Hôtel St-Georges she'd been reconciled for years to her barren state; they lived with it, or so she thought. The letter changed everything. The letter frightened her; she should have known.

'We need the window-cleaners one of them days,' Marietta says, dipping a biscuit into her coffee. 'Shocking, the upstairs panes is.'

'I'll ring them.'

'Didn't mind me mentioning it, dear? Only with the build-up it works out twice the price. No saving really.'

'Actually, I forget. I wasn't trying to –'

'Best done regular I always say.'

'I'll ring them this afternoon.'

Mrs Lethwes said nothing in the Hôtel St-Georges and she hasn't since. He doesn't know she knows; she hopes that nothing ever shows. She sat for an hour on the terrace of the hotel, working it out. Say something, she thought, and as soon as she does it'll be in the open. The next thing is he'll be putting it gently to her that nothing is as it should be. Gently because he always has been gentle, especially about her barren state; sorry for her, dutiful in their plight, tied to her. He'd have had an Eastern child, any little slit-eyed thing, but when she hadn't been able to see it he'd been good about that too.

'Sets the place off when the windows is done, I always say.'

'Yes, of course.'

He came back from his swim; and the letter from a woman who played an instrument in an orchestra was already torn into little pieces and in a waste-bin in the car park, the most distant one she could find. 'Awfully good, this,' she said when he came and sat beside her. *Some Do Not* was the book she laid aside. He said he had read it at school.

'I'll do the window-sills when they've been. Shocking with flies, July is. Filthy really.'

'I'll see if I can get them next week.'

There hadn't been an address, just a date: September 4th. No need for an address because of course he knew it, and from the letter's tone he had for ages. She wondered what that meant and couldn't think of a time when a change had begun in his manner towards her. There hadn't been one; and in other ways, too, he was as he always had been: unhurried in his movements and his speech, his square healthy features the same terracotta shade, the grey in his hair in no way diminishing his physical attractiveness. It was hardly surprising that someone else found him attractive too. Driving up through France, and back again in England, she became used to pretending in his company that the person called Elspeth did not exist, while endlessly conjecturing when she was alone.

'I'll do the stairs down,' Marietta says, 'and then I'll scoot, dear.'

'Yes, you run along whenever you're ready.'

'I'll put in the extra Friday, dear. Three-quarters of an hour I owe all told.'

'Oh, please don't worry –'

'Fair's fair, dear. Only I'd like to catch the twenty-past today, with Bernardo anxious for his dinner.'

'Yes, of course you must.'

The house is silent when Marietta has left, and Mrs Lethwes feels free again. The day is hers now, until the evening. She can go from room to room in stockinged feet, and let the telephone ring unanswered. She can watch, if the mood takes her, some old black-and-white film on the television, an English one, for she likes those best, pretty girls' voices from the 1940s, Michael Wilding young again, Ann Todd.

She doesn't have much lunch. She never does during the week: a bit of cheese on the Ritz biscuits she has a weakness for, gin and dry Martini twice. In her spacious sitting-room Mrs Lethwes slips her shoes off and stretches out on one of the room's two sofas. Then the first sharp tang of the Martini causes her, for a moment, to close her eyes with pleasure.

Silver-framed, a reminder of her wedding day stands on a round inlaid surface among other photographs near by. August 26th 1974: the date floats through her midday thoughts. 'I *know* this'll work out,' her mother – given to speaking openly – had remarked the evening before, when she met for the first time the parents of her daughter's fiancé. The remark had caused a silence, then someone laughed.

She reaches for a Ritz. The soft brown hair that's hardly visible beneath the bridal veil is blonded now and longer than it was, which is why she wears it gathered up, suitable in middle age. She was pretty then and is handsome now; still loose-limbed, she has put on only a little weight. Her teeth are still white and sound; only her light-blue eyes, once brilliantly clear, are blurred, like eyes caught out of focus. Afterwards her mother's remark on the night before the wedding became a joke, because of course the marriage had worked out. A devoted couple; a perfect marriage, people said – and still say, perhaps – except for the pity of there being no children. It's most unlikely, Mrs Lethwes believes, that anyone much knows about his other woman. He wouldn't want that; he wouldn't want his wife humiliated, that never was his style.

Mrs Lethwes, who smokes one cigarette a day, smokes it now as she lies on the sofa, not yet pouring her second drink. On later September holidays there had been no letters, of that she was certain. Some alarm had been raised by the one that didn't find its intended destination: dreadful, he would have considered it, a liaison discovered by chance, and would have felt afraid. 'Please understand. I'm awfully sorry,' he would have said, and Elspeth would naturally have honoured his wishes, even though writing to him when he was away was precious.

'No more. That's all.' On her feet again to pour her second drink, Mrs Lethwes firmly makes this resolution, speaking aloud since there is no one to be surprised by that. But a little later she finds herself rooting beneath underclothes in a bedroom drawer, and finding there another bottle of Gordon's and pouring some and adding water from a bathroom tap. The bottle is returned, the fresh drink carried downstairs, the Ritz packet put away, the glass she drank her two cocktails from washed and dried and returned to where the glasses are kept. Opaque, blue to match the bathroom paint, the container she drinks from now is a toothbrush beaker, and holds more than the sedate cocktail glass, three times as much almost. The taste is different, the plastic beaker feels different in her grasp, not stemmed and cool as the glass was, warmer on her lips. The morning that has passed seems far away as the afternoon advances, as the afternoon connects with the afternoon of yesterday and of the day before, a repetition that must have a beginning somewhere but now is lost.

He is with her now. They are together in the flat she shares with no one, being an independent girl. At three o'clock, that is Mrs Lethwes's thought. Excuses are not difficult; in his position in the office, he would not even have to make them. Lunch with the kind of business people he often refers to, lunch in the Milano or the Petit Escargot, and then a taxi to the flat that is a second home. 'Surprise!' he says on the doorstep intercom, and takes his jacket off while she makes tea. 'I'll not be back this afternoon,' is all he has said on the phone to his bespectacled and devoted secretary.

They sit by the french windows that open on to a small balcony and are open now. It is a favourite place in summer, geraniums blooming in the balcony's two ornamental containers, the passers-by on the street below viewed through the metal scrolls that decorate the balustrade, the drawn-back curtains undisturbed by breezes. The teacups are a shade of pink. The talk is about the orchestra, where it is going next, how long she'll be away, the dates precisely given because that's important. In winter the imagined scene is similar, except that they sit by the gas fire beneath the reproduction of *Field of Poppies*, the curtains drawn because it's darkening outside even as early as this. In winter there's Mahler on the CD player, instead of the passers-by to watch.

Why couldn't it be? Mrs Lethwes wonders at ten past five when a film featuring George Formby comes to an end. Why couldn't it be that he would come back this evening and confess there has been a miscalculation? 'She is to have a child': why shouldn't it be that he might say simply that? And how could Elspeth, busy with her orchestra, travelling to Cleveland and Chicago and San Francisco, to Rome and Seville and Nice and Berlin, possibly be a mother? And yet, of course, Elspeth would want his child, women do when they're in love.

Vividly, Mrs Lethwes sees this child, a tiny girl on a rug in the garden, a sunshade propped up, Mr Yatt bent among the dwarf sweetpeas. And Marietta saying in the kitchen, 'My, my, there's looks for you!' The child is his, Mrs Lethwes reflects, pouring again; at least what has happened is halfway there to what might have been if the child was hers also. Beggars can't be choosers.

At fifteen minutes past five, fear sets in, the same fear there was on the terrace of the Hôtel St-Georges when the letter was still between her fingers. He will go from her; it is pity that keeps him with a barren woman; he will find the courage, and with it will come the hardness of heart that is not naturally his. Then he will go.

Once, not long ago – or maybe it was a year or so ago, hard to be accurate now – she said on an impulse that she had been wrong to resist the adoption of an unwanted child, wrong to say a child for them must only be his and hers. In response he shook his head. Adoption would not be easy now, he said, in their middle age, and that was that. Some other day, on the television, there was a woman who took an infant from a pram, and she felt sympathy for that woman then, though no one else did. Whenever she saw a baby in a pram she thought of the woman taking it, and at other times she thought of that girl who walked away with the baby she was meant to be looking after, and the woman who took one from a hospital ward. When she told him she felt sympathy he put his arms around her and wiped away her tears. This afternoon, the fear lasts for half an hour; then, at a quarter to six, it is so much nonsense. Never in a thousand years would he develop that hardness of heart.

'I have to go now,' he says in his friend's flat. They cease their observation of the passers-by below. Again they embrace and then he goes. The touch of her lips goes with him, her regretful smile, her fragile fingers where for so long that afternoon they rested in his hand. He drives through traffic, perfectly knowing the way, not having to think. And in the flat she plays her music, and finds in it a consolation. It is his due to have his other woman: on the hotel terrace she decided that. In the hour she sat there with the letter not yet destroyed everything fell into place. She knew she must never say she had discovered what she had. She knew she didn't want him ever not to be there.

Lovers quarrel. Love affairs end. What life is it for Elspeth, scraps from a marriage he won't let go of? Why shouldn't she tire of waiting? 'No,' he says when Elspeth cheats, allowing her pregnancy to occur in order to force his hand. Still he says he can't, and all there is is a mess where once there was romance. He turns to his discarded wife and there between them is his confession. 'She travels, you see. She has to travel, she won't give up her music.' How quickly should there be forgiveness? Should there be some pretence of anger? Should there be tears? His friend set a trap for him, his voice goes on, a tender trap, as in the song: that is where his weakness has landed him. His voice apologizes and asks for understanding and for mercy. His other woman has played her part although she never knew it; without his other woman there could not be a happy ending.

She sets the table for their dinner, the tweed mats, the cutlery, the pepper-mill, the German mustard, glasses for wine because he deserves a little wine after his day, Châteauneuf-du-Pape. The bottle's on the table, opened earlier because she knows to do that from experience: it's difficult later on to open wine with all the rush of cooking. And the wine should breathe: years ago he taught her that.

In the kitchen she begins to cut the fat off the pork chops she bought that morning, a long time ago it seems now. Marietta's recipe she's intending to do: pork chops in tomato sauce, onions and peppers. On the mottled working surface the blue toothbrush beaker is almost full again, reached out for often. The meat slides about although, in actual fact, it doesn't move. It is necessary to be careful with the knife; her little finger is wrapped in a band-aid from a week ago. On the radio Humphrey Lyttelton asks his teams to announce the Late Arrivals at the Undertakers Ball.

'Of course,' Mrs Lethwes says aloud. 'Of course, we'll offer it a home.'

At five to seven, acting instinctively as she does every evening at about this time, Mrs Lethwes washes the blue plastic beaker and replaces it in the bathroom. Twice, before she hears the car wheels on the tarmac, she raises the gin bottle directly to her lips, then pours herself, conventionally, a cocktail of Gordon's and Martini. She knows it will happen tonight. She knows he will enter with a worry in his features and stand by the door, not coming forward for a moment, that then he'll pour himself a drink, too, and sit down slowly and begin to tell her. 'I'm sorry,' is probably how he'll put it, and she'll stop him, telling him she can guess. And after he has spoken for twenty minutes, covering all the ground that has been lost, she'll say, of course: 'The child must come here.'

The noisy up-and-over garage door falls into place. In a hurry Mrs Lethwes raises the green bottle to her lips because suddenly she feels the need of it. She does so again before there is the darkness that sometimes comes, arriving suddenly today just as she is whispering to herself that tomorrow, all day long, she'll not take anything at all and thinking also that, for tonight, the open wine will be enough, and if it isn't there's always more that can be broached. For, after all, tonight is a time for celebration. A schoolgirl on a summer's day, just like the one that has passed, occupies the upper room where only visitors sleep. She comes downstairs and chatters on, about her friends, her teachers, a worry she has, not understanding a poem, and together at the kitchen table they read it through. Oh, I do love you, Mrs Lethwes thinks, while there is imagery and words rhyme.

On the mottled worktop in the kitchen the meat is where Mrs Lethwes left it, the fat partly cut away, the knife still separating it from one of the chops. The potatoes she scraped earlier in the day are in a saucepan of cold water, the peas she shelled in another. Often, in the evenings, it is like that in the kitchen when her husband returns to their house. He is gentle when he carries her, as he always is.

Marrying Damian

'I'm going to marry Damian,' Joanna said.

Claire wasn't paying attention. She smiled and nodded, intent on unravelling a ball of garden twine that had become tangled. I said:

'Well, that's nice, of course. But Damian's married already.'

It didn't matter, Joanna said, and repeated her resolve. Joanna was five at the time.

Twenty-two years later Damian stood on the wild grass, among the corn-flowers and the echiums and the lavatera, under the cricket-bat willow that had been a two-foot shrub when Joanna made her announcement. He was wearing blue sunglasses and a powder-blue suit that looked new. In contrast, his tie – its maroon and gold stripes seeming to indicate membership of some club to which almost certainly Damian did not belong – was lank, and the collar of his shirt was frayed. We hadn't been expecting him; we hadn't heard from Damian for years. Since the spring of 1985, Claire later calculated, the year of his second divorce, from an American widow in upstate New York. After that there was an English-woman who lived in Venice, about whom we were never told very much. When Joanna had declared her childhood intention Damian had been still married to the only one of his three wives Claire and I actually knew: a slender, pretty girl, the daughter of the Bishop of Killaloe. We had known her since the wedding; I'd been Damian's best man.

I was actually asleep when Damian walked into our garden all those years later, and I think Claire was too. We were lolling in deck-chairs, Claire's spaniels stretched out under hers, avoiding the afternoon sun.

'Yes,' Damian said. 'It's Damian.'

We were surprised, but perhaps not much: turning up out of the blue had always been his habit. He never telephoned first or intimated his intention by letter or on a postcard. Over the years he had arrived in all seasons and at varying times of day, once rousing us at two o'clock in the morning. Invariably he brought with him details of a personal disaster which had left him with the need to borrow a little money. These loans were not paid back; even as he accepted them he made no pretence that they would be.

'Damian.' Claire hugged him, laughing, playfully demanding to know what he was doing in that awful suit. I asked him where he'd been and he said oh, a lot of places – Vancouver, Oregon, Spain. Claire made him sit down, saying she was going to make some tea, inviting him to stay a while. He was the tonic we needed, Claire said, for she's always afraid that we'll slump into dullness unless we're careful. A woman, somewhere, had given him the suit: we both guessed that.

'I wasn't all that well in Spain,' Damian said. 'Some kind of sunstroke.'

We are the same age, Damian and I, not young any more; that day, as we sat together in the garden, we were sixty and a bit, Claire five years younger. She's tall and slim, and I can't believe she'll ever be anything but elegant, but of course I know I may be wrong. When we married she came to live in the country town I've always known, acquiring an extra identity as the doctor's wife and the receptionist at the practice, as the mother of a daughter and a son, the organizer of a playgroup, the woman who first taught the illiterate of the town to read.

Damian, at the first opportunity, fled this neighbourhood. On his return to it the time before this one he had carried – clearly an affectation – a silver-topped cane, which was abandoned now, no doubt because it drew attention to its own necessity, and Damian inclines towards vanity. Although he sat down briskly in the chair Claire had vacated for him, the protest of a joint caused him, for a single instant, to wince. His light, fair hair is grey in places now, and I don't suppose he cares for that either, or that his teeth have shrivelled and become discoloured, nor that the freckles on the backs of his hands form blobs where they have spread into one another, or that the skin of his forehead is as dry as old vellum. But that day there was nothing about his eyes to suggest a coming to terms with a future destined to be different from the past, no hint of a hesitation about what should or should not be undertaken: in that sense Damian remains young.

Even as a boy his features were gaunt, giving the impression then of undernourishment. He was angular, but without any of the awkwardness sometimes associated with that quality. In spite of whatever trouble he was having with a joint, he could still, I noticed that day, tidy himself away with natural ease. As always at the beginning of a visit, he was good-humoured; moodiness – sometimes a snappish response to questions, or silence – was apt to set in later.

If, in terms of having a profession, Damian is anything, he is a poet, although in all the time I've known him he has never shown me more than a verse or two. Years ago someone told us that he once had a coterie of admirers and was still, in certain quarters, considered to possess 'a voice' that should be more widely heard. A volume entitled *Slow Death of a Pigeon* – its contents sparse, Claire and I always assumed, for nothing about Damian suggests he is profligate with his talent – appears to represent all he has so far chosen for posterity. In time we would receive a copy of *Slow Death of a Pigeon*, he promised on one of his visits, but none arrived.

'Well, yes, it was that. Something like it,' he was saying, slightly laughing, when I returned with another deck-chair after Claire had brought out the tea things. He had repeated all he'd told me about his sunstroke and the lack of anything of interest in Vancouver. Yes, he was confessing now, a relationship with a woman had featured in his more recent travels, had somehow been the reason for them. There was no confirmation that the powder-blue suit had been a gift. Damian wouldn't have considered that of interest.

'I thought I'd maybe die,' he said, returning to the subject of his sunstroke, but when I asked him what he'd taken for it, what treatment there had been, he was vague.

'Bloody visions,' he said instead. 'Goya stuff.' In any case, he confidently pronounced, Spain was overrated.

Had the woman been Spanish? I wondered, and thought of dancers, white teeth and a rosebud that was red, black skirts swirling, red ribbons in black hair. I have doctor colleagues who farm a bit, who let the wind blow away the mixture of triviality and death that now and again makes our consulting rooms melancholy places. Others collect rare books, make cabinets, involve themselves in politics, allow gardening or some sport to become a way of life to skulk in. For me, Damian's infrequent visits, and wondering about him in between, were such a diversion. Not as efficacious as afternoons on a tractor or searching out a Cuala Press edition of Yeats, but then by nature I'm lazy.

'A chapter closed?' Claire was saying.

'Should never have been opened.'

Later, in the kitchen, I decanted the wine and Claire said the lamb would be enough, with extra potatoes and courgettes. We heard Joanna's car and then her voice exclaiming in surprise and Damian greeting her.

I carried a tray of drinks to the garden. Damian's small black suitcase, familiar to us for many years, was still on the grass beside his deck-chair. I can see it now.

The visit followed a familiar pattern. In the small suitcase there were shirts and underclothes and socks in need of laundering; and when they had been through the washing-machine most of them were seen to be in need of repair. Damian, besides, was penniless; and there was the request that if anyone telephoned him – which was, he said, unlikely since, strictly speaking, no one knew his whereabouts – his presence in our house should be denied.

When we were children, Damian and I had played together at Doul, the grey, half-derelict house where his Aunt Una had brought him up. Doul is no longer there, having been sold to a builder for the lead of its roof, and later razed to the ground. Damian's Aunt Una had drunk herself to death in a caravan. I was actually there when her head jerked suddenly to one side on the pillow, the visible indication of her demise. She'd been, in our childhood, a vague presence in that old house and its lost garden, tall and handsome yet somehow like a ghost of someone else: it was said that she was Damian's mother. People who remembered her advent, with an infant, in the neighbourhood, said the house had been bought for her by the man who'd made her pregnant, buying her silence also.

I learned all that later. When Damian and I were eight his Aunt Una was known to me as his aunt and there was never a reason, afterwards, to doubt that she was. He and I were sent away to different schools – the seducer from the past said to have obliged in this way, also, where Damian's boarding fees were concerned – but our friendship none the less continued. Damian – like a scarecrow sometimes because it was never noticed by his Aunt Una that he grew out of his clothes – was easy company, hard to dislike, an antidote to the provincial respectability I grew up in. We wandered about the countryside; we hung about point-to-points; when we were older we went to Friday dance-halls if one of us had money; we dreamed of romance with Bettina Nowd, clerk in the Munster and Leinster Bank. Abruptly, our ways parted, and remained so for a long time: when Damian, at nineteen, left the neighbourhood he did not return for fourteen years, by which time his Aunt Una was dead and her house gone. It was said he hadn't written to her, or communicated in any way during that time, which was surprising because he was always fond of her. But as I heard nothing from him either it's perhaps less odd than it seems. For Damian, perhaps, the vacuum of people's absence cannot be filled by any other means. During that fourteen years he and I met only once, at Killaloe at the first of his weddings.

'You know, I'd like to see Doul again,' he said the day after he'd appeared in his powder-blue suit. So we went there, where there was nothing to see, not even the caravan his Aunt Una died in. Beneath the brambles that grew everywhere, and the great swathes of nettles, there might have been remains of some kind, but if there were the naked eye could not discern them. When we walked on a bit there were the walls of the kitchen garden, ivy-clad in places, fallen away in others.

'You couldn't build Doul again,' I pointed out when he said he'd like to. 'Not without a fortune, Damian.'

He muttered something, and for the first time sounded disagreeable. There was some kind of complaint, a protest about his continuing lack of means, and then: 'The avenue . . . the gates . . .'

A fragment from a poem? I wondered. Sometimes in Damian's conversation words stand isolated and out of context, as though they do not belong in conversation at all.

'The house,' I began.

'Oh, not the house as it was.'

Claire's spaniels sniffed about for rabbits. As we stood there, the September sun felt hot. Damian believes in the impossible and when we were younger occasionally inspired me with his optimism: that nothing could be easier than poaching salmon, that a bookie or a publican would accept an IOU, that Bettina Nowd had the love-light in her eyes. It was an endearing quality then; I wasn't so sure about its being one that had endearingly endured. I felt uneasy about this talk of coming back. During the companionship of our youth there had never been an attempt to borrow money, since there was none to lend; nor was advantage taken of small politenesses, since politeness was not then readily on offer. The threat of a neighbour with a fly-by-night's presumptions was just a little alarming.

'Who owns it now?' he asked, and I told him: the son of the builder who had stripped the roof of its lead.

The cawing of rooks and the occasional bark of the dogs were the only sounds. It had always been quiet at Doul; that tall, beautiful woman floating about from room to room or picking the last of the mulberries; bees in the honeysuckle.

'What?' I said, again unable to catch Damian's murmur. Still moody, he did not directly reply, but seemed to say that the Muse would not be silent here.

I had ceased to practise on my sixtieth birthday, feeling the time had come, although previously I had imagined I could go on more or less for ever, as my father had in this same house, to his dying day. 'What'll it be like?' Damian used to ponder when we were young, the world for him an excitement to investigate after a small, familiar town in south-west Ireland. Both of us, of course, knew what it would be like for me: we knew my father's house, its comfortably crowded rooms, its pleasant garden; we knew the narrow main street, the shopkeepers, priests and beggars, the condensed-milk factory, the burnt-out cinema, the sleepy courthouse, the bright new hospital, the old asylum, the prison. But neither of us could conjecture a single thing about what lay ahead for Damian.

'It's all right, is it?' Damian asked me on the way back from Doul that day, his mood gregarious again, suddenly so, as if he had remembered who I was. 'Doing nothing these days is all right?'

'Yes, it's all right.'

In fact, it was more than that: all sorts of things were easier in retirement. People weren't patients any more. Met by chance on the street, they conversed with less embarrassment; while privately I registered that Raynaud's was at work or that Frolich's syndrome would not now be reversed. In ordinary chat, awkward secrets were not shared with me; more likely I was shown an adolescent's face and then reminded I'd been the first to see it as an infant's; or informed of athletic achievements in children who had grown up, or of success in other ways, and weddings that were planned. Worries were held back, not coinage for me now, as bad backs weren't, or stitched wounds or blood pressure, the smell of sickness in small back bedrooms.

'Yes, it's fine,' I said in the bar of Traynor's Hotel. 'And you?' I added. 'Nowadays, Damian?'

Again he became morose. He shrugged and did not answer. He stared at the back of a man who was standing at the bar, at the torn seam of a jacket. Then he said:

'I used to think about Doul. Wherever I was, I'd come back to that.'

From his tone, those thoughts about the place of his youth had been a comfort, occurring – the implication was – at times of distress or melancholy. Then Damian said, as if in response to a question I had not asked:

'Well yes, an inspiration.'

He had finished the whiskey in his glass. I went to the bar, and while the drinks I ordered were poured I was asked by Mr Traynor about our son, now a doctor in New South Wales, and about Joanna, who had returned to the town six months ago to work in the prison. 'You'd be delighted she's back here,' Mr Traynor conjectured, and I agreed, although pointing out that sooner or later she would move away again. I smiled, shrugging that away, my mind not on the conversation. Could Doul have been a poet's inspiration for all these years? I wondered. Was that the meaning I was supposed to find in what had been so vaguely stated?

'I thought I recognized him,' Mr Traynor next remarked, his voice kept low, after I had answered his query about who Damian was. 'How're you doing these times?' he called out, and Damian called back that none of us was getting younger.

'God, that's the truth in it,' Mr Traynor agreed, wagging his head in a pretence that this hadn't occurred to him before.

I picked up my change and made my way back to the table where we sat.

'Nothing grand,' Damian said, as if my absence hadn't interrupted what we'd been saying. 'Any little hovel that could be knocked together. There are things . . .' He let the sentence trail away. 'I have the time now.'

I sipped my drink, disguising amusement: all his life Damian had had time. He ran through time, spending it as a spendthrift, wallowing in idleness. Perhaps poets always did, perhaps it was the way they had to live; I didn't know.

'Stuff accumulates,' Damian confided, 'unsaid. Oh, it's just a thought,' he added, and I concluded, with considerable relief, that this was probably the last we'd hear of his morning's whim. After all, there was no sign whatsoever of his being in possession of the necessary funds to build the modest dwelling he spoke of, and personal loans could be resisted. 'Silly old Damian,' Claire murmured when I told her, with the indulgent smile that talk of Damian always drew from her.

Then, quite suddenly, everything was different. Perhaps in the same moment – at dinner two days later – Claire and I were aware that our daughter was being charmed all over again by the man she had once picked out as the man she would like to marry. To this day, I can hear their two voices in my dining-room, and Damian laughing while Claire and I were numbed into silence. To this day I can see the bright flush in Joanna's cheeks.

'And are you settled, Joanna?' Damian asked. 'Here?'

'For the time being,' Joanna said.

The prison is two miles outside the town, a conglomeration of stark grey buildings behind high grey walls, which occasionally I have visited during an epidemic. *Ad sum ard labor*, a waggish inmate has carved on a sundial he made for the governor, a tag that is a talking point when visitors are led around. Joanna has worked in prisons in Dublin and in England; she came here because from conversations she has had with me she was aware that rehabilitation – which is her territory – wasn't being much bothered with. It was a challenge that here on the doorstep of the town she was born and grew up in were circumstances that professionally outraged her.

'I remember sharing a railway carriage with a man who'd just been released from gaol,' Damian said. 'He robbed garages.'

In Joanna's view a spell in prison was the offer of another chance for the offender, a time to come to terms with the world and with oneself. She was an optimist; you had to be, she insisted.

'Lonely wayside garages,' Damian said. 'A child working the pumps.'
'Did he say —'
'All he said was that he didn't intend to get caught the next time.'

Beneath these exchanges there was something else, a tremor that was shared; a tick answered another tick, fingers touched although a dinner table separated them. I pushed my knife and fork together; and Claire said something that nobody heard and went to the kitchen.

Joanna is small and dark-haired, and pretty. She has had admirers, a proposal of marriage from a map-maker, a longish affair with an ornithologist, but her passionate devotion to her work has always seemed to make her draw back when there was pressure that a relationship should be allowed the assumption of permanence. It was as though she protected her own dedication, as though she believed she would experience a disloyalty in herself if she in any way devoted less time and energy to her work. Recidivists, penitents, old lags, one-time defaulters, drug pushers, muggers, burglars, rapists: these were her lovers. She found the good in them, and yet, when telling us about them, did not demand that we should too. It has never been her way to lecture, or stridently to insist, and often people are surprised at the intensity of her involvement, at the steel beneath so soft a surface. Neither Claire nor I ever say so, but there is something in our daughter that is remarkable.

Across the dinner table that evening she became demure. There was obedience in her glance, and respect for every ordinary word our visitor uttered, as though she would blindly have acted as he dictated should his next words express a desire. I followed Claire into the kitchen, carrying plates and dishes. 'I always wanted to,' Joanna was saying, drawn out by Damian in a way that was not usual in his conversation. 'I never thought of doing anything else.'

We didn't speak, Claire and I, in the kitchen. We didn't even look at one another. It was our fault; we had permitted this stroke of fate to stake its claim. The suitable admirers – the dark-haired map-maker, the ornithologist, and others – were not what a retriever of lost causes, a daily champion of down-and-outs, had ever wanted. In the dining-room the voices chatted on, and in the kitchen we felt invaded by them, Claire and I, she tumbling raspberries into a blue glass bowl, I spooning coffee into the filter. 'I remember hearing you'd been born,' Damian was saying in the dining-room when we returned.

It was I who had told him. I delivered Joanna myself; Claire and I heard her first cry in the same moment. 'A girl,' I said when Damian arrived six months later for one of his visits, and we drank my whiskey on a bitter January night. 'How nice to have a daughter!' he murmured when we gazed down at the cot by Claire's bedside. And he was right: it was nice having a girl as well as a boy, nice being a family. Even then, two different personalities were apparent: our son's easy-going, rarely ruffled, Joanna's confident. At five and six, long-legged and determined, she won the races she ran because insistently she believed she could. Oh no, she wouldn't, she asserted when it was pointed out that she would tire of looking after the unattractive terrier she rescued after tinkers left it behind. And for years, until the creature died in old age, she did look after it.

'It was snowing outside,' Damian reminisced in the dining-room. 'Black Bush was what we drank, Joanna, the night your father and I wet the baby's head.'

His fingernails were rimmed: ash from the cigarettes he was smoking, as he always does, between courses. Once upon a time, years ago, he affected a cigarette-holder. He had sold it, he told Claire when she asked, and we guessed it had been another gift from a woman, sold when the affair was over.

'Raspberries, Damian?' Claire offered.

He smiled his acceptance. He placed his cigarette, still burning, on a side plate, and poured cream on the fruit. I wondered if children had been born to him; I hadn't wondered that before. I imagined, as I often had, his public-house life in London, some places he could not enter because of debts, late-night disagreements turning sour. I had a feeling that his travels – so often mentioned – had always been of brief duration, that London was where he had mostly belonged, in seedy circumstances. I imagined lodgings, rent unpaid, possessions pawned. How often had there been flits in the small hours? Were small dishonesties a poet's right? And yet, I thought as well, he was our friend and almost always had been. He'd cheered our lives.

'Damian's tired of London,' Joanna said. 'He's going to live at Doul again.'

In the night, believing me to be asleep, Claire wept. I whispered, trying to console her. We didn't say to one another that shock came into this, that we must allow a little time to calm us. We lay there, remembering that not much longer than twenty-four hours ago Claire had said our friend was the tonic we needed. On all his visits we'd never been dismayed to see him, and he couldn't help being older now, less handsome than he had been, his grubbiness more noticeable. He was, at heart, as he had always been. It was unfair to say he wasn't, just because he had cast a spell in our house. We'd always known about those spells. We'd read between the lines, we hadn't been misled.

Marriage was what we dreaded, although neither of us used the word. It was not because Damian had so often confessed he liked to marry that our melancholy threw up this stark prediction; it was because Joanna was Joanna. We might be wrong, we felt each other thinking; a tawdry love affair might be enough. But we did not believe it and neither of us suggested the consolation of this lesser pain. Nor did we remind one another that Joanna, all her life, had been attracted by the difficult, nor did we share it with one another when in the dark we were more certainly aware that there had been no challenge in her relationship with the map-maker or the ornithologist, or with any of her suitable admirers. Perhaps, that night, we knew our daughter a little better, and perhaps we loved her just a little more. She would succeed where other women had failed: already we could hear her offering this, already we sensed her not believing that the failure could lie anywhere but with those other women. 'I'm going to marry Damian,' the childish silliness brightly echoed, and with it our amusement.

Had he come to us this time with a purpose? Claire asked when she ceased to weep. Did he intend our daughter to earn his living for him, to tend him in the place of his childhood, cosseting his old man's frailties? Had his future lit up suddenly on a London street, the years ahead radiant as a jewel in his imagination? 'I'll tell them,' had our daughter said already, planning to sit us down, to pour out drinks in celebration? She would break the news that was not news, and we'd embrace her, not pointing out that Damian couldn't help destroying his achievements. And she would hurry to him when he next appeared and they would stand together as lovers do. We could not foretell the details after that, and quite suddenly the form the relationship might take in time hardly seemed to matter any more: enough of it was there already. 'Are we being punished?' Claire asked, and I didn't know if we were or not, or why we should be punished, or what our sin was.

We didn't want that night to end. We didn't want to feel, again, the excitement that had crept into our house, that passed us by and was not ours. It was not in Damian's nature to halt an adventure that was already under way, not in his nature to acquire from nowhere the decency that would forbid it to proceed. His bedroom would not be empty when morning came, the small suitcase gone, a note left on his bedside table. 'Remember the others?' Claire whispered in the dark, and I knew whom she meant without having to think – the daughter of the Bishop of Killaloe, the widow from upstate New York, the Englishwoman in Venice, and other nameless women mentioned by our friend in passing.

Ill-suited, we said, when we learned that the first of his marriages had fallen apart, and were too busy in those busy days to be more than sorry. We had hardly wondered about the fate of the bishop's daughter, and not at all about the American widow, except to say to one another that it was typical of Damian to make the same mistake twice. And when the Englishwoman left him it was a joke. Old reprobate, we said. Incorrigible.

The first streaks of dawn came flickering in, the birds began. We lay there silent, not trusting ourselves to comment on this past that the present had thrown up. The bishop's daughter – younger than Joanna was now – smiled in her wedding dress, and I felt again the warm touch of her cheek when I kissed it, and heard her reply to my good wishes, her shy voice saying she was happier than she deserved to be. And a face from a photograph we'd once been shown was the oval face of the American, dark hair, dark eyes, lips slightly parted. And the face of the Englishwoman was just a guess, a face contorted in a quarrel, made bitter with cold tears. The shadows of other men's wives, of lovely women, girls charmed, clamoured for attention, breaking from their shadows, taking form. Old reprobate.

'I think I'll go and talk to her.' Claire's voice was hushed in the twilight, but she didn't move, and I knew that already she had changed her mind; talking would make everything worse. Eighty-one, Claire said: he would be eighty-one when Joanna was forty-eight.

I didn't calculate. It didn't matter. I thought we might quarrel, that tiredness might bring something like that on, but we didn't. We didn't round on each other, blaming in order to shed guilt, bickering as we might have once, when upsets engendered edginess. We didn't because ours are the dog days of marriage and there aren't enough left to waste: dangerous ground has long ago been charted and is avoided now. There was no point in saying, either, that the damage we already sensed would become entertainment for other people, as damage had for us.

'I'll make tea,' I said, and descended the stairs softly as I always do at this early hour so as not to wake our daughter. Some time today Damian and I might again call in at Traynor's; I might, in sickening humility, ask for mercy. I heard my own voice doing so, but the sound was false, wrong in all sorts of ways; I knew I wouldn't say a thing. To ensure that our daughter had a roof over her head I would lend whatever was necessary. A bungalow would replace the fallen house at Doul.

The *Irish Times* was half pushed through the letter-box; I slipped it out. I brought the tray back to our bedroom, with gingersnap biscuits on a plate because we like them in the early morning. We read the paper. We didn't say much else.

Later that morning Joanna hurried through cornflakes and a slice of toast. Her car started, reversed, then dashed away. Damian appeared and we sat outside in the September sunshine; Claire made fresh coffee. It was too late to hate him. It was too late to deny that we'd been grateful when our stay-at-home smugness had been enlivened by the tales of his adventures, or to ask him if he knew how life had turned out for the women who had loved him. Instead we conversed inconsequentially.

Three People

On the steps of the Scheles' house, stained glass on either side of the brown front door, Sidney shakes the rain from his plastic mackintosh, taking it off to do so. He lets himself into the small porch, pauses for a moment to wipe the rain from his face with a handkerchief, then rings the bell of the inner door. It is how they like it, his admission with a key to the porch, then this declaration of his presence. They'll know who it is: no one else rings that inner bell.

'Good afternoon, Sidney,' Vera greets him when the bolts are drawn back and the key turned in the deadlock. 'Is it still raining, Sidney?'

'Yes. Getting heavy now.'

'We did not look out.'

The light is on in the hall, as it always is except in high summer.

Sidney waits while the bolts are shot into place again, the key in the deadlock turned. Then he hangs his colourless plastic coat on the hall-stand pegs.

'Well, there the bathroom is,' Vera says. 'All ready.'

'Your father —'

'Oh, he's well, Sidney. Father is resting now. You know: the afternoon.'

'I'd hoped to come this morning.'

'He hoped you would, Sidney. At eleven maybe.'

'The morning was difficult today.'

'Oh, I don't mind, myself.'

In the bathroom the paint tins and brushes and a roller have been laid out, the bath and washbasin covered with old curtains. There is Polyfilla and white spirit, which last week Sidney said he'd need. He should have said Polyclens, he realizes now, instead of the white spirit; better for washing out the brushes.

'You'd like some tea now, Sidney?' Vera offers. 'You'd like a cup before you begin?'

Vera has sharp cheek-bones and hair dyed black because it's greying. The leanness in her face is everywhere else too; a navy-blue skirt is tight on bony hips, her plain red jumper is as skimpy as a child's, clinging to breasts that hardly show. Her large brown eyes and sensuous lips are what you notice, the eyes expressionless, the lips perhaps a trick of nature, for in other ways Vera does not seem sensuous in the least.

'Tea later.' Sidney hesitates, glancing at Vera, as if fearing to offend her. 'If that's all right?'

And Vera smiles and says of course it's all right. There is a Danish pastry, she says, an apricot Danish pastry, bought yesterday so she'll heat it up.

'Thanks, Vera.'

'There's Father, waking now.'

Lace Cap is the colour chosen. Sidney pours it into the roller dish and rolls it on to the ceiling, beginning at the centre, which a paint-shop man advised him once was the best way to go about it. The colour seems white but he knows it isn't. It will dry out a shade darker. A satin finish, suitable for a bathroom.

'The tiling,' Mr Schele says in the doorway when Sidney has already begun on the walls. 'Maybe the tiling.'

Clearing away his things – his toothbrush and his razor – Mr Schele noticed the tiling around the washbasin and the bath. In places the tiling is not good, he says. In places the tiles are perhaps a little loose, and a few are cracked. You hardly notice, but they are cracked when you look slowly, taking time to look. And the rubber filler around the bath is discoloured. Grubby, Mr Schele says.

'Yes, I'll do all that.'

'Not the tiling before the paint, heh? Not finish the tiling first maybe?'

Sidney knows the old man is right. The tile replacement and the rubber should be done first because of the mess. That is the usual way. Not that Sidney is an expert, not that he decorates many bathrooms, but it stands to reason.

'It'll be all right, Mr Schele. The tiling's not much, two or three to put in.'

While the undercoat on the woodwork is drying he'll slip the new tiles in. He'll cut away the rubber and squeeze in more of it, a tricky business, which he doesn't like. He has done it only once before, behind the sink in the kitchen. While it's settling he'll gloss the woodwork.

'You're a good man, Sidney.'

He works all afternoon. When Vera brings the Danish pastry and tea, and two different kinds of biscuits, she doesn't linger because he's busy. Sidney isn't paid for what he does, as he is for all his other work – the club, delivering the leaflets or handing them out on the street, depending on what's required. He manages on what he gets; he doesn't need much because there is no rent to pay. Just enough for food, and the gas he cooks it on. The electricity he doesn't have to pay for; clothes come from the charity shop.

They let him live above the club because there's a room. At night he takes the ticket money, protected in his kiosk by Alfie and Harry at the door; in the daytime he cleans up after the night before and takes the phone messages. All the club's facilities are his to make use of, which he appreciates. Sidney is thirty-four now, thirty-four and one week and two days. He had just turned twenty when he first helped Vera.

In Mr Schele's house they do not ever mention that. They do not talk about a time that was distressing for Vera, and for Mr Schele too. But when Sidney's not in the house, when he's private and on his own, in his room above the club, he talks to himself about it. 'Shining armour,' he repeats because it said that in the paper; still says it if he wants to look. *Knight in Shining Armour*, all across the page. Sometimes, when he's trying to get to sleep, he lies there polishing the armour, laying all the pieces out, unfolding cloths, setting out the Duraglit and the Goddard's.

'Sidney, you stay with us for supper tonight?' There is enough, Vera assures him. Another cup of rice will make it enough, and she recites this Saturday's menu: chicken cooked her way and her good salad, strudel and just a little cream. Then *Casualty* on the TV, five past eight.

It is a plea, occasionally made when Sidney is in the house as late as this. Vera begs for company with her invitation, Sidney finds himself reflecting; for another presence besides her elderly father. Vera would have been glad when he didn't come in the morning because he'd have finished earlier, too long before supper, and staying to lunch is never the same.

'I should be getting on.'

'Oh, do stay with us.'

And Sidney does. He sits with Mr Schele in the sitting-room and there's an appetizer, salty little pretzels Vera has bought. No drink accompanies these. Mr Schele talks about his childhood.

'The big rosebush has blown down,' Sidney interrupts, standing by the window now. 'This wind has taken it.'

Mr Schele comes to look and sorrowfully shakes his head. 'Maybe the roots are holding,' he suggests. 'Maybe a little can be done.'

Sidney goes through the kitchen to the garden. 'No,' he says when they all three sit down to eat: the roots have snapped in the fall. The news upsets Mr Schele, who remembers the rose being planted, when Vera was a child. He'll not see another rose grown to that size in the garden, he predicts. He blames himself, but Vera says no and Sidney points out that even roses come to an end.

A strudel enriched with sultanas follows the chicken cooked Vera's way and her good salad, and then they stand in the bathroom doorway, surveying Sidney's work. The bathroom is as new, Mr Schele says, greatly cheered by the sight of it. It is the bathroom as it was the day the house was built. Everything except the linoleum on the floor, which has been there since 1951, Mr Schele calculates.

'A nice new vinyl,' Mr Schele suggests, and Vera adds that not much is necessary. Two metres and three-quarters, a metre wide: she measured it this morning. 'You lay it down, Sidney?' Mr Schele enquires. 'You lay it for us?'

They know he will. If Vera chooses what she wants and brings the piece back to the house he'll lay it. There is adhesive left over from the time he laid the surround in Mr Schele's small bedroom. In windy weather draughts came up through the cracks between the floorboards, the bedroom being on the ground floor. There's been no trouble since Sidney cut out the vinyl surround and stuck it down, except that Mr Schele still can't get used to the colour, shades of marbled orange.

'For a bathroom,' he states his preference now, 'we keep to pale, heh?'

To go with the Lace Cap, Vera agrees. Maybe even white, to go with the bath and washbasin and the tiles. A flush of pink has crept into Vera's hollow cheeks, and Sidney – knowing Vera well – knows it is there in anticipation of the treat that lies ahead: choosing the floor material, the right weight for bathroom use, a shade to match the paint or the porcelain.

'You can wait another minute, Sidney?' Vera says, and briefly goes away, returning with a piece of card she has torn from a cornflakes packet. 'You brush the paint on that for me, Sidney?' she requests, and Sidney does so and washes out the brush again. His Stanley knife slipped when he was cutting the orange vinyl for the bedroom; he had to have three stitches and a tetanus injection.

'Time for the hospital programme,' Mr Schele reminds Vera, who's disappointed when Sidney shakes his head. Not this Saturday, he explains, because he's on early turn at the club.

'You're good to come, Sidney,' Vera says in the porch, whispering as she always does when she says that. She's older than Sidney, forty-one; she was twenty-seven when he first helped her, the time of her distress.

'It's nothing,' he says before he leaves, his unchanging valediction.

They took Vera in because in the end they didn't believe her story about an intruder while she was at the cinema. They had accepted it at first, when everything hung together – the kitchen window forced open, the traces of dry mud on the draining-board and again by the door, where the shoes had been taken off. Forty-eight pounds and ninepence had been taken, and medals and a silver-plated stud-box. The hall door and the porch door were both wide open when Vera returned to the house; Mr

Schele, employed in those days in a radio and television shop, was still at work. They took Vera in because there was something that didn't seem right to them about the entry through the kitchen window, no sign on the path outside of the dried mud, no sign of it on the window-sill. There was something not quite right about only a stud-box and medals taken, not other small objects that were lying about; and no one could remember Vera at the cinema. Then, in the garden, a dog sniffed out part of a glove that had been burnt on the garden fire, and the wool matched the fibres found in the room upstairs. Odd, it seemed, that gloves had been burnt, even if they were old and done for.

All that passes through Sidney's thoughts, as it usually does when he walks away from the house. He isn't late for his Saturday duties at the club; he doesn't hurry. After an afternoon inside, the air is good. The wind that blew away the rain is noisy in the empty trees, lifts off a dustbin lid and plays with plastic flowerpots in the small front gardens. He'll walk until it rains again, then take a bus.

'Come, Angus! Angus!' a woman calls her dog, a Pomeranian. 'What a wind!' she calls out, going by, and Sidney says what wind indeed. He knows the woman from meeting her and her dog on this particular stretch. Several times a day she's out.

Walking through the ill-lit suburban avenues and crescents, leaves scattered on the pavements or gathered into corners by the wind, Sidney remembers the photograph of Vera, her big lips a little parted, her hair – blonde then – falling almost to her shoulders, her eyes innocent and lovely. She was in custody when he saw the photograph; her solicitors, not she, were appealing for anyone who'd seen her entering or leaving the cinema to come forward.

Sidney passes into streets with closed shops and minimarkets, dentists and chiropodists advertised, the Regina take-away, the Queen's Arms at a corner, Joe Coral's betting shop. Then there is a quiet neighbourhood, the yellow caravan still parked in the garden, the open space that's not quite a park, litter sodden on its single path. The film was *French Connection 2*. He went to see it as soon as he saw the photograph, so that he knew the plot.

On the bus Sidney feels like sleep because last night, being Friday, was one of his late ones. But he doesn't sleep because he hates waking up on a bus. Once he went past his stop and had to pay the extra, but that hasn't happened since. Something wakes him, some worry about having to pay the extra again; one stop before his own he always wakes now, but even so he'd rather not sleep. He closes his eyes though, because he wants to go back in his thoughts, to run it again, to make sure it's all still there: usually after he has been to the Scheles' he does that. 'The ice-cream girl was going round,' he said, and every word was written down. 'The lights were up.'

He needn't have sat next to her but he did, he explained. He wanted to; soon's he saw the hair he wanted to, soon's he looked along the row and saw her lips, moving as it happened, sucking a sweet maybe, or chocolate. 'You make a practice of this, Sidney?' the sergeant asked. Well, once or twice before, he said, a woman he liked the look of.

The bus draws in again, three people get off, two men and a girl, the men much older, as if one of them's her father. 'You're certain, Sidney?' the sergeant pressed him, and he said the ice-cream girl took her time, not that anyone was buying from her, a good five minutes it was the lights were up. And there was afterwards too, of course. No way he wasn't certain, he said. 'Definitely,' he said. 'Oh, yes.' The other man came in then, and asked the same questions all over again. 'You tell us what clothes she was wearing, Sidney? Take your time now, son.' It said in the paper about the clothes, and he remembered because he'd learnt it off.

The club is in darkness when he reaches it, but he turns the lights on as soon as he's inside. He tidied this morning, the time he always tidies. Everything is ready. Alfie and Harry arrive, and he makes them Maxwell House the way they like it, and they sit there, drinking it and smoking. Tomorrow he'll go back, Sidney says to himself, tidy up that rose that's come down.

The Sunday bells of a church are sounding for an early service when Vera glances from the kitchen window and there he is, cutting up the big rosebush that the wind brought down. A warmth begins in Vera, spreading from some central part of her to her shoulders and her thighs, tingling in her arms and legs. It is the warmth of Vera's passion, heat in her blood that such an unexpected glimpse always inspires. He came to help yesterday. Why today also? The blown-down rosebush could have waited.

'Sidney's come,' her father says, having looked out too. 'Twenty-five years, that rosebush. High as a tree and now we must begin again.'

'Oh, I'm not sorry it's gone. It darkened the garden. Sidney, you like some coffee?' Vera calls from the back door and Sidney waves and says in a minute.

'Is Sidney wearing the garden gloves?' Mr Schele fusses. 'You need the gloves with a rose.'

'Sidney knows.'

Once, working in the garden, sawing up old planks of wood, he got a splinter under a thumbnail and Vera saw to it: Sidney's hand laid flat on the kitchen worktop, a light brought specially in, a needle sterilized in a match flame, TCP and tweezers. In her night-time fantasies she has comforted Sidney, whispering to him, asking him to talk to her. Sometimes, when he has worked all through a weekend morning, she turns the immersion heater on early in case he'd like to have a bath before he goes. The time he cut his hand she staunched the blood flow with a tourniquet.

'Ready, Sidney,' Vera calls from the back door. 'Coffee.'

Mr Schele senses something in the air. His thoughts reflect Vera's: unsightly though it is, the thicket of twisted branches on the grass could easily have stayed there for a week. It is Sidney's pretext, Mr Schele tells himself; it is a reason to come back so soon. He pours hot milk on to his bran flakes and stirs the mixture with his spoon, softening the flakes because he does not like them crispy. Is this, at last, the Sunday of the proposal? He watches Vera at the stove. She remembers her fluffy slippers and hurries away to change them. The glass disc rattles in the milk saucepan and Mr Schele rises to attend to that. He cannot last for ever; each day, at seventy-eight, is borrowed time. What life is it for a woman alone?

Moving the saucepan to one side of the gas jet, Mr Schele accepts that when he is gone Vera will have no one. Going out with chaps – and there used to be quite a few – has been a thing of the past since the trouble. Vera will be alone for the rest of her days: he understands that, although the subject is never mentioned. He understands that her luck might even change for a while, before some new chap she makes friends with has second thoughts, even though at the time she walked away without a stain. That is how things happen, Mr Schele knows, and knows that Vera has worked it out too. Sidney is different because of coming forward, and in a sense he has been coming forward ever since, as good a friend to Vera as he was at the time, a saviour really: in Mr Schele's opinion that word is not too strong. It took time for the opinion to form, as naturally it would in a father, the circumstances as they were.

'It's good of Sidney. Just because that rose blew down.'

'Yes, it is.'

Vera nods, saying that, lending the words a little emphasis. Her father knows what other people know, no more. He came in at his usual time, just after half past six. He saw the white police cars outside and was in a state before he passed through the porch. 'You sit down now,' she said, and told him, and the policewoman brought him tea. 'It can't be,' he kept saying. Later on, she had kippers to boil in the bag, but they didn't want them. She folded up the wheelchair and put it in the cupboard under the stairs, not wanting to look at it. Best to get it out of the house, she decided when everything quietened down, a month gone by, and they got a fair price for it.

'You take your chances, Vera.'

She knows what he means, but Sidney's not going to propose marriage, this morning or any other time, because marriage isn't on the cards and never has been. The intruder would not have guessed there was anyone in that room because when he'd watched the house he'd only ever seen two people coming and going: the policemen explained all that. An intruder always sussed a place, they explained, he didn't just come barging in. Her father out all day from eight-fifteen on, and the villain would have followed her to the cinema and seen her safely in. Cinemas, funerals, weddings: your house-thief loves all that. 'Oh no, that's crazy,' her father kept muttering when they changed their minds, suddenly taking a different line. He had always thought it was crazy, their groundless probing, as he put it. He had always believed their case would fall to bits because it didn't make sense.

'You know what I'm saying, Vera? You take your chances.'

She nods. Changing her slippers for shoes because Sidney had come, she decided as well to change her drab Sunday skirt for her dog-tooth. She stood in front of the long wardrobe looking-glass the way she used to in the old days. She liked to be smart in the old days and she still does now. Sometimes a man looks at her in a supermarket or on the street. And Sidney does, when he thinks she isn't noticing. She heats the milk again and is ready to make fresh coffee.

'You like an egg, Sidney?' she offers when Sidney comes in. 'Poached egg? Maybe scrambled?'

'No, honestly. Thanks, Vera.' It's too windy to risk burning the rose-bush, he says, but he has clipped it up, ready for a calmer day.

There's a leaf in his hair, and Vera draws his attention to it. 'You just sit down.'

'Only a cup of coffee, Vera.'

That morning Sidney woke when it was half past six, the light just beginning. He thought at once about Vera, although it had been a particularly rough night in the club and usually that comes into his mind first thing. Harry and Alfie had had to separate youths who began to fight, one of them with a knife. Later, after two, a girl who was a stranger in the club collapsed. But in spite of the intervention of that excitement, this morning it was Vera he woke up to, her face as it was when her hair was blonde. Fleshy you'd have called her face then, soft was what he'd thought when he first saw the photograph, in the *Evening Standard* someone had left behind in the club. It doesn't matter that Vera is leaner now, it doesn't matter that her hair is different. Vera's the same, no way she isn't.

'Dried out a lovely shade,' Mr Schele says. 'The bathroom.'

'There's half that tin left for touching up.' The coffee cup is warm in Sidney's cold hands. He likes that skirt. He'd like to see it folded on a chair and Vera standing in her slip, her jersey still on. The jersey's buttons are at the top, along one shoulder, four red buttons to match the wool. In the photograph it was a jacket, and white dots on her shirt. A loving sister, the paper said.

'Anything on the News, Sidney?'

He shakes his head, unable to answer the question because this morning he didn't turn the radio on. Some expedition reached a mountain top, Vera says.

'Bad night in the club,' Sidney says, and tells them. He'd had to fish light bulbs and tins out of the toilet when he was closing up, but he doesn't mention that. The girl who'd collapsed was on Ecstasy, the ambulance men said. There is some way they can tell an Ecstasy collapse, now that they've got used to them. Sidney doesn't know what it is.

'Out of control,' Mr Schele comments, hearing that. 'The whole globe out of control.'

'Maybe how they sweat. There's different ways a person sweats, an ambulance man told me. According to what's taken.'

The blow left scarcely a contusion. It was to the neck, the paper said, the side of the neck, no more than a smack. The intruder had lost his head; he'd walked into a room where he wasn't expecting anyone to be, and there was a figure in a wheelchair. He'd have been seen at once, but what he didn't know was that he couldn't ever have been described. Probably he struck the blow to frighten; probably he said if a description was given he'd be back. The room is empty now, even the bed taken away; two years ago Sidney painted out the flowery wallpaper with satin emulsion – Pale Sherbet – the woodwork to match in gloss.

'One thing I hate,' he says, 'is when an ambulance has to come.'

God did not make another man in all His world as gentle: often Vera thinks that, and she thinks it now. His voice was gentle when he said about an ambulance coming to take away the Ecstasy girl, the hands that grasp the coffee cup are gentle. 'Short of a slate or two,' they said when they told her a man had come forward. 'But crystal clear in his statements.'

The first time she saw him in court his shabby jacket needed a stitch. Yes, what he said was true, she agreed when it was put to her, and was told to speak up.

'You see the world at that club, Sidney,' her father says.

When she walked free, when she came back to the house, her father didn't look at her at first. And when he did she could see him thinking that a man who was a stranger to her, whose face she had not even noticed,

had reached out to her in the darkness of a cinema, and that she had
acquiesced. With her looks, she could have had anyone: that, too, her
father didn't say.

'Yeah, a lot come into the club. Though Monday's always light. Not
much doing on a Monday.'

She knew he'd visit. She knew in court, something about him, something about the pity that was in his eyes. Nearly a year went by but still
she guessed she'd open the porch door and there he'd be, and then he was.
He came when he knew her father would be out at work. He stood there
tongue-tied and she said come in. 'I couldn't face him,' her father said
when she told him, but in the end he did, so much was owing; and now he
waits for a proposal. Step by step, time wore away the prejudice any father
would have.

'You try that new biscuit, Sidney.' She pushes the plate towards him
and then fills up his coffee cup. Nicer than the ones with the peel in them,
she says.

'I met that woman with the dog again. Last night.'

They don't know who the woman is. Must be she lives the other side
of the green, her father has said when she was mentioned before. On his
own walks he has never run into her, preferring to go the other way.

'You think we put in another rose, Sidney?' her father asks.

'It's empty, the way it is. You'd notice that.'

'I thought it maybe would be.'

Mr Schele goes to see for himself, changing his shoes in the shed by the
back door. The first time he faced Sidney he kept looking at his hands,
unable to keep his eyes off them. He kept thinking of Vera when she was
little, when her mother was alive, Mona already confined. Vera always
looked out for him, and ran down the garden path to meet him when he
came home, and he lifted her up high, making her laugh, the way poor
Mona never could, not all her life. The first time he faced Sidney he had to
go out and get some air, had stood where he is standing now, near to where
the rosebush was. It wasn't wrong that Vera had left Mona on her own
that afternoon. Ever since their mother died he'd kept saying to Vera that
she couldn't be a prisoner in the house. One sister should not imprison
another, no matter what the circumstances were; that was not ever meant.
The shopping had to be done; and no one could begrudge an hour or so in
a cinema. And yet, he thought the first day he faced Sidney, why did it have
to be the way it was, poor Mona's head fallen sideways as though her
neck'd been cracked, while that was happening in the cinema's dark?

'I'm sorry there was that trouble,' Vera says in the kitchen, referring to
the fight in the club, and the girl for whom an ambulance had come.

'On a Saturday you expect it.' And Sidney says he doesn't know why that is. Often on a Thursday or a Friday the club's as full. 'I like a Sunday,' he says, quite suddenly, as if he has for the first time realized that. 'There's church bells somewhere near the club. Well, anyway they carry. Could be a mile off.'

On Sunday evenings Vera goes to church, a Baptist place, but anywhere would do. She says she's sorry when she kneels, and feels the better for saying it in a church, with other people there. And afterwards she wonders what they'd think if they knew, their faces still credulous following their hour of comfort. She makes herself go through it when she's on her knees, not permitting the excuses. She wants to draw attention to how awful it was for so long, ever since their mother died, how awful it would always be, the two of them left together, the washing, the dressing, the lifting from the wheelchair, the feeding, the silent gaze. All that, when praying, Vera resists in her thoughts. 'You want to get turned off?' a boy said once, she heard him in the play yard when she was fourteen. 'You take a look at the sister.' And later, when the wheelchair was still pushed out and about, proposals didn't come. Later still, when there were tears and protestations on the street, the wheelchair was abandoned, not even pushed into the garden, since that caused distress also: Mona was put upstairs. 'Vera, take your friend up,' her father, not realizing, suggested once: an afflicted sister's due to stare at visitors to the house. On her knees – kneeling properly, not just bent forward – Vera makes herself watch the shadow that is herself, the sideways motion of her flattened hand, some kind of snap she felt, the head gone sideways too.

'The wind's dropped down. You stay to lunch, Sidney? You could have your fire, eh?'

In the courtroom people gazed at both of them. Asked again, she agreed again. 'Yes, that is so,' she agreed because a man she didn't know wanted her to say it: that for as long as the film lasted they were lovers.

'I'll have the fire,' he says, and when he moves from the window he sees her father, standing by the empty place where the rosebush was. His belief protects them, gives them their parts, restricts to silence all that there is. When her father goes to his grave, will his ghost come back to tell her his death's the punishment for a bargain struck?

'A loin of lamb,' Vera says, and takes it from the fridge, a net of suet tied in place to make it succulent in the roasting. Parsnips she'll roast too, and potatoes because there's nothing Sidney likes more.

'I left my matches at the club.'

She takes a box from a cupboard, swinging back the door that's on a level with her head, reaching in. *Cook's Matches* the label says. She hands them to him, their fingers do not touch. In the garden her father has not moved, still standing where his rosebush was. He's frail, he suffers from the ailments of the elderly. More often than he used to he speaks of borrowed time.

'I'll get it going now,' Sidney says.

There'll be a funeral, hardly different from her mother's, not like Mona's. Their time is borrowed too, the punishment more terrible because they know it's there: no need for a ghost to spell it out.

She smears oil on the parsnips she has sliced, and coats with flour the potatoes she has already washed and dried. Sidney likes roast potatoes crispy. There is nothing, Vera sometimes thinks, she doesn't know about his likes and dislikes. He'll stand there at the funeral and so will she, other people separating them. The truth restored, but no one else knowing it.

'Colder now,' her father says when he comes in. The wind turned, and left a chill behind when it dropped.

He warms himself by standing close to the gas stove, massaging his fingers. Without his presence, there would be no reason to play those parts; no reason to lose themselves in deception. The darkness of their secrets lit, the love that came for both of them through their pitying of each other: all that might fill the empty upstairs room, and every corner of the house. But Vera knows that, without her father, they would frighten one another.

Of the Cloth

He was out of touch, and often felt it: out of touch with the times and what was happening in them, out of touch with two generations of change, with his own country and what it had become. If he travelled outside Ireland, which he had never done, he knew he would find the same new *mores* everywhere, the different, preferred restrictions by which people now lived their lives; but it was Ireland he thought about, the husk of the old, the seed of the new. And often he wondered what that new would be.

The Rev. Grattan Fitzmaurice, Ennismolach Rectory, his letters were addressed, the nearest town and the county following. His three Church of Ireland parishes, amalgamated over the years, were in a valley of pasture land in the mountains, three small churches marking them, one of them now unattended, each of them remote, as his rectory was, as his life was.

The town that was nearest was thirteen miles away, where the mountain slope became a plain and the river that flowed through the townland of Ennismolach was bridged. The rectory was reached from Doonan crossroads by taking the road to Corlough Gap and turning right three miles farther on at the Shell petrol pump. A few minutes later there was the big Catholic Church of the Holy Assumption, solitary and splendid by the roadside, still seeming new although it had been there for sixty years. Over the brow of the next hill were the gates to Ennismolach Rectory, its long curving avenue years ago returned to grass.

This was granite country and Grattan Fitzmaurice had a look of that grey, unyielding stone, visible even in the pasture land of the valley. Thin, and tall, he belonged to this landscape, had come from it and had chosen to return to it. Celibacy he had chosen also. Families had spread themselves in the vast rectory once upon a time; now there was only the echo of his own footsteps, the latch of the back door when Mrs Bradshaw came in the mornings, the yawning of his retriever, the wireless when he turned it on. Emptily, all sound came twice because an echo added a pretence of more activity than there was, as if in mercy offering companionship.

There was, as well, the company of the past: the family Grattan remembered here was his own, his father the rector of Ennismolach before him, his mother wallpapering the rooms and staining the floorboards to freshen them up, his sisters. The rectory had always been home, a vigour there in his childhood, the expectation that it would continue. Change had come before his birth, and the family was still close to revolution and civil war. The once impregnable estates had fallen back to the clay, their people gone away, burnt-out houses their memorial stones. Rectories escaped because in Ireland men of the cloth would always have a place: as the infant nation was nurtured through the 1930s, it seemed in Ennismolach that ends would forever be made to meet in the lofty rooms, that there would forever be chilblains in winter, cheap cuts from the butcher at Fenit Bridge, the Saturday silence while a sermon was composed. And even as a child Grattan had wanted to follow his father's footsteps in this parish.

His father died in 1957, his mother in that year also. By then the congregation at Ennismolach church had dwindled, the chapel of ease near Fenit Bridge hadn't been made use of for years, and melancholy characterized other far-flung parishes in the county. The big houses, which had supported them, tumbled further into ruin; the families who had fled did not return; and from farm and fields, from townlands everywhere, emigration took a toll. 'It'll get worse,' Grattan's father said a few weeks before he died. 'You realize it'll get worse?' It wasn't unexpected, he said, that the upheaval should bring further, quieter upheaval. The designation of the Protestant foundation he served, the 'Church of Ireland', had long ago begun to seem too imposing a title, ludicrous almost in its claim. 'We are a remnant,' Grattan's father said.

It was an irony that they should be, for their Protestant people of the past – Wolfe Tone and Thomas Davis, Emmet and Parnell, the Henry Grattan after whom Grattan was named – had in their different ways and in their different times been the inspiration for the Ireland that had come about, and Grattan knew that its birth was Ireland's due no matter how, in the end, it had happened. Yet it was true: they were a remnant. While Church of Ireland notice-boards still stood by old church gates, gold letters on black giving details of what services could be offered, there was a withering within that Church that seemed a natural thing. Risen from near suppression, the great Church of Rome inherited all Ireland.

In a dream when he was old, Grattan rode on horseback from Ennismolach Rectory, and walked slowly to an altar between crowded pews. The dream came often and he knew it did so because the past was never far from his thoughts. He knew, as well, that the pages could not be turned back, that when the past had been the present it had been uneasy with shortcomings and disappointments, injustice and distress. He did not in any way resent the fact that, while his own small churches fell into disrepair, the wayside Church of the Holy Assumption, with its Virgin's grotto and its slope of new graves, was alive and bustling, that long lines of cars were parked on the verges and in gateways for its Sunday Masses, that there was Father MacPartlan as well as Father Leahy, that large sums were gathered for missions to the African heathen. Father MacPartlan and Father Leahy praised and rejoiced and celebrated, gave absolution, gave thanks. The simplicity of total belief, of belonging and of being in touch, nourished – or so it seemed to Grattan – Father MacPartlan's ruddy features and Father Leahy's untroubled smile.

A man called Con Tonan, who had lost the use of an arm in a tractor accident, worked in the garden of Ennismolach Rectory, his disablement rendering him unfit for employment as a farm labourer, which had always been the source of his livelihood. Unable to pay more than a pittance, Grattan took him on when he'd been out of work for a year. Con Tonan, still young then, knew nothing about gardening, but the six-mile bicycle journey to Ennismolach Rectory, and doing what he could to release the choked shrubs and restore the flowerbeds that had all but disappeared, gave a pattern to his day three times a week. Mrs Bradshaw, one of Grattan's flock at Glenoe, began to come to the rectory when Con Tonan was just beginning to understand the garden. Twice a week she drove over from Glenoe in a small, old Volkswagen, a woman who was as warm-hearted as she was dutiful.

That was the household at Ennismolach, Mrs Bradshaw ill-paid also, her arrival on Tuesdays and Thursdays as much an act of charity on her part as the employment of a one-armed man was on Grattan's. Sometimes Con Tonan brought one of his children with him, skilfully balancing the child on the crossbar of his bicycle in spite of the absence of an arm.

For twenty-eight years Con Tonan came to the rectory and then, before one winter began, he decided the journey was too much for him. 'Arrah, I'm too old for it now,' was all he said when he broke the news of his intentions. It was perhaps because his pension had come through, Mrs Bradshaw suggested, but Grattan knew it wasn't. It was because Con Tonan was as old as he was, because he was tired.

Mrs Bradshaw was younger. Plump and respectable, she knew all about the greater world, delighting in its conveniences as much as she deplored its excesses. She and Grattan would sit together at the kitchen table on Tuesdays and Thursdays, exchanging the scraps of news she brought for those he had heard that morning on the radio, which she herself rarely turned on.

He sensed her fondness for him – an old man who was a legend in the neighbourhood simply because he'd been a part of it for so long – and sometimes asked her if it was ever said that he was going on beyond his time. Was it said that he was ineffective in his vocation, that he managed ineffectively what remained of his Church's influence in the amalgamated parishes? He was always reassured. No one wanted him to go, no one wanted some bright young curate to come out from one of the towns on alternate Sundays, to breathe life into what was hardly there.

'Mr Fitzmaurice,' a red-cheeked, red-haired youth said, arriving at the rectory on a day in the early summer of 1997. 'My father died.'

Grattan recognized the bicycle the boy dismounted from as the big old Rudge that had once so regularly been pedalled up and down the rectory avenue. He hadn't seen a child of Con Tonan's for years, since one by one they'd all become too heavy to be carried on their father's crossbar.

'Oh, Seamus, I'm sorry. Come in, come in.'

His one-time gardener had died of a stroke, a mercy he hadn't lingered: the boy was articulate, slow but clear in delivering the sombre message.

'He was speechless a day, Mr Fitzmaurice. Then that was the end of it.'

His mother had sent him over, and Grattan was touched that he'd been remembered. The funeral was on Monday.

'I'll be there of course, Seamus.'

He made tea and put out biscuits. He asked Seamus if he'd like a boiled egg, but Seamus said no. They talked for a while, until the tea he'd poured was cool and then drunk. Seamus was working for Kelly Bros., who were building two bungalows at Fenit Bridge.

'Are you all right yourself, Mr Fitzmaurice?' he enquired before he mounted the bicycle that now was his. It was serving its third generation, having passed on in the same way to his father.

'Ah, I am, Seamus, I am.'

'I'll be off so.'

Mrs Bradshaw brought the same tidings the next morning. A decent, quiet man, she said, which she had not said in Con Tonan's lifetime. A humble man, who had accepted without bitterness the tragedy that had changed his life. 'Sure, wasn't he happy here?' her comment was, her tone adding one finality to another. She washed their coffee cups at the sink and stacked away the two saucers. She'd brought eggs, she said, the hens beginning to lay again.

On Monday he attended the funeral. He held back afterwards outside the big church that still seemed new, waiting his turn with the widow. He did not know her well; he could remember meeting her only once before, a long time ago.

'He loved going over to the rectory,' she said, and as if something in the clergyman's expression indicated surprise she said it again, her hands grasping one of his. 'Oh, he did, Mr Fitzmaurice, he did,' she insisted. 'It was a good thing in the end, he used say. If he hadn't had the accident he wouldn't have got to know Ennismolach Rectory. He wouldn't have got to know yourself, sir.'

Grattan Fitzmaurice drove away from the funeral, warmed by what had been said to him. Walking with his dog about the garden that had deteriorated in the last few years, although was not as neglected as it had been before he had help in it, he thought about the man who had died, who had become a friend. Con Tonan hadn't known what a daphne was when first he came, nor what choisya and ceanothus were called. He'd been amazed that raspberry canes were cut down to the ground in the autumn. He'd learnt how to rid the roses of suckers and when to clip the yew hedge, and not to burn the leaves that came down in autumn but to let them decay into mould to enrich the soil. The two men had talked about ordinary things: the weather, and sometimes what a new government intended to do, pondering over which promises would be easy to keep, which would have to be abandoned. In other ways they were separated, but that never mattered.

When Grattan had fed his dog on the evening of the funeral, when he'd boiled himself the couple of eggs he always had at a quarter past seven, with toast and a pot of tea, there was the sound of a car. He opened the front door a few minutes later to the younger of the two priests who had conducted the service. Smiling, hand out, Father Leahy said, 'I thought I'd come over.'

He said it easily, as if he were in the habit of calling in regularly at the rectory, as if he knew from long experience that this was a good moment. But neither he nor Father MacPartlan had ever driven up to Ennismolach Rectory before.

'Come in, come in,' Grattan invited. The curate's handshake had been firm, the kind you can feel the friendliness in.

'Isn't that a lovely evening, Mr Fitzmaurice? Are we in for a heatwave?'

'I'd say we might be.'

In the big drawing-room all the furniture was old but not old enough to be valuable: armchairs and a sofa shabby from wear, plant stands and rickety little tables with books and ornaments on them, sun-browned wallpaper cluttered with pictures and photographs, a tarnished looking-glass huge above the white marble mantelpiece, a card-table with a typewriter on it. The long curtains – once two shades of blue – were almost colourless now and in need of repair.

'You'll take a cup of tea, Father?'

'Ah no, no. Thanks though, Mr Fitzmaurice.'

'Well, we've lost poor Con.'

'God rest him.'

'I missed him when coming out here was too much for him in the end.'

Glancing beside him as he sat down, Grattan noticed the *Irish Times*, where earlier he had placed it on the table by his armchair. His eye had been caught then, as it was now, by the grinning countenance of Father Brendan Smyth being taken into custody by a grim-faced detective. *Paedophile Priest is Extradited*, the headline ran. He reached out and turned the newspaper over.

'You'd miss Con, of course.' There was a pause, and then Father Leahy added, 'You're a long way from the world here.'

'I'm used to that.'

He wondered if his gesture with the paper had been noticed. He had meant it as a courtesy, but a courtesy could be offensive. Long way from the world or not, it was impossible not to be aware of the Norbertine priest's twenty-year-long persecution of children in Belfast. One sentence already served in Magilligan Prison in County Derry, he was now on his way to face seventy-four similar charges in Dublin. All day yesterday the News had been full of it.

'It was good of you to attend the funeral, Mr Fitzmaurice.'

'I was fond of Con.'

The funeral service had impressed him. There'd been confidence in its ceremony and its ritual, in the solemn voice of Father MacPartlan, in Father Leahy's, in the responses of the congregation. It was there again in the two priests' gestures, hands raised to give the blessing, in the long line of communicants and the coffin borne away, the graveside exhortations. Founded on a rock, Grattan had thought: you felt that here. The varnished pews were ugly, the figure in the Stations of the Cross lifeless, but still you felt the confidence and the rock.

'Mrs Tonan said the same thing, that it was good of you to come. 'Tis difficult sometimes for a parishioner to understand that someone of your Church would want to.'

'Ah well, of course I would.'

'That's what I'm saying.'

There was a silence. Then Father Leahy said:

'That's a great dog.'

'I'd be lost without Oisín.'

'You always had a dog. I always associate a dog with you in the car.'

'Company.' And Grattan thought you didn't often see a priest with a dog. Maybe once in a while you would, but not often. He didn't say so in case it sounded intrusive. He remembered Father Leahy as a child, one of the Leahys from the white farmhouse on the Ballytoom road. Three brothers he remembered, swinging their legs on a whitewashed wall, waving at him whenever he drove past. The priest would be the youngest, the youngest in all the family, someone told him once. Four girls there were as well.

'We neither of us moved far off,' he said, and Father Leahy nodded, affirming his understanding of how the conversation had drifted in this direction.

'We didn't, right enough,' he said.

Grattan wondered why the curate had come. Had he decided to pay the visit when he saw the lone figure at the funeral? Had he come to offer half an hour of companionship, maybe out of pity? Had the two priests said after the service that perhaps the occasion had been hard to bear for a Protestant clergyman, with nothing of a flock left?

'Your family scattered?' He kept the conversation going, feeling that was required of him.

'Mostly.'

The farm was still run by the brother who'd inherited it, Young Pat. There was another brother in Cleveland, Ohio. The sisters had all gone, married in different parts of the country, two in Cork.

'We used meet up at Christmas, a few of us anyway. They'd come back to the farm, but then the girls have families of their own now. They don't want to be travelling.'

'I remember you sitting on that wall.'

'We used learn off the car numbers. Not that there were many, maybe two a day. ZB 726.'

'Was that my old Morris?'

'The slopey-back green Morris. You used put out one of your indicators when you went by, waving at us. D'you remember that? The little orange yoke?'

'I bought that car from Mr Keane in the Bank of Ireland. Would you have known Mr Keane?'

'I would, of course. Wasn't it Keane himself lent my father the price of the milking parlour? A decent man.'

Protestants were often called decent. You knew where you were with Protestants: that was said often in those days. Straight-dealing was what was meant, the quality not begrudged. The bank manager had been the churchwarden at Ennismolach.

'Father MacPartlan remembers your father. Your mother too.'

Grattan imagined Father MacPartlan mentioning them, telling his curate about the old days, how the big houses had been burnt down, the families driven from them, how the rectories had escaped. 'Wouldn't you call round on the old fellow one of these evenings?' he imagined Father

MacPartlan urging. 'If it wouldn't be taken wrong?' And the bluff tones of the older priest continued to disturb Grattan's thoughts, instructing the curate in mercy and understanding, reminding him of the spirit of the different times. After all, it was said also, all three of them shared the cloth.

'Would you care for a stroll in the garden, Father?'

'Well, that would be grand.'

Dusk had settled in. With the dog a few paces behind them, the two men passed from path to path, going slowly, shrubs and flowers pointed out. Father Leahy, like Con Tonan once, knew the names of hardly anything.

'Con knocked the garden into shape for me.'

'His wife was saying you taught him the way of it.'

'Oh, at first of course. He ended knowing more than I did myself. He loved the old garden before he was done with it.'

'He was a long time here.'

'He was.'

'Near enough the time Father MacPartlan entered the priesthood it would have been when he came to you.'

The air was fragrant with the scent of night stock, there was the sound of Oisín rooting in the undergrowth. Rabbits came into the garden, and one scuttled away now.

'Father MacPartlan came off a farm, like I did myself. A lot of priests in Ireland came off a farm.'

'They still do, I'm told.'

'Simple enough lads at first.'

'Yes.'

It seemed to Grattan that they were talking about something else. Nothing was ever entirely as it seemed, he found himself thinking, and didn't know why he did.

'Different for yourself, I'd say, Mr Fitzmaurice.'

Grattan laughed. 'Oh, I knew what I was in for.'

They stood by the barbed-wire fence at the bottom of the garden, looking out into the shadows of pasture land beyond. Heifers were grazing there, but you could hardly see them now. Shadowy themselves, the two black-clad figures turned and walked back the way they'd come. It didn't seem likely, a sudden realization came to Grattan, that the priests had spoken in the way he'd thought, that the curate had been instructed in mercy and understanding. When you imagined, you were often wrong, and again he wondered why his visitor was here.

'It's a big old house,' Father Leahy said. 'It would always have been a rectory, would it?'

'Oh, it was built as a rectory all right. 1791.'

'It'll see a few years yet.'

'A lot of the clergy would prefer something smaller these days.'

'But not yourself?'

'You're used to a place.'

In front of the house again, twilight giving way to the dark now, they stood by Father Leahy's car, a silence gathering, the small talk of the conversation running out. Oisín ambled over the gravel and settled himself patiently on the front-door steps. Father Leahy said:

'I never knew a place as peaceful.'

'Any time you're near by come in again, Father.'

There was the flare of a match, then the glow of the priest's cigarette, tobacco pleasant on the evening air, mingling with the flowers.

'It wasn't easy, I dare say.' Father Leahy's face was lost in the dark now, only the glow of the cigarette's tip moving, his voice trailing off.

'Easy, Father?'

'I meant for yourself.'

It seemed to Grattan that it was possible to say that in the dark, when it hadn't been before, that truth could flourish in the dark, that in the dark communication was easier.

'Time was, a priest in Ireland wouldn't read the *Irish Times*. Father MacPartlan remarks on that. But we take it in now.'

'I thought maybe that picture –'

'There's more to it all than what that picture says.'

Something about the quiet tone of voice bewildered Grattan. And there were intimations beneath the tone that startled him. Father Leahy said:

'It's where we've ended.'

So softly that was spoken, Grattan hardly heard it, and then it was repeated, increasing his bewilderment. Why did it seem he was being told that the confidence the priests possessed was a surface that lingered beyond its day? Why, listening, did he receive that intimation? Why did it seem he was being told there was illusion, somewhere, in the solemn voices, hands raised in blessing, the holy water, the cross made in the air? At Ennismolach, long ago, there had been the traps and the side-cars and the dog-carts lined up along the Sunday verges, as the cars were lined up now outside the Church of the Holy Assumption. The same sense of nourishment there'd been, the safe foundation on a rock that could not shatter. Why did it seem he was being reminded of that past?

'But surely,' he began to say, and changed his mind, leaving the two words uselessly on their own. He often read in the paper these days that in the towns Mass was not as well attended as it had been even a few years ago. In the towns marriage was not always bothered with, confession and absolution passed by. A different culture, they called it, in which restraint and prayer were not the way, as once they had been. Crime spread in the different culture, they said, and drugs taken by children, and old women raped, and murder. A plague it was, and it would reach the country too, was reaching it already. The jolly Norbertine man of God grinned from the newspaper photograph in village shops and farmhouse kitchens, on cottage dressers, propped up against milk jugs at mealtimes, and he grinned again on television screens. Would he say that all he ever did was to reach out and gather in his due, that God had made him so? In the different culture Christ's imitation offered too little.

'I often think of those monks on the islands,' Father Leahy said. 'Any acre they'd spot out on the sea they would row off to to see could they start a community there.'

'They would.'

'Cowled against the wind. Or cowled against what's left behind. Afraid, Father MacPartlan says. When Father MacPartlan comes in to breakfast you can see the rims of his eyes red.'

An image of the older priest was vivid for a moment in Grattan's recall, his mourning black, the collar cutting into pink flesh, hair that had thinned and gone grey over the years of their acquaintanceship. That this man wept in the night was barely credible.

'I never left Ireland,' Father Leahy said. 'I have never been outside it.'

'Nor I.' The silence after that was part of the dark, easily there, not awkward. And Grattan said, 'I love Ireland.'

They loved it in different ways: unspoken in the dark, that was another intimation. For Grattan there was history's tale, regrets and sorrows and distress, the voices of unconquered men, the spirit of women as proud as empresses. For Grattan there were the rivers he knew, the mountains he had never climbed, wild fuchsia by a seashore and the swallows that came back, turf smoke on the air of little towns, the quiet in long glens. The sound, the look, the shape of Ireland, and Ireland's rain and Ireland's sunshine, and Ireland's living and Ireland's dead: all that.

On Sundays, when Mass was said and had been said again, Father Leahy stood in a crowd watching the men of Kildare and Kerry, of Offaly and Meath, yelling out encouragement, deploring some lack of skill. And afterwards he took his pint as any man might, talking the game through. For Father Leahy there was the memory of the cars going by, his bare feet on the cobbles of the yard, the sacrifice he had made, and his faithful coming to him, the cross emblazoned on a holy robe. Good Catholic Ireland, a golden age.

'Anywhere you'd be,' Grattan said, 'there's always change. Like day becoming night.'

'I know. Sure, I know of course.'

Father Leahy's cigarette dropped on to the ground. There was the sound of his shoe crunching away the spark left in the butt, then his footsteps began on the gravel. A light came on when he opened the car door.

'You're not left bereft, you know,' Grattan said.

'Father MacPartlan looked over the table tonight after he'd put sugar in his tea. What he said to me was you'd given Con Tonan his life back. Even though Con Tonan wasn't one of your own.'

'Ah, no, no, I didn't do that.'

'D'you know the way it sometimes is, you want to tell a person a thing?'

The curate's hand was held out in the little pool of light, and there was the same friendliness in the clasp before he started the car's engine.

'Father Leahy called in last night,' Grattan heard himself reporting to Mrs Bradshaw. 'The first time a priest ever came to the rectory that I remember.' And Mrs Bradshaw, astonished, would think about it all morning while she worked, and would probably say before she left that the curate calling in was an expression of the ecumenical spirit they were all on about these days. Something like that.

For a few more minutes Grattan remained outside, a trace of tobacco smoke still in the garden, the distant hum of the curate's car not quite gone. The future was frightening for Father Leahy, as it had been for the monks who rowed away from Ireland once, out on to their rocks; as it had been for his father on his deathbed. But the monks and his father had escaped, mercy granted them. The golden age of the bishops was vanishing in a drama that was as violent as the burning of the houses and the fleeing of the families, and old priests like Father MacPartlan were made melancholy by their loss and passed their melancholy on.

'Come on, Oisín,' Grattan called, for his dog had wandered in the garden. 'Come on now.'

He had paid Con Tonan what he could; he'd been glad of his company. He had never thought of Con Tonan in his garden as a task he'd been given, as a single tendril of the vine to make his own. But the priest had come this evening to say it had been so, and by saying it had found a solace for himself. Small gestures mattered now, and statements in the dark were a way to keep the faith, as the monks had kept it in an Ireland that was different too.

Good News

'Hi,' the bald man with the earrings said. 'I'm Roland.'

He looked at Bea from behind small, round spectacles. She watched his gaze passing slowly over her features, over her shoulders and her chest, her hands on the table between them. Bea was nine, with dark hair that was long, and brown eyes with a dreamy look that was sometimes mistaken for sadness.

'You're going to show us, Leah?' the man with earrings said, and the girl who stood beside him, in a navy-blue jumper and jeans, ran a finger down a list on her clipboard and told him the name was Bea.

'Take your time, Leah,' the man said.

Bea had practised, the curtains drawn so that it was dark, Iris suddenly switching on the table lamp. Waking up on the sofa, wondering where she was, was what was marked on the script as the bit they would ask her to do.

She crossed to where two chairs were drawn close together to represent the sofa. She lay down on them and waited for the girl with the clipboard to say she'd switched the light on, as she'd said she would. Bea's hands went up then, shielding her eyes, not making too much of the gesture, not milking it, as Iris had explained you never should, subtlety being everything.

'Quite nice,' the man with the earrings said.

Iris was Bea's mother. Iris Stebbing she'd been born, but she'd turned that into Iris Orlando for professional purposes, and Iris Adams she'd become when she married Dickie. It was several years since she had gone for a part herself – 'woman in massage parlour' – which they'd said at the last minute she wasn't quite right for. Occasionally she still rang up about a forthcoming production she'd read about in *The Stage* and they always promised to bear her in mind. But they never rang back.

Bea was different, with everything ahead of her. And Bea had talent, Iris was certain of that. She could see her one day as Ophelia, or the young just-married in *Outward Bound*, which she had played herself, or Rachel-Elizabeth in *Bring on the Night*. Iris had taught Bea all she knew.

Another child came in to wait, with a stout young woman who was presumably a mother too, unhealthy-looking, Iris considered. The child was timid, which of course was what they wanted, but rabbity in appearance, which Iris doubted they'd want, not for a minute. Bea was quiet, always had been, but she didn't look half dead. More to the point, she didn't have teeth like that.

'Hi,' the mother said.

Iris wrinkled her lips a bit, the smile she gave to strangers. There would be others, of course. Every fifteen minutes, they'd keep coming all morning. She knew the drill.

Iris was not a young mother herself. She hadn't wanted to have children, but when she reached forty she had suddenly felt panicky, which of course – she readily admitted – was her all over. She had a part in the hospital serial then, but she'd begun to think she'd never have another one. The last year in Wanstead it was. Dickie was still on the road, office stationery.

Another mother and another child came in, the mother even younger than the fat one, the child brazen-faced, not right at all. They liked to be early, half an hour at least, and this time there was no greeting, nothing said, no smiles. Competitiveness had taken over; Iris could feel it in herself, a mounting dislike of those she shared the small waiting-room with.

'There we are,' the girl in the navy-blue jumper and jeans said, bringing Bea back. 'You like to come in now?' she invited the rabbity child, and shook her head when the mother attempted to accompany her. 'We'll call you this evening,' she said to Iris, 'if Bea has been successful. After five it'll be. All right, after five?'

Iris said it would be, handing Bea her coat. They didn't say 'Don't ring us' any more, a joke it had become. But she remembered when it wasn't.

A mother and child were on the way in as they left and Iris stared quickly at the child: lumpy, you couldn't call her anything else, and thin hair with a grey tinge.

'Let's have a coffee,' Iris said on the street.

Bea was thinking about Dickie. When Iris had come off the phone and said there'd be an audition she had thought about him; and ever since, while they were practising and going through the script, he'd kept coming into her mind. It was two years since the quarrel about the shirts, when Iris said she'd had enough and Dickie went off, the summer before last, a Monday.

'They say they liked you?' Iris asked in the café. 'They say anything?'

Bea shook her head, then pushed back her hair where it had fallen over her forehead. John's the café was called, all done out in green, which Bea liked because it was her favourite colour. They sat at a counter that ran along the windows and a girl brought them cappuccinos.

'They only said about the waking up,' Bea said.

When she'd told Dickie about the audition he'd stopped suddenly as they were walking across the dusty grass in the Wild Park. She'd told him then because Iris said she should, the Sunday after it was all fixed up. He'd stood perfectly still, looking into the trees in the distance, then he turned and looked down at her. That was marvellous, he said.

'They wanted you to do it with the movements?' Iris asked. 'Like I showed you?'

Bea shook her head. They didn't want movements, she said. The man called her Leah, she said.

'Leah? My God, he thought you were one of the others! My God!'

'He didn't understand "Bea".'

She'd known what was passing through Dickie's thoughts when he heard the news in the Wild Park. She'd known because of the other times there'd been good news – when Iris won fifteen pounds in the milkman's draw, when Dickie was in work again one time, when Iris's aunt died and there was the will. Dickie had been invited in the Sunday after the milk-man's draw and there'd been a bottle of wine. 'He still holding on to that job?' Iris would ask, but he hadn't, not for long; and the will had brought only the fish cutlery. But even so, good news when it came always bright-ened things up where Dickie and Iris were concerned, and one of these days it wouldn't just go away again. Quite often Bea felt sure of that.

'You told that man, though? You said about the name?'

'The girl knew.'

'You said it to her? You're sure?'

'She had it written down.'

It was July, warm and airless, no sign of the sun. It pleased Bea that all this had occurred when the summer holidays were about to start and no one in her class would have to know she was in an audition for a TV thing. 'Of course you'll have to say,' Iris had said, 'if you get the part. On account they'll see you when it comes on.'

Bea thought she probably wouldn't. It could even be they wouldn't recognize her, which was what she'd like. She didn't know why she wanted that, at the same time wanting so much to get the part because of Dickie. 'So what kind of a story is it?' Dickie had asked in the Wild Park and she said a woman was murdered in it.

'Practise a bit?' Iris said when they were back in the flat, after they'd had clam chowder and salad.

Bea didn't want to, now that the audition was over, but Iris said it would pass the time. So they practised for an hour and then sat by the open window, listening to the sound of the traffic coming from Chalmers

Street, watching the people going by, the afternoon turned sunny at last. 'Don't be disappointed,' Iris kept saying, and when the telephone rang at a quarter to six she said it could be anyone. It could be Dickie about tomorrow, or the telephone people, who often rang at this time on a Saturday to explain some scheme or other, offering free calls if you did what they wanted you to do.

But it was the girl in the navy-blue jumper to say that Bea had got the part.

The rehearsals took place in an army drill-hall. Iris had to be there too, and at the studios where the set was, and on location. She had arranged to take her holiday specially; and it worried Bea that she intended to call in sick when the holiday time ran out. 'I *know* this place!' she cried, excitedly looking round the drill-hall when they walked into it the first morning.

'A while ago now,' Bea heard her telling the woman who'd said she was playing the bag-lady. She'd had great ambitions, Iris said, but then the marriage and all that had been a setback. He'd been out of work for six years as near's no matter, and then again later of course. A regular thing it became and she'd had to take what was going in a typing pool. Ruinous that was, as she'd known it would be, as anyone in the profession could guess.

'The kiddie'll make it up to you,' the bag-lady predicted. 'Definitely,' she added, as if making up herself for not sounding interested enough.

'When the call came I couldn't believe it. "Ring Dickie," I said. Well, it's only fair, no matter what the past.'

'A father'd want to know. Any father would.'

'She's had to have her hair cut off.'

Bea listened to these exchanges because there was nothing else to do. When she'd rung Dickie to tell him he'd said immediately that he was over the moon and she knew he was. 'You say well done to Iris for me,' he'd said, and immediately she had imagined him coming back to the flat, as sometimes she did, arriving with his two old suitcases. 'Well, what d'you know!' he'd kept saying on the phone. 'Well, I never!'

He liked Bea to call him Dickie because she called Iris Iris; he liked the warmth of it, he said. 'Remember the time we stayed in the hotel?' he often reminded her, having once taken her to Brighton for a night. 'Remember the day we saw the accident, the bus going too fast? Remember the first time in the Wild Park?'

He was big and awkward, given to knocking things over. He had another child, dark-skinned, who didn't live with him either. 'You tell her good old Iris,' he said on the phone, giving credit where it was due because he knew Iris had been trying for this for years. 'You won't forget now, old girl?'

Any excuse, he'd be back. When he said he was over the moon it was because this was the kind of chance that could change everything. Bea saw him once a fortnight, a week on Sunday the next time was and he'd said he couldn't wait.

'Hi, Bea,' the man called Roland said, getting her name right when they were all sitting down at the drill-hall's long trestle-table. The girl in the navy-blue jumper had a walkie-talkie attached to her clipboard, and a badge with *Andi* on it. A boy with fuzzy hair was handing round biscuits, and coffee in paper cups. 'Best coffee in London,' he kept saying and sometimes someone laughed.

Bea watched while the scripts were leafed through, some of them being marked with a ballpoint. She turned the pages of hers, finding page fourteen, which was where she came into it, even though in the whole script she didn't actually speak. 'Mr Hance,' the man who came to sit in the chair next to hers introduced himself as, giving the name of the character he played. He was thin and lank, with milky eyes beneath a squashed forehead, his grey suit spotted a bit, his tie a tight knot in an uncomfortable-looking collar. 'You've dressed the part,' Bea had heard Andi saying to him.

'From the top,' Roland called out, and the drill-hall went silent. Then the voices began.

It was the old woman with the dyed red hair who was murdered. In the drill-hall her elderliness was disguised with bright crimson lipstick and the henna in her hair. Mr Hance put the poison in the yoghurt carton that was left with her milk on Wednesdays and Fridays. Iris had explained all that, but Bea understood it better when she heard the voices in the drill-hall.

Not that she understood everything. In the script it said that Mr Hance played marbles with her, which was a game no one Bea knew played or had an interest in. 'That's a very lonely man,' Iris had said, but it seemed peculiar to Bea that a lonely person wouldn't go to the pub or some billiard hall instead of playing marbles with a child in a car park. In the script she was meant to be lonely herself; 'Little Miss Latchkey' Mr Hance called her because there was never anyone at home to let her in. In the script it said the old woman had tidy white hair, and a walking-stick because she couldn't manage without one.

Iris was happy from the moment they entered the drill-hall: Bea could tell. She remembered it all so well, Bea heard her telling the bag-lady and later Ann-Marie, the newsagent's daughter. The gossip of the profession, the knitting while you waited for your cue, the puffing at a cigarette you didn't want when something wasn't going right: Iris was back where she belonged, among the friends she might have had.

In the late afternoon there was the funeral scene: the clergyman's words ringing out, the mourners standing round a chalked rectangle on the floor, the old woman who was dead completing the *Daily Telegraph* crossword. When the burial was over the boy with the fuzzy hair was given the task of showing Bea and Mr Hance how to play marbles.

'All right then, Bea?' Andi asked a few times, and Bea said she was. It was probably not being tall, she thought, that gave Andi the heavy look she had heard her complaining about earlier. She was on a slimming course, she'd said, but it didn't seem to be doing any good. Bea liked her best of all the people in the drill-hall.

'From the top one more time,' Roland called out when Bea thought the rehearsing must surely be over, and they went through the whole script again. She hadn't shared her mother's pleasure in the day. She hadn't known what to expect, any more than she'd known what to expect at the audition. When the script had come in Iris said that the only disappointment was that Bea didn't ever get to speak. She had remarked as much to Ann-Marie while the funeral scene was going on, mouthing it so as not to interrupt. And Ann-Marie, who was pussy-faced, Bea thought, but very pretty, waited until the funeral scene was over to say that Bea's part was all the more telling for being silent. Bea had been glad she didn't have to say anything, but she wondered now if it might perhaps be less boring if she had to say just a little.

'How's it going, Beasie?'

Dickie's brown jacket needed a stitch at the pocket that was nearer to her, on a level with her eyes when she looked. It needed more of a stitch than it had two Sundays ago, which was the last time she'd seen it. He was incapable of attending to his clothes, Iris said.

'OK,' Bea said. Three weeks had passed since the first day in the drill-hall and the drill-hall had long ago been left behind. They'd moved into the set at the studios, and there'd been days of filming on location.

'You tell Iris what I said that time, Beasie? You say I said well done?'

She nodded, cold on the street where they were walking even though it was August. She dug her hands into the pockets of the coat Iris had said to take in case it rained. The Sunday before last she'd said she'd told Iris.

'I told her,' she said again.

He hadn't seen Iris today. He hadn't seen her the last Sunday either.

He'd rung the bell and Bea had called down on the intercom and he'd waited for her, the same both times.

'All these years,' he said on the street, '*The Stage*'s been her Bible.'

'Yes.'

And in the end it was *The Stage* that came up trumps. Dickie went on talking about that, and Bea imagined her mother inviting him in. One Sunday or another, she said to herself, sooner or later. 'We must tell Dickie,' Iris had kept saying during the three weeks that had passed – about Ann-Marie being half asleep in the early morning and letting the piles of newspapers she'd just opened fall off the counter, and how she put back the different sections any old how; about Mr Hance and the marbles; about the caged canary still singing when the old woman lay dead.

'Doesn't worry you, any of that stuff?' Dickie had said in the Wild Park when she'd shown him in the script where the murder was. 'If it worries you, you say, old girl.'

She never would. She didn't tell Iris when she dreamed about the dog on the garbage tip, the microbes you could see moving through its entrails in the film sequence. In the viewing-room, with the red light showing outside, she had sat with the others, not knowing what it was the police were looking for on the tip, watching while the camera crept slowly over the entrails of the dog. She didn't know why the old woman kept rapping with her stick on the window, why she kept sitting there and then rapping again. 'She's a peeper,' was all Mr Hance said in the script, and in the long waits when Bea wasn't involved the confusion made the boredom worse.

'What's that Hance like?' Dickie asked.

'All right.' Bea didn't say she didn't like him. She said it was a joke that he was always called Mr Hance. Extra pages had gone into his script, yellow pages at first, the second batch pink. She hadn't been given any herself, but she could see the colours showing at the edges when he sat beside her in the coach, on the way to the studios or the locations. He always sat beside her. Getting to know her, Iris said.

'Iris think he's good?' Dickie asked.

'Oh, yes.'

They all did. He took pains, they said; he found his way. 'She wasn't very nice, you know,' he said about the old woman, talking about her in the room where Bea had to wake up on the sofa. He often didn't look at you when he spoke and because of his whispery voice you sometimes couldn't hear. Bea didn't know why Mr Hance made her nervous, why he had even on the first day, why most of all he did when he sat beside her in the coach, one of his fingers tracing over and over again the outline of the little label that was sewn into the edge of his plain brown scarf. On every journey his milky eyes turned away from the coach window before the journey ended and his fingers became still. He gazed at her, saying nothing, and at first she thought he was practising the part. She'd seen them doing that, trying something out, hearing one another's lines, but in the coach it didn't seem like practising. The room with the sofa in it was in his house, where he took her after the old woman was dead, the sofa all sagging and old, two empty milk bottles on the window-sill, cat litter on the floor beneath it. They kept having to do the scene in which she woke up, getting it right.

'We take in a film today?' Dickie suggested. '*Meet Me in St Louis*'s come back.' In the cinema, listening to the songs, Bea tried not to think about being bored again tomorrow or Mr Hance making her nervous in the coach. She tried not to see the moisture on his squashed forehead when he knelt down by the sofa and asked her to forgive him. She tried not to hear him saying something she couldn't hear in the coach, or not saying anything when he gazed at her.

'Wasn't that grand!' Dickie said when Judy Garland sang for the last time and *The End* went up on the screen. 'I've got some hot-cross buns,' he said when they were on the street, although it wasn't Easter, the wrong time of year by ages. In his bedsitting-room they toasted the hot-cross buns because they were a bit on the stale side. They squatted on the floor, each of them with a fork, poking their buns at the bar of the electric fire.

It was warm in the bedsitting-room, Dickie's overcoat hanging from the hook on the back of the door, his bed under the sloping windows, a curtain drawn over so you wouldn't know the sink was there. He had little sachets of jam, blackcurrant and strawberry, and he offered her a choice.

'There's Swiss roll,' he said, and he laughed. What was left of one, he meant. He'd kept it for her. 'Iris busy this evening?' he asked when they had finished everything. 'Going out, is she?'

Bea shook her head, but when they got to the flat Iris didn't ask him in. Iris wasn't sure yet, Bea said to herself, and later on, when she was in bed, she went over the signs there'd been – Iris saying they must tell Dickie about the audition and then about Ann-Marie and the newspapers, and the canary singing. But when Bea fell asleep it wasn't Dickie being back that came into her dreams. In the room with the milk bottles on the window-sill Mr Hance was showing her the label on his scarf and she kept saying she must go now. She kept trying to get up from the sofa but she couldn't.

*

'It's like you pity Mr Hance,' Roland said, turning a chair round so that he was facing Bea in the viewing-room. He dangled a leg over one of the chair's arms, which was his favourite way of sitting. His earrings were crucifixes, Bea noticed, which she hadn't before. 'The piece is about stuff like that, chick.'

Yesterday on the screen Mr Hance had walked away from the funeral and then walked on, through the streets by the river and the gasometers. In a startling way his features had suddenly filled the screen, tears glistening on his lean cheeks.

'We're into compassion here,' Roland said.

Bea tried to blank out Mr Hance's weeping face, which she could still see even though the screen was empty now. The tears ran down to the corners of his mouth, droplets becoming snagged there or slipping on, into the crevices of his chin.

'Like some poor wounded bird,' Roland said. 'Some little sparrow with a smashed-up wing. And you'd be sorry for it because maybe the other sparrows would be quicker and take the crumbs. You're with us here, Bea?'

Her mother looked sharply at her, which quite reminded her of a sparrow's beady gaze. Bea knew Iris was being sharp because she didn't want her to say she didn't like feathers, that they never put crumbs out because of that. The time in Trafalgar Square the pigeons were frightening the way they rushed by you, their wings crashing into your face. 'Never again,' Dickie had promised. 'You give your nuts to that little boy there.' But she hadn't wanted even to do that. She didn't want to have the nuts in her hand for a minute longer.

'Try for it, shall we?' Roland said. 'The pity thing?'

Bea began to nod. 'Why'd he have to murder her?' she asked, because she had always wondered that.

'Because the friendship's going to be taken from him.' Roland swung his leg off the arm of the chair. 'Because the old lady's got the wrong end of the stick. OK, chick?'

Bea said it was, because there didn't seem much point in saying anything else. She had asked Iris where the dog's carcass on the tip came into it, if the dog had been the old woman's or what, and Iris said they would understand that when the film was put together. They would understand where Ann-Marie arranging the newspapers came into it, and the bag-lady looking in the lamp-post bins for any food that was thrown away, and the workmen repairing a pavement, and the man in a maroon-coloured car. The trouble was, Iris said, that the scenes hadn't been shot in the right order, which naturally made it difficult. The yoghurt the poison had been put in was banana and guava, and Bea said to herself that never in her whole life would she eat banana and guava yoghurt again. One morning on the coach Mr Hance asked her what colour her school uniform was and she felt panicky when he did although she didn't know why, just a simple question it was. She wanted to get up, to find some place else to sit, but moving about the coach would draw attention to her and she didn't want that. 'It's all just pretend,' Mr Hance said another day. 'Only pretend, Bea.' It seemed strange to say that, to say what she already knew, and she wondered if she'd misheard because of Mr Hance's quiet voice.

Once when the coach drew up and they all got out, when Bea was walking with Iris to the location, she wanted so much to say she was frightened of Mr Hance that she almost did. She began to, but Iris luckily wasn't listening. Bea realized at once that it was lucky. Everything would have been ruined.

'Let's go for it this time, chick,' Roland said on the last day, going for the final take. Bea could hear the soft whirring of the camera when the fuzzy-haired boy had given the take number and clapped the clapperboard. They had practised the scene before the coffee break and again after it, when Roland had repeated all he'd said about pity.

Bea couldn't do it in the take any more than she'd been able to when they'd practised. 'Cut!' the fuzzy-haired boy had to keep exclaiming, and Roland came on to the set and talked to Bea again, and Iris came on because he asked her to. 'Sorry,' Bea kept saying.

The make-up girls came on in the end. They gave her artificial tears, and the cameraman said that was better by a long chalk. The lighting man changed the lighting, softening it considerably.

'We'll go for it this time,' Roland said, and the fuzzy-haired boy held up the clapperboard and called out another number. 'One more time,' Roland said when Bea had lost count of the takes.

They ran fifteen minutes into the lunch break before they dispersed and made their way to the mobile canteen. Over a chicken salad with chips, Iris recalled for the bag-lady and the police inspector the part she'd had – a child herself then – in an episode of *Z Cars*, 1962 it was. Bea had heard this a few times before and, since she didn't like the bean-and-sausage bake she'd helped herself to, she looked around for somewhere to get rid of it without anyone, especially Iris, noticing. Iris always said to eat well at the mobile canteen so that there wouldn't have to be much cooking when they got back to the flat. But there was no convenient vase or fire bucket into which to tip the load on Bea's cardboard plate. Outside, where the cars were parked, she found the dustbins.

After that she didn't want to go back to where the mobile canteen was set up because they'd see she wasn't eating anything and press a lot of stuff she didn't want on her. She walked about the empty set, which she had never had to herself before. She wandered from room to room, thinking it was a pity that soon it would all be dismantled when the homeless who slept in doorways could do with it, even if only for a night.

'Hullo,' a voice said just before Bea heard Mr Hance's footstep, and she knew he had come looking for her.

That evening Dickie came to the party. 'You ask your father,' Iris had said. 'Only fair.' Dickie had said yes at once.

'Under time, under budget!' Roland announced in his speech of gratitude to the cast, and everyone clapped.

They were all there on the set – the bag-lady, Ann-Marie, the police inspector, the old woman, the man in the maroon car, the workmen who'd been repairing a pavement, the policemen who'd searched the tip, Mr Hance.

They made a fuss of Mr Hance. It was his piece, they said, his show. 'I've heard a lot about you,' Dickie said to him, and Bea thought he hadn't really, but Dickie was good at being polite. The tear by his jacket pocket hadn't been repaired. Bea had seen Iris noticing it when Dickie came over to say hullo.

'So what's next on the agenda?' the police inspector asked Bea. 'Another part lined up, have we?'

'Spoilt for choice,' Iris said, but Bea wondered about that, and Dickie said what's this then? A certain little lady on her way was what, the police inspector said.

All the technicians and production people were at the party – the sound man, the cameraman and the assistant cameraman, the set designer, the make-up girls, the costume girls, the continuity girl. They drank wine, red or white, and there was Coca Cola or orange juice to go with the plates of cold food. Dickie asked who the big woman with the glasses on a chain was and Iris said the producer. 'Remember that producer on *Emergency Ward 10*?' Dickie said.

'Oh, my God, don't!'

Music began. Bea showed Dickie about the set: Mr Hance's room with the cat litter still there, the stairs, the hall with the antlers, the living-room of the other house, where the old woman rapped the window with her walking-stick. 'Marvellous,' Dickie kept saying. One part of the set had been dismantled already and Iris came along to explain all that.

Andi and the boy with fuzzy hair brought round the wine and the food. Roland knocked on the floor with the old woman's walking-stick: early as it was, he said, he had to be going. They'd been great, he complimented everyone. Pure electricity this production was, the Good Housekeeping Seal.

There was laughter, and more applause. Roland waved good-bye with the walking-stick, then handed it to Andi. After he'd gone someone turned the music up.

When no one was looking, Bea opened the sandwich she had taken. There seemed to be scrambled egg in it so she dropped it into an empty cardboard box beside where she was standing. She was alone there, obscured by the pot plants that had been gathered together on a table, ready to go back to *Flowers Etc*, which was what was scrawled on a piece of paper tied around one of them. She could see Dickie and Iris and Mr Hance, the sound man seeming to be telling them a story. When he came to the end of it they laughed, Iris particularly, throwing back her head in a way she had. Still pouring wine, the boy with the fuzzy hair looked to where the laughter had come from and laughed himself, then moved over to fill their glasses up.

Peeping through the fleshy green leaves, Bea watched Mr Hance earnestly talking now, Dickie's head bent to listen. A moment ago Iris had held on to Dickie's arm, just for a second when one of her high heels let her down. She had reached out and clutched at him and he had smiled at her and she had smiled herself. Where they were standing was quite near where Bea had been when Mr Hance had said hullo that afternoon.

Across the set the old woman was sitting on her own, a cigarette alight, her wine glass half full. With her painted features and bright dyed hair she didn't at all look like the old woman by the window, but in spite of that she still was, and suddenly Bea wanted to go over to her and say she'd been right. She wanted her to know. She wanted just one person to know.

'Hi, Bea,' Andi said. 'That your dad, then?'

'Yes.'

'He looks nice. Nice way he has.'

'Yes.'

'Not in the profession, though? Not like your mum?' Andi reached out to feel one of the leaves, softly caressing it between forefinger and thumb. 'He could get a walk-on, your dad. You never know.'

Andi seemed forlorn without her clipboard and mobile telephone, wearing the same blue jumper she'd worn for all six weeks of the production. She wasn't drinking wine; she wasn't eating anything, but that would be because of her slimming.

'You going for it, Bea? You reckon?' She'd gone for it herself only it hadn't worked out. She wasn't right for the acting side of the business, although it was what she'd wanted at first. 'Different for you,' Andi said.

'Yes.'

It would be better to tell Andi. It would be easier to say it had to be a secret, that all she wanted was one person to know. It seemed mean not to tell Andi when she'd come over specially to be friendly.

'Maybe our paths'll cross again,' Andi said. 'Anyway I hope they do.'

'Yes.'

'You did fine.'

Bea shook her head. Through the foliage she saw Mr Hance's hand held out, to her mother and then to Dickie. They smiled at him, and then he made his way through the other people at the party, stepping over the electrical cables that stretched from one room of the set to another. Occasionally he stopped to shake hands or to be embraced. The old woman laughed up at him, sharing some joke.

'I must make my farewells.' Andi kissed Bea and said again she hoped their paths would cross some time.

'So do I.' Bea tried to tell Andi then. But if Andi knew it might show in her face even if she didn't want it to. It mightn't be easy for her not to let it, and when someone asked her what the matter was it could slip out when she wasn't thinking.

'Cheers,' Andi said.

The bag-lady was going also. In the corner where the cameras still were, outside the set itself, Ann-Marie was dancing with one of the policemen. Dickie was holding up Iris's see-through plastic mackintosh, waiting for Iris to step into it. 'See you on the ice,' the fuzzy-haired boy called after Mr Hance, and Mr Hance waved back at him before he walked out of the brightness that was the party.

On the train Iris told Dickie who everyone was, which part each had played, who was who among the technicians. Dickie asked questions to keep her going.

It was the first time Bea had made the journey in from the studios by train. There had always been the coach before, to the studios and back, to whatever the location was. The train was nicer, the houses that backed on to the railway line lit up, here and there people still in their gardens even though it was dark. Sometimes the train stopped at a suburban station, the passengers who alighted seeming weary as they made their way along the platform. 'I must say, I enjoyed that,' Dickie said.

They got the last bus to Chalmers Street and walked, all three of them, to the flat. 'Come in, Dickie?' Iris invited.

She'd got in the cereal he liked and it was there on the kitchen table, ready for breakfast. Bea saw him noticing it.

'Good night, old girl,' he said, and Bea kissed him, and kissed Iris too, for Iris had said she was too tired to come in to say good-night.

Bea washed, and folded her clothes, and brushed her teeth. She turned the light out, wondering in what way her dreams would be different now, reminding herself that she mustn't cry out in case, being sleepy, she ruined everything.

The Mourning

In the town, on the grey estate on the Dunmanway road, they lived in a corner house. They always had. Mrs Brogan had borne and brought up six children there. Brogan, a council labourer, still grew vegetables and a few marigolds in its small back garden. Only Liam Pat was still at home with them, at twenty-three the youngest in the family, working for O'Dwyer the builder. His mother – his father, too, though in a different way – was upset when Liam Pat said he was thinking of moving further afield. 'Cork?' his mother asked. But it was England Liam Pat had in mind.

Dessie Coglan said he could get him fixed. He'd go himself, Dessie Coglan said, if he didn't have the wife and another kid expected. No way Rosita would stir, no way she'd move five yards from the estate, with her mother two doors down. 'You'll fall on your feet there all right,' Dessie Coglan confidently predicted. 'No way you won't.'

Liam Pat didn't have wild ambitions; but he wanted to make what he could of himself. At the Christian Brothers' he'd been the tidiest in the class. He'd been attentive, even though he often didn't understand. Father Mooney used to compliment him on the suit he always put on for Mass, handed down through the family, and the tie he always wore on Sundays. 'The respect, Liam Pat,' Father Mooney would say. 'It's heartening for your old priest to see the respect, to see you'd give the boots a brush.' Shoes, in fact, were what Liam Pat wore to Sunday Mass, black and patched, handed down also. Although they didn't keep out the wet, that didn't deter him from wearing them in the rain, stuffing them with newspaper when he was home again. 'Ah, sure, you'll pick it up,' O'Dwyer said when Liam Pat asked him if he could learn a trade. He'd pick up the whole lot – plumbing, bricklaying, carpentry, house-painting. He'd have them all at his fingertips; if he settled for one of them, he wouldn't get half the distance. Privately, O'Dwyer's opinion was that Liam Pat didn't have enough upstairs to master any trade and when it came down to it what was wrong with operating the mixer? 'Keep the big mixer turning and keep Liam Pat Brogan behind it,' was one of O'Dwyer's good-humoured catch-phrases on the sites where his men built houses for him. 'Typical O'Dwyer,' Dessie Coglan scornfully pronounced. Stay with

O'Dwyer and Liam Pat would be shovelling wet cement for the balance of his days.

Dessie was on the estate also. He had married into it, getting a house when the second child was born. Dessie had had big ideas at the Brothers'; with a drink or two in him he had them still. There was his talk of 'the lads' and of 'connections' with the extreme republican movement, his promotion of himself as a fixer. By trade he was a plasterer.

'Give that man a phone as soon as you're there,' he instructed Liam Pat, and Liam Pat wrote the number down. He had always admired Dessie, the easy way he had with Rosita Drudy before he married her, the way he seemed to know how a hurling match would go even though he had never handled a hurley stick himself, the way he could talk through the cigarette he was smoking, his voice becoming so low you couldn't hear what he was saying, his eyes narrowed to lend weight to the confidential nature of what he passed on. A few people said Dessie Coglan was all mouth, but Liam Pat disagreed.

It's not bad at all, Liam Pat wrote on a postcard when he'd been in London a week. *There's a lad from Lismore and another from Westmeath*. Under a foreman called Huxter he was operating a cement-mixer and filling in foundations. He got lonely was what he didn't add to his message. *The wage is twice what O'Dwyer gave*, he squeezed in instead at the bottom of the card, which had a picture of a guardsman in a sentry-box on it.

Mrs Brogan put it on the mantelpiece. She felt lonely herself, as she'd known she would, the baby of the family gone. Brogan went out to the garden, trying not to think of the kind of place London was. Liam Pat was headstrong, like his mother, Mr Brogan considered. Good-natured but headstrong, the same red hair on the pair of them till her own had gone grey on her. He had asked Father Mooney to have a word with Liam Pat, but the damn bit of good it had done.

After that, every four weeks or so, Liam Pat telephoned on a Saturday evening. They always hoped they'd hear that he was about to return, but all he talked about was a job finished or a new job begun, how he waited every morning to be picked up by the van, to be driven halfway across London from the area where he had a room. The man who was known to Dessie Coglan had got him the work, as Dessie Coglan said he would. 'A Mr Huxter's on the lookout for young fellows,' the man, called Feeny, had said when Liam Pat phoned him as soon as he arrived in London. In his Saturday conversations – on each occasion with his mother first and then, more briefly, with his father – Liam Pat didn't reveal that when he'd asked Huxter about learning a trade the foreman had said take what was

on offer or leave it, a general labourer was what was needed. Liam Pat
didn't report, either, that from the first morning in the gang Huxter had
taken against him, without a reason that Liam Pat could see. It was Huxter's way to pick on someone, they said in the gang.

They didn't wonder why, nor did Liam Pat. They didn't know that a
victim was a necessary compensation for the shortages in Huxter's life –
his wife's regular refusal to grant him what he considered to be his bedroom rights, the failure of a horse or greyhound; compensation, too, for
surveyors' sarcasm and the pernicketiness of fancy-booted architects. A
big, black-moustached man, Huxter worked as hard as any of the men
under him, stripping himself to his vest, a brass buckle on the belt that
held his trousers up. 'What kind of a name's that?' he said when Liam Pat
told him, and called him Mick instead. There was something about Liam
Pat's freckled features that grated on Huxter, and although he was well
used to Irish accents he convinced himself that he couldn't understand
this one. 'Oh, very Irish,' Huxter would say even when Liam Pat did
something sensible, such as putting planks down in the mud to wheel the
barrows on.

When Liam Pat had been working with Huxter for six weeks the man
called Feeny got in touch again, on the phone one Sunday. 'How're you
doing?' Feeny enquired. 'Are you settled, boy?'

Liam Pat said he was, and a few days later, when he was with the two
other Irish boys from the gang, standing up at the bar in a public house
called the Spurs and Horse, Feeny arrived in person. 'How're you doing?'
Feeny said, introducing himself. He was a wizened-featured man with
black hair in a widow's peak. He had a clerical look about him but he
wasn't a priest, as he soon made clear. He worked in a glass factory, he
said.

He shook hands with all three of them, with Rafferty and Noonan as
warmly as with Liam Pat. He bought them drinks, refusing to let them
pay for his, saying he couldn't allow young fellows. A bit of companionship was all he was after, he said. 'Doesn't it keep the poor exile going?'

There was general agreement with this sentiment. There were some
who came over, Feeny said, who stayed no longer than a few days. 'Missing the mam,' he said, his thin lips drawn briefly back to allow a laugh
that Rafferty remarked afterwards reminded him of the bark of a dog. 'A
young fellow one time didn't step out of the train,' Feeny said.

After that, Feeny often looked in at the Spurs and Horse. In subsequent conversations, asking questions and showing an interest, he learnt
that Huxter was picking on Liam Pat. He didn't know Huxter personally,
he said, but both Rafferty and Noonan assured him that Liam Pat had

cause for more complaint than he admitted to, that when Huxter got going he was no bloody joke. Feeny sympathized, tightening his mouth in a way he had, wagging his head in disgust. It was perhaps because of what he heard, Rafferty and Noonan deduced, that Feeny made a particular friend of Liam Pat, more than he did of either of them, which was fair enough in the circumstances.

Feeny took Liam Pat to greyhound tracks; he found him a better place to live; he lent him money when Liam Pat was short once, and didn't press for repayment. As further weeks went by, everything would have been all right as far as Liam Pat was concerned if it hadn't been for Huxter. 'Ah, no, I'm grand,' he continued to protest when he made his Saturday telephone call home, still not mentioning the difficulty he was experiencing with the foreman. But it had several times crossed his mind that one Monday morning he wouldn't be there, waiting for the van to pick him up, that he'd had enough.

'What would you do though, Liam Pat?' Feeny asked in Bob's Dining Rooms, where at weekends he and Liam Pat often met for a meal.

'Go home.'

Feeny nodded; then he sighed and after a pause said it could come to that. He'd seen it before, a bullying foreman with a down on a young fellow he'd specially pick out.

'It's got so's I hate him.'

Again Feeny allowed a silence to develop. Then he said:

'They look down on us.'

'How d'you mean?'

'Any man with an Irish accent. The way things are.'

'You mean bombs and stuff?'

'I mean, you're breathing their air and they'd charge you for it. The first time I run into you, Liam Pat, weren't your friends saying they wouldn't serve you in another bar you went into?'

'The Hop Poles, that is. They won't serve you in your working clothes.'

Feeny leaned forward, over a plate of liver and potatoes. He lowered his voice to a whisper. 'They wash the ware twice after us. Plates, cups, a glass you'd take a drink out of. I was in a launderette one time and I offered a woman the machine after I'd done with it. "No, thanks," she said soon's I opened my mouth.'

Liam Pat had never had such an experience, but people weren't friendly. It was all right in the gang; it was all right when he went out with Rafferty and Noonan, or with Feeny. But people didn't smile, they didn't nod or say something when they saw you coming. The first woman he rented a room from was suspicious, always in the hall when he left the house, as if she thought he might be doing a flit with her belongings. In the place Feeny had found for him a man who didn't live there, whose name he didn't know, came round every Sunday morning and you paid him and he wrote out a slip. He never said anything, and Liam Pat used to wonder if he had some difficulty with speech. Although there was other people's food in the kitchen, and although there were footsteps on the stairs and sometimes overhead, in the weeks Liam Pat had lived there he never saw any of the other tenants, or heard voices. The curtains of one of the downstairs rooms were always drawn over, which you could see from the outside and which added to the dead feeling of the house.

'It's the same the entire time,' Feeny said. 'Stupid as pigs. Can they write their names? You can see them thinking it.'

Huxter would say it straight out. 'Get your guts put into it,' Huxter shouted at Liam Pat, and once when something wasn't done to his liking he said there were more brains in an Irish turnip. 'Tow that bloody island out into the sea,' he said another time. A drop of their own medicine, he said.

'I couldn't get you shifted,' Feeny said. 'If I could I would.'

'Another gang, like?'

'Maybe in a couple of weeks there'd be something.'

'It'd be great, another gang.'

'Did you ever know McTighe?'

Liam Pat shook his head. He said Feeny had asked him that before. Did McTighe run a gang? he asked.

'He's in with a bookie. It'd be a good thing if you knew McTighe. Good all round, Liam Pat.'

Ten days later, when Liam Pat was drinking with Rafferty and Noonan in the Spurs and Horse, Feeny joined them and afterwards walked away from the public house with Liam Pat.

'Will we have one for the night?' he suggested, surprising Liam Pat because they'd come away when closing time was called and it would be the same anywhere else. 'No problem,' Feeny said, disposing at once of this objection.

'I have to get the last bus out, though. Ten minutes it's due.'

'You can doss where we're going. No problem at all, boy.'

He wondered if Feeny was drunk. He'd best get back to his bed, he insisted, but Feeny didn't appear to hear him. They turned into a side street. They went round to the back of a house. Feeny knocked gently on a window-pane and the rattle of television voices ceased almost immediately. The back door of the house opened.

'Here's Liam Pat Brogan,' Feeny said.

A bulky middle-aged man, with coarse fair hair above stolid, reddish features, stood in the rectangle of light. He wore a black jersey and trousers.

'The hard man,' he greeted Liam Pat, proffering a hand with a cut healing along the edge of the thumb.

'Mr McTighe,' Feeny completed his introduction. 'We were passing.'

Mr McTighe led the way into a kitchen. He snapped open two cans of beer and handed one to each of his guests. He picked up a third from the top of a refrigerator. Carling it was, Black Label.

'How're you doing, Liam Pat?' Mr McTighe asked.

Liam Pat said he was all right, but Feeny softly denied that. More of the same, he reported: a foreman giving an Irish lad a hard time. Mr McTighe made a sympathetic motion with his large, square head. He had a hoarse voice, that seemed to come from the depths of his chest. A Belfast man, Liam Pat said to himself when he got used to the accent, a city man.

'Is the room OK?' Mr McTighe asked, a query that came as a surprise. 'Are you settled?'

Liam Pat said his room was all right, and Feeny said:

'It was Mr McTighe fixed that for you.'

'The room?'

'He did of course.'

'It's a house that's known to me,' Mr McTighe said, and did not elucidate further. He gave a racing tip, Cassandra's Friend at Newton Abbot, the first race.

'Put your shirt on that, Liam Pat,' Feeny advised, and laughed. They stayed no more than half an hour, leaving the kitchen as they had entered it, by the door to the back yard. On the street Feeny said:

'You're in good hands with Mr McTighe.'

Liam Pat didn't understand that, but didn't say so. It would have something to do with the racing tip, he said to himself. He asked who the man who came round on Sunday mornings for the rent was.

'I wouldn't know that, boy.'

'I think I'm the only lodger there at the moment. There's a few shifted out, I'd say.'

'It's quiet for you so.'

'It's quiet all right.'

Liam Pat had to walk back to the house that night; there'd been no question of dossing down in Mr McTighe's. It took him nearly two hours, but the night was fine and he didn't mind. He went over the conversation that had taken place, recalling Mr McTighe's concern for his well-being, still bewildered by it. He slept soundly when he lay down, not bothering to take off his clothes, it being so late.

Weeks went by, during which Liam Pat didn't see Feeny. One of the other rooms in the house where he lodged was occupied again, but only for a weekend, and then he seemed once more to be on his own. One Friday Huxter gave Rafferty and Noonan their cards, accusing them of skiving. 'Stay if you want to,' he said to Liam Pat, and Liam Pat was aware that the foreman didn't want him to go, that he served a purpose as Huxter's butt. But without his friends he was lonely, and a bitter resentment continuously nagged him, spreading from the foreman's treatment of him and affecting with distortion people who were strangers to him.

'I think I'll go back,' he said the next time he ran into Feeny, outside the Spurs and Horse one night. At first he'd thought Feeny was touchy when he went on about his experience in a launderette or plates being washed twice; now he felt it could be true. You'd buy a packet of cigarettes off the same woman in a shop and she wouldn't pass a few minutes with you, even though you'd been in yesterday. The only good part of being in this city was the public houses where you'd meet boys from home, where there was a bit of banter and cheerfulness, and a sing-song when it was permitted. But when the evening was over you were on your own again.

'Why'd you go back, boy?'

'It doesn't suit me.'

'I know what you mean. I often thought of it myself.'

'It's no life for a young fellow.'

'They've driven you out. They spent eight centuries tormenting us and now they're at it again.'

'He called my mam a hooer.'

Huxter wasn't fit to tie Mrs Brogan's laces, Feeny said. He'd seen it before, he said. 'They're all the same, boy.'

'I'll finish out the few weeks with the job we're on.'

'You'll be home for Christmas.'

'I will.'

They were walking slowly on the street, the public houses emptying, the night air dank and cold. Feeny paused in a pool of darkness, beneath a street light that wasn't working. Softly, he said:

'Mr McTighe has the business for you.'

It sounded like another tip, but Feeny said no. He walked on in silence, and Liam Pat said to himself it would be another job, a different foreman. He thought about that. Huxter was the worst of it, but it wasn't only

Huxter. Liam Pat was homesick for the estate, for the small town where people said hullo to you. Since he'd been here he'd eaten any old how, sandwiches he bought the evening before, for breakfast and again in the middle of the day, burger and chips later on, Bob's Dining Rooms on a Sunday. He hadn't thought about that before he'd come – what he'd eat, what a Sunday would be like. Sometimes at Mass he saw a girl he liked the look of, the same girl each time, quiet-featured, with her hair tied back. But when he went up to her after Mass a few weeks back she turned away without speaking.

'I don't want another job,' he said.

'Why would you, Liam Pat? After what they put you through?'

'I thought you said Mr McTighe –'

'Ah no, no. Mr McTighe was only remembering the time you and Dessie Coglan used distribute the little magazine.'

They still walked slowly, Feeny setting the pace.

'We were kids though,' Liam Pat said, astonished at what was being said.

'You showed your colours all the same.'

Liam Pat didn't understand that. He didn't know why they were talking about a time when he was still at the Brothers', when he and Dessie Coglan used to push the freedom magazine into the letter-boxes. As soon as it was dark they'd do it, so's no one would see them. Undercover stuff, Dessie used to say, and a couple of times he mentioned Michael Collins.

'I had word from Mr McTighe,' Feeny said.

'Are we calling in there?'

'He'll have a beer for us.'

'We were only being big fellas when we went round with the magazine.'

'It's remembered you went round with it.'

Liam Pat never knew where the copies of the magazine came from. Dessie Coglan just said the lads, but more likely it was the barber, Gaughan, an elderly man who lost the four fingers of his left hand in 1921. Liam Pat often noticed Dessie coming out of Gaughan's or talking to Gaughan in his doorway, beneath the striped barber's pole. In spite of his fingerless hand, Gaughan could still shave a man or cut a head of hair.

'Come on in,' Mr McTighe invited, opening his back door to them. 'That's a raw old night.'

They sat in the kitchen again. Mr McTighe handed round cans of Carling Black Label.

'You'll do the business, Liam?'

'What's that, Mr McTighe?'

'Feeny here'll show you the ropes.'

'The thing is, I'm going back to Ireland.'

'I thought maybe you would be. "There's a man will be going home," I said to myself. Didn't I say that, Feeny?'

'You did of course, Mr McTighe.'

'What I was thinking, you'd do the little thing for me before you'd be on your way, Liam. Like we were discussing the other night,' Mr McTighe said, and Liam Pat wondered if he'd had too much beer that night, for he couldn't remember any kind of discussion taking place.

Feeny opened the door of the room where the curtains were drawn over and took the stuff from the floorboards. He didn't switch the light on, but instead shone a torch into where he'd lifted away a section of the boards. Liam Pat saw red and black wires and the cream-coloured face of a timing device. Child's play, Feeny said, extinguishing the torch.

Liam Pat heard the floorboards replaced. He stepped back into the passage off which the door of the room opened. Together he and Feeny passed through the hall and climbed the stairs to Liam Pat's room.

'Pull down that blind, boy,' Feeny said.

There was a photograph of Liam Pat's mother stuck under the edge of a mirror over a wash-basin; just above it, one of his father had begun to curl at the two corners that were exposed. The cheap brown suitcase he'd travelled from Ireland with was open on the floor, clothes he'd brought back from the launderette dumped in it, not yet sorted out. He'd bought the suitcase in Lacey's in Emmet Street, the day after he gave in his notice to O'Dwyer.

'Listen to me now,' Feeny said, sitting down on the bed.

The springs rasped noisily. Feeny put a hand out to steady the sudden lurch of the headboard. 'I'm glad to see that,' he said, gesturing with his head in the direction of a card Liam Pat's mother had made him promise he'd display in whatever room he found for himself. In the Virgin's arms the infant Jesus raised two chubby fingers in blessing.

'I'm not into anything like you're thinking,' Liam Pat said.

'Mr McTighe brought you over, boy.'

Feeny's wizened features were without expression. His priestly suit was shapeless, worn through at one of the elbows. A tie as narrow as a bootlace hung from the soiled collar of his shirt, its minuscule knot hard and shiny. He stared at his knees when he said Mr McTighe had brought Liam Pat from Ireland. Liam Pat said:

'I came over on my own though.'

Still examining the dark material stretched over his knees, as if fearing damage here also, Feeny shook his head.

'Mr McTighe fixed the room. Mr McTighe watched your welfare. "I like the cut of Liam Pat Brogan." Those were his words, boy. The day after yourself and myself went round to him the first time wasn't he on the phone to me, eight a.m. in the morning? Would you know what he said that time?'

'No, I wouldn't.'

'"We have a man in Liam Pat Brogan," was what he said.'

'I couldn't do what you're saying all the same.'

'Listen to me, boy. They have no history on you. You're no more than another Paddy going home for Christmas. D'you understand what I'm saying to you, Liam Pat?'

'I never heard of Mr McTighe till I was over here.'

'He's a friend to you, Liam Pat, the same way's I am myself. Haven't I been a friend, Liam Pat?'

'You have surely.'

'That's all I'm saying to you.'

'I'd never have the nerve for a bomber.'

'Sure, is there anyone wants to be? Is there a man on the face of God's earth would make a choice, boy?' Feeny paused. He took a handkerchief from a pocket of his trousers and passed it beneath his nose. For the first time since they'd entered Liam Pat's room he looked at him directly. 'There'll be no harm done, boy. No harm to life or limb. Nothing the like of that.'

Liam Pat frowned. He shook his head, indicating further bewilderment.

'Mr McTighe wouldn't ask bloodshed of anyone,' Feeny went on. 'A Sunday night. You follow me on that? A Sunday's a dead day in the city. Not a detail of that written down, though. Neither date nor time. Nothing I'm saying to you.' He tapped the side of his head. 'Nothing, only memorized.'

Feeny went on talking then. Because there was no chair in the room, Liam Pat sat on the floor, his back to the wall. Child's play, Feeny said again. He talked about Mr McTighe and the mission that possessed Mr McTighe, the same that possessed every Irishman worth his salt, the further from home he was the more it was there. 'You understand me?' Feeny said often, punctuating his long speech with this query, concerned in case there was incomprehension where there should be clarity. 'The dream of Wolfe Tone,' he said. 'The dream of Isaac Butt and Charles Stewart Parnell. The dream of Lord Edward Fitzgerald.'

The names stirred classroom memories for Liam Pat, the lay teacher Riordan requesting information about them, his bitten moustache disguising a long upper lip, a dust of chalk on his pinstripes. 'Was your man Fitzgerald in the Flight of the Earls?' Hasessy asked once, and Riordan was contemptuous.

'The massacre of the innocents,' Feeny said. 'Bloody Sunday.' He spoke of lies and deception, of falsity and broken promises, of bullying that was hardly different from the bullying of Huxter. 'O'Connell,' he said. 'Pearse. Michael Collins. Those are the men, Liam Pat, and you'll walk away one of them. You'll walk away ten feet high.'

As a fish is attracted by a worm and yet suspicious of it, Liam Pat was drawn into Feeny's oratory. 'God, you could be the Big Fella himself,' Dessie Coglan complimented him one night when they were delivering the magazines. He had seen the roadside cross that honoured the life and the death of the Big Fella; he had seen the film only a few weeks back. He leaned his head against the wall and, while staring at Feeny, saw himself striding with Michael Collins's big stride. The torrent of Feeny's assurances and promises, and the connections Feeny made, affected him, but even so he said:

'Sure, someone could be passing though.'

'There'll be no one passing, boy. A Sunday night's chosen to make sure of it. Nothing only empty offices, no watchmen on the premises. All that's gone into.'

Feeny pushed himself off the bed. He motioned with his hand and Liam Pat stood up. Between now and the incident, Feeny said, there would be no one in the house except Liam Pat. Write nothing down, he instructed again. 'You'll be questioned. Policemen will maybe get on the train. Or they'll be at the docks when you get there.'

'What'll I say to them though?'

'Only that you're going home to County Cork for Christmas. Only that you were nowhere near where they're asking you about. Never in your life. Never heard of it.'

'Will they say do I know you? Will they say do I know Mr McTighe?'

'They won't have those names. If they ask you for names say the lads in your gang, say Rafferty and Noonan, say any names you heard in public houses. Say Feeny and McTighe if you're stuck. They won't know who you're talking about.'

'Are they not your names then?'

'Why would they be, boy?'

Liam Pat's protestation that he couldn't do it didn't weaken at first, but as Feeny went on and on, the words becoming images in Liam Pat's vision, he himself always at the centre of things, he became aware of an excitement. Huxter wouldn't know what was going to happen; Huxter would look at him and assume he was the same. The people who did not say hullo when he bought cigarettes or a newspaper would see no difference either. There was a strength in the excitement, a vigour Liam Pat had never experienced in his life before. He would carry the secret on to the site every morning. He would walk through the streets with it, a power in him where there'd been nothing. 'You have a Corkman's way with you,' Feeny said, and in the room with the drawn curtains he showed Liam Pat the business.

Sixteen days went by before the chosen Sunday arrived. In the Spurs and Horse during that time Liam Pat wanted to talk the way Feeny and Mr McTighe did, in the same soft manner, mysteriously, some private meaning in the words he used. He was aware of a lightness in his mood and confidence in his manner, and more easily than before he was drawn into conversation. One evening the barmaid eyed him the way Rosita Drudy used to eye Dessie Coglan years ago in Brady's Bar.

Liam Pat didn't see Feeny again, as Feeny had warned him he wouldn't. He didn't see Mr McTighe. The man didn't call for the rent, and for sixteen days Liam Pat was the only person in the house. He kept to his room except when he went to take up the sawn-through floorboards, familiarizing himself with what had to be done, making sure there was space enough in the sports bag when the clock was packed in a way that was convenient to set it. He cooked nothing in the kitchen because Feeny had said better not to. He didn't understand that, but even so he obeyed the command, thinking of it in that way, an order, no questions asked. He made tea in his room, buttering bread and sprinkling sugar on the butter, opening tins of beans and soup, eating the contents cold. Five times in all he made the journey he was to make on the chosen Sunday, timing himself as Feeny had suggested, becoming used to the journey and alert to any variations there might be.

On the Saturday before the Sunday he packed his suitcase and took it across the city to a locker at Euston Station, still following Feeny's instructions. When he returned to the house he collected what tins he'd opened and what food was left and filled a carrier bag, which he deposited in a dustbin in another street. The next day he had a meal at one o'clock in Bob's Dining Rooms, the last he would ever have there. The people were friendlier than they'd been before.

Nothing that belonged to him remained in his room, or in the house, when he left it for the last time. Feeny said to clean his room with the Philips cleaner that was kept for general use at the bottom of the stairs. He said to go over everywhere, all the surfaces, and Liam Pat did so, using the little round brush without any extension on the suction tube. For his own protection, that was. Wipe the handles of the doors with a tissue last thing of all, Feeny had advised, anywhere he might have touched.

Shortly after seven he practised the timing again. He wanted to smoke a cigarette in the downstairs room, but he didn't because Feeny had said not to. He zipped up the sports bag and left the house with it. Outside, he lit a cigarette.

On the way to the bus stop, two streets away, he dropped the key of the house down a drain, an instruction also. When Feeny had been advising him about cleaning the surfaces and making sure nothing was left that could identify him, Liam Pat had had the impression that Mr McTighe wouldn't have bothered with any of that, that all Mr McTighe was interested in was getting the job done. He went upstairs on the bus and sat at the back. A couple got off at the next stop, leaving him on his own.

It was then that Liam Pat began to feel afraid. It was one thing to have it over Huxter, to know what Huxter didn't know; it was one thing to get a smile from the barmaid. It was another altogether to be sitting on a bus with a device in a sports bag. The excitement that had first warmed him while he listened to Feeny, while he sat on the floor with his head resting against the wall, wasn't there any more. Mr McTighe picking him out felt different now, and when he tried to see himself in Michael Collins's trench-coat, with Michael Collins's stride, there was nothing there either. It sounded meaningless, Feeny saying he had a Corkman's way with him.

He sat with the sports bag on the floor, steadied by his feet on either side of it. A weakness had come into his arms, and for a moment he thought he wouldn't be able to lift them, but when he tried it was all right, even though the feeling of weakness was still there. A moment later nausea caused him to close his eyes.

The bus lurched and juddered through the empty Sunday-evening streets. Idling at bus stops, its engine vibrated, and between his knees Liam Pat's hand repeatedly reached down to seize the handles of the sports bag, steadying it further. He wanted to get off, to hurry down the stairs that were beside where he was sitting, to jump off the bus while it was still moving, to leave the sports bag where it was. He sensed what he did not understand: that all this had happened before, that his terror had come so suddenly because he was experiencing, again, what he had experienced already.

Two girls came chattering up the stairs and walked down the length of the bus. They laughed as they sat down, one of them bending forward, unable to control herself. The other went on with what she was saying, laughing too, but Liam Pat couldn't hear what she said. The conductor came for their fares and when he'd gone they found they didn't have a light for their cigarettes. The one who'd laughed so much was on the inside, next to the window. The other one got up. 'Ta,' she said when she had asked Liam Pat if he had a lighter and he handed her his box of matches. He didn't strike one because of the shaking in his hands, but even so she must have seen it. 'Ta,' she said again.

It could have been in a dream. He could have dreamed he was on a bus with the bag. He could have had a dream and forgotten it, like you sometimes did. The night he'd seen Feeny for the last time, it could have been he had a dream of being on a bus, and he tried to remember waking up the next morning, but he couldn't.

The girl next to the window looked over her shoulder, as if she'd just been told that he'd handed her friend the box instead of striking a match for her. They'd remember him because of that. The one who'd approached him would remember the sports bag. 'Cheers,' the same one said when they both left the bus a couple of stops later.

It wasn't a dream. It was the *Examiner* spread out on the kitchen table a few months ago and his father shaking his head over the funeral, sourly demanding why those people couldn't have been left to their grief, why there were strangers there, wanting to carry the coffin. 'My God! My God!' his father savagely exclaimed.

It hadn't worked the first time. A Sunday night then too, another boy, another bus. Liam Pat tried to remember that boy's name, but he couldn't. 'Poor bloody hero,' his father said.

Another Dessie Coglan had done the big fella, fixing it, in touch with another Gaughan, in touch with the lads, who came to parade at the funeral. Another Huxter was specially picked. Another Feeny said there'd be time to spare to get to Euston afterwards, no harm to life or limb, ten exactly the train was. The bits and pieces had been scraped up from the pavement and the street, skin and bone, part of a wallet fifty yards away.

Big Ben was chiming eight when he got off the bus, carrying the sports bag slightly away from his body, although he knew that was a pointless precaution. His hands weren't shaking any more, the sickness in his stomach had passed, but still he was afraid, the same fear that had begun on the bus, cold in him now.

Not far from where Big Ben had sounded there was a bridge over the river. He'd crossed it with Rafferty and Noonan, his first weekend in London, when they'd thought they were going to Fulham only they got it all wrong. He knew which way to go, but when he reached the river wall he had to wait because there were people around, and cars going by. And when the moment came, when he had the bag on the curved top of the wall, another car went by and he thought it would stop and come back, that the people in it would know. But that car went on, and the bag fell with hardly a splash into the river, and nothing happened.

O'Dwyer had work for him, only he'd have to wait until March, until old Hoyne reached the month of his retirement. Working the mixer it would be again, tarring roofs, sweeping the yard at the end of the day. He'd get on grand, O'Dwyer said. Wait a while and you'd never know; wait a while and Liam Pat could be his right-hand man. There were no hard feelings because Liam Pat had taken himself off for a while.

'Keep your tongue to yourself,' Mrs Brogan had warned her husband in a quiet moment the evening Liam Pat so unexpectedly returned. It surprised them that he had come the way he had, a roundabout route when he might have come the way he went, the Wexford crossing. 'I missed the seven train,' he lied, and Mrs Brogan knew he was lying because she had that instinct with her children. Maybe something to do with a girl, she imagined, his suddenly coming back. But she left that uninvestigated, too.

'Ah sure, it doesn't suit everyone,' Dessie Coglan said in Brady's Bar. Any day now it was for Rosita and he was full of that. He never knew a woman get pregnant as easy as Rosita, he said. He didn't ask Liam Pat if he'd used the telephone number he'd given him, if that was how he'd got work. 'You could end up with fourteen of them,' he said. Rosita herself was one of eleven.

Liam Pat didn't say much, either to O'Dwyer or at home or to Dessie Coglan. Time hung heavy while old Hoyne worked out the few months left of his years with O'Dwyer. Old Hoyne had never risen to being more than a general labourer, and Liam Pat knew he never would either.

He walked out along the Mountross road every afternoon, the icy air of a bitterly cold season harsh on his hands and face. Every day of January and a milder February, going by the rusted gates of Mountross Abbey and the signpost to Ballyfen, he thought about the funeral at which there'd been the unwanted presence of the lads, and sometimes saw it as his own.

All his life he would never be able to tell anyone. He could never describe that silent house or the stolid features of Mr McTighe or repeat Feeny's talk. He could never speak of the girls on the bus, how he hadn't been able to light a match, or how so abruptly he realized that this was the second attempt. He could never say that he'd stood with the sports bag on the river wall, that nothing had happened when it struck the water. Nor that he cried when he walked away, that tears ran down his cheeks and on to his clothes, that he cried for the bomber who might have been himself.

He might have left the bag on the bus, as he had thought he would. He might have hurried down the stairs and jumped off quickly. But in his fear he had found a shred of courage and it had to do with the boy: he knew that now and could remember the feeling. It was his mourning of the boy, as he might have mourned himself.

On his walks, and when he sat down to his meals, and when he listened to his parents' conversation, the mourning was still there, lonely and private. It was there in Brady's Bar and in the shops of the town when he went on his mother's messages. It would be there when again he took charge of a concrete-mixer for O'Dwyer, when he shovelled wet cement and worked in all weathers. On the Mountross road Liam Pat didn't walk with the stride of Michael Collins, but wondered instead about the courage his fear had allowed, and begged that his mourning would not ever cease.

A Friend in the Trade

They fell in love when *A Whiter Shade of Pale* played all summer. They married when Tony Orlando sang *Tie a Yellow Ribbon Round the Old Oak Tree*. These tunes are faded memories now, hardly there at all, and they've forgotten Procol Harum and Suzi Quatro and Brotherhood of Man, having long ago turned to Brahms.

The marriage has managed well, moving with ease through matrimony's stages, weathering its storms. It seems absurd to Clione when she looks back that she fussed so because at their first dinner party her husband of a month innocently remarked that she hadn't made the profiteroles herself. It was ridiculous in turn, James has apologized, that he banged out of the house when coffee was spilt over Pedbury's *The Optimistic Gardener*, ridiculous that he had not been calm when they missed the night train at the Gare de Lyon, ridiculous that they'd rowed about it when the workmen laid the wrong tiles.

The intensity of passion, and touchiness surfacing quickly, gave way to familial pleasure and familial pressures – three children growing up, their grandparents growing old. Tranquillity came when the children grew up a little more, when a Sunset Home took in a grandfather, a Caring Fold a grandmother. Give and take ruled the middle years; the marriage took on the odds and won. Passed through the battle, surviving dog days' ennui, love now seems surer than before.

Clione is still as slender as ever she was, with wide blue eyes that still, occasionally, have a startled look. Beauty has not finished with her: her delicately made features – straight classic nose and sculptured lips – are as they always were, and cobweb wrinkles have an attraction of their own. She is glad she did not marry someone else and could not ever have considered being unfaithful. She knows – she doesn't have to ask – that her husband has not been faithless either.

He deals in first editions and manuscripts. As well, he and Clione run the Asterisk Press together, publishing the verse of poets who are in fashion, novellas, short stories, from time to time a dozen or so pages of reminiscence by a writer whose standing guarantees the interest of collectors. Their business is conducted from home, an old suburban house in south-west London, not far from the river. Provincial auctions are

attended in pursuit of forgotten tomes and the letters of the literati, alive
or dead. The demands of the Asterisk Press – the choosing of typefaces
and bindings, paper of just the right shade and weight, mail-order sales
– provide a contrast. A catalogue that combines both sources of livelihood is published every six months or so.

Years ago, the trade in first editions and other rarities threw up Michingthorpe, who specializes mainly in what he calls nineteenth-century
jottings. A 'trade friend' James calls him, but there is more to it than this
designation implies. Since before the children were born, before the funerals of the grandparents, Michingthorpe has been a regular presence in the
house near the river. He has brought with him the excitement of jottings
that are special; a discovery that defies or contradicts the agreed opinion
of academe delights him most of all. But anything will do, for everything
is special, or becomes so in Michingthorpe's possession. Scraps of letters
are lovingly laid out; the beginning of a Dickens chapter that was not
proceeded with; frustrated Coleridge lines, scratched out, begun again; a
note to a tailor; initials on a bill. All have been offered to James and
Clione for perusal and admiration.

Michingthorpe talks mostly about himself. In remarking on the particular way a great Victorian author had of looping his I's or y's, he manages
to make the matter personal to himself, going on to relate that he loops his
own letters in that way too, or does not. Responding to a comment or
prediction about the weather, he recalls how when he was in Venice once
– on the track of a John Cross jotting – rain for six days caused the canals
to rise, trapping him in his hotel with nothing better to re-read than Ches-
terton's life of Browning, which he had not cared for the first time. If frost
is forecast, he recalls that it brings on an ailment. He had an uncle who
perished in a storm, struck by the bough of a cherry tree.

Michingthorpe was already running to youthful fat when he first
became a trade friend; he is fatter now. The flesh that smudges the con-
tours of his face is pale. Eyes, behind spectacles, are slate-coloured and
small. His hair was conventionally short when he was younger; now its
grey mat obscures his ears in so distinctive a manner that Clione has
heard her waggish son likening Michingthorpe to a New Testament dis-
ciple. Had Michingthorpe himself heard that, he would not have minded
but possibly would have recalled that as a schoolboy he wrote an essay on
the subject of the Last Supper and was awarded a prize for it. He welcomes it when he is spoken of, adverse comments being rarely recognized
as such.

When her middle child was three years old, Clione came into the sitting-
room one day to hear Michingthorpe explaining why it was that oysters

did not agree with him. He recounted occasions, before he was aware that they did not, when disaster had occurred. Still on the subject of his digestion, he next spoke of a dressmaker who had taken a liking to him in his own childhood, always having rock buns ready when he called in to see her. The rock buns had no ill effects, even though on one occasion he had eaten seven. Changing the subject, though without alteration of expression or tone, he reported that when he first wore spectacles everything tilted – whole rooms, and lamp-posts, the pavement when he walked on it. This led to a memory of someone saying, 'We see God's world as God would wish us to.' Once in a zoo he watched a gorilla escape. He recognized on the street one day the late Boris Karloff. Often he speaks of waiters – how skilled or careless one was last week, what he had eaten on that occasion, whose company he was in. His mealtime companions are always from the trade, business conducted over soup and entrée and pudding.

In the past Michingthorpe appeared to dress more ordinarily: clothes that were hardly noticeable in youth – jeans and T-shirts – are more emphatic with his long grey hair, as if they seek to make a point or perpetuate some illusion. There are chunky jerseys to go with them, horn buttons down the front.

'I dare say we all are someone else's unpresentable friend,' Clione has said, causing her husband and children to laugh, because Clione herself is not in the least unpresentable.

The children, who are adults now – the waggish boy, two younger girls – have ages ago come to regard Michingthorpe as they do the familiar items of furniture in their parents' house. He is something that has been there for as long as the buttoned sofa in the hall has been, and the ugly picture of mules drawing carts on the stairway wall, the davenport on the first-floor landing. For all the children's lives he has come and gone, expected or not expected, some detail at once related about the journey he has made. 'Oh, God, that man!' the children have cried, when young, when older. Not that Michingthorpe has ever noticed them much, seeming not ever to have established which is which. Among themselves they still wonder, as they always have, how it is that he continues to be a welcome visitor in their parents' house. The fact bewilders them, but then is packed away as one of the small mysteries that haunt the separation of generations.

The children are visitors themselves now, coming back to the house when they are ill or unhappy in a love affair, though often leaving again without mentioning anything; or coming back because they are, all three, affectionately disposed towards both their mother and their father. Their mother's fifty-first birthday draws them for Sunday lunch one damp February weekend, the last time it will be celebrated in this house, for after nearly twenty-five years there is to be a move. 'We rattle about like two ageing peas,' Clione has said, 'now that you have left us on our own.' Two days ago an offer was made for a converted oast-house in Sussex. Tomorrow it will be known if it has been accepted.

Clione has privately resolved that if it isn't she'll somehow find the extra and pay the asking price. Her childhood was passed in the country, and already she has wondered about keeping a dog – a spaniel – as once she did. Time has been on her hands since her children's going; she wants to grow her own vegetables again, to have asparagus beds, to cosset anemones and clematis and hellebores. Some intuition tells her she'll delight in that.

This prospect cheers Clione after her children have left, all together in the late afternoon, and the house in which all of them were born has gone quiet again. She wears a dress she bought specially for her birthday lunch, two shades of green, a silk scarf with an ivy pattern at her throat. Her presents clutter the sitting-room and there are torn cardboard packages on the floor, four different kinds of shiny coloured paper waiting to be folded: at Christmas it can be used again. Her cards are on the mantelpiece. A Rösel pepper-grinder is on the hearthrug beside her where she kneels, her new yellow coffee-maker on the armchair she usually sits in, Mahler's Sixth Symphony on disc beside it. The glow of smokeless fuel throws back a little heat at her.

Clione misses her children. It is missing them that drew her to the oast-house, to thoughts of vegetables and plants. And the chances are that her children will be drawn to it too, that they'll come there more often than to the house in London, that they'll delight in the summer countryside and weekend walks about the lanes, in winter bleakness, the trees skeletal, brown empty hedges. She longs for her children sometimes, wanting to set the time back to when there were children's worries, so very easy to comfort, to when her children gave her what a husband can't, not even the most generous. That a child was stillborn is never spoken of by James or by herself; their living children do not know.

She pushes away a surge of melancholy and thinks again about the changing seasons in a garden that does not yet quite exist, about fitting in all the paraphernalia of the Asterisk Press in the upstairs rooms. No longer kneeling, she leans back against the seat of an armchair, her legs slipped more comfortably to one side. Her eyelids droop.

There is something about Michingthorpe's way of ringing a doorbell that indicates, in this house at least, who it is: a single short ring, shorter than most people's and never repeated. Michingthorpe knows the sound can be heard in all the rooms, that if the summons is not answered no one is in, even though some lights are on.

Her doze disturbed, Clione imagines him already in the room and bearing, as her children have, a brightly wrapped gift. The unlikely, sleepy fantasy goes on a little longer. She sees herself in gratitude embracing Michingthorpe – which she has never done – and hears her voice exclaiming over what their visitor has brought.

Dusk is giving way to darkness. She shovels more coal on to the fire, then pulls the curtains over all three windows. The hall door bangs downstairs. Minutes later, in his long black overcoat, Michingthorpe is giftless in the sitting-room doorway.

'I knew of course that it was there.' He speaks to the air, as he always does, addressing no one. 'The funeral two months ago, disposal of the library on the eighth. They'd no idea. All that stuff and they'd no idea. I had the pickings to myself.'

He doesn't take his overcoat off. He has a way of sometimes not doing that. He sits down, still talking, saying he spent the night before in the temperance hotel of the town he visited, the only hotel there was. He and a local bookseller were the only dealers, and all the bookseller wanted was the Hardy. Sluggish on the sofa, Michingthorpe polishes his glasses and carefully replaces them as he speaks.

'Frightful journey. Change twice and a tree down on the line at Immington. Of course I had the Grossmith stuff to annotate.'

Pouring drinks, James nods. His fair hair has gone non-descript and is receding; in fawn corduroy trousers, checked winter shirt, fawn pullover, he is a little stooped.

'Clione's birthday,' he says, offering Michingthorpe a Kir.

But nothing that is outside himself, or part of other people, ever influences Michingthorpe. His surface runs deep, for greater knowledge of him offers nothing more than what initially it presents. Roaming the Internet is his hobby, he sometimes says.

Still feeling a little woozy from the wine at lunchtime, Clione shakes her head at the offer of a drink and tidies the room instead. Michingthorpe says he has formed the opinion that Conrad conducted a correspondence with a woman called Rosa Hoogwerf.

'Then residing in Argentina, though why remains a mystery. I've floated the name on the Net.'

Clione wonders if he noticed that she has carried a yellow coffee-maker across the room, or registers that she is now gathering up the remains of cardboard packages from the floor. She clears away the birthday cards from the mantelpiece.

'Some woman in Hungary,' Michingthorpe is saying. 'By the sound of her, Rosa Hoogwerf's granddaughter.'

He has accepted the drink that has been poured for him, and Clione wonders why he is here, then realizes it is to tell about the journey he has made and the prize that has come his way. Someone who once visited his flat saw the refrigerator open, with only a single bottle of milk in it, and uncooked sausages on a plate and butter still in its foil. Michingthorpe is unmarried, has apparently never had with anyone – man or woman – what could be called a relationship. That is generally assumed, but assumed with confidence, and is not contradicted by the known facts.

Clione sits down again. The conversation dims to a grey murmur she doesn't listen to. She doesn't dislike Michingthorpe, she never has; he isn't an enemy of any kind. Sometimes she considers he isn't even a bore, simply a presence with small slate eyes and teenager's hair that has a biblical look. She isn't aware of how she knows he loves her.

'Not that I feel my age,' she suddenly hears now, and wonders if he has finally acknowledged that there has been a birthday in the house and has said when his is, in August, as he has said before. 'Miskolc is where that woman is. She has a little English.'

He has never, that Clione can remember, met her eye, for he doesn't go in for that with anyone; yet still she knows. For several years – and before, for she senses that it has been longer – there has been something that even now seems extraordinary: it is incredible that Michingthorpe can love anyone; incredible too that he can be mysterious. Burning the cardboard she has collected, continuing not to listen to what is said, she wonders yet again if he is aware that she senses his attachment.

'We can sell the house at last.'

She hears James passing this information on and looks to see the vagueness it inspires in Michingthorpe's plump features, as happens when something utterly without interest requires his attention.

'We've found an oast-house,' she says herself.

There is a different reaction now. For the first time in Clione's entire acquaintance with him, Michingthorpe allows his mouth to open in what appears to be shock. Nor does it close. His small eyes stare harshly at the air. He sits completely still, one hand grasping the other, both pressed into his chest.

'This is the country?'

'Well, yes. Sussex.'

There is a pause, and then recovery. Michingthorpe stands up. 'Originally my family came from Sussex. But a long time ago. Michingthorpe Ales.'

'We shall miss you.' Clione notices herself sounding as mischievous as

one of her children. There is no protestation that they'll be missed themselves. For a long moment their empty-handed visitor is silent. But before
he goes there's more about the Internet.

Pouring coffee at breakfast five days later, Clione waits to hear the content of an early-morning telephone call: only Michingthorpe gets in touch
at five to eight. It has occasionally been earlier.

'He has been to see it.'

'What? Seen what?'

'The oast-house. He's been down there. Well, he was near, I think.
Anyway, he has looked it over.'

'But why on earth?'

'It's decidedly unlike him, but even so he has. I think I told him where
it was. Not that he asked.'

'You mean, he went along and bothered those people for no reason?'

'He just said he'd looked it over.'

A flicker of unease disturbs Clione. It might have amused her if ever
she had confessed that Michingthorpe has feelings for her; but to have
confessed as well that he has never displayed them, that her woman's
intuition comes in here, would have led too easily on to a territory of
embarrassment. Could it all not be imagination on her part? Or put more
cruelly, a fading beauty's yearning for attention? 'Oh, but surely,' Clione
has heard James's objection, the amusement all his now. Better just to
leave it, she has always considered.

'He knows our offer has been accepted?'

'Oh, yes, he knows.'

Two days later, in the early afternoon, they visit again the house they
have bought, received there by an elderly man – a Mr Witheridge whom
they have not met before, whose daughter and son-in-law showed them
around. They are permitted to take measurements, and in whispers speak
of structural changes they hope to make.

'Nice that your friend liked it too,' the old man says, waiting downstairs with teacups on a tray when they have finished.

Profuse apologies are offered, and explanations that sound lame. Some
silly muddle, James vaguely mutters.

'Oh, good heavens, no! Oast-houses are in Mr Michingthorpe's family,
it seems. Michingthorpe Ales, he mentioned.'

The garden is little more than a field with a few shrubs in it. The
present occupants came in 1961; Mr Witheridge moved in when his wife
died. All this is talked about over cups of tea, and how mahonias do well,
and winter heathers. But there are no heathers, of any season, that Clione

and James can see, and herbs have failed in brick-edged beds in the cobbled yard.

'Martins nest every year but they aren't a nuisance,' the old man assures them. 'I'd stay here for ever, actually.' He nods, then shrugs away his wish. 'But we need to be nearer to things. Not that we're entirely cut off. No, I don't want to go at all.'

'We're sorry to take it from you.' James smiles, again apologetic.

'Oh, good heavens, no! It's just that it's a happy place and we want you to be happy here, too. There's a bus that goes by regularly at the bottom of the lane. I explained that to your friend when he said he didn't drive.'

'Yes, I dare say he'll visit us.' Clione laughs, but doubts – and notices James doubting it too – that Michingthorpe often will, not being the country kind. The long acquaintanceship seems already over, the geography of their lives no longer able to contain it.

'Your friend was interested in the outhouses.'

'You're intending to live with us?' Clione stares into the puffy features, but the slaty eyes are blank, as everything else is. His voice is no more lifeless than it usually is when he explains that he happened to be in the neighbourhood of the oast-house, a library he had to look over at Nettleton Court.

'Not fifteen minutes away. Nothing of interest. A wasted journey, I said to myself, and that I hate.'

'You mentioned converting the outhouses to that old man.'

'I have a minikin's lifestyle. I like a certain smallness, I like things tidy around me. I throw things out, I do not keep possessions by me. That's always been my way, I've been quite noted for it.'

'We've no intention of converting the outhouses.'

Michingthorpe does not respond. He takes his spectacles off and looks at them, holding them far away. He puts them on again and says:

'What d'you think I got for the Madox Ford? Remember the Madox Ford?'

'We've never talked about your living with us.'

It is impossible to know if this is acknowledged, if there is a slight gesture of the head. Michingthorpe Ales were brewed at Maresfield, Clione learns, but that was long ago. In the 1730s, then for a generation or two.

'I never took much interest. Just chance that I stumbled across the family name. In Locke's *Provincial Byeways*, I believe it was.'

'We'll move down there in May.'

Quite badly foxed, the Ford, the frontispiece gone. 'Well, you saw yourself. Six five, would you have thought it?'

*

Later, Clione passes all that on. The faint unease she experienced when she heard that Michingthorpe had been to Sussex is greater now. For more than twenty years he has had the freedom of a household, been given the hospitality a cat which does not belong to it is given, or birds that come to a window-sill. Has he seen all this as something else? It seems to Clione that it must be so, that what appears to her children and her husband to have come out of the blue is a projection of what was there already. Michingthorpe's clumsy presumption is the presumption of an innocent, which is what his unawareness makes him. She should say that, but finds she cannot.

She listens to family laughter and when the children are no longer there says she is to blame, that she should have anticipated that something like this would one day happen.

'Of course you're not to blame.'

'It was my fault that he presumed so.'

'I don't see how.'

She tells because at last she has to, because what didn't matter matters now. A misunderstanding, she calls it. She knew and she just left it there, permitting it.

'Oh, but surely this can't be so? Surely not?'

'I've always thought of it as harmless.'

'You couldn't have imagined it?'

She does not let a stab of anger show. Her husband is smiling at her, standing by the windows of the sitting-room they soon will leave for ever. His smile is kind. He is not mocking or being a tease.

'No, I haven't imagined it.'

'Poor bloody fool!'

'Yes.'

She does not confess that after her recent conversation with Michingthorpe she felt sorry she'd been cold, that bewilderingly she dreamed these last few nights of his shadow thrown on snow that had fallen in the oast-house garden, his shadow on sunlit grass, an imprecise reflection in a pool on the cobbles where the outhouses were. His fleshy palms were warmed by a coffee mug while his talk went on, while she beat up a soufflé, while again he recalled the dressmaker who had made him rock buns.

'It's horrid,' she says. 'Dropping someone.'

'I know.'

James does know; she is aware of that, drawn into his thoughts, as their closeness so often allows. Dropping someone is not in James's nature, yet why should they pander to the awkward selfishness of an oddity? There are the memories that go back to *A Whiter Shade of Pale*, the settlements and compromises of the marriage they were determined to make work. Her friends have not always been her husband's kind, nor his hers, and there were other differences that, with time, didn't matter either. The intimacy they have come to know is like a growth of roots, spreading and entangling, making them almost one. Why should there be embarrassment now?

'For it would be like that,' she hears James say. 'Day after day.'

'He has a nothing life.'

She pleads before she knows she's doing so, and realizes then that she has done so before. In the car when they drove away after the revelation in the oast-house she suggested that the old man might have misheard, that it was probably gratuitous information on his part about the buses passing near, not the answer to a question. You can pity a child, Clione finds herself thinking, no matter what a child is like.

'It's a different kind of love,' she murmurs, hesitating over every word.

'It's fairly preposterous, whatever it is.'

'For all the time we've known him we have looked after him. You as much as I.'

'My dear, we can't play fantasies with a fully grown man.'

She sees again the shadow from her dream, distorted when it crosses the cobbles from the outhouses, cast bulkily on the kitchen floor, taking sunlight from the table spread with her cooking things. Being a shadow suits him, as being a joke once did.

'It was just a thought he had,' she says.

On a cool May morning, piece by piece, the furniture is carried across the pavement to the removal vans. The men are given cups of tea, the doors of the vans are closed. Clione passes from one room to the next through the emptiness of the house where her three children were born, the house in which they grew up and then left, leaving her too. Who will listen to him now? Who'll watch him talking to the air? Who'll not want to know what a splendid find he has come across at another auction? Who'll not want to know that oysters don't agree with him?

He is there when they drive off but does not wave, as if already he does not know them, as if he never did. 'Oh, he'll latch on to someone else,' the children have said, each of them putting it in that same way. 'He won't mind your going much.' She cannot guess how he'll mind, what form his minding will take, where or how the pain will be. But the pain is there, for she can feel it.

Their unpresentable friend won't come, not even once. Because he does not drive, because there is no point in it, because the pain would be too much. She does not know why he will not come, only that he won't. She does not know why the pity she feels is so intensely there, only that it is and that his empty love is not absurd.

Low Sunday, 1950

She put the wine in the sun, on the deep white window-sill, the bottle not yet opened. It cast a flush of red on the window-sill's surface beside the porcelain figure of a country girl with a sheaf of corn, the only ornament there. It felt like a celebration, wine laid out to catch the last of the warmth on a Sunday evening, and Philippa wondered if her brother could possibly have forgotten what Sunday it was when he brought the bottle back from Findlater's on Friday.

There was no sound in the house. Upstairs, Tom would be reading. At this time of day at weekends he always read for a while, as she remembered him so often as a child, comfortable in the only armchair his bedroom contained. He had been tidier in the armchair then, legs tucked beneath him, body curled around his book; now the legs that had grown longer sprawled, spilt out from the cushions, while one arm dangled, a cigarette smouldering from the fingers that also turned the pages.

Philippa was petite by comparison, fair-haired, her quiet features grave in repose, a prettiness coming with animation. She took care with her clothes rather than dressed well. Her blouse today was two striped shades of green, one matching her skirt, the other her tiny emerald earrings. She was thirty-nine in the Spring of 1950, her brother three years older.

They did not regret, either of them, the fruits of the revolution that by chance had changed their lives in making them its casualties. They rejoiced in all that had come about and even took pride in their accidental closeness to the revolution as it had happened. They had been in at a nation's birth, had later experienced its childhood years, unprosperous and ordinary and undramatic. That a terrible beauty had transformed the land they had not noticed.

In the garden Philippa picked lily tulips and bluebells, and sprigs of pink hazel. Tom's vegetable beds were raked and marked to indicate where his seeds had not yet come up, but among the herbs the tarragon was sprouting, and apple mint, and lovage. Chives were at their best, sage thickening with soft fresh growth. Next weekend, he'd said, they should weed the long border, turn up the caked soil.

On the long wooden draining-board in the kitchen she began to arrange the flowers in two vases. Tom always bought the wine in Findlater's, settling the single bottle into the basket strapped to the handlebars of his bicycle. They didn't make much of Sunday lunch – a way of arranging the day that went back to their Aunt Adelaide's lifetime – and only on Sundays was there ever wine at supper. In the other house – before Philippa and her brother had come to Rathfarnham – decanters of whiskey and sherry had stood on the dining-room sideboard, regularly replenished, not there for appearance's sake. 'What you need's a quick one,' her father had said on the Sunday of which today was yet another anniversary, and poor little Joe Paddy hadn't been able to say anything in response, shivering from head to toe as if he had the flu. 'What d'you say to a sharpener?' had been another way of putting it – when Mr Tyson or Mr Higgins came to the house – or sometimes, 'Will we take a ball of malt?' When the outside walls were repainted, the work complete, the men packing up their brushes and their ladders, they had been brought in to have glasses filled at the sideboard. A credit to Sallymount Avenue, her father had said, referring to the work that had been done, and the glasses were raised to it.

'Well, I've finished that,' Tom said, knowing where to find her.

'What happened?'

'She married the naval fellow.'

'They'll manage.'

'Of course.'

She felt herself watched. Clipping the stems to the length she wanted each, shaping the hazel, she heard the rattle of his matches and knew if she turned her head she would see cigarettes and matches in one hand, the ashtray in the other. Players he smoked, though once it had been Woodbines, what he could afford then. 'You've been smoking, Tom!' Aunt Adelaide used to cry, exasperated. 'Tom, you are *not* to smoke!'

He came further in to the kitchen, tipped the ashtray into the waste bucket beneath the sink, washed it under the tap and put it aside to carry back upstairs later.

'Where's the old dog?' he asked. 'Come back, has he?'

She shook her head and then, together, they heard their dog in the garden, the single bark that indicated his return from the travels they could not control. She glanced up, through the window above the sink, and there he was, panting on the grass, a black and white terrier, his smooth coat wringing wet.

'He's been in the Dodder,' she said. 'Or somewhere.'

'He'll be the death of me, that dog.'

The word could be used; they neither of them flinched. It had a different resonance when applied so lightly to the boldness of their dog. Different again when encountered in lines of poetry. Even the Easter Passion

– recently renewed for both of them in the Christ Church service on Good Friday evening – gave death a hallowed meaning, and softened it through the miracle of the Resurrection. But death as it had affected their lives was still raw, the moment of its awful pain still terrible if they let it have its way.

'I'll be an hour or so,' Tom said.

He scolded the exhausted dog on the lawn, and the dog was sheepish, hunching himself in shame and only daring then to wag his tail. Philippa watched from the window and guessed – and was right – that, exhaustion or not, Tom would be accompanied on his walk.

'No hurry.' She unlatched the window to call out, to smile because she realized, quite suddenly, that she hadn't during their conversation. This year she would go, she thought. She would go, and Tom would live his life.

Rathfarnham had hardly changed in all the years he'd known it; that was yet to come. This evening no one was about, the few small shops closed, the Yellow House – where he sometimes had a drink on weekdays – not open either. Low in the sky, the sun cast shadows that were hardly there.

'We're invited to Rathfarnham for tea,' Tom remembered his mother so often announcing in Sallymount Avenue, her tone reflecting the pleasure she knew the news would bring. The tram and then the long walk, for which it had to be fine or else, at the last minute, they wouldn't go. 'Oh, Aunt Adelaide'll know why,' their mother would say, and it was always only a postponement. Twice, Tom remembered, that happened, but probably there had been another time, now forgotten. The great spread on the dining-room table, the mysterious house – for it was mysterious then – were what the pleasure of those announcements had been about. Aunt Adelaide made egg sandwiches and sardine sandwiches, and two kinds of cake – fruit and sponge – and there were little square buns already buttered, and scones with raisins in them. In the garden, among the laurels, there was a secret place.

Perfectly obedient now, the dog trotted without a sign of weariness, as close to Tom's legs as he could manage. 'Well, wasn't that a grand day, sir?' an old man Tom didn't know remarked, and the dog went to sniff his trousers. 'Oh, I've seen you about all right,' the old man said, patting the black head.

What a *bouleversement* it had been in Aunt Adelaide's life! In a million years she couldn't have guessed that the two children who had occasionally come to tea, who had crept about upstairs, opening doors they knew they should not, who had whispered and pretended in the laurels, would every day and every night be there, her house their home, all mystery gone. Often on his weekend walks Tom thought about that; often on his return he and Philippa shared the remorse those thoughts engendered. How careless they had been of the imposition, how casual, how thoughtless! 'I shall have to lie down,' Aunt Adelaide used to say and Nelly, her maid and her companion, would angrily explain that that was because of rowdiness or some quarrel there had been. Murphy, who did the garden, who came every day – there being no shortages in Aunt Adelaide's spinster life – told them the blackly moustached figure, silver-framed on the drawing-room window-table, stern and unsmiling, was an admirer of long ago. They'd often wondered who he was.

Tom's sister had been wrong in assuming he could not possibly have forgotten what this Sunday was when he bought the wine. Tom had forgotten because, he supposed, he wanted to; dismounting from his bicycle outside Findlater's on Friday evening, he had been thinking of their summer holiday and so the aberration had occurred. Within a minute he had realized, but would have felt foolish handing the bottle back, and when he reached the house he felt it would have been underhand not to have brought the wine to the kitchen, as he always did if he'd bought a bottle. There had of course been Philippa's surprise, but it was natural between them that they did not comment.

When he had passed the last short terrace of cottages before he reached the countryside, Tom softly sang the first few lines of 'She is Far from the Land'. The song always came to him in the territory of the lovers it celebrated; here it was that Robert Emmet and Sarah Curran had walked too. Far ahead of him, the last of the sun no longer brightened the gorse on the slopes of Kilmashogue, where their stifled romance had been a happiness. Fiery, handsome Robert Emmet, foolish insurgent; gentle Sarah. In their company, Tom thought of them as friends – here or in the deerpark below the distant gorse slopes. They had sat in its summer-house, talking of Ireland as it would one day be, and of themselves, how they'd be too. They had wandered in the future, as Tom now wandered in the past to eavesdrop in pretence. Part of today it was, the walk and being with them.

He lit a cigarette. In loving because she could not help herself, Sarah too had been a casualty of chance, beyond the battlefield yet left to bear the agony of scars you could not see. They hanged defiant Robert Emmet.

This past filled Tom's reflections as he walked on. If beauty had come to Ireland, tranquillity was its form: a quietness in Ireland's dark, a haven these lovers had not known. His pity was for them.

*

Philippa set the table, spreading first the bleached linen tablecloth. It had come from the house in Sallymount Avenue, as the extra knives and forks had, and the Galway glasses, and the table in the hall. But anything large – the dining-table with the leaves that could be added, the dining chairs, the carpets, the wardrobes, the sideboard – had had to go for auction because their aunt's rooms were on the crowded side already. 'A mistake,' Aunt Adelaide called what had happened, as if offering that as a consolation, since there was nothing else. Often she repeated it in that same way, and she would repeat it, too, when some visitor came, someone new to the district or from the far-off past: an explanation for the presence of two children in her house. 'A terrible mistake.'

Sausages they were having, Hafner's of course, which Philippa had gone specially in for yesterday, saying she had things to do in Henry Street. Sausages and mashed potatoes, and glazed carrots, which recently she had learned how to do. Then steamed fig pudding, which had been steaming for an hour already, and custard. Often Philippa wondered how it would be different, cooking for a husband. She sensed it would be, as she sensed Tom's return to the house every day would be different, but she did not know how. 'He's more than a brother to her,' their aunt had always lowered her voice to inform a visitor. 'Well, being older, of course.'

She made up mustard, mixing it in the small blue glass that lined the silver container. They'd listened at the banisters when Joe Paddy came knocking wildly at the door. Supposed to be in bed, they crouched there, and their father said what Joe Paddy needed was a drink, Joe Paddy shouting all the while that a man was after him, their mother calming him, saying the Troubles were all over now. He'd been in himself to see, their father said: Dublin had gone quiet after the carnage. He had stood and seen the surrender in the name of peace; there was nothing to be frightened of now. But Joe Paddy kept saying a man was after him.

She pricked the sausages and laid them on the fat that had gone liquid in the pan. 'If the man comes we'll explain to him,' their mother said. 'We'll explain you weren't in any of it, Joe Paddy.' And then the voices became murmurs, passing from the hall. She was asleep when there was shouting in the garden and she couldn't remember what anything was about. They went to the window to look out and there the man was, in a soldier's uniform. 'We'll explain,' their mother repeated, in the hall again. 'You stay where you are, boy,' their father said. 'You take another drink.'

The sausages fried slowly. She put the potatoes on. Tom would mash them when they were ready, and add a butter pat and chives. 'I'm going to try for the Bank of Ireland,' Tom had said, pleasing Aunt Adelaide because their father, too, had tried for the Bank of Ireland, and been employed for all his adult life in the architectural splendour of the College Green office, as Tom was now. 'You'll have the house, of course,' Aunt Adelaide had said, months before she died.

From the kitchen window Philippa saw Tom in the garden again. He often returned from a walk like that, by the side door, not coming into the house at once, strolling about, dead-heading if the season called for that. She washed the parsley he'd earlier picked for her, and chopped it finely, ready for the carrots, the two bright colours of the tricolour – she'd never noticed that until Tom said one suppertime. He'd taken her away from the window and she'd whispered, 'Poor Joe Paddy!' because she was confused, and he said no, it wasn't Joe Paddy who'd been shot. She asked him then and he said: because he had to, because she had to know. He hadn't let her look.

'Would you like a sherry?' Tom was suddenly there, as earlier he'd been when he'd told her he'd finished his book.

'Sherry would be nice,' she said.

Anglesea Street, she thought, a little flat in Anglesea Street, plumb in the middle of Dublin. She'd always been attracted by that narrow street, not far from Tom's office, not far from Jury's Hotel, where sometimes they met for a cup of coffee in his lunchtime. They'd still do that, of course, and as often as she was welcome she'd visit Rathfarnham – at weekends, Saturday lunch, whatever was convenient. She could say so now; it was a time to do so, while they drank their sherry.

'There was an old man I don't remember seeing before,' Tom said. 'By the bridge.'

'He's come to live with the Mulcahys. Her father.'

'Ah.'

Children would run about the garden again. There would be their laughter, and family birthdays. She would bring her presents, and with the years Tom would slip into their father's role and be like him too, easy-going, with jokes to tell. The children would tell her things, have secrets with her, as sometimes children did with an aunt.

She heard the clink of the decanter's stopper, the sherry poured, and then Tom brought the two glasses from the dining-room. It was extraordinary that the officer who came had wept in front of them. He had alarmed them, weeping so suddenly, so unnaturally, the brick-hued flesh of his heavy face crumpling into dismay and grief. 'The waste of it,' he mumbled. 'The waste of it.' The soldier who had gone berserk in mistaking Joe Paddy for someone else had suffered shell-shock. His officer – in charge of him, responsible, he wretchedly insisted – could hardly explain, so clogged with emotion his voice was. He did not know, for it did not concern him, that Joe Paddy's connection with the house he'd sought refuge in when he was pursued through the streets was as tenuous as the unbalanced soldier's was with Joe Paddy: once every two months or so Joe Paddy came to clean its windows. Madness and death: that's how it was in war, this big, ruddy officer had said. As long as he lived, he made a kind of promise, he would not be able to forget what had happened in a suburban garden.

'We're nearly ready,' Philippa said in the kitchen, but her brother made her pause for a moment to sip her sherry while he mashed the potatoes and sprinkled in the chopped-up chives.

'Tom,' she said and found it difficult to continue, and he smiled at her as if he perfectly divined her thoughts. He even slightly shook his head, although she was not entirely sure about that and perhaps he didn't. Intent upon his task again, he turned away and she did not continue.

She imagined, in a small low-ceilinged sitting-room a coal fire spluttering a bit, a single blue flame among insipid spurts of orange. People didn't live much in Anglesea Street, it wasn't that kind of street, but that would suit her – the sound of handcarts down below, voices faintly calling out.

'Thank you,' she said, finishing her sherry when she saw that Tom had finished his. She rinsed the glasses. Thirty-four years, she calculated; she would be seventy-three when the same time had passed again, Tom would be seventy-six. 1984 it would be, sixteen years from the century's end, as 1916 had been from the beginning.

He helped her carry the dishes into the dining-room and then he poured the wine. It did not seem an error now, that he had bought it. The wine would make it easier to say, the sherry and the wine together.

'There's talk of a new road,' he said. 'Out near Marley.'

'I hadn't heard that.'

'Oh, some time well into the future they're talking of.'

'Maybe it won't happen.'

Once on this Sunday he had predicted more war and more war had come; he had predicted Ireland's wise neutrality and had been right. He would hate a big new road out there. He hated the motorcycles that roared up Tibradden, that crashed through fern and undergrowth and little woods, that muddied the streams. One day the crawl of lorries would take the freshness from the air.

'Tom,' she said again. She was wondering, she began, and paused, a natural pause it seemed. *13 Anglesea St*, it said on an envelope, and they crossed College Green from Trinity, and then she heard their footsteps on the stairs. She made them coffee because coffee was what they liked, and cut the Bewley's cake, ready for them. Why thirteen? she wondered, and

wondered then if even now there was an empty flat there, if some premo-
nition had winkled that out for her. Long legs her nephew had, like his
father; her niece was beautiful already.

'This summer?' Tom said. 'Port-na-Blagh, d'you think?' He had been
patient, not saying anything. A kindness that was, and his smile was a
kindness too. 'Port-na-Blagh?' he said again.

She nodded, making herself because he had been kind. She talked
about the summer because he wanted to. Three weeks away from Dublin
and Rathfarnham, the sands at Port-na-Blagh unchanged, the white
farmhouse, the hens that pecked about its yard. She loved it too, as much
as he did, when they locked up and went away to Donegal. Even when it
rained and her summer dresses remained unpacked, when they gazed
from the windows at their ruined days or crunched over pebbles that
never dried. They always brought more books than they could read,
denuding the shelves of the Argosy Lending Library, owing a bit on them
when they returned.

'Or somewhere else, d'you think?' he said.

They'd gone to Glandore once, another year to Rossleague, but Port-
na-Blagh they still liked best. 'I wonder what became of those widowed
brothers,' Tom said, and she knew at once whom he meant: two Guin-
ness clerks who'd been widowed in the same year, who hardly spoke in the
boarding-house dining-room; on Achill that was. And the school inspector who spoke in Irish came for a few nights to Glandore.

'July again?' she said.

'I'm afraid so.'

'It's often fine enough.'

He nodded, and she could tell he was longing for a cigarette. But it
wasn't his way to smoke during a meal; she'd never seen him doing that.

'Yes, of course it is,' he said.

He saw, again, the effort in her eyes, and sensed her saying to herself that
it would not be difficult, that he would listen, that the words were simple.
Once, a while ago, maybe as long ago as fifteen years, she had said it; and
again, more recently, had come closer to saying it than she had tonight.

'Low Sunday it is called, you know,' he said.

'Yes, I did know.'

He poured the last of the wine in the silence that had gathered. Once
she had wept when he was not there; he knew because her smile was different when he returned, the marks of tears powdered over. Now, it was
easier. Only Low Sunday held them in its thrall, her head pressed into the
wool of his jersey, his voice not letting her look. Pity for his romantic

ghosts still kept the moment at bay; she had her fantasy of the future. Fragments of intuition were their conversation, real beneath the unreal words. No one else would understand: tomorrow, she would once more know that.

They gathered the dishes and the plates from the table and took them to the kitchen. He washed up, as he always did at weekends. She put things away. The tired dog lay sleeping in his kennel. The downstairs lights were one by one extinguished.

The past receded a little with the day; time yet unspent was left to happen as fearfully as it would. Night settled, there was no sound. Tranquil 1950 was again a haven in Ireland's dark.

Le Visiteur

Once a year, when summer was waning, Guy went to the island. And once a year, as his visit drew to a close, he took Monsieur and Madame Buissonnet out to dinner at the hotel. He had not always done so, for he had first received the Buissonnets' invitation to visit them when he was seven. He was thirty-two now, no longer placed by his mother in the care of the ferryman for the journey from Port Vevey and by Madame Buissonnet for the journey back. For thirteen years there had been the tradition of dinner at the hotel, the drive from the farm in the onion truck, Madame Buissonnet in her grey and black, Monsieur Buissonnet teasingly not taking off his boatman's cap until they were almost in the restaurant, then stuffing it into his pocket. *Loup de mer*: always the same for both of them, and as often as not for Guy also. *Soupe de langoustines* to start with.

'Well, now,' Madame Buissonnet said, as she always did when the order had been given, the Macon Fuissé tasted. 'Well, now?' she repeated, for dinner at the hotel was the occasion for such revelations as had not yet been divulged during Guy's stay.

'Gérard married,' he said. 'Jean-Claude has gone to Africa.'

'*Africa?*'

'Maybe for ever. I miss him.'

Monsieur Buissonnet listened less intently than his wife did, his eye roving about the restaurant, lingering occasionally on a beautiful face. Sometimes he softly sighed. 'Your mother?' he had enquired in a private moment on the first afternoon of Guy's visit, as every year he did. As far as Madame Buissonnet was concerned, Guy's mother might not have existed.

'And you are promoted a step higher, Guy?' she asked now.

'It is once in three years, that.'

'Ah, yes.'

'My dear.' Monsieur Buissonnet placed a hand over one of his wife's, his endearment gently reassuring her that it didn't matter if she had forgotten promotion did not come every single year.

'How agreeable it is here,' she murmured, turning her palm upward for a moment and smiling a smile she reserved for such moments. Guy felt not included in this occasion of communication between the couple, even though he was responsible for their presence here. A silence fell, then Monsieur Buissonnet said:

'It was nothing once, this place.'

'It has made a *milliard* since,' his wife reminded him. Or two, he agreed. A man who knew how to make money was Perdreau. Yet every dish you ate in his restaurant was worth its francs.

White-haired, a shock still falling over his forehead, Monsieur Buissonnet possessed the remnants of handsome features, as his wife did of beauty. Nothing would be regained by either of them; the disturbances of time and sun were there for ever. Yet the toll was softened: the whiteness of their hair, and its abundance, was an attraction in old age; that he was leaner than he had ever been brought out in Monsieur Buissonnet qualities of distinction that had not been evident before; his wife's fragility complemented the slenderness she had never lost.

'And now what else?' she enquired when *les amuse-gueules* were finished.

Guy talked about Club 14 because he could think of nothing else. It was odd, it always seemed to him, what was said and what was not; and not just here, not only by the Buissonnets. His mother had never asked a single thing about the island, or even mentioned the Buissonnets except, in his childhood, to say when September was half over that it was time for him to visit them again. Once he had tried to tell her of the acre or two Monsieur Buissonnet and his labourers had reclaimed for cultivation during the year that had passed, how *oliviers* or vines had been planted where only scrub had grown before, how a few more metres had been marked out for irrigation. His mother had never displayed an interest. 'Oh, it is because they have no children of their own,' she'd said when he asked why it was that the Buissonnets invited him. 'It is so sometimes.'

Not that Guy objected to being invited. He was as fond of the farm and the island as he was of the Buissonnets themselves. He delighted in the dry, parched earth, the *crêtes*, the unsafe cliffs. Dust coated the vegetation, the giant cacti, the purple or scarlet ipomoea with which the villagers decorated their walls, the leaves of brambles and oleander. It invaded cypresses and heather and the rock roses that Guy had never seen in flower. Only the huge stones and well-washed pebbles of the little bays escaped its grey deposit. Only the eucalyptus trees and the plane trees rose above it.

The accompaniments of the *soupe de langoustines* came, the waiter unfamiliar, new this season as the waiters often were. He placed the dishes he brought where they might easily be reached by all three diners, then ladled out the soup. He poured more Macon Fuissé.

'What style!' Madame Buissonnet whispered when he had passed on to another table, and then, 'How good you are to take us here again, Guy!'

'It's nothing.'

'Oh, but yes, it is, my dear.'

The restaurant of the hotel had views over a valley to a lush growth of trees, unusual on the island. A carpet of grass, broken by oleander beds, formed the valley's base, far below the level of the restaurant itself. This was shadowy now in the September twilight, the colour drained from its daytime's splendour. The lengths of blue and white awning that earlier had protected the lunchtime diners from the sun had been rolled in, the sliding glass panels closed against mosquitoes. Thirty tables, a stiff white tablecloth on each, were widely separated in the airy, circular space, a couple of them unoccupied tonight. Monsieur Perdreau, the hotel's proprietor for as long as Guy and the Buissonnets had been dining in its restaurant, was making his evening tour, pausing at each table to introduce himself or to ensure that everything was in order.

The Buissonnets knew him well, and by now so did Guy. He stayed a while, receiving compliments, bowing his gratitude, giving some details of his season, which had, this year, been particularly good, even if the restaurant was not quite full tonight. The hotel itself was, he explained: it was just that at the moment there were fewer yachts moored at the harbour.

'You are getting to be my oldest client, Guy,' he said, shaking hands before he went away.

It was then that Guy noticed that the girl two tables away had been joined by a companion. She was in white, fair-haired, slight; the man was bulky, in a bright blue suit. Guy had noticed the girl earlier and had thought it singular that being on her own she should want to occupy so prominent a table.

'Splendid!' Monsieur Buissonnet exclaimed when the waiter returned with the soup tureen.

The evening advanced, pleasurably and easily, as in previous Septembers so many others had. The *loup de mer* was as good as ever; glasses of Margaux accompanied the cheese. Madame Buissonnet's disappointment that Guy had been unable to report a new relationship in his life was kept in check. She asked about Colette, who for a time had been Guy's fiancée, and bravely smiled when she heard that Colette had become engaged to André Délespaul. Monsieur Buissonnet talked about the olive harvest, the coldest November he could remember on the island because of the bitter wind, how it had suddenly got up and remained for weeks, a mistral out of season. But none the less the harvest had been a good one.

Vanilla ice-cream came, a mango *coulis*. The little *boules* were so elegantly arranged on the green, yellow-rimmed plates that Madame Buissonnet said it was a pity to disturb them. The man in the blue suit had again left his companion on her own. She sat very still, eating nothing now. Coffee was brought to her but she did not pour it out. A cup and saucer were placed for her companion, beside his crumpled napkin.

'They are a pest sometimes,' Monsieur Buissonnet said, an observation he now and again made about the tourists who came to the island, 'even if they bring a bit of life.'

The tourists hired bicycles at the harbour or in the village and rode about the sandy tracks. They came for the day or lodged in one of the small village hotels if not in Monsieur Perdreau's rather grander one. The only vehicles that were permitted on the island were the farm trucks, the tractors, the delivery vans, and the minibus that delivered and collected guests. Cigarettes were forbidden in wooded areas because of the risk of fire.

'Oh, we enjoy the tourists,' Madame Buissonnet commented. 'Of course we do.'

One by one, the tables were deserted. When the waiter whom Madame Buissonnet considered stylish brought chocolates and coffee, only a few were still occupied — the one at which the girl sat alone, a corner one at which Italian was spoken, a third at which a couple now stood up. The man in the blue suit returned, his progress unsteady and laboured, an apologetic smile thrown about, as if he were unaware that the chairs he circumvented were empty. He sat down noisily and at once stood up again, seeming to seek the attention of a waiter. When one approached he waved him away but, still on his feet, filled his glass and spilt it as he sat down. The girl poured coffee. She did not speak.

'*È oritologo*,' someone said at the Italian table, a woman's voice carrying across the restaurant. '*Scrive libri sugli uccelli.*'

The man in the blue suit stood up and again looked around him. He pulled at the knot of his tie, loosening it. He groped beneath it for the buttons of his shirt. His companion stared at the tablecloth. Was she weeping? Guy wondered. Something about her bent head suggested that she might be.

There was a glisten of sweat on the man's forehead and his cheeks. He raised his glass in the direction of the Italians, smiling at them foolishly. One of them — a man in a suede jacket — bowed stiffly.

The waiters stood back, perfectly discreet. Amused at first by the scene,

Madame Buissonnet now glanced away from what was happening. They should be going, she said.

'*Mi dà i brividi*,' one of the Italians exclaimed quite loudly, and they all got up, the women gathering handbags and shawls, one of the men lighting a fresh cigarette.

Watching them go, Guy realized that all evening he had been stealing glances at the girl who shared the drunk man's table. Especially when she was alone he had kept glancing at her, unable to prevent himself. She was very thin. He had never seen a girl as thin. All the time he had talked about Gérard and Jean-Claude, and André Délespaul and Colette, all the time he had listened to the details of the olive harvest, while he'd shaken Monsieur Perdreau's hand and laughed at his joke, he had imagined being with her in the little bay where he swam and at Le Nautic or the Café Vert in the village. He had looked for a wedding ring, and there it was.

The drunk man laughed. He waved at the Italians, his laughter louder, as if he and they shared some moment of comedy. The one who'd just lit a cigarette waved back.

'Hi!' the drunk man called after them, and lurched across the restaurant, knocking into the chairs and tables, apologizing to people who weren't there. He stopped suddenly, as if his energy had failed him. He was confused. He frowned, shaking his head.

It wasn't a real smile when the girl smiled at Guy; it was too joyless for that, with a kind of pleading in it. She smiled because all evening she had been aware he'd been unable to take his eyes off her. Had she really once married this man? Guy wondered. Could they really be husband and wife?

'Thank you, Guy,' Madame Buissonnet said, as she always did when the evening ended. The bill came swiftly when he gestured for it. He signed the *carte bancaire*.

'Yes,' Monsieur Buissonnet said. 'Thank you.'

It was then that the man fell down. He fell on to an unlaid table and slithered sideways to the ground. Waiters came to help him up, but he managed to scramble to his feet by himself. His wife didn't look. Guy was certain now she was his wife.

'Hi!' the man shouted at the Buissonnets. 'Hi!'

He was laughing again and he shouted something else but Guy couldn't understand what it was because the man spoke in either English or German; it was difficult to distinguish which because his voice was slurred. He clattered down, into the chair he'd been sitting on before. He spread his arms out on the tablecloth and sank his head into them. The girl said something, but he didn't move.

Guy didn't let his anger show. He was good at that; he always had been. It could happen like this that you fell in love, that there was some moment you didn't notice at the time and afterwards couldn't find when you thought back. It didn't matter because you knew it was there, because you knew that this had happened.

'I talked to those people on my walk today.' It seemed hardly a lie, just something it was necessary to say. Anything would have done.

Madame Buissonnet displayed no surprise, accepting Guy's claim without a knowing smile. A man of the world in such matters, Monsieur Buissonnet said the key to the farmhouse would be where it always was when it was left outside: in the dovecot. 'Madame must have her beauty sleep,' he added, tucking his wife's arm into his.

'It is no trouble.'

Again Guy imagined being with her in the little bay, and telling her in Le Nautic or the Café Vert why he was on the island, explaining about the Buissonnets, explaining why it was that he had been in the restaurant when first they saw one another, how he had told the Buissonnets a lie, how they had guessed it was a lie, and how that didn't matter.

'Madame,' a waiter murmured, offering help, repeating what Guy had said – that it was no trouble – pretending that nothing much had happened.

The man in the blue suit was awake and on his feet, squeezing his eyes closed, as if to clear what was faulty in his vision, blinking them open again. Guy and the waiter helped him across the restaurant, across the foyer to the lift. The girl who had been humiliated whispered her gratitude, seeming not to have the confidence to raise her voice. She looked even thinner, even frailer, when she was on her feet.

On Sunday, on the last of the evening ferries, Guy would leave the island, his visit over. Even sooner she might go herself, first thing in the morning, hurrying off with her companion because of the shame they shared. In the lift there was no embarrassment when they touched, her shoulder pressed on Guy's because the lift was small. He felt panic spreading, affecting his heartbeat, a dryness in his mouth. Yet how could she go so swiftly when she had pleaded so? Where had the pleading come from if not from their being aware of one another? Alone at her table when her boorish husband left her to fend for herself, she had been disturbed by a stranger's gaze and had not rejected it. Why had she not unless she'd known as certainly as he? Even before they heard one another's voices, there had been that certainty of knowing. All intuition, all just a feeling across a distance, and yet more than they had ever known before.

'*Voilà!*' the waiter murmured, producing the key of the couple's room

from one of the man's pockets. A moment before there had been conster-
nation when it could not be found.

Love was conversation: Gérard had said that, and Guy had never
understood until tonight. They would sit on the rocks and their conversation would spread itself around them, their two lives tangling, as in a
different way they had already begun to. Club 14, Gérard, Jean-Claude,
Jean-Pierre, Colette, Michelle, Dominique, Adrien, the walk from the rue
Marceau to the Café de la Paix after a badminton game, his mother, and
all the rest of what there was: tomorrow and Saturday were not enough.
Well, of course they did not have to be.

She gave the waiter a hundred-franc note when the man had been
dumped on the bed. The waiter put the room key on the writing-table.
When he went he did not seem surprised that Guy did not go also, perhaps sensing something of what had come about. Only once in a whole
lifetime, Guy thought, fate offered two people this. 'How much a visitor
you are!' Michelle said once, and truth to tell he had always felt so, not
quite belonging in the group, not even with his mother. And with the
Buissonnets, of course, he was a visitor too. All that would come into the
conversation; everything would in the end.

'Thank you,' she said, speaking in English, and then in French in case
he had not understood. But he could manage a little English, and wondered if these were Americans or English people. On the bed the man was
snoring.

'Please,' she said, opening the minibar and gesturing toward its array
of little bottles. 'Please have something.'

He wanted to say she mustn't feel embarrassed. He wanted to reassure
her absolutely, to say that what had occurred downstairs was of no possible consequence. He wanted to talk of all the other matters immediately, to tell her that years ago he had guessed that Monsieur Buissonnet
was his father, that he was certain he owed his position in the Crédit
Lyonnais to Monsieur Buissonnet's influence. He wanted to tell her that
nothing was ever said – not a word – by Madame Buissonnet about his
mother, or by his mother about Madame Buissonnet, that he had long
ago guessed his mother had been a woman in Monsieur Buissonnet's life
before his marriage. It would have been before his marriage; it was not
Monsieur Buissonnet's style to be unfaithful.

'Oh, then, a cognac,' he said.

It was not ever said that the farm would one day be his. That was why
Monsieur Buissonnet talked so often and so much about it, why Madame
Buissonnet asked if this was right, or that, when she chose the colours for
a room she wanted to have repainted.

Guy took the glass that was held out to him and for a second his fingers brushed the fingers of the girl he had fallen in love with. He had not known until tonight that it was something you could tell in minutes, even seconds, when you first loved somebody.

'You have been kind,' she said. She sat in a low armchair beside the minibar and Guy sat by the writing-table. She flattened the skirt of her white dress over her knees. So much about her was like a child, he thought: her hands as they passed over the white material, the outline of her knees, her feet in high-heeled shoes. Her fair hair fell tidily, framing an image of features in which he believed he could still detect the lingering of the hurt she'd suffered. Her eyes were blue, as pale as the sky there'd been that day.

'Are you American?' he asked, carefully speaking English, translating the question from the French.

'Yes, American.'

It was awkward, the man being there, even though he was asleep. His mood might not be pleasant if he woke up, yet it did not seem to matter; it was only awkward. Guy said:

'I have only been in the restaurant of the hotel before. Not in a room.'

'You are not staying here?'

'No, no.'

She went to the bed and pushed the man on to his side, exerting herself to do so. The snoring ceased.

'I come every year to the island,' Guy said. 'The Buissonnets have a farm.'

'The people you were with?'

'Yes.'

'I have never been here before.'

'People find it tranquil.'

'Yes, it's that.'

When she sat down again the gaze they held one another in was as bold as for each of them it had been downstairs, as open and as confident. Guy hadn't realized then that this confidence had been there, and the openness. He wondered if – until she smiled – he had assumed that in the unobtrusive lighting of the restaurant she had failed to notice his obsessive interest. He couldn't remember what he had assumed and it didn't seem to be important. He wondered what she was thinking.

'We came by chance here,' she said. 'To the island.'

'Yes.'

'Please don't get up and go.'

He shook his head. She smiled and he smiled back. He would show her everything on the island, and when the moment for it came he would tell her that he loved her. He would tell her that never before had he loved a girl like this, had only been attracted in the more ordinary way. That could be because he was what Michelle had called a visitor, always a little on his own. It could have to do with the circumstances of his birth, so little being said, nothing whatsoever really. Who can tell? Guy wondered. Who can tell what makes a person what he is?

'May I ask your name?'

'It's Guy.'

She didn't give hers. Guy was nice, she said, especially as it was said in France. It suited him, the French way of saying it.

'Some more?' she offered.

He had hardly drunk a drop. He shook his head. She reached out to close the door of the minibar, shutting away the light that through its array of bottles had been falling on the thin calves of her legs. They would have a marriage like the Buissonnets'; in the farmhouse it would be like that. Slowly she reached down and took her shoes off.

The jaw of the man on the bed had fallen open. An arm hung down, fingers trailing the carpet quite close to where they were.

'Guy,' she whispered, her white dress in a bundle on the floor, one of her shoes on its side. 'My dear,' she whispered.

There was an urgency in her resistance to his drawing back from the act that was pressed upon him. There were no whispers now, and no caresses. Instinctively Guy knew there was no pleasure for her. She laughed when it was over, a soundless laugh, different from her husband's yet it echoed that.

The room was stifling, the air gone stale, infected by the rank breath of the man who slept. Naked, she stood above him, looking down at his slumbering features, at the stubble that was beginning on his chin and neck, a dribble running from a corner of his mouth. She touched his shoulder, and for an instant his eyes opened. She said nothing, and he slept again. For all this – for what had happened, for what was happening still – she had returned a stranger's gaze. Destruction was present in the room; Guy was aware of that.

She turned away, from the bed where her husband lay, from Guy. The drink she'd poured herself had not been touched. Guy watched her cross the room and close a door behind her. He heard the running of her bath.

He dressed, separating his clothes from hers. He might go to her, now that these minutes had elapsed. Tomorrow, he might say. In the Café Vert at half past ten, ten if it suited better. He would show her the island, he would show her the farm; she would tell him about herself. It could not be forgotten, what had happened, there could be no pretence; yet when they talked, when their conversation began, what had happened would not belong in it.

He laid her dress, with her underclothes, on a chair, arranged her shoes one beside the other on the floor. He drank the cognac, leaving none of it, wanting it because she'd poured it for him. Then he tapped on the door she'd closed.

Her voice came at once, harsh and loud, as it had not been before.

'I'm having a bath. You'll have to wait.'

She spoke in English. Guy understood the first sentence, but had to think about the second, and in thinking realized that it was the sleeping man who was addressed, that he himself should already have gone away. About to reply, to correct this misunderstanding, he hesitated.

'Look about you while you're waiting.' Mockery was added to the other qualities that had come into her voice. 'Why not do that?'

She would have liked it better had he woken up properly when she touched his shoulder; it was second best, her clothes thrown about, the two glasses where they'd been left. It was second best but even so it was enough. And the room's impressions of what had taken place still hung about it.

Guy's footsteps were soundless on the carpet as he moved away. He glanced as he passed the bed at the man in the bright blue suit, some spillage of food whitening a lapel, cheeks and forehead florid. He wondered what his name was, hers too, before he left the room.

The night air was cold, already the air of autumn. Slowly progressing on the dusty track, Guy wondered what the Buissonnets had said to one another. They might mention the incident in the morning, or might have decided that they should not.

The sea lapped softly over the pebbles of the bay where he swam. He sat down among the rocks, wondering if he would ever tell anyone, and if he did how exactly he would put it. It was how they lived, he might say; it was how they belonged to one another, not that he understood. In the cold bright moonlight he felt his solitude a comfort.

The Virgin's Gift

A gentle autumn had slipped away, sunny to the end, the last of the butterflies still there in December, dozing in the crevices of the rocks. The
lingering petals of the rock flowers had months before faded and fallen
from their stems; the heather was in bloom, the yellow of the gorse had
quietened. It was a miracle, Michael often thought, a summer marvel that
the butterflies came to his place at all.

Feeling that he had walked all Ireland – an expression used often in the
very distant past that was his time – Michael had arrived at Ireland's most
ragged edge. He knew well that there was land to the north, and to the
west and east, which he had not travelled, that no man could walk all
Ireland's riverbanks and tracks, its peaks and plains, through every spin-
ney, along every cliff, through every gorge. But the exaggeration of the
expression offered something in the way of sense; his journey, for him,
had been what the words implied. Such entanglements of truth and falsity – and of good and evil, God and the devil – Michael dwelt upon in
the hermitage he had created, while the seasons changed and the days of
his life were one by one extinguished.

The seasons announced themselves, but for the days he kept a calendar
– as by rule they had at the abbey – his existence shaped by feast days and
fasting days, by days of penance and of rest. Among the rocks of his island,
time was neither enemy nor friend, its passing no more than an element
that belonged with the sea and the shores, the garden of vegetables he had
cultivated, the habitation he had made, the gulls, the solitude. He sensed
the character of each one of the seven days and kept alive the different feeling that each inspired, knowing when he awoke which one it was.

When the fourth day in December came it was St Peter Chrysologus's.
There was more dark than light now, and soon rain and wind would take
possession of the craggy landscape. At first, in winter, he had lost his way
in the mists that came at this time too, when all that was familiar to him
became distorted; now, he knew better than to venture far. In December
each day that was not damp, each bitter morning, each starry night, was
as welcome as the summer flowers and butterflies.

When he was eighteen Michael's vocation had been revealed to him, an
instruction coming in a dream that he should leave the farm and offer

himself at the abbey. He hardly knew about the abbey then, having heard it mentioned only once or twice in conversation, and was hazy as to its purpose or its nature. 'Oh, you'd never want to,' Fódla said when he told her, for ever since they'd first embraced he had told her everything. 'You'd go there when you're old,' she hopefully conjectured, but her dark eyes were sad already, a finger twisting a loop of hair, the way she did when she was unhappy. 'A dream's no more'n a dream,' she whispered in useless protestation when he repeated how the Virgin had appeared, bearing God's message.

Cutting new sods for his roof on the morning of St Peter Chrysologus's day, Michael remembered Fódla's tears. They had played together since they were infants – on the earthen floor of the outside house where the feed was boiled, on the dug-out turf bogs while the donkeys patiently waited to have their panniers filled, on the stubble of the cornfield where her father and his worked together to raise the stooks, their mothers too, her brothers when they were old enough. 'I have to,' he said when Fódla wept, and near to where they walked a bird warbled for a moment, as if to mock her sorrow. Her hand slipped out of his, their friendship over. Her life, too, she said.

'God has spoken for you.' His father took a different view that same evening. 'And by that He has honoured you. Do not have doubt, Michael.'

He did not have doubt, only concern that God's honouring of him would one day mean the farm's decline: he was an only child.

'He will provide,' his father reassured, sturdy and confident, in the prime of his life. 'He surely will.'

Michael carried from the other side of his island the first sods of scrappy grass he had cut. Back and forth he went all morning, until he had a stack beside his shelter. Then he lifted the sods into place, twelve rows of six on the two slight inclines of the roof, beating them together with the long, flat stone he kept for the purpose. Three sides of his shelter were constructed as he had long ago learned to build a field wall, the stones set at an angle. The fourth was a natural hollow in the rock-face, and the frame on which he laid the sods was of branches lashed together, door and door-frame made similarly.

He had soothed with dock leaves Fódla's arms when they were stung. When she was frightened of the orchard geese he had taken her from them and soon after that she was frightened of nothing. She would be married now, children and grandchildren born to her, the friendship of so far back forgotten: he accepted that. His mother would be eighty years old, his father older still. Or they would not be there at all, which was more likely.

Michael saved the salt of the sea, and in summer preserved with it the fish he caught. The grain he had first cultivated from the seed he brought from the abbey continued year by year. There were the hurtleberries, the patch of nettles he had encouraged and extended, the mossy seaweed that ripened in the sun, the spring that never failed, the herbs he'd grown from roots brought from the abbey also. 'Find solitude,' the Virgin had instructed the second time, after he had been seventeen years at the abbey, and again it seemed like punishment, as it had on the morning of Fódla's tears.

When it was twilight and the task of repairing his roof was complete, Michael climbed to the highest crag of the island to look across at the mainland cliffs he had so long ago waded away from, with all he had brought with him held above his head. From the sky he predicted tomorrow's weather; it would still be fine. Skimpy tails of cloud did not disturb the trail of amber left behind after the sun had slipped away. The sea was placid as a lake.

Often on evenings as tranquil as this Michael imagined he could hear the Angelus bell at the abbey, although he knew that was impossible. In his time there he had come to love the discipline and the order, the simplicity of the few pleasures there had been, the companionship. The dawn processing from the cloisters to the high cross in the pasture, the evening lamps lit, the chanting of the psalter, the murmur of the Mass – all that, even now, he missed. Brother Luchan knew the saints and told their stories: how St Mellitus refused to give the Blessed Sacrament to the king's sons, how wolves and bears were obedient to St Marcian, how St Simeon scourged himself on pillars. In their cells Cronan and Murtagh illuminated the Scriptures, compounding inks and cutting pens. Ioin had a lazy eye, Bernard was as tubby as a barrel, Fintan fresh-cheeked and happy. Diarmaid was the tallest, Conor the best at conversation, Tomás the most forgetful, Cathal the practical one. 'Never lose your piece of glass,' Cathal warned in his farewell. 'Never be without the means of fire.'

Did they see him, as he could still see them – his tattered habit, his tonsure gone, beard trimmed as well as he could manage, bare feet? Did they imagine the cross scratched on the stone above the ledge that was his bed? Did they hear in their mind's ear the waves, and the wailing of the gulls while he hauled over the rocks the seaweed to his garden plot? Did they guess he still visited in his thoughts the little pond beyond the coppice, and watched the decorating of a verse, the play of creatures arrested by Cronan's pen, fish and birds, snakes coiled about a letter's stem?

It was as Murtagh had represented her that the Virgin came to him the second time, not as she had been before, which was in a likeness that was almost his mother's. He had not understood, that second time, why there should again be disruption in his life. He understood now. At the abbey he had learned piety, had practised patience, been humbled by his companions' talents, strengthened by their friendship. But in his solitude he was closer to God.

Still standing on the crag that rose above the others, he knew that with a certainty that came freshly to him in the evening of every day. During all his time here he had not seen another person, had spoken only to God and to himself, to animals and birds and the butterflies that so strangely arrived, occasionally to an insect. The figments that congregated in his imagination did not create an alien mood; nostalgia was always checked. This evening, as he prepared his food and ate it, it pleased him that he had cut the roof sods and settled them into place while it was fine. That was a satisfaction, and he took it with him when he lay down to rest.

Colour came from nowhere, brightening to a vividness. There was a fluttering of wings closing after flight, scarlet birds of paradise, yellow-breasted, green. Archways receded into landscape; faint brown and pink were washed through the marble tracery of a floor. Rays of sunlight were like arrows in the sky.

The Virgin's dress was two shades of blue, her lacy halo hardly there. This time her features were not reminiscent of what Michael's mother's once had been, nor of a gospel illumination: there was such beauty as Michael had never before beheld in a human face or anywhere in nature – not in the rock flowers or the heather, not in the delicacy of the seashore shells. Pale, slender hands were raised in a gesture of affection.

'Michael,' the Virgin said and there was a stillness until, unkempt and ragged, he stood before her, until he said:

'I am content here.'

'Because you have come to love your solitude, Michael.'

'Yes.'

'In this month of the year you must leave it.'

'I was content on my father's farm. I was content at the abbey. This is my place now.'

Through denial and deprivation he had been led to peace, a destination had been reached. These words were not spoken but were there, a thought passing through the conversation.

'I have come to you the last time now,' the Virgin said.

She did not smile and yet was not severe in the serenity that seemed to spread about her. Delicately, the fingers of her hands touched and parted, and then were raised in blessing.

'I cannot understand,' Michael said, struggling to find other words and remaining silent when he could not. Then it was dark again, until he woke at dawn.

It was a Thursday. Michael sensed that in nervous irritation. The day of the week was irrelevant when, this morning, there was so much else. 'Blessed among women,' he beseeched. 'Our Lady of grace, hear me.'

He begged that his melancholy might be lifted, that the confusion which had come in the night might be lightened with revelation. These were the days of the year when his spirits were most joyful, when each hour that passed brought closer the celebration of the Saviour's birth. Why had this honouring of a season been so brutally upset?

'Blessed among women,' Michael murmured again, but when he rose from his knees he was still alone.

The greyness of early morning made his island greyer than it often was, and the images of the dream – brightly lingering – made it greyer still. 'A dream's no more'n a dream,' Fódla's young voice echoed from the faraway past, and Michael saw his own head shaking a denial. Though feeling punished after the previous occasions of the Virgin's presence, he had not experienced the unease of irritation. He had not, in all his life, experienced it often. At the abbey there had been the dragging walk of Brother Andrew, his sandals flapping, a slow, repetitive sound that made you close your eyes and silently urge him to hurry. Every time Brother Justus stood up from the refectory table he shook the crumbs from the lap of his habit, scattering them so that the floor would have to be swept again. There was old Nessan's cough.

This morning, though, Michael's distress was bleaker than any mood engendered by such pinpricks of annoyance. The prospect of moving out of his solitude was fearful. This was his place and he had made it so. In his fifty-ninth year, it would enfeeble him to travel purposelessly. He would not bear a journey with the fortitude he had possessed in his boyhood and in his middle age. If he was being called to his death, why might he not die here, among his stones, close to his heather and his gorse, close to his little garden of lettuces and roots?

Slowly, when a little more time had passed, he made his way to the different shores of the island. He stood in the mouth of the cave where he had lived before he built his shelter. Then – twenty-one years ago – he had thought he would not survive. He had failed when he tried to trap the fish, had not yet developed a taste for the sloes that were the nourishment his fastness offered. He had tried to attract bees, but no bees came. He had hoped a bramble might yield blackberries, but it was not the kind to do so. Before he found the spring he drank from a pool in the bog.

From the cave he could see the stunted oak trees of the island's head-land, bent back to the ground, and he remembered how at first they had seemed sinister, the wind that shaped them hostile. But this morning they were friendly and the breeze that blew in from the sea was so slight it still did not disturb the water's surface. The waves lapped softly on the shin-gle. For years the gulls had not feared him and they alighted near him now, strutting a little on the rocks and then becoming still.

'I am content here,' Michael said aloud, saying it again because it was the truth. Head bent in shame, shoulders hunched beneath the habit that no longer offered much warmth or protection, eyes closed and seeing nothing, Michael struggled with his anger. Had his obedience not been enough? Had he been vain, or proud? Should he not have taken even one egg from the gulls' nests?

No answer came, none spoken, none felt, and he was surly when he sought forgiveness for questions that were presumptuous.

He crossed to the cliffs when the tide was low enough, wading through the icy water that soaked him up to his breast. He took his habit off and shivered as he squeezed the sea out of it, laying it on a rock to catch the sun. He beat at his body with his arms and clenched his fingers into his palms to restore the circulation.

He waited an hour, then dressed again, all he put on still damp. He felt himself watched by the gulls, and wondered if they sensed that some-thing was different about the place he'd shared with them. He climbed the cliff-face, finding footholds easily, hauling himself up by grasping the spiky rock. At the top there was a ridge of bitten grass and then the gorse began, and became so dense he thought at first he would not be able to make a way through it. The thorns tore at his legs and feet, drawing blood, until he came upon a clearing where the vegetation had failed. It narrowed, then snaked on ahead of him, like a track.

He walked until it was dark, stopping only to pick crabapples and to drink from a stream. He lay down to rest on a growth of ferns, placing over him for warmth those he had rooted up. He slept easily and deeply, although he had thought he would not.

The next morning he passed a tower that was deserted, with nothing left of its one-time habitation. He passed a dwelling outside which a jen-net was tethered. In a field a young man and woman were weeding a winter crop. They told him where he was, but he had never heard of the neighbourhood they mentioned, nor of a town two hours further on. He asked for water and they gave him milk, the first he had tasted since he left the abbey. They gave him bread and black pudding that had a herb in it, marjoram, they said. They guessed he was a *seanchaí* but he said no, not adding that the only story he had to tell was his own, wondering how they would respond if he revealed that Our Lady had three times appeared to him in a dream.

'Are you walking all Ireland?' the young man asked, making conversation with that familiar expression. Their hoes laid down, the two sat with him on a verge of grass while he ate and drank.

'I have walked it before,' he replied. 'In the way you mean.'

'Not many pass us here.'

They spoke between themselves, establishing when last there had been a visitor on the way that was close to them. They had the field and the jennet, they said when he asked. It wouldn't be long before an infant was born to them.

'You are prosperous so.'

'Thanks be to God, we are.'

He was a wandering beggar: they could not tell that what he wore had been a monk's habit once, or that a tonsure had further marked his calling. They would have considered him blasphemous if he had divulged that he was angry with Our Lady, that he resented the mockery of this reward for his compliance in the past, that on his journey bitterness had spread in him. 'Am I your plaything?' he gruffly demanded as he trudged on and, hearing himself, was again ashamed.

He passed through a forest, so dark at its heart it might have been night. Hour upon hour it took before the trees began to dwindle and the faint light of another evening dappled the gloom. He passed that night on the forest's edge, covering himself again with undergrowth.

'I will go back,' he muttered in the morning, but knew immediately that this petulance was an empty threat: he would not find the way if he attempted to return; wild boars and wolves would come at night. Even though the gorse had drawn blood, he knew he was protected while he was obedient, for in the dark of the forest he had not once suffered from a broken branch spiking his head or face, had not once stumbled on a root.

So, testily, he went on. The hoar-frost that whitened grass and vegetation was lost within an hour each morning to the sun. St Sabas's day came, St Finnian's, St Lucy's, St Ammon's. In other years they had occurred in all weathers, but on Michael's journey it still did not rain. He cracked open nuts, searched where there was water for cresses and wild parsley. He remembered, on St Thomas's day, Luchan telling of Thomas's finger placed on the wound and of his cry of anguish as his doubt was exposed, and his Saviour's chiding. 'It is only that I cannot understand,' Michael pleaded, again begging for the solace of forgiveness.

Often he did not rest but walked on when darkness fell, and sometimes he did not eat. The strength to walk remained, but there was a lightness in his head and, going on, he wondered about his life, whether or not he had wasted the time given to him on earth. He begged at the door of a great house and was brought in, to warmth and food. The lady of the house came to the kitchen to pour wine for him and ask if he'd seen badgers and foxes the way he had come. He said he had. Her dark hair and the olive skin of her face put him in mind of Fódla once and that night, when he lay in a bed as comfortable as he had ever known, he thought about his childhood friend: her skin would be rough now, and lined, her hands ingrained from a lifetime's work. More anger was kindled in him; he was no longer penitent. Why should it have been that Fódla bore the children of another man, that she had come to belong to someone else, that he had been drawn away from her? His melancholy thoughts frightened him, seeming like a madness almost. Since first he had dreamed his holy dreams had there been some folly that controlled him, a silliness in his credulity? Had he been led into what Cathal called confusion's dance? Cathal would have spoken on that, Diarmaid too, and Ioin. There would have been their arguments and their concern, and the wisdom of Brother Beocca. But alone and lost in nowhere there was only a nagging that did not cease, a mystery that mocked and taunted, that made of him in his fifty-ninth year a bad-tempered child.

Mass was said in the house in the morning, and the lady of the house came to him when he was given breakfast.

'Do not hasten on,' she begged, 'if you do not have to. These days of the year, we would not wish to see you without a roof.'

Stay, she urged, until St Stephen's day, offering her hospitality with a smile touched by sorrow. She was a widow, he had heard in the kitchen.

They would clothe him, although it was not said. They would burn the old habit that was no longer recognizable as to its origin. He had told them nothing about himself; they had not asked.

'You are welcome in my house,' he heard the invitation repeated. 'And the weather may turn bitter.'

It would be pleasant to stay. There was the bed, the kitchen fireside. He had watched the spicing of beef the evening before; he had seen poultry hanging in the cold rooms, and fruits laid out in jars.

'I am not allowed to stay,' he said, and shook his head and was not pressed.

It was soon after he left the house, still in the same hour, that his cheerless mood slipped from him. As he walked away in the boots he had been given, he sensed with startling abruptness – not knowing why he did –

that he had not failed himself, either as the young man he once had been or the old man he had become; and he knew that this journey was not the way to his death. Faithful to her prediction, the Virgin had not come to him again, but in a different way he saw her as she might have been before she was holy. He saw her taken aback by the angel's annunciation, and plunged into a confusion such as he had experienced himself. For her, there had been a journey too. For her, there had been tiredness and apprehension, and unkind mystery. And who could say there had not been crossness also?

Like blood flowing again, trust trickled back and Michael felt as he had when first he was aware he would survive among the rocks of his island. There was atonement in the urgency of his weary travail for three more days; and when the fourth day lightened he knew where he was.

The abbey was somewhere to the east, the pasture land ahead of him he had once walked. And closer, there was the hill on which so often he had watched over his father's sheep. There was the stream along which the alders grew, their branches empty of leaves now. No flock grazed the slopes of the hill, nor were there geese in the orchard, nor pigs rooting beneath the beech tree. But the small stone farmhouse was hardly changed.

There was no sound when he went nearer, and he stood for a moment in the yard, glancing about him at the closed doors of the outside houses, at the well and the empty byre. Grass grew among the roughly hewn stones that cobbled the surface beneath his feet. Ragwort and nettles withered in a corner. A roof had fallen in.

They answered his knock and did not know him. They gave him bread and water, two decrepit people he would not have recognized had he met them somewhere else. The windows of their kitchen were stuffed with straw to keep the warmth in. The smoke from the hearth made them cough. Their clothes were rags.

'It is Michael,' suddenly she said.

His father, blind, reached out his hand, feeling in the air. 'Michael,' he said also.

There was elation in their faces, joy such as Michael had never seen in faces anywhere before. The years fell back from them, their eyes were lit again with vigour in their happiness. A single candle burned in celebration of the day, its grease congealed, holding it to the shelf above the hearth.

Their land would not again be tilled; he was not here for that. Geese would not cry again in the orchard, nor pigs grub beneath the beech trees. For much less, and yet for more, he had been disturbed in the contentment of his solitude. So often he had considered the butterflies of his rocky fastness his summer angels, but if there were winter angels also they were here now, formless and unseen. No choirs sang, there was no sudden splendour, only limbs racked by toil in a smoky hovel, a hand that blindly searched the air. Yet angels surely held the cobweb of this mercy, the gift of a son given again.

Death of a Professor

The roomful of important men expectantly await the one whom another has already dubbed the party's ghost. In some, anticipation is disguised, in others it is a glint in an eye, a flushed cheek, the flicker of a smile that comes and goes. Within their disciplines it is their jealously possessed importance that keeps those gathered in the room going, but for once, this morning, their disciplines do not matter. Shafts of insult remain unlaunched, old scores can wait as the Master's Tio Pepe makes the rounds. Gossip is in command today.

'Oh, just a – a jape, they say?' little McMoran mutters, excusing cruelty with a word he has to search for. His sister's school stories of forty years ago were full of japes – *The Girls of the Chalet School, Jo Finds a Way, The Terrible Twins.* No point in carrying on about it, McMoran mutters also: they'll never find the instigator now. A bit of fun, still mischievously he adds.

Seeming almost twice McMoran's size, Linderfoot sniffs into his empty glass, his great pate shiny in bright winter light. Oh, meant as fun, he quite agrees. No joke, of course, if it comes your way. No joke to be called dead before your time.

'It hasn't come your way, though,' McMoran scratchily points out, and wonders what the obituarists have composed already about this overweight, obtuse man, for he has always considered Linderfoot more than a little stupid even though he holds a Chair, which McMoran doesn't. Obedient, it would seem, to the devilment of some jesting or malicious student, four newspapers this morning have published their obituarists' tributes to the professor who has not yet arrived for the Master's midday drinks.

'Kind on the whole,' Quicke remarks to a colleague who does not respond, being one of several in the room who likes to keep a private counsel. 'Oh, kind, of course. No, I would not say less than kind.'

Grinning through bushy sideburns that spread on to his cheeks, Quicke offers variations of his thought, recalling an attack made on the historian Willet-Horsby after his death – disguised, of course, but none the less an attack. '1956. Unusual on an obituary page, but there you are.'

Quicke is the untidiest of the men in the room, his pink corduroy suit having gone without the attentions of an iron for many weeks, the jacket shabby, lapels touched here and there with High Table droppings. A virulent red tie – assertion of Quicke's political allegiance – does not quite hide the undone buttons of his checked lumberjack's shirt. He is a hairy, heavily made man, his facial features roughly textured, who in his sixties is still the *enfant terrible* of College junketings and gatherings such as this one.

'Ormston has taken it in his stride,' he finishes his observations now, guessing this to be far from so. 'He is a man of humour.'

'Ormston's nothing of the sort.' The tallest man in the room, skinny as a tadpole, Triller peers down at the Master's wife to contradict what both have overheard. Triller is courteous but given on occasion to sharpness, tweedily one of the old school, with a pipe that this midday remains unlit in the Master's drawing-room.

'It is a most appalling thing,' the Master's wife, the only woman in the room, asserts. 'I doubt that Professor Ormston will turn up.'

'You've had no word?'

'Not a thing.'

'Oh, then he'll come. Unlike him not to.'

'It's going too far, don't you think, this? Why is it that everything must go too far these days?'

'Your husband, I'm perfectly certain, intends to do what is necessary.'

The Master is lax, Triller's private view is. Tarred with the Sixties' brush, the Master long ago let the reins slip away. What better can be expected now? A show of strength is necessary, and Triller adds:

'Not for an instant do I doubt the Master's intention to supply it. How odd, though, that the victim should be Ormston.'

'I didn't myself realize Professor Ormston was unpopular. No, not at all.'

'He does not suck up.' Professor Triller glances briefly at Wirich's back and is pleased when the Master's wife acknowledges his allusion with one of her faint smiles. 'I don't suppose Ormston has ever worn leathers in his life.'

This elicits laughter, a tinkle in the noise of conversation. Though not attired so now, Wirich is given to leather – jackets and tight leather trousers, studded belts, occasionally a choker. He rides a motorcycle, a big Yamaha.

'Could this not simply be carelessness?' the Master's wife suggests. 'Newspapers have a way, these days, of being careless.'

'Not four different obituary departments, I'd have thought. I rather fear it was deliberate.'

Plump, with spectacles dangling, the Master's wife retorts that no matter how the unpleasantness has come about it is unacceptable in an older university. She's cross because what clearly excites her guests does not excite her, nor the Master himself. Something has been taken from them, she feels. Today should belong to them.

'I considered telephoning Ormston,' the Master reveals to the author of *Tribal Organization in the Karakoram Foothills* and to a classicist who considers the investigation of foothill tribes a waste of time. 'But then I rather thought that would simply highlight the thing, so I didn't.'

Nods greet this. They would have resisted telephoning too, a joint indication is, both men reflecting that the Master's role is not one they could ever take to, with irritating decisions endlessly to consider.

'I really am disturbed.' Given to booming, the Master lowers his voice to indicate the seriousness of his state. 'I truly am.'

Before his time, by as much as fifteen years, there was the business of Batchett's extra-mural lecture, and longer ago still the mocking of T. L. Hapgood, which now is in the annals, although no one in the Master's drawing-room this midday knew T. L. Hapgood in his lifetime or is aware of what he looked like. More recently, one morning, there was the delivery of a pig to Dr Kindly, and that same evening four dozen take-away pizzas. Batchett had presented himself at a famous public school to lecture to the Geographical Society on land lines, only to discover that not only had some sort of mid-term break emptied the school of his anticipated audience but that there was, in fact, no Geographical Society and never had been.

'The Hapgood riddle was never solved?' the Karakoram foothills man hazards. 'I've never known.'

'No, they didn't get to the bottom of it. Years later, identities often surface after such nuisances, but none did then. Some disaffected bunch.'

The bunch who took against T. L. Hapgood – by general consent because his sarcasm hurt – based their jape on the professor's disdain for the stream of consciousness in the literature of his time. Other academics were written to in Professor Hapgood's name, announcing his authorship of a forthcoming study of James Joyce's life and works. *I feel my task will be incomplete and greatly lacking without the inclusion of your views on the great Irishman, and in particular, perhaps, on his subtle and enlightening use of what we have come to call the 'stream of consciousness'. Anything from a paragraph to thirty or so pages would be welcome from your pen, with prompt reward either in cheque form or our own good claret, whichever is desired. I am most reluctant to go to press without your voice, inimitable in its perception and its sagacity.* For eighteen months Professor Hapgood received contributions from Europe, America, Japan and the antipodes. Later, demands for reimbursement became abusive.

'I didn't know Ormston in his youth wanted to be a cabinet-maker,' the classicist remarks. 'It said that in one of them this morning.'

'Affectionately, though,' the Master hurriedly interjects. 'The point was affectionately made.'

'Oh yes, affectionately.'

Historians and philosophers and breezy sociologists, promoters of literature and language, of medieval lore and the Internet, they stand about and talk or do not talk. In different ways the diversion draws them from their shells, even those who have decided that comment on any matter can be a giveaway. Some wonder about the absent victim, others about his younger wife – a flibbertigibbet in Triller's view, the price you pay for beauty. To McMoran it seems like fate's small revenge that Ormston should be struck down before his time: his own wife has long ago given in to dowdiness and fat.

At twenty-five past twelve there is a lull in the drawing-room conversations, occurring as if for a reason, although there isn't one. For a moment only Quicke's rather high voice can be heard, repeating to someone else that Ormston is a man of humour. A snigger is inadequately suppressed.

'My dear, there are empty glasses,' the Master's wife murmurs in her husband's ear.

As he looks about him, wondering where he left the decanter, the conversational lull seems not to have been adventitious after all, but a portent. The doorbell sounds. Professor Ormston has come at last.

Someone once said – the precise source of a much-repeated observation long ago lost – that in her heyday Vanessa Ormston's beauty recalled Marilyn Monroe's. Over the years, inevitably has come the riposte that she still possesses the film star's brain. Photographs show a smiling girl with bright fair hair, slender to the point of slightness, her features lit with the delicate beauty of a child. At forty-eight – younger by sixteen years than her husband – she seems thin rather than slender and has retained her beauty to the same degree that the flowers she presses between the leaves of books have. Ormston's wife – as she is often designated among her husband's colleagues – has a passion for flowers. Significance has been found in her preservation of blooms beyond their prime, the venom of envy spilt a little in college cloisters or at High Table.

Very early on the morning of the Master's sherry do – that racy term racily approved in academe – Vanessa read the obituary of her husband, whom ten minutes ago she had left alive in the twin bed next to hers. Arrested by the grainy photograph – head and shoulders, caught at Commencements five years ago – her instinct was to hurry upstairs to make sure everything was all right, that time had not played tricks on her. Was it somehow another day? Had amnesia kindly erased the facts of tragedy? But then she heard her husband's footfall and his early-morning cough. Mistily, she read – a revelation – that he was well loved by his students. She read that he was 'distinguished in his small world' and knew he would not care for that. None of them recognized that his world was small.

The electric kettle came to the boil while Vanessa read on; and then, alarmed anew, she hurried upstairs. He was propped up on his pillows after his brief absence from the bed, what showed of him almost a replica of the photographed head and shoulders on the fawn Formica surface of the kitchen table. 'Won't be a tick,' she managed to get out and hurried off again to make their seven o'clock tea, the tray prepared the night before, gingersnap biscuits in the round tin with 'The Hay Wain' on it. The newspaper should accompany all this, his turn to scan it then.

Vanessa lost her head, as in difficult moments she tended to. She could not possibly hand the paper to him and wait for him to arrive at his recorded death. His companions on the page – no doubt correctly there – were a backing singer of a pop group, a bishop, born in Stockport, and a lieutenant colonel. *Professor A. R. Ormston*, it said, the space allocated to him less than that of the others, less particularly than the backing singer's. The bishop's photograph was small, but generous text made up for that; the lieutenant colonel married Anne Nancy Truster-Ede in 1931 and lost an arm in Cyprus. Gazing at his soldier's brave old eyes and the bishop's murky likeness, the raddled babyface of the singer, metal suspended from lobe and nostril, Vanessa again said to herself that she could not possibly commit this cruelty. Being crammed into what space remained was horrible.

The obituaries were on the inside of the last page. There had been a time when the paperboy jammed the paper into the letter-box, tearing that page quite badly. *Please leave the newspapers on the window-sill*, her husband had instructed on a square of cardboard which he suspended from the brass hall-door handle. He kept the square of cardboard by him, displaying it each time the paperboy changed.

Vanessa tore the bottom of the page and bundled away what she could not bring herself to reveal. She dropped the ball of paper into the waste-bucket beneath the sink, pushing it well down, under potato peelings and a soup tin. Then she carried the tray upstairs.

'We need to hang out your notice again,' she said, pouring tea and adding milk. 'It's a different boy.'

'What boy's that, dear?'

'The one with the papers.'

What on earth else could I do? she wildly asked herself, dipping a gingersnap into her tea. She had needed time to think, but now that she had it could think of nothing. Her worried features, private behind the cover of the magazine that had been delivered also, were a blankness that filled eventually with a consideration of the consequences of her subterfuge. It did not occur to her that this was anything but an error in a single newspaper. More on her mind was that her protection could not possibly last, that when the moment of truth arrived no explanation could soften the harshness of an obituarist's mistake. She might have tried to speak, to lead on gently to a confession, but still she could not.

'Whatever's a stealth fighter?' came an enquiry from the other bed, the question answered almost as soon as it was asked. An F117 Stealth Fighter was an aeroplane, she was told, and also told that there was going to be trouble with the postal unions, and then that there was not much news today. 'Oh, little do you know!' her own voice cried, though only to herself. She turned the pages of her magazine, seeing nothing of them. Her desperation misled her: friends and colleagues would rally round in humane conspiracy, their instinct to protect, as hers had been. When letters arrived from those who could not know the truth she would reply, explaining. They would, in the nature of things, be addressed to her. That some undergraduate, when the new term began, might say, 'Sir, surely you are dead?' did not enter Vanessa's bewildered thoughts. He was well loved by his students, after all. They, too, would surely respect his dignity.

But minutes later, when Professor Ormston's wife stood in the bedroom with her dressing-gown and nightdress slipped off, the moment before her underclothes every morning felt cold on her skin, she knew she had again done the wrong thing, as so often she had in her marriage and in her life. And as so often also, she had compounded it by creating an unreal wonderland: they would take pleasure, all of them, in this amusement.

'What shall today bring?' the Professor wondered from his bed, words familiar in the bedroom at this time.

She thought to tell him then. She could have gone to him half dressed, and offered consolation with her young wife's body. 'I am ridiculous,' instead her own voice echoed, soundless in the room, ridiculous because she did not have the courage to cause pain.

She boiled his egg and made his toast. She heated milk for their coffee. To come were the leisurely hours of this Saturday morning, while still he would not know. And hopelessly again she wondered why, for once, it should not be different, why at the Master's sherry do they should not be merciful.

'This matter shall be dealt with,' is the Master's greeting. 'Have no doubt on that score.'

He says no more, only nods through what he takes to be Ormston's embarrassment but is, in fact, bewilderment. It seems to the Master that Ormston intends to ride the storm, disdaining comment. And in that, of course, he must be honoured. 'Is this what's called insouciance?' McMoran mutters, struck also by Ormston's calm.

Alone in a corner a medievalist, Kellfittard, regards Ormston with a distaste that reaches into hatred. 'The Quicke and the dead,' Kellfittard hears coming from his left when for a moment the man declared to be no longer alive is in the company of the pinkly corduroyed professor. Kellfittard cares for neither of them, but has more reason to dislike the one he imagined until an hour ago had left his wife a widow. Kellfittard's bachelor status has everything to do with Vanessa Ormston, who is of an age with him and wasted, so he believes, on a dry old man. Dry himself, he is one of the professors who are economical with their utterances, an inclination in him that played against his chances where Vanessa was concerned, allowing his rival to get in first. Hours ago in his cheerless college rooms he gazed in disbelief and wonder, and then in pure delight, at the likeness on the obituary page, went out to buy the three other newspapers he guessed might carry the same happy tidings, and there they were. Fantasies began at once: theatre visits with Vanessa Ormston, quiet dinners at The Osteria, a discreet weekend, and in Salzburg before the autumn term began the honeymoon that should have taken place years ago. It wasn't until he arrived at the Master's house that Kellfittard realized some prankster had been at work.

Quicke's donkey roar reaches him in his corner. It mocks him, as the faces all around him do – McMoran's wizened, Linderfoot's a blob of fat, the one that has been to the Karakoram foothills sunburnt, Wirich's beaky, the Master's square and heavy, Triller's long and tidy. Kellfittard himself shares with the man who nineteen years ago snatched beauty from him a pallor without a trace of pink, and rimless spectacles. Both men are grey-haired; both are sparely made. In the course of his morning's thoughts it seemed rational to Kellfittard that, in marrying again, a wife would choose, the second time, a physical repetition. Though in no other way, those same thoughts adamantly insisted, was there a similarity.

'Impossible to know how it was done. One of our names taken in vain, I have no doubt.'

It is Linderfoot who makes that pronouncement, approaching Kellfittard in his chummy way. What Linderfoot maintains – idiotically, it seems to Kellfittard – is that some undergraduate has simply acted a part on the telephone, proffering the news of a professor's death.

'Your name or mine,' Linderfoot presses, 'would seem to have been enough.'

'No,' another man joins in to say. 'That would not have been enough.'

'Then what?' Linderfoot purses his big lips as if to whistle, his habit when a conversation palls. The man who has butted in says:

'This was done from within a news agency. It must have been.'

'A *news* agency?'

'One of Ormston's old students. Forgiveness does not come cheaply always.'

'But Ormston –'

'We all offend.'

'Ormston appears to be pretending it hasn't happened.' Kellfittard breaks his silence with that. He does not say he rejoiced to know the man was dead. He does not believe that he himself in any way offends his students, but he keeps that back also.

'Extraordinary,' Linderfoot interjects, pursing his lips again. 'Extraordinary.'

It is known to the others, but not to Linderfoot – who takes no interest in such matters – that Kellfittard feels he should have married Vanessa Ormston, that he has married no one else because a passion has lingered. It's understandable, in Linderfoot's opinion, that Ormston should choose to ignore the embarrassment of what has happened to him. He blunders about the room, seeking other conversations, unaware of the prevailing disappointment that Ormston has not appeared among them a broken man, that there has been this anticlimax.

'An inside job,' Quicke remarks eventually, determined to exact something from the let-down. Leaving the house with Ormston, he offers his opinion as they make their way on the Master's wide garden path. 'On the media front, an inside job, so they are saying now.'

He touches one nostril and then the other with a red spotted handkerchief, causing Ormston to look away. Quicke's manner implies particular comradeship between the two, a lowered tone suggests concern. The comradeship does not exist, the concern's unreal.

'What are you talking about?' Ormston asks and in a roundabout way, the information larded with commiseration, he learns of what has occurred.

*

Passing on his left the grey-brown stone of porters' lodge and deeply recessed library windows, Ormston remembers the torn back page of his morning paper. The face of the pop-group singer, which briefly he glanced at, is as briefly repeated in his recall. What was missing from that page was what was left hanging when the Master said the matter would be dealt with. The Master's wife was awkward in her greeting, McMoran smug. Triller's vague air disguised something else; Wirich stared; Linderfoot was excited; Kellfittard looked the other way. Every one of them knows.

As others already have, Ormston knits together an explanation that is similar to theirs except in detail. When he was young himself an unpopular Senior Dean suffered the indignity of being approached by a police constable, following information that confused his identity with a draper's elderly assistant who hung around public lavatories. A youth called Tottle was sent down for that; and Ibbs and Churchman suffered the same fate less than a term later for stealing the Master's clothing, confining him miserably when he should have been delivering the Hardiman lecture in the presence of a member of the Royal Family. All one year there'd been a spate of that kind of thing, chamber pots on spires, false charges laid, old Purser's bicycle dismantled more than a dozen times.

Why should he be a victim now? He is not arrogant that he's aware of, or aloof among his students; he does not seek to put them in their place. Lacking the ambition of his colleagues, he is a scholar as scholars used to be, learned in an old-fashioned sense. Has all this jarred and irritated without his knowing? Still walking slowly, Professor Ormston shakes his head. He is not a fool, of course he would have sensed unpopularity.

Noticing the green and black hanging sign of the St Boniface public house, he considers entering it and a moment later does so instead of passing by. He has rarely in his life been in a public house, maybe a dozen times in all, he estimates as the swing doors close behind him. Blue plush banquettes along the walls are marked with cigarette burns, as are the low tables arranged in front of them, each with a glass ashtray advertising a brand of beer and small round mats bearing similar insignia. Unwashed glasses have been collected and are still on trays; busy ten minutes ago with Saturday-morning trade, the place is empty now.

'Sir?' a man behind the bar greets Professor Ormston, looking up from a plate of minced meat with a topping of potato.

'Might I have a glass of whisky?'

'You could of course, sir.'

Warmly steaming, smeared with tomato sauce, the food smells of the grease it has been cooked in. On a radio somewhere a disc jockey is gabbling incomprehensibly.

'Would I make that a double, sir?'

As if aware that his customer is unused to public-house measures, the barman holds the glass up to display how little whisky there is in it.

'Yes, please do.'

'Decent enough bit of weather.'

'Yes, it is.'

'There you go, sir.'

'Thanks.'

He pays and takes the drink to one of the tables by the windows. 'Kind,' was how Quicke put it; all four obituarists were kind in Quicke's opinion. 'Quite right, of course.' And he was able to nod, not up to pretending aloud that yes, the notices were kind enough. A dare, Quicke said, young men have dares. They think up these things and the one who is eventually in a position to do so sees something through. A bet it might have been, and probably was. There'd be apologies from all four editors, Quicke was certain about that.

A child appears behind the bar, only the top of her head visible. The man tells her to go away, but then he reaches for a glass and pours a Pepsi Cola into it while continuing to eat. He tells the girl she'll be the ruin of him.

'This'll make me drunk,' Professor Ormston tells himself, whisky on top of Tio Pepe before lunch. And yet he wants to stay here. The newspaper beside the trays of unwashed glasses on the bar is not the kind that has obituaries. Again the torn page stirs in his recall, only half of the backing singer there, the name of the army colonel not known to him, as the bishop's wasn't either. Of course a popular entertainer took precedence. The way things are these days, that stands to reason.

'I'm sorry,' he says at the bar after he has sat for a while longer, apologizing because the man hasn't finished his food. But the man is cheerful, Irish by the sound of him. Professor Ormston has read somewhere that the Irish make good publicans, a touch of the blarney not out of place.

'Sure, and what am I here for, sir? Wouldn't I be negligent to eat me dinner with a man going thirsty?'

'Thank you so much.'

He carries the replenished glass back to where he has been sitting. *Survived by his wife, Vanessa.* It would have said that, Vanessa mentioned once. No children, acquaintances of long ago would notice. And students who did not know he'd ever married would be surprised, he not being the sort, they might in their day have assumed. When they took her on as secretary in the department there had hardly been enough work to justify it and she was bored at first, until it was suggested she should be shared with McMoran. When she left, three years ago, it was because she didn't like McMoran.

She has done what she thought best. He knows that in her; and sipping more whisky, he tries to understand. Apart altogether from McMoran's spikiness, she had never been happy in the department, as later she confessed. 'You think this girl's up to it?' he asked when they first considered her, not even noticing her beauty then. This city, not a human attribute, was what he'd thought of when he thought of beauty, the grey-brown columns and façades, carved figures in their niches, the lamplight coming on in winter. Seven hours have passed, he calculates: she came up with the tea and gingersnaps, prevaricating although prevarication does not come naturally to her.

Another man comes in, who doesn't have to order what he wants. The barman knows and pours a bottle of Adnams' beer. 'Floating Voter,' the barman says. 'You'll get him at nines.'

The others kept it to themselves when she left the department, unable to criticize her because she was his wife. McMoran muttered something, feeling more let down because he had relied on her more, but what he said wasn't audible. It doesn't interest any of them that she is happier now, that she has given her life up to her flowers and to her hospital charity work, amusing children while they wait on cysticfibrosis days, or children undergoing leukaemia treatment, or hole-in-the heart children. 'I don't know how she does it,' he might have said, but never has because they wouldn't be interested in the charity work of someone's wife. She wanted children; he could not give her them.

The trawl through his life that she has withheld from him would not, of course, record that. Nor would it touch upon his occasional testiness, his cold appraisal of examination answers, the orderly precision that enhances his work and affects him as a husband, the melancholy that comes from nowhere. Other human-interest decoration might enliven a drab account, with liberties taken for the casual reader. *His wife was younger by sixteen years* most certainly would not be written. Nor *as lovely in her day as Marilyn Monroe.*

The whisky has dried his mouth. In the Master's drawing-room he would have seemed a figure of silliness, not saying anything: those of them who have wives would now be passing that across their lunch tables. They'd be amused to know that he is surreptitiously drinking in a public house.

The house is silent. Wintry sunshine dwindles in the kitchen, on the places laid at the oval table, each of the two plates of tongue covered with another plate, for the sun has made the window a haven for the last of autumn's flies. A salad, the oil and vinegar dressing not yet added, is covered also.

Whoever the perpetrators are, Vanessa feels she belongs with them, that she has added something to their cruelty. 'I couldn't think, I didn't know what I was doing': all that is ready, and has been for longer than the food she has prepared. 'Panic,' she must also say, for that word belongs. 'I went all blank.' No need to say a wife should have the courage to bear bad news.

He'll know because it will, of course, have all come out; and then he'll see her reddened eyes and know the rest as well. A nest of vipers the Master and his simpering wife gather round them on these occasions. Who has a chance in a nest of vipers?

'My God!' Vanessa's mother exclaimed in open horror when, nineteen years ago almost to the month, she learned of her daughter's engagement to a fusty academic who was just old enough to be her father. 'My God!' she said again after their first encounter, when Vanessa brought him for the weekend to her mother's flat. 'Has he money?' she asked, unable to find some other reason for what she termed an unattractive marriage. 'Just what he earns,' Vanessa replied, and two months later married him.

His key turns in the hall-door Yale. While waiting for him, it has occurred to Vanessa that there would be the other newspapers. She has imagined him in a newsagent's, giving the right money because he likes to if he can, taking the papers to where he can peruse them undisturbed.

The hall door bangs softly; he does not call her name. There's the pause that means he's hanging up his overcoat and scarf, the papers placed on the table beneath the picture of a café scene. There are his footsteps then.

'I have to tell you,' her husband says, 'that I believe I'm drunk.'

His voice is quiet, the words not slurred. He does not look drunk; he is the same. He doesn't smile, but then he often doesn't when he comes in. 'A sobersides,' her mother said. 'Wizened,' she added, although that wasn't true.

'I looked in at the St Boniface,' he says. 'Understandably, I believe.'

'I'm awfully sorry.'

'Oh Lord, it's not your fault.'

'I –'

'I know, I know.'

'I couldn't think.'

'I couldn't when I heard, myself.'

'They mentioned it?'

'Quicke couldn't resist a little mention. It didn't matter. Sooner or later someone would.'

'Yes.'

'The culprits will be exposed, the Master's view is. Of course he's wrong.'

'You don't seem drunk in the least.' Relief has slipped through Vanessa during these exchanges. For a reason that is obscure to her, and for the first time since she turned the pages of the newspaper while waiting for the early-morning kettle to boil, she feels that nothing is as terrible as it seemed in those awful moments.

'To the best of my knowledge I have never in my life been drunk before. The man poured three double whiskies, and that on top of sherry.'

She lifts the plates that cover their cold meat. She stirs the oil and vinegar, shakes the salad about when she has added a few spoonfuls, then pours on the rest. Perhaps they'll go away, Vanessa's thought is, perhaps he'll take an early retirement, as one of them so unexpectedly did last year. She'd pack up at once, she wouldn't hesitate. Liguria, or Sansepolcro, where his favourite paintings are. Hers, too, they have become. 'I could live here happily,' he has said, over coffee in Sansepolcro.

'I can tell you how this has happened,' he says. 'If you would care to know.'

'Panic,' she begins to say, and ceases when he shakes his head, grey hair as smooth as a helmet.

'An act of compassion,' he corrects.

'But it was stupid. To try to suppress what cannot be suppressed –'

'Why cannot an act of compassion be a stupid one? I can tell you,' he repeats exactly, 'how this has happened. If you would care to know.'

'Some horrid, wretched student.'

'I am not the sort to inspire a grudge. I am too shadowy and grey, too undramatic. I annoy too little, I do not attack.'

She watches the buttering of a piece of baguette, the knife laid down, the meticulous loading of tongue and salad on to a fork, the smear of mustard. She pours his coffee; he likes it with his food at this time of day, with French bread in particular, he has often said. My God, Vanessa thinks, it might be true. He might not be here now.

'Imagine Kellfittard opening his paper this morning. Imagine his happy hour or two.'

For a moment she is confused, thinking he means Kellfittard is responsible for this. He says, 'And then the rug pulled out from under him. Generations have suffered from Kellfittard's wit. It passes for that, you know. So much we fusties say passes for wit.'

'But you –'

'They would not mind about me. Whoever they are who got this going would not think twice about reaping me in before I'm due. What's famous here is Kellfittard's abiding passion for someone else's wife.'

The last time Kellfittard stopped to talk to her yesterday's garlic was on his breath. Stopping to talk to her has always been his ploy, and smiling in a secretive way – as if, by doing so, secrets are created.

'Fall-guy, do they call it?' she hears her husband say. 'I am the fall-guy.'

He has winkled out the truth, sitting in the public house he gave the name of, which she has often passed. The truth doesn't make much difference, and certainly is no consolation. Yet for her older husband it had to be established, if only because it's there somewhere. Students who are no longer students have got their own back. He is an incidental figure, and so is she.

'Well, that is that,' he says. 'Four notices in all, Quicke said. Space to spare on a Saturday.'

'There will be letters.'

'Oh, and apologies will be printed. So Quicke says too.'

Something in his tone, or in what he has said, causes her to realize that she was wrong when she imagined him buying the newspapers. He has not done so. He asks about the coffee and she says Kenya.

He nods. The coffee's good, he says. The other matter's over, he does not add, but Vanessa knows it is. Once Kellfittard gave her a box of chocolates, Bendicks' Peppermints because he knew she liked them. 'I bought these by mistake,' he said, the lie so damaging the gesture that the gesture lost its point. It would have been silly not to accept them.

'Linderfoot's put on another stone, I'd say. How fortunate the wives are to be left at home!'

His wisdom was what she loved when first she loved him, when she was still a girl. She called it that, though only to herself. Not brains, they all had brains. Not skill. Not knowing everything, for they knew less than they imagined. His wisdom is almost indefinable, what a roadworker might have, a cinema usher or a clergyman, or a child. Her mother would not understand, and he himself would deny that he is wise. Of course the papers are not on the hall table; of course he hasn't read a word – the subtle slights wrapped up as worthiness, and qualities he did not possess made his because it is the thing to do, all of valediction's clichés.

'No, no, a blunder,' she hears him say when the telephone rings, the first time it has today, the house of mourning left to itself until this moment. 'No, most ridiculous,' he says. 'I'm sorry if I startled you.'

He laughs, replacing the receiver, and Vanessa does not say she loves him, although she wants to. Absurd, to have thought of hiding away in Italy, packing everything up, leaving for ever his beautiful city just because they have been involved in someone else's hoax.

He has worn the better of the two, Vanessa reflects. Age in his features was always there; her beauty loses a little every day. 'I love your wisdom,' she wants to say, but still is shy to use that word, fearing a display of her naïvety would make her foolish.

'My dear,' he murmurs in the calmness they have reached, and holds her as he did the day he first confessed his adoration. It is the wedding of their differences that protects them, steadfast in the debris of the storm.

Against the Odds

Mrs Kincaid decided to lie low. There had been a bit of bother, nothing much but enough to cause her to change her address. From time to time she was obliged to do so.

She wondered about Portrush. It was May, which meant that the holiday accommodation would still be available at low-season terms. She wondered about Cushendall, which she would have preferred because she liked the air there, but only three years had passed since her last visit and somehow three years didn't feel quite long enough. Cushendun, Ballygalley, Portstewart, Ardglass, Bangor, Kilkeel: Mrs Kincaid had breathed the air in all of them.

This time, though, she decided on an inland town. She knew many of these also, Armagh and Lisburn in particular, but Ballymena, Magherafelt, Lurgan and Portadown almost as well. She was a Belfast woman herself, but long ago had made all the territory of the Six Counties her business ground. Only once, in 1987, had she strayed outside the North of Ireland, taking the Larne crossing to Stranraer, then travelling on to Glasgow, an episode in her life she regretted and preferred not to dwell upon. Equally regretted was a suspended sentence in the Derry courts in 1981, since it had ruled out as a place to do business in a city she was particularly fond of.

Mrs Kincaid – with no claim to that name other than her occasional use of it – was just over eleven stone, and tall. Although well covered, she gave no impression of plumpness; no bloated or sagging flesh seemed superfluous beneath her clothes. Her arms were sturdy, her legs looked strong. In her own opinion her biggish face was something she got away with, no feature in it particularly objectionable, neither a fallen-away chin nor protruding teeth. Modest in her dress, careful not to overdo her use of perfume and make-up, she was sixty years old, admitting to fifty-one. Her easy smile worked wonders.

'Well, isn't that great?' she remarked to the driver of the Ulsterbus that was taking her to the inland town she had finally chosen, one she neither knew nor was known in. Her display of elation as she entered the bus had to do with the declaration of peace in the Six Counties. A double cease-fire had been announced in the thirty years' war that was not called a war;

politicians from within the North of Ireland and from London and Dublin, advisers from America, had drawn up a long agenda that had since been agreed to by referendum on both sides of the Border. Mrs Kincaid had not herself suffered more than inconvenience during the years of conflict; the trouble in her life had been a personal one. Yet the havoc that occurred with such weary repetition and for so long had naturally impinged; she would be glad to see its end.

'Great?' the bus driver responded to her optimism.

'The peace.'

'There's maybe something in their bits of paper.' Nonchalantly, the driver turned on the ignition. Windscreen wipers lumbered across the curved glass in front of him, clearing away a few drops of rain. 'We'll see,' he said, a reminder in his tone that whatever agreements had been reached, whatever pledges given, there were gunmen who had not gone away, who still possessed their armoury and were used to calling the tune. 'We'll see,' he said again.

'Hope for the best.'

'Aye.'

'Isn't it cold, though, for May? Whenever I looked out first thing I said you'll be needing your wool, Mabel.'

The bus driver agreed that the weather was unseasonable before starting his engine. Mrs Kincaid passed on to a seat. She never liked leaving Belfast. Its streets were hers, its intonations always a pleasure to hear again when she returned from an exile never made through choice. The bombs that had battered its buildings, blown its motor-cars to pieces, maimed and killed its citizens, had never, in thirty years, caused her to wish to live elsewhere. Child of a Belfast boarding-house, she had salted away the wealth that property had fetched when she inherited it, only later to be parted from her gains, which was the personal circumstance that had coloured her life since.

She sat alone on the bus, her two brown suitcases on the rack above her. As always, she travelled light. Rented rooms with furniture supplied were what she liked, someone else's taste. She lived in that way, and although she guessed that in the town she was going to there wouldn't be a soul who did so too, she would manage not to stand out. Not yet composed, whatever story came to her on her journey would see to that for her.

Blakely crushed the peas beneath his fork, then mixed them into a mush of potato and gravy. There was one piece of meat left, its size calculated to match what was left of the potatoes and peas. Since first being on his own he had got into this way of eating, of gauging forkfuls in advance, of precisely combining the various items on his plate. It was a substitute for conversation, for invariably, these days, Blakely ate alone.

Six days a week he drove in from the farm and sat down at the same table in Hirrel's Café, never looking at a menu but taking whatever was on specially for that day. On Sundays he sat down with the Reverend Johnston in the manse, having brought with him whatever eggs he could spare, or butter-milk, which the Reverend Johnston was partial to, once a month a turkey. In December he supplied Hirrel's with turkeys also.

The *Belfast Telegraph*, folded and propped up against two Yorkshire Relish bottles, was full of the recent political developments and the prospect for the future. Fourteen years ago Blakely's wife and daughter had been killed in error, a bomb attached to a car similar in make and colour to the would-be victim's, the registration number varying by only a single digit. Promptly, he had received an apology, a telephone call of commiserations that sounded genuine. Two wreaths were sent.

He pushed his knife and fork to the side of the plate, and a few minutes later Mrs Hirrel brought him a plate of rhubarb and custard and a pot of tea. He thanked her, folding the newspaper away. The men of violence were still in charge, no doubt about it. He'd said that to Mrs Hirrel the time the cease-fires were predicted, and she'd agreed with him. They'd talked about it for a long while; today, as yesterday and the day before, there was nothing left to say on the subject. Mrs Hirrel remarked instead that the rhubarb was all young shoots, grown under plastic, the first that had come up out the back. 'See to that woman, Nellie,' she called out to her waitress, for a woman had entered the café, bringing with her a stream of bitterly cold air.

All the tables were taken, as they always were at this time. Shop people came to Hirrel's at lunchtime, commercial travellers took advantage of being in the town in the middle of the day. Toomey from the Northern Bank was always there, with the lady clerk he was doing a line with. Van drivers, occasionally a lorry driver, looked in.

'Can you wait a wee minute?' Nellie enquired of the newcomer. 'There's several finishing up.'

'D'you know who that is, Mr Blakely?' Mrs Hirrel asked him, and he said he didn't, and Mrs Hirrel said nor did she. 'Would she sit there a minute with you while you drink your tea?'

Sometimes this happened because of the empty chair opposite him. He never minded. Travellers in drapery or hardware items would fall into conversation with him, giving him some idea of the current ups and downs of the commercial world, usually asking him what line he was in himself.

'Are you sure?' Led to the table, Mrs Kincaid was hesitant before she sat down. 'I wouldn't want to butt in on you.'

'You're doing rightly,' Blakely reassured her. He was a nervous man with strangers and often expressed himself not quite as he meant to in order to get out any words at all. His tea was hot and he would have liked to pour it on to the saucer. But that wouldn't do in Hirrel's.

'Homey,' Mrs Kincaid remarked, looking around her at a familiar aspect – the laminate tabletops, cheap knives and forks, plates of bread and butter, faces intent on mastication, a toothpick occasionally spearing trapped shreds: many times she had frequented cafés like this. The man opposite her at least had taken off his cap, which often men didn't when they ate in such places. He had tufty grey hair cut short and a lean, narrow face with a deep flush in both cheeks. A healthy-looking, outside man, well enough dressed, with a collar and tie. In Mrs Kincaid's childhood if a man not wearing a collar and tie came to the boarding-house after a room he was turned away at once.

'Isn't it chilly today, though?' she remarked, noticing that a plate of rhubarb and custard had been finished quite tidily, a little left behind, spoon and fork kept together. Late fifties, she put him down as; fingernails a little grimed but nothing to write home about.

'There's a few more days of it,' he said, and then the waitress was there, asking her what she'd like, saying the mutton was finished. Mrs Kincaid ordered a plate of bread and butter, and tea.

'Have we peace at last?' she asked and the man replied civilly enough that you wouldn't know. His own opinion was that there was a long way to go, and she could feel him being careful about how he put it, in how he chose his words. Not knowing about her, not knowing which foot she dug with, as her father used to say, he held back. He poured himself another cup of tea, added milk and stirred in sugar, two spoonfuls of granulated.

'Ach, it's been going on too long,' she said.

'Maybe it's the end so.'

He folded his newspaper into a side pocket of his jacket. The jacket was of dark tweed and needed a press, a thread hanging down where a button had come off. You could tell from his way with the waitress that he was a regular. He counted out the money for his bill and left a 5p piece and some coppers as a tip. 'Good day,' he said before he went to pay at the counter.

From force of habit rather than anything else, Mrs Kincaid continued to wonder about Blakely after he'd gone. She wondered if he could be a road surveyor, since something about him reminded her of a road surveyor she'd once briefly known. She imagined him with a road gang, a smell of tar in the air, fresh chippings still pale on the renovated surface. Then Mrs Kincaid reminded herself that she wasn't here to interest herself in a man she didn't know, far from it. She had left her two suitcases in the newsagent's shop where the bus had put her down. When she'd had something to eat and had made enquiries she'd go back and collect them.

'Try Bann Street,' the waitress said. 'There's a few that lets rooms there.'

Leave it, Mrs Kincaid warned herself again when she noticed Blakely coming out of Hirrel's Café four days later, repeating her reminder to herself that she was not here for anything like that. She'd stay a month, she had decided; from experience a month was long enough for any bit of trouble to quieten. Talk of solicitors' letters, of walking straight round to a police station, threats of this and that, all simmered away to nothing when a little time went by. Frayed tempers mended, pride came to terms with whatever foolishness she'd taken advantage of in the way of business. Not that much had mended in her own case, not that pride had ever recovered from the dent it had received, but her own case was different and always had been. Eighty-four thousand pounds the boarding-house had realized in 1960, more like ten times that it would be now. 'We'd put the little enterprise in your name,' the man she'd thought of as her fiancé had said. 'No hanky-panky.' But somehow in the process of buying what he always called the little enterprise the eighty-four thousand had slipped out of her name. Soon after that it disappeared and he with it. The little enterprise it was to purchase was a bookmaker's in Argyle Street, an old bookie retiring, two generations of goodwill. A chain took it over a couple of months later.

These days Mrs Kincaid did her best to take the long view, telling herself that what had happened was like a death and that you couldn't moan about a death for ever, not even to yourself. In her business activities she did not seek vengeance but instead sought to accumulate what was rightfully hers, keeping her accounts in a small red notebook, always with the hope that one day she would not have to do so, that her misfortune in the past would at last free her from its thrall.

Walking against a steady east wind on the day she saw Blakely for the second time, she recalled his lean face very clearly, his tufty hair, the hanging thread on his jacket where a button had come off. He'd be a bachelor or a widower, else he wouldn't be taking his dinner in a café every day. You could tell at once the foot he dug with, as decent a Protestant foot as her own, never a doubt about that.

The room she had taken – not in Bann Street but above a butcher's shop in Knipe Street – smelt of meat and suet. She had an electric ring to cook on, a sink for the washing of clothes and dishes, lavatory and bathroom a flight up. There was a television, a gas fire, a single bed under the window, and when she fried something on the electric ring the butchery smell disappeared for a while. Mrs Kincaid had been in worse places.

She brought back from the shops a bar of Kit-Kat, *Woman's Own*, *Hello!*, *The Lady*, and a film magazine. She ate the chocolate bar, read a story about a late flowering of romance, made tea, slipped out of her skirt and blouse, slept, and dreamed she had married a clergyman to whom she'd once sold back the letters he'd written her. When she woke she washed herself, fried rashers and an egg, and went out again.

She sat alone at a table in the bar of Digby's Hotel, listening to tunes of the fifties, all of which she was familiar with. Occasionally someone smiled at her, a man or a woman, the girl behind the bar, but generally they just went by. She heard talk about a dance. She would have gone on her own when she was younger, but those days were over now. She drank vodka with no more than a colouring of port in it, which was her tipple. She bought a packet of cigarettes, although as a general rule she didn't smoke any more. She wasn't going to be able to resist what had been put in her path: she knew that perfectly.

She knew it again when she woke up in the middle of the night and lay for a while awake in the darkness. The smell from the shop below had come back, and when she dropped back into sleep she dreamed that the man she had met in the café was in butcher's clothes, separating lamb chops with a cleaver.

There was a traveller on his own by the table at the window, but that was the smallest table in the café and he had his samples' case on the other chair, out of the way of people passing. Otherwise, Blakely's was the only table that wasn't shared.

'Only she said go on over,' the same woman who'd shared it with him before said.

'You're welcome. Sure, there's nowhere else.'

'Isn't that the bad news?' She nodded at the headline in his paper. A taxi-driver had been shot dead the evening before, the first murder since the cease-fires.

'Aye,' Blakely said. 'It is that.'

She was dressed as she'd been before, in shades of fawn and brown – a skirt and cardigan, cream blouse, under the coat she'd taken off. There was a brooch, made to look like a flower, in her blouse.

'The plate's hot, Mr Blakely,' Nellie warned, placing roast beef and potatoes and cabbage in front of him. She wiped the edge of the plate where gravy had left a residue.

'Bread and butter and tea, Nellie,' Mrs Kincaid ordered, remembering the name from the last time. 'I don't take much,' she informed Blakely, 'in the middle of the day. And jam,' she called after the waitress.

'It's my main meal,' Blakely explained, a note of mild justification in his tone.

'Convenient, to go out for it.'

'Ach, it is.'

'You live in the town, Mr Blakely?'

'A bit out.'

'I thought maybe you would. You have the look of the open air.'

'I'm a turkey farmer.'

'Well, there you are.'

He worried a piece of beef into shreds, piled cabbage and potato on to his fork, soaking up a little gravy before conveying the lot to his mouth.

'Not bad,' he responded when he was asked if turkeys were fetching well.

'Time was when turkeys were a Christmas trade and no more. Amn't I right? Not that I know a thing about poultry.'

'Oh, you're right enough.'

'I like the brown of a turkey. I'm told that's unusual.'

'It's all white flesh they go for those times.'

'You'd supply the supermarkets, would you?'

'The most of it goes that way all right. Though there's a few outlets locally.'

'I have a room above Beatty's.'

'I sell to Beatty for Christmas.'

'Well, there's a coincidence for you!'

'He's a decent man, Henry Beatty.'

'It's not a bad little room.'

Further details were exchanged – about the room and then about the rearing, slaughtering and plucking of turkeys, the European regulations there were as regards hygiene and refrigeration. Divulging that she was a Belfast woman, Mrs Kincaid talked about the city. Blakely said he hadn't been there since he lost his wife. She used to go for the shopping, he said. Brand's, he said.

'Oh, a great store, was Brand's. You were always on the farm, Mr Blakely?'

'Aye, I was.'

'I was sorry to hear there about your wife.'

'Aye.'

The plate of bread and butter arrived, with tea, and a small glass dish of gooseberry jam.

'I'm a widow myself,' Mrs Kincaid said.

'Ah, well —'

'I know, I know.'

That comment, spoken in a whisper, contrived to make one of the two widowings, contrived to isolate with quiet poignancy a common ground. There was for an instant the feeling at the table that death had struck almost simultaneously. This feeling, for Mrs Kincaid, was a theatrical effect, since in her case no death, no widowing, had occurred. For Blakely, it was real. He finished the food he had been brought. Jelly with sponge-cake in it was placed before him, with a pot of tea.

'Are you far out of the town?' Mrs Kincaid asked.

'Ah, no. Not far.'

'I sometimes come to a quiet town for a rest. A resort most times. But this time of year they're lonely enough yet.'

'They would be surely.'

Shortly after that Blakely folded his newspaper into the side pocket of his jacket. He picked up his cap from the knob at the top of his chair. He said good-bye to Mrs Kincaid and went to pay his bill at the counter.

'Who is she, that woman?' Mrs Hirrell asked him in a whisper, and he said that Mrs Kincaid was lodging above Beatty's butcher's shop. He didn't know her name, he said, a Belfast woman in the town for a rest.

After that, Blakely found himself running into Mrs Kincaid quite often. She sat at his table in Hirrell's Café even when on one occasion there was an empty table just inside the door. She was in Blundell's News and Confectionery when he went in for his paper one day. Another time she was a mile out on the road when he was driving back to the farm and he waved at her and she waved back. A few days later she was there again with an umbrella up and he stopped, feeling he should offer her a lift.

'Well, now, that's very nice of you,' she said.

'Where're you heading?'

Mrs Kincaid said nowhere in particular. Just a daunder, she said, to fill in the afternoon. 'My name's Mrs Kincaid,' she added, since this information had not been given before, and went on to enquire if he ever felt that afternoons hung heavy.

Blakely replied that any hour of the day was the same to him. He tried to sound polite, picking out the right words, not wishing to seem brusque. 'That's Madole's,' he said as they passed a field with the gate wide open.

Spring ploughing was in progress, Madole's man, Quin, on the tractor. Madole had a lot of land, Blakely explained, some of it stretching right back to the town's outskirts.

'Here's my own few acres,' he said when his pink-washed roadside farmhouse and turkey sheds came into view. 'Would I drop you? I'd say the rain's stopped.' Specks had come on to the windscreen after he'd turned off the wipers five minutes ago, but already they were drying away. There used to be a Kincaid in Lower Bridge Street one time, a dentist, before the present man came.

'It'll be a nice walk back,' she said, getting out of the car when Blakely drew it up before turning into his yard. She thanked him. 'What's on ahead, though?'

'Loughdoon. Three-quarters of a mile.'

'I'll take a look at it.'

'It's only small.'

'I like a small place.'

The Lacky sisters – twins of forty-five – were in the plucking shed, with the birds that were ready strung up along a rafter. The sisters were in their similar black and grey overalls, their similarly crowded teeth hugely exposed as soon as their employer entered the shed, their reddish hair bulging out of the cloth caps they wore. They had been plucking Blakely's turkeys for him for twenty-nine years, since their childhood. Quin came over when Madole gave him his time off, to help around the place in any way that was necessary.

Blakely nodded at the two women. They'd done well. He counted the prepared turkeys, sixteen of them. Two dozen were to be ready for the carrier when he called at four and they'd easily make that. The Lacky sisters threw back their heads and acknowledged his compliment by laughing shrilly. They couldn't have seen the woman he'd given a lift to, they wouldn't have heard the voices. People would be talking in Hirrel's about the way she always sat at his table, but what could he do about it? And he couldn't have passed her by on the road with rain falling. He put the car away in the lean-to and set off to repair a fence that had been in need of attention for a long while. His two sheepdogs went with him, loping along at his heels.

The job took longer than he'd estimated. By the time he'd finished it the carrier had been and the Lackys had gone home. The dogs began to bark when he was mixing the evening feed.

'Now that's for you,' Mrs Kincaid said, holding out something in a brown-paper bag. It was raining lightly, but she'd taken her umbrella down. 'I sheltered in Mullin's,' she said. 'That's a comfy wee bar he has there.'

Blakely stared at the bag she held out to him. 'What is it?' he said.

She smiled, shaking her head to indicate he'd have to find out himself. 'Cheer you up, Mr Blakely.'

He didn't want to accept a present from her. There was no call for her to give him a present. There was no call for her to come into the yard, looking for him.

'No need,' he said, taking a bottle of Bushmills whiskey from the damp paper bag. 'No,' he protested. The two sheepdogs, which he had pointed into a corner, had begun to creep forward on their haunches. 'Ah, no,' he said, handing back the bottle and the bag. 'Ah no, no.'

The rain was getting heavier. 'Would you mind if I stood in your turf shed for a minute?' she said. 'You get on with your work, Mr Blakely. The little offering's for your kindness, letting me share your table and that. Mullin said you took a glass like the next man.'

'I can't take this from you.'

'It's nothing, Mr Blakely.'

'Come into the kitchen till it clears.'

She said she didn't want to interrupt him, but he led the way into the house, not saying anything himself. In the kitchen he pulled the damper out on the Rayburn to warm the place up. The bottle and the bag were on the table.

'You're looking frozen, Mr Blakely,' she said, surprising him by taking two glasses from the dresser. She opened the bottle and poured whiskey for both of them. It was nothing, she said again.

It wasn't an evening when Quin came, which Blakely was glad about. The Lackys couldn't have missed her on the road, but they wouldn't have known who she was and they'd never have guessed she'd turn in to the yard.

'He told me about you,' she was saying now. 'Mr Mullin did.'

'I go in there the odd time.'

'He told me about the loss of your wife. How it was. And your daughter, of course.'

Blakely didn't say anything. The whiskey was warm in his chest. In spite of what Mullin had said he wasn't a drinking man, but he appreciated a drop of Bushmills. A going-away present, she said.

'You're going back soon?' he asked, not pressing the question, keeping it casual.

She had taken her coat off. She was wearing a blue dress with tiny flashes of red in it, like pencil dots. There was a scarf, entirely red, tucked in at the top. At the table one leg was crossed over the other, both knees shiny because the stocking material was taut. Her umbrella was cocked up on the flags to dry.

'Sooner or later,' she said. 'Cheers!'

She added more to both their glasses when he'd taken another mouth-ful. She looked round the kitchen and said it was lovely. 'Mabel,' she said.

'What?'

'Mabel Kincaid.'

The rain was heavy now, rattling on the window panes. The Rayburn had begun to roar. He got up to push the damper in a bit.

'That's the mother and father of a shower,' she said.

'Yes.'

'You never smile, Mr Blakely.'

Blakely was embarrassed by that. 'I think maybe I'm a dour kind of man.'

'You're not at all. But after what I heard I wouldn't blame you.'

She asked if he had always lived in this house, and he said he had. His father bought the few fields from Madole, farming pigs in those days. It was the Madoles who'd built the house and they'd built it without foun-dations, which his father didn't know until after he'd bought it, didn't know that was why he'd got it cheap.

'A big family was it, Mr Blakely?'

He shook his head. A family of four, he said, one more than his own family, later on. 'I have a brother, Willie John.'

As soon as he mentioned Willie John's name Willie John laughed silently in Blakely's recall, his big jaw split, the freckles around his eyes merging as the flesh puckered. Huge and ungainly, ham-fisted their father called him before the first fruits of those same hands were completed – a twin-engined Dewoitine 510, built from a kit.

'We used to fly them out in the fields.' He didn't know why he told her; he hadn't meant to, but sometimes, with whiskey, he was garrulous, even though he still hadn't drunk much. Drink had a way of bringing things to life for him and he felt it doing that now. A Messerschmitt came to rest in a clump of nettles and Willie John gingerly rescued it, noting the damage to the tail-piece and one of the wings. His own Black Widow took off, airborne until the lighter fuel in the engine ran out. It glided down on to the cropped grass. Bloody marvellous, Willie John said.

'Just the two of you,' she said. 'I was an only myself.'

'Willie John got out when the troubles began. I get a card, Christmas time. Denver, Colorado.'

The telephone rang in the hall. It was Nathan Smith from Ulsterfare with the order for next week. When they finished talking about the tur-keys Nathan said his daughter had got herself engaged.

'I heard it. Isn't that great, Nathan?'

'It is surely. All we need now is the quiet'll last for the wedding. Thursday will we say for the order?'

'No problem, Nathan.'

In the kitchen she was on her feet with the frying-pan in her hand. The frying-pan had the breakfast fat congealed on it. She'd taken rashers out of the fridge and had lifted up one of the covers of the Rayburn. There were knives and forks on the table.

'I was hoping you'd be longer,' she said. 'I had a surprise planned.'

'Oh, look –'

'Sit down and take another drop. It's still at it cats and dogs. You have sausages in there. Would you take a couple?'

'The rain's no worry. I can run you back.'

She shook her head. She'd never ask a man who'd been drinking to drive. She spread four rashers on the fat of the pan and put the pan on the heat. She pricked four sausages on the draining-board. 'Have you eggs?' she said.

He brought in a bowl of eggs from the scullery. A woman hadn't cooked in the kitchen since Hetty and Jacqueline died. He couldn't remember that a woman had even been in the house since the last of the funeral guests stepped out of it, certainly not the Lackys. He shouldn't have talked about Willie John like that. Talk had encouraged her. He shouldn't have taken the Bushmills.

'When it clears up I'll walk it,' she said. 'I'm only filling in the time, Mr Blakely.'

'I'll drive you in,' he insisted. 'I'm well known. They won't stop me.'

Mrs Kincaid undressed herself, thinking about him. He was a finished man. The man in the bar had said as much. He'd been destroyed by the troubles, but even so he kept going, with his turkeys and the two queer-looking women she'd met on the road working for him, feathers all over their overalls. His dinner every day in a café that overcharged you, his memories of toy aeroplanes, the wife and daughter never talked about: that was it for him. A Christmas card from Denver kept his spirits up.

Removing the last of her underclothes, Mrs Kincaid guessed that he was thinking about her also, that he might even be seeing her as she was in this very minute. Finished or not, there was always a spark that could be kindled. An old hand at that, Mrs Kincaid didn't have to ask herself whether or not, today, she had done so. She had broken her resolve and she wondered as she buttoned her nightdress if she had the will to draw back now, to move on tomorrow, before things went any further. She lay for a moment with the bedside light on, then reached out and turned it off. She felt as she had often felt when she got to this stage in a bit of business – that some shadow of herself was having its way with her, that if eighty-four thousand pounds hadn't been lifted off her she'd be a different woman entirely.

'Left high and dry,' she murmured in the darkness, applying the expression to the turkey farmer, dozily remembering that it was the one she had used about herself when she'd suffered her calamity.

On the morning after the evening of Mrs Kincaid's visit to his house Blakely was aware of not minding if people had seen her in his car when he'd driven her to her room above Beatty's shop. Her company in his kitchen had not, in the end, been disagreeable. She had washed up the dishes from which they had eaten the food she'd cooked. She had been sympathetic about several matters, and before they left he had shown her the plucking and dressing sheds even though he'd told himself he shouldn't. 'Isn't it lonely for you?' she'd said.

She wasn't in Hirrel's that day, nor the next. She'll have gone, Blakely thought. She had bought him the bottle and now she'd gone back to Belfast. He hadn't been welcoming; he'd been cagey and suspicious, worried in case the Lackys knew she'd cooked his food, worried in case Quin walked in. He was thinking about her when he heard the dogs barking and her voice quietening them.

'I was passing by,' she said.

The friendship that began for Blakely when the Bushmills was poured again and when for the second time a meal was shared in his kitchen was later remarked upon in Hirrel's and in the turkey sheds. Because of his trouble in the past people were pleased, and pleased again when the two were seen together on the steps of the Stella Four-Screen. Reports went round that they'd danced, one Friday night, in the Crest Ballroom; a corner of the bar in Digby's Hotel became known as theirs.

Soon after that the Lackys met Mrs Kincaid, and Quin did. She was brought to Sunday lunch with the Reverend Johnston. One morning Blakely woke up aware of a deep longing for Mrs Kincaid, aware of a gentleness when he thought about her, of an impatience with himself for not declaring his feelings before this.

'Oh no, dear, no.'

She said he was too good for her. Too good a man, she said, too steady a man, too well-set-up, too decent a man. She could bring nothing, she said, she would be coming empty-handed and that was never her way.

Kincaid had left her no more than a pittance, she said, not expecting to be taken so soon, as no man would in the prime of his life. A few years ago Mrs Kincaid had heard talk of a Belfast man who'd electrocuted himself drilling holes in an outside wall: as the cause of Kincaid's demise, that did well enough.

'No, I never could,' she repeated, surveying the astonishment she had known would appear in the lean features, the flush of the cheeks darkening. 'You have your life the way it is,' she said. 'You have your memories. I'd never upset the way things are with you.'

He went silent. Was he thinking he'd made a fool of himself? she wondered. Would he finish his drink and that would be the end of it?

'I'm on my own,' he said.

They were in the bar of the hotel, the quiet time between six and seven. The day before she'd said she'd definitely be off at the end of the week. Refreshed and invigorated, she'd said.

'I'm alone,' he repeated.

'Don't I know you are? Didn't I say you'd be lonely?'

'What I'm saying to you –'

'I know what you're saying to me. What I'm saying to yourself is you're set in your ways. You're well-to-do, I haven't much. Isn't it about that too?'

'It's not money –'

'There's always money.'

The conversation softly became argument. Affection spread through it, real and contrived. It had been great knowing him, Mrs Kincaid said. You come to a place, you gain a friend; nothing was nicer. But Blakely was stubborn. There were feelings in this, he insisted; she couldn't deny it.

'I'm not. I'm not at all. I'm only trying to be fair to you. I have a Belfast woman's caution in me.'

'I'm as cautious myself as any man in Ulster. I have a name for it.'

'You're trusting the unknown all the same. Fair and square, hasn't that to be said?'

'You're never unknown to me.'

'When the cards are down I'm a woman you don't know from a tinker.'

Blakely denied that with a gesture. He didn't say anything. Mrs Kincaid said:

'If I asked you for money, why would you give it to me? I wouldn't do it, but if I did. Who'd blame you for shaking your head? If I said write me a cheque for two thousand pounds who'd blame you for saying no? No man in his senses would say anything else. If I said to you I'd keep that cheque by me, that I'd never pass it into the bank because it was only there as a bond of trust between us, you wouldn't believe me.'

'Why wouldn't I trust you?'

'That's what I'm saying to you. I'm a woman turned up in the town to get away for a little while from the noise and bustle of the city. Who'd blame you if you'd say to yourself I wouldn't trust her as far as an inch? When there's trust between us, is what I'm saying, we'll maybe talk about the other. D'you understand me, dear?'

'We know each other well.'

'We do and we don't, dear. Bad things have happened to us.'

Mrs Kincaid spoke then of the trouble in her past, speaking only the truth, as always she did at this stage in the proceedings.

Blakely felt in the inside pocket of his jacket and took out a Northern Bank cheque-book. He wrote the cheque. He dated it and signed it and tore it out. He handed it to her. She took it, staring at it for as long as a minute. Then she tore it up.

'Please,' he said. 'I mean it.'

'I never knew a straighter man,' Mrs Kincaid said, and for a moment longer the open cheque-book lay between them on the bar-room table. When he reached for it again she said, 'I bank under my maiden name.' She gave him a name, which he added to the *Mabel* he had written while she was speaking. 'That will never be cashed,' she said. 'I promise you that.'

They would not correspond, she laid down. They would wait two months and then they would meet again at the table they were at now, the table they had made their own. They chose a date and a time, a Tuesday at the end of July.

The cheque was for the amount Mrs Kincaid had mentioned. She paid it into her bank as soon as she was back in Belfast and recorded the amount in her notebook. Two days later it reached Blakely's bank and was covered by his standing instruction that if his current account ever did not have sufficient funds in it a transfer should be made from his deposit account. He received his next bank statement sixteen days later.

She could have married the man. The clergyman she'd been introduced to would have done the job. She could have been the wife of a turkey farmer for the rest of her days and she wondered about that – about waking in the farmhouse and the sheepdogs in the yard, about conversations there might have been, their common ground as the victims of gangsters.

Regret nagged Mrs Kincaid then. She felt she had missed a chance she hadn't even known was there. Her instinct was to write a letter, although what she might say in it she didn't know. The more she wondered if she should or not, the more her confidence grew that inspiration would come to her, that in the end she would fill a page or two as easily as she made an entry in her notebook. Time would pass, and she had faith in the way time had of softening anything which was distressful. Naturally the poor man would have been distressed.

Sadness afflicted Blakely, which eased a little while that time went by. Resignation took its place. It was his fault; he had been foolish. His resistance had been there, he had let it slip away. But even so, on the day they had arranged to meet, he put on his suit and went along to Digby's Hotel.

He waited for an hour in their corner of the bar, believing that against the odds there might somehow be an explanation. Then he went away.

Somewhere in him as he drove out of the town there was still a flicker of optimism, although he did not know where it came from or even if what it promised was sensible. He did not dwell upon his mood; it was simply there.

The troubles had returned since Mrs Kincaid had travelled back to Belfast. There had been murder and punishment, the burning of churches, the barricades at Drumcree, the destruction of the town of Omagh. Yet belief in the fragile peace persisted, too precious after so long to abandon. Stubbornly the people of the troubles honoured the hope that had spread among them, fierce in their clamour that it should not go away. In spite of the quiet made noisy again, its benign infection had reached out for Blakely; it did so for Mrs Kincaid also, even though her trouble was her own. Weary at last of making entries in a notebook, she wrote her letter.

The Telephone Game

Since the conventional separation of the sexes on the evening before a wedding did not appeal to Liese, Tony agreed that there should be a party to which both sides of the wedding came instead. A party was necessary because the formalities of the day would not allow for much of a reunion with friends they had not seen for some time, but they did not wish the reception to be an occasion that went on and on in order to cater for this: they wanted to be in Venice in time for the first dinner of their marriage. So in Tony's flat, already re-arranged for married life, his friends and Liese's mixed jollily in advance, while wine flowed generously and there was background music that was danced to, while tomorrow's bride and groom learnt a little more about one another from what was said. Friendships here were longer than their own.

Tonight, there was a solemnity about Liese's manner that softened further the beauty of her features: her mind was on her marriage. Smooth, pale as wheat, her hair fell to her shoulders; her light-blue eyes were a degree less tranquil than usually they were, but when she smiled all that tranquillity came back. 'Oh, Tony, you are lucky,' a cousin who had not met Liese before remarked, and Tony said he knew it. He was fair-haired too, by nature insouciant and humorous, handsome in his way.

In Germany Liese's father was a manufacturer of gloves. In England Tony had been looked after by an aunt ever since his parents died in the worst air disaster of 1977 – the runway collision of two jumbo-jets – when Tony was six, an only child. Nineteen years later he and Liese had met by chance, in a bustling lunchtime restaurant, not far from Victoria Station. 'D'you think we could meet again?' he had pleaded, while a tubby, middle-aged waitress, bringing their coffee in that moment, approved of his boldness and let it show. 00178 was the number on the back of the driver's seat in the first taxi they sat in together, black digits on an oval of white enamel. Afterwards, romantically, they both remembered that, and the taxi-driver's conversation, and the tubby waitress.

Already in love, Liese had heard about the tragedy in 1977, Tony about the gloves that had been the source of livelihood in Liese's family for generations, lambskin and pigskin, goatskin and doeskin. Hand-stitching and dyeing skills, a different way with gussets for the different leathers, were talked about when for the first time Tony visited Schelesnau, when he was shown the long rows of templates and the contented workforce, the knives and thonging tools tidily on their racks. In Schelesnau, driven by love, he played the part required of him, asking questions and showing an interest. Liese was nervous in anticipation before meeting Tony's aunt, who was getting on a bit now in a small South Coast resort with a distant view of the ferries plying back and forth to France. But Liese needn't have been apprehensive. 'She's lovely,' Tony's aunt said, and in Schelesnau – where there were Liese's two younger sisters and a busy family life – Tony was considered charming. There was at first – in Schelesnau and in England – a faint concern that the marriage was taking on a burden that marriage did not always have to, that would have been avoided if Liese had chosen to marry a German or Tony an English girl: after all, there had been enmity in two terrible wars. It was a vague feeling, very much at odds with the sentiments of the time, and although it hovered like some old, long-discredited ghost, it failed in the end to gain a place in the scheme of things. What did, instead, was the telephone game.

On the night before the wedding it was Tony who suggested playing it. Afterwards, he hardly knew why he did, why he had imagined that Germans would understand the humour of the game, but of course he'd had a certain amount to drink. For her part, Liese wished she had insisted that her wedding party wasn't an occasion for this kind of diversion. 'Oh, Tony!' was her single, half-hearted protest, and Tony didn't hear it.

Already he had explained to Liese's sisters – both of whom were to be bridesmaids – that strangers were telephoned, that you won if you held a stranger in conversation longer than anyone else could. The information was passed around the bewildered Germans, who politely wondered what was coming next.

'I am in engine boats,' a man who had been a classmate of Liese's in Fräulein Groenewold's kindergarten was saying when the music was turned off. 'Outboards, you say?'

He, and all the others – more than thirty still left at the party – were asked to be silent then. A number was dialled by Tony's best man and the first of the strangers informed that there was a gas leak in the street, asked to check the rooms of his house for a tell-tale smell, then to return to the phone with information as to that. The next was told that an external fuse had blown, that all electrical connections should be unplugged or turned off to obviate danger. The next was advised to close and lock his windows against a roving polecat.

'The Water Board here,' Tony said when his turn came. 'We're extremely sorry to ring you so late. We have an emergency.'

Some of the German visitors were still perplexed. 'So they are all your friends?' a girl with a plait asked, in spite of what had been said. 'This is a joke with friends?'

Liese explained again that the people who were telephoned were just anyone. The game was to delay, to keep a conversation going. She whispered, in case her voice should carry to Tony's victim. '*Was? Stimmt irgendwas nicht?*' her friend whispered back, and Liese said it was all just for fun. The last call had lasted three and three-quarter minutes, the one before only a few seconds.

'What we would like you to do,' Tony said, 'is to make your way to the water tanks in your loft and turn off the inlet tap. This tap is usually red, madam, but of course the colour may have worn off. What we're endeavouring to do is to prevent the flooding of your house.'

'Flooding?' the woman he spoke to repeated, her voice drowsy with sleep. 'Eh?'

'One of our transformer valves has failed. We have a dangerously high pressure level.'

'I can't go up into the loft at this hour. It's the middle of the night.'

'We're having to ask everyone in the area, madam. Perhaps your husband –'

'I ain't got no husband. I ain't got no one here. I'm seventy-three years of age. How d'you think I'd know about a tap?'

'We're sorry for the inconvenience, madam. We naturally would not ask you to do this if it were not necessary. When a transformer valve goes it is a vital matter. The main articulated valve may go next and then of course it is too late. When the articulated valve goes the flood-water could rise to sixteen feet within minutes. In which case I would advise you to keep to the upstairs rooms.'

Tony put the palm of his hand over the mouthpiece. She had beetled off to get a stepladder, he whispered, and a flashlight. He listened again and said there was the mewing of a cat.

'It'll be all right now?' another German girl leaned forward to ask Liese, and the German who was in outboard engines, who perfectly understood the game, gestured with a smile that it would be. The game was amusing, he considered, but not a game to play in Schelesnau. It was sophisticated. It was the famous English sense of humour.

Tony heard the shuffle of footsteps, a door closing in the distance, and in the distance also the mewing of the cat again. Then there was silence.

Tony looked round his guests, some of them, as he was, a little drunk. He laughed, careless now of allowing the sound to pass to the other

house, since its lone occupant was presumably already in her loft. He put
the receiver down beside the directories on the narrow telephone table,
and reached out with a bottle of Sancerre to attend to a couple of empty
glasses. A friend he'd been at school with began to tell of an occasion
when a man in Hoxton was sent out on to the streets to see if a stolen blue
van had just been parked there. He himself had once posed as the proprietor of a ballroom-dancing school, offering six free lessons. Some of the
Germans said they must be going now.

'Shh.' Listening again, Tony held up a hand. But there was no sound
from the other end. 'She's still aloft,' he said, and put the receiver down
beside the directories.

'Where're you staying?' the best man asked, his lips brushing the cheek
of the girl with the plait as they danced, the music there again. The telephone game had run its course.

'In Germany,' it was explained by the man in outboard motors, 'we
might say this was *Ärgernis*.'

'Oh, here too,' an English girl who did not approve of the telephone
game said. 'If that means harassment.'

Those who remained left in a bunch then, the Germans telling about
Wasservexierungsport, a practical joke involving jets of water. You put
your ten pfennigs into a slot machine to bring the lights on in a grotto and
found yourself drenched instead. 'Water-vexing,' the outboard-motors
man translated.

'You could stay here, you know,' Tony said when he and Liese had collected the glasses and the ashtrays, when everything had been washed and
dried, the cushions plumped up, a window opened to let in a stream of
cold night air.

'But I have yet to finish packing up my things. The morning will be
busy.'

They walked about the flat that soon would be their home, going
from room to room, although they knew the rooms well. Softly, the
music still played, and they danced a little in the small hall, happy to be
alone now. The day they'd met there had been an office party in the busy
lunchtime restaurant, a lot of noise, and a woman in a spotted red dress
quarrelling with her friend at the table next to theirs. How cautious
Liese had been that day was afterwards remembered; and how cautious
she'd been – much later – when Tony said he loved her. Remembered,
too, with that same fondness was how both of them had wanted marriage, not some substitute, how they had wanted the binding of its
demands and vows and rigours. London was the city of their romance

and it was in London – to the discomfort and annoyance of her parents, defying all convention – that Liese had insisted the marriage should take place.

While they danced, Tony noticed that his telephone receiver was still lying beside the directories. More than half an hour ago he had forgotten about it. He reached to pick it up, bringing their dance to an end. He said:

'She hasn't put hers back.'

Liese took the receiver from him. She listened, too, and heard the empty sound of a connected line. 'Hullo,' she said. 'Hullo.'

'She forgot. She went to bed.'

'Would she forget, Tony?'

'Well, something like it.'

'She give a name? You have the number still?'

Tony shook his head. 'She didn't give a name.' He had forgotten the number; he'd probably never even been aware of it, he said.

'What did she say, Tony?'

'Only that she was without a husband.'

'Her husband was out? At this time?'

They had drawn away from one another. Tony turned the music off. He said:

'She meant she was widowed. She wasn't young. Seventy-three or something like that.'

'This old woman goes to her loft –'

'Well, I mean, she said she would. More likely, she didn't believe a word I said.'

'She went to look for a stepladder and a flashlight. You told us.'

'I think she said she was cold in her nightdress. More likely, she just went back to bed. I don't blame her.'

Listening again, Liese said:

'I can hear the cat.'

But when she passed the receiver over, Tony said he couldn't hear anything. Nothing whatsoever, he said.

'Very far away. The cat was mewing, and suddenly it stopped. Don't put it back!' Liese cried when Tony was about to return the receiver to its cradle. 'She is there in her loft, Tony.'

'Oh, honestly, I don't think so. Why should she be? It doesn't take long to turn a stop-cock off.'

'What is a stop-cock?'

'Just a way of controlling the water.'

The mewing of the cat came faintly to him, a single mew and then another. Not knowing why he did so, Tony shook his head again, silently denying this sound. Liese said:

'She could have fallen down. It would be hard to see with her flashlight and she could have fallen down.'

'No, I don't think so.' For the first time in the year and a half she had known him Liese heard a testiness in Tony's voice. There was no point in not replacing the receiver, he said. 'Look, let's forget it, Liese.'

Solemnly, but in distress, Liese gazed into the features of the man she was to marry in just over twelve hours' time. He smiled a familiar, easy smile. No point, he said again, more softly. No point of any kind in going on about this.

'Honestly, Liese.'

They had walked about, that first afternoon. He had taken her through Green Park, then down to the river. She was in London to perfect her English; that afternoon she should have been at another class. And it was a quarter past five before Tony explained, untruthfully, his absence from his desk. The next day they met again.

'Nothing has happened, Liese.'

'She could be dead.'

'Oh, Liese, don't be silly.'

At once, having said that, Tony apologized. Of course she wasn't silly. That game was silly. He was sorry they'd played it tonight.

'But, Tony —'

'Of course she isn't dead.'

'Why do you think you can be sure?'

He shook his head, meaning to indicate that he wasn't claiming to be sure, only that reason implied what he suggested. During the months they were getting to know one another he had learnt that Liese's imagination was sometimes a nuisance; she had said so herself. Purposeless and dispensable, she said, a quirk of nature that caused her, too often, to doubt the surface of things. Music was purposeless, he had replied, the petal of a flower dispensable: what failed the market-place was often what should be treasured most. But Liese called her quirk of nature a pest; and experiencing an instance of it for the first time now, Tony understood.

'Let's not quarrel, Liese.'

But the quarrel — begun already while neither noticed — spread, insidious in the stillness that the silent telephone, once more passed from hand to hand, seemed to inspire. Neither heard the mewing of the cat again, and Tony said:

'Look, in the morning she'll see that receiver hanging there and she'll remember she forgot to put it back.'

'It is morning now. Tony, we could go to the police.'

'The *police*? What on earth for?'

'They could find out where that house is.'

'Oh, none of this makes sense!' And Tony, who happened just then to be holding the telephone receiver, would again have replaced it.

Liese snatched it, anger flushing through her cheeks. She asked him why he'd wanted to do that, and he shrugged and didn't answer. He didn't because all this was ridiculous, because he didn't trust himself to say anything.

'The police couldn't find out,' he said after a silence had gone on. The police wouldn't have a telephone number to go on. All they could tell the police was that in a house somewhere in London there was an old woman and a cat. All over London, Tony said, there were old women and cats.

'Tony, try to remember the number.'

'Oh, for God's sake! How can I remember the bloody number when I didn't even know it in the first place?'

'Well, then it will be in the computers.'

'What computers?'

'In Germany all calls go into the computers.'

Liese didn't know if this was so or not. What she knew was that they could do nothing if he had put the receiver back. Why had he wanted to?

'Darling, we can't,' he was saying now. 'We can't just walk round to a police station at nearly three o'clock in the morning to report that an old woman has gone up to her loft. It was a harmless game, Liese.'

She tried to say nothing, but did not succeed. The words came anyway, unchosen, ignoring her will.

'It is a horrible game. How can it not be horrible when it ends like this?'

The old woman lies there, Liese heard her own voice insist. And light comes up through the open trapdoor, and the stepladder is below. There are the dusty boards, the water pipes. The cat's eyes are pinpricks in the gloom.

'Has she struck her head, Tony? And bones go brittle when you're old. I'm saying what could be true.'

'We have no reason whatsoever to believe any of this has happened.'

'The telephone left hanging –'

'She did not replace the telephone because she forgot to.'

'You asked her to come back. You said to do what you asked and to tell you if it was done.'

'Sometimes people can tell immediately that it's a put-up thing.'

'Hullo! Hullo!' Liese agitatedly shouted into the receiver. 'Hullo . . .
Please.'

'Liese, we have to wait until she wakes up again.'

'At least the cat will keep the mice away.'

Other people will see the lights left on. Other people will come to the
house and find the dangling telephone. Why should an old woman in her
night clothes set a stepladder under a trapdoor? The people who come
will ask that. They'll give the cat a plate of milk and then they'll put the
telephone back, and one of them will climb up the ladder.

'I wish it had happened some other night.'

'Liese —'

'You wanted to put the receiver back. You wanted not to know. You
wanted us for ever not to know, to make a darkness of it.'

'No, of course I didn't.'

'Sometimes a person doesn't realize. A person acts in some way and
doesn't realize.'

'Please,' Tony begged again and Liese felt his arms around her. Tears
for a moment smudged away the room they were in, softly he stroked her
hair. When she could speak she whispered through his murmured consolation, repeating that she wished all this had happened sooner, not tonight.
As though some illness had struck her, she experienced a throbbing ache,
somewhere in her body, she didn't know where. That came from muddle
and confusion was what she thought, or else from being torn apart, as if
she possessed two selves. There was not room for quarrels between them.
There had not been, there was not still. Why had it happened tonight, why
now? Like a hammering in Liese's brain, this repetition went on, began
again as a persistent roundabout. Imagining was Gothic castles and her
own fairytales made up when she was in Fräulein Groenewold's kindergarten, and fantasies with favourite film stars later on. It became a silliness
when reality was distorted. Of course he was right.

'I can't help thinking of her,' Liese whispered none the less. 'I cannot
help it.'

Tony turned away, and slowly crossed to the window. He wanted to be
outside, to walk about the streets, to have a chance to think. He had been
asked to reason with Liese when she wanted her wedding to be in London. A longish letter had come from Schelesnau, pleading with him to
intervene, to make her see sense. It was inconvenient for everyone; it was
an added and unnecessary expense; it was *exzentrisch* of her.

Tonight Liese had learnt that Tony had been daring as a boy, that he
had walked along a ledge from one dormitory window to another, eighteen feet above the ground. She had delighted in that — that he had not told

her himself, that he was courageous and did not boast of it. Yet every-thing seemed different now.

'It is a feeling,' Liese said.

At the window, Tony stared down into the empty street. The artificial light had not yet been extinguished and would not be for hours. Yet dawn had already crept in, among the parked cars, the plastic sacks brought up from basements the night before, bicycles chained to railings. What did she mean, a feeling?

'Honestly, there is no reason to be upset.'

As he spoke, Tony turned from the window. Liese's face was tight and nervous now, for a moment not beautiful. The air that came into the room was refreshingly cold, and again he wanted to be walking in it, alone somewhere. She did not love him was what she meant, she had been taken from him. He said so, staring down into the street again, his back to her.

'Oh no, I love you, Tony.'

All over London, sleeping now, were tomorrow's wedding guests – her mother and her father, her friends come all the way from Schelesnau. Her sisters' bridesmaids' dresses were laid out. Flowers had been ordered, and a be-ribboned car. The grass of the hotel lawns was trimmed for the reception. In her house by the sea Tony's aunt had ironed the clothes she'd chosen, and Liese imagined them waiting on their hangers. The morning flights would bring more guests from Germany. She had been stubborn about the city of their romance. There would have been no old woman's sleep disturbed in Schelesnau, no ugly unintended incident. Why did she know that the dead were carried from a house in a plain long box, not a coffin?

'We are different kinds of people, Tony.'

'Because you are German and I am English? Is that it? That history means something after all?'

She shook her head. Why did he think that? Why did he go off so much in the wrong direction, seizing so readily a useful cliché?

'We are not enemies, we are friends.' She said a little more, trying to explain what did not seem to her to be complicated. Yet she felt she made it so, for the response was bewilderment.

'Remember that office party?' Tony said. 'The quarrelling woman in red? The waitress smiling when we went off together? 00178. Remember that?'

She tried to, but the images would not come as clearly as they usually did. 'Yes, I remember,' she said.

The doubt in their exchanges brought hesitation, was an inflexion that could not be disguised. Silences came, chasms that each time were wider.

'This has to do with us, not with the past we did not know.' Liese shook her head, firm in her emphasis.

Tony nodded and, saying nothing, felt the weight of patience. He wondered about it in a silence that went on for minutes, before there was the far-off rattle of the human voice, faint and small. He looked from the window to where Liese had laid the receiver on the table. He watched her move to pick it up.

They stood together while a clergyman repeated familiar lines. A ring was passed from palm to palm. When the last words were spoken they turned to walk away together from the clergyman and the altar.

The wedding guests strolled on tidy hotel lawns. A photographer fussed beneath a bright blue sky. 'You are more beautiful than I ever knew,' Tony whispered while more champagne was drunk and there was talk in German and in English. 'And I love you more.'

Liese smiled in the moment they had purloined, before another speech was called for, before her father expressed his particular joy that the union of two families brought with it today the union of two nations. 'We are two foolish people,' Tony had said when at last the telephone receiver was replaced, after the journey to the loft had been retailed in detail, an apology offered because carrying out the instructions had taken so long. They had embraced, the warmth of their relief sensual as they clung to one another. And the shadow of truth that had come was lost in the euphoria.

'I'm sorry,' Liese said in the next day's sunshine. 'I'm sorry I was a nuisance.'

Glasses were raised to greater happiness than the happiness of the day. Together they smiled and waved from the car when it came to take them away. Then private at last, they let their tiredness show, each reaching for a hand. Their thoughts were different. He had been right. Yet again, for Tony, that conclusion repeated itself: not for an instant in the night had he doubted that he'd been right. Did love spawn victims? Liese wondered. Had they been warned off a territory of unease that did not yet seem so? Why was it that passing incidents seemed more significant in people's lives and their relationships than the enmity or amity of nations? For a moment Liese wanted to speak of that, and almost did before deciding not to.

The Hill Bachelors

In the kitchen of the farmhouse she wondered what they'd do about her, what they'd suggest. It was up to them; she couldn't ask. It wouldn't be seemly to ask, it wouldn't feel right.

She was a small woman, spare and wiry, her mourning clothes becoming her. At sixty-eight she had ailments: arthritis in her knuckles and her ankles, though only slightly a nuisance to her; a cataract she was not yet aware of. She had given birth without much difficulty to five children, and was a grandmother to nine. Born herself far from the hills that were her home now, she had come to this house forty-seven years ago, had shared its kitchen and the rearing of geese and hens with her husband's mother, until the kitchen and the rearing became entirely her own. She hadn't thought she would be left. She hadn't wanted it. She didn't now.

He walked into the hills from where the bus had dropped him on the main road, by Caslin's petrol pumps and shop across the road from the Master McGrath Bar and Lounge, owned by the Caslins also. It was mid-day and it was fine. After four hours in two different buses he welcomed the walk and the fresh air. He had dressed himself for the funeral so that he wouldn't have to bring the extra clothes in a suitcase he'd have had to borrow. Overnight necessities were in a ragged blue shopping bag which, every working day, accompanied him in the cab of the lorry he drove, delivering sacks of flour to the premises of bakers, and cartons of pre-packed bags to retailers.

Everything was familiar to him: the narrow road, in need of repair for as long as he had known it, the slope rising gently at first, the hills in the far distance becoming mountains, fields and conifers giving way to marsh and a growth that couldn't be identified from where he walked but which he knew was fern, then heather and bog cotton with here and there a patch of grass. Not far below the skyline were the corrie lakes he had never seen.

He was a dark-haired young man of twenty-nine, slightly made, pink cheeks and a certain chubbiness about his features giving him a genial, easygoing air. He was untroubled as he walked on, reflecting only that a drink and a packet of potato crisps at the Master McGrath might have been a good idea. He wondered how Maureen Caslin had turned out; when they were both fifteen he'd thought the world of her.

At a crossroads he turned to the left, on to an unmade-up boreen, scarcely more than a track. Around him there was a silence he remembered also, quite different from the kind of silence he had become used to in or around the midland towns for which, eleven years ago, he had left these hills. It was broken when he had walked another mile by no more than what seemed like a vibration in the air, a faint disturbance that might have been, at some great distance, the throb of an aeroplane. Five minutes later, rust-eaten and muddy, a front wing replaced but not yet painted, Hartigan's old red Toyota clattered over the potholes and the tractor tracks. The two men waved to each other and then the ramshackle car stopped.

'How're you, Paulie?' Hartigan said.

'I'm all right, Mr Hartigan. How're you doing yourself?'

Hartigan said he'd been better. He leaned across to open the passenger door. He said he was sorry, and Paulie knew what he meant. He had wondered if he'd be in luck, if Hartigan would be coming back from Drunbeg this midday. A small, florid man, Hartigan lived higher up in the hills with a sister who was more than a foot taller than he was, a lean, gangling woman who liked to be known only as Miss Hartigan. On the boreen there were no other houses.

'They'll be coming back?' Hartigan enquired above the rasping noise of the Toyota's engine, referring to Paulie's two brothers and two sisters.

'Ah, they will surely.'

'He was out in the big field on the Tuesday.'

Paulie nodded. Hartigan drove slowly. It wasn't a time for conversation, and that was observed.

'Thanks, Mr Hartigan,' Paulie said as they parted, and waved when the Toyota drove on. The sheepdogs barked at him and he patted their heads, recognizing the older one. The yard was tidy. Hartigan hadn't said he'd been down lending a hand but Paulie could tell he had. The back door was open, his mother expecting him.

'It's good you came back,' she said.

He shook his head, realizing as soon as he had made it that the gesture was too slight for her to have noticed. He couldn't not have come back. 'How're you doing?' he said.

'All right. All right.'

They were in the kitchen. His father was upstairs. The others would come and then the coffin would be closed and his father would be taken to the church. That was how she wanted it: the way it always was when death was taken from the house.

'It was never good between you,' she said.

'I'd come all the same.'

Nothing was different in the kitchen: the same green paint, worn away to the timber at two corners of the dresser and around the latch of the doors that led to the yard and to the stairs; the same delft seeming no more chipped or cracked on the dresser shelves, the big scrubbed table, the clutter on the smoky mantel-shelf above the stove, the uncomfortable chairs, the flagged floor, the receipts on the spike in the window.

'Sit with him a while, Paulie.'

His father had always called him Paul, and he was called Paul in his employment, among the people of the midland towns. Paul was what Patsy Finucane called him.

'Go up to him, Paulie. God rest him,' she said, a plea in her tone that bygones should be bygones, that the past should be misted away now that death had come, that prayer for the safe delivery of a soul was what mattered more.

'Will they all come together?' he asked, still sitting there. 'Did they say that?'

'They'll be here by three. Kevin's car and one Aidan'll hire.'

He stood up, his chair scraping on the flagstones. He had asked the questions in order to delay going up to his father's bedside. But it was what she wanted, and what she was saying without saying it was that it was what his father wanted also. There would be forgiveness in the bedroom, his own spoken in a mumble, his father's taken for granted.

He took the rosary she held out to him, not wishing to cause offence.

Hearing his footsteps on the brief, steeply pitched stairs, hearing the bedroom door open and close, the footsteps again in the room above her, then silence, she saw now what her returned son saw: the bloodless pallor, the stubble that had come, eyelids drawn, lips set, the grey hair she had combed. Frances had been the favourite, then Mena; Kevin was approved of because he was reliable; Aidan was the first-born. Paulie hadn't been often mentioned.

There was the sound of a car, far back on the boreen. A while it would take to arrive at the farmhouse. She set out cups and saucers on the table, not hurrying. The kettle had boiled earlier and she pushed it back on to the hot plate of the stove. Not since they were children had they all been back at the same time. There wouldn't be room for them for the two nights they'd have to spend, but they'd have their own ideas about how to manage that. She opened the back door so that there'd be a welcome.

*

Paulie looked down at the stretched body, not trusting himself to address it in any way. Then he heard the cars arriving and crossed the room to the window. In the yard Frances was getting out of one and the other was being backed so that it wouldn't be in the way, a white Ford he'd never seen before. The window was open at the top and he could hear the voices, Kevin saying it hadn't been a bad drive at all and Aidan agreeing. The Ford was hired, *Cahill of Limerick* it said on a sticker; picked up at Shannon it would have been.

The husbands of Paulie's sisters hadn't come, maybe because of the shortage of sleeping space. They'd be looking after the Dublin children, and it seemed that Kevin's Sharon had stayed behind with theirs in Carlow. Aidan had come on his own from Boston. Paulie had never met Aidan's wife and Sharon only once; he'd never met any of the children. They could have managed in a single car, he calculated, watching his brothers and sisters lifting out their suitcases, but it might have been difficult to organize, Kevin having to drive round by Shannon.

His brothers wore black ties, his sisters were in mourning of a kind, not entirely, because that could wait till later. Mena looked pregnant again. Kevin had a bald patch now. Aidan took off the glasses he had worn to drive. Their suitcases weren't heavy. You could tell there was no intention to stay longer than was necessary.

Looking down into the yard, Paulie knew that an assumption had already been made, as he had known it in the kitchen when he sat there with his mother. He was the bachelor of the family, the employment he had wasn't much. His mother couldn't manage on her own.

He had known it in Meagher's back bar when he told Patsy Finucane he had a funeral to go to. The death had lost him Patsy Finucane: it was her, not his father, he thought about when he heard of it, and in Meagher's the stout ran away with him and he spoke too soon. 'Jeez,' she said, 'what would I do in a farmhouse!'

Afterwards – when the journey through the hills had become a funeral procession at the edge of the town, when the coffin had been delivered to its night's resting place, and later when the burial was complete and the family had returned to the farmhouse and had dispersed the next morning – Paulie remained.

He had not intended to. He had hoped to get a lift in one of the two cars, and then to take a bus, and another bus, as he had on his journey over.

'Where is it they'll separate?' his mother asked in the quietness that followed the departure.

He didn't know. Somewhere that was convenient; in some town they would pull in and have a drink, different now that they weren't in a house of mourning. They would exchange news it hadn't seemed right to exchange before. Aidan would talk about Boston, offering his sisters and his brother hospitality there.

'Warm yourself at the fire, Paulie.'

'Wait till I see to the heifers first.'

'His boots are there.'

'I know.'

His brothers had borrowed the gum boots, too; wherever you went, you needed them. Kevin had fixed a fence, Aidan had got the water going again in the pipe up to the sheep. Between them, they'd taken the slack out of the barbed wire beyond the turf bog.

'Put on a waterproof, Paulie.'

It wasn't going to rain, but the waterproof kept the wind out. Whenever he remembered the farmhouse from his childhood it was windy – the fertilizer bags blowing about in the yard, blustery on the track up to the sheep hills, in the big field that had been the family's mainstay ever since his father had cleared the rocks from it, in the potato field. Wind, more than rain or frost, characterized the place, not that there wasn't a lot of rain too. But who'd mind the rain? his father used to say.

The heifers didn't need seeing to, as he had known they wouldn't. They stood, miserably crouched in against the wall of a fallen barn, mud that the wind had dried hanging from them. His father had taken off the roof when one of the other walls had collapsed, needing the corrugated iron for somewhere else. He'd left the standing wall for the purpose the heifers put it to now.

Paulie, too, stood in the shelter of the wall, the puddles at his feet not yet blown dry, as the mud had on the animals. He remembered the red roof lifted down, piece by piece, Kevin waiting below to receive it, Aidan wrenching out the bolts. He had backed the tractor, easing the trailer close to where they were. 'What's he want it for?' he'd asked Kevin, and Kevin said the corrugated iron would be used for filling the gaps in the hedges.

Slowly, Paulie walked back the way he had come. 'D'you think of coming back?' Aidan had said, saying it in the yard when they were alone. Paulie had known it would be said and had guessed it would be Aidan who'd say it, Aidan being the oldest. 'I'm only mentioning it,' Aidan had said. 'I'm only touching on it.'

Blowing at the turf with the wheel-bellows, she watched the glow spread, sparks rising and falling away. It hadn't been the time to make arrangements or even to talk about them. Nothing could have been more out of place, and she was glad they realized that. Kevin had had a word with Hartigan after the funeral, something temporary fixed up, she could tell from the gestures.

They'd write. Frances had said she would, and Aidan had. Sharon would write for Kevin, as she always did. Mena would. Wherever it was they stopped to say good-bye to one another they'd talk about it and later on they'd write.

'Sit down, Paulie, sit down,' she said when her son came in, bringing the cold with him.

She said again that Father Kinally had done it beautifully. She'd said so yesterday to her daughters in the car, she'd said it to Kevin and to Aidan this morning. Paulie would have heard, yet you'd want to repeat it. You felt the better for it.

'Ah, he did,' Paulie said. 'He did of course.'

He'd taken over. She could feel he'd taken over, the way he'd gone out to see were the heifers all right, the way it was he who remembered, last evening and this morning, that there was the bit of milking to do, that he'd done it without a word. She watched him ease off the gum boots and set them down by the door. He hung the waterproof on the door hook that was there for it and came to the fire in his socks, with his shoes in one hand. She turned away so that he wouldn't notice she'd been reminded of his father coming into the kitchen also.

'Aren't the heifers looking good?' she said.

'Oh, they are, they are.'

'He was pleased with them this year.'

'They're not bad, all right.'

'Nothing's fetching at the minute, all the same.'

He nodded. He naturally would know times were bad, neither sheep nor cattle fetching what they were a year ago, everything gone quiet, the way you'd never have believed it.

'We're in for the night so,' she said.

'We are.'

She washed the eggs Mena had collected earlier, brushing off the marks on them, then wiped the shells clean before she piled them in the bowl. The eggs would keep them going, with the rashers left over and half a saucepan of stew in the fridge. 'You've enough for an army!' Kevin had said, looking into the deep-freeze, and she reminded him you had to have enough in case the weather came in bad.

'What'd we do without it?' she said now, mentioning the deep-freeze. They'd had half a pig from the Caslins, only a portion of the belly used up so far. 'And mutton till Doomsday,' she said.

'How're they these days, the Caslins? I didn't notice Maureen at the funeral.'

'Maureen married a man in Tralee. She's there since.'

'Who's the man?'

'He's in a shoe shop.'

They could have gone to the wedding only it had been a period of the year when you wouldn't want to spare the time. The Hartigans had gone. They'd have taken her but she'd said no.

'Hartigan came back drunk, you should have seen the cut of him! And herself with a frost on her that would have quenched the fire!'

'He's driving down in the morning. He'll pick me up.'

Rashers and black pudding and fried bread were ready on the pan. She cracked two eggs into the fat, turned them when they were ready because he liked them turned. When she placed the plate in front of him he took a mouthful of tea before he ate anything. He said:

'You couldn't manage. No way.'

'It wasn't a time to talk about it, Paulie.'

'I'll come back.'

He began to eat, the yolk of the eggs spreading yellow on the plate. He left the black pudding and the crisp fat of the bacon until last. He'd always done that.

'Hartigan'd still come down. I'm all right on the bit of milking. I'm all right on most things. The Caslins would come up.'

'You couldn't live like that.'

'They're neighbours, Paulie. They got help from himself if they wanted it. I looked over and saw Kevin having a word with Hartigan in the grave-yard. It won't be something for nothing, not with Hartigan. Kevin'll tell me later.'

'You'd be dependent.'

'You have your own life, Paulie.'

'You have what there is.'

He ate for several minutes in silence, then he finished the tea that had been poured for him.

'I'd have to give in notice. I'd have to work the notice out. A month.'

'Think it over before you'll do anything, Paulie.'

Paulie harboured no resentment, not being a person who easily did: going back to the farmhouse was not the end of the world. The end of the world had been to hear, in Meagher's back bar, that life on a farm did not attract Patsy Finucane.

As soon as he'd mentioned marriage that day he knew he shouldn't have. Patsy Finucane had taken fright like a little young greyhound would. She'd hardly heard him when he said, not knowing what else to say, 'Ah well, no matter.' It was a nervousness mixed in with the stout that had caused him to make the suggestion, and as soon as he had there was no regaining her: before she looked away that was there in her soft grey eyes. 'I won't go back so,' he'd said, making matters worse. 'I won't go back without you.'

When they sat again in Meagher's back bar after the funeral Paulie tried to put things right; he tried to begin again, but it wasn't any good. During the third week of his working out his notice Patsy Finucane began to go out with a clerk from the post office.

In the yard she threw down grains for the hens and remembered doing it for the first time, apprehensive then about what she'd married into. Nor had her apprehension been misplaced: more than she'd imagined, her position in the household was one of obedience and humility, and sometimes what was said, or incidents that occurred, left a sting that in private drew tears from her. Yet time, simply in passing, transformed what seemed to be immutable. Old age enfeebled on the one hand; on the other, motherhood nurtured confidence. In the farmhouse, roles were reversed.

She didn't want distress like that for any wife Paulie would eventually bring to the kitchen and the house. She would make it easier, taking a back seat from the start and be glad to do so. It was only a pity that Maureen Caslin had married the shoe-shop man, for Maureen Caslin would have suited him well. There were the sisters, of course.

During the weeks that followed Paulie's departure, the anticipated letters came from Mena and Frances and from her daughter-in-law Sharon on behalf of Kevin, and from Aidan. The accumulated content was simple, the unstated expectation stated at last, four times over in different handwriting. Aidan said he and Paulie had had a talk about it. *You are good to think of me*, she wrote back, four times also.

Hartigan continued to come down regularly and a couple of times his sister accompanied him, sitting in the kitchen while he saw to any heavy work in the yard. 'Would Mena have room for you?' she enquired on one of these occasions, appearing to forget that Paulie was due to return when he'd worked out his notice. Miss Hartigan always brought sultana bread when she came and they had it with butter on it. 'I only mentioned Mena,' she said, 'in case Paulie wouldn't be keen to come back. I was thinking he maybe wouldn't.'

'Why's that, Miss Hartigan?'

'It's bachelors that's in the hills now. Like himself,' Miss Hartigan added, jerking her bony head in the direction of the yard, where her brother was up on a ladder, fixing a gutter support.

'Paulie's not married either, though.'

'That's what I'm saying to you. What I'm saying is would he want to stop that way?'

Miss Hartigan's features were enriched by a keenness to say more, to inform and explain, to dispel the bewilderment she had caused. She did so after a pause, politely reaching for a slice of sultana bread. It might not have been noticed that these days the bachelors of the hills found it difficult to attract a wife to the modest farms they inherited.

'Excuse me for mentioning it,' Miss Hartigan apologized before she left.

It was true, and it had been noticed and often remarked upon. Hartigan himself, twenty years ago, was maybe the first of the hill bachelors: by now you could count them – lone men, some of them kept company by a mother or a sister – on the slopes of Coumpeebra, on Slievenacoush, on Knockrea, on Luirc, on Clydagh.

She didn't remember putting all that from her mind when Paulie had said he would come back, but perhaps she had. She tried not to think about it, comforting herself that what had been said, and the tone of Miss Hartigan's voice, had more to do with Miss Hartigan and her brother than with the future in a neighbouring farmhouse. Nor did it necessarily need to be that what had already happened would continue to happen. The Hartigans' stretch of land was worse by a long way than the land lower down on the hill; no better than the side of Slievenacoush, or Clydagh or Coumpeebra. You did the best you could, you hoped for warm summers. Paulie was a good-looking, decent boy; there was no reason at all why he wouldn't bring up a family here as his father had.

'There's two suitcases left down with the Caslins,' he said when he walked in one Saturday afternoon. 'When I get the car started I'll go down for them.'

They didn't embrace; there'd never been much of that in the family. He sat down and she made tea and put the pan on. He told her about the journey, how a woman had been singing on the first of the two buses, how he'd fallen asleep on the second. He was serious the way he told things, his expression intent, sometimes not smiling much. He'd always been like that.

'Hartigan started the car a while back,' she said, 'to make sure it was in form.'

'And it was? All right?'

'Oh, it was, it was.'

'I'll take a look at it later.'

He settled in easily, and she realized as he did so that she had never known him well. He had been lost to her in the family, his shadowy place in it influenced by his father's lack of interest in him. She had never protested about that, only occasionally whispering a surreptitious word or two of comfort. It was fitting in a way that a twist of fate had made him his father's inheritor.

As if he had never been away, he went about his daily tasks knowledgeably and efficiently. He had forgotten nothing – about the winter feed for the heifers, about the work around the yard or where the fences might give way on the hills or how often to go up there after the sheep, about keeping the tractor right. It seemed, which she had not suspected before, that while his presence was so often overlooked he had watched his father at work more conscientiously than his brothers had. 'He'd be proud of you these days,' she said once, but Paulie did not acknowledge that and she resisted making the remark again. The big field, which had been his father's pride, became his. There was another strip to the south of it that could be cleared and reclaimed, he said, and he took her out to show her where he would run the new wall. They stood in the sunshine on a warm June morning while he pointed and talked about it, the two sheepdogs obedient by him. He was as good with them as his father ever had been.

He drove her, as his father had, every three weeks down to Drunbeg, since she had never learned to drive herself. His father used to wait in the car park of Conlon's Supermarket while she shopped, but Paulie always went in with her. He pushed the trolley and sometimes she gave him a list and he added items from the shelves. 'Would we go and see that?' he suggested one time when they were passing the Two-Screen Rialto, which used to be just the Picture House before it was given a face-lift. She wouldn't be bothered, she said. She'd never been inside the cinema, either in the old days or since it had become a two-screen; the television was enough for her. 'Wouldn't you take one of the Caslin girls?' she said.

He took the older of them, Aileen, and often after that he drove down in the evenings to sit with her in the Master McGrath. The relationship came to an end when Aileen announced that her sister in Tralee had heard of a vacancy in a newsagent and confectioner's, that she'd been to Tralee herself to be looked over and in fact had been offered the position.

'And did you know she had intentions that way?' Paulie's mother asked him when she heard, and he said he had, in a way. He didn't seem put about, although she had assumed herself that by the look of things Aileen Caslin – stolid and on the slow side – would be the wife who'd come to the farmhouse, since her sister Maureen was no longer available. Paulie didn't talk about it, but quite soon after Aileen's departure he began to take an interest in a girl at one of the pay-outs in Conlon's.

'Wouldn't you bring Maeve out one Sunday?' his mother suggested when the friendship had advanced, when there'd been visits to the two-screen and evenings spent together drinking, as there'd been with Aileen Caslin. Maeve was a fair bit livelier than Aileen; he could do worse.

But Maeve never came to the farmhouse. In Conlon's Paulie took to steering the trolley to one of the other pay-outs even when the queue at hers was shorter. His mother didn't ask why. He had his own life, she kept reminding herself; he had his privacy, and why shouldn't he? 'Isn't he the good boy to you?' Father Kinally remarked one Sunday after Mass when Paulie was turning the car. 'Isn't it grand the way it's turned out for you?'

She knew it was and gratefully gave thanks for it. Being more energetic than his father had been at the end, Paulie worked a longer day, far into the evening when it was light enough.

'I don't know did I ever speak a word to her,' she said when he began to go out with the remaining Caslin daughter. Sensible, she looked.

'Ah, sure, anything,' the youngest of the three Caslin girls always said when Paulie told her what films were on and asked which she'd like to see. When the lights went down he waited a bit before he put an arm around her, as he always had with her sisters and with Maeve. He hadn't been able to wait with Patsy Finucane.

The sensible look that Paulie's mother had noted in Annie Caslin was expressed in a matter-of-fact manner. Sentiment played little part in her stalwart, steady nature. She was the tallest and in a general way the biggest of the three Caslin girls, with black hair that she curled and distinctive features that challenged one another for dominance – the slightly large nose, the wide mouth, the unblinking gaze. Paulie took her out half a dozen times before she confessed that what she wanted to do was to live in a town. She'd had the roadside Master McGrath, she said; she'd had serving petrol at the pumps. 'God, I don't know how you'd stand it up in the bogs,' she said before Paulie had a chance to ask her if she'd be interested in coming up to the farmhouse. Even Drunbeg would do her, she said, and got work six months later in the fertilizer factory.

Paulie asked other girls to go out with him, but by then it had become known that what he was after was marriage. One after another, they made excuses, a fact that Hartigan was aware of when he pulled up the Toyota one morning beside a gateway where Paulie was driving in posts. He didn't say anything, but often Hartigan didn't.

'Will it rain, Mr Hartigan?' Paulie asked him.

'The first time I saw your mammy,' Hartigan said, rejecting a discussion about the weather, 'she was stretching out sheets on the bushes. Six years of age I was, out after a hare.'

'A while ago, all right.'

'Amn't I saying it to you?'

Not understanding the conversation, Paulie vaguely shook his head. He struck the post he was easing into the ground another blow. Hartigan said:

'I'd take the big field off you.'

'Ah no, no.'

That was why he had stopped. It might even have been that he'd driven down specially when he heard the thud of the sledgehammer on the posts, saying to himself that it was a good time for a conversation.

'I wouldn't want to sell the field, Mr Hartigan.'

'But wouldn't you do well all the same if you did? Is it a life at all for a young fellow?'

Paulie didn't say anything. He felt the post to see if it was steady yet. He struck it again, three times before he was satisfied.

'You need a bit of company, boy,' Hartigan said before he backed into the gateway and drove up the hill again.

What she had succeeded in keeping at bay since Miss Hartigan had spoken of it was no longer possible to evade. When Paulie told her about Patsy Finucane she was pleased that he did, glad that he didn't keep it to himself. She knew about everything else: it was all of a piece that Hartigan was trying to get the land cheap by taking advantage of the same circumstances that had left him a bachelor himself. Who could blame him? she said to herself, but even so she wondered if Paulie – so agreeable and good-hearted – would become like that in his time; if he'd become hard, as his father had been, and as grasping as Hartigan.

'I'll go to Mena,' she said. 'There's room there.'

'Ah, there isn't.'

'They'd fit me in.'

'It's here there's room.'

'You want to be married, Paulie. Any man does.'

'He'd take a day shifting a boulder with the tractor. He'd put a ditch through the marsh to gain another half yard. He never minded how long a thing took.'

'It's now we're talking about, Paulie.'

'There'd be sheep in this house within a twelvemonth if Hartigan had it, the doors taken off and made use of, and the next thing is the wind'd be shifting the slates. There'd be grazing taken out of the big field until there wasn't a blade of grass left standing. The marsh'd come in again. No one'd lift a finger.'

'You didn't know what you were coming back to.'

'Ah, I did. I did.'

Obligingly, he lied. You'd say to yourself he was easygoing. When he'd told her about the Finucane girl he'd said it was the way things were. No matter, he'd said. Often you'd forget he wasn't easygoing at all; often she did.

'There's no need, Paulie.'

'There is.'

He said it quietly, the two words hanging there after he had spoken, and she realized that although it was her widowhood that had brought him back it wasn't her widowhood that made him now insist he must remain. She could argue for ever and he would not go now.

'You're good, Paulie,' she said, since there was nothing else left to say.

He shook his head, his dark hair flopping from side to side. 'Arrah, no.'

'You are. You are, Paulie.'

When her own death came, her other children would return, again all at the same time. The coffin would be carried down the steep stairs, out into the van in the yard, and the funeral would go through the streets of Drunbeg, and the next day there'd be the Mass. They'd go away then, leaving Paulie in the farmhouse.

'Wait till I show you,' he said, and he took her out to where he was draining another half yard. He showed her how he was doing it. He showed her the temporary wall he had put up, sheets of red corrugated that had come from the old shed years ago.

'That's great,' she said. 'Great, Paulie.'

A mist was coming in off the hills, soft and gentle, the clouds darkening above it. The high edge of Slievenacoush was lost. Somewhere over the boglands a curlew cried.

'Go in out of the drizzle,' he said, when they had stood there for a few minutes.

'Don't stay out long yourself, Paulie.'

Guilt was misplaced, goodness hardly came into it. Her widowing and the mood of a capricious time were not of consequence, no more than a flicker in a scheme of things that had always been there. Enduring, unchanging, the hills had waited for him, claiming one of their own.

Sitting with the Dead

His eyes had been closed and he opened them, saying he wanted to see the stable-yard.

Emily's expression was empty of response. Her face, younger than his and yet not seeming so, was empty of everything except the tiredness she felt. 'From the window?' she said.

No, he'd go down, he said. 'Will you get me the coat? And have the boots by the door.'

She turned away from the bed. He would manage on his own if she didn't help him: she'd known him for twenty-eight years, been married to him for twenty-three. Whether or not she brought the coat up to him would make no difference, any more than it would if she protested.

'It could kill you,' she said.

'The fresh air'd strengthen a man.'

Downstairs, she placed the boots ready for him at the back door. She brought his cap and muffler to him with his overcoat. A stitch was needed where the left sleeve met the shoulder, she noticed. She hadn't before and knew he wouldn't wait while she repaired it now.

'What're you going to do there?' she asked, and he said nothing much. Tidy up a bit, he said.

He died eight days later, and Dr Ann explained that tidying the stable-yard with only a coat over his pyjamas wouldn't have hastened anything. An hour after she left, the Geraghtys came to the house, not knowing that he was dead.

It was half past seven in the evening then. At the same time the next morning, Keane the undertaker was due. She said that to the Geraghtys, making sure they understood, not wanting them to think she was turning them away for some other reason. Although she knew that if her husband had been alive he wouldn't have agreed to have the Geraghtys at his bedside. It was a relief that they had come too late.

The Geraghtys were two middle-aged women, sisters, the Misses Geraghty, who sat with the dying. Emily had heard of them, but did not know them, not even to see: they'd had to give their name when she opened the door to them. It had never occurred to her that the Geraghtys would attempt to bring their good works to the sick-room she had lived with herself for the last seven months. They were Legion of Mary women, famed for their charity, tireless in their support of the Society of St Vincent de Paul and their promulgation of the writings of Father Xavier O'Shea, a local priest who, at a young age in the 1880s, had contracted malaria in the mission fields of the East.

'We only heard of your trouble Tuesday,' the thinner and smaller of the two apologized. 'It does happen the occasional time we wouldn't hear.'

The other woman, more robust and older, allowed herself jewellery and make-up and took more care with her clothes. But it was her quiet, sharp-featured sister who took the lead.

'We heard in MacClincy's,' she said.

'I'm sorry you've had a wasted journey.'

'It's never wasted.' There was a pause, as if a pause was necessary here. 'You have our sympathy,' was added to that, the explanation of why the journey had not been in vain.

The conversation took place entirely at the hall door. Dusk was becoming dark, but over the white-washed wall of the small front garden Emily still could see a car drawn up in the road. It was cold, the wind gone round to the east. They meant well, these women, even if they'd got everything wrong, driving out from Carra to visit a man who wouldn't have welcomed them and then arriving too late, a man whose death had spared them an embarrassment.

'Would you like a cup of tea?' Emily offered.

She imagined they'd refuse and then begin to go, saying they couldn't disturb her at a time like this. But the big, wide-shouldered one glanced at her sister, hesitating.

'If you're alone,' the smaller one said, 'you'd be welcome to our company. If it would be of help to you.'

The dead man had been without religion. Anyone could have told them that, Emily reflected, making tea. He would have said that there was more to their sitting at the bedsides of the ill than met the eye, and she wondered if that could possibly be so. Did they in their compassionate travels hope for the first signs of the belief that often came out of nowhere when death declared its intention? Did they drive away from the houses they visited, straight to a presbytery, their duty done? She had never heard that said about the Geraghtys and she didn't want to believe it. They meant well, she said to herself again.

When they left, she wouldn't go back upstairs to look at the dead features. She'd leave him now to Keane in the morning. In the brief time that had elapsed a day had been settled for the funeral, Thursday of next week; in the morning she would let a few people know; she'd put a notice in the *Advertiser*. No children had been born: when Thursday had passed everything would be over except for the unpaid debts. She buttered slices of brack and stirred the tea in the pot. She carried in the tray.

They hadn't taken their coats off, but sat as still as statues, a little apart from one another.

'It's cold,' she said, 'I'll light the fire.'

'Ah no. Ah no, don't bother.' They both protested, but she did anyway, and the kindling that had been in the grate all summer flared up at once. She poured their tea, asking if they took sugar, and then offering the brack. They began to call her Emily, as if they knew her well. They gave their own names: Kathleen the older sister, and Norah.

'I didn't think,' Kathleen began to say, and Norah interrupted her.

'Oh, we know all right,' she said. 'You're Protestant here, but that never made a difference yet.'

They had sat with the Methodist minister, the Reverend Wolfe, Kathleen said. They'd read to him, they'd brought in whatever he wanted. They were there when he went.

'Never a difference,' Norah repeated, and in turn they took a slice of brack. They commented on it, saying it was excellent.

'It isn't easy,' Kathleen said when the conversation lapsed. 'The first few hours. We often stay.'

'It was good of you to think of him.'

'It's cheerful with that fire, Emily,' Kathleen said.

They asked her about the horses because the horses were what they'd heard about, and she explained that they'd become a thing of the past. She'd sell the place now, she said.

'You'd find it remote, Emily,' Kathleen said. Her lipstick had left a trace on the rim of the teacup and Norah drew her attention to it with a gesture. Kathleen wiped it off. 'We're town people ourselves,' she said.

Emily didn't consider the house she'd lived in for nearly thirty years remote. Five minutes in the car and you were in the middle of Carra. Mangan's Bridge, in the other direction, was no more than a minute.

'You get used to a place,' Emily said.

They identified for her the house where they lived themselves, on the outskirts of Carra, on the Athy road. Emily knew it, a pleasant creeper-covered house with silver railings in front of it, not big but prosperous-looking. She'd thought it was Corrigan's, the surveyor's.

'I don't know why I thought that.'

'We bought it from Mr Corrigan,' Norah said, 'when we came to Carra three years ago.' And her sister said they'd been living in Athy before that.

'Carra was what we were looking for,' Norah said.

They were endeavouring to lift her spirits, Emily realized, by keeping things light. Carra had improved in their time, they said, and it would again. You could tell with a town; some of them wouldn't rise out of the doldrums while a century'd go by.

'You'd maybe come in to Carra now?' Kathleen said.

'I don't know what I'll do.'

She poured more tea. She handed round the brack again. Dr Ann had given her pills to take, but she didn't intend to take them. Exhausted as she was, she didn't want to sleep.

'He went out a week ago,' she said. 'He got up and went out to the yard with only a coat over his pyjamas. I thought it was that that hurried it on, but seemingly it wasn't.'

They didn't say anything, just nodded, both of them. She said he had been seven months dying. He hadn't read a newspaper all that time, she said. In the end all the food he could manage was cornflour.

'We never knew your husband,' Norah said, 'any more than yourself. Although I think we maybe met him on the road one day.'

A feeling of apprehension began in Emily, a familiar dread that compulsively caused one hand to clench the other, fingers tightly locking. People often met him, exercising one of the horses. A car would slow down for him but he never acknowledged it, never so much as raised the crop. For a moment she forget that he was dead.

'He was often out,' she said.

'Oh, this was long ago.'

'He sold the last of the horses twelve months ago. He didn't want them left.'

'He raced his horses, we're to understand?' Kathleen said.

'Point-to-points. Punchestown the odd time.'

'Well, that's great.'

'There wasn't much success.'

'It's an up and down business, of course.'

Disappointment had filled the house when yet again a horse trailed in, when months of preparation went for nothing. There had never been much reason for optimism, but even so expectation had been high, as if anything less would have brought bad luck. When Emily married, her husband had been training a string of yearlings on the Curragh. Doing well, he'd said himself, although in fact he wasn't.

'You never had children, Emily?' Kathleen asked.

'No, we never did.'

'I think we heard that said.'

The house had been left to her by an aunt on her mother's side. Forty-three acres, sheep kept; and the furniture had been left to her too. 'I used come here as a child. A Miss Edgill my aunt was. Did you hear of her?'

They shook their heads. Way before their time, Kathleen said, looking around her. A good house, she said.

'She'd no one else to leave it to.' And Emily didn't add that neither the property nor the land would ever have become hers if her aunt had suspected she'd marry the man she had.

'You'll let it go though?' Kathleen pursued her enquiries, doing her best to knit together a conversation. 'The way things are now, you were saying you'd let it go?'

'I don't know.'

'Anyone would require a bit of time.'

'We see a lot of widowing,' Norah murmured.

'Nearly to the day, we were married twenty-three years.'

'God took him because He wanted him, Emily.'

The Geraghtys continued to offer sympathy, one following the other in what was said, the difference in tone and manner continuing also. And again – and more often as more solace was pressed upon her – Emily reflected how fortunate it was that they had escaped the awkwardness of attempting to keep company with her husband. He would have called her back as soon as she'd left them with him. He would have asked her who they were, although he knew; he would have told her to take them away. He'd never minded what he said – the flow of coarse language when someone crossed one of the fields, every word shouted out, frighteningly sometimes. It was always that: raising his voice, the expressions he used; not once, not ever, had there been violence. Yet often she had wished that there had been, believing that violence would have been easier to bear than the power of his articulated anger. It was power she had always felt coming from him, festering and then released, his denial of his failure.

'The horses. Punchestown. The world of the race-course,' Kathleen said. 'You've had an interesting life, Emily.'

It seemed to Emily that Norah was about to shake her head, that for the first time the sisters were on the verge of a disagreement. It didn't surprise her: the observation that had been made astonished her.

'Unusual is what my sister means.' Norah nodded her correction into place, her tone softening the contradiction.

'There's many a woman doesn't get out and about,' Kathleen said.

Emily poured more tea and added turf to the fire. She had forgotten to draw the curtains over and she did so now. The light in the room was dim; he'd been particular about low-wattage electric bulbs. But the dimness made the room cosy and it seemed wrong that anywhere should be so while he lay only a few hours dead. She wondered what she'd do when another bulb went, either here or somewhere else, if she would replace it with a stronger one or if low-wattage light was part of her now. She wondered if her nervousness was part of her too. It didn't seem that it had always been, but she knew she could be wrong about that.

'I didn't go out and about much,' she said because a silence in the conversation had come. Both visitors were stirring sugar into their tea. When their teaspoons were laid down, Norah said:

'There's some wouldn't bother with that.'

'He was a difficult man. People would have told you.'

They did not contradict that. They did not say anything. She said:

'He put his trust in the horses. Since childhood what he wanted was to win races, to be known for it. But he never managed much.'

'Poor man,' Kathleen murmured. 'Poor man.'

'Yes.'

She shouldn't have complained, she hadn't meant to: Emily tried to say that, but the words wouldn't come. She looked away from the women who had visited her, gazing about her at the furniture of a room she knew too well. He had been angry when she'd taken the curtains down to wash them; everyone staring in, he'd said, and she hadn't known what he'd meant. Hardly anyone passed by on the road.

'He married me for the house,' she said, unable to prevent herself from saying that too. The women were strangers, she was speaking ill of the dead. She shook her head in an effort to deny what she'd said, but that seemed to be a dishonesty, worse than speaking ill.

The women sipped their tea, both lifting the cups to their lips in the same moment.

'He married me for the forty acres,' Emily said, compelled again to say what she didn't want to. 'I was a Protestant girl that got passed by until he made a bid for me and I thought it was romantic, like he did himself – the race cards, the race ribbons, the jockeys' colours, the big crowd there'd be. That's how it happened.'

'Ah now, now,' Kathleen said. 'Ah now, dear.'

'I was a fool and you pay for foolishness. I was greedy for what marriage might be, and you pay for greed. We'd a half acre left after what was paid back a year ago. There's a mortgage he took out on the house. I could have said to him all the time he was dying, "What'll I do?" But I didn't, and he didn't say anything either. God knows what his last thoughts were.'

They told her she was upset. One after the other they told her any widow would be, that it was what you had to expect. Norah said it twice. Kathleen said she could call on them in her grief.

'There's no grief in the house you've come to.'

'Ah now, now,' Kathleen said, her big face puckered in distress. 'Ah, now.'

'He never minded how the truth came out, whether he'd say it or not. He didn't say I was a worthless woman, but you'd see it in his eyes. Another time, I'd sweep the stable-yard and he'd say what use was that. He'd push a plate of food away untouched. We had two collies once and they were company. When they died he said he'd never have another dog. The vet wouldn't come near us. The man who came to read the meter turned surly under the abuse he got for driving his van into the yard.'

'There's good and bad in everyone, Emily.' Norah whispered that opinion and, still whispering, repeated it.

'Stay where you are, Emily,' Kathleen said, 'and I'll make another pot of tea.'

She stood up, the teapot already in her hand. She was used to making tea in other people's kitchens. She'd find her way about, she said.

Emily protested, but even while she did she didn't care. In all the years of her marriage another woman hadn't made tea in that kitchen, and she imagined him walking in from the yard and finding someone other than herself there. The time she began to paint the scullery, it frightened her when he stood in the doorway, before he even said a thing. The time she dropped the sugar bag and the sugar spilt out all over the floor he watched her sweeping it on to the dustpan, turf dust going with it. He said what was she doing, throwing it away when it was still fit to stir into your tea? The scullery had stayed half-painted to this day.

'He lived in a strangeness of his own,' Emily said to the sister who was left in the room with her. 'Even when he was old, he believed a horse could still reclaim him. Even when the only one left was diseased and fit for nothing. When there was none there at all he scoured the empty stables and got fresh straw in. He had it in mind to begin all over again, to find some animal going cheap. He never said it, but it was what he had in mind.'

The house wasn't clean. It hadn't been clean for years. She'd lost heart in the house, and in herself, in the radio that didn't work, her bicycle with the tyres punctured. These visitors would have noticed that the summer flies weren't swept up, that nowhere was dusted.

'Three spoons and one for the pot,' Kathleen said, setting the teapot down in the hearth. 'Is that about right, Emily? Will we let it draw a minute?'

She had cut more brack, finding it on the breadboard, the bread saw beside it, the butter there too. She hoped it wasn't a presumption, she hoped it wasn't interference, she said, but all that remained unanswered.

'He'd sit there looking at me,' Emily said. 'His eyes would follow me about the kitchen. There was a beetle got on the table once and he didn't move. It got into the flour and he didn't reach out for it.'

'Isn't it a wonder,' Norah said, 'you wouldn't have gone off, the way things were, Emily? Not that I'm saying you should have.'

Emily was aware that that question was asked. She didn't answer it; she didn't know why she hadn't gone off. Looking back on it, she didn't. But she remembered how when she had thought of going away what her arguments to herself had been, how she had wondered where she could go to, and had told herself it would be wrong to leave a house that had been left to her in good faith and with affection. And then, of course, there was the worry about how he'd manage.

'Will you take another cup, Emily?'

She shook her head. The wind had become stronger. She could hear it rattling the doors upstairs. She'd left a light burning in the room.

'I'm wrong to delay you,' she said.

But the Geraghtys had settled down again, with the fresh tea to sustain them. She wasn't delaying them in any way whatsoever, Kathleen said. In the shadowy illumination of the single forty-watt bulb the alarm clock on the mantelpiece gave the time as twenty past eleven, although in fact it was half an hour later.

'It's just I'm tired,' Emily said. 'A time like this, I didn't mean to go on about what's done with.'

Kathleen said it was the shock. The shock of death changed everything, she said; no matter how certainly death was expected, it was always a shock.

'I wouldn't want you to think I didn't love my husband.'

The sisters were taken aback, Kathleen on her knees adding turf to the fire, Norah pouring milk into her tea. How could these two unmarried women understand? Emily thought. How could they understand that even if there was neither grief nor mourning there had been some love left for the man who'd died? Her fault, her foolishness from the first it had been; no one had made her do anything.

The talk went on, back and forth between the widow and the sisters, words and commiseration, solace and reassurance. The past came into it when more was said: the wedding, his polished shoes and shiny hair, the party afterwards over on the Curragh, at Jockey Hall because he knew the man there. People were spoken of, names known to the Geraghtys, or people before their time; occasions were spoken of – the year he went to

Cheltenham, the shooting of the old grey when her leg went at Glanbyre point-to-point. The Geraghtys spoke of their growing up in Galway, how you wouldn't recognize the City of the Tribes these days so fashionable and lively it had become; how later they had lived near Enniscorthy; how Kathleen had felt the draw of the religious life at that time but then had felt the receding of it, how she had known ever since that she'd been tested with her own mistake. In this way the Geraghtys spread themselves into the conversation. As the night went on, Emily was aware that they were doing so because it was necessary, on a bleak occasion, to influence the bleakness in other ways. She apologized for speaking ill of the dead, and blamed herself again. It was half past three before the Geraghtys left.

'Thank you,' she said, holding open the hall door. The wind that had been slight and then had got up wasn't there any more. The air was fresh and clean. She said she'd be all right.

Light flickered in the car when the women opened the doors. There was the red glow of the tail-light before the engine started up, a whiff of exhaust before the car moved slowly forward and gathered speed.

In the room upstairs, the sheet drawn up over the raddled, stiffening features, Emily prayed. She knelt by the bedside and pleaded for the deliverance of the husband who had wronged her for so long. Fear had drained to a husk the love she had spoken of, but she did not deny that remnant's existence, as she had not in the company of her visitors. She could not grieve, she could not mourn; too little was left, too much destroyed. Would they know that as they drove away? Would they explain it to people when people asked?

Downstairs, she washed up the cups and saucers. She would not sleep. She would not go to bed. The hours would pass and then the undertaker's man would come.

The headlights illuminated low stone walls, ragwort thriving on the verges, gorse among the motionless sheep in gated fields. Kathleen drove, as she always did, Norah never having learnt how to. A visit had not before turned out so strangely, so different from what had been the sisters' familiar expectation. They said all that, and then were silent for a while before Kathleen made her final comment: that what they had heard had been all the more terrible to listen to with a man dead in an upstairs room.

Hunched in the dark of the car, Norah frowned over that. She did not speak immediately, but when they'd gone another mile she said:

'I'd say, myself, it was the dead we were sitting with.'

*

In the house the silence there had been before the visitors disturbed it was there again. No spectre rose from the carnal remains of the man who was at last at peace. But the woman sitting by the turf fire she kept going was aware, as dawn lightened the edges of the curtains, of a stirring in her senses. Her tiredness afflicted her less, a calm possessed her. In the neglected room she regretted nothing now of what she had said to the women who had meant well; nor did it matter if, here and there, they had not quite understood. She sat for a while longer, then pulled the curtains back and the day came in. Hers was the ghost the night had brought, in her own image as she once had been.

Traditions

They came in one by one as they always did. Hambrose, then Forrogale; Accrington, Olivier, Macluse, Newcombe, Napier. Each in turn saw the jackdaws dead on the earthen floor: seven, as there were seven of them.

'It's Leggett,' Macluse said and the others were silent. Only Napier also suspected Leggett. The others were bewildered, except for Olivier. The birds' necks had been snapped, one of the heads twisted off. Lying in the dust, their feathers already had a lank look; their beady gaze had dulled. 'Some bloody people,' Newcombe said flatly, his tone empty of protest or emotion. Olivier knew it was the girl.

A bell was chiming, calling them to Chapel. In the morning there was never longer than those few minutes, just time enough to get to the barn and make sure the birds were all right. Usually the chiming started when the seven were already on the way back. Earlier they'd had their morning smoke.

'Oh, *God!*' Macluse spat out as they hurried. Forrogale and Accrington said they now agreed: it was Leggett. No one else said anything.

They taught their birds to talk. Generations had before them. They enticed the very young ones; they clipped their wings and tamed them. There were other places where they might have kept them but the barn was the most suitable, spacious and empty, chicken-wire drawn over the aperture that was a kind of window, tacked on to the bottom of the doors. It was used for no other purpose, derelict and forgotten until a reminder that this whole area was out-of-bounds was again issued – an edict that regularly became forgotten also. So it had been for generations. But never before had there been a slaughter.

The jackdaws did not speak clearly when they were taught. They did not converse with one another, nor even release a single utterance that might be called a word. The sounds that came from them after hours of instruction were approximate, meaning interpreted by the listener. More satisfactory results might have been obtained, it was said, if the tongues were slit, and in the past that had been done, but not for many years now. It was felt to be not quite the thing.

With scarcely a minute to spare the seven boys arrived at the Chapel precincts, passed the line of masters waiting to make an entrance from the cloisters, and took their places, all of them sitting together. That something was wrong this morning was at once apparent to their peers; curiosity was whetted as prayers were mumbled, and hymns sung with roistering enthusiasm. The grave-faced chaplain conducted the service, briefly touching upon the temptations in the wilderness, since it was the time of year to do so. His gravity was a familiar quality in him, in no way caused by what had occurred in the night, which he did not know about. 'For it is written,' he quoted, 'He shall give his angels charge over thee.' Tidily with that, he brought his exposition to an end. As boys and masters, all formally gowned, filed back into the fresh air, the organ voluntary was by Handel.

There was a general dispersal while, increasing in volume, talk began. Boys went several ways, to widely scattered classrooms, the masters in one direction only, to collect from their common-room what books were immediately needed. Hambrose and Accrington remained together, as did Macluse and Napier and Newcombe, all three of whom belonged in a cleverer set. Forrogale had a piano lesson; Olivier had been summoned by the Headmaster. Each of the seven had on his mind the outrage that had occurred, and neither resentment nor anger had receded.

Forrogale practised while he waited, since he had not practised much in the time that had passed since he and Mr Hancock last had met. In the Headmaster's house the blue light above the drawing-room door was extinguished when the school butcher and handyman, Dynes, left the room. He winked at Olivier in a sinister manner, implying that he knew more than he did about Olivier's summons. The winking went unacknowledged, since it was one of Dynes's usual ploys. Olivier rapped lightly on a panel of the door and was told to come in.

'I am disappointed,' the Headmaster declared at once, leading the way from the fire against which he had been warming himself to a small adjoining room untidy with books and papers and confiscated objects. A burly, heavily made man, he sat down behind a desk while Olivier stood. 'Disappointed to note,' he went on, 'that you have failed to come up to scratch in any one of the three scientific subjects. Yet it seems you yourself had chosen the scientific side of things.' He broke off to peer at a piece of paper he had drawn towards him. 'Your ambitions are in that direction?'

'I was curious to know more about science, sir.'

'Sit down, Olivier.'

'Thank you, sir.'

'You say curious?'

'Yes, sir.'

'Now tell me why you are curious in that way. Remember I have a duty

– and a conscience if I knowingly release upon the innocent world the ignorant and the inept. The fees at this school are high, Olivier. They are high because expectations are high. Your housemaster has said this to you. You are here this morning to be made aware of the seriousness we attach to it. When you went on to the scientific side you were not driven by vocation?'

'No, sir.'

'You indulged a curiosity. You indulged yourself: that can be dangerous.'

Why did the man have to speak in that pompous, prissy way? Olivier asked himself. If it was self-indulgence simply to wish to learn more since he knew so little, then it was self-indulgence. In what way dangerous? he wondered, but did not ask. That he had failed to perform adequately in the laboratory had not surprised him, nor did it now.

He said he was sorry, and the Headmaster spoke of the school's belief in tradition, which he did on all convenient occasions. What he extolled had little, if anything at all, to do with Olivier's failure. That this was so was a tradition in itself, all deviations from required behaviour assumed to have a source in careless disregard of time-hardened precepts and mores. This Headmaster's predecessors had in their day advocated such attention to the past, to the achievements of boys when they became men, to the debts they owed. In turn, Olivier's predecessors had listened with the same degree of scepticism and disdain.

'Shall we put it like this,' the present Headmaster suggested, 'that you promise me this morning to knuckle down? That we review the circumstances in, say, five weeks' time?'

'Or I could give up science, sir.'

'Give up? I hardly like the sound of that.'

'I made a mistake, sir.'

'Do not compound it, Olivier. Failure is a punishment in itself. Perhaps you might dwell on that?'

With this suggestion Olivier was dismissed. In the great stone-paved hall beyond the study and the drawing-room he forgot at once all that had been said and returned to the subject of the slaughtered birds. Again he reached the conclusion he had reached already: that the culprit was not another boy. Leggett would be seized after the games practices this afternoon and accused under duress. Dawdling on the journey to his classroom, Olivier anticipated that unfair revenge but knew he would still not reveal what he suspected. There was pleasure in not doing so, in holding things back, in knowing what others didn't.

*

Wednesdays until tea were hers. They always had been and she would have hated a change. That middle-of-the-week day she had come to regard as her private Sunday – when her alarm didn't go off, when the Chapel bell and First School bell, sounding in the distance, could be ignored. Even her unconscious knew what to do: to sleep on until the morning was half gone. It was ragged sleep, made restless with dreams that were always vivid at this time, but that never mattered. Nothing was more luxurious than Wednesday mornings, than imagining between dozing and waking the untidy after-breakfast dining hall, and the silence that came suddenly when classes began, the cutlery carried to the pantries, polished clean there, carried back again, the big oak tables laid for lunch. She had Saturday evening off as well but it wasn't the same, nothing much really and often she stood in for one of the others, not even wanting to be paid back.

She rose this morning at half past ten, her usual Wednesday time. She read a colour supplement while the kettle boiled. She opened the back door and stood there in her nightdress, shooing away the cat that was a nuisance. Stacpoole used to come to her on Wednesday mornings, the only one who ever had, the only one who in all the years had ever managed to have a free period then, eleven to a quarter to twelve. She remembered Stacpoole returning to the school long afterwards with a woman they said would be his wife, pointing out to her this place or that. She remembered wondering if she'd been pointed out herself.

She stood a little longer, relishing the soft, fresh air. Then the smell of toast drew her back into her kitchen.

They made coffee in the quarry and drank it out of jampots. They drank it very sweet but without milk because milk was a nuisance. Then, lying on their backs in the sun, they smoked.

Leggett, meanwhile, crept back to his House, simulating lameness for as long as he estimated he could be seen. He thought he had a cracked rib but Forrogale, claiming medical knowledge, had said no, having poked it with his fingers. 'Definitely not,' Forrogale had said, but Leggett was not sure about that. They'd picked on him because he was underhand: they'd said so, and Leggett knew he was. None the less, he was innocent. He wouldn't have touched one of their hideous jackdaws, much less taken in his hand a head with a beak that could snap at you.

'He didn't do it,' Accrington said, breaking a long silence, and one at a time the others agreed. Not that duffing up Leggett was in the least to be regretted.

'Who?' Napier asked, and Olivier didn't say the girl.

'Unless it was Dynes,' Macluse said.

They all thought about that except Olivier. Dynes was outside the order of things; they could not duff him up or in any way harass him; they could not so much as speak to him about the matter, for although the handyman was aware that jackdaws were kept he would most likely counter the accusation by revealing what he had previously been silent about. He was a touchy man.

'I doubt in any case it was Dynes,' Accrington said. 'This doesn't have Dynes's fingerprints.'

Some years ago a boy had hanged himself but had not succeeded in taking his life. It was established afterwards that he had not intended to, since the noose he had prepared had never tightened, one foot pressed into a hollow in the tree he'd chosen taking all the weight. The boy had not, though, remained at the school but had been sent home, considered unbalanced. This was spoken of now, since it was surely some similar individual who had killed the birds. The names of the unstable were bandied about, recent behaviour of new suspects discussed. Olivier remained silent. He was the smallest of the boys though not the youngest, his dark hair in a fringe above a sallow complexion. His looks stood out among those of his companions, a delicacy about him that the others could not claim. There was – or so it seemed when Olivier was there as an example of how it might be better done – a carelessness in how the others had been made. Adolescence was marked in them by jacket sleeves too short, unruly hair and coarsened voices, blemished skin beneath beginners' stubble. Yet none particularly noticed that Olivier had escaped this prelude to man's estate, the gangling awkwardness that his friends accepted without regret for what was left behind.

The last of the coffee was drunk, cigarette butts thrown into the embers of the fire before the charred remains of sticks were scattered. In a body, the boys returned to the school, then to the barn that had been their jackdaws' home. Hambrose, who knew the conventions of the school's farm through assisting in the work there, made a detour to collect a spade and advised on where it was best to dig a common grave. One by one the birds were dropped into it. Macluse piled back the clay and then the capturing of replacement birds began.

Long before Olivier came to the school there had been incidents in the past that word of mouth had since made famous: the ringing of the Chapel bell in the middle of the night; the removal of a Renoir print – 'Young Girl Reading' – from its place between the windows in one of the prefects' common-rooms; the purloining of a cigarette lighter and a pipe from a pocket of Dobie-Gordon's overcoat; the mysterious collapse of the central-heating system. Occurring over many years, the incidents had in common only that no culprit had ever been brought to book; nor did it seem possible that the same hand could have been responsible for any two of the occurrences – let alone all of them – since the length of a boy's stay at the school did not allow it. Seven years ago – long before Olivier's arrival – there'd been the trouble in the bicycle sheds: the random deflating of tyres. Then nothing had happened until the killing of the jackdaws.

It was purely intuition that caused Olivier to suspect the girl, not just of the latest outrage but of the others too. And though certain that he was right, so sure was his instinct, so unassailable his sensing of a purpose in all this, he could not think why one of the dining-hall maids should wish to alert the school to fire at one o'clock in the morning or what possible use she could have had for Dobie-Gordon's pipe. Somewhere here there was revenge, he had conjectured when first he'd had his idea, but had since rejected the speculation, for he considered it too pat and obvious. He thought so again on the day of Leggett's duffing up when at teatime he stared at the girl, trying to catch her when she wasn't looking. He was skilled at breaking into privacies without the knowledge of the person observed; he prided himself on that, but twice, or even three times, he suddenly had to drop his scrutiny, taken unawares by having his gaze returned. Bella this maid's name was, but 'the girl' identified her in the dining hall and beyond it.

Along one arm, plates touching to keep them balanced, the dining-hall maids could carry five at a time, each bearing a sausage roll, or toast with beans or scrambled eggs. Today it was sausage roll, two sausages in each envelope of pastry, the pastry dark brown and flaky. At St Andrew's Second Table you passed your sausage roll to Chom, who ate it for you. Elsewhere in the dining hall more usual conventions prevailed, unwanted sausage rolls disposed of later.

Olivier's place this evening at St David's Third Table was on the prefect's right, a position that recurred every twelve days, each boy but for the prefect moving on a place each day. The prefect did not speak except to request the salt or pepper or jam; it was his privilege to be aloof. The warm plates were passed along each row of boys, the prefect's fetched at the last moment and mustard brought with it.

The maid who interested Olivier did not serve this table. He watched her at the far end of the dining hall, where the St Patrick's tables were, where Accrington and Newcombe and Hambrose sat. Only Olivier, among the boys who tamed jackdaws, was in St David's. Forrogale and Macluse and Napier were in St George's, the House renowned for games.

The noise in the dining hall was considerable, but the only snatches of conversation that reached Olivier were from his own table, all else being lost in the general din. The Saturday-evening debate this week was to be about the existence or otherwise of ghosts. This was talked about in advance; and an item of national news – the conviction of a medical doctor who had murdered a number of his female patients – was discussed, the death penalty advocated or opposed. Olivier drank his tea and passed his cup and saucer to where a large metal teapot was in the charge of the two boys at the table's other end. Then he watched the maid again. Waiting for the moment when the clearing away of plates and cutlery began, she stood now in a line with the other maids in front of the high table, which was unoccupied during this meal.

She was a girl in name only, a designation that carried from the past, from when she had been the youngest of the maids by many years. It honoured a celebrity she had enjoyed, when her fresh beauty had time and again inspired passion in the dining hall. Such facts came into the mystery of the incidents, Olivier felt himself guessing; but did not know how. She did not mind being observed: that, too, was there.

'Olivier,' the prefect interrupted the blankness that followed these reflections. 'Jam.'

Olivier reached for the dish of apple jam, apologizing. She was a woman in late middle age now, tall, with grey hair tied back behind her cap, her features still touched with a trace of the beauty other boys had known. Olivier understood – had come to understand when first he'd been interested in her – why she was different from the other maids. It was not just the tales that lingered from the past, nor the reminder in her features that these were not exaggerated, nor her preference for silence when the other maids chattered in carefully guarded dining-hall whispers. There was something else, belonging only to her. Again her glance caught his, too far away for Olivier to be certain that it did so intentionally, but he was certain anyway.

The grey sausage meat within his pastry smelt a bit; not that it was bad, Olivier knew, for the smell was of sausage and of meat; only that the cooking had drawn some excess of natural odour from it. The first time she'd looked in his direction he hadn't recognized her and would have passed her by because she wasn't in her uniform. Often since, he'd noticed her on the back drive, alone on her afternoon off or when her duties for the day were done, not in a bunch as the others usually were. She never smiled, nothing like that, and he didn't himself.

There was the clatter of standing up, the benches pushed back from the tables, the shuffling of shoes on polished boards. '. . . *per Christum Dominum nostrum*,' the Senior Prefect intoned and then there were the evening's announcements, the duty master hurrying off, the prefects going when the announcements finished, one falling in behind another, interrupted conversations picked up as the dining hall emptied but for the maids.

It would not be the birds again. There was always a variation, and Olivier had once tried to guess what the next transgression would be, but had failed hopelessly. He would not be here when it occurred, and he imagined returning for some Old Boys' event and hearing something casually mentioned. He imagined not quite knowing what had happened and having to ask outright in the end. For a moment he wanted to reassure his friends that the new birds were safe, that there would not be a repetition. But he desisted. It was a time for cigarettes again, and the seven trooped off to the stone hut they had built for that purpose, out of sight in a corner of a field.

That evening the Headmaster himself spoke at compline, which on rare occasions he did. He told a parable of his own invention: how a man, repeating every day of his life a certain pattern of behaviour, made the pattern richer. He told of how, in a dream, this man had deviated once from his chosen way and been harshly judged by God, and punished with failure where all his life there had been success before.

Olivier recognized in the words a faintly apposite note and wondered if inspiration for them had perhaps come from his own deviation, and subsequent failure, in the realm of science. In ending his address, the Headmaster did not omit to include a reference to the value of tradition, claiming for it and for the school it ruled a potency that must surely be the approval of the God who punished when displeased. The Headmaster's philosophy did not vary except in the allegorical garb of his discourse. It was a circle that came full, ending where it had begun: with the school and its time-worn customs, tried and true, that made men of boys.

Later, in scanning a Horace ode with the aid of a Kelly's Key, Olivier found himself distracted, in turn, by the Headmaster's overwhelming confidence in the established rites of passage through his school and by the dining-hall maid's transgressions. Were her sins the weaponry of insurrection, intended as such or simply so because they happened? What passed through her thoughts as she implemented another disturbance or discomfort? And why was it that the Headmaster's beliefs and a woman's recidivistic stratagems seemed now to cling together like proximate jig-saw pieces? *Angustam amice pauperiem pati, robustus acri militia puer condiscat*, Horace had written; and Olivier matched Latin and English as best he could, his key's translation not being word for word.

Of course, the Headmaster did not know – as authority before him had not known – that the dining-hall maid had in her girlhood been, her-self, a fragment of tradition, supplying to boys who now were men a service that had entered the unofficial annals. There was that too, Olivier reminded himself, before he returned to winkling out which word went with which.

At the end of the day the dining-hall maids, and the dormitory maids, and those with diverse duties, went home, some sharing the available space in the cars that a few of them drove, others on bicycles, some on foot to the village. Among those who walked was the girl who was now a woman. She smoked on the leafy back drive, a little behind two of her colleagues, one of whom lit the way with a torch. The skin of the boy she admired was still as smooth as porcelain though not as white, and with-out the blush of pink that porcelain flesh went in for. She loved the sallow tinge, the dark eyes gazing out of it, the fringe that so perfectly followed the forehead's contour.

His image filled her consciousness as she walked on, his voice the voice of boys who had long ago tenderly spoken her name. He knew, as she had guessed he would be the one to know, because he was the kind. She'd always known the kind.

The first of the late bells sounded, rhythmically clanging. Younger boys gathered up their books, and then their footsteps were muffled in the cor-ridors, no conversation exchanged because noise was forbidden while the Upper and Middle School classes continued their preparation. Olivier read *Cakes and Ale*, the orange-backed book hidden from view behind *Raleigh and the British Empire* and a guide to laboratory experiments. *Was it Chapman, do you think?* a note interrupted this, passed along the row of desks to him. *Maybe*, he scribbled and passed the scrap of paper back to Newcombe. You had to lie. They'd be suspicious if you kept denying it whenever they mentioned anyone.

Someone would guess: one after another she had caused the incidents to happen so that someone would guess. As certain as he was about every-thing else, so he was certain that this last conjecture was not fanciful. He knew no more; he doubted that he ever would. In his mind's eye he saw her as once or twice he had when he'd been out and about at this time himself: in her navy-blue coat, the belt tied loosely, a headscarf with horses on it.

'Cheers, Bella,' the two in front called out, one after the other, as they turned into Parsley Lane. 'Cheers.'

She loathed that cheap word, so meaningless, used all the time now. 'Good night,' she called back.

Voices and the occasional laugh accompanied the bobbing torchlight in Parsley Lane. She went a different way and heard only the hooting of an owl. She came to the Railwayman, where there were voices and laughter again, and then the television turned loud in Mrs Hodges' front room.

Her mother, still alive, would be in her bed: she pretended that. And he would be silent among the churchyard yews, and would say nothing while she went by. Then when she had brought the tea upstairs and had sat a while to watch the old eyelids droop, she'd slide back the wooden bolt and move the curtain an inch to the right, leaving it for just a moment. He would come in without a knock.

Someone leaving the Railwayman called after her, saying good night, and she called back. She could have had any of them; she still could, for all she knew. My God, she thought, the stifled life it would have been, with any one of them!

She didn't mind the short cut by the churchyard, not any more. She'd passed through the lines of gravestones too often, the Greshams' great family vault damaged and open in one place, the smashed, forgotten wreaths eerie when there was moonlight. The odour she'd once associated with the dead was old leaves rotting.

The cottage where all her life she'd lived was the last in the village. Her father had left it every morning of her childhood to go to work at the quarry; he'd died upstairs, where her mother had too. A boy had come on the day her mother died and she'd had to send him away, head of St Andrew's he'd been, Tateman. *La même chose*: it was he who'd taught her that, and *chacun à son goût*, making her pout her lips to get the sounds. Long afterwards she'd imagined travelling with him, all over France and Germany, saying *la même chose* herself when she was offered a dessert, wanting what he'd had. Fair-haired he'd been, not at all like the present one, whose name she did not know.

She turned the latchkey in her front door and drew the curtains in the room she'd walked straight into, the heavy one over the door to keep the draught out. Two bars of the electric fire warmed her ankles when she sat down, with tea and Petit Beurre. The secret side of it they'd always relished, as much as the other in a way. And she had, too – not quite as much but almost.

When the dormitory had quietened Olivier thought about her again. He wondered how, when she was young, her expression had changed when her mood did. He imagined her demure, for there was about her some-times in the dining hall a trace of that as she stood waiting for Grace to be said, while the others were impatient. Conjecturing again, he saw her in a different coat, without a headscarf, hair blown about. He saw her uniform laid out, starched and ready on an ironing board, a finger damped before the iron's heat was tested. He saw her stockinged feet and laughter in her eyes, and then her nakedness.

Justina's Priest

Only Justina Casey made sense, Father Clohessy reflected yet again, shaking his head over the recurrence of the thought, for truth to tell the girl made no sense at all. The contradiction nagged a little in a familiar way, as it did whenever Justina Casey, sinless as ever, made her confession. It caused Father Clohessy to feel inadequate, foolish even, that he failed to understand something that as a priest he should have.

Leaving the confessional she had just left herself, he looked around for her: at the back, near the holy-water stoup, she trailed her rosary through her fingers. 'Father, I'm bad,' she had insisted and, allotting her her penance, he had been again aware that she didn't even know what badness was. But without the telling of her beads, without the few Hail Marys he had prescribed, she would have gone away unhappy. Of her own volition, every few days she polished the brass of the altar vases and the altar cross. She would be there on Saturday evening, a bucket of scalding water carried through the streets, the floor mop lifted down from its hook in the vestry cupboard. On Fridays she scraped away the week's accumulation of candle grease and arranged to her satisfaction the out-of-date missionary leaflets.

Fifty-four and becoming stout, his red hair cut short around a freckled pate, Father Clohessy watched while Justina Casey dipped the tips of her fingers in the holy water and blessed herself before she left the church. Her footsteps were soft on the tiles, as if her devotion demanded that, as if she were of less importance than the sacred ground she walked on, less than the burning candles and the plaster Virgin, less even than the unread missionary leaflets. He remembered her at her First Communion, standing out a bit from the other children, a scraggy bunch of lily-of-the-valley pressed close to her. It was afterwards that she'd asked him if she could look after the brass.

The door of the church closed soundlessly behind her and Father Clohessy was aware of an emptiness, of something taken from him.

Justina dawdled, examining the goods in the shop windows. There were the tins of sweets in Hehir's, and the glass jars in a row behind them, half full of the mixtures, the jelly babies and bull's-eyes, soft-centred fruits, toffees. There were the fashions in Merrick's, the window changed only a week ago, meat in Cranly's, delft and saucepans in Natton's. A fine dust had gathered on the dry goods in MacGlashan's, on packets of Barry's tea and the advertisements for Bisto and chicken-and-ham paste. Cabbage drooped outside Mrs Scally's, the green fringe of the carrots was tinged with yellow.

'How's Justina?' Mrs Scally enquired from the doorway, the flowered overall that encased her girth crossed over on itself beneath her folded arms. She always had her arms folded, Justina's thought was as she stopped to hear what else Mrs Scally had to say. One shoulder taking the weight against the door-jamb, a single curler left in her hair, slippers on her feet and the folded arms: that was Mrs Scally unless she was weighing out potatoes or wrapping a turnip. 'All right,' Justina said. 'I'm all right, Mrs Scally.'

'I have apples in. Will you tell them up in the house I have apples in?'
'I will.'
'There's a few tins of peaches that's dinged. I wouldn't charge the full.'
'You told me that, Mrs Scally.'
'Did you mention it in the house?'
'I did surely.'

Justina passed on. She had spoken to Maeve about the peaches and her sister hadn't said anything. But Mr Gilfoyle had heard her saying it and he'd laughed. When Micksie came in he said that if the dinge in the tin caused rust you'd have to be careful. Micksie was Maeve's husband, Mr Gilfoyle was his father. Diamond Street was where they lived, where Maeve ruled the small household and most of the time was unable to hide the fact that she resented its composition. Capable and brisk of manner, a tall, dark-haired childless woman, Maeve considered that she'd been caught: when their mother had died there had been only she to look after Justina, their mother being widowed for as long as either of them could remember. And Maeve had been caught again when her father-in-law, miserable with the ailments of old age, had to be taken in; and again in not realizing before her marriage that Micksie had to be kept out of the pubs. 'Oh, I have children all right,' was how she often put it when there was sympathy for her childlessness.

Justina bought an ice-cream in the Today Tonight shop. The evening papers had just come off the Dublin bus. *No-vote a Winner*, the headline said and she wondered what that meant. People she knew were gathering items from the shelves, minerals in bottles and tins, frozen food from the central refrigerator, magazines from the racks. She walked about, licking at her ice-cream, nibbling the edge of the cone. Up one aisle and down another, past shoe polish and disinfectant and fire-lighters, carton soups reduced, everything handy in case you'd forgotten to get it in Superquinn.

'You're a great girl,' one of two nuns remarked, reaching out for Kerrygold and dropping it into her wire basket. Older and more severe, the other nun didn't say anything.

'Ah, I'm not,' Justina said. She held out her ice-cream, but neither nun licked it. 'No way I'm great,' Justina said.

'What kept you?' Maeve asked in the kitchen.

'Mrs Scally was on about the peaches. Sister Agnes and Sister Lull were in the Today Tonight.'

'What'd you go in there for?'

'Nothing.'

Justina paused for an instant and then she told about the ice-cream and Maeve knew it was because her sister had suddenly considered it would be a lie to hold that back.

'God, will you look at the cut of you!' She shouted, furious, unable to help herself. 'Aren't there jobs to do here without you're streeling about the town?'

'I had to make my confession.'

'Oh, for heaven's sake!'

'What's up, Maeve?'

Maeve shook her head. She could feel a weariness in her eyes which made her want to close them, and then felt it spreading through her body. She returned to what she'd been doing before Justina came in, slicing cooked potatoes.

'Lay the table,' she said. 'Take your anorak off and lay the table.'

'I got a letter from Breda,' Justina said.

She had closed the back door behind her but hadn't come further into the kitchen. She had a way of doing that, just as she had a way of standing by the sink, not getting on with what she was there for, as if she'd forgotten everything. All their lives, for as long as Maeve could remember, she had been irritated by this shortcoming in her sister, as she was by Justina's bringing back messages from the shopkeepers to say this or that commodity had come in or that there was a new bargain line, as she was by the telephone calls that came from a farmer nearly six miles from the town to say that Justina was again feeding his bullocks bunches of grass. Not that he objected, the man always said, only the bullocks could be frisky and maybe crowd her.

'Will you read me Breda's letter, Maeve?'

'You keep away from that one, d'you hear me?'

'Sure, Breda's gone.'
'And she'll stay where she is.'
'Will I lay the table, Maeve?'
'Didn't I ask you to?'
'I'll lay it so.'

Father Clohessy walked in the opposite direction from the one taken by
Justina. The sense of loss that had possessed him when she left the church
had given way to a more general feeling of deprivation that, these days,
he was not often without. The grandeur of his Church had gone, leaving
his priesthood within it bleak, the vocation that had beckoned him less
insistent than it had been. He had seen his congregations fall off and
struggled against the feeling that he'd been deserted. Confusion spread
from the mores of the times into the Church itself; in combating it, he
prayed for guidance but was not heard.

A familiar melancholy, not revealed in his manner, accompanied
Father Clohessy in the minutes it took him to reach the limestone figure
of the rebel leader in the square that was the centre of the town. That he
considered it necessary to keep private his concern about the plight of
his Church did nothing to lighten the burden of his mood, any more
than the temporary absence from the parish of Father Finaghy did. At
present undergoing a period of treatment after a car accident, Father
Finaghy was extrovert and gregarious, a priest who carried his faith on
to the golf-course, where it was never a hindrance. 'Arrah, sure we do
our best,' Father Finaghy was given to remarking. Father Clohessy missed
his companionship; almost a protection it seemed like sometimes.

'Have you change, Father?' a young woman begged from a doorway, a
baby asleep in a shawl beside her. 'A few coppers at all today?'

She said she'd pray for him and he thanked her, finding the coins she
hoped for. He knew her; she was usually there. He might have asked her
when he'd see her at Mass, but he didn't bother.

Music blared across the small square from Mulvany's Electrical and
TV, giving way to the careless whine of Bob Dylan. Mulvany had established for himself a tradition of celebrating the birthdays of popular
entertainers by playing a tribute: today Bob Dylan was sixty. Although
one song only was played on these occasions, and no more than once during the day it related to, Father Clohessy considered it a disturbance in a
quiet town and had once approached Mulvany about it. But Mulvany
had argued that it was nostalgic for the older citizens to hear the likes of
Perry Como or Dolly Parton coming out of the blue at them, and exciting
for the youngsters to have the new arrivals on the music scene honoured.

That a priest's protest had been so summarily dismissed was par for the course, an expression often used by Father Finaghy in his own unprotesting acceptance of the decline of clerical influence. The times they were a-changing, Bob Dylan's reminder was repeated yet again before there was silence from Mulvany's loudspeakers.

'Isn't that a grand day, Father?' a woman remarked to him and he agreed that it was and she said thank God for it. He wondered if she knew, if any of them knew, that when he preached he was angry because he didn't know what to say to them, that he searched for ways to disguise his distress, stumbling about from word to word. 'How's Father Finaghy?' the woman asked him. 'Have you heard, Father?'

He told her. Father Finaghy was making good progress; he'd heard that morning.

'Wouldn't it be the prayers said for him?' the woman suggested, and he agreed with that, too, before he resumed his journey through the town to where he and Father Finaghy lodged.

His tea was ready for him there. Comeraghview, called after the mountains in the faraway distance, was a grey detached house with a handkerchief tree in a front garden protected from the main road by grey iron railings. It was he and Father Finaghy who had decided that the presbytery could be put to better use, who with their bishop's permission, and in the end with his blessing, had given it over to become the youth centre the town had long been in need of.

'I have ham and a salad for you,' Father Clohessy's landlady said, placing this food in front of him.

'I will of course,' Mr Gilfoyle said when Justina asked him to read Breda Maguire's letter to her. 'Have you it there?'

Justina had, and Mr Gilfoyle suggested that they'd take it out the back where they'd be private. His daughter-in-law went ballistic at any mention of Breda Maguire these days, never mind having to hear of her doings in Dublin. Time was when someone who'd take her sister off her hands was a relief for Maeve, but now that the two girls were grown up and Breda Maguire had gone off the rails it was naturally different.

'*I'm living in a great joint!*' he read aloud in the small flowerless back garden that had become a depository for the abandoned wash-basins and lavatory bowls and perforated ballcocks that his son had replaced in his work as a plumber. Nettles had grown up around cast-iron heating radiators and a bath; dandelions and docks flourished. Mr Gilfoyle had cleared a corner, where he kept a chair from the kitchen; on sunny mornings he read the newspaper there.

He was a moustached man, grey-haired, once burly and on the stout side, less so now, since time had established in him the varying character-istics of advancing years. His pronounced stoop, an arthritic shoulder, trouble with gallstones, fingers distorted by Dupuytren's Disease had made another man of him. In his day he, too, had been a plumber.

'*The kind of house you wouldn't know about,*' *he read out, imagining what was described: a place where theatre people lived, coffee always on the go, late mornings. Mr Gilfoyle found it hard to believe that Breda Maguire had been given accommodation there, but he supposed it could be true.*

Justina, sitting on the edge of the bath, had no such difficulty. She accepted without demur all that was related. She saw her friend in the green-and-blue kimono that was described. '*Like a dragon wrapped round me,*' Mr Gilfoyle had read out and explained that a kimono was Japanese. He felt what he believed to be a gallstone changing position inside him somewhere, a twitch of pain that was only to be expected at his age he'd been told by the doctor he visited regularly.

'*Davy Byrne's you'd never see only it's jammed to the doors. The racing crowd, all that kind of thing.*' Breda Maguire was on the streets, Mr Gil-foyle said to himself. She had money, you could tell she had, nothing made up about that. The house she said she was stopping in was out Island-bridge way and again there was an echo of the truth in that, handy for the quays. The quays were where you'd find them, a bricklayer told him once, maybe fifty years ago, and it could still be where a man would go to look for a street woman. '*I have a friend takes me out,*' he read. '*Billy.*'

'Will you listen to that!' Justina whispered. The name of a hotel where there were dances was mentioned, shops, cinemas. A wrist bangle had been bought, and Justina saw her friend and Billy at a counter with a glass top like the one in Hennessy's the Clock Shop, necklaces and ban-gles laid out for them. She saw them in a café, a waitress bringing grills, the same as Justina had seen people eating in Egan's, a chop and chips, bacon, egg and sausage. Billy was like the air pilot in the film she and Breda had watched on the television only the day before Breda went off. '*How's tricks with yourself?*' Mr Gilfoyle's voice continued.

It would be impossible for Justina to respond to that because her learn-ing difficulty deprived her of any communication that involved writing words down. But Breda had remembered, as naturally she would. '*I'll maybe give you a call one of these days,*' Mr Gilfoyle read out. The pain had shifted, had gone round to the back, like a gallstone maybe would.

'Isn't Billy great, the way he'd give her things?' Justina said.

'He is, Justina.'

'Isn't Billy a great name?'

'It is.'

Covering a multitude of sins, Mr Gilfoyle assumed, a stand-in name for names Breda didn't know, the presents another way of putting it that money had changed hands in some quayside doorway.

'I'll dream about Breda and Billy,' Justina said, slipping down from the edge of the bath.

Father Clohessy listened when Justina put it into her confession that Maeve was cross with her because Breda telephoned. She put it into her confession that she went into the kitchen to tell what Breda had said and Maeve wouldn't listen; and the next thing was she let drop a cup she was drying. It was then that Maeve began to cry, tears streaming down her cheeks, down her neck into the collar of her dress. As if it wasn't nuisance enough, an old man who didn't know how to make his bed forever on about his ailments. As if it wasn't enough, Micksie in and out of the pubs, a girl with learning trouble, the back garden a tip. Was there a woman in Ireland could put up with more, when on top of everything a hooer the like of Breda Maguire got going again after they thought they'd seen the back of her?

All that Justina put into her confession. She was bad, she said. One minute she was laughing with Breda on the phone; the next, Maeve was crying in the kitchen. Breda said come up to Dublin and they'd have great gas. Get the money however, Breda said. Get it off Mr Gilfoyle, anything at all. Take the half-two bus, the same as she'd got herself. Come up for the two days, what harm would it do anyone? 'I'll show you the whole works,' Breda said.

The fingers of Father Clohessy's hands were locked together as he listened, that being his usual pose in the confessional, head turned so that one ear could pick up the revelations that were coming through the gauze of the grille. Among his confessants, it was only Justina he ever interrupted and he did so now.

'Ah no, Justina, no,' he said.

'Will I say a Hail Mary for Maeve, Father?'

'You wouldn't want to go up to Dublin, Justina. You wouldn't want to upset your sister more.'

'It's only Breda's gone up there.'

'I know, I know.'

When they were no more than five or six he remembered the two of them playing in Diamond Street, Justina's black hair cut in a fringe and curling in around her face, Breda as thin as a weasel. She'd been the bane

of the nuns when she'd attended the convent, sly and calculating, all
knowing talk and unspoken defiance. She'd plastered herself with lipstick
when she was older; in the end she'd worn a T-shirt with an indecency on
it.

'Would it be bad to go up on the bus, Father?'

'I think maybe it would. Have you anything else to confess, Justina?'

'Only Maeve was crying.'

'Light a candle when you'll leave the confessional. Do the floor on Saturday, do the brasses.'

Again he remembered her standing on her own by the shrine outside
the church after her First Communion, her face held up to the sunshine,
the lily-of-the-valley tightly clenched. Before she left the confessional he
murmured a prayer for her, knowing that was what she liked to hear best
of all. It frightened him that she might visit her friend, that she might
forget what he had said, that somehow she might acquire the bus fare,
that she'd go, not telling anyone.

Two days later, when Justina was washing the church floor, Father
Clohessy called at the house in Diamond Street.

'Come in, Father, come in,' Mr Gilfoyle said.

He led the way into a room where a football match was in progress on
the television, Aston Villa and Arsenal. His son had been watching it, Mr
Gilfoyle said, but then a call had come through, a tank overflowing on the
McCarron estate. Mr Gilfoyle turned the football off. Maeve had gone
out for rashers. She'd be back in no time, he said.

They talked about a job Mr Gilfoyle had done years ago in the church,
putting in a sink in the vestry. Father Clohessy said it was still going
strong; in use all the time, he said.

'A Belfast sink,' Mr Gilfoyle said. 'A Belfast sink was the name we had
for that fellow. You wouldn't see the better of it.'

'No.'

'Sit down, Father. I have to sit down myself. I have trouble in the old
legs.'

A sound came from the kitchen. Mr Gilfoyle called out to his daughter-
in-law that Father Clohessy was here and when Maeve came in, still in her
coat, a scarf tied round her hair, Father Clohessy said:

'I wanted a word about Justina.'

'She's being a nuisance to you?'

'Ah no, no.'

'She lives in that church.'

'Justina's welcome, Maeve. No, it's only she was mentioning Breda

Maguire. I'm concerned in case Justina might try to make her way to Dublin.'

There was a silence then. The priest was aware of Mr Gilfoyle being about to say something and changing his mind, and of Maeve's unbelieving stare. He watched while she restrained herself: once or twice before, she had been abrupt to the point of rudeness when he'd been concerned about her sister. He didn't say anything himself; the silence went on.

'She never would,' Maeve said at last.

Successful in controlling her irritation, she failed to keep an errant note of hope out of her tone. It flickered in her eyes and she shook her head, as if to deny that it was there.

'How could she, Father?'

'The bus goes every day.'

'She'd need money. She spends every penny soon as she gets it.'

'I just thought I'd say. So you could keep an eye on her.'

Maeve did not respond to that. Mr Gilfoyle said Justina would never board that bus. He'd walk down to the square himself and keep a look-out where the bus drew in.

'It would be worse if she got a lift off someone.'

Wearily, Maeve closed her eyes when Father Clohessy said that. She sighed and turned away, struggling with her anger, and Father Clohessy felt sorry for her. It wasn't easy, she did her best.

'We'll keep an eye on her,' she said.

That night, when Father Clohessy closed his church after the late Saturday Mass, he wondered if he had become prey to despair, the worst sin of all in the canon that was specially a priest's. At street corners, in the square, men stood in conversation, lit cigarettes, argued the chances of Offaly the next day. Women linked arms, talking as they strolled. Children carried away chips from O'Donnell's. The grandeur might have gone from his church, his congregations dwindling, his influence fallen away to nothing, but there was money where there'd been poverty, ambition where there'd been humility. These were liberated people who stood about in ways that generations before them had not. They wore what they wished to wear, they said what they wished to say, they stayed or went away. Was it much of a price to pay that the woman he had visited would rid herself of a backward sister if she could? It was on a Saturday evening little different from this one that he had first read the legend on Breda Maguire's T-shirt, bold yellow letters on black, simple and straightforward: *Fuck Me.*

On the streets of the town he had always known, people spoke to him, warmly, with respect. They wished him good night, they wished him well.

He could not blame them if in his sermons he didn't know what to say to them any more. He should apologize, yet knew he must not. In the square, he entered the Emmet Bar, between the old Munster and Leinster Bank, now an AIB branch, and Mulvany's television shop. Father Finaghy always called in on Saturdays after they closed the church, and he sometimes did himself – to drink a couple of glasses of Beamish's stout and smoke a couple of cigarettes while he talked to two men with whom he had attended the Christian Brothers' forty years ago. Both had done well enough in the new prosperity, had fathered children and seen them educated, were decent men. He liked them as much as he always had, even sometimes was envious of their uncomplicated lives. They, not he, did the talking in the Emmet Bar, always sensitive to the cloth he wore. They neither of them had mentioned it when a few years ago a well-loved bishop had been exposed as the begetter of a child, nor when there had been other misdemeanours on the part of other clergymen.

'Bring us the same, Larry,' the bulkier of the two called out, a brightly coloured tie loosened in his collar, freckles darkening his forehead. Clumsy hands pushed the empty glasses across the bar. 'And one for the Father.'

'I wouldn't see Offaly victorious,' his companion remarked, tidier, wiry, a salesman of agricultural implements. 'No way.'

Music was faint in the crowded bar, as if coming from some other room or conveyed through apparatus that was faulty; laughter exploded in guffaws, or rippled, hardly heard.

'Thanks,' Father Clohessy said, reaching for the glass that had been filled for him.

There would be embarrassment if he mentioned the Church's slow collapse. There would be an awkwardness; best not said, his friends' opinion would be. Sometimes you had to close your mind down.

A sense of isolation, often creeping up on him during a Saturday evening in the Emmet Bar, did so again. Centuries of devotion had created a way of life in which the mystery of the Trinity was taken for granted, the Church's invincible estate a part of every day, humility part of it, too, instead of rights plucked out of nowhere, order abandoned in favour of confusion. What priests and bishops had been – their strength and their parish people's salvation – was mocked in television farces, deplored, presented as absurdity. That other priests in other towns, in cities, in country parishes, were isolated by their celibacy, by the mourning black of their dress, had been a consolation once, but that source of comfort had long ago dried up.

The Offaly flags would be hoisted all right if Ger Toibin had been fit, his companions were agreeing. The final score was predicted; he joined in that, the talk went on. Houses were to be built on the Tinakilty road where the old cement works had been. Madden's Hotel would be closed for six months while improvements were put in. There were rumours of a fertilizer outfit taking over Williamson's Yard.

'Are you off so?' Father Clohessy heard himself asked when half an hour had passed, then heard it said that he would surely have another.

He shook his head, finishing his second cigarette and stubbing out the butt. There were a few more exchanges, before he pushed his way through the drinkers, his hand shaken once or twice, salutes of farewell.

In the darkening streets of the town his reverie continued. A kind of truth it was, somewhere at the heart of his vocation, that there should be awareness of the holy world that was lost – yet he could not ever deny that vocation claimed its postulants as it wished. Companionable and easy, Father Finaghy led the singsongs in the Emmet Bar on a Saturday evening, a little tipsy and none the worse for that.

Slowly, as Father Clohessy walked on, these wellworn reflections were left behind in the town that was half closed down for the night. Nothing replaced them for a while, before the careful hands of Justina Casey lifted down the altar ornaments, her polishing rags and Brasso pads tidily laid out. She touched away from a lily a petal that had gone brown. She scraped off the candle grease that had accumulated on the candleholders. She re-arranged the missionary leaflets.

It was what there was; it was what he had, whether he understood it or not. Justina Casey would stay in the town because Mr Gilfoyle would make sure she didn't get on the Dublin bus; Maeve would keep an eye on her; after a time Breda Maguire would forget about her. In the confined space of the confessional there would again be the unnecessary confessions, again the granting of absolution. Then happiness would break in the face that saw God in his own.

An Evening Out

In the theatre bar they still talked, not hurrying over their drinks although an announcement had warned that the performance would begin in two minutes. There were more people in the bar than it could comfortably accommodate, crushed close against the bar itself and in the corners, some just beginning to make their way through the several doorways to the auditorium.

'The performance will begin in one minute,' the peremptory Tannoy voice reminded, and quite suddenly the bar was almost empty.

The barman was a character, gloomy-faced, skin and bone, bespectacled; lank like old string, he said himself. The barmaid was younger by quite a bit, and cheerfully plump.

'Oh, look,' she said. 'That woman.'

One woman had not left with the others and showed no sign of doing so. She was in a corner, sitting at one of the few tables the bar provided. All around her, on the shelf that ran around the walls, on the seats of chairs, there were empty glasses. Her own was three-quarters full of gin and tonic.

'Deaf, d'you think?' the barman wondered and the barmaid remarked that the theatre was never a place for the hard of hearing, it stood to reason. It could be of course that a deaf-aid had been temporarily turned off and then forgotten.

The woman they spoke of was smartly dressed, two shades of green; a coat that was tweed on one side and waterproof on the other was draped over the other chair at her table. The remains of beauty strikingly lit her features, seeming to be there less casually, less incidentally, than beauty might have been earlier in her life. Touches of grey were allowed in her fair hair, adding a distinction that went with the other changes time had wrought.

'Excuse me, madam,' the barman said, 'but the performance has begun.'

What a city London is! Jeffrey thought, staring up at the dark bronze features of Sir Henry Havelock beneath the sprinkling of pigeon droppings that lightened the soldier's crown. The last of an April twilight was slipping away, the city at its best, as it also was – in Jeffrey's view – when dawn was turning into day. In Trafalgar Square the traffic was clogged, a crawl of lumbering red buses and patient taxis, a cyclist now and again weaving through. People gathered at the crossing lights, seeming to lose something of themselves in each small multitude while obediently they waited to move forward when the signal came. Pigeons swooped above territory they claimed as theirs, and landed on it to waddle after tit-bits, or snapped at one another, flapping away together into the sky, still in dispute.

Jeffrey turned away from it all, from Sir Henry Havelock and the pigeons and the four great lions, the floodlights just turned on, illuminating the façade of the National Gallery. 'Won't do to keep her waiting,' he murmured, causing two girls who were passing to snigger. He kept her waiting longer, for when he reached it he entered the Salisbury in St Martin's Lane and ordered a Bell's, and then called out that it had better be a double.

He needed it. Truth to tell, he needed a second but he shook away the thought, reprimanding himself: neither of them would get anywhere if he was tipsy. On the street again he searched the pockets of his mackintosh for the little plastic container that was rattling somewhere, and when he found it in his jacket he took two of his breath fresheners.

Evelyn drew back slightly from the barman's elderly, untidy face, from cheeks that fell into hollows, false teeth. He said again that the performance had begun.

'Thank you,' she said. 'Actually, I'm waiting for someone.'

'We could send your friend in if you liked to go on ahead. If you have your ticket. They're sometimes not particular about a disturbance before a play's got going.'

'No, actually we're just meeting here. We're not going to the theatre.'

She read, behind heavily rimmed lenses, bewilderment in the man's eyes. It was unusual, she read next, the thought flitting through his confusion. He settled for that, a conclusion reached.

'You didn't mind my asking? Only I said to my colleague where's the need for both of them to be late if they have their tickets on them?'

'It's very kind of you.'

'Thank you, madam.'

Near to where she sat he cleared the shelf of glasses, wiped it down with a damp grey cloth, moved on, expertly balancing the further glasses he collected. 'Lady's waiting for her friend,' he said to the barmaid, who was washing up at a sink behind the bar. 'They're not attending the show tonight.'

Evelyn was aware of the glances from behind the bar. Speculation would come later, understandable when there was time to kill. For the moment she was no more than a woman on her own.

'D'you think I could have another?' she called out, suddenly deciding to. 'When you have a minute?'

She speculated herself then, wondering about whoever was destined to walk in. Oh, Lord! she so often had thought when an unsuitable arrival had abruptly brought such wondering to an end. 'Oh no,' she had even murmured to herself, looking away in a futile pretence that she was expecting no one. Doggedly they had always come – the Lloyd's bank manager, the choral-music enthusiast, the retired naval officer who turned out to be a cabin steward, the widowed professor who had apologized and gone away, the one who made up board games. Even before they spoke, their doggedness and their smiles appeared to cover a multitude of sins.

She had all her life been obsessively early for appointments, and waiting yet again she made a resolution: this time if it was no good there wouldn't be a repetition. She'd just leave it; though of course a disappointment, it might be a relief.

Her drink came. The barman didn't linger. She shook her head when he said he'd bring her change.

'That's very kind of you, madam.'

She smiled that away, and was still smiling when a man appeared in the open doorway. He was hesitant, looking about him as if the place were crowded and there were several women to choose from, his nervousness not disguised. When he came closer he nodded before he spoke.

'Jeffrey,' he said. 'Evie?'

'Well, Evelyn actually.'

'Oh, I'm awfully sorry.'

His mackintosh was worn in places but wasn't grubby. His high cheekbones stood out, the skin tight where they stretched it. He didn't look at all well nourished. His dark hair, not a fleck of grey in it, was limp and she wondered if perhaps he was recovering from flu.

'Would you like your drink topped up?' he offered in a gentlemanly way. 'Nuts? Crisps?'

'No, I'm happy, thanks.'

He was fastidious, you could tell. Was there a certain vulnerability beneath that edgy manner? She always stipulated well-spoken and on that he could not be faulted. If he was recovering from even a cold, he'd naturally look peaky; no one could help that. He took off his mackintosh and a blue muffler, revealing a tweed jacket that almost matched the pale brown of his corduroy trousers.

'My choice of rendezvous surprise you?' he said.

'Perhaps a little.'

It didn't now that she had met him, for there was something about him that suggested he thought things out: theatre bars were empty places when a performance was on; there wouldn't be the embarrassment of approaches made by either of them to the wrong person. He didn't say that, but she knew. Belatedly he apologized for keeping her waiting.

'It doesn't matter in the least.'

'You're sure I can't bring you another drink?'

'No, really, thank you.'

'Well, I'll just get something for myself.'

At the bar Jeffrey asked about wine. 'D'you have white? Dry?'

'Indeed we do, sir.' The barman reached behind him and lifted a bottle from an ice bucket. 'Grinou,' he said. 'We like to keep it cool, being white.'

'Grinou?'

'It's what the wine's called, sir. La Combe de Grinou. The label's a bit washed away, but that's what it's called. Very popular in here, the Grinou is.'

Jeffrey took against the man, the way he often did with people serving him. He guessed that the barmaid looked after the man in a middle-aged daughterly way, listening to his elderly woes and ailments, occasionally inviting him to a Christmas celebration. Her daytime work was selling curtain material, Jeffrey surmised; the man had long ago retired from the same department store. Something like that it would be, the theatre bar their real world.

'All right, I'll try a glass,' he said.

They talked for a moment about the weather and then about the bar they were in, commenting on the destruction of its Georgian plasterwork, no more than a corner of the original ceiling remaining. From time to time applause or laughter reached them from the theatre's auditorium. Gingerly in their conversation they moved on to more personal matters.

Forty-seven they'd said he was. *Photographer* they'd given as his profession on the personal details' sheet, and she had thought of the photographers you saw on television, a scrum of them outside a celebrity's house or pushing in at the scene of a crime. But on the phone the girl had been reassuring: a newspaper photographer wasn't what was meant. 'No, not at all like that,' the girl had said. 'Nor weddings neither.' Distinguished in his field, the girl had said; there was a difference.

She tried to think of the names of great photographers and could remember only Cartier-Bresson, without a single image coming into her mind. She wondered about asking what kind of camera he liked best, but asked instead what kind of photographs he took.

'Townscapes,' he said. 'Really only townscapes.'

She nodded confidently, as if she caught the significance of that, as if she appreciated the attraction of photographing towns.

'Parts of Islington,' he said. 'Those little back streets in Hoxton. People don't see what's there.'

His lifetime's project was to photograph London in all its idiosyncrasies. He mentioned places: Hungerford Bridge, Drummond Street, Worship Street, Brick Lane, Wellclose Square. He spoke of manhole covers and shadows thrown by television dishes, and rain on slated roofs.

'How very interesting,' she said.

What she sought was companionship. Sometimes when she made her way to the Downs or the coast she experienced the weight of solitude; often in the cinema or the theatre she would have liked to turn to someone else to say what she'd thought of this interpretation or that. She had no particular desire to be treated to candle-lit dinners, which the bureau – the Bryanston Square Introduction Bureau – had at first assumed would be a priority; but she would not have rejected such attentions, provided they came from an agreeable source. Marriage did not come into it, but nor was it entirely ruled out.

People she knew were not aware that she was a client at the Bryanston Square Bureau, not that she was ashamed of it. There would perhaps have been some surprise, but easily she could have weathered that. What was more difficult to come to terms with, and always had been, was the uneasy sense that the truth seemed to matter less than it should, both in the agency itself and in the encounters it provided. As honestly as she knew how, she had completed the personal details' sheet, carefully deliberating before she so much as marked, one way or the other, each little box, correctly recording her age, at present fifty-one; and when an encounter took place she was at pains not to allow mistaken impressions to go unchecked. But even so there was always that same uneasiness, the nagging awareness that falsity was natural in what she was engaged upon.

'You drive?' he asked.

He watched her nod, covering her surprise. It always took them aback, that question; he couldn't think why. She seemed quite capable, he thought, and tried to remember what it said on the information he'd been sent. Had she been involved with a language school? Something like that came back to him and he mentioned it.

'That was a while ago,' she said.

She was alone now; and, as Jeffrey understood it, devoted some of her time to charity work; he deduced that there must be private means.

'My mother died in nineteen ninety-seven,' she said. 'I looked after her during her last years. A full-time occupation.'

Jeffrey imagined a legacy after the mother's death; the father, he presumed, had departed long before.

'I'm afraid photography is something I don't know much about,' she said, and he shrugged, vaguely indicating that that was only to be expected. A tooth ached a bit, the same one as the other night and coming on as suddenly, the last one on the right, at the bottom.

'You found it interesting,' he said, 'languages and that?'

She was more promising than the insurance woman, or the hospital sister they'd tried so hard to interest him in. He'd said no to both, but they'd pressed, the way they sometimes did. He'd been indifferent this time, but even so he'd agreed. While he prodded cautiously with his tongue he learnt that passing on a familiarity with foreign languages was, in fact, not a particularly interesting way of making a living. He wondered if the barman kept aspirin handy; more likely, though, the barmaid might have some; or the Gents might run to a dispenser.

'Excuse me a sec,' he said.

'Oh yes, there's something in the Gents,' the old barman said when the barmaid had poked about in her handbag and had shaken her head. 'Just inside the door, sir.'

But when Jeffrey put a pound in nothing came out. Too late he saw – scrawled on a length of perforated stamp paper and stuck too high to be noticed – *Out of order*. He swore hotly. If the woman hadn't been there he'd have created a scene, demanding his pound back, even claiming he had put in two.

'You have a car?' he enquired quite bluntly when he returned to the theatre bar, because on the way back from the Gents it had occurred to him that she had only said she could drive. *Driver?* it enquired on the wretchedly long-winded personal data thing, but he always asked, just to be sure. He was modest in his expectations where the Bryanston Square Introduction Bureau was concerned. He sought no more than a car-owner who would transport him and his photographic equipment from one chosen area of London to another, someone who – as privately he put it to himself – would be drawn into his work. He imagined a quiet person, capable after instruction of unfolding and setting up a tripod, of using a simple light-meter, of making notes and keeping a record, who would enjoy becoming part of things. He imagined conversations that were all to do with the enterprise he had undertaken; nothing more was necessary. He naturally had not revealed any of these details on the Bryanston Square application form he had completed eighteen months ago, believing that it would be unwise to do so.

'It's just I wondered,' he said in the theatre bar, 'if you possessed a car?'

He watched her shaking her head. She'd had a car until a year ago, a Nissan. 'I hardly ever used it,' she explained. 'I really didn't.'

He didn't let his crossness show, but disappointment felt like a weight within him. It wearied him, as disappointment had a way of doing. The nearest there'd ever been was the social worker with the beaten-up Ford Escort, or ages before that the club receptionist with the Mini. But neither had lasted long enough to be of any real help and both had turned unpleasant in the end. All that wasted effort, this time again; he might as well just walk away, he thought.

'My turn to get us a drink,' she said, taking a purse from her handbag and causing him to wonder if she had an aspirin in there too.

He didn't ask. He'd thought as he set out that if yet again there was nothing doing there might at least be the consolation of dinner – which references to toothache could easily put the kibosh on. He wondered now about L'Etape. He'd often paused to examine the menu by the door.

'Wine, this was.' He handed her his glass and watched her crossing the empty space to the bar. She wasn't badly dressed: no reason why she shouldn't be up to L'Etape's tariff.

She listened while he went through his cameras, giving the manufacturers' names, and details about flash and exposure. Nine he had apparently, a few of them very old and better than any on the market now. His book about London had been commissioned and would run to almost a thousand pages.

'Gosh!' she murmured. Halfway through her third gin and tonic, she felt pleasantly warm, happy enough to be here, although she knew by now that none of this was any good. 'Heavens, you'll be busy!' she said. His world was very different from hers, she added, knowing she must not go on about hers, that it would be tedious to mention all sorts of things. Why should anyone be interested in her rejection more than twenty years ago of someone she had loved? Why should anyone be interested in knowing that she had done so, it seemed now, for no good reason beyond the shadow of doubt there'd been? A stranger would not see the face that she still saw, or hear the voice she heard; or understand why, afterwards, she had wanted no one else; or hear what, afterwards, had seemed to be a truth – that doubt played tricks in love's confusion. And who could expect

a stranger to want to hear about the circumstances of a mother's lingering illness and the mercy of her death in a suburban house? You put it all
together and it made a life; you lived in its aftermath, but that, too, was
best kept back. She smiled at her companion through these reflections,
for there was no reason not to.

'I was wondering about L'Etape,' he said.

Imagining this to be another camera, she shook her head, and he said
that L'Etape was a restaurant. It was difficult then, difficult to say that
perhaps they should not begin something that could not be continued,
which his manner suggested had been his conclusion also. They were not
each other's kind: what at first had seemed to be a possibility hadn't
seemed so after three-quarters of an hour, as so often was the way. So
much was right: she would have liked to say so; she would have liked to
say that she'd enjoyed their encounter and hoped he'd shared that with
her. Her glass was nowhere near empty, nor was his; there was no hurry.

'But then I'd best get back,' she said. 'If you don't mind.'

She wondered if in his life, too, there had been a mistake that threw a
shadow, if that was why he was looking around for someone to fill a gap
he had never become used to. She smiled in case her moment of curiosity
showed, covering it safely over.

'It was just a thought,' he said. 'L'Etape.'

The interval curtain came down at an emotional moment. There was
applause, and then the first chattering voices reached the bar, which filled
up quickly. The noise of broken conversation spread in the quiet it had
disturbed, until the Tannoy announcement warned that three minutes
only remained, then two, and one.

'I'm afraid we shut up shop now,' the elderly barman said and the
plump barmaid hurried about, collecting the glasses and pushing the
chairs against one wall so that the cleaners could get at the floor when
they came in the morning. 'Sorry about that,' the barman apologized.

Jeffrey considered making a fuss, insisting on another drink, since the
place after all was a public bar. He imagined waking up at two or three in
the morning and finding himself depressed because of the way the evening
had gone. He would remember then the stern features of Sir Henry Havelock in Trafalgar Square and the two girls giggling because he'd said
something out loud. He would remember the *Out of order* sign in the
Gents. She should have been more explicit about the driving on that
bloody form instead of wasting his time.

He thought of picking up a glass and throwing it at the upside-down
bottles behind the bar, someone's leftover slice of lemon flying through the

air, glass splintering into the ashtrays and the ice-bucket, all that extra for them to clear up afterwards. He thought of walking away without another word, leaving the woman to make her peace with the pair behind the bar. Ridiculous they were, ridiculous not to have an aspirin somewhere.

'It was brilliant, your theatre-bar idea,' she said as they passed through the foyer. The audience's laughter reached them, a single ripple, quietening at once. The box office was closed, a board propped up against its ornate brass bars. Outside, the posters for the play they hadn't seen wildly proclaimed its virtues.

'Well,' he said, though without finality; uncertain, as in other ways he had seemed to be.

Yet surely she hadn't been mistaken; surely he must have known also, and as soon as she had. She imagined him with one of his many cameras, skulking about the little streets of Hoxton. There was no reason why a photographer shouldn't have an artistic temperament, which would account for his nerviness or whatever it was.

'I don't suppose,' he said, 'you'd have an aspirin?'

He had a toothache. She searched her handbag, for she sometimes had paracetamol.

'I'm sorry,' she said, still rummaging.

'It doesn't matter.'

'It's bad?'

He said he would survive. 'I'll try the Gents in L'Etape. Sometimes there's a vending machine in a Gents.'

They fell into step. It wasn't why he'd suggested L'Etape, he said. 'It's just that I felt it would be nice,' he said. 'A regretful dinner.'

When they came to a corner, he pointed up a narrower, less crowded street than the one they'd walked along. 'It's there,' he said. 'That blue light.'

Feeling sorry for him, she changed her mind.

The hat-check girl brought paracetamol to their table, since there wasn't a vending machine in the Gents. Jeffrey thanked her, indicating with a gesture that he would tip her later. At a white grand piano a pianist in a plum-coloured jacket reached out occasionally for a concoction in a tall lemonade glass, not ceasing to play his Scott Joplin medley. A young French waiter brought menus and rolls. He made a recommendation but his English was incomprehensible. Jeffrey asked him to repeat what he'd said, but it was hopeless. Typical, that was, Jeffrey thought, ordering lamb, with peas and polenta.

'I'm sorry about your toothache,' she said.

'It'll go.'

The place was not quite full. Several tables, too close to the piano, were still unoccupied. Someone applauded when the pianist began a showy variation of 'Mountain Greenery'. He threw his head about as he played, blond hair flopping.

'Shall I order the wine?' Jeffrey offered. 'D'you mind?' He never said beforehand that he intended not to pay. Better just to let it happen, he always thought.

'No, of course I don't mind,' she said.

'That's kind of you.' He felt better than he had all evening, in spite of the nagging in his lower jaw and that, he knew, would lessen when the paracetamol got going. It was always much better when they said yes to a regretful dinner, when the disappointment began to slip away. 'We'll have the Lamothe Bergeron,' he ordered. 'The '95.'

She was aware that a woman at a distant table, in a corner where there were potted plants, kept glancing at her. The woman was with two men and another woman. She seemed faintly familiar; so did one of the men.

'*Madame*,' the young waiter interrupted her efforts to place the couple, arriving with the escalope she'd ordered. '*Bon appétit, madame.*'

'Thank you.'

She liked the restaurant, the thirties' style, the pale blue lighting, the white grand piano, the aproned waiters. She liked her escalope when she tasted it, and the heavily buttered spinach, the little out-of-season new potatoes. She liked the wine.

'Not bad, this place,' her companion said. 'What d'you think?'

'It's lovely.'

They talked more easily than they had in the theatre bar and it was the theatre bar they spoke about, since it was their common ground. Odd, they'd agreed, that old barman had been; odd, too, that 'barmaid' should still be a common expression, implying in this case someone much younger, the word hanging on from another age.

'Oh, really . . .' she began when a second bottle of wine was suggested, and then she thought why not? They talked about the Bryanston Square Bureau, which was common ground too.

'They muddle things up,' he said. 'They muddle people up. They get them wrong, with all their little boxes and their questionnaires.'

'Yes, perhaps they do.'

The woman who'd kept glancing across the restaurant was listening to one of the men, who appeared to be telling a story. There was laughter when he finished. The second man lit a cigarette.

'Heavens!' Evelyn exclaimed, although she hadn't meant to.

Jeffrey turned to look and saw, several tables away, four smartly dressed people, one of the two women in a striped black and scarlet dress, the other with glasses, her pale blonde hair piled elaborately high. The men were darkly suited. Like people in an advertisement, he thought, an impression heightened by the greenery that was a background to their table. He knew the kind.

'They're friends of yours?' he asked.

'The woman in red and the man who's smoking have the flat above mine.'

She'd sold some house or other, he heard; a family house, it then became clear. She'd sold it when her mother died and had bought instead the flat she spoke of, more suitable really for a person on her own. Pasmore the people she had suddenly recognized were called. She didn't know them.

'But they know you, eh?'

He felt quite genial; the diversion passed the time.

'They've seen me,' she said.

'Coming and going, eh?'

'That kind of thing.'

'Coffee? Shall we have coffee?'

He signalled for a waiter. He would go when the wine was finished; usually he went then, slipping off to the Gents, then picking up his coat. Once there had been a complaint to the bureau about that but he'd said the woman had invited him to dinner – Belucci's it was that time – and had become drunk before the evening finished, forgetting what the arrangement had been.

'I'll hold the fort,' he said, 'if you want to say hullo to your friends.'

She smiled and shook her head. He poured himself more wine. He calculated that there were four more glasses left in the bottle and he could tell she'd had enough. The coffee came and she poured it, still smiling at him in a way he found bewildering. He calculated the amount she'd had to drink: two gin and tonics he'd counted earlier, and now the wine, a good four glasses. 'I wouldn't even know the Pasmores' name,' she was saying, 'except that it's on their bell at the downstairs door.'

He moved the wine bottle in case she reached out for it. The pianist, silent for a while, struck up again, snatches from *West Side Story*.

'It's lovely here,' she murmured, and Jeffrey would have sworn her eyes searched for his. He felt uneasy, his euphoria of a few moments ago slipping away; he hoped there wasn't going to be trouble. In an effort to distract her mood, he said:

'Personally, I shan't be bothering the Bryanston Square Bureau again.'

She didn't appear to hear, although that wasn't surprising in the din that was coming from the piano.

'I don't suppose,' she said, 'you have a cigarette about you?'

Her smile, lavish now, had spread into all her features. She'd ticked *Non-smoker* on the information sheet, she said, but all that didn't really matter any more. He pressed a thumbnail along the edge of the transparent cover of the Silk Cut packet he had bought in the Salisbury and held it out to her across the table.

'I used to once,' she said. 'When smoking was acceptable.'

She took a cigarette and he picked up a little box of matches with *L'Etape* on it. He struck one for her, her fingers touching his. He lit a cigarette for himself.

'How good that is!' She blew out smoke, leaning forward as she spoke, cheeks flushed, threads of smoke drifting in the air. 'I used to love a cigarette.'

She reached a hand out as if to seize one of his, but played instead with the salt-cellar, pushing it about. She was definitely tiddly. With her other hand she held her cigarette in the air, lightly between two fingers, as Bette Davis used to in her heyday.

'It's a pity you sold your car,' he said, again seeking a distraction.

She didn't answer that, but laughed, as if he'd been amusing, as if he'd said something totally different. She was hanging on his words, or so it must have seemed to the people who had recognized her, so intent was her scrutiny of his face. She'll paw me, Jeffrey thought, before the evening's out.

'They're gathering up their things,' she said. 'They're going now.'

He didn't turn around to see, but within a minute or so the people passed quite close. They smiled at her, at Jeffrey too. Mr Pasmore inclined his head; his wife gave a little wave with her fingers. They would gossip about this to the residents of the other flats if they considered it worthwhile to do so: the solitary woman in the flat below theirs had something going with a younger man. No emotion stirred in Jeffrey, neither sympathy nor pity, for he was not given to such feelings. A few drinks and a temptation succumbed to, since temptation wasn't often there: the debris of all that was nothing much when the audience had gone, and it didn't surprise him that it was simply left there, without a comment.

When a waiter came, apologetically to remind them that they were at a table in the no-smoking area, she stubbed her cigarette out. Her features settled into composure; the flush that had crept into her cheeks drained away. A silence gathered while this normality returned and it was she in the end who broke it, as calmly as if nothing untoward had occurred.

'Why did you ask me twice if I possessed a car?'

'I thought I had misunderstood.'

'Why did it matter?'

'Someone with a car would be useful to me in my work. My gear is heavy. I have no transport myself.'

He didn't know why he said that; he never had before. In response her nod was casual, as if only politeness had inspired the question she'd asked. She nodded again when he said, not knowing why he said it either:

'Might our dinner be your treat? I'm afraid I can't pay.'

She reached across the table for the bill the waiter had brought him. In silence she wrote a cheque and asked him how much she should add on.

'Oh, ten per cent or so.'

She took a pound from her purse, which Jeffrey knew was for the hat-check girl.

They walked together to an Underground station. The townscapes were a weekend thing, he said: he photographed cooked food to make a living. Hearing which tins of soup and vegetables his work appeared on, she wondered if he would add that his book of London would never be completed, much less published. He didn't, but she had guessed it anyway.

'Well, I go this way,' he said when they had bought their tickets and were at the bottom of the escalators.

He'd told her about the photographs he was ashamed of because she didn't matter; without resentment she realized that. And witnessing her excursion into foolishness, he had not mattered either.

'Your toothache?' she enquired and he said it had gone.

They did not shake hands or remark in any way upon the evening they'd spent together, but when they parted there was a modest surprise: that they'd made use of one another was a dignity compared with what should have been. That feeling was still there while they waited on two different platforms and while their trains arrived and drew away again. It lingered while they were carried through the flickering dark, as intimate as a pleasure shared.

Graillis's Legacy

He hadn't meant to break his journey but there was time because he was early, so Graillis made a detour, returning to a house he hadn't visited for twenty-three years. A few miles out on the Old Fort road, devoured by rust, the entrance gates had sagged into undergrowth. The avenue was short, twisting off to the left, the house itself lost behind a line of willows.

When the woman who'd been left a widow in it had sold up and gone to Dublin, a farmer acquired the place for its mantelpieces and the lead of its roof. He hadn't ever lived there, but his car had been drawn up on the gravel when the house was first empty and Graillis had gone back, just once. Since then there'd been talk of everything falling into disrepair, not that there hadn't been signs of this before, the paint of the windows flaking, the garden neglected. The woman on her own hadn't bothered much; although it had never otherwise been his nature to do so, her husband had seen to everything.

Graillis didn't get out of his car, instead turned it slowly on the grass that had begun to grow through the gravel. He drove away, cautious on the pot-holed surface of the avenue, then slowed by the bends of a narrow side-road. A further mile on, a signpost guided him to the town he had chosen for his afternoon's business. An hour's drive from the town he lived in himself, it was more suitable for his purpose because he wasn't known there.

Still with time to spare, he parked and took a ticket from a machine. He locked his car and went to look for Davitt Street, where he enquired in a newsagent's and was told that Lenehan and Clifferty's office was four doors further on, what used to be the old Co-op Hardware.

'Mr Clifferty won't keep you a minute,' the girl assured him in the spacious reception area where the day's newspapers were laid out. Only last week's *Irish Field* had been unfolded.

'You were recommended to us, Mr Graillis?' Clifferty asked, having apologized because there'd been a wait of much longer than a minute. He was a man in a tweed suit, with a tie of the same material, and garnet cufflinks. He was stylish for a country solicitor, his considerable bulk crowned by a full head of prematurely white hair. Graillis was less at ease in comparison, more humbly attired in corduroy trousers and an imitation suede jacket. He was an angular, thin man of fifty-nine, his fair hair receding and touched with grey.

'You're in the Golden Pages,' he responded to the solicitor's query.

He passed the envelope he'd brought with him across the green leather surface of a tidy desk that was embossed with a pattern at the corners. Clifferty extracted a folded sheet of writing paper and when he'd read its contents made a single note on a pad, then read the letter again.

'She was a woman a while back,' Graillis said.

'Well, if I've got this right, you're not attempting anything illegal, Mr Graillis. A legacy can be rejected.'

'It's that I was wondering about.'

Clifferty returned the letter to its envelope but didn't hand it back. 'These people are a reputable firm of solicitors. We do some business with them. I can write to say the inheritance is an embarrassment if that's what you'd like me to do. The estate would be wound up in the usual way, with the proposed bequest left in as part of it.'

'I wouldn't want to turn my back on the thought that was there. Since I'm mentioned in the will I wouldn't want to do that.'

'You're more than mentioned, Mr Graillis. From what's indicated in the notification you received, no one much else is. Besides charities.'

Sensing the content of the solicitor's thoughts, Graillis was aware of an instinct to contradict them. It was understandable that the interest of a country solicitor should be fed by what he assumed, that the routine of family law in a provincial town should make room for a hint of the dramatic. Graillis might have supplied the facts, but did not do so.

'Maybe some small memento,' he said. 'Maybe an ornament or a piece of china. Anything like that.'

'You've been left a sum of money that's not inconsiderable, Mr Graillis.'

'That's why I drove over, though – to see could I accept a little thing instead.'

There'd been an ashtray with a goldfinch on it, but in case it had since been broken, he didn't like to mention it. And there were dinner plates he'd always liked particularly, with a flowery edging in two shades of blue.

'Just something, was what I thought. If it would be possible.'

When the snowdrops spread in clumps beneath the trees, she'd said he might like some and would have given him what she had picked already. Wrapped in damp newspaper, they would keep their freshness, she said, and he tried to remember how it was she broke off what she was saying when she realized her suggestion wasn't possible. She had tried to settle the stems back in the water of the vase she'd taken them from but it was difficult, and then the floor was scattered with flowers gone limp already. It didn't matter, she could pick some more, she said.

'Oh, it would be possible, I'm sure,' Clifferty said, 'to have what you want. I only mention the other.'

The solicitor had a way of smoothing the wiry, reddish thicket of his eyebrows, a leisurely attention given first to one and then the other. He allowed himself this now, before he continued:

'But I should tell you I would require a sight of the will before advising you on any part of it.'

'Would they send it down from Dublin?'

'They'd send a copy.'

Clifferty nodded saying that, the conversation over. He asked Graillis what line he was in and Graillis said he was in charge of the branch library in the town where he lived. He added that a long time ago he had been employed in the Munster and Leinster Bank there, in the days when the bank was still called that. He stood up.

'Make an appointment with the girl outside for this day week, Mr Graillis,' Clifferty said before they shook hands.

He drove slowly through flat, unchanging landscape and stopped when he had almost reached the town he was returning to. No other car was drawn up outside the Jack Doyle Inn, no bicycle leant against the silver-painted two-bar railings that protected its windows. Inside, the woman who served him called him by his name.

She went away when, pouring him a John Jameson, she'd asked him how he was these days. 'Give a rap on the counter if you'll want something more,' she said, a smell of simmering bacon beginning to waft in from the cooking she returned to. There was no one else in the bar.

He should have explained to the solicitor that he was a widower, that there was no marriage now to be damaged by a legacy that might seem to indicate a deception in the past. He should have explained that his doubts about accepting so much, and travelling to seek advice in another town, had only to do with avoiding curiosity and gossip in his own. He didn't know why he hadn't explained, why it hadn't occurred to him that Clifferty had probably taken it upon himself to pity a wronged wife who was now being wronged again, that subterfuge and concealment were again being called upon.

He took his whiskey to a corner. It would not have seemed unusual to speak about his marriage, about love's transformation within it, about his grief when it was no longer there, about the moments and occasions it had since become. Caught in the drift of memory, he saw – as vividly as if it were still the time when love began – a girl in a convent uniform, green and blue, shyness in her bright, fresh face. Half smiling, she turned her head away, made to blush by her friends when the gawky junior from the Munster and Leinster Bank went by on the street. And she was shy again when, grown up, she walked for the first time into the bank with her father's weekly cheques and takings. In her middle age, the mother she had twice become made her only a little different, made her the person she remained until there was the tragedy of a winter's night, on an icy road three years ago.

Graillis sipped his whiskey and lit a cigarette and slowly smoked, then drank some more. Beneath his professional rectitude, the solicitor would naturally have been more interested in the woman of the legacy than in the wife. *In her sixty-eighth year* was the only tit-bit the letter he'd been given to read revealed: she'd been an older woman, he would have realized.

The whiskey warmed Graillis, the cigarette was a comfort. He hadn't explained because you couldn't explain, because there was too little to explain, not too much. But even so he might have said he was a widower. He sat a little longer, eyeing an ornamental sign near the door – white letters on blue enamel – *You May Telephone From Here*. 'A small one,' he said when his rapping on the surface of the counter brought a sleek-haired youth he remembered as a child. The girl in Lenehan and Clifferty's reception had given him a card with his next week's appointment noted on it, and the telephone number of Lenehan and Clifferty as well. It wasn't too late, a few minutes past five.

'If it's possible,' he said when the same girl answered. 'Just something I forgot to say to Mr Clifferty.'

Waiting, he lit another cigarette. His glass was on a shelf in front of him, beside an ashtray with *Coca-Cola* on it. 'Mr Clifferty?' he said when Clifferty said hullo.

'Good evening, Mr Graillis.'

'It's just I wanted to clear up a detail.'

'What detail's that, Mr Graillis?'

'I don't think I explained that I'm widowed.'

The solicitor made a sympathetic sound. Then he said he was sorry, and Graillis said:

'It's just if you thought my wife's alive it would have been misleading.'

'I follow what you're saying to me.'

'I didn't want a misunderstanding.'

'No.'

'It's difficult, a thing like this coming out of the blue.'

'I appreciate that, Mr Graillis, and I have your instruction. I'm sanguine it can be met. If there's anything else, if there's a worry at all, bring it with you when you come over next week.'

'It's only I wanted you to know what I told you just now. There's nothing else.'

'We'll say goodbye so.'

'Who'd get what I'm handing back?'

'Whoever's in line for it. Some grand-nephew somewhere, I'd hazard. There's often a grand-nephew.'

'Thanks,' Graillis said and, not knowing what else to do, returned the receiver to its hook.

He picked up his glass and took it back to the table he'd been sitting at. He had thought he would feel all right after he'd seen a solicitor, and had thought so again when the telephone sign had given him the idea of ringing up. But still there was the unease that had begun when the letter about the legacy came. He didn't know why he'd gone to the house; he didn't know why he'd got into a state because he hadn't told a man who was a stranger to him that he was widowed. It had been the whiskey talking when he'd said he wanted to clear up a detail; it was whiskey courage that had allowed him to dial the number. He was bewildered by the resurrection of a guilt that long ago had softened away to nothing. In that other time no pain had been caused, no hurt; he had managed the distortions that created falsity, the lies of silence; what he had been forgiven for was not seeming to be himself for a while. A crudity still remained in the solicitor's reading of the loose ends that still were there: the wronged wife haunting restlessly from her grave, the older woman claiming from hers the lover who had slipped away from her.

'God, we never had it worse!'

'Oh, we will, boy, we will.'

Deploring the fall in sheep prices, two men settled themselves at the bar. The sleek-haired youth returned to serve them, and then an older man came in, with a white greyhound on a leash. The youth poured Smithwick's for him and said the *Evening Herald* hadn't been dropped off the bus yet. 'Shocking,' the old man grumbled, hunching himself over the *Tullamore Tribune* instead.

Graillis finished what was left of his whiskey. After the accident, when the notice had appeared in the obituary columns of the *Irish Times*, no lines of condolence had come from the woman whose half-ruined house he had visited. He had thought there might be a note and then had thought it was not appropriate that there should be. She would have thought so too.

He stubbed out his second cigarette. He never smoked at home, continuing not to after he'd found himself alone there, and smoking was forbidden in the branch library, a restriction he insisted upon himself. But in the drawing-room he had sat in so often in the autumn of 1979 and during the winter and spring that followed it, a friendship had developed over cigarettes, touches of lipstick on the cork tips that had accumulated in the ashtray with the goldfinch on it. That settled in his thoughts, still as a photograph, arrested with a clarity that today felt cruel.

He carried his glass back to the bar. He talked for a moment about the weather to the sleek-haired youth before he left. 'Take care, Mr Graillis,' the boy called after him, and he said he would.

Driving on, he tried to think of nothing, not of the girl who had become his wife when he was still a junior in the Munster and Leinster Bank, not of the woman he'd got to know when she borrowed novels from his branch library. The landscape he passed through was much the same as the landscape had been before he'd called in at the public house. It didn't change when a sign in Irish and English indicated the town ahead, only doing so when the town's outskirts began: the first few bungalows, summer blossom in their trim gardens. Cars with prices on their windscreens crowded Riordan's forecourt, *Your Nissan Dealer* a reminder of the franchise. He passed the electricity works and then the rusty green Raleigh sign, the two figures and their bicycles only there in places.

Evening traffic slowed his progress on the town's main street. He wound down the window beside him and rested his elbow on it. He had intended to go straight to where he lived but changed his mind and instead turned into Cartmill Street, where the branch library was. No traffic disturbed the quiet here. Sometimes boys rattled up and down on their skate-boards, but there were no boys now, and hardly a pedestrian. He parked beneath the lime trees where the walk by the river began and crossed the street to a small building crouched low among the abandoned warehouses that ran the length of Cartmill Street and gave it character, as the lime trees and the river did.

Today he had closed the library at one o'clock, the only weekday it was shut in the afternoon, when some of the main-street shops were also. He turned a key in the deadlock, another in the Yale, then pushed the pale-blue door open. It was a Mr Haverty – failed grocer of Lower North Street, lifelong bachelor, aficionado of Zane Grey among Wild West storytellers – who had nagged the county library service into letting the town have a branch library, who had become, in fact, its first librarian. Since those early days, when he was a borrower himself, Graillis had felt at home in these modest premises, the walls entirely shelves, a narrow counter near the door. He had been the branch library's most frequent visitor then, and when galloping arthritis made Mr Haverty's duties increasingly a burden it was Mr Haverty who nominated him as his successor, enticing him away from the superior prospects of the bank. And Graillis said yes before he had a chance to dwell on all the disadvantages. 'But why on earth?' the girl he'd married cried out in bewilderment and disappointment. His safe employment had been taken for granted; in time promotion would mean occupancy of a squat grey landmark in the town, the house above the bank, with railings and a grained hall door. She had married into that; books had never been an interest they shared, had never been, for her, a need.

The woman for whom they were had often been noticed by Graillis about the town, coming out of a shop, getting into her car, not the kind of woman he would ever have known. Tall, and beautiful in her way, there was a difference about her, suggested by her composure and her clothes, and she seemed more different still when vaguely she wondered where Mr Haverty was, not knowing he had retired. She smiled when they talked then, and Graillis hadn't seen her smile before. The next time they talked for longer, and after that more easily. When she asked him which novelists he recommended he introduced her to Proust and Malcolm Lowry, to Forster and Madox Ford, and Mrs Gaskell and Wilkie Collins. He got in another copy of *Dubliners* for her because the existing copy had been left out in the rain and rendered unintelligible. He drew her attention to *Brighton Rock* and *Tender is the Night*. She found Elizabeth Bowen for herself.

In her tidy drawing-room he poured the wine at lunchtime. Not feeling careless themselves, for they were not, they talked about the careless people of Scott Fitzgerald, about the Palace Flophouse, and Hangover Square and Dorlcote Mill. The struggles of Jude acquired new small dimensions, the goodness of Joe Gargery marked a day, as Mrs Proudie did and Daisy Miller. Ellen Wedgeworth died, Dermot Trellis slept. Maurice Bendrix embraced the wife of his friend.

They did not go in for telling one another the story of their lives. Their conversation was not like that, yet almost without their knowing it their lives were there, in a room made different by their friendship. They did not touch upon emotions, nor touch upon regret or anything that might have been; they did not lose control of words. They did not betray, she her finished past, he what still was there. She brought in coffee, he turned from gazing out at rain or cold spring sunshine, they spoke again of Wildfell Hall. Her front door wide behind her, she stood on the steps, and was there in his driving-mirror until the willow trees were there instead.

There was the beginning of gossip: his car seen on that road, people noticing that she came often to the library. It was not much but would become so; he knew that and so did she; they did not say it. When the days began to lengthen there had been three seasons. In summer they would sit outside, at the white table on the lawn, but summer did not come.

Graillis replaced on the shelves what had been returned earlier today, *The Garden of Allah* still read by someone, crime stories more popular, Georgette Heyer holding her own. Sunburnt spines enclosed a world that the smell of old paper made what it was. She had said she envied him this place.

He looked about him before he left. A poster hung from the counter by the door, advertising the Strawberry Festival in June. Above the door, in straw, there was St Brigid's Cross. It was on the evening of the day the removal vans had clattered empty through the town and later lumbered away full of her possessions that she'd said she envied him. They'd had to wait until *Seven Pillars of Wisdom* was stamped for Mrs Garraher before they said goodbye, a Tuesday it had been.

He locked the door behind him and drove away.

Hearts were forming in the lettuces of his vegetable beds. He cut one, and chives and parsley. He walked about before he collected what he'd left on the path that ran beside his vegetables, adding a tomato that had ripened beneath a cloche. He had never become used to the emptiness of this return to his garden and his house, and he supposed he never would. In his kitchen he opened tins of soup and sardines. He washed the lettuce.

'He phoned me afterwards,' he imagined Clifferty saying now, standing in a kitchen doorway, going through his day, his solicitor's caution estimating how much he could pass on. 'I don't know what that man's trouble was,' Clifferty said, and added that there hadn't been much else today.

There was whiskey somewhere; Graillis looked for it and found it among the kitchen bottles. He poured a little, mixed oil and vinegar for his salad. On the radio there was agricultural news, the latest from the markets, and then a brash disc-jockey pumped out his chatter before a cacophony began. Silence was a pleasure after that.

Laying out a knife and fork on the kitchen table, Graillis wondered if either of his children would phone tonight. There was no reason why one of them should. There'd been nothing wrong, no cause for concern, when he'd heard from both of them not long ago. He poured more whiskey, not wanting to eat yet. He couldn't remember any other time when he'd drunk alone in this house. He kept the whiskey for people who dropped in.

Taking his glass with him, he walked about his garden, among penstemons and roses and crocosmia not yet in bud. The row of artichokes he'd planted in February stood as high as empty sunflowers. Lavender scented the warm twilight.

The whiskey talk was private now, a whisper from his orderly remembering that no longer nurtured panic. In visiting the solicitor, in going to the house, he had touched what should not be touched except in memory, where everything was there for ever and nothing could be changed. Retirement from a branch library would not bring much and so there'd been a gesture. A stranger's interpretation of that – what curiosity hatched or gossip spun – was neither here nor there. Again, instead, there was the fresh, bright face, the gentle shyness. Again, instead, the older woman lifted to her lips a tan-tipped cigarette touched with crimson. Again there was the happiness of marriage, again embraces were imagined.

There was no more, nor would there be. Not even an ornament, for that would cheat reality. Not even a piece of china, and he would write to say so. The winter flowers lay scattered in the shadow of a secret, deception honouring a silent love.

Solitude

I reach the lock by standing on the hall chair. I open the hall door and pull the chair back to the alcove. I comb my hair in the hallstand glass. I am seven years old, waiting for my father to come downstairs.

Our house is a narrow house with a blue hall door, in a square, in London. My father has been away and now he is back. *The first morning we'll go to the café.* Ages ago my mother read what he had written for me on the postcard. 'They're called the Pyramids,' she said when I pointed at the picture. And then: 'Not long before he's back.' But it was fifty days.

I hear him whistling on the stairs, 'London Bridge Is Falling Down', and then he hugs me, because he has come in the night when I was asleep. He doesn't believe it, he says, how I have grown. 'I missed you terribly,' he says.

We walk together, across the square to where the traffic and the streets are. 'Coffee,' my father says in the café. 'Coffee, please, and a slice of Russian cake for you-know-who.'

But all the time there is what happened and all the time I know I mustn't say. A child to witness such a thing was best forgotten, Mrs Upsilla said, and Charles nodded his long black head. No blame, Charles said; any child would play her games behind a sofa; all they'd had to do was look. 'No skin off my nose,' Charles said. 'No business of a poor black man's.' And not knowing I was still outside the kitchen door, Mrs Upsilla said it made her sick to her bones. Well, it was something, Charles reminded her, that my mother wouldn't take her friend to the bedroom that was my father's too. At least there was the delicacy of that. But Mrs Upsilla said what delicacy, and called my mother's friend a low-down man.

'You're learning French now?' my father says in the café. 'Do you like French?'

'Not as much as history.'

'What have you learnt in history?'

'That William the Conqueror's son also got an arrow in his eye.'

'Which eye? Did they say which eye?'

'No, I don't think so.'

In the café the waitress is the one who always comes to us. My father says that is because we always sit at the same table. He says our waitress has Titian hair; he says that's what that colour is. My father is always commenting on people, saying they have this or that, guessing about them, or asking questions. Often he falls into conversation with people who enquire the way on the street, and beggars, anyone who stops him, anyone in shops. 'Rich as a candy king,' I heard someone in the café say once, and my father laughed, shaking his head.

All the time in the café I want to tell him, because I tell him everything when he comes back from a journey. I want to tell him about the dream I had that same night, all of it happening again. 'Oh, horrid nightmare,' my mother comforted me, not knowing what it was about because I didn't say, because I didn't want to.

'The picture gallery?' my father suggests when we have had our coffee. 'Or the dolls' museum today? Look, I have this.'

He spreads out on the table a handkerchief he has bought, all faded colours, so flimsy you can see through it in places. Old, he says, Egyptian silk. There is a pattern and he draws his forefinger through it so that I can see it too. 'For you,' he says. 'For you.'

In the bus, on the way to the dolls' museum he talks about Egypt. So hot it could make your skin peel off, so hot you have to lie down in the afternoon. One day he'll bring me with him; one day he'll show me the Pyramids. He takes my hand when we walk the last bit.

I know the way, but when we get there the doll I like best isn't on her shelf. Unwell, the man says, getting better in hospital. It's his way of putting it, my father says. He asks the man: that doll, the Spanish doll, will be back next week. 'Well, we can come again,' my father promises. 'Who's going to stay up for the party?' he says when we're back in the house.

The party is tonight. In the kitchen the wine bottles are laid out, two long rows all the length of the table, and other bottles on trays, and glasses waiting to be filled. Charles comes specially early to help when there is a party. There always is when my father returns.

'You sit down there and have your sandwich.' Mrs Upsilla's grey head is bent over what she's cooking; she's too busy to look up. Charles winks at me and I try to wink back but I can't do it properly. He passes close to where I'm sitting and then the sandwich I don't want isn't there any more. 'Oh, there's a good girl,' Mrs Upsilla says when she asks if I've eaten it and I say yes. And Charles smiles. And Davie giggles and Abigail does.

Abigail and Davie aren't real, but most of the time they're there. They were that day, when the door opened and my mother and her friend came into the drawing-room. 'It's all right,' my mother said. 'She's not here.' And Davie giggled and Abigail did too and I made them be quiet.

'My, my,' Charles says in the kitchen when Mrs Upsilla calls me a good girl. He says it so often it annoys Mrs Upsilla. 'Why's he saying that?' she asks me every time. 'What's he on about?' And Charles always laughs.

I thank Mrs Upsilla for the sandwich I haven't eaten because she likes me to thank her for things. On the way upstairs I remember that when the person in the café said *as rich as a candy king* I heard my father repeating that to my mother afterwards; he said that maybe what the person meant was he was rich to have so beautiful a wife. Or you could take it differently, Mrs Upsilla said when I told her: the person in the café could have been referring to my mother's inheritance.

Upstairs, my father is standing at the door of their bedroom, my mother is tidying the bed. He has brought her a handkerchief too, bigger than mine, and already she wears it as a scarf. 'So beautiful you are!' my father says and my mother laughs, a sound that's like the tinkling of a necklace he gave her once. The bath taps are dribbling in the bathroom, turned low for my mother's bath. 'Who's going to help me take the corks out?' my father says, and my mother asks him to open the window at the top. Her lips are soft when she kisses my forehead, her scent makes me want to close my eyes and always be able to smell it. 'Good darling,' she whispers.

In the kitchen my father draws out the corks and I make a pile of them, and count them. The red bottles are really green, he says, but you can't see that until they're empty. He cuts away the shiny covering over each cork before he puts the corkscrew in. 'Well, that's all done,' he says and asks how many and I say thirty-six. 'You take me to the picture gallery next time?' he says, and the dancing ladies come into my head, and the storm at the cricket match, and Saint Catherine, and the portrait of the artist. 'That to look forward to,' my father says before he goes upstairs again.

We play a game in my room, Abigail and Davie and I. We pretend we are in Egypt, climbing up a pyramid, and Abigail says we should be wearing our cotton sun hats because the sun can burn your head even through your hair. So we go down for them but then it's cooler so we walk about the streets. We buy things in a market, presents to bring home, rings and brooches and jars of Egyptian peaches, and Egyptian chocolate and Egyptian rugs for the floor. Then I go back to the kitchen.

Charles has gone out for ice. 'You going to keep me company?' Mrs Upsilla says, still busy with her cooking. 'You'll trip on those laces,' she says, allowing the electric mixer to operate on its own for a moment. A nasty accident there could be, and she ties my laces. Always double-tie a shoelace, she says, and I go away.

In the drawing-room the bowls of olives and tit-bits are laid out; the fire is blazing, the wire net of the fire-guard drawn down. I watch the raindrops sliding on the window-panes. I watch the people in the square, hurrying through the rain, a woman holding an umbrella over her dog, Charles returning with the ice. The cars go slowly, the street lights have come on.

I sit in the armchair by the fire, looking at the pictures in the books, the old woman who kept children in a cage, the giants, the dwarfs, the Queen's reflection in the looking-glass. I look out into the square again: my mother's friend is the first to come. He waits for a car to pass before he crosses the square, and then there is the doorbell and his footsteps on the stairs.

'Have one of these,' he says in the drawing-room: cheese straws that Mrs Upsilla has made. 'Time for your dancing lesson,' and he puts the music on. He shows me the same steps again because I never try, because I don't want to try. 'How are they?' he asks and I know he means Davie and Abigail; ever since my mother mentioned them to him he asks about them. I might have told him they were there that afternoon, but instead I just say they're all right. Then other people come and he talks to them. I hate him so much I wish he could be dead.

I listen from one of the window-seats, half behind the curtain. A man is telling about a motor race he has taken part in. One of these days he'll win, a woman says. In his white jacket, Charles offers the drinks.

Other people come. 'Well, goodness me!' Mr Fairlie smiles down at me, and then he sits beside me. Old and tired, he says, not up to this gallivanting. He asks me what I did today and I tell him about the dolls' museum. He manages on his own, Mrs Upsilla told me, since his wife died. My mother went to the funeral, but he doesn't talk about that now. 'Poor old boy,' Charles said.

You can hardly hear the music because so many people are talking. Every time Charles passes by with another tray he waves to me with a finger and Mr Fairlie says that's clever. 'Well, look at you two!' a woman says and she kisses Mr Fairlie and kisses me, and then my father comes. 'Who's sleepy?' he says and he takes me from the party.

It will be ages before he goes away again: he promises that before he turns the light out, but in the dark it's like it was in the dream. He'll go away and he won't come back, not ever wanting to. There'll never be the picture gallery again, our favourite picture the picnic on the beach. There'll never be the café again, there'll never be the dolls' museum. He'll never say, 'Who's sleepy?'

In the dark I don't cry although I want to. I make myself think of something else, of the day there was an accident in the square, of the day a man came to the door, thinking someone else lived in our house. And then I think about Mr Fairlie on his own. I see him as clearly as I did when he was beside me on the window-seat, the big freckles on his forehead, his wisps of white hair, his eyes that don't look old at all. 'A surgeon in his day,' Mrs Upsilla told Charles the morning my mother went to the funeral. I see Mr Fairlie in his house although I've never been there. I see him cooking for himself as best he can, and with a Hoover on the stairs. 'Who'd mind being cut up by Mr Fairlie?' Charles said once.

The music's so faint it sounds as if it's somewhere else, not in our house, and I wonder if they're dancing. By ten o'clock the party will be over, Mrs Upsilla said, and then they'll go off to different restaurants, or maybe they'll all go to the same one, and some will just go home. It's that kind of party, not lasting for very long, not like some Mrs Upsilla has known. 'Here?' Charles asked, surprised when she said that. 'Here in this house?' And she said no, not ever an all-night party here, and Charles nodded in his solemn way and said you'd know it. He'll stay for an hour or so when everyone has gone, helping Mrs Upsilla to clear up. I've never been awake then.

Davie says it was some kind of game. Fun, he says, but Abigail shakes her head, her black plaits flying about. I don't want to talk about it. A Wednesday it was, Mrs Upsilla gone off for the afternoon, Charles tending the flowerbeds in the square.

I try to think about Mr Fairlie again, having to make his bed, doing all the other things his wife did, but Mr Fairlie keeps slipping away. My mother's dress was crumpled on the floor and I could see it when I peeped out, her necklace thrown down too. Afterwards, she said they should have locked the door.

The music is still far away. The noise of the people isn't like people talking, more like a hum. I push the bedclothes back and tip-toe to the stairs to look down through the banisters. Mrs Upsilla is dressed specially for the party, and Charles is carrying in another tray of glasses. Mrs Upsilla goes in too, with two plates of tit-bits. Bacon wound round an apricot she makes, and sandwiches no bigger than a stamp. People come out and stand about on the landing. My mother and her friend are there for a moment, before she goes into the drawing-room again. He stays there, his shoulder against the wall by the window, the red curtains drawn over. 'The child's on to it,' was what he said the day before my father came back.

I don't want to go back to bed because the dream will be there even if I'm not asleep, Mrs Upsilla saying my father's gone for ever, that of course he had to. When I look for it, the leather suitcase he takes on his travels won't be there and I'll know it never will be again. I'll take out the Egyptian handkerchief and I'll remember my father spreading it on the café table, showing me the pattern. 'Our café,' he calls it.

My mother's friend looks up from the landing that's two flights down. He waves and I watch him coming up the stairs. There's a cigarette hanging from his mouth but he hasn't lit it and he doesn't take it out when he puts a finger to his lips. 'Enough to make them drunk,' Charles said when he saw the bottles opened on the kitchen table, and I wonder if my mother's friend is drunk because he takes another cigarette from his packet even though he hasn't lit the first one.

When he sways he has to reach out for the banister. He laughs, as if that's just for fun. I can see the sweat on his face, like raindrops on his forehead. His eyes are closed when he takes another step. Slowly he goes on coming up, another step and then another and another. There's a fleck of spit at the edge of his mouth, the two cigarettes have fallen on to the stair carpet. When I reach out I can touch him. My fingertips are on the dark cloth of his sleeve and I can feel his arm beneath, and everything is different then.

There is his tumbling down, there is the splintered banister. There is the thud, and then another and another. There is the stillness, and Mrs Upsilla looking up at me.

I watch them from my window, coming separately to the table they have chosen for breakfast in the garden of the hotel. They place their gifts by my place. They speak to one another, but I never know what they say in private. I turn from the window and powder over the coral lipstick I have just applied. On my seventeenth birthday nothing of my reflection is different in an oval looking-glass.

Downstairs, the salon I pass through is empty, the shutters half in place against the glare of sun that will be bothersome to the hotel guests later in the day.

'*Bonjour, mademoiselle,*' a waiter greets me in the garden.

Even in the early morning the air is mellow. Chestnuts have begun to fall; bright crimson leaves are shrivelling. The sky is cloudless.

'Well, old lady,' my father says. There is a single rose, pink bled with scarlet, which he has picked for me. On my birthday he always finds a rose somewhere.

'What shall we do today?' my mother asks when she has poured my coffee and my father remembers the year of the Pilgrims' Way, when he took me on his back because I was tired, when we met the old man who told us about Saint Sisinnius. He remembers the balloon trip and the year of the casino. Birthdays are always an occasion, my mother's in July, my father's in May, mine in October.

We live in hotels. We've done so since we left the house in the square, all kinds of hotels, in the different countries of Europe, a temporary kind of life it seemed at first, acquiring permanence later.

'So what shall we do?' my mother asks again.

It is my choice because of the day and after I've opened the presents they've given me, after I've embraced them and thanked them, I say that what I'd like to do is to walk through the birch woods and have a picnic where the meadows begin.

'*Moi, je suis tous les sports*,' a man is telling his friend at the table next to ours. '*Il n'y en a pas un seul auquel je ne m' intéresse pas*.'

I can hear now, thirty-five years later, that man's rippling voice. I can see the face I glimpsed, bespectacled and pink, and hear his companion ordering *thé de Ceylan*.

'It will be lovely, that walk today,' my mother says, and we choose our picnic and after breakfast go to buy the different items and put our lunch together ourselves.

'Why do you always find a rose for me?'

I ask that on our walk, when my mother is quite far ahead of my father and myself. I have not chosen the moment; it is not because my mother isn't there; there's never anything like that.

'Oh, there isn't a reason for a rose, you know. It's just that sometimes a person wants to give one.'

'You make everything good for me.'

'Because it is your birthday.'

'I didn't mean only on my birthday.'

My mother has reached the meadows and calls back to us. When we catch up with her the picnic is already spread out, the wine uncorked.

'When your father and I first met,' she says once lunch has begun, 'he was buying a film for his camera and found himself short. That's how we met, in a little shop. He was embarrassed so I lent him a few coins from my purse.'

'Your mother has always had the money.'

'And it has never made a difference. An inheritance often does; but by chance, I think, this one never has.'

'No, it has never made a difference. But before we say another word we must drink a toast to today.'

My father pours the wine. 'You must not drink yourself, Villana. That isn't ever done.'

'Then may I have a toast to you? Is that ever done?'

'Well, do it and then it shall be.'

'Thank you for my birthday.'

In the sudden manner he often has my father says:

'Marco Polo was the first traveller to bring back to Europe an account of the Chinese Empire. No one believed him. No one believed that the places he spoke of, or the people – not even Kublai Khan – existed. That is the history lesson for today, old lady. Or history and geography all in one. It doesn't matter how we think of it.'

'In German "to think" is *denken*,' my mother interposes. 'And in Italian?'

'*Pensare*. And *credere* of course.'

'This ham is delicious,' my father says.

They took me from England because that was best. I never went to school again. They taught me in their way, and between them they knew a lot: they taught me everything. My father's ambitions as an Egyptologist fell away. Once upon a time when he went on his travels – always determined to make discoveries that had not been made before – he scrimped and saved in order to be independent in his marriage, and in Egypt often slept on park benches. But after we left the house in the square my father had no profession; he became the amateur he once regarded as a status he despised. His books did not remain unwritten, but he did not ever want to publish them.

'Oh, how good this is!' he says, his soft voice hardly heard when my birthday picnic is over, the wine all drunk. We lie, all three of us, in the warm autumn sun, and then I pack the remains of the picnic into the haversack and think that my father is right, that this is good, even that it is happiness.

'I worry sometimes he does not get enough exercise,' my mother remarks on our journey back, going by a different way, my father's turn now to be a little ahead. Often, it seems to me, it is deliberately arranged that I should always be in the company of one or other of them.

'Doesn't he get enough?'

'Well, it could be more.'

'Papa's not ill?'

'No, not at all. Not at all. But in the nature of things . . .'

She does not finish what she might have said, but I know what follows. In the nature of things neither she nor my father will always be there. I sense her guessing that I have finished her sentence for her, for that is how we live, our conversations incomplete, or never begun at all. They have between them created an artefact within which our existence lies, an artefact as scrupulously completed as a masterpiece on a mosaicist's table. My father accepts what he has come to know – which I believe is everything – of my mother's unfaithfulness. There is no regret on my mother's part that I can tell, nor is there bitterness on his; I never heard a quarrel.

They sacrifice their lives for me: the change of surroundings, constantly repeated, the anonymous furniture of hotels, nothing as it has been – for my sake, no detail is overlooked. In thanking them I might say my gratitude colours every day, but they do not want me to say that, not even to mention gratitude in such a manner because it would be too much.

'*Quel après-midi splendide!*'

'*Ah, oui! on peut le dire.*'

'*J'adore ce moment de la journée.*'

Often my mother and I break into one of the languages she has taught me; as if, for her, a monotony she does not permit is broken. Does she – do they – regret the loss of the house in London, as I do? Do they imagine the changes there might be, the blue hall door a different colour, business plates beside it, a voice on the intercom when one of the bells is rung? What is the drawing-room now? Is there a consulate in the ground-floor rooms, stately men going back and forth, secretaries with papers to be signed? All that I know with certainty – and they must too – is that the violets of my bedroom wallpaper have been painted away to nothing, that gone from the hall are the shipyard scenes in black and white, the Cries of London too. They may even wonder, as I do, if the chill of the past is in that house, if the ghosts of my childhood companions haunt its rooms, for since leaving England I have never been able to bring them to life again.

'*C'est vraiment très beau là-bas,*' my mother says when we catch up with my father, who has already begun to gather chestnuts. We watch a bird which he says is something rare, none of us knowing what it is. There is a boy at the hotel to whom we'll give the chestnuts, each of us knowing as we do so that this will become another birthday memory, spoken of, looked back to.

'Ernest Shackleton was a most remarkable man,' my father comments in his abrupt way. 'Maybe the finest of all those men who were remarkable for making the freezing winds a way of life, and ice a landscape, whose grail was the desolation at the end of the world's most terrible journeys. Can you imagine them, those men before him and all who followed later? Secrets kept from one another, ailments hidden, their prayers, their disappointments? Such adversity, yet such spirit! We are strangely made, we human beings, don't you think?'

It doesn't matter that he hasn't taken me to see the Pyramids, not in the least does it matter, but even so I do not ever say I understand why he hasn't. For that, of course, is best not said. I, too, prevaricate.

'We've never brought you to Heiligenberg,' he muses as we walk on.

The last of the autumn wild flowers would still be in bloom at Heiligenberg, and the hellebores out all winter. The hotel they know – the Zeldenhof – would be grander since their day, my mother says.

We'll spend the winter in Heiligenberg, they decide, and I wonder if at Heiligenberg a letter might come from Mrs Upsilla. Now and again, not often, one arrives at some hotel or is discovered at a *Poste Restante*. Once I saw what I knew I should not have: the cramped handwriting I remembered, the purple ink Mrs Upsilla always favoured. Such letters that come are never opened in my presence; once when I looked in my mother's belongings none had been kept.

'We stayed at the Zeldenhof when we were married a month,' my father says. 'I photographed your mother at the refuge.'

I ask about that, and I ask where the little shop was where they met, when my father was buying a film for his camera.

'Italy,' my mother says. 'The front at Bordighera.'

There is a photograph.

The ticket collector's beard is flecked with grey, his uniform in need of attention. I know him well, for often I travel on his train.

'*Grazie, signora.*' He hands my ticket back, reminding me to change in Milan and Genoa. In the early afternoon the string of little seaside towns will begin, the train unhurried then, slowing, halting, juddering on, gathering speed again. That part of the journey I like best.

I wear blue because it suits me best, often with green, although they say the two are difficult to combine. My hair's well tended, the style old-fashioned. 'You're an old-fashioned lady,' my father used to say, not chiding me for that, his tone as light as ever. She liked my old-fashionedness, my mother said when I was very young. I'm in my fifty-third year now, a woman who has settled down at last in the forgotten Italian seaside resort where they met. In nineteen forty-nine that was, I calculate.

They died, he first – in his eighties – she less than a year later; and I, who should have known them better than anyone, did not know them at all, even though my mother did not release my hand all during her last night. The second funeral was conducted with the same simple formality as the first, the coffin placed beside the other in the small graveyard they had chosen, the place remembered from the summers we often spent in the Valle Verzasca. I walked away from both of them through cold winter air, snow on the ground but no longer falling.

A month or so later, calling in at the *Poste Restante* at Bad Mergentheim, as we had always done in their lifetime, I found a letter from Mrs Upsilla. Addressed as usual to my mother, it had been lying there for almost a year.

. . . I only write because it is so long now since I have heard from you. I am concerned but perhaps it is all right and you have been so kind to an old woman. The summer has not been good in Brighton but I struggle on, the season very poor. Several other landladies have given up and I read the writing on the wall and think how different life was once, those days in London! Well, I must not say it but there you are. I only write because I have not heard.

I knew at once that my mother had paid Mrs Upsilla all these years. Charles too, I imagined. The rich's desperate bid for silence: I think of it as that; but no, I do not blame my mother. I replied to Mrs Upsilla, simply saying that my mother had died and asking her to pass this information on to Charles if she happened to be in touch with him. No acknowledgement ever found its way to me from either of them, but it was hearing from Mrs Upsilla that first made me want to honour my father and mother. For Mrs Upsilla would die too, and Charles would, and I myself in time: who then, in all the world, would be aware of the story that might be told?

In the hotel where I live, in Bordighera's Regina Palace, my friends are the dining-room waiters, and the porters in the hall, and the bedroom maids; I do not turn away such friendship and I have myself for company too. Yet when my face is there in the glass of my compact, or reflected in shop windows when the sun is right, or glimpsed in public mirrors, I often think I do not know that woman. I wonder when I gaze for a moment longer if what I see is the illusion imposed by my imagination upon the shadow a child became, if somehow I do not entirely exist. I know that this is not so, yet still it seems to be. Confusion has coloured my life since my mother's death; and the waking hours of my solitude are nagged by the compulsion to make known the goodness of two people. Obsessively there, beyond my understanding, that has become the insistent orderer of how things should be. Not ever finding the courage to make it known in the corridors and lounges of the Regina Palace, for years I travelled from my shabby old town by the sea to distant cities where I might be anonymous. Again and again I searched among strangers for a listener who would afterwards pass on as a wonder the beneficence of those two people, a marvel to be repeated at family gatherings, at dinner tables, in bars and shops, interrupting games of cards and chess, spreading to other cities, to villages and towns, to other countries.

Each time I found my listener, each time across a teashop table or in a park, there was politeness; and moments later there was revulsion. Some traveller killing tedious time in a railway waiting-room would look away and mumble nothing; or on a tram, or in a train, would angrily push past a nuisance. And the whisper of my apology would not be heard.

In my foolishness I did not know what I since have learnt: that the truth, even when it glorifies the human spirit, is hard to peddle if there is something terrible to tell as well. Dark nourishes light's triumphant blaze, but who should want to know? I accept, at last, that I am not to be allowed the mercy of telling what is mine to tell. The wheels of my suitcase rattle on the surface of the railway platform at Bordighera and outside the station the evening is bright with sunshine. The taxidriver knows my destination without having to ask. I might say, in making conversation, that there will not be another journey but enquire instead about the family he often tells me about.

'*Buona sera, signora. Come sta?*' The afternoon porter welcomes me in the empty hall of the Regina Palace, appearing out of nowhere.

'*Sto bene, Giovanni. Bene.*'

Small and pallid, an elaborate uniform dwarfing him, Giovanni keeps the Regina Palace going, as much as Signor Valazza, its manager, does; or the stoutly imperious Signora Casarotti, who knew it from her Reception counter in its glory days. Fashion has long ago lifted its magic from what fashion once made gracious, leaving behind flaking paint and dusty palms. Masonry crumbles, a forgotten lift is out of order. But Camera Ventinove, the room I have always returned to from the failure of my journeys, has a view of the sea as far as the horizon.

'We miss you always, *signora*,' Giovanni tells me, practising his English, as he likes to in our conversations. 'Was fine, your travel, *signora?*'

'Was fine, Giovanni, was fine.'

The door of Camera Ventinove is unlocked as that lie is told. Giovanni stands aside, I go in first. There is a little more to the ceremony of my return, not much: the opening of the shutters, the view again remarked upon, the giving and receiving of the tip. Then Giovanni goes.

I hang some of the clothes I have travelled with in the wardrobe and write the list to accompany those that must be laundered. Unhurriedly, I have a bath and, downstairs for a while, finish the easy book I bought for my journey. I leave it with the newspapers in case it interests someone else.

I walk by the sea, my thoughts a repetition, imagining on this promenade the two people who have been rejected, who did not know one another well when they walked here too. The bathing huts of the photograph have gone.

'*Buona sera, signora.*'

It is not an unusual courtesy for people to address one another on this promenade, even for a man who is not familiar to her to address a woman. But still this unexpected voice surprises me, and perhaps I seem a little startled.

'I'm sorry, I did not mean to . . .' The man's apology trails away.

'It's quite all right.'

'We are both English, I think.' His voice is soft, pleasant to hear, his eyes quite startling blue. He is tall, in a pale linen suit, thin and fair-haired, his forehead freckled, the blue of his eyes repeated in the tie that's knotted into a blue-striped shirt. Some kindly doctor? Schoolmaster? Horticulturalist? Something about him suggests he's on his own. Widowed? I wondered. Unmarried? It is impossible to guess. His name is d'Arblay, he reveals, and when I begin to walk on, it seems only slightly strange that he changes direction and walks with me.

'Yes, I am English,' I hear myself saying, more warmly than if I had not hesitated at first.

'I thought you might be. Well, I knew. But even so it was a presumption.' The slightest of gestures accompanies this variation of his apology. He smiles a little. 'My thoughts had wandered. I was thinking as I strolled of a novel I first read when I was eighteen. *The Good Soldier*.'

'I have read *The Good Soldier* too.'

'The saddest story. I read it again not long ago. You've read it more than once?'

'Yes, I have.'

'There's always something that wasn't there before when you read a good novel for the second time.'

'Yes, there is.'

'I have been re-reading now the short stories of Somerset Maugham. Superior to his novels, I believe. In particular I like "The Kite".'

'They made a film of it.'

'Yes.'

'I never saw it.'

'Nor I.'

There is no one else on the promenade. Neither a person nor a dog. Not even a seagull. We walk together, not speaking for a moment, until I break that silence, not to say much, but only that I love the sea at Bordighera.

'And I.'

Our footsteps echo, or somehow do I imagine that? I don't know, am only aware that again the silence is there, and that again I break it.

'A long time ago I lived in a house in a square in London . . .'

He nods, but does not speak.

'My father was an Egyptologist.'

Taped music reaches me in the bar, where once there was the chatter of cocktail drinkers and the playing of a palm-court quartet. I order Kir, and when the barman has poured it he leaves me on my own, as every night he does, since he has other things to do. I guessed this would be so and for company I've brought with me the temperate features of the Englishman on the promenade. 'So much is chance,' he said, and with no great difficulty I hear his distinctive voice again. 'So much,' he says.

I take that with me when I cross the hall to the struggling splendours of the Regina Palace's dining-room. I take with me Mr d'Arblay's composure, his delicate hands seeming to gesture without moving, the smile that is so slight it's hardly there. Royalty has celebrated in this vast dining-room, so Signor Valazza claims. But tonight's reflection in its gilded mirrors is a handful of travellers, shadowy beneath the flickering chandeliers. There is a man with a yellow pipe on the table beside him, and a couple who might be on their honeymoon, and two ageing German *fräuleins* who might be schoolmistresses just retired. Little stoves keep warm *filetto di maialino* and *tortelli di pecorino*. But all reality is less than Mr d'Arblay.

'*Si, signora.*' Carlo jots down my order: the consommé, the turbot. '*E Gavi dei Gavi. Subito, signora.*'

My mother gathered her dress from the floor, her necklace too, where she had thrown them down. The drawing-room was heavy with her scent and her friend put a record on the gramophone. The voice still sang when they had gone. And Charles came in then, and knew, and took me out to the square to show me the flowerbeds he'd been tending.

'*Prego, signora. Il vino.*'

The Gavi is poured, but I do not need to taste it, and simply nod.

'*Grazie, signora.*'

Mr d'Arblay has walked through our square; more than once he remembers being there. It is not difficult for him to imagine the house as it was; he does not say so, but I know. He can imagine; he is the kind that can.

'*Buon appetito, signora.*'

A child's light fingertips on a sleeve, resting there for no longer than an instant. So swift her movement then, so slight it might not have occurred at all: that, too, Mr d'Arblay can imagine and he does. The unlit cigarettes are crushed beneath a shoe. There is the crash of noise, the splintered banister. There are the eyes, looking up from far below. There is the rictus grin.

The man on his own presses tobacco into his yellow pipe but does not light it. Ice-cream is brought to the German schoolmistresses. The honeymoon couple touch glasses. Three late arrivals hesitate by the door.

'*Il rombo arrosto, signora.*'

'*Grazie, Carlo.*'

'*Prego, signora.*'

Three lives were changed for ever in that instant. Whatever lies my father told were good enough for people at a party, the silence of two servants bought. My mother wept and hid her tears. But some time during that sleepless night was she – my father too – touched by the instinct to abandon the child who had been born to them? Was it more natural that they should, and do no more than call what had happened evil?

'It is natural too,' Mr d'Arblay replied while we walked, 'to find the truth in the agony of distress. The innocent cannot be evil: this was what, during that sleepless night, they came to know.'

It was enough, Mr d'Arblay diffidently insisted, that what there is to tell, in honouring the dead, has now been told between two other people and shall be told again between them, and each time something gained. The selfless are undemanding in their graves.

I do not taste the food I'm eating, nor savour the wine I drink. I reject the *dolce* and the cheese. They bring me coffee.

'Theirs was the guilt,' Mr d'Arblay says again, 'his that he did not know her well enough, hers that she made the most of his not knowing. Theirs was the shame, yet their spirit is gentle in our conversation: guilt is not always terrible, nor shame unworthy.'

Petits fours have been brought too, although I never take one from the plate. One night she may, is what they think in the kitchen, and even say to one another that one night when she sits down at this same table, as old as she will ever become, she will be lonely in her solitude. How can they know that in the dining-room where royalty has dined she is not alone among the tattered drapes and chandeliers abandoned to their grime? They cannot know, they cannot guess, that in the old hotel, and when she walks by the sea, there is Mr d'Arblay, as in another solitude there were her childhood friends.

Sacred Statues

They would manage, Nuala had always said when there had been difficulties before. Each time it was she who saw the family through: her faith
in Corry, her calmness in adversity, her stubborn optimism were the
strengths she brought to the marriage.

'Would you try Mrs Falloway?' she suggested when, more seriously
than ever in the past, their indigence threatened to defeat them. It was a
last resort, the best that desperation could do. 'Wouldn't you, Corry?'

Corry said nothing and Nuala watched him feeling ashamed, as he had
begun to these last few weeks. It wouldn't be asking much of Mrs Falloway,
she said. Tiding them over for a year while he learnt the way of it in the
stoneyard wouldn't be much; and after that he'd be back on wages. The
chance in the stoneyard was made for him; didn't O'Flynn say it himself?

'I couldn't go near Mrs Falloway. I couldn't at all.'

'Only to put it to her, Corry. Only to say out what's the truth.'

'It came to nothing, what she was doing that time. Why'd she be interested in us now?'

'All she saw in you'll be lost if we don't get assistance, Corry. Why
wouldn't she still take an interest?'

'It's all in the past, that.'

'I know. I know.'

'I'd be embarrassed going over there.'

'Don't I know that too, Corry?'

'There's work going on the roads.'

'You're not a roadworker, Corry.'

'There's things we have to do.'

Deliberately Nuala let a silence gather; and Corry broke it, as she knew
he would.

'I'd be a day going over there,' he said, and might have added that
there'd be the bus fare and something to pay for the loan of a bicycle in
Carrick, but he didn't.

'A day won't hurt, Corry.'

They were a couple of the same age – thirty-one – who'd known one
another since childhood, Corry tall and bony, Nuala plumper and smaller,
with a round, uncomplicated face, her fair hair cut shorter than it had

been when she'd first become a wife. The youngest of their children, a girl, took after her in appearance; the boys were both as lean and gangling as their father.

'You always did your best, Corry.' The statement hung there, concluding their conversation, necessary because it was true, its repetition softening the crisis in their lives.

Corry's workshop was a shed, all his saints in a row on a shelf he had put up. Beneath them were his Madonnas, his John the Baptist, and a single Crucifixion. His Stations were there too, propped against the rough concrete wall. Limewood and ash the woods were, apple and holly and box, oak that had come from a creamery paddle.

When the children left the house in the mornings to be picked up at Quirke's crossroads and driven on to school, when Corry was out looking for work on a farm, Nuala often took pride in her husband's gift; and in the quiet of his workshop she wondered how it would have been between them if he did not possess it, how she would feel about him if he'd been the master in a school or a counter-hand in one of the shops in Carrick, or permanently on a farm.

Corry's saints had become her friends, Nuala sometimes thought, brought to life for her, a source of sympathy, and consolation when that was necessary. *And Jesus Fell the Second Time* were the words beneath the Station that was her favourite. Neither saints nor Stations belonged in a concrete shed, any more than the figures of the Virgin did, or any of the other carvings. They belonged in the places they'd been created for, the inspiration of their making becoming there the inspiration of prayer. Nuala was certain that this was meant to be, that in receiving his gift Corry had been entrusted with seeing that this came about. 'You were meant for other times, Corry,' a priest had remarked to him once, but not unkindly or dismissively, as if recognizing that even if the present times were different from those he spoke of, Corry would persevere. A waste of himself it would be otherwise, a waste of the person he was.

Nuala closed the shed door behind her. She fed her hens and then walked through the vegetable patch she cultivated herself. Mrs Falloway would understand; she had before, she would again. The living that Corry's gift failed to make for him would come naturally when he had mastered the craft of cutting letters on head-stones in O'Flynn's yard. The headstones were a different kind of thing from his sacred statues but they'd be enough to bring his skill to people's notice, to the notice of bishops and priests as well as anyone else's. Sooner or later everyone did business in a stoneyard; when he'd come to the house to make the offer O'Flynn had said that too.

In the field beyond Nuala's vegetable garden the tethered goat jerked up its head and stared at her. She loosened the chain on the tether post and watched while the goat pawed at the new grass before eating it. The fresh, cool air was sharp on her face and for a moment, in spite of the trouble, she was happy. At least this place was theirs: the field, the garden, the small, remote house that she and Corry had come to when Mrs Falloway lent them the asking price, so certain was she that Corry would one day be a credit to her. While still savouring this moment of elation, Nuala felt it slipping away. Naturally, it was possible that Corry would not succeed in the mission she had sent him on: optimist or not, she was still close to the reality of things. In the night she had struggled with that, wondering how she should prepare him, and herself, for the ill fortune of his coming back empty-handed. It was then that she had remembered the Rynnes. They'd come into her thoughts as she imagined an inspiration came to Corry; not that he ever talked like that, but still she felt she knew. She had lain awake going over what had occurred to her, rejecting it because it upset her, because it shocked her even to have thought of it. She prayed that Mrs Falloway would be generous, as she had been before.

When he reached the crossroads Corry waited at the petrol pumps for the bus to Carrick. It was late but it didn't matter, since Mrs Falloway didn't know he was coming. On the way down from the house he'd considered trying to telephone, to put it to her if she was still there what Nuala had put to him, to save himself the expense of the journey. But when first she'd brought the subject up, Nuala had said that this wasn't something that could be talked about on the phone even if he managed to find out Mrs Falloway's number, which he hadn't known in the past.

In Carrick, at Hosey's bicycle shop, he waited while the tyres of an old Raleigh were pumped up for him. New batteries were put in the lamp in case he returned after dark, although he kept assuring young Hosey that it wouldn't be possible to be away for so long: the bus back was at three.

It was seven miles to Mountroche House, mostly on a flat bog road bounded by neither ditches nor fencing. Corry remembered it from the time he and Nuala had lived in Carrick, when he'd worked in the Riordans' joinery business and they'd had lodgings in an upstairs room at her mother's. It was then that he began to carve his statues, his instinctive artistry impressing the Riordan brothers, and Mrs Falloway when the time came. It surprised Corry himself, for he hadn't known it was there.

Those times, the first few years of marriage, cheered him as he rode swiftly on. It could be that Nuala was right, that Mrs Falloway would be pleased to see him, that she'd understand why they hadn't been able to pay anything back. Nuala had a way of making good things happen, Corry considered; she guessed what they might be and then you tried for them.

The road was straight, with hardly a curve until the turf bogs eventually gave way to hills. Hedges and trees began, fields of grass or crops. Mountroche House was at the end of an unkempt avenue that continued for another three-quarters of a mile.

The Rynnes lived in a grey, pebble-dashed bungalow at the crossroads, close to the petrol pumps they operated, across the main road from Quirke's SuperValu. They were well-to-do: besides the petrol business, there was Rynne's insurance agency, which he conducted from the bungalow. His wife attended to the custom at the pumps.

When Nuala rang the doorbell the Rynnes answered it together. They had a way of doing that when both of them were in; and they had a way of conducting their visitors no further than the hall until the purpose of the interruption was established. An insurance matter was usually enough to permit further access.

'I was passing by,' Nuala said, 'on my way to the SuperValu.'

The Rynnes nodded. Their similar elongated features suggested that they might be brother and sister rather than man and wife. They both wore glasses, Rynne's dark-rimmed and serious, his wife's light and pale. They were a childless couple.

'Is it insurance, Nuala?' Rynne enquired.

She shook her head. She'd just looked in, she said, to see how they were getting on. 'We often mention you,' she said, taking a liberty with the facts.

'Arrah, we're not bad at all,' Rynne said. 'Game ball, would you say, Etty?'

'Oh, I would, I would.'

The telephone rang and Rynne went to answer it. Nuala could hear him saying he was up to his eyes this morning. 'Would tomorrow do?' he suggested. 'Would I come up in the evening?'

'I'm sorry, Etty. You're busy.'

'It's only I'm typing his proposals. God, it takes your time, and the pumps going too! Twenty-six blooming pages every one of them!'

In spite of its plaintive note, it was cheerful talk, relegating to its place beneath the surface what had been disguised when Rynne said they were game ball: neither Etty Rynne's failure to become pregnant nor the emotional toll it had taken of both husband and wife was ever mentioned by them, but the fact and its consequences were well known in the neighbourhood. It was even said that dishearteningly fruitless enquiries had been made regarding the possibility of adoption.

'Goodbye so, Etty.' Nuala smiled and nodded before she left, the sympathy of a mother in her eyes. She would have liked to commiserate, but spoken words would have been tactless.

'You're all well above, Nuala?'

'We are.'

'Tell Corry I was asking for him.'

'I will of course.'

Nuala wheeled her bicycle across the road and propped it against the side wall of Quirke's SuperValu. While she was shopping – searching for the cheap lines with a sell-by date due, bundling the few items she could afford into a wire basket – she thought about the Rynnes. She saw them almost as visibly as she had ten minutes ago seen the faraway, sorrowful look in Etty's pale-brown eyes; she heard the unvoiced disappointment that, in both husband and wife, dwindled into weariness. They had given up already, not knowing that they needn't yet: all that, again, passed through Nuala's reflections.

She went on thinking about the Rynnes as she rode away from the crossroads, up the long hill to her house. They were decent people, tied into themselves only because of their childlessness, because of what the longing had done to them. She remembered them as they'd been when first they'd married, the winter card parties they invited people to, Etty like a fashion-plate for each occasion, the stories Rynne brought back from his business travels.

'Would it be wrong?' Nuala whispered to herself, since there was no one there to hear. 'Would it be against God?'

Unhooking her shopping bags from the handlebars when she reached the house, she asked herself the same questions again, her voice loud now in the stillness. If Corry did well with Mrs Falloway there wouldn't be a need to wonder if it would be wrong. There wouldn't even be a need – when years had gone by and they looked back to the bad time there'd been – to mention to Corry what had come into her mind. If Mrs Falloway came up trumps you'd make yourself forget it, which was something that could be done if you tried.

It was a white house for the most part, though grey and green in places where the colourwash was affected. Roches had lived at Mountroche for generations, until the family came to an end in the 1950s; Mrs Falloway had bought it cheaply after it had been empty for seventeen years.

Corry heard the bell jangling in the depths, but no one answered the summons. On the bus and as he rode across the bog he had worried in case Mrs Falloway had gone, in case years ago she had returned to England; when he jerked the bell-pull for the third time he worried again. Then there was a sound somewhere above where he stood. A window opened and Mrs Falloway's voice called down.

'Mrs Falloway?' He stepped backwards on to the gravel in order to look up. 'Mrs Falloway?'

'Yes, it's me. Hullo.'

'Hullo, Mrs Falloway.'

He wouldn't have recognized her and wondered if she recognized him after so long. He said who he was.

'Oh, of course,' Mrs Falloway said. 'Wait a minute for me.'

When she opened her hall door she was welcoming. She smiled and held a hand out. 'Come in, come in.'

They passed through a shabby hall and sat in a drawing-room that smelt of must. The cold ashes of a fire were partly covered with dead hydrangeas, deposited there from a vase. The room seemed choked with what littered its surfaces: newspapers and magazines, drawings, books face downward as if to mark a place, empty punnets, bric-à-brac in various stages of repair, a summer hat, a pile of clothes beside a work-basket.

'You've come on a bicycle, Corry?' Mrs Falloway said.

'Only from Carrick. I got the bus to Carrick.'

'My dear, you must be exhausted. Let me give you tea at the very least.'

Mrs Falloway was gone for nearly twenty minutes, causing Corry some agitation when he thought of the three o'clock bus. He and Nuala had sat waiting in this room when they'd come to the house the first time, after Corry got the letter. They'd sat together on the sofa that was a receptacle for oddments now; the room had been tidier then, Mrs Falloway had been brisker. She'd talked all the time, full of her plans, a table laid in the big bow window to which she brought corned beef and salad, and toast that was moist with the butter she'd spread, and Kia-Ora orange, and tea and fruitcake.

'Not much, I'm afraid,' she said now, returning with a plate of biscuits, and cups and saucers and a tea-pot. The biscuits were decorated with a pink mush of marshmallow and raspberry jam.

Corry was glad of the tea, which was strong and hot. The biscuit he took had gone soft, but even so he liked it. Once in a while Nuala bought the same kind for the children.

'What a lovely surprise!' Mrs Falloway said.

'I wondered were you still here.'

'I'm here for ever now, I think.'

A dismal look had crept into her face, as if she knew why he had come. If she'd thought about it, she would have guessed long ago about the plight they were in. He wasn't here to say it was her fault; he hoped she didn't think that, because of course it wasn't. All the blame was his.

'I'm sorry we didn't manage to pay anything back,' he said.

'You weren't expected to, Corry.'

She was a tall woman, seeming fragile now. When she'd been younger her appearance had been almost intimidating: determination had influenced the set of her features and seemed to be there again in her wide mouth and saucer eyes, in her large hands as they gestured for attention. Swiftly her smile had become stern or insistent; now it was vaguely beseeching; her piled-up hair, which Corry remembered as black with a few strands of grey, had no black left in it. There was a tattered look about her that went with the room they were in.

'You have children now, Corry?'

'We have three. Two boys and a girl.'

'You're finding work?'

He shook his head. 'It never got going,' he said. 'All that.'

'I'm sorry, Corry.'

Soon after Mrs Falloway bought Mountroche House and came to live there she had attended the funeral of the elderly widow who'd been the occupant of the Mountroche gate-lodge. Being, as she put it, a black Protestant from England, who had never, until then, entered an Irish Catholic church, she had not before been exposed to such a profusion of plaster statues as at that funeral Mass. *I hope you do not consider it interference from an outsider*, she wrote in her first letter to Bishop Walshe, *but it is impossible not to be aware of the opportunity there is for young craftsmen and artists*. With time on her hands, she roved Bishop Walshe's diocese in her Morris Minor, taking photographs of grottoes that featured solitary Virgin Marys or *pietàs*, or towering crucifixions. How refreshing it would be, she enthused to Bishop Walshe when eventually she visited him, to see the art of the great high crosses of Ireland brought into the modern Church, to see nativities and annunciations in stained glass, to have old lecterns and altar furniture replaced with contemporary forms. She left behind in the Bishop's hall a selection of postcards she had obtained from Italy, reproductions of the bas-reliefs of Mino da Fiesole and details from the pulpit in Siena cathedral. When she had compiled a list of craftsmen she wrote to all of them, and visited those who lived within a reasonable distance of Mountroche House. To numerous priests and bishops she explained that what was necessary was to bring wealth and talent together; but for the most part she met with opposition and indifference. Several bishops wrote back crossly, requesting her not to approach them again.

Breaking in half another biscuit, Corry remembered the letter he had received himself. 'Will you look at this!' he had exclaimed the morning it arrived. Since he had begun to carve figures in his spare time at the joinery he had been aware of a vocation, of wishing to make a living in this particular way, and Mrs Falloway's letter reflected entirely what he felt: that the church art with which he was familiar was of poor quality. 'Who on earth is she?' he wondered in bewilderment when he'd read the letter through several times. Less than a week later Mrs Falloway came to introduce herself.

'I've always been awfully sorry,' she repeated now. 'Sorrier than I can say.'

'Ah, well.'

When it was all over, all her efforts made, her project abandoned, Mrs Falloway had written in defeat to a friend of her distant schooldays. *Well, yes, I am giving up the struggle. There is a long story to tell, which must wait until next you come for a few summer weeks. Enough to say, that everything has changed in holy Ireland.* Mrs Falloway spoke of that to Corry now, of her feelings at the time, which she had not expressed to him before. The Church had had enough on its hands, was how she put it; the appearance of things seemed trivial compared with the falling away of congregations and the tide of secular attack. Without knowing it, she had chosen a bad time.

'It was guilt when I gave you that poor little house, Corry. I'd misled you with my certainties that weren't certainties at all. A galumphing English woman!'

'Ah no, no.'

'Ah yes, I'm afraid. I should have restrained you, not urged you to give up your employment in the joinery.'

'I wanted to.'

'You're hard up now?'

'We are a bit, to tell the truth.'

'Is that why you've come over?'

'Well, it is.'

She shook her head. There was another pause and then she said: 'I'm hard up myself, as things are.'

'I'm sorry about that.'

'Are you in a bad way, Corry?'

'O'Flynn'll give me a place in the stoneyard at Guileen. He's keen because I'd learn the stone quickly, the knowledge I have with the wood. It's not like he'd be taking on a full apprentice. It's not like the delay there'd be until some young fellow'd get the hang of it.'

'You'd be lettering gravestones?'

'I would. He'd put me on wages after a twelve-month. The only thing is, I'd be the twelve-month without a penny. I do a few days on a farm here and there if there's anything going, but I'd have to give that up.'

'The stoneyard seems the answer then.'

'I'd be in touch with anyone who'd maybe be interested in the statues. I'd have them by me in the yard. A priest or a bishop still looking for something would maybe hear tell I could do a Stations. O'Flynn said that to Nuala.'

They went on talking. Mrs Falloway poured out more tea. She pressed Corry to have another biscuit.

'I'd have the wages steady behind me,' Corry said, 'once we managed the year. I'd ride over to Guileen every morning on the bike we have, no problem at all.'

'I haven't money, Corry.'

There was a quietness in the room then, neither of them saying anything, but Corry didn't go at once. After a few moments they talked about the time in the past. Mrs Falloway offered to cook something, but Corry said no. He stood up as he did so, explaining about the three o'clock bus.

At the hall door Mrs Falloway again said she was sorry, and Corry shook his head.

'Nuala's tried for work herself only there's nothing doing. There's another baby coming,' Corry said, feeling he should pass that on also.

When Nuala heard, she said it had been a forlorn hope anyway, and when Corry described the state of Mountroche House she felt sorry for Mrs Falloway, whose belief in Corry had always seemed to Nuala to be a confirmation of the sacred nature of his gift, as if Mrs Falloway had been sent into their lives to offer that encouragement. Even though her project had failed, it was hardly by chance that she had come to live only fourteen miles from Carrick at a time when Corry was employed in the Riordans' joinery; and hardly by chance that she'd become determined in her intentions when she saw the first of his saints. He'd made the little figure of St Brigid for Father Ryan to set in the niche in St Brigid's parish hall even though Father Ryan couldn't pay him anything for it. Whenever Nuala was in Carrick she called in at the parish hall to look again at it, remembering her amazement – similar to Mrs Falloway's – when she'd first seen it. 'He has a right way with a chisel,' O'Flynn said when he'd made his offer of employment in the stoneyard. 'I don't know did I ever see better.' For Nuala it was all of a piece – the first of the saints, and Mrs Falloway coming to live near by, and O'Flynn's offer when they'd nearly given up hope. She could feel it in her bones that that was how it was.

'Rest yourself,' she urged Corry in the kitchen, 'while I'll get the tea.'

'They all right?'

They were out playing in the back field, she said; they'd been no trouble since they'd come in. She spread out rashers of streaky bacon on the pan that was warming on the stove. She'd gone down to the SuperValu, she said, and Corry told her how he'd nearly missed the bus back.

'He was drawing away. I had to stop him.'

'I shouldn't have sent you over on that awful old trek, Corry.'

'Ah no, no. To tell you the truth, it was good to see her. Except she was a bit shook.'

He talked about the journey on the bus, the people on it when he was coming back. Nuala didn't mention the Rynnes.

'Glory be to God!' Etty Rynne exclaimed. She felt shaky so she sat down, on a chair by the hallstand. 'I don't think I understood you,' she said, although she knew she had.

She listened, not wanting to, when Nuala went into it. 'It'd be April,' Nuala said and repeated the sum of money she had mentioned already. Late April, she thought, maybe just into May. She'd never been early, she said.

'Himself would say it was against the law, Nuala. I'd wonder was it, myself.'

The daylight in the hall had blurs of blue and pink in it from the coloured panes on either side of the front door. It was a dim, soft light because of that, and while she tried to gather her thoughts together Etty Rynne found herself thinking that its cloudiness was suitable for the conversation that was being conducted – neither of them able to see the other's face clearly, her own incomprehension.

'It would be confidential between us,' Nuala said, 'that there was money.'

Not meaning to, and in a whisper, Etty Rynne repeated that. A secret was what was meant: a secret kept for ever among the four of them, a secret that was begun already because Nuala had waited for the car to drive off, maybe watching from the SuperValu's windows. She'd have seen him walking out of the bungalow; when the car had gone she'd have crossed the road.

'Listen to me, Etty.'

Corry's statues came into what Nuala said, the wooden figures he made, the Blessed Virgin and the saints, St Brigid in the St Brigid's Hall in Carrick. And Nuala trying for work in the SuperValu and anywhere she could think of came into it. With the baby due she'd be tied down, but she'd have managed somehow if there was work, only there wasn't. How Corry had drawn a blank with a woman whose name was unfamiliar came into it. And O'Flynn who had the stoneyard at Guileen did.

'O'Flynn has his insurances with us.' For a moment in her mind's eye Etty Rynne saw the bulky grey-haired stonemason, who always dropped the premiums in himself in case they went astray, who afterwards drew his Peugeot pick-up in at the pumps for a fill-up. It was a relief when all that flickered in Etty Rynne's memory, after the shock that had left her weak in the legs and wanting to gasp and not being able to.

'It's a long time since you put the room ready, Etty.'

'Did I show it to you?'

'You did one time.'

She used to show it to people, the small room at the back of the bungalow that she'd painted a bright buttercup shade, the door and window-sills in white gloss.

'It's still the same,' she said.

'That's what I was thinking.'

She'd made the curtains herself, blue that matched the carpet, dolls playing ring-a-roses on them. They'd never bought furniture for the little room. Tempting Providence it would be, he said.

'There'd be no deception,' Nuala said. 'No lie, nothing like that. Only the money side kept out of it.'

Etty nodded. Like a dream, it was disordered and peculiar: the ring at the door and Nuala smiling there, and standing in the hall with Nuala and having to sit down, her face going red and then the blood draining out of it when Nuala asked if she had savings in the bank or in a credit society, and mentioning the sum that would be enough.

'I couldn't take your baby off of you, Nuala.'

'I wouldn't be deprived. I'd have another one, maybe two or three. A bit of time gone by and people would understand.'

'Oh God, I doubt they would.'

'It isn't against the law, Etty. No way.'

'I couldn't. I never could.' Pregnancy made you fanciful sometimes and she wondered if it was that that had got at Nuala. She didn't say it in case it made things worse. Slowly she shook her head. 'God, I couldn't,' she said again.

'Nowadays if a man and woman can't have a baby there's things can be done.'

'I know, I know.'

'Nowadays –'

'I couldn't do what you're saying, Nuala.'

'Is it the money?'

'It's everything, Nuala. It's what people'd say. He'd blow his head off if he knew what you're after suggesting. It would bring down the business, he'd say. Nobody'd come near us.'

'People –'

'They'd never come round to it, Nuala.'

A silence came, and the silence was worse than the talk. Then Nuala said:

'Would we sit down to a cup of coffee?'

'God, I'm sorry. Of course we will.'

She could feel sweat on the sides of her body and on her neck and her forehead. The palms of her hands were cold. She stood up and it was better than before.

'Come into the kitchen.'

'I didn't mean to upset you, Etty.'

Filling the kettle, spooning Nescafé into two cups, pouring in milk, Etty Rynne felt her jittery unease beginning to recede, leaving her with stark astonishment. She knew Nuala well. She'd known her since they were six, when first they'd been at school together. There had never been any sign whatsoever of stuff like this: Nuala was what she looked like, down-to-earth and sensible, both feet on the ground.

'The pregnancy? Would it be that, Nuala?'

'It's no different from the others. It's just that I thought of the way things are with you. And with Corry, talking about going to work on the roads.'

Two troubles, Etty Rynne heard then, and something good drawn out of them when you'd put them together. That's all it was, Nuala said; no more than that.

'What you said will never go outside these four walls,' Etty Rynne promised. 'Nor mentioned within them either.' It was a woman's thing, whatever it was. Wild horses wouldn't drag the conversation they'd had out of her. 'Didn't you mean well? Don't I know you did?'

The coffee calmed their two different moods. They walked through the narrow hall together and a cold breeze blew in when the front door was opened. A car drew up at the petrol pumps and Etty Rynne hurried to attend to it. She waved when Nuala rode away from the crossroads on the bicycle she shared with her husband.

*

'It's how it is,' Corry said when he rejected O'Flynn's offer of a place in the stoneyard, and he said it again when he agreed to work on the roads.

Stubbornly, Nuala considered that it needn't be how it was. It was ridiculous that there should live within a mile of one another a barren wife and a statue-maker robbed by adverse circumstances of his purpose in God's world. It was stupid and silly and perverse, when all that had to be done was to take savings out of a bank. The buttercup-yellow room so lovingly prepared would never now be occupied. In the tarmac surfaces he laid on roads Corry would see the visions he had betrayed.

Nuala nursed her anger, keeping it to herself. She went about her tasks, collecting eggs from where her hens had laid, preparing food, kneading dough for the bread she made every second day; and all the time her anger nagged. It surely was not too terrible a sin, too redolent of insidious presumption, that people should impose an order of their own on what they were given? Had she been clumsy in her manner of putting it to Etty Rynne? Or wrong not to have revealed her intentions to Corry in the hope that, with thought, he would have accepted the sense of them? But doubt spread then: Corry never would have; no matter how it had been put, Etty Rynne would have been terrified.

Corry bought new boots before he went to work on the roads. They were doing a job on the quarry boreen, he said, re-surfacing it because of the complaints there'd been from the lorry drivers. A protective cape was supplied to him in case there'd be rain.

On the night before his new work began Nuala watched him applying waterproof stuff to the boots and rubbing it in. They were useless without it, he'd been told. He took it all in his stride.

'Things happen differently,' he said, as if something in Nuala's demeanour allowed him to sense her melancholy. 'We're never in charge.'

She didn't argue; there was no point in argument. She might have confessed instead that she had frightened Etty Rynne; she might have tried to explain that her wild talk had been an effort to make something good out of what there was, as so often she had seen the spread of angels' wings emerging from roughly sawn wood. But all that was too difficult, so Nuala said nothing.

Her anger was still merciless when that day ended; and through the dark of the night she felt herself oppressed by it and bleakly prayed, waiting for a response that did not come. She reached out in the morning dusk to hold for a moment her husband's hand. Had he woken she would have told him all she had kept to herself, unable now to be silent.

But it was Corry's day that was beginning, and it was he who needed sympathy and support. Making breakfast for him and for her children,

Nuala gave him both as best she could, banishing from her mood all outward traces of what she knew would always now be private. When the house was empty again but for herself, she washed up the morning's dishes and tidied the kitchen as she liked to have it. She damped the fire down in the stove. Outside, she fed her hens.

In Corry's workshop she remained longer than she usually did on her morning visit to the saints who had become her friends: St Laurence with his gridiron, St Gabriel the messenger, St Clare of Assisi, St Thomas the Apostle and blind St Lucy, St Catherine, St Agnes. Corry had made them live for her and she felt the first faint slipping away of her anger as they returned her gaze with undisturbed tranquillity. Touched by it, lost in its peace, she sensed their resignation too. The world, not she, had failed.

Rose Wept

'How nice all this is!' Rose's mother cried, with dishes on the way to the dinner table Rose had laid. 'What weather, Mr Bouverie, don't you think? Please sit here next to me.'

Obediently Mr Bouverie did so, replying to the comment about the weather.

'Can't stand a heatwave,' Mr Dakin cheerfully grumbled.

Rose's father – Mrs Dakin's better half, so she insisted – was bluff and genial. He spoke with a hoarseness, always keeping his voice down as if saving it for professional use, he being an auctioneer. Apart from her shrillness, there was a similarity about his wife: both were large and shared an ease often to be found in people of their girth and stature. This evening Mr Dakin was sweating, as he tended to in summer; he had taken his jacket off and undone the buttons of the waistcoat he always wore no matter what the temperature.

His daughter sweltered in her guilt. Rose was eighteen and wished, this evening, she could be somewhere else. She wished she didn't have to meet Mr Bouverie's weary eyes or watch him being polite, listening with inclined head to her mother, smiling at her father's bonhomie. The occasion was a celebration: Rose was to go to university, Mr Bouverie had had a hand in her success. As a tutor, he had made borderline cases his business for more than thirty years, but intended to no longer, Rose being his last. *My God, this is appalling*, she thought. She had begged her mother not to issue this invitation but Mrs Dakin had insisted that they must. Mr Bouverie had attempted to refuse but had then been offered a choice of evenings.

'How I adore the asparagus season!' Rose heard her mother cry in her vivacious way, pressing a dish of the vegetable, well buttered, on their visitor.

Mr Bouverie smiled and murmured his appreciation. He was a man of sixty-odd. Strands of faded hair were hardly noticeable on the freckled pate of his head. There were freckles, also, on the backs of his hands, on old worn skin like dried-out chamois. He wore a pale suit and one of his colourful Italian bow ties.

'And how is your world, Mr Bouverie?' Mr Dakin civilly enquired.

'Shrinking,' Mr Bouverie replied. 'That is something you notice as you age.'

Mrs Dakin bubbled into good-sort laughter. Mr Dakin poured claret.

'You shrink yourself of course.' Mr Bouverie obligingly pursued the subject, since it was clear that the Dakins liked to have a conversation going. He smiled at Rose. Half his teeth were still his own, grey and sucked away to crags.

'Good tidings for the obese,' mumbled Mr Dakin, his features screwed up as they often were when he made a joke. Directed against himself, his banter caused his wife to exclaim:

'Oh, Bobo, you're not obese!'

'I used to be six foot and half an inch,' Mr Bouverie laboured on. 'I'm nothing like that now.'

'But otherwise all is well?' Mr Dakin enquired.

'Oh, yes, indeed.'

Mrs Dakin had had her dining-room papered blue, a dark stripe and a lighter one. Curtains matched, the paintwork was white. Mrs Dakin enjoyed this side of things and often said so: leafless delphiniums patterned her drawing-room; her hall and staircase were black and gold.

'I say, this is awfully good.' Mr Dakin complimented his wife on what she had done with the turkey slices that accompanied the asparagus.

'Delicious,' Mr Bouverie affirmed.

Rose wore a slate-grey dress, with a collar that folded back. Unlike her parents, Rose was petite, her fair hair cut short, a fringe following the curve of her forehead, her eyes a forget-me-not shade of blue. Her guilt, this evening, silenced her, and her smile came fleetingly and not often. When it did, her lower lip lost its bee-sting look and for an instant her white, irregular teeth appeared. She felt awkward and unpretty at the dinner table, sick of herself.

'We cultivate it late in our garden,' her mother was saying, still talking about the asparagus, of which Rose had taken only a single shoot. 'Our season runs almost to September.'

What kind of an ordeal was it for him? Rose wondered. They had invited his wife as well but a message had come the day before to say that Mrs Bouverie was unwell. Rose knew that wasn't true. His wife had seized the opportunity; she'd said to him she couldn't be bothered, but that wasn't true either. His wife would be naked now, Rose thought.

'Extraordinary, what you read on cars' rear windows,' her mother suddenly remarked, the subject of a particular season for asparagus now exhausted. '*Baby on Board*, for instance. I mean, why on earth should a total stranger be interested in that?'

'I think you're being told not to drive too close,' Rose's father suggested.

Tinkling with unmalicious social laughter, her mother pointed out that it was an enticement to drive too close in order to read what was said.

'They haven't thought of that, my dear.'

In all her chosen subjects Rose had been a borderline case and every Thursday afternoon, for almost a year, had gone to Mr Bouverie's house, where they had sat together in the bow window that looked out into the garden. Mrs Bouverie brought tea as soon as Rose arrived and while they drank it Mr Bouverie didn't attempt to teach but instead talked about the past, about his own life when he had been about to go to university himself, and later being interviewed for a position in the worsted-cloth business. He had tried the worsted trade for a while and then had turned to schoolmastering. But something about the form of discipline and the tedium of 'hobbies time' – when the boys put together model aeroplanes – caused him to give it up after a year. Ever since, he had received pupils in his house, deciding only a month or so ago that Rose should be the last of them. 'Anno Domini,' he'd said, but Rose knew that wasn't the reason. During all those teatimes he had spun his life out, like a serial story.

'But it's odd,' Mrs Dakin lightly persisted. 'Don't you agree with me, Mr Bouverie?'

The old man hesitated, and Rose could see he had momentarily lost track of the conversation. She knew her mother would notice also and not be dismayed. Smoothly her mother said:

'All those personal declarations on motor cars – whom people love, where they've been, who occupies the two front seats.'

'Sharon and Liam usually,' Mr Dakin guffawed.

Mrs Bouverie, ten years younger than her husband and seeming more, had a lover. Mrs Bouverie, slim and silky, with long legs and a wrinkled pout, too well made up, received a visitor on Thursday afternoons because her husband was occupied with the last of his pupils then, concentrating on a borderline case's weaknesses. Mrs Bouverie's visitor came softly, but there were half-muffled sounds, like shadows passing through the house, a pattern of whispers and footfalls, a gently closed door, and always – ten minutes or so before Rose was due to leave the house herself – the lightest of footsteps on the stairs and in the hall. It was a pattern that belonged with Mrs Bouverie's placing the tea tray on the pale mahogany of the window table, her scent lingering after she left the room, the restlessness in her eyes. But Rose hadn't entirely guessed the nature of the weekly rendezvous until the afternoon she went to fetch a handkerchief from her coat pocket

on the hallstand, and saw a sallow-faced man with a latchkey in his hand
breathlessly closing the hall door. Seeing her in turn, he smiled, a brightly
secret smile. 'Younger than her?' Rose's friend Caroline, sharp on detail,
wanted to know, and Rose said no, not much, but beautifully turned out
in a brown linen suit, a grey-haired man, and elegant. 'Not come to mend
something?' suggested Daisy, who could not help being sceptical when
someone else claimed the limelight. Her doubts were scorned at once by
Angela and Liz, for why should a repairer of washing machines or television sets be in possession of a latchkey and be dressed so? Why should he
come so regularly? Why should he smile a secret smile? In the Box Tree
Café where the five girls gossiped and complained of this and that, where
they talked about sex and other private matters, where Daisy and Caroline
smoked, Mrs Bouverie's Thursday lover became the subject of intense and
specific speculation. He was married, Caroline said, which was why he
had to come to her house: in illicit love affairs there was always the difficulty of finding somewhere to go. He came on Thursdays because, Rose
being the last of Mr Bouverie's pupils, there was no other time when Mr
Bouverie was fully occupied as perhaps there had been in the past, when
there were other pupils. 'That kind of thing and she's *fifty?*' Daisy frowned
through the words, but Angela said fifty was nothing. 'I do not intend to
be unfaithful,' Liz romantically declared, but the others weren't interested
in that, any more than they wished to dwell for long on the advanced age
of Mrs Bouverie. What fascinated all of them, Daisy too in the end, was
that while Rose sat in a room that had been described to them – a long
low-ceilinged room that had once been two, with sofas and armchairs and
a circular mirror over the mantelpiece – in a room upstairs a man and a
woman got into bed together. 'I would love to see him,' Caroline said.
'Even a glance.' Was it like, each of them wondered in the Box Tree Café,
the lovemaking you saw on the television or in the cinema? Or was, somehow, the real thing quite different? They argued about that. 'I would not
hesitate to be unfaithful,' Caroline said, 'if things went stale.' Caroline
was like that, her matter-of-factness sometimes sounding hard. Angela –
long black hair, brown eyes, rarely smiling because of her dental wires –
was the victim kind, and accident-prone. Liz gave too much, generosity
part of her romantic nature. Daisy, red-haired and bespectacled, distrusted
the world. Liz was the prettiest of the five, with neat features and flaxen
hair in a ponytail and a film star's mouth, nothing particularly special
except for deep-blue eyes, but still the prettiest. Rose thought of herself as
ordinary, too quiet, too shy and nervous: Mrs Bouverie and her Thursday
visitor were a godsend in her relationship with her friends.

'How nice all this is!' Mrs Dakin enthused for the second time, the subject of notices on motor cars having run its course. 'How hugely grateful to you we are, Mr Bouverie!'

Rose watched him shaking his head, and heard him saying that the credit must wholly go to her.

'No, truly, Mr Bouverie,' her father insisted with a solemn intonation.

'All her young life before her,' her mother threw in.

Rose hadn't told them, nor told her brother. It wasn't the sort of thing that was talked about within this family. She would have been embarrassed and would have caused embarrassment – a very different reception from the one there'd been when she had passed the information on in the Box Tree Café with its green-topped tables. After the first time, her friends had always been expectant. 'It could be any of our mothers,' Liz whispered, awestruck, once. They had sat there, coffee drunk, Caroline and Daisy with their cigarettes, dwelling upon that, imagining Rose's sallow-skinned man arriving in the surroundings that had been described to them. 'Beautifully pressed, his linen suit,' Rose said. 'And a plain green shirt.'

Around the dinner table the conversation, still powered by Mrs Dakin, had changed again. '*The Kindest Cut*,' she was saying now, drawing Mr Bouverie's attention to the droll wit of hairdressers as exemplified in the titles chosen for their premises. '*Nutters* I saw the other day!'

This evening, for the very last time, he would be there. Mr Bouverie did not normally go out to dinner; he'd said as much when joining in the celebratory mood on his arrival. No tea tray had been carried to the window table since Rose had ceased to visit the house. The invitation for this evening must have seemed like a gift, naughtily wrapped, for slim Mrs Bouverie. 'It's a Mr Azam,' her husband had said on the last but one of their Thursdays. 'In case you are interested in his name.'

Mr Dakin poured the wine again. He said they'd had the glasses as a wedding present, only four of them left so they couldn't use them often.

'The Mitages,' Mrs Dakin murmured softly, the shrillness that whistled through her voice gone from it now, inappropriate because the Mitages were no longer alive. She paused in her eating, inclining her head in memory, slanting it a little to the left, a wistful smile enlivening her reddened lips. Mr Dakin sighed; then death passed on, and Mrs Dakin picked up her fork again and the wine bottle was replaced on its little silver tray, another wedding gift, although this was not said.

'Cuckold.' In the Box Tree Café the ugly word, spoken first by Caroline, had formed in their minds, its sound acquiring shape and colour. Only Rose knew what Mr Bouverie looked like but he, really, scarcely came into it. It was not an old man who had once planned a future in the cloth trade and had ended as a tutor that was of interest. He was no rival for the darkened bedroom above the room that had once been two, or for the scent of Mrs Bouverie or her lover's suit draped on a chair, or smears of lipstick left on sallow flesh. No one ever interposed a comment while Rose spread out for the delectation of her friends another Thursday harvest. Once, music softly played, 'Smoke Gets in Your Eyes'. Once the telephone rang and was not answered by Mr Bouverie, although the receiver was only yards from where they sat. Sooner than if he had crossed to it the ringing ceased, answered at the bedside. Not always, but now and again, Mrs Bouverie appeared on the stairs when Rose was putting her coat on at the hallstand; or in summer, when there was no coat, she sometimes called down goodbye when she heard the voices of her husband and his pupil. 'Vicious,' Liz said. 'That's a vicious woman.' But Rose said no, you couldn't call Mrs Bouverie vicious; she didn't strike you as that. 'More significant that she's childless,' Daisy said. 'Or at least it could be.' Caroline disagreed.

'Oh, my golly gosh!' Rose's father exclaimed with his auctioneer's jolliness when gooseberry fool was placed in front of him. Mrs Dakin said the gooseberries had been picked from her own bushes.

'Delicious,' Mr Bouverie for the second time remarked, and the talk was of gooseberries for a while, of different varieties, one favoured for this purpose, another for that.

'Mr Azam,' Rose had announced in the Box Tree Café and Daisy had gone at once to the telephone directory to look the name up. 'Hundreds,' she'd said, returning. 'Hundreds of Azams.' In her absence the conversation had advanced in another direction, the name agreed to be a foreign one and then abandoned as a subject for discussion. 'When a husband knows,' Caroline said, 'he's not so much a cuckold as complaisant.' And they talked about the fact that while Mr Bouverie dealt with the last of his borderline cases he knew what was occurring all around him – the nature of the creaking stairs and closing doors, the light tap of footsteps not his wife's, the snatch of music hushed. 'Did he seem different when he said the name?' Caroline sharply asked, and Rose said no.

Her brother Jason arrived. Like his parents, he was well covered, with a jowl that was identically his father's and with his mother's small fat hands, bland in his manner. It was because of Jason that Mr Bouverie had been discovered, for Jason in his time had been a borderline case also. They greeted one another now, shaking hands and enquiring about one another's well being.

'How did it do?' Jason asked Mr Dakin when all that was over.

'Oh, well enough. The Chippendale fetched a price. A happy day's business,' Mr Dakin reported, smiling.

'How very nice!' His wife glanced round the table, seeking to share her exultation in the day's success. 'All right, dear?' she asked when her gaze lighted on her daughter. 'All right, Rose?'

Rose nodded, lying. 'I do mind, as a matter of fact,' he had said, as if he knew all about the Box Tree Café and the audience of five crowding the same green-topped corner table, as if he had listened to every word. Guilt had come then, beginning in that moment. His spectacles had slipped to one side and he adjusted them as soon as he had spoken. The cuffs of his blue tweed jacket were trimmed with leather. 'Yes,' she'd said, not knowing what else to say, the waves of guilt already a sickness in her stomach. 'Yes.' It was as though for all the months that had passed they, too, had shared a secret, the secret of knowing everything that was happening and not saying. When her Thursday visits came to an end a way of life would finish for him also, for Rose knew that Mr Azam would not just come to the house and march upstairs while the old cuckold sighed and blinked. That would not be: all of it had to do with pretence, and deception of a kind. 'I'm sorry,' she had wanted to say, and did not know why she would have given anything not to have blurted out so much in the Box Tree Café. She had longed to share his confidences with him, but had betrayed him even before he offered them.

In the lovers' bedroom Rose saw Mrs Bouverie close her eyes in ecstasy, while the gooseberry fool was finished and Jason spoke of a function he had attended, how one man had gone on and on. Coffee came and was poured at the table. 'Don't go yet. Oh, love, don't go,' Mrs Bouverie pleaded, and Mr Azam said he didn't ever want to go.

Across the table, all that was in Mr Bouverie's face, as so much had been when he gave the man a name and later when he said he minded. It was there behind the spectacles, in the tired skin touched with two crimson wine-blurs above the cheekbones. They shared it, yet they did not. Their sharing was a comfort for him, yet the comfort was as false as his wife's voice on the stairs.

'All right, dear?' her mother asked again, and by way of response Rose reached out for her coffee.

A frown began to knit Mr Dakin's forehead. Jason coughed and touched his face with a handkerchief, then folded it into his top pocket and began again about the function he had attended, referring to a commercial prospect he had advanced. His father nodded, thankfully diverted. Mrs Dakin tidied the surface up, murmuring to Mr Bouverie that probably he'd never guess she'd been shy herself at Rose's age.

'I'm confident we'll pick it up,' Jason said. 'I'll write tomorrow, see if we can't clinch.'

Mrs Bouverie clung to her lover, saying no this couldn't be the last time, sobbing over him, noisily exclaiming that something better was their due. But Mr Azam only shook his head. He was not a man to cause a wife who had borne his children to suffer. 'We have our dignity, you and I,' he said. 'We have been given this much.' Mr Azam drew on his green shirt, and brushed his hair with a hairbrush on the dressing-table, and saw that the lipstick smears were gone. 'I saw the pupil once,' he said, but the woman he spoke to had turned her face to the wall.

'Sounds promising,' Mr Dakin complimented Jason. 'Sure to work out, I'd say.'

Mrs Dakin poured more coffee. She spoke of names, how it had struck her this afternoon that names can inspire the quality they suggest. She described a Prudence she had known when she was Rose's age, and a Verity. 'Remember Ernest Calavor?' she prompted Mr Dakin, and he said yes indeed. Bitter chocolates were passed round in a slim red box. When she'd refused one Rose offered it across the table to Mr Bouverie.

'Thank you, Rose.'

The lover's footsteps were on the stairs, and then the front door closed and he was gone.

'It's been so good of you,' Mr Bouverie said. 'So very kind of you to have me.'

'I hope your wife,' Mrs Dakin began.

'She was so sorry to miss an evening out.'

'There'll be another time. We'll keep in touch.'

'Always good to see you,' Mr Dakin added. 'Cheers us no end.'

The old man hesitated before he rose to go. Had he not done so Rose might not have wept. But Mr Bouverie hesitated and Rose wept to exclamations of concern, and fuss and embarrassment, while Mr Bouverie stood awkwardly. She wept for his silent suffering, for his having to accept a distressing invitation because of her mother's innocent insistence. She wept for the last golden opportunity the occasion provided for two other people, for the woman whose sinning caused her in the end to turn her face to the wall, for the man whom duty bound to a wife. She wept for the *modus vivendi* that was left in the house no pupil or lover would visit again, for the glimpse she had had of it, enough to allow her a betrayal. She wept for her friends – for the unfaithful when things turned stale, and for the accident-prone; for the romantic, who gave too much, and the mistrustful. She wept for the brittle surface of her mother's good-sort laughter and her father's jolliness, and Jason settling into a niche. She wept for all her young life before her, and other glimpses and other betrayals.

Big Bucks

Fina waited on the pier, watching the four men dragging the boat on the shingle. She watched while the catch was landed and some damage to the nets examined. At the top of the steps that brought them near to where she stood the men parted and she went to John Michael.

'Your mother,' Fina said, and she watched him guessing that his mother was dead now. 'I'm sorry, John Michael,' she said. 'I'm sorry.'

He nodded, silent, as she knew he would be. It was cold and darkening as they walked together to the cottage where his mother was. Grey on grey, swiftly blown clouds threatened rain. They could go now, Fina's thought was. They could make a life for themselves.

'Father Clery was there,' she said.

'Have you plans?' John Michael's uncle – his mother's brother – enquired after the funeral. Plans were necessary: John Michael's father had drowned when John Michael was an infant, his fisherman's cottage then becoming his widow's by right for her lifetime. In a different arrangement – John Michael being a fisherman himself – a cottage would become his in time, but not yet, he being the youngest, the only young one among older men.

'I'll go,' he said in reply to his uncle's question.

Fina heard that said, the confirmation given that John Michael had been waiting only for the death. Going was a tradition, time-honoured, the chance of it coming in different ways, the decision long dwelt upon before it was taken. Bat Quinn – who had stayed – had a way of regretfully pointing over the sea to the horizon beyond the two rocks that were islands in the bay. 'Big bucks,' he'd say, and name the men of his own generation who had gone in search of them: Donoghue and Artie Hiney and Meagher and Flynn, and Big Reilly and Matt Cready. There were others who'd gone inland or to England, but they hadn't done as well.

'A thing I'll put to you,' John Michael's uncle was saying now, 'is the consideration of the farm.'

'The farm?'

'When I'm buried myself.'

'What about the farm?'

'I'm saying it'll be left.'

Still listening, Fina heard a statement made through what was being left out: the farm would pass to John Michael, since there was no one else to inherit it.

'I get a tiredness those days,' John Michael's uncle said. His wasted features and old man's bloodshot eyes confirmed this revelation. Two years ago he'd been widowed; after a childless marriage he was alone.

'There's a while in you yet,' John Michael said.

'I can't manage the acres.'

They could be on the farm already was what was being suggested, and it wouldn't be hard to pull the place together. Inland from the sea, where the air was softer and you didn't live in fear of what the sea would take from you, they could make a life there. The heart had gone from the old man, but he wasn't difficult. He wouldn't be a burden in the time that was left to him.

'Ah, no, no.' John Michael shook his head, his rejection not acknowledging in any other way what was being offered. America was what he and Fina wanted, what they'd always talked about. That evening John Michael said he had the fare saved.

The plans that could not be made in the lifetime of John Michael's mother were made now. John Michael would go soon. In May he would return for the wedding, and take Fina back with him. He didn't know what work he'd get, but according to Bat Quinn it had never mattered to the men who'd gone before that fishing was all they knew. 'Leave it open till you'll get there, boy,' Bat Quinn advised, the same advice he had been giving for forty years. Matt Cready came back, the only one who did, his big bucks spent like pennies every night in the bar of the half-and-half. 'Look at that, boy,' Bat Quinn invited, displaying for John Michael the dollar bill he kept in an inside pocket. Bat Quinn had a niece, a nun in Delaware, and had had a sister in Chicago until her death two years ago. Slouched heavily at the bar of the grocery and public house that Fina's family kept, his great paunch straining his clothes, his small eyes watery from drink, Bat Quinn showed everyone his dollar. 'I'll send you back another,' John Michael always promised, and Fina always giggled.

They knew one another well, had gone together to school, picked up on the pier every morning by the bus, the only two from the village at that time. Concerned about the adventure that was being embarked upon, Fina's father had protested more than once that they were still no more than the children they'd been then. 'Oh, John Michael'll fall on his feet,' her mother predicted, fond of John Michael, optimistic on his behalf. 'But isn't he welcome to move in with us all the same?' Fina's father had offered when John Michael's mother died, and Fina passed that on, knowing that John Michael wouldn't ever consider serving in the half-and-half, drawing pints or checking the shelves for which grocery items were running out.

'Sure, we have to go,' was all John Michael said himself. Fina's own two brothers had gone, one to Dublin, the other to England. One or other of them would have had the inheritance of the half-and-half but both had turned their backs on it.

A few evenings before they were to be parted, they walked through the twilight on the strand, talking about what they intended to reject for ever: the sea and the fishing, or John Michael being beholden in the half-and-half, his uncle's farm. Eleven miles away, beyond the town of Kinard – which had a minimarket, a draper's, five public houses, a hardware, and Power's Medical Hall – the farmhouse was remote, built without foundations according to John Michael. Slated and whitewashed, it was solitary where it stood except for the yard sheds, its four fields stretching out behind it, as far as the boglands that began with the slope of the mountain. The mountain had no name, John Michael said, or if it had it was forgotten now, and there wasn't a gate that swung. Old bedsteads blocked the holes in the hedges, there was a taste of turf on the water you drank. Damp brought on mildew in the rooms.

'Even if you could get the place up on its feet again,' John Michael said, 'it's never what we want.'

'No way.' Vehemently Fina shook her head, reassurance and agreement bright in her eyes. 'No way,' she said again.

Physically, there was a similarity about them, both of them slightly made, John Michael hardly a head taller. Both were dark-haired, with a modesty in their features, as there was in their manner. They seemed more vulnerable when they were together than when they were on their own.

'Did you ever think it, though, Fina? That we'd be on our way?'

Her hand was warm in his, and his felt strong, although she knew it wasn't particularly. Since they were children they had belonged to one another. On this same strand two years ago, in the twilight of an evening also, they had first spoken of love.

'I only wish I'd be going with you,' she said now.

'Ah sure, it's not long.'

He was gone, quite suddenly. For two hundred and one days they would be parted: already Fina had counted them. She thought at first that maybe at the last moment he'd be sent back, that the immigration-control men at Shannon wouldn't let him on to the plane because he didn't possess a work permit. But he'd said he'd be ready for that and he must have been. You had to be up to the tricks, he'd said.

The first day without him passed and when it was the evening of the next one Bat Quinn was talking about big bucks again, his small eyes squinting at Fina from the red fat of his face. Only Jamesie O'Connor was ever sent back, he said, on account of his dead leg. 'Don't worry, girl,' Bat Quinn consoled, and began about the schooner that was pitched up on the rocks when he was five years old, twelve foreign men taken in for burial. 'Sure, what's here for John Michael only the like of that? And isn't he safe with the mighty dollar to watch over him?' Bat Quinn had more talk in him than anyone who ever came into the half-and-half. If exile or shipwrecks weren't his subject it would be the Corpus Christi he had walked to in his childhood, twenty-three miles to Kinard, twenty-three miles back again, or how an old priest used to bless the hurley sticks of the team he favoured, or the firing of Lisreagh House. Bat Quinn had been a fisherman himself, going out with the boats for more than fifty years. He'd never worn a collar or tie in his life, he shaved himself once a week and had never had the need of a wife; he washed his clothes when they required it. All that Bat Quinn would tell you, having told you most of it before. He had stayed at home when the others went, but even so he insisted that Boston's long, straight streets were a wonder when the evening sun shone down them. You'd go into McDaid's and there was shamrock in pots and a photo of Christy Ring. He had it as a fact that Donoghue got to be a candy king before he went to his grave in a green-upholstered coffin. Artie Hiney made his stack in the wheatfields of Kansas. Big Reilly rose high in the Frisco police force and ran it in the end.

I missed you the minute I left, John Michael wrote. There was a lot to tell her, his first letter went on, but even so it was short. He wasn't used to writing letters, he'd said before he went away, he'd do his best. *I have work with a gang*, he wrote when three weeks had gone by, and unable to help herself Fina thought of gangsters. She laughed, as though John Michael were there to laugh with her.

There were tourists here last week, she wrote herself. *Italian people who asked Mary Doleen would there be fish today. They came into the shop and we thought they were German but they said Italian. They'd be back for fish in the morning, they said, but they never came. Bat Quinn was on the pier waiting, wanting to know was it Rome they were from. There were never Italians here before, he said, the time of the wreck it was Spaniards washed up. He was down on the pier the next few mornings, but they never came back.*

John Michael replied directly to that, saying he was working with an Italian but he didn't know his name. It was labouring work, he said. 'Give him time, girl,' Bat Quinn advised, but when more weeks went by there was no mention of the streets of Boston or the Kansas wheatlands. Then a letter came that asked Fina not to write because there wouldn't be an address to write to for a while. John Michael said he'd let her know when he had one again.

In this way Fina and John Michael began to lose touch. You had to lodge where you could, John Michael had explained; you wouldn't earn a penny if you paid regular rent. Fina didn't entirely understand this. She couldn't see that you could lodge anywhere without paying rent, and it was too late now to ask. John Michael had to take what he could get, she of course could see that. He had to move about if it was the only way; if he said so it must be right.

A cold, sunny November began, but the pattern of the days themselves didn't change much. Fina served in the shop, slicing rashers on the machine, adding up bills, unpacking the items that were delivered – the jams and meat pastes and tinned goods, the porridge meal and dried goods, the baking ingredients in their bulky cartons. O'Brien's bread van brought the bread from Kinard on Tuesdays and Fridays, milk came on alternate days and there was the longlife if it was held up, which sometimes it was. Experience had taught the family of the half-and-half the business, what to order and when, what to keep in stock both in the shop and in the bar. You could be caught out if you didn't know what you were doing, Fina's mother used to say; you could have stuff on the shelves for a generation or find yourself running out because you hadn't looked ahead. Her mother ran the shop and took a rest in the evenings when the men came into the bar and Fina's father was in charge. Her mother was as lightly made as Fina was, small and busy, with a certain knowledge of where everything was on the crowded shelves of the grocery, quick with figures, spectacles suspended on a chain. Fina's father – assisted in the bar by Fina, as her mother was in the shop – was a big man, slow of movement and thought, silver-haired, always in his shirtsleeves, the sleeves themselves rolled up. He put on a black suit to go to Mass, and a tie with a tiepin, and wore a hat for the walk through the village. Fina's mother dressed herself carefully also, in a coat and hat that were not otherwise worn. The three of them went together on Sundays and separately at other times, to confession or confraternity.

John Michael didn't write when he had no address, and Fina fell back on her imagination. The world of America, which she and John Michael had talked about and wondered about for so long, was spiced with the yarns of Bat Quinn, his exaggeration and fantasy steadied by facts remembered from the days when Mr Horan unrolled the map of the continent and hung it on the blackboard. On the glossy surface the states were shown in shades of brown and green and yellow, the Great Lakes blue. Iron came from Minnesota and Michigan and Pennsylvania, uranium from Colorado. Cotton and tobacco belonged to the south.

The tip of Mr Horan's cane moved in a straight line, horizontally, up and down, dividing Nebraska from South Dakota, Oregon from Idaho. It rapped the dates of admission to the Union, it traced the course of the long Mississippi, it touched the Rockies. You listened because you had to, stifling yawns of tedium, thankfully forgetting what the Louisiana Purchase was. The scissor-tailed flycatcher was the state bird of Oklahoma, the peony was the flower of Indiana. It was in Milwaukee that Donoghue became a candy king.

The tattered schoolroom cane picking out the facts had failed to create much of a reality. Bat Quinn's second-hand information didn't inspire Fina as it did John Michael. But America lived for both of them on the screen high up above the bar of the half-and-half or the one in John Michael's kitchen. For two years before she died his mother had to be helped to go to bed and as often as she could Fina assisted. Afterwards she sat with John Michael in the kitchen, with tea and pink Mikado biscuits and the sound turned low. They watched America, they heard its voices. Its ballgame heroes battled, rigid in their padding and their helmets. Steam swirled above the night-time gratings of its city streets. Legs wide, eyes dead, its gangsters splayed their fingers on precinct walls.

Fina liked it when the doormen greeted the yellow cabs, and the quick talk in the skyscraper lifts, and Christmas in the stores. She liked the lone driver on the highway, music on his radio, the wayside gas station he drew up at, its attendant swatting flies. She liked the boy who drilled for oil too near the old-time ranch, everything changing because the gush of oil was what mattered now, the boy in the end a bigtime millionaire. College days, Thanksgiving, Robert E. Lee: she liked all that. 'You want to?' John Michael would whisper and Fina always nodded, never hesitating.

I got work in a laundry, the next letter said, slow in coming. Bat Quinn wagged his head in admiration when he heard. There were big bucks in the laundry business, no doubt about it. The President's shirts would have to go to a laundry, and Bat Quinn twisted round on his barstool, exclaiming loudly that John Michael Gallagher was in charge of the shirts of the President of the United States. 'I'll tell you a thing, girl, you hit it lucky with John Michael Gallagher.'

Fina put all that in a letter, making a joke of it, as they would have in the past. It was a long letter, with bits of news saved up from the period when they'd been out of touch: O'Brien's bread van breaking down, the boats unable to go out for four days, the widow dancing at Martin Shaul's wake. She wondered if John Michael had an accent now, like Bat Quinn said Matt Cready acquired.

A Christmas card came in January and a fortnight later a letter with an address, 2a Beaver Street, a room that was big enough for both of them. *I painted it out*, John Michael wrote. *I cleaned the windows*. Ninety-one days had passed and the ones that were passing now had begun to lengthen. In Kinard a week ago Fina had chosen the material for her dress. She kept telling herself it wouldn't be all that long before the first banns were called.

The morning the letter about the room came there was an iciness in the air when she walked on the strand, thinking about the banns and thinking about Beaver Street. She imagined a fire escape zig-zagging on an outside wall, a big metal structure she had seen in a film, windows opening on to it. She imagined a poor neighbourhood because that was what John Michael could afford, spindly trees struggling to grow along a sidewalk. She wouldn't object to a poor neighbourhood, she knew he'd done his best.

The strand was empty that morning. The fishing boats were still out, there had been no one on the pier when she went by it. New shells were embedded in the clean, damp sand where she walked, washed by the waves that lapped softly over them. Once upon a time, so the story was told in the village, a woman had walked all the way to Galway, going after the man she loved. Missing John Michael more than ever, even though the time was shortening with every day, Fina understood that now. Slowly, she made her way back to the village, the room he had found for them more vivid in her consciousness than anything she saw.

She knew when her father called her. She had heard the ringing of the telephone above the clatter of voices in the bar, and her father's surprise when he responded. 'Well, b'the holy farmer! How are you at all?' She pushed the glass she'd just filled across the counter. 'Wait'll I get Fina for you,' she heard her father say, and when she picked the receiver up John Michael's voice was there at once.

'Hullo, Fina.'

He didn't sound distant, only unusual, because in all the time of their friendship they had never spoken on the telephone to one another.

'John Michael!'

'Did you get my letter, Fina? About the room?'

'I got it yesterday.'

'Are you OK, Fina?'

'Oh, I am, I am. Are you, yourself?' There wouldn't be telephone calls, he'd said before he went, and she agreed: telephone calls would eat up what he earned. But hearing his voice was worth every penny they'd lose.

'I'm good, Fina.'

'It's great to hear you.'

'Listen, Fina, there's a thing we have to think about.' He paused for a second or two. 'A difficulty about May, Fina.'

'Difficulty?'

'About coming back.'

He paused again, and then he had to repeat some of what he said because she couldn't follow it. It was why he had phoned. Because he knew it would sound complicated, but actually it wasn't: it was best he didn't come back in May for the wedding. It was best because once you'd got to where he was now, once you'd got into steady work, it wasn't easy to come and go. He shouldn't be working at all, he said. Like hawks, he said they were.

'You understand, Fina?'

She nodded in the darkened shop, where the telephone was. There was a smell of bacon, and of stout and spirits drifting in from the other side of the half-and-half. The deep-freeze began to sound, registering its periodic intake of electricity. *Chef Soups*, a point-of-sale inducement read, close enough to discern, the rest of its message lost in the gloom.

'If I was to come over I wouldn't get back in again.'

It would be better to be married in America. It would be better if she came over and he stayed where he was. He asked her if she understood and she felt as if she were stumbling about, in some kind of a dream without sense in it, but even so she said she understood.

'I think of you all the time, John Michael. I love you.'

'It's the same way with me. We'll work something out. Only it's different than we thought.'

'Different?'

'All the time you're thinking would you be sent back.'

'We'll be married in America, John Michael.'

'I think of you too, Fina. I love you too.'

They would work something out, he said again, and then there was the click of the receiver replaced. Fina wondered where he was, in what kind of room, and if he was still standing as she was, beside the telephone. Once there had been voices in the background. It would be half past four, still daylight there, and she wondered if he was at work in the laundry and if he'd taken a risk, using the phone like that.

'How's John Michael Gallagher?' Bat Quinn asked, slouched in his corner, on the stool that over the years had become his own. In the dimly illuminated bar the expression on his face was as lost as the words on the Chef point-of-sale had been, but Fina could guess at what was there – the small eyes would be reflecting his excitement because all those miles away John Michael Gallagher had touched success.

'He's doing well, girl. Isn't it grand for the pair of ye?'

By the door of the bar there was a game of twenty-one. The men John Michael had fished with were silent, as they often were. Fina's father washed glasses at the sink.

'He can't come back for the wedding,' Fina said to Bat Quinn. She moved closer to him, drawn to him because with his knowledge of America he would know about the anxiety that was worrying John Michael.

'It's understandable,' Bat Quinn said.

The porter he was drinking was drained away, the glass edged toward her on the scrubbed surface of the bar. Fina refilled it and scooped up the coins that had been counted out.

'It's never as easy as they think,' Bat Quinn said.

Chance had always played a part, ever since the Famine years, that first great exodus from the land, the ships called coffin ships. As often as the good side of it was there, so were misfortune and desperation and failure.

'Never was easy, never will be, girl.'

'Will they take it back?' Fina's mother wondered about the wedding-dress material. All but the yard she had begun to cut the arms out of was untouched. Scally wouldn't return the full price because what was left would have to be sold as a remnant. You couldn't expect the full price from a draper like Scally, but an agreement might be reached to make up for the disappointment. Fina's mother had sat for a while not saying anything when she heard the news, and then she sighed and cheered up, for that was her way. She'd assumed at first that she'd finish the dress anyway, that Fina would need it when she married John Michael in America. But Fina explained it wouldn't be that kind of wedding now.

'They gave an amnesty a while back,' Fina's father said. He remembered a figure, something like a hundred and twenty thousand Irish immigrants outside the system in New York. But it could be a while before there'd be an amnesty again. 'Go easy now, Fina,' he advised, not elaborating on that. 'John Michael'll fix something,' her mother said.

Ten days later John Michael phoned again. He'd thought more about it, he said; and listening to him, Fina realized he wasn't just talking about not coming home for the wedding.

'Don't you want me?' she asked, meaning to add something to that, to ask if he'd changed his mind about her coming over. But she left it as she'd said it, and John Michael reassured her. It was just that he was wondering would it be too much for them, the uncertainty there'd be, the hole-in-corner existence; too much for any wife, was what he was wondering. It was all right for some young fellow on his own, who could scuttle around, dodging the bit of trouble. If she was there with him now she'd see what he meant, and Fina imagined that, being with him in the room with the clean windows and the freshly painted walls, all of it ready for her.

'I'll come back,' John Michael said.

'But you said –'

'I'll come back altogether. I'll come back and we'll stay where we are.'

She couldn't say anything. She tried to, but the words kept becoming muddled before she got them out. John Michael said:

'I love you, Fina. Isn't it that that matters? The two of us loving one another?'

It was, she agreed. Of course it was.

'I'll work out the time I'm taken on for.'

They said goodbye. It was a shock for her, he said, and he was sorry. But it was better, no way it wasn't better. Again he said he loved her, and then the line went dead.

It would be his uncle's farm. She guessed that; it hadn't been said. They'd pull the place together; his uncle would stay there with them until he died. John Michael would rather that than going on with the fishing. He'd prefer it to being beholden in the half-and-half.

'There's the odd one comes back all right,' Bat Quinn said, having listened to Fina's side of the telephone conversation.

Fina nodded, not saying anything, and that same week she went out to the farm. She took the Kinard bus and walked the last two miles from where it dropped her off. Sheepdogs barked when she turned in to the yard, but the barking was ignored by John Michael's uncle, as if it didn't matter to him that someone had come, as if all curiosity about visitors had long ago expired. Grass grew through the cobbles, a solitary hen pecked at the edge of a dung pile.

'I was wondering how you were,' Fina said in the kitchen, and the haggard countenance that the farm had defeated was lifted from a perusal of *Ireland's Own*. Boiled potatoes had been tumbled out on to a newspaper, the skins of those eaten in a pile, peas left in a tin. A plate with a knife and fork on it was pushed to one side.

'Sit down, Fina,' the old man invited. 'Wait till I make a cup of tea.'

Life seemed to return to him while he half filled a kettle and put it on a ring of his electric stove. He spooned tea into an unheated pot and set out cups and saucers, and milk in a milking can. He offered bread but Fina shook her head. He took a heel of butter from a safe on the dresser.

'John Michael went over,' he said.

'Yes, he did. A while back.'

'He's settled so.'

'He hasn't the right papers,' Fina said.

She watched while the butter was spread on a slice of bread, and sugar sprinkled over it. It wouldn't take long to set the kitchen to rights. It wouldn't take long to paint over the dingy ceiling, to take up the linoleum from the floor and burn it, to wash every cup and knife and fork, to scrub the grease from the wooden tabletop, to fix the taps that were hanging from the wall, to replace the filthy armchair.

'You were never here before,' the old man said, and led her upstairs to dank bedrooms, an image of Our Lady on the wall opposite each bed. A forgotten cat rushed, hissing, from a windowsill. Electric wire hung crookedly from a fallen-in ceiling, mould was grey on the faded flowers of wallpaper. Downstairs, ivy crept over panes of glass.

A digger would take out those rocks, Fina thought, surveying the fields. Half a day it would take with a digger. John Michael's uncle said they'd be welcome if it was something they'd consider. When the wedding would be over, he said, when they'd have gathered themselves together.

'It's different why you'd go into exile these days,' Bat Quinn said in the half-and-half. 'A different approach you'd have to it.'

You made a choice for yourself now. The way the country was doing well, you could stay where you were or you could travel off. A different thing altogether from the old days, when you had no choice at all.

'Yes,' Fina said.

I went over to see the farm, she wrote. *No way we wouldn't be able to get it up and going. He'd be no trouble to us.* Her mother finished the wedding dress. Fina imagined John Michael, any day now, walking in with the red holdall they'd bought together in Kinard. They'd bought her own at the same time, the same colour and size. She imagined going back with him to Scally's and explaining to Scally that they wouldn't want it now. John Michael would be better at that than she'd be.

Fina's feelings bewildered her. She kept hoping that out of the blue the phone would ring and John Michael would say it was all right, that he'd wangled a work permit, that the boss he was working for had put a word in, that there'd been a further amnesty. But then another while would pass and there'd be no hope at all. John Michael would walk in and she'd be shy of him, the way she'd never been. She imagined herself on the farm as she used to imagine herself in the room John Michael had described, the silence of the fields instead of the noise on the streets and the yellow cabs flashing by. When she wondered if she still loved John Michael, she told herself not to be a fool. He was right when he said that it was loving one another that mattered. But then the confusion began again.

No phone call came. *We'll sort things out when I'm back*, another letter said. *We'll have it done before the wedding.* The banns had long ago been called. The half-and-half would be closed for the day. People had been invited to the house. If she had a number, she would telephone herself, Fina thought, not that she'd say anything about how she felt. She woke up in the middle of one night feeling afraid. In the dark she knew she didn't love John Michael.

It's only I'm ruining everything for you, she wrote when there was hardly time for him to receive the letter before he'd have to set out. *I have it on my mind, John Michael.* Alone on the strand, she had decided on that way of putting things. Five days later, two before he was due back, John Michael phoned. He'd got her letter, he said, and then he said he loved her.

'I always will, Fina.'

He could tell: she heard it in his voice. Always quick on the uptake, always receptive of her emotions, even in a letter, even on the long-distance telephone, he knew more than she did herself.

'I don't know what it is,' she said.

'You're uncertain.'

She began to say it wasn't that, but she stumbled and hesitated. She wanted to cry.

'You have to be guided by yourself, Fina. You're doubtful about the wedding.'

She said what she had in her letter, that she was ruining things for him. 'It wouldn't be right to wait until you got here.'

'Better to wait all the same,' he said. 'It's not long.'

'I don't want you to come.'

'You don't love me, Fina?'

He asked that again when she didn't reply.

'I don't know,' she said.

*

John Michael did not come back. For Fina, the pain lasted for the empty weeks that followed the day that had been set for the wedding, and then for all the summer. September was balmy, thirty days of a clear blue sky, the days gently slipping away as they shortened. In October a year had passed since the death of John Michael's mother. By October John Michael's scant letters didn't come any more.

'I'd say he'd walk in in the time ahead,' Bat Quinn said on a night his intake had exceeded what he allowed himself. Squinting blearily up at Fina, he added, as if the two observations somehow belonged together: 'Haven't you the delicate way with you, pouring that stout, girl?'

'Oh, I have all right.'

Bat Quinn was right. It was likely enough that in the time ahead, when John Michael had made his money, he would return, to look about him and remember.

'An amnesty'll bring him,' Bat Quinn said, heaving himself off his stool to lead the exodus from the bar. 'Good night to you so, girl.'

She was better at pouring the stout than her father was, even though he'd been at it for longer. Her hands were steadier, not yet roughened. She had the delicacy of the young, she'd heard her mother say when the disappointment about John Michael had become known.

'Good night, Fina,' the men called out, one after another before they left, and when the last of them had gone she bolted the door and urged her father to go upstairs to bed. She cleared up the glasses and knocked the contents of the ashtrays into a bowl. She wondered if they were sorry for her, Bat Quinn and the men John Michael had fished with, her mother and her father. Did they think of her as trapped among them, thrown there by the tide of circumstances, alone because she had misunderstood the nature of her love?

They could not know she had come to realize that she was less alone than if she were with John Michael now. The long companionship, their future planned, their passion and their embraces, were marked in memory with a poignancy from which the sting had been drawn. It was America they had loved, and loved too much. It was America that had enlivened love's fantasies, America that had enriched their delight in one another. He'd say that too if he came back when he'd made his money. They would walk again on the strand, neither of them mentioning the fragility of love, or the disaster that had been averted when they were young.

On the Streets

Arthurs ordered liver and peas and mashed potatoes in Strode Street. When it came, the liver didn't taste good. A skin of fat was beginning to congeal on the surface of the gravy where the potato hadn't soaked it up. The bright green peas were more or less all right.

He was a dark-haired man in his mid-fifties, with a widow's peak and lean features that matched his spare frame, bony wrists protruding from frayed white cuffs. He wore a black suit, its black trousers being a requirement for a breakfast waiter beneath a trim white jacket.

'You want a pot of tea with that?' the elderly woman who had brought him his plate of liver enquired. She came back to his table to ask him that, her only customer at this time in the afternoon.

Arthurs said yes. The woman wasn't a proper waitress; she didn't have a uniform, just a flowered overall folded over, tight on her stomach. Nearly seventy she'd be, he estimated, a woman who should be sitting by a fire somewhere, the heat bringing out crimson rings on her legs. He could sense her exhaustion, and wondered if she'd talk about it, if a conversation might develop.

'Finishing soon?' he said when she brought the tea, speaking as if he knew her well, his tone suggesting that there'd been a past in their relationship, which there had not.

'I go at three-thirty.'

'Stop in tonight, will you?'

'Eh?' She looked at Arthurs with something like alarm in her tired eyes. Her hair was dyed yellowish, dewlaps of fat rolled over her neck. Widowed, he imagined.

'Reckon I'll stop in myself,' he said. 'Best if you're feeling dull.'

The woman answered none of that. He wondered if he should follow her when she finished for the day. It was twenty past three now and he'd be ready to go himself by half past. He broke the Garibaldi biscuit she'd brought with the tea. Since childhood he had followed people on the streets, to find out where they lived, to make a note of the address and add a few details that would remind him of the person. The compulsion was still insistent sometimes, but he could tell it wasn't going to be today.

'There's the television of course,' he said, 'if you're feeling not up to much.'

'No more'n rubbish these times,' the woman said, allowing herself that single comment only.

'Sends you to an early bed, does it?'

Again anxiety invaded the woman's eyes. She passed the tip of her tongue over her lips and wiped away the coating of saliva it left. Silent, she stumped off.

A pound and a few pence the bill came to when she brought it, food cheaper here when the busy lunchtime hours had passed. He'd known it would be cheaper, Arthurs reminded himself.

Mr Warkely came in and said don't start another batch or there'll be a clog-up in the dispatch room. So Cheryl turned the machine off and saw Mr Warkely glancing at the clock and noting the time on his pad. Finishing a quarter of an hour early would naturally have to be taken into account at the end of the week.

The Warkelys' business was in a small way, established three years ago in a basement, the retailing of scenic cards. Cheryl's task was to work the machine that encased in strong plastic wrapping each selection of six, together with the one that displayed in miniature the scenes each pack contained. It was part-time work, two hours three days a week; there was also, mornings only, the Costcutter checkout, office cleaning evenings.

The Warkelys employed no one else: Mrs Warkely attended to the accounts, the addressing of labels, and all correspondence; Mr Warkely packed the packaged selections into cardboard boxes and drove a van with *WPW Greetings Cards* on it. What was called the dispatch room was where television was watched, with the Warkelys' evening meal on two trays, evidence of their business stacked around the walls.

'See you Thursday,' Cheryl said before she went, and Mrs Warkely called out from somewhere and Mr Warkely grunted because his ballpoint was in his mouth. 'Thanks,' Cheryl said, which was what she always said when she left the basement. She didn't know why she did, but somehow that expression of gratitude seemed to round off the couple of hours better than just saying goodbye.

She banged the door behind her and climbed the steps to the street, a thin, smallish woman, grey in her hair now, lines gathering around her eyes and lips. She had been pretty once and still retained more than a vestige of those looks at fifty-one. Shabby in a maroon coat that once she'd been delighted to own and now disliked, her high-heeled shoes uncomfortable, she hurried on the street. There was no reason to hurry.

She knew there was not and yet she hurried, her way of walking it had become.

'You getting on all right?' The voice came from behind her, the question asked by the man she'd once been married to, whom she'd thought of since as the error in her life. Always the same question it was when he was suddenly there on the street. She turned around.

'D'you want something?' She spoke sharply and he walked away at once, her tone causing offence. She knew it was that because it had happened often before. She had never told him what her hours at the Warkelys' were but he knew. He knew where her cleaning work was, he knew which Costcutter it was. Five months the marriage had lasted, before she packed her belongings and went, giving up a full-time position in a Woolworth's, because she'd thought it better to move into another district.

She stood where he had left her, watching him in the distance until he turned a corner. 'I don't think you should have married me,' she'd said, more or less what Daph, who shared her counter in Woolworth's, had been remorselessly repeating ever since the marriage had taken place, not that she'd admitted to Daph that things weren't right, not wanting to.

On the pavement she realized she was in the way of two elderly women who were trying to pass. 'I'm sorry,' she apologized and the women said it didn't matter.

She walked on, more slowly than she'd been walking before. When they married she had moved upstairs to his two rooms, use of kitchen and bath, the rooms freshly painted by him in honour of the change in both their lives, old linoleum replaced by a carpet. The paint had still been fresh when she left, the carpet unstained; she'd never begun to call herself Mrs Arthurs.

Later that afternoon, although he was not a drinking man, Arthurs entered a public house. Like the café in which he had earlier had a meal, it was not familiar to him: he liked new places.

He took the beer he ordered to a corner of the almost empty saloon bar, where the fruit machines were at rest, the music speakers silent. There was a griminess about the place, a gloom that inadequate lighting did not dispel. At the bar, on barstools, two men morosely sat without communicating. A shirtsleeved barman turned the pages of the *Star*.

The dullness Arthurs had mentioned in the café possessed him entirely now, an infection it almost felt like, gathering and clinging to him, an unhealthy tepidness about it. He sipped the beer he'd ordered, wondering why he had come in here, wondering why he wasted money. Time was when he'd have gone to a racetrack, the dogs at Wimbledon or White City.

In the crowd, with his mind on something else, he could have shaken off the mood. Or he might have rid himself of it by getting into conversation with a tart. Not that a tart had ever been much good, any more than the elderly waitress would have been. He closed his eyes, squeezing back disappointment at being asked if he wanted something when all he was doing was being friendly. They might have sat down somewhere, on a seat in a park, the flowerbeds just beginning to be colourful, birds floating on the water. She knew how it had been; she knew he'd gone there at last, today. In their brief encounter, she had guessed.

People began to come into the saloon bar, another lone man, couples. Arthurs watched them, picking out the ones he immediately disliked. He wondered about phoning up Mastyn's and saying he wouldn't be in in the morning. A stomach upset, he'd say. But the hours would hang heavy, because he'd wake anyway at twenty past five, being programmed to it. And there'd be nothing to replace the walk to the Underground, and the Underground itself, and walking the last bit to the hotel; and nothing to replace the three and a half hours in the dining-room until at half past ten he could hang up his white jacket and unhook his black bow tie. Since the hours of his employment at Mastyn's had been reduced, his earnings solely as a breakfast waiter were not enough to live on, but he made up the shortage in other ways. Since childhood he had stolen.

There was a telephone across the bar from where he sat, half obscured by a curtain drawn back from the entrance to the Ladies. Noticing it, he was tempted again. But whoever answered at the Reception would grumble, would say leave it until the morning, see how he was then. The conversation would be unsatisfactory, any message he left for the dining-room probably forgotten, and blame attached to him when he didn't turn up even though he'd done what was required of him. None of that was worth it.

Why had she spoken to him like that? Why had her voice gone harsh, asking him if he wanted something? He had never asked her for money, not once, yet the way she'd spoken you'd think he'd been for ever dropping hints. Music began, turned down low but noisy anyway because that was what it was, more a noise than anything else. The last couple who'd come in were noisy too, laughter that could have been kept quieter, both wearing dark glasses although there hadn't been sunshine all day. What he'd wanted to say was maybe they could go to a café for a few minutes. No more than that, ten minutes of her time.

Arthurs stared into the beer he hadn't drunk, at the scummy froth becoming nothing. The sympathy she could call upon was a depth in her, surprising in a woman who wasn't clever. He had been aware of it the first day on the stairs, when they'd got into conversation because he happened to be passing by. 'You like a cup of tea or something?' she'd offered, her key already in the lock of the door; and he'd said tea, two sugars, when they were in her room. He told her about the lunchtime complaint in the dining-room of Mastyn's because it was a natural thing to do; she said she'd wondered why he looked upset and then said anyone would be, a horrible thing to happen. He repeated the remarks that had been made, how he'd stood there having to listen, how the man had demanded the manager, how he'd said, 'We apologize for troubling you' when Mr Simoni came. Mr Simoni had held his hand out but they hadn't taken it.

Arthurs wondered for a moment if, that first day or later, he'd told her this too – that Mr Simoni's outstretched hand had been ignored. He couldn't remember saying it. A dotted bow-tie the man had been wearing, white dots on red, a chalk-striped shirt. The pepper had been ground over her risotto with a mutter that sounded insolent, the woman said. The coffee had been cold. 'Well, there'll certainly be no charge for the coffee,' Mr Simoni's immediate response was. Something special, this lunch should have been, the man said, and the woman called the lunch a misery before she threw her napkin down. They'd gone away, not knowing what they left behind. 'Breakfasts only after this,' Mr Simoni murmured while bowing and scraping to the people who'd gone silent at the other tables. 'Take it or not.' Beneath the thrown-down napkin there was a shopping list on a letter that had been half written and then abandoned, the shopping items pencilled on the space remaining. *Dear Sirs, An electric fire I purchased from you is faulty* had a jagged line drawn through it; there was a date in the same handwriting, and an address embossed in blue at the top of the single sheet.

Arthurs reached into an inside pocket and took from it this same writing paper, now folded to a quarter of its size. Frayed at the edges, it was dog-eared and soiled, one of the folds beginning to give way, and he didn't open it out for fear of damaging it further: it was enough to hold it for a moment between thumb and forefinger, to know that it was what he knew it was, kept by him always. A year ago he'd gone into a Kall-Kwik and had had it photographed twice, nervous in case one day the original might, somehow, not be there: he did not trust, and never had, any time that was yet to come or what might happen in it. He knew the address by heart, even in his sleep, in dreams; but who could tell what might happen to memory? Not that it mattered now, of course.

He returned the folded paper to his pocket and stood up. Seven o'clock she finished in the offices, ten past she was out on the streets again. Five to six it was and he sat for a little longer, thinking about her. For a long time before the day she'd asked him into her room he'd seen her coming and going. They had passed often on the stairs of the house where his own two rooms were a flight above hers, cheaper than the other rooms because of their bad state of repair. He hadn't known she was a widow, thinking her to be unmarried ever since she'd come to the house a year or so ago. A ticket man on the Underground apparently her husband had been.

He left his beer, pushing the glass away in case a sleeve caught it while he was putting his overcoat on. He buttoned the coat slowly – black like his suit – then crossed the saloon bar and stepped out into the darkening twilight. The folded paper was not something to keep, not any more, but even so he knew he could not destroy it. There was that, too, to tell her: that the shopping list would always be a memento.

Her encounter with her ex-husband had not particularly upset Cheryl: she was too used to his sudden appearances for that. As she emptied waste-paper baskets and gathered up plastic cups, uncoiled the long flex of her vacuum cleaner and began on the floors, she yet again blamed herself. She had been foolish. Lonely, she supposed, missing what death had taken from her, she had seen the man differently; it had felt natural, saying yes. Daph had been a witness in the register office, with a man they'd fetched in from the street. Afterwards they'd sat with Daph in the back bar of the Queen's Regiment and when a few people from the house turned up later they'd gone in a crowd to Bruce's Platter, above the Prudential Office. They'd kept calling her Mrs Arthurs, making a joke of it once the wine got going, but all that time he was very quiet until she heard him telling Daph about the lunchtime complaint, and every few minutes Daph – outspoken when she'd had a few too many – saying people like that didn't deserve a life. 'You hear that?' he said afterwards. 'What your friend remarked?'

At the time it had seemed ordinary enough that he should mention the complaint to someone else, that that terrible lunchtime should nag so, the wound of humiliation slow to heal. She had urged him to leave Mastyn's Hotel, to find another post in a restaurant or another hotel, but for whatever reason he wouldn't, stoically maintaining that being a lowly breakfast waiter was what he would remain now. She didn't understand that, although she accepted that when you married someone you took on his baggage, and one day the healing would be complete.

But on the night of her second marriage the baggage she'd taken on was suddenly more complicated. When they returned from the celebrations in the Queen's Regiment and Bruce's Platter her husband of half a day didn't want to go to bed. He said it was hardly worth it, since he had to get up soon after five. But it was not yet eleven when he said that.

Still vacuuming the office floors, Cheryl remembered the unflurried timbre of his voice when he offered this explanation, a matter-of-factness that, quite suddenly, made her feel cold. She remembered turning on the single bar of the electric fire she had brought upstairs from the room she no longer occupied. She remembered lying awake, wondering if the darkness of the bedroom would draw him to her, wondering if he was a man like that, not that she had ever heard of being like that before. But nothing happened except what was happening in her mind, the realization that she had made a mistake.

As she slid her vacuum cleaner into corners and under desks, all that was there again, as often it was when, on the streets, her ex-husband once more attempted to enter her life. A man who was hurt was what he'd seemed to be during the time they had been getting to know one another. She'd told him about times in her childhood, about her marriage, and the shock of widowhood; he'd spoken of the censure he'd always felt himself subjected to, culminating in the lunchtime complaint he'd taken so hard. Small rebukes, reproof, blame in its different forms affected him – she was sure – more than ever was intended: from the first she had known that, when each new shade of his accumulated pain was revealed to her. Then, too, she had believed that the pain would ease, as it seemed to when she was with him. But even before she packed her things to go, Daph said, 'Your guy's doolally.'

Cheryl turned the cleaner off and wound the flex back into place. She straightened the chairs she had had to move out of the way, finishing one office at a time and closing the door of each behind her. She took her coat and scarf from the hooks in the passage and carried downstairs the black plastic bag in which she'd collected the waste-paper. She re-set the night alarm. She banged the door behind her and began to walk away.

'They ignored Mr Simoni,' he said in the empty dark. 'Mr Simoni tried to shake hands with them but he needn't have bothered.'

She looked at him with nothing in her eyes. There was no flicker that they were man and wife, as if she had forgotten. She had been everything to him; she could have sensed it from the way he'd been with her. When they'd gone for a walk together, the second time they had, she'd put a hand on his arm. A Sunday that had been, a cold afternoon and she'd been wearing gloves, red and blue. Just a touch of pressure from her fingers, no more than that, nothing forward, but he'd felt the understanding there was. A waiter could tell you how people were, he had explained to her another time. She hadn't known it; she hadn't known how you could feel insulted, the amount people left beside a plate. Not that a breakfast waiter got anything at all.

'I don't want to stand here listening to you,' she said, and then she said he should see someone; she said she had asked him to leave her alone.

'It's just I wondered if I'd ever told you that, how Mr Simoni held out his hand.'

'Please leave me alone,' she said, walking on.

Every plea she made was a repetition, already stale before she made it, and sounding weary when she did. She had lost touch with Daph when she'd moved to another district but Daph had made her promise to go to the police if she became frightened.

'You could tell she was the kind of woman who complained,' he said. He'd put the coffee ready for her to pour out, but when he walked away she called after him that it was cold. You didn't expect there'd be a waiter with soiled cuffs in this dining-room, she said when Mr Simoni came.

Cheryl tried not to see when he rooted in a pocket for his wallet. It was worst of all, the grubby paper taken from his wallet and carefully unfolded, its tattered edges and the blue letters of the address offered to her as a gift might be. *Dear Sirs, I believe an electric fire I purchased . . .* In the dark she couldn't see but she knew the words were there, as the shopping list had been there too, before its pencilled items had all but disappeared.

'Please leave me alone,' she said.

Walking with her, he said the café by the launderette was always open, people waiting there for their washing to be ready. 'Quiet,' he said. 'Never less than quiet, that café.'

She could tell from his movements beside her that the paper was being folded again and then returned to the right compartment of his wallet. His wallet was small, black, its plastic coating worn away in places.

'It's hardly out of your way,' he said.

They were alone on the street; they had been since she'd heard his voice behind her saying that the people who'd complained had ignored Mr Simoni's wish to shake hands with them. He always spoke first from behind her on a street, his footsteps silent.

'I thought I might run into you today,' he said. 'She'll want to know about this morning, I thought.'

He mentioned tea and she said she didn't want tea at this hour. And then she thought that in a café she could raise her voice, drawing attention to his harassing of her. But she didn't want to go to a café with him. When she'd found things he'd stolen he'd said nothing, not even shaking his head. When she'd packed her belongings he'd been silent too, as if expecting nothing better, humiliation self-inflicted now.

'Straight after I'd done at the hotel I went out there,' he said. 'This morning.'

He told her about the hotel people who'd had breakfast, a slack morning, being a Monday. He remembered the orders; he always could afterwards, even on a busy day, a waiter's skill, he called it. He told her about the bus he'd taken, out through Shepherd's Bush and Hammersmith and then the green of trees and grass beginning when Castelnau was left behind. Someone called out for the Red Rover and the driver shouted back that the Red Rover had gone years ago. There was a traffic hold-up at Upper Richmond Road and he got off and walked a bit. He'd been out there before, he said: Priory Lane, then left by a letter-box. A dozen times, he said, he'd checked it out.

They turned a corner and she could see the lit-up window of the launderette. She remembered the café he was talking about then, a little further along with a 7-Up sign in the window.

'I've something to get washed,' he said.

She didn't go into the launderette with him. While he was there she could have hurried on, past the café, to where the buses ran. Any bus would have done, even one going in the wrong direction. But in the café, where an elderly man and two women on their own were the only customers, she carried from the counter a pot of tea and two glass cups and saucers, and went back for milk.

She waited then, blankly staring at the tea she'd poured, taking the first sip, tasting nothing. No thoughts disturbed her. She did not feel she was in a café, only that she was alone, anywhere it could have been; and then her thoughts began again. She had been drawn to him; that reminder echoed, hardly anything else made sense.

She watched him coming in, the door slipping closed behind him. He looked about, knowing she would be there, knowing she wouldn't have disappeared.

On the table he laid out what he had taken from the pockets of his jacket before he'd put it into a washing machine: keys, his wallet, a ballpoint. He had thought she would ask about his jacket, where it was, why he wasn't wearing it, but she didn't. He stirred the tea she'd poured for him. It didn't matter that she didn't ask; his overcoat was open, she could see the jacket wasn't there.

'Three hours ago he'll have found her,' he said. 'A quarter past seven every evening he gets back to that house.'

Cheryl stared at a cigarette burn on the table's surface while he told her. He had rung the bell, he said, and the woman hadn't recognized him when she opened the door. He'd said he'd come to read the meter, not saying which one. The gas man had been, no longer than a week ago, the woman had said, and he'd apologized for not having his badge on display. He'd pulled aside his overcoat to show the electricity badge on his left lapel. The woman hadn't closed the door when he walked into the hall. A good ten minutes it was open before his hands were free to close it.

'I blame myself,' he said, 'for being stupid like that.' He added that he didn't blame himself for anything else; he had stood there, not blaming himself, remembering the woman saying that his cuffs were grimy, complaining that the coffee was cold. He had stood there, hearing her voice, and the telephone rang on a small table near the hallstand. When it stopped he went to wash his hands in the downstairs lavatory, where coats and the man's hats and a cap hung on hooks. In the hall he draped a tissue over the Yale latch before he turned it; and afterwards dropped the scrunched-up tissue into a waste-bin on a lamp post.

Cheryl didn't say anything; she never did. She watched while his overcoat was buttoned again after she'd seen he wasn't wearing his jacket. A dribble of blood from the woman's mouth had got on to his sleeve, he said, the kind of thing that was discernible beneath a microscope, easy to overlook.

Once he'd shown her a bruise he'd acquired on a finger while he was committing his crime, another time he'd shown her the tissue he had draped over the Yale, forgotten in his pocket all day. Once he'd said the second post had come while he was there, brown envelopes mostly, clattering through the letter-box. While the woman was on the floor there'd been the postman's whistling and his footsteps going away.

'I didn't take a bus,' he said. 'I didn't want that, sitting on a bus. The first food I had afterwards was liver and peas.'

The last time it had been a packet of crisps; another time, a chicken burger. Still silent, Cheryl listened while his voice continued, while he explained that ever since this morning he'd felt she was his only friend, ever since he'd washed his hands, with the man's coats on coat-hangers and the scented soap on its own special little porcelain shelf. A cat had jumped on to the windowsill outside and begun to mew, as if it knew what had occurred. He had thought of opening the back door to let it in, so that it would be in the hall when the man returned, and its bloody footsteps all over the house.

She had never told Daph that it wasn't fear she experienced when she was with him, that it wasn't even disquiet. She had never said she knew there was cunning in his parade of what hadn't happened, yet that it hardly seemed like cunning, so little did he ask of her. She had never said she knew it was her nature that had drawn her to go for walks with him and to accept his reticent embrace, that her pity was his nourishment. She had never wanted to talk to Daph about him. The Warkelys didn't know he existed.

He lifted the glass cup to his lips. She still did not speak. It was not necessary to speak, only to remain a little longer, the silence an element in being with him. He did not follow her when she walked away.

He would finish his tea and pour another cup: on the streets again she imagined that. In the launderette he would open the door of a machine and release his sodden jacket from where it clung to the drum. He would spread out the sleeves and pull the material back into shape before he began his journey to the rooms where so briefly they had lived together. He would not, tonight, be offended by the glare of neon beneath which she now walked herself. Nor by the cars that loitered in their search for what the night had to offer. Nor by the voices of the couples pressed close to one another as they went by. Her tears, tonight, allowed him peace.

The Dancing-Master's Music

Brigid's province was the sculleries, which was where you began if you were a girl, the cutlery room and the boot room if you weren't. Brigid began when she was fourteen and she was still fourteen when she heard about the dancing-master. It was Mr Crome who talked about him first, whose slow, lugubrious delivery came through the open scullery door from the kitchen. Lily Geoghegan said Mr Crome gave you a sermon whenever he opened his mouth.

'An Italian person, we are to surmise. From the Italian city of Naples. A travelling person.'

'Well, I never,' Mrs O'Brien interjected, and Brigid could tell she was busy with something else.

The sculleries were low-ceilinged, with saucepans and kettles hanging on pot-hooks, and the bowls and dishes and jelly-moulds which weren't often in use crowding the long shelf that continued from one scullery to the next, even though there was a doorway between the two. Years ago the door that belonged in it had been taken off its hinges because it was in the way, but the hinges were left behind, too stiff to move now. Flanked with wide draining-boards, four slate sinks stretched beneath windows that had bars on the outside, and when the panes weren't misted Brigid could see the yard sheds and the pump. Once in a while one of the garden boys drenched the cobbles with buckets of water and swept them clean.

'Oh, yes,' Mr Crome went on. 'Oh, yes, indeed. That city famed in fable.'

'Is it Italian steps he's teaching them, Mr Crome?'

'Austria is the source of the steps, we have to surmise. I hear Vienna mentioned. Another city of renown.'

Mr Crome's sermon began then, the history of the waltz step, and Brigid didn't listen. From the sound of the range dampers being adjusted, the oven door opened and closed, she could tell that Mrs O'Brien wasn't listening either.

Nobody listened much to Mr Crome when he got going, when he wasn't cross, when he wasn't giving out about dust between the banister supports or the fires not right or a staleness on the water of the carafes. You listened then all right, no matter who you were.

Every morning, early, Brigid walked from Glenmore, over Skenakilla Hill to Skenakilla House. She waited at the back door until John or Thomas opened it. If Mr Crome kept her on, if she gave satisfaction and was conscientious, if her disposition in the sculleries turned out to be agreeable, she would lodge in. Mr Crome had explained that, using those words and expressions. She was glad she didn't have to live in the house immediately.

Brigid was tall for her age, surprising Mr Crome when she told him what it was. Fair-haired and freckled, she was the oldest of five, a country girl from across the hill. 'Nothing much in the way of looks,' Mr Crome confided in the kitchen after he'd interviewed her. Her mother he remembered well, for she had once worked in the sculleries herself, but unfortunately had married Ranahan instead of advancing in her employment, and was now – so Mr Crome passed on to Mrs O'Brien – brought low by poverty and childbirth. Ranahan was never sober.

Brigid was shy in the sculleries at first. The others glanced in when they passed, or came to look at her if they weren't pressed. When they spoke to her she could feel a warmth coming into her face and the more she was aware of it the more it came, confusing her, sometimes making her say what she didn't intend to say. But when a few weeks had gone by all that was easier, and by the time the dancing-master arrived in the house she didn't find even dinnertime the ordeal it had been at first.

'Where's Naples, Mr Crome?' Thomas asked in the servants' dining-room on the day Mr Crome first talked about Italy. 'Where'd it be placed on the map, Mr Crome?'

He was trying to catch Mr Crome out. Brigid could see Annie-Kate looking away in case she giggled, and Lily Geoghegan's elbow nudged by the tip of John's. Nodding and smiling between her mouthfuls, deaf to all that was said, but with flickers of ancient beauty still alive in her features, Old Mary sat at the other end of the long table at which Mr Crome presided. Beside him, Mrs O'Brien saw that he was never without mashed potato on his plate, specially mashed, for Mr Crome would not eat potatoes served otherwise. The Widow Kinawe, who came on Mondays and Thursdays for the washing and was sometimes on the back avenue when Brigid reached it in the mornings, sat next to her at the table, with Jerety from the garden on the other side, and the garden boys beside him.

'Naples is washed by the sea,' Mr Crome said.

'I'd say I heard a river mentioned, Mr Crome. It wouldn't be a river it's washed by?'

'What you heard, boy, was the River Danube. Nowhere near.' And Mr Crome traced the course of that great river, taking a chance here and there in his version of its itinerary. It was a river that gave its name to a waltz, which would be why Thomas heard it mentioned.

'Well, that beats Banagher!' Mrs O'Brien said.

Mrs O'Brien often said that. In the dining-room next to the kitchen the talk was usually of happenings in the house, of arrivals and departures, news received, announcements made, anticipations: Mrs O'Brien's expression of wonderment was regularly called upon. John and Thomas, or the two bedroom maids, or Mr Crome himself, brought from the upper rooms the harrowings left behind after drawing-room conversation or dining-room exchanges, or chatter anywhere at all. 'Harrowings' was Mrs O'Brien's word, servitude's share of the household's chatter.

It was winter when Brigid began in the sculleries and when the dancing-master came to the house. Every evening she would return home across the hill in the dark, but after the first few times she knew the way well, keeping to the stony track, grateful when there was moonlight. She took with her, once in four weeks, the small wage Mr Crome paid her, not expecting more until she was trained in the work. When it rained she managed as best she could, drying her clothes in the hearth when she got home, the fire kept up for that purpose. When it rained in the mornings she could feel the dampness pressed on her all day.

The servants were what Brigid knew of Skenakilla House. She heard about the Master and Mrs Everard and the family, about Miss Turpin and Miss Roche, and the grandeur of the furniture and the rooms. She imagined them, but she had not ever seen them. The reality of the servants when they sat down together at dinnertime she brought home across Skenakilla Hill: long-faced Thomas, stout John, Old Mary starting conversations that nobody kept going, Lily Geoghegan and Annie-Kate giggling into their food, the lugubriousness of Mr Crome, Mrs O'Brien flushed and flurried when she was busy. She told of the disappointments that marked the widowhood of the Widow Kinawe, of Jerety wordless at the dinner table, his garden boys silent also.

'Ah, he's no size at all. Thin as a knife-blade,' was the hearsay that Brigid took across Skenakilla Hill when the dancing-master arrived. 'Black hair, like Italians have. A shine to it.'

At one and the same time he played the piano and taught the steps, Mr Crome said, and recalled another dancing-master, a local man from the town, who had brought a woman to play the piano and a fiddler to go with her. Buckley that man was called, coming out to the house every morning in his own little cart, with his retinue.

'Though for all that,' Mr Crome said, 'I doubt he had the style of the Italian man. I doubt Buckley had the bearing.'

Once Brigid heard the music, a tinkling of the piano keys that lasted only as long as the green, baize-covered door at the end of the kitchen passage was open. John's shoulder held it wide while he passed through with a tray of cups and saucers. At the time, Annie-Kate was showing Brigid how to fill the oil lamps in the passage, which soon would become one of her duties if Mr Crome decided she was satisfactory. Until that morning she had never been in the passage before, the sculleries being on the other side of the kitchen wing. 'That same old tune,' Annie-Kate said. 'He never leaves it.' But Brigid would have listened for longer and was disappointed when the baize door closed and the sound went with it. It was the first time she had heard a piano played.

Three days later, at dinnertime, Mr Crome said:

'The Italian has done with them. On Friday he'll pack his traps and go on to Skibbereen.'

'Can they do the steps now, Mr Crome?' Annie-Kate asked, in the pert manner she sometimes put on at the dinner table when she forgot herself. Once Brigid heard Mrs O'Brien call it cheek, giving out to Annie-Kate in the kitchen, and Annie-Kate came into the sculleries afterwards, red-faced and tearful, dabbing at her face with her apron, not minding being seen by Brigid, the way she would by the others.

'That is not for us to know,' Mrs O'Brien reprimanded her, but Mr Crome pondered the question. It was a safe assumption, he suggested eventually, that the dancing-master wouldn't be leaving unless the purpose of his visit had been fulfilled. He interrupted a contribution on the subject from John to add:

'It's not for that I mention it. On Thursday night he is to play music to us.'

'What d'you mean, Mr Crome?' Mrs O'Brien was startled by the news, and Brigid remembered hearing Lily Geoghegan once whispering to Annie-Kate that Mrs O'Brien was put out when she wasn't told privately and in advance anything of importance in Mr Crome's news.

'I'll tell you what I mean, Mrs O'Brien. It's that every man jack of us will sit down upstairs, that John and Thomas will carry up to the drawing-room the chairs we are occupying this minute and arrange them as directed by myself, that music will be played for us.'

'Why's that, Mr Crome?' Annie-Kate asked.

'It's what has been arranged, Annie. It's what we're being treated to on Thursday evening.'

'We're never sitting down with the Master and Mrs Everard? With the girls and Miss Turpin and Miss Roche? You're having us on, Mr Crome!' Annie-Kate laughed and Lily Geoghegan laughed, and John and Thomas. Old Mary joined in.

But Mr Crome had never had anyone on in his life. For the purpose of the dancing-master's recital, the drawing-room would be vacated by the family, he explained. The family would have heard the music earlier that same day, in the late afternoon. It was a way of showing gratitude to the dancing-master for his endeavours that he was permitted to give his performance a second time.

'Is it the stuff he's always hammering out we'll have to listen to?' Annie-Kate asked. 'The waltz steps, is it, Mr Crome?'

Mr Crome shook his head. He had it personally from Miss Turpin that the music selected by the dancing-master was different entirely. It was music that was suitable for the skill he possessed at the piano, not composed by himself, yet he knew every note off by heart and didn't need to read off a page.

'Well, I never!' Mrs O'Brien marvelled, mollified because all that Mr Crome said by way of explanation had been directly addressed to her, irrespective of where the queries came from.

On that Thursday evening, although Brigid didn't see the Master or Mrs Everard, or the girls, or Miss Turpin or Miss Roche, she saw the drawing-room. At the end of a row, next to the Widow Kinawe, she took her place on one of the round-bottomed chairs that had been arranged at Mr Crome's instruction, and looked about her. A fire blazed at either end of the long, shadowy room and, hanging against scarlet wallpaper, there were gilt-framed portraits, five on one wall, four on another. There were lamps on the mantelpiece and on tables, a marble figure in a corner, the chairs and the sofa the family sat on all empty now. A grand piano had pride of place.

Brigid had never seen a portrait before. She had never seen such furniture, or two fires in a room. She had never seen a piano, grand or otherwise. On the wide boards of the floor, rugs were spread, and in a whisper the Widow Kinawe drew her attention to the ceiling, which was encrusted with a pattern of leaves and flowers, all in white.

Small, and thin as a knife-blade, just as she had described him herself, the dancing-master brought with him a scent of oil when he arrived, a lemony smell yet with a sweetness to it. He entered the drawing-room, closed the door behind him, and went quickly to the piano, not looking to either side of him. He didn't speak, but sat down at once, clasped his hands together, splayed his fingers, exercising them before he began. All the time he played the music, the scent of oil was there, subtle in the warm air of the drawing-room.

There had been a fiddler at the wake of Brigid's grandmother. He was an old man who suffered from the coldness, who sat close in to the hearth and played a familiar dirge and then another and another. There was keening and after it the tuneless sound continued, the fiddler hunched over the glow of the turf, Brigid's grandmother with her hands crossed on her funeral dress in the other room. But while the lamplight flickered and the two fires blazed, the dancing-master's music was different in every way from the fiddler's. It scurried and hurried, softened, was calm, was slow. It danced over the scarlet walls and the gaze of the portrait people. It lingered on the empty chairs, on vases and ornaments. It rose up to reach the white flowers of the encrusted ceiling. Brigid closed her eyes and the dancing-master's music crept about her darkness, its tunes slipping away, recalled, made different. There was the singing of a thrush. There was thunder far away, and the stream she went by on Skenakilla Hill, rushing, then babbling. The silence was different when the music stopped, as if the music had changed it.

The dancing-master stood up then and bowed to the congregated servants, who bowed back to him, not knowing what else to do. He left the drawing-room, still without saying anything, and the round-bottomed chairs were carried back to where they'd come from. Brigid caught a glimpse of Lily Geoghegan and John kissing while she was getting herself ready for the walk across the hill. 'Well, there's skill in it all right,' was Mr Crome's verdict on the dancing-master's performance, but Thomas said he'd been looking forward to a few jigs and Annie-Kate complained that she'd nearly died, sitting on a hard chair for an hour and a half. The Widow Kinawe said it was great to see inside a room the like of that, twenty-three pieces of china she'd counted. Old Mary hadn't heard a thing, but still declared she'd never spent a better evening. 'Who was that man at all?' she asked Mrs O'Brien, whose eyes had closed once or twice, but not as Brigid's had.

That February night on the stony hillside track there was frost in the air and the sky was blazing with stars that seemed to Brigid to be a further celebration of the music she'd heard, of beauty and of a feeling in herself. The tunes she tried for eluded her, but somehow it was right that they should, that you couldn't just reach out for them. The hurrying and the slowness and the calm, the music made of the stream she walked by now, weren't perfect, as when she'd closed her eyes in the drawing-room. But crossing Skenakilla Hill, Brigid took with her enough of what there had been, and it was still enough when she woke in the morning, and still enough when she worked again in the sculleries.

Mr Crome said at dinnertime that the dancing-master had left the house after breakfast. One last time he'd gone through the waltz steps. Then he left for Skibbereen.

*

Only once in the weeks and months that followed did the Italian dancing-master come up in conversation. Mrs O'Brien wondered where his travels had taken him, which caused Mr Crome to draw on his conversations with Miss Turpin and Miss Roche. The dancing-master, true enough, was a wandering stone. The chances were that he was in England or perhaps in France; and Spain and India had been spoken of. One fact that could be stated with confidence, Mr Crome assured his fellow-servants: long ago the dancing-master would have shaken the dust of Skibbereen from his heels. 'And who'd blame him?' Thomas muttered, chewing hard on gristle until surreptitiously he took it from his mouth.

That was the last time in the dining-room next to the kitchen, or anywhere else where the servants conversed, that the visit of the dancing-master to Skenakilla House was talked about. The event passed into the shadows of their memory, the gathering in the drawing-room touched in the recall of some with tedium. Other instances more readily claimed attention: heatwaves and storms, winter nights that froze the pump in the yard, props made for two of the cherry trees.

But for Brigid the music kept faith with her and she with it. The dancing-master splayed his fingers while the two fires burned in the drawing-room and the eyes looked down from the walls. In the sculleries where no man loved her as John loved Lily Geoghegan, the music rose on a crescendo and settled to a whisper. She brought it to the bedroom that in time she came to share with Lily Geoghegan and Annie-Kate. She brought it to the garden where, every day, her task was to cut whatever herbs were wanted. On Sunday afternoons when she walked to Glenmore through the solitude of Skenakilla Hill, the stars that had lit a February sky were still a celebration.

Advancing in her employment, Brigid was permitted to know the house and the family, and always stopped whatever she was doing in another room when the sound of the piano reached her. She heard it with pleasure, but nothing in it haunted her or stayed with her afterwards, even vaguely or uncertainly. At first she hoped that the same piano would one day bring her the dancing-master's music, but she was glad in the end that the music was not played by someone else.

It belonged with the dancing-master on his travels, and Brigid imagined great houses in England and France, seeing them as clearly as looking at pictures in a book. Grey elephants ambled through the bright heat of India, pale palaces in Spain echoed with the dancing-master's skill. There was the church of the dancing-master's city, and the priests waiting with the Host.

A time came when there was no longer a reason for Brigid to walk to

Glenmore on Sunday afternoons, there being no one left in Glenmore to visit. In that same year Mr Crome gave up his position to a new man who had come; not long after that one of the garden boys took over from Mr Jerety. Old Mary had gone long ago; one morning Mrs O'Brien was found dead.

A time came later when the fortunes of the family declined. The trees were felled for timber. Slates blown from the roof were left where they lay. In forgotten rooms cobwebs gathered; doors were closed on must and mildew. The servants' dining-room was abandoned because there weren't servants enough to sit round the table.

With great sadness, Brigid witnessed the spread of this deterioration, the house gone quiet in its distress, the family broken. But as if nothing had happened, as if no change had occurred, the dancing-master's music did not cease. It was there in the drawing-room where the vases were empty of flowers and the ceiling dark with smoke and the covers of the sofas marked by the sun. Untouched, unaffected, it cheered the sculleries and the kitchen and the yard. It danced over dust and decay in the hall and the passageways, on landings and stairs. It was there with the scents of the herb garden, tarragon and thyme half stifled.

No longer possessing the strength to stroll on Skenakilla Hill, Brigid looked out from the windows of the house to where tree stumps were the remnant of the hillside woods. As old now as she remembered Old Mary being, it was with difficulty that she discerned the stream and the track, but each time she looked from the windows she managed to do so in the end. She knew with the certainty of instinct that the dancing-master's music was there too. She knew it would be there when she was gone, the marvel in her life a ghost for the place.

A Bit on the Side

In the Japanese café he helped her off with her coat and took it to the line of hooks beneath the sign that absolved the management of responsibility for its safety. They weren't the first in the café, although it was early, ten past eight. The taxi-driver who came in most mornings was reading the *Daily Mail* in his usual corner. Two of the music students had arrived.

He hung up the coat, which still carried a faint trace of scent. Light-weight, and black, its showerproof finish was protection enough today, since the forecast they'd both heard – she in her kitchen an hour ago, he while he shaved in Dollis Hill – confidently predicted that the fine weather was here for another few days. He hadn't brought a coat himself and he didn't wear a hat in summer.

From the table they always sat at, side by side so that they could see the street where the office workers were beginning to hurry by, she watched him patting a pocket of his jacket, making sure his cigarettes and lighter were there. Something was different this morning; on the walk from Chiltern Street she had sensed, for an instant only, that their love affair was not as it had been yesterday. Almost always they met in Chiltern Street, their two journeys converging there. Neither ever waited: when one or other was late they made do with meeting in the café.

'All right?' she asked. 'All right?' She kept anxiety out of her tone; no need for it, why should there be? She knew about the touchiness of love: almost always, it was misplaced.

'Absolutely,' he said, and then their coffee came, his single croissant with it, the Japanese waitress smiling. 'Absolutely,' he repeated, breaking his croissant in half.

Another of the music students arrived, the one with the clarinet case. Then a couple from the hotel in George Street came in, Americans, who sat beneath the picture of the sea wave, whose voices – ordering scrambled eggs and ham – placed them geographically. The regular presence of such visitors from overseas suggested that breakfast in the nearby hotel was more expensive than it was here.

The lovers who had met in Chiltern Street were uneasy, in spite of efforts made by both of them. Discomfiture had flickered in his features when he'd been asked if everything was all right: now, at least, that didn't show. She hadn't been convinced by his reassurance and, within minutes, her own attempt to reassure herself hadn't made much sense: this, in turn, she kept hidden.

She reached out to flick a flake of croissant from his chin. It was the kind of thing they did, he turning up the collar of her coat when it was wrong, she straightening his tie. Small gestures made, their way of possessing one another in the moments they made their own, not that they ever said.

'I just thought,' she began to say, and watched him shake his head.

'How good you look!' he murmured softly. He stroked the back of her hand with his fingertips, which he often did, just once, the same brief gesture.

'I miss you all the time,' she said.

She was thirty-nine, he in his mid-forties. Their relationship had begun as an office romance, before computers and their software filched a living from her. She had moved on of necessity, he of necessity had remained: he had a family to support in Dollis Hill. These days they met as they had this morning, again at lunchtime in the Paddington Street Gardens or the picture gallery where surreptitiously they ate their sandwiches when it was wet, again at twenty to six in the Running Footman.

He was a man who should have been, in how he dressed, untidy. His easy, lazily expansive gestures, his rugged, often sunburnt features, his fair hair stubborn in its disregard of his intentions, the weight he was inclined to put on, all suggested a nature that would resist sartorial demands. In fact, he was quite dressily turned out, this morning in pale lightweight trousers and jacket, blue Eton shirt, his tie striped blue and red. It was a contradiction in him she had always found attractive.

She herself, today, besides the black of her showerproof coat, wore blue and green, the colours repeated in the flimsy silk of her scarf. Her smooth black hair was touched with grey which she made no attempt to disguise, preferring to make the most of what the approach of middle age allowed. She would have been horrified if she'd put on as much as an ounce; her stratagems saw to it that she didn't. Eyes, nose, mouth, cheeks, unblemished neck: no single feature stood out, their combination necessary in the spare simplicity of her beauty. Good earrings – no more than dots, and never absent – were an emphasis that completed what was already there.

'Have your cigarette,' she said.

He slipped the cellophane from a packet of Marlboro. They talked about the day, predicting what it would bring. She was secretary to a businessman, the managing director of a firm that imported fashion clothes, he an accountant. A consignment of Italian trouser-suits had failed to reach the depot in Shoreditch, had still been missing the evening before. She spoke of that; he of a man called Bannister, in the patio business, who had been under-declaring his profits, which meant he would have to be dismissed as a client. He had been written to yesterday: this morning there'd be an outraged telephone call in response.

The taxi-driver left the café, since it was almost half past eight now and the first of the traffic wardens would be coming on. From where they sat they watched him unlock his cab, parked across the street. With its orange light gleaming, he drove away.

'You're worried,' she said, not wanting to say it, pursuing what she sensed was best left.

He shook his head. Bannister had been his client, his particularly, he said; he should have known. But it wasn't that and she knew it wasn't. They were lying to one another, she suddenly thought, lies of silence or whatever the term was. She sensed their lies although she hardly knew what her own were, in a way no more than trying to hide her nervousness.

'They suit you,' he said. 'Your Spanish shoes.'

They'd bought them, together, two days ago. She'd asked and the girl had said they were Spanish. He'd noticed them this morning in Chiltern Street, the first time she'd worn them. He'd meant to say they suited her then, but the bagwoman who was usually in Chiltern Street at that time had shuffled by and he'd had to grope in his pocket for her twenty pence.

'They're comfortable,' she said. 'Surprisingly so.'

'You thought they mightn't be.'

'Yes, I did.'

It was here, at this same table, that she had broken the news of her divorce, not doing so – not even intimating her intentions – until her marriage's undoing was absolute. Her quiet divorce, she had called it, and didn't repeat her husband's protest when the only reason she had offered him was that their marriage had fallen apart. 'No, there is no one else,' she had deftly prevaricated, and hadn't passed that on either. 'I would have done it anyway,' she had insisted in the café, though knowing that she might not have. She was happier, she had insisted too. She felt uncluttered, a burden of duty and restriction lifted from her. She'd wanted that.

'Wire gauze, I suppose,' he said, the subject now a cat that was a nuisance, coming in the bedroom windows of his house.

Although such domestic details were sometimes touched upon – his house, his garden, the neighbourhood of Dollis Hill – his family remained mysterious, never described or spoken of. Since the divorce, he had visited the flat her husband had moved out of, completing small tasks for her, a way of being involved in another part of her life. But her flat never seemed quite right, so used had they become to their love affair conducted elsewhere and differently.

He paid and left a tip. He picked up his old, scuffed briefcase from where he'd leant it against a leg of their table, then held her coat for her. Outside, the sun was just becoming warm. She took his arm as they turned from Marylebone High Street into George Street. These streets and others like them were where their love affair belonged, its places – more intimately – the Japanese café and the Paddington Street Gardens, the picture gallery, the Running Footman. This part of London felt like home to both of them, although her flat was miles away, and Dollis Hill further still.

They walked on now, past the grey bulk of the Catholic church, into Manchester Square, Fitzhardinge Street, then to her bus stop. Lightly they embraced when the bus came. She waved when she was safely on it.

Walking back the way they'd come, he didn't hurry, his battered briefcase light in his right hand, containing only his lunchtime sandwiches. He passed the picture gallery again, scaffolding ugly on its façade. A porter was polishing the brass of the hotel doors, people were leaving the church.

Still slowly, he made his way to Dorset Street, where his office was. When she'd worked there, too, everyone had suspected and then known – but not that sometimes in the early morning, far earlier than this, they had crept together up the narrow stairs, through a dampish smell before the air began to circulate in the warren that partitions created. The waste-paper baskets had usually been cleared the night before, perfunctory hoovering had taken place; a tragedy it always was if the cleaners had decided to come in the morning instead and still were there.

All that seemed long ago now and yet a vividness remained: the cramped space on the floor, the hurrying, footsteps heard suddenly on the stairs, dust brushed from her clothes before he attended to his own. Even when she was no longer employed there they had a couple of times made use of the office in the early morning, but she had never wanted to and they didn't any more. Too far away to be visited at lunchtime, her flat had never come into its own in this way after the divorce. Now and again, not often, he managed a night there, and it was then that there were the tasks she had saved up for him, completed before they left together in the morning.

He thought about her, still on her bus, downstairs near the back, her slim black handbag on her lap, her Spanish shoes. What had she noticed? Why had she said, 'All right?' and said it twice? Not wanting to, and trying not to, he had passed on a mood that had begun in him, the gnawing of a disquiet he didn't want to explain because he wasn't able to, because he didn't understand it. When she'd said she missed him all the time, he should have said he missed her in that same way, because he did, because he always had.

When he had settled himself in the partitioned area of office space allocated to him, when he had opened the window and arranged in different piles the papers that constituted the work he planned for the morning, the telephone rang.

'Hey!' the voice of the patio-layer, Bannister, rumbustiously protested. 'What's all this bloody hoo-ha then?'

'It would have been Tuesday,' she said. 'Tuesday of last week. The twenty-fourth.'

There was silence, a muffled disturbance then, a hand placed over the receiver.

'We'll ring you back,' someone she hadn't been talking to before promised. 'Five minutes.'

The consignment of trouser suits had gone to York, another voice informed her when she telephoned again. There was ninety per cent certainty about that. The Salvadore dresses had been on their way to York; the trouser suits must somehow have taken that route too.

Hours later, when the morning had passed, when there'd been further telephone calls and faxes sent and faxes received, when the missing trouser-suits had definitely been located in York, when they'd been loaded on to a van and conveyed at speed to London, the crisis was recounted in the Paddington Street Gardens. So was the fury of the patio-layer Bannister, the threats of legal action, the demands that fees already charged and paid should in the circumstances be returned.

'Could he have a case?' Not just politely, she took an interest, imagining the anger on the telephone, the curt responses to it, for naturally no sympathy could be shown.

Listening, she opened the plastic container of the salad she had picked up on her way from the Prêt à Manger in Orchard Street. He had already unwrapped his sandwiches, releasing a faint whiff of Marmite. Edges of lettuce poked out from between slices of white bread. Not much nourishment in that, she'd thought when first she'd seen his sandwiches, but had not said. There usually was egg or tomato as well, which was better; made for him that morning in Dollis Hill.

Small and sedate – no walking on the grass – the Gardens were where a graveyard once had been, which for those who knew added a frisson to the atmosphere. But bright with roses today, there was nothing sombre about the place for those who didn't. Girls sunbathed in this brief respite from being inside, men without their jackets strolled leisurely about. A lawnmower was started up by a young man with a baseball cap turned back to front. Escaping from a Walkman, jazz for an instant broke the Gardens' rule and was extinguished swiftly.

She didn't want the salad she was eating. She wanted to replace the transparent lid and carry the whole thing to one of the black rubbish bins, and then sit down again beside him and take his hand, not saying anything. She wanted them to sit there while he told her what the trouble was, while all the other office people went away and the Gardens were empty except for themselves and the young mothers with their children in the distant playground. She wanted to go on sitting there, not caring, either of them, about the afternoon that did not belong to them. But she ate slowly on, as he did too, pigeons hovering a yard away.

It was the divorce, she speculated; it was the faltering at last of his acceptance of what she'd done. It wasn't difficult to imagine him lying awake at nights, more and more as time went by, for longer and longer, feeling trapped by the divorce. He would hear the breathing of his wife, a murmur from a dream; a hand would involuntarily reach out. He would watch light breaking the dark, slivers at first at the edges of the curtains through which marauding cats had been known to pass. He would try to think of something else, to force into his consciousness a different time of his life, childhood, the first day in an office and all the strangeness there had been. But always, instead, there was what there was.

'It's over, isn't it?' she said.

He screwed up the foil that had wrapped his sandwiches and lobbed it into the bin nearest to where they sat. He nearly always didn't miss. He didn't now.

'I'm using up your life,' he said.

Her unfinished salad was on the seat between them, where his briefcase was too. When they'd been employed in the same office their surreptitious lunches among the dozy attendants in the picture gallery hadn't been necessary when it rained; there'd been the privacy of his partitioned space, a quietness in the building then, sometimes a transistor playing gently behind a closed door, usually not even that. But always they had preferred their picnic in the Gardens.

'It's what I want,' she said.

'You deserve much more.'

'Is it the divorce?' And in the same flat tone she added, 'But I wanted that too, you know. For my own sake.'

He shook his head. 'No, not the divorce,' he said.

*

'No end to the heatwave they can't see,' Nell the tea-woman remarked, pouring his tea from a huge metal teapot, milk already added, two lumps of sugar on the saucer. She was small and wiry, near the end of her time: when she went there'd be a drinks machine instead.

'Thanks, Nell,' he said.

It wasn't the divorce. He had weathered the tremors of the divorce, had admired – after the shock of hearing what so undramatically she had done – her calm resolve. He had let her brush away his nervousness, his alarm at first that this was a complication that, emotionally, might prove too much for both of them.

Sipping his milky tea, he experienced a pang of desire, sharp as a splinter, an assault on his senses and his heart that made him want to go to her now, to clatter down the uncarpeted stairs and out into the fresh summer air, to take a taxi-cab, a thing he never did, to ask for her in the much smarter office building that was hers, and say when she stepped out of the lift that of course they could not do without one another.

He shuffled through the papers that were his afternoon's work. *I note your comments regarding Section TMA (1970)*, he read, *but whilst it is Revenue policy not to invoke the provisions of Section 88 unless there is substantial delay it is held that when the delay continues beyond the following April 5 these provisions are appropriate. Under all the circumstances, I propose to issue an estimated assessment which will make good an apparent loss of tax due to the Crown.*

He scribbled out his protest and added it to the pile for typing. She was the stronger of the two, stoical, and being stoical was what he'd always loved. Deprived of what they had, she would manage better, even if the circumstances suggested that she wouldn't.

He wasn't in the Running Footman when she arrived. He usually was, and no matter what, she knew he'd come. When he did, he bought their drinks, since this evening it was his turn. He carried them to where she had kept a seat for him. Sherry it was for her, medium dry. His was the week's red wine, from Poland. Muzak was playing, jazzy and sentimental.

'I'm sorry,' he said before he said anything else.

'I'm happy, you know.' She intended to say more. She'd thought all that out during the afternoon, her sentences composed and ready. But in his company she was aware that none of that was necessary: it was he, not she, who had to do the talking. He said, again, that she deserved much more; and repeated, too, that he was using up her life.

Then, for the forty minutes that were theirs, they spoke of love: as it had been for them, as it still was, of its confinement, necessarily so, its intensity too, its pain, the mockery it had so often felt like, how they had never wasted it by sitting in silence in the dark of a cinema, or sleeping through the handful of nights they'd spent together in her flat. They had not wasted it in lovers' quarrels, or lovers' argument. They did not waste it now, in what they said.

'Why?' she murmured when their drinks were almost finished, when the Running Footman was noisier than it had been, other office workers happy that their day was done. 'Please.'

He did not answer, then dragged the words out. It was in people's eyes, he said. In Chiltern Street it was what the bagwoman he gave alms to saw, and the taxi-driver in the Japanese café, and their waitress there, and the sleepy attendants of the picture gallery, and people who glanced at them in the Gardens. In all the places of their love affair – here too – it was what people saw. She was his bit on the side.

'I can't bear it that they think that.'

'It doesn't matter what people think. Come to the flat now.'

He shook his head. She'd known he would: impulses had never been possible. It was nothing, what he was saying; of course it didn't matter. She said so again, a surge of relief gathering. More than anything, more than ever before in all the time they'd been in love, she wanted to be with him, to watch him getting his ticket for the tube, to walk with him past the murky King and Queen public house at the corner of India Street, the betting shop, the launderette. Four times he'd been to the flat: two-day cases, in Liverpool or Norwich. She'd never wanted to know what he said in Dollis Hill.

'I don't mind in the least,' she said, 'what people think. Really I don't.' She smiled, her hand on his arm across the table, her fingers pressing. 'Of course not.'

He looked away and she, too, found herself staring at the brightly lit bottles behind the bar. 'My God, I do,' he whispered. 'My God, I mind.'

'And also, you know, it isn't true.'

'You're everything to me. Everything in the world.'

'Telephone,' she said, her voice low, too, the relief she'd felt draining away already. 'Things can come up suddenly.' It had always been he who had made the suggestion about his visiting her flat, and always weeks before the night he had in mind. 'No, no,' she said. 'No, no. I'm sorry.'

She had never asked, she did not know, why it was he would not leave his marriage. His reason, she had supposed, was all the reasons there usually were. They would not walk this evening by the murky public house, or call in at the off-licence for wine. She would not see him differently in her flat, at home there and yet not quite. It was extraordinary that so much should end because of something slight. She wondered what it would feel like, waking up in the night, not knowing immediately what the dread she'd woken to was, searching her sudden consciousness and finding there the empty truth and futile desperation.

'It's no more than an expression,' she said.

He knew she understood, in spite of all her protestations; as he had when when she arranged her divorce. It had become an agitation for her, being married to someone else, but he had never minded that she was. A marriage that had died, and being haunted by how people considered the person you loved, were far from the heart of love itself; yet these had nagged. They would grow old together while never being together, lines ravaging her features, eyes dulled by expectation's teasing. They would look back from their rare meetings as the years closed over this winning time and take solace from it. Was that there, too, in the bagwoman's eyes, and idly passing through strangers' half-interested reflections?

'I haven't explained this well,' he said, and heard her say there was tomorrow. He shook his head. No, not tomorrow, he said.

For longer than just today she had been ready for that because of course you had to be. Since the beginning she had been ready for it, and since the beginning she had been resolute that she would not attempt to claw back fragments from the debris. He was wrong: he had explained it well.

She listened while again he said he loved her, and watched while he reached out for the briefcase she had so often wanted to replace and yet could not. She smiled a little, standing up to go.

Outside, drinkers had congregated on the pavement, catching the last of the sun. They walked through them, her coat over his arm, picked up from where she'd draped it on the back of her chair. He held it for her, and waited while she buttoned it and casually tied the belt.

In the plate-glass of a department-store window their reflection was arrested while they embraced. They did not see that image recording for an instant a stylishness they would not have claimed as theirs, or guessed that, in their love affair, they had possessed. Unspoken, understood, their rules of love had not been broken in the distress of ending what was not ended and never would be. Nothing of love had been destroyed today: they took that with them as they drew apart and walked away from one another, unaware that the future was less bleak than now it seemed, that in it there still would be the delicacy of their reticence, and they themselves as love had made them for a while.

The Dressmaker's Child

Cahal sprayed WD-40 on to the only bolt his spanner wouldn't shift. All the others had come out easily enough but this one was rusted in, the exhaust unit trailing from it. He had tried to hammer it out, he had tried wrenching the exhaust unit this way and that in the hope that something would give way, but nothing had. Half five, he'd told Heslin, and the bloody car wouldn't be ready.

The lights of the garage were always on because shelves had been put up in front of the windows that stretched across the length of the wall at the back. Abandoned cars, kept for their parts, and cars and motor-cycles waiting for spares, and jacks that could be wheeled about, took up what space there was on either side of the small wooden office, which was at the back also. There were racks of tools, and workbenches with vices along the back wall, and rows of new and reconditioned tyres, and drums of grease and oil. In the middle of the garage there were two pits, in one of which Cahal's father was at the moment, putting in a clutch. There was a radio on which advice was being given about looking after fish in an aquarium. 'Will you turn that stuff off?' Cahal's father shouted from under the car he was working on, and Cahal searched the wavebands until he found music of his father's time.

He was an only son in a family of girls, all of them older, all of them gone from the town – three to England, another in Dunne's in Galway, another married in Nebraska. The garage was what Cahal knew, having kept his father company there since childhood, given odd jobs to do as he grew up. His father had had help then, an old man who was related to the family, whose place Cahal eventually took.

He tried the bolt again but the WD-40 hadn't begun to work yet. He was a lean, almost scrawny youth, dark-haired, his long face usually unsmiling. His garage overalls, over a yellow T-shirt, were oil-stained, gone pale where their green dye had been washed out of them. He was nineteen years old.

'Hullo,' a voice said. A man and a woman, strangers, stood in the wide open doorway of the garage.

'Howya,' Cahal said.

'It's the possibility, sir,' the man enquired, 'you drive us to the sacred Virgin?'

'Sorry?' And Cahal's father shouted up from the pit, wanting to know who was there. 'Which Virgin's that?' Cahal asked.

The two looked at one another, not attempting to answer, and it occurred to Cahal that they were foreign people, who had not understood. A year ago a German had driven his Volkswagen into the garage, with a noise in the engine, so he'd said. 'I had hopes it'd be the big end,' Cahal's father admitted afterwards, but it was only the catch of the bonnet gone a bit loose. A couple from America had had a tyre put on their hired car a few weeks after that, but there'd been nothing since.

'Of Pouldearg,' the woman said. 'Is it how to say it?'

'The statue you're after?'

They nodded uncertainly and then with more confidence, both of them at the same time.

'Aren't you driving, yourselves, though?' Cahal asked them.

'We have no car,' the man said.

'We are travelled from Ávila.' The woman's black hair was silky, drawn back and tied with a red and blue ribbon. Her eyes were brown, her teeth very white, her skin olive. She wore the untidy clothes of a traveller: denim trousers, a woollen jacket over a striped red blouse. The man's trousers were the same, his shirt a nondescript shade of greyish blue, a white kerchief at his neck. A few years older than himself, Cahal estimated they'd be.

'Ávila?' he said.

'Spain,' the man said.

Again Cahal's father called out, and Cahal said two Spanish people had come into the garage.

'In the store,' the man explained. 'They say you drive us to the Virgin.'

'Are they broken down?' Cahal's father shouted.

He could charge them fifty euros, Pouldearg there and back, Cahal considered. He'd miss Germany versus Holland on the television, maybe the best match of the Cup, but never mind that for fifty euros.

'The only thing,' he said, 'I have an exhaust to put in.'

He pointed at the pipe and silencer hanging out of Heslin's old Vauxhall, and they understood. He gestured with his hands that they should stay where they were for a minute, and with his palms held flat made a pushing motion in the air, indicating that they should ignore the agitation that was coming from the pit. Both of them were amused. When Cahal tried the bolt again it began to turn.

He made the thumbs-up sign when exhaust and silencer clattered to the ground. 'I could take you at around seven,' he said, going close to where the Spaniards stood, keeping his voice low so that his father would not hear. He led them to the forecourt and made the arrangement while he filled the tank of a Murphy's Stout lorry.

When he'd driven a mile out on the Ennis road, Cahal's father turned at the entrance to the stud farm and drove back to the garage, satisfied that the clutch he'd put in for Father Shea was correctly adjusted. He left the car on the forecourt, ready for Father Shea to collect, and hung the keys up in the office. Heslin from the court-house was writing a cheque for the exhaust Cahal had fitted. Cahal was getting out of his overalls, and when Heslin had gone he said the people who had come wanted him to drive them to Pouldearg. They were Spanish people, Cahal said again, in case his father hadn't heard when he'd supplied that information before.

'What they want with Pouldearg?'

'Nothing only the statue.'

'There's no one goes to the statue these times.'

'It's where they're headed.'

'Did you tell them, though, how the thing was?'

'I did of course.'

'Why they'd be going out there?'

'There's people takes photographs of it.'

Thirteen years ago, the then bishop and two parish priests had put an end to the cult of the wayside statue at Pouldearg. None of those three men, and no priest or nun who had ever visited the crossroads at Pouldearg, had sensed anything special about the statue; none had witnessed the tears that were said to slip out of the downcast eyes when pardon for sins was beseeched by penitents. The statue became the subject of attention in pulpits and in religious publications, the claims made for it fulminated against as a foolishness. And then a curate of that time demonstrated that what had been noticed by two or three local people who regularly passed by the statue – a certain dampness beneath the eyes – was no more than raindrops trapped in two over-defined hollows. There the matter ended. Those who had so certainly believed in what they had never actually seen, those who had not noticed the drenched leaves of overhanging boughs high above the statue, felt as foolish as their spiritual masters had predicted they one day would. Almost overnight the weeping Virgin of Pouldearg became again the painted image it had always been. Our Lady of the Wayside, it had been called for a while.

'I never heard people were taking photographs of it.' Cahal's father shook his head as if he doubted his son, which he often did and usually with reason.

'A fellow was writing a book a while back. Going around all Ireland, tracking down the weeping statues.'

'It was no more than the rain at Pouldearg.'

'He'd have put that in the book. That man would have put the whole thing down, how you'd find the statues all over the place and some of them would be okay and some of them wouldn't.'

'And you set the Spaniards right about Pouldearg?'

'I did of course.'

'Drain the juice out of young Leahy's bike and we'll weld his leak for him.'

The suspicions of Cahal's father were justified: the truth had no more than slightly played a part in what Cahal had told the Spanish couple about Pouldearg. With fifty euros at the back of his mind, he would have considered it a failure of his intelligence had he allowed himself to reveal that the miracle once claimed for the statue at Pouldearg was without foundation. They had heard the statue called Our Lady of Tears as well as Our Lady of the Wayside and the Sacred Virgin of Pouldearg by a man in a Dublin public house with whom they had drifted into conversation. They'd had to repeat this a couple of times before Cahal grasped what they were saying, but he thought he got it right in the end. It wouldn't be hard to stretch the journey by four or five miles, and if they were misled by the names they'd heard the statue given in Dublin it was no concern of his. At five past seven, when he'd had his tea and had had a look at the television, he drove into the yard of Macey's Hotel. He waited there as he'd said he would. They appeared almost at once.

They sat close together in the back. Before he started the engine again Cahal told them what the cost would be and they said that was all right. He drove through the town, gone quiet as it invariably did at this time. Some of the shops were still open and would remain so for a few more hours – the newsagents' and tobacconists', the sweet shops and small groceries, Quinlan's supermarket, all the public houses – but there was a lull on the streets.

'Are you on holiday?' Cahal asked.

He couldn't make much of their reply. Both of them spoke, correcting one another. After a lot of repetition they seemed to be telling him that they were getting married.

'Well, that's grand,' he said.

He turned out on to the Loye road. Spanish was spoken in the back of the car. The radio wasn't working or he'd have put it on for company. The car was a black Ford Cortina with a hundred and eighty thousand miles on the clock; his father had taken it in part-exchange. They'd use it until the tax disc expired and then put it aside for spares. Cahal thought of telling them that in case they'd think he hadn't much to say for himself, but he knew it would be too difficult. The Christian Brothers had had him labelled as not having much to say for himself, and it had stuck in his memory, worrying him sometimes in case it caused people to believe he was slow. Whenever he could, Cahal tried to give the lie to that by making a comment.

'Are you here long?' he enquired, and the girl said they'd been two days in Dublin. He said he'd been in Dublin himself a few times. He said it was mountainy from now on, until they reached Pouldearg. The scenery was beautiful, the girl said.

He took the fork at the two dead trees, although going straight would have got them there too, longer still but potholes all over the place. It was a good car for the hills, the man said, and Cahal said it was a Ford, pleased that he'd understood. You'd get used to it, he considered; with a bit more practising you'd pick up the trick of understanding them.

'How'd you say it in Spanish?' he called back over his shoulder. 'A statue?'

'*Estatua*,' they both said, together. '*Estatua*,' they said.

'*Estatua*,' Cahal repeated, changing gear for the hill at Loye.

The girl clapped her hands, and he could see her smiling in the driving mirror. God, a woman like that, he thought. Give me a woman like that, he said to himself, and he imagined he was in the car alone with her, that the man wasn't there, that he hadn't come to Ireland with her, that he didn't exist.

'Do you hear about St Teresa of Ávila? Do you hear about her in Ireland?' Her lips opened and closed in the driving mirror, her teeth flashing, the tip of her tongue there for a moment. What she'd asked him was as clear as anyone would say it.

'We do, of course,' he said, confusing St Teresa of Ávila with the St Teresa who'd been famous for her humility and her attention to little things. 'Grand,' Cahal attributed to her also. 'Grand altogether.'

To his disappointment, Spanish was spoken again. He was going with Minnie Fennelly, but no doubt about it this woman had the better of her. The two faces appeared side by side in his mind's eye and there wasn't a competition. He drove past the cottages beyond the bridge, the road twisting and turning all over the place after that. It said earlier on the radio there'd be showers but there wasn't a trace of one, the October evening without a breeze, dusk beginning.

'Not more than a mile,' he said, not turning his head, but the Spanish was still going on. If they were planning to take photographs they mightn't be lucky by the time they got there. With the trees, Pouldearg was a dark place at the best of times. He wondered if the Germans had scored yet. He'd have put money on the Germans if he'd had any to spare.

Before they reached their destination Cahal drew the car on to the verge where it was wide and looked dry. He could tell from the steering that there was trouble and found it in the front offside wheel, the tyre leaking at the valve. Five or six pounds it would have lost, he estimated.

'It won't take me a minute,' he reassured his passengers, rummaging behind where they sat, among old newspapers and tools and empty paint tins, for the pump. He thought for a moment it mightn't be there and wondered what he'd do if the spare tyre was flat, which sometimes it was if a car was a trade-in. But the pump was there and he gave the partially deflated tyre a couple of extra pounds to keep it going. He'd see how things were when they reached Pouldearg crossroads.

When they did, there wasn't enough light for a photograph, but the two went up close to the Wayside Virgin, which was more lopsided than Cahal remembered it from the last time he'd driven by it, hardly longer than a year ago. The tyre had lost the extra pressure he'd pumped in and while they were occupied he began to change the wheel, having discovered that the spare tyre wasn't flat. All the time he could hear them talking in Spanish, although their voices weren't raised. When they returned to the car it was still jacked up and they had to wait for a while, standing on the road beside him, but they didn't appear to mind.

He'd still catch most of the second half, Cahal said to himself when eventually he turned the car and began the journey back. You never knew how you were placed as regards how long you'd be, how long you'd have to wait for people while they poked about.

'Was she all right for you?' he asked them, turning on the headlights so that the potholes would show up.

They answered in Spanish, as if they had forgotten that it wouldn't be any good. She'd fallen over a bit more, he said, but they didn't understand. They brought up the man they'd met in the public house in Dublin. They kept repeating something, a gabble of English words that still appeared to be about getting married. In the end, it seemed to Cahal that this man had told them people received a marriage blessing when they came to Pouldearg as penitents.

'Did you buy him drinks?' he asked, but that wasn't understood either.

They didn't meet another car, nor even a bicycle until they were further down. He'd been lucky over the tyre: they could easily have said they wouldn't pay if he'd had them stranded all night in the hills. They weren't talking any more; when he looked in the mirror they were kissing, no more than shadows in the gloom, arms around one another.

It was then, just after they'd passed the dead trees, that the child ran out. She came out of the blue cottage and ran at the car. He'd heard of it before, the child on this road who ran out at cars. It had never happened to himself, he'd never even seen a child there any time he'd passed, but often it was mentioned. He felt the thud no more than a second after the headlights picked out the white dress by the wall and then the sudden movement of the child running out.

Cahal didn't stop. In his mirror the road had gone dark again. He saw something white lying there but said to himself he had imagined it. In the back of the Cortina the embrace continued.

Sweat had broken on the palms of Cahal's hands, on his back and his forehead. She'd thrown herself at the side of the car and his own door was what she'd made contact with. Her mother was the unmarried woman of that cottage, many the time he'd heard that said in the garage. Fitzie Gill had shown him damage to his wing and said the child must have had a stone in her hand. But usually there wasn't any damage, and no one had ever mentioned damage to the child herself.

Bungalows announced the town, all of them lit up now. The Spanish began again, and he was asked if he could tell them what time the bus went to Galway. There was confusion because he thought they meant tonight, but then he understood it was the morning. He told them and when they paid him in Macey's yard the man handed him a pencil and a notebook. He didn't know what that was for, but they showed him, making gestures, and he wrote down the time of the bus. They shook hands with him before they went into the hotel.

In the very early morning, just after half past one, Cahal woke up and couldn't sleep again. He tried to recall what he'd seen of the football, the moves there'd been, the saves, the yellow card shown twice. But nothing seemed quite right, as if the television pictures and snatches of the commentary came from a dream, which he knew they hadn't. He had examined the side of the car in the garage and there'd been nothing. He had switched out the lights of the garage and locked up. He'd watched the football in Shannon's and hadn't seen the end because he lost interest when nothing much was happening. He should have stopped; he didn't know why he hadn't. He couldn't remember braking. He didn't know if he'd tried to, he didn't know if there hadn't been time.

The Ford Cortina had been seen setting out on the Loye road, and then returning. His father knew the way he'd gone, past the unmarried woman's cottage. The Spaniards would have said in the hotel they'd seen the Virgin. They'd have said in the hotel they were going on to Galway. They could be found in Galway for questioning.

In the dark Cahal tried to work it out. They would have heard the bump. They wouldn't have known what it was, but they'd have heard it while they were kissing one another. They would remember how much longer it was before they got out of the car in Macey's yard. It hadn't been a white dress, Cahal realized suddenly: it trailed on the ground, too long for a dress, more like a nightdress.

He'd seen the woman who lived there a few times when she came in to the shops, a dressmaker they said she was, small and wiry with dark inquisitive eyes and a twist in her features that made them less appealing than they might have been. When her child had been born to her the father had not been known – not even to herself, so it was said, though possibly without justification. People said she didn't speak about the birth of her child.

As Cahal lay in the darkness, he resisted the compulsion to get up in order to go back and see for himself; to walk out to the blue cottage, since to drive would be foolish; to look on the road for whatever might be there, he didn't know what. Often he and Minnie Fennelly got up in the middle of the night in order to meet in the back shed at her house. They lay on a stack of netting there, whispering and petting one another, the way they couldn't anywhere in the daytime. The best they could manage in the daytime was half an hour in the Ford Cortina out in the country somewhere. They could spend half the night in the shed.

He calculated how long it would take him to walk out to where the incident had occurred. He wanted to; he wanted to get there and see nothing on the road and to close his eyes in relief. Sometimes dawn had come by the time he parted from Minnie Fennelly, and he imagined that too, the light beginning as he walked in from the country feeling all right again. But more likely he wouldn't be.

'One day that kid'll be killed,' he heard Fitzie Gill saying, and someone else said the woman wasn't up to looking after the kid. The child was left alone in the house, people said, even for a night while the woman drank by herself in Leahy's, looking around for a man to keep her company.

That night, Cahal didn't sleep again. And all the next day he waited for someone to walk into the garage and say what had been found. But no one did, and no one did the next day either, or the day after that. The Spaniards would have gone on from Galway by now, the memories of people who had maybe noticed the Ford Cortina would be getting shaky.

And Cahal counted the drivers whom he knew for a fact had experienced similar incidents with the child and said to himself that maybe, after all, he'd been fortunate. Even so, it would be a long time before he drove past that cottage again, if ever he did.

Then something happened that changed all that. Sitting with Minnie Fennelly in the Cyber Café one evening, Minnie Fennelly said, 'Don't look, only someone's staring at you.'

'Who is it?'

'D'you know that dressmaker woman?'

They'd ordered chips and they came just then. Cahal didn't say anything, but knew that sooner or later he wasn't going to be able to prevent himself from looking around. He wanted to ask if the woman had her child with her, but in the town he had only ever seen her on her own and he knew that the child wouldn't be there. If she was it would be a chance in a thousand, he thought, the apprehension that had haunted him on the night of the incident flooding his consciousness, stifling everything else.

'God, that one gives me the creeps!' Minnie Fennelly muttered, splashing vinegar on to her chips.

Cahal looked round them. He caught a glimpse of the dressmaker, alone, before he quickly looked back. He could still feel her eyes on his back. She would have been in Leahy's; the way she was sitting suggested drunkenness. When they'd finished their chips and the coffee they'd been brought while they were waiting, he asked if she was still there.

'She is, all right. D'you know her? Does she come into the garage?'

'Ah no, she hasn't a car. She doesn't come in.'

'I'd best be getting back, Cahal.'

He didn't want to go yet, while the woman was there. But if they waited they could be here for hours. He didn't want to pass near her, but as soon as he'd paid and stood up he saw they'd have to. When they did she spoke to Minnie Fennelly, not him.

'Will I make your wedding-dress for you?' the dress-maker offered. 'Would you think of me at all when it'll be the time you'd want it?'

And Minnie Fennelly laughed and said no way they were ready for wedding-dresses yet.

'Cahal knows where he'll find me,' the dressmaker said. 'Amn't I right, Cahal?'

'I thought you didn't know her,' Minnie Fennelly said when they were outside.

Three days after that, Mr Durcan left his pre-war Riley in because the hand-brake was slipping. He'd come back for it at four, he arranged, and said before he left: 'Did you hear that about the dressmaker's child?'

He wasn't the kind to get things wrong. Fussy, with a thin black moustache, his Riley sports the pride of his bachelor life, he was as tidy in what he said as he was in how he dressed.

'Gone missing,' he said now. 'The gardaí are in on it.'

It was Cahal's father who was being told this. Cahal, with the cooling system from Gibney's bread van in pieces on a workbench, had just found where the tube had perished.

'She's backward, the child,' his father said.

'She is.'

'You hear tales.'

'She's gone off for herself anyway. They have a block on a couple of roads, asking was she seen.'

The unease that hadn't left him since the dressmaker had been in the Cyber Café began to nag again when Cahal heard that. He wondered what questions the gardaí were asking; he wondered when it was that the child had taken herself off; although he tried, he couldn't piece anything together.

'Isn't she a backward woman herself, though?' his father remarked when Mr Durcan had gone. 'Sure, did she ever lift a finger to tend that child?'

Cahal didn't say anything. He tried to think about marrying Minnie Fennelly, although still nothing was fixed, not even an agreement between themselves. Her plump honest features became vivid for a moment in his consciousness, the same plumpness in her arms and her hands. He found it attractive, he always had, since first he'd noticed her when she was still going to the nuns. He shouldn't have had thoughts about the Spanish girl, he shouldn't have let himself. He should have told them the statue was nothing, that the man they'd met had been pulling a fast one for the sake of the drinks they'd buy him.

'Your mother had that one run up curtains for the back room,' his father said. 'Would you remember that, boy?'

Cahal shook his head.

'Ah, you wouldn't have been five at the time, maybe younger yet. She was just after setting up with the dressmaking, her father still there in the cottage with her. The priests said give her work on account she was a charity. Bedad, they wouldn't say it now!'

Cahal turned the radio on and turned the volume up. Madonna was singing, and he imagined her in the get-up she'd fancied for herself a few years ago, suspenders and items of underclothes. He'd thought she was great.

'I'm taking the Toyota out,' his father said, and the bell from the fore-court rang, someone waiting there for petrol. It didn't concern him, Cahal told himself as he went to answer it. What had occurred on the evening of Germany and Holland was a different thing altogether from the news Mr Durcan had brought, no way could it be related.

'Howya,' he greeted the school-bus driver at the pumps.

The dressmaker's child was found where she'd lain for several days, at the bottom of a fissure, partly covered with shale, in the exhausted quarry half a mile from where she'd lived. Years ago the last of the stone had been carted away and a barbed-wire fence put up, with two warning notices about danger. She would have crawled in under the bottom strand of wire, the gardaí said, and a chain-link fence replaced the barbed wire within a day.

In the town the dressmaker was condemned, blamed behind her back for the tragedy that had occurred. That her own father, who had raised her on his own since her mother's early death, had himself been the father of the child was an ugly calumny, not voiced before, but seeming now to have a natural place in the paltry existence of a child who had lived and died wretchedly.

'How are you, Cahal?' Cahal heard the voice of the dressmaker behind him when, early one November morning, he made his way to the shed where he and Minnie Fennelly indulged their affection for one another. It was not yet one o'clock, the town lights long ago extinguished except for a few in Main Street. 'Would you come home with me, Cahal? Would we walk out to where I am?'

All this was spoken to his back while Cahal walked on. He knew who was there. He knew who it was, he didn't have to look.

'Leave me alone,' he said.

'Many's the night I rest myself on the river seat and many's the night I see you. You'd always be in a hurry, Cahal.'

'I'm in a hurry now.'

'One o'clock in the morning! Arrah, go on with you, Cahal!'

'I don't know you. I don't want to be talking to you.'

'She was gone for five days before I went to the guards. It wouldn't be the first time she was gone off. A minute wouldn't go by without she was out on the road.'

Cahal didn't say anything. Even though he still didn't turn round he could smell the drink on her, stale and acrid.

'I didn't go to them any quicker for fear they'd track down the way it was when the lead would be fresh for them. D'you understand me, Cahal?'

Cahal stopped. He turned round and she almost walked into him. He told her to go away.

'The road was the thing with her. First thing of a morning she'd be running at the cars without a pick of food inside her. The next thing is she'd be off up the road to the statue. She'd kneel to the statue the whole day until she was found by some old fellow who'd bring her back to me. Some old fellow'd have her by the hand and they'd walk in the door. Oh, many's the time, Cahal. Wasn't it the first place the guards looked when I said that to the sergeant? Any woman'd do her best for her own, Cahal.'

'Will you leave me alone!'

'Gone seven it was, maybe twenty past. I had the door open to go into Leahy's and I seen the black car going by and yourself inside it. You always notice a car in the evening time, only the next thing was I was late back from Leahy's and she was gone. D'you understand me, Cahal?'

'It's nothing to do with me.'

'He'd have gone back the same way he went out, I said to myself, but I didn't mention it to the guards, Cahal. Was she in the way of wandering in her night-dress? was what they asked me and I told them she'd be out the door before you'd see her. Will we go home, Cahal?'

'I'm not going anywhere with you.'

'There'd never be a word of blame on yourself, Cahal.'

'There's nothing to blame me for. I had people in the car that evening.'

'I swear before God, what's happened is done with. Come back with me now, Cahal.'

'Nothing happened, nothing's done with. There was Spanish people in the car the entire time. I drove them out to Pouldearg and back again to Macey's Hotel.'

'Minnie Fennelly's no use to you, Cahal.'

He had never seen the dressmaker close before. She was younger than he'd thought, but still looked a fair bit older than himself, maybe twelve or thirteen years. The twist in her face wasn't ugly, but it spoilt what might have been beauty of a kind, and he remembered the flawless beauty of the Spanish girl and the silkiness of her hair. The dressmaker's hair was black too, but wild and matted, limply straggling, falling to her shoulders. The eyes that had stared so intensely at him in the Cyber Café were bleary. Her full lips were drawn back in a smile, one of her teeth slightly chipped. Cahal walked away and she did not follow him.

That was the beginning; there was no end. In the town, though never again at night, she was always there: Cahal knew that was an illusion, that she wasn't always there but seemed so because her presence on each occasion meant so much. She tidied herself up; she wore dark clothes, which people said were in mourning for her child; and people said she had ceased to frequent Leahy's public house. She was seen painting the front of her cottage, the same blue shade, and tending its bedraggled front garden. She walked from the shops of the town, and never now stood, hand raised, in search of a lift.

Continuing his familiar daily routine of repairs and servicing and answering the petrol bell, Cahal found himself unable to dismiss the connection between them that the dressmaker had made him aware of when she'd walked behind him in the night, and knew that the roots it came from spread and gathered strength and were nurtured, in himself, by fear. Cahal was afraid without knowing what he was afraid of, and when he tried to work this out he was bewildered. He began to go to Mass and to confession more often than he ever had before. It was noticed by his father that he had even less to say these days to the customers at the pumps or when they left their cars in. His mother wondered about his being anaemic and put him on iron pills. Returning occasionally to the town for a couple of days at a weekend, his sister who was still in Ireland said the trouble must surely be to do with Minnie Fennelly.

During all this time – passing in other ways quite normally – the child was lifted again and again from the cleft in the rocks, still in her nightdress as Cahal had seen her, laid out and wrapped as the dead are wrapped. If he hadn't had to change the wheel he would have passed the cottage at a different time and the chances were she wouldn't have been ready to run out, wouldn't just then have felt inclined to. If he'd explained to the Spaniards about the Virgin's tears being no more than rain he wouldn't have been on the road at all.

The dressmaker did not speak to him again or seek to, but he knew that the fresh blue paint, and the mourning clothes that were not, with time, abandoned, and the flowers that came to fill the small front garden, were all for him. When a little more than a year had passed since the evening he'd driven the Spanish couple out to Pouldearg, he attended Minnie Fennelly's wedding when she married Des Downey, a vet from Athenry.

The dressmaker had not said it, but it was what there had been between them in the darkened streets: that he had gone back, walking out as he had wanted to that night when he'd lain awake, that her child had been there where she had fallen on the road, that he had carried her to the quarry. And Cahal knew it was the dressmaker, not he, who had done that.

He visited the Virgin of the Wayside, always expecting that she might be there. He knelt, and asked for nothing. He spoke only in his thoughts, offering reparation and promising to accept whatever might be visited upon him for associating himself with the mockery of the man the Spaniards had met by chance in Dublin, for mocking the lopsided image on the road, taking fifty euros for a lie. He had looked at them kissing. He had thought about Madonna with her clothes off, not minding that she called herself that.

Once when he was at Pouldearg, Cahal noticed the glisten of what had once been taken for tears on the Virgin's cheek. He touched the hollow where this moisture had accumulated and raised his dampened finger to his lips. It did not taste of salt, but that made no difference. Driving back, when he went by the dressmaker's blue cottage she was there in the front garden, weeding her flowerbeds. Even though she didn't look up, he wanted to go to her and knew that one day he would.

The Room

'Do you know why you are doing this?' he asked, and Katherine hesitated, then shook her head, although she did know.

Nine years had almost healed a soreness, each day made a little easier, until the balm of work was taken from her and in her scratchy idleness the healing ceased. She was here because of that, there was no other reason she could think of, but she didn't say it.

'And you?' she asked instead.

He was forthcoming, or sounded so; he'd been attracted by her at a time when he'd brought loneliness upon himself by quarrelling once too often with the wife who had borne his children and had cared for him.

'I'm sorry about the room,' he said.

His belongings were piled up, books and cardboard boxes, suitcases open, not yet unpacked. A word-processor had not been plugged in, its flexes trailing on the floor. Clothes on hangers cluttered the back of the door, an anatomical study of an elephant decorated one of the walls, with arrows indicating where certain organs were beneath the leathery skin. This grey picture wasn't his, he'd said when Katherine asked; it came with the room, which was all he had been able to find in a hurry. A sink was in the same corner as a wash-basin, an electric kettle and a gas-ring on a shelf, a green plastic curtain not drawn across.

'It's all a bit more special now that you're here,' he said.

When she got up to put on her clothes, Katherine could tell he didn't want her to go. Yet he, not she, was the one who had to; she could have stayed all afternoon. Buttoning a sleeve of her dress, she remarked that at least she knew now what it felt like to deceive.

'What it had felt like for Phair,' she said.

She pulled the edge of the curtain back a little so that the light fell more directly on the room's single looking-glass. She tidied her hair, still brown, no grey in it yet. Her mother's hadn't gone grey at all, and her grandmother's only when she was very old, which was something Katherine hoped she wouldn't have to be; she was forty-seven now. Her dark eyes gazed back at her from her reflection, her lipstick smudged, an emptiness in her features that had not to do with the need to renew her makeup. Her beauty was ebbing – but slowly, and there was beauty left.

'You were curious about that?' he asked. 'Deception?'

'Yes, I was curious.'

'And shall you be again?'

Still settling the disturbances in her face, Katherine didn't answer at once. Then she said: 'If you would like me to.'

Outside, the afternoon was warm, the street where the room was – above a betting shop – seemed brighter and more gracious than Katherine had noticed when she'd walked the length of it earlier. There was an afternoon tranquillity about it in spite of shops and cars. The tables were unoccupied outside the Prince and Dog, hanging baskets of petunias on either side of its regal figure and a Dalmatian with a foot raised. There was a Costa Coffee next to a Prêt à Manger and Katherine crossed to it. '*Latte,*' she ordered from the girls who were operating the Gaggia machines, and picked out a florentine from the glass case on the counter while she waited for it.

She hardly knew the man she'd slept with. He'd danced with her at a party she'd gone to alone, and then he'd danced with her again, holding her closer, asking her her name and giving his. Phair didn't accompany her to parties these days and she didn't go often herself. But she'd known what she intended, going to this one.

The few tables were all taken. She found a stool at the bar that ran along one of the walls. *Teenagers' Curfew!* a headline in someone else's evening paper protested, a note of indignation implied, and for a few moments she wondered what all that was about and then lost interest.

Phair would be quietly at his desk, in shirtsleeves, the blue-flecked shirt she'd ironed the day before yesterday, his crinkly, gingerish hair as it had been that morning when he left the house, his agreeable smile welcoming anyone who approached him. In spite of what had happened nine years ago, Phair had not been made redundant, that useful euphemism for being sacked. That he'd been kept on was a tribute to his success in the past, and of course it wasn't done to destroy a man when he was down. 'We should go away,' she'd said, and remembered saying it now, but he hadn't wanted to, because running away was something that wasn't done either. He would have called it running away, in fact he had.

This evening he would tell her about his day, and she would say about hers and would have to lie. And in turn they'd listen while she brought various dishes to the dining-table, and he would pour her wine. None for himself because he didn't drink any more, unless someone pressed him and then only in order not to seem ungracious. 'My marriage is breaking up,' the man who'd made love to her in his temporary accommodation had confided when, as strangers, they had danced together. 'And yours?'

he'd asked, and she'd hesitated and then said no, not breaking up. There'd never been talk of that. And when they danced the second time, after they'd had a drink together and then a few more, he asked her if she had children and she said she hadn't. That she was not able to had been known before the marriage and then become part of it – as her employment at the Charter-house Institute had been until six weeks ago, when the Institute had decided to close itself down.

'Idleness is upsetting,' she had said while they danced, and had asked the man who held her closer now if he had ever heard of Sharon Ritchie. People often thought they hadn't and then remembered. He shook his head and the name was still unfamiliar to him when she told him why it might not have been. 'Sharon Ritchie was murdered,' she'd said, and wouldn't have without the few drinks. 'My husband was accused.'

She blew on the surface of her coffee but it was still too hot. She tipped sugar out of its paper spill into her teaspoon and watched the sugar darkening when the coffee soaked it. She loved the taste of that, as much a pleasure as anything there'd been this afternoon. 'Oh, suffocated,' she'd said, when she'd been asked how the person called Sharon Ritchie had died. 'She was suffocated with a cushion.' Sharon Ritchie had had a squalid life, living grandly at a good address, visited by many men.

Katherine sat a while longer, staring at the crumbs of her florentine, her coffee drunk. 'We live with it,' she had said when they left the party together, he to return to the wife he didn't get on with, she to the husband whose deceiving of her had ended with a death. Fascinated by what was lived with, an hour ago in the room that was his temporary accommodation her afternoon lover had wanted to know everything.

On the Tube she kept seeing the room: the picture of the elephant, the suitcases, the trailing flexes, the clothes on the back of the door. Their voices echoed, his curiosity, her evasions and then telling a little more because, after all, she owed him something. 'He paid her with a cheque once, oh ages ago. That was how they brought him into things. And when they talked to the old woman in the flat across the landing from Sharon Ritchie's she recognised him in the photograph she was shown. Oh yes, we live with it.'

Her ticket wouldn't operate the turnstile when she tried to leave the Tube station and she remembered that she had guessed how much the fare should be and must have got it wrong. The Indian who was there to deal with such errors was inclined to be severe. Her journey had been different earlier, she tried to explain; she'd got things muddled. 'Well, these things happen,' the Indian said, and she realized his severity had not been meant. When she smiled he didn't notice. That is his way too, she thought.

She bought two chicken breasts, free-range, organic; and courgettes and Medjool dates. She hadn't made a list as she usually did, and wondered if this had to do with the kind of afternoon it had been and thought it probably had. She tried to remember which breakfast cereals needed to be replenished but couldn't. And then remembered Normandy butter, and Braeburns and tomatoes. It was just before five o'clock when she let herself into the flat. The telephone was ringing and Phair said he'd be a bit late, not by much, maybe twenty minutes. She ran a bath.

The tips of his fingers stroked the arm that was close to him. He said he thought he loved her. Katherine shook her head.

'Tell me,' he said.

'I have, though.'

He didn't press it. They lay in silence for a while. Then Katherine said: 'I love him more, now that I feel so sorry for him too. He pitied me when I knew I was to be deprived of the children we both wanted. Love makes the most of pity, or pity does of love, I don't know which. It hardly matters.'

She told him more, and realized she wanted to, which she hadn't known before. When the two policemen had come in the early morning she had not been dressed. Phair was making coffee. 'Phair Alexander Warburton,' one of them had said. She'd heard him from the bedroom, her bath water still gurgling out. She'd thought they'd come to report a death, as policemen sometimes have to: her mother's or Phair's aunt, who was his next of kin. When she went downstairs they were talking about the death of someone whose name she did not know. 'Who?' she asked, and the taller of the two policemen said Sharon Ritchie and Phair said nothing.

'Your husband has explained,' the other man said, 'that you didn't know Miss Ritchie.' A Thursday night, the eighth, two weeks ago, they said: what time – could she remember – had her husband come in?

She'd faltered, lost in all this. 'But who's this person? Why are you here?' And the taller policeman said there were a few loose ends. 'Sit down, madam,' his colleague put in and she was asked again what time her husband had come in. The usual misery on the Northern line, he'd said that night, the Thursday before last. He'd given up on it, as everyone else was doing, then hadn't been able to get a taxi because of the rain. 'You remember, madam?' the taller policeman prompted, and something made her say the usual time. She couldn't think; she couldn't because she was trying to remember if Phair had ever mentioned Sharon Ritchie. 'Your husband visited Miss Ritchie,' the same policeman said, and the other man's pager sounded and he took it to the window, turning his back to them.

'No, we're talking to him now,' he mumbled into it, keeping his voice low but she could hear.

'Your husband has explained it was the day before,' his colleague said. 'And earlier – in his lunchtime – that his last visit to Miss Ritchie was.'

Katherine wanted to stay where she was now. She wanted to sleep, to be aware of the man she did not know well beside her, to have him waiting for her when she woke up. Because of the heatwave that had begun a week ago, he had turned the air-conditioning on, an old-fashioned contraption at the window.

'I have to go,' he said.

'Of course. I won't be long.'

Below them, another horse-race had come to its exciting stage, the commentary faintly reaching them as they dressed. They went together down uncarpeted, narrow stairs, past the open door of the betting shop.

'Shall you come again?' he asked.

'Yes.'

And they arranged an afternoon, ten days away because he could not always just walk out of the office where he worked.

'Don't let me talk about it,' she said before they parted. 'Don't ask, don't let me tell you.'

'If you don't want to.'

'It's all so done with. And it's a bore for you, or will be soon.'

He began to say it wasn't, that that was what the trouble was. She knew he began to say it because she could see it in his face before he changed his mind. And of course he was right; he wasn't a fool. Curiosity couldn't be just stifled.

They didn't embrace before he hurried off, for they had done all that. When she watched him go it felt like a habit already, and she wondered as she crossed the street to the Costa café if, with repetition, her afternoons here would acquire some variation of the order and patterns of the work she missed so. 'Oh, none at all,' she'd said when she'd been asked if there were prospects yet of something else. She had not said it was unlikely that again she'd make her morning journey across London, skilful in the overcrowded Tube stations, squeezing on to trains that were crowded also. Unlikely that there'd be, somewhere, her own small office again, her position of importance, and generous colleagues who made up for a bleakness and kept at bay its ghosts. She hadn't known until Phair said, not long ago, that routine, for him, often felt like an antidote to dementia.

She should not have told so much this afternoon, Katherine said to herself, sitting where she had sat before. She had never, to anyone else, told anything at all, or talked about what had happened to people who knew. I am unsettled, she thought; and, outside, rain came suddenly, with distant thunder, ending the heat that had become excessive.

When she'd finished her coffee Katherine didn't leave the café because she didn't have an umbrella. There had been rain that night too. Rain came into it because the elderly woman in the flat across the landing had looked out when it was just beginning, the six o'clock news on the radio just beginning too. The woman had remembered that earlier she had passed the wide-open window half a flight down the communal stairway and gone immediately to close it before, yet again, the carpet was drenched. It was while she was doing so that she heard the downstairs hall door opening and footsteps beginning on the stairs. When she reached her own door the man had reached the landing. 'No, I never thought anything untoward,' she had later stated apparently. Not anything untoward about the girl who occupied the flat across the landing, about the men who came visiting her. 'I didn't pry,' she said. She had turned round when she'd opened her front door and had caught a glimpse of the man who'd come that night. She'd seen him before, the way he stood waiting for the girl to let him in, his clothes, his hair, even his footfall on the stairs: there was no doubt at all.

The café filled up, the doorway crowded with people sheltering, others queuing at the counter. Katherine heard the staccato summons of her mobile phone, a sound she hated, although originally she'd chosen it herself. A voice that might have been a child's said something she couldn't understand and repeated it when she explained that she couldn't, and then the line went dead. So many voices were like a child's these days, she thought, returning the phone to her handbag. 'A fashion, that baby telephone voice,' Phair had said. 'Odd as it might seem.'

She nibbled the edge of her florentine, then opened the spill of sugar. The light outside had darkened and now was brightening again. The people in the doorway began to move away. It had rained all night the other time.

'Nothing again?' Phair always enquired when he came in. He was concerned about what had been so arbitrarily and unexpectedly imposed upon her, had once or twice brought back hearsay of vacancies. But even at his most solicitous, and his gentlest, he had himself to think about. It was worse for Phair and always would be, that stood to reason.

Her mobile telephone rang again and his voice said that in his lunch hour he'd bought asparagus because he'd noticed it on a stall, looking good and not expensive. They'd mentioned asparagus yesterday, realizing it was the season: she would have bought some if he hadn't rung. 'On the way out of the cinema,' she said, having already said that she'd just seen

La Strada again. He'd tried for her an hour ago, he said, but her phone had been switched off. 'Well, yes, of course,' he said.

Six months was the length of an affair that took place because something else was wrong: knowing more about all this than Katherine did, the man she met in the afternoons said that. And, as if he had always been aware that he would, when a little longer than six months had passed he returned to his wife. Since then, he had retained the room while this reunion settled – or perhaps in case it didn't – but his belongings were no longer there. The room looked bigger, yet dingier, without them.

'Why do you love your husband, Katherine? After all this – what he has put you through?'

'No one can answer that.'

'You hide from one another, you and he.'

'Yes.'

'Are you afraid, Katherine?'

'Yes. Both of us are afraid. We dream of her, we see her dead. And we know in the morning if the other one has. We know and do not say.'

'You shouldn't be afraid.'

They did not ever argue in the room, not even mildly, but disagreed and left it there. Or failed to understand and left that too. Katherine did not ask if a marriage could be shored up while this room was still theirs for a purpose. Her casual lover did not press her to reveal what she still withheld.

'I can't imagine him,' he said, but Katherine did not attempt to describe her husband, only commented that his first name suited him. A family name, she said.

'You're fairly remarkable, you know. To love so deeply.'

'And yet I'm here.'

'Perhaps I mean that.'

'More often than not, people don't know why they do things.'

'I envy you your seriousness. It's that I'd love you for.'

Once, when again he had to go, she stayed behind. He was in a hurry that day; she wasn't quite ready. 'Just bang the door,' he said.

She listened to his footsteps clattering on the boards of the stairs and was reminded of the old woman saying she had recognized Phair's. Phair's lawyer would have asked in court if she was certain about that and would have wondered how she could be, since to have heard them on previous occasions she would each time have had to be on the landing, which surely was unlikely. He would have suggested that she appeared to spend more time on the communal landing than in her flat. He would have wondered that a passing stranger had left behind so clear an impression of his features, since any encounter there had been would have lasted hardly more than an instant.

Alone in the room, not wanting to leave it yet, Katherine crept back into the bed she'd left only minutes ago. She pulled the bedclothes up although it wasn't cold. The window curtains hadn't been drawn back and she was glad they hadn't. 'I didn't much care for that girl,' Phair said when the two policemen had gone. 'But I was fond of her in a different kind of way. I have to say that, Katherine. I'm sorry.' He had brought her coffee and made her sit there, where she was. Some men were like that, he said. 'We only talked. She told me things.' A girl like that took chances every time she answered her doorbell, he said; and when he cried Katherine knew it was for the girl, not for himself.

'Oh yes, I understand,' she said. 'Of course I do.' A sleazy relationship with a classy tart was what she understood, as he had understood when she told him she could not have children, when he'd said it didn't matter, although she knew it did.

'I've risked what was precious,' he whispered in his shame, and then confessed that deceiving her had been an excitement too. Risk came into it in all sorts of ways; risk was part of it, the secrecy of concealment, stealth. And risk had claimed its due.

The same policemen came back later. 'You're sure about that detail, madam?' they asked and afterwards, countless times, asked her that again, repeating the date and hearing her repeat that ten to seven was the usual time. Phair hadn't wanted to know – and didn't still – why she had answered as she had, why she continued to confirm that he'd returned ninety minutes sooner than he had. She couldn't have told him why, except to say that instinct answered for her, as bewilderment and confusion had when first she'd heard the question. She might have said she knew Phair as intimately as she knew herself, that it was impossible to imagine his taking the life of a girl no matter what his relationship with her had been. There was – she would have said if she'd been asked – the pain of that, of their being together, he and the girl, even if only for conversation. 'You quarrelled, sir?' the tall policeman enquired. You could see there'd been a quarrel, he insisted, no way you could say there hadn't been a disagreement that got out of hand. But Phair was not the quarrelling sort. He shook his head. In all his answers, he hadn't disputed much except responsibility for the death, had not denied he'd been a visitor to the flat, gave details as he remembered them. He accepted that his fingerprints were there, while they accepted nothing. 'You're sure, madam?' they asked again, and her instinct hardened, touched with apprehension, even though their implications were ridiculous. Yes, she was sure, she said. They said their spiel and then arrested him.

Katherine slept and when she woke did not know where she was. But only minutes had passed, fewer than ten. She washed at the basin in the corner, and slowly dressed. When he was taken from her, in custody until the trial's outcome, it was suggested at the Institute that they could manage without her for a while. 'No, no,' she had insisted. 'I would rather come.' And in the hiatus that followed – long and silent – she had not known that doubt began to spread in the frail memory of the elderly woman who in time would be called upon to testify to her statements on oath. She had not known that beneath the weight of importance the old woman was no longer certain that the man she'd seen on that wet evening – already shadowy – was a man she'd seen before. With coaching and encouragement, she would regain her confidence, it must have been believed by those for whom her evidence was essential: the prosecution case rested on this identification, on little else. But the long delay had taken a toll, the witness had been wearied by preparation, and did not, in court, conceal her worries. When the first morning of the trial was about to end, the judge calmed his anger to declare that in his opinion there was no case to answer. In the afternoon the jury was dismissed.

Katherine pulled back the curtains, settled her make-up, made the bed. Blame was there somewhere – in faulty recollection, in the carelessness of policemen, in a prosecution's ill-founded confidence – yet its attribution was hardly a source of satisfaction. Chance and circumstance had brought about a nightmare, and left it to a judge's invective to make a nonsense of it. He did so, but words were not enough: too much was left behind. No other man was ever charged, although of course there was another man.

She banged the door behind her, as she'd been told to. They had not said goodbye, yet as she went downstairs, hearing again the muffled gabble of the racecourse commentator, she knew it was for the last time. The room was finished with. This afternoon she had felt that, even if it had not been said.

She did not have coffee and walked by the Prince and Dog without noticing it. In her kitchen she would cook the food she'd bought and they would sit together and talk about the day. She would look across the table at the husband she loved and see a shadow there. They would speak of little things.

She wandered, going nowhere, leaving the bustling street that was gracious also, walking by terraced houses, lace-curtained windows. Her afternoon lover would mend the marriage that had failed, would piece by piece repair the damage because damage was not destruction and was not meant to be. To quarrel often was not too terrible; nor, without love, to be unfaithful. They would agree that they were up to this, and friendly time would do the rest, not asked to do too much. 'And she?' his wife one day might wonder, and he would say his other woman was a footnote to what had happened in their marriage. Perhaps that, no more.

Katherine came to the canal, where there were seats along the water. This evening she would lie, and they would speak again of little things. She would not say she was afraid, and nor would he. But fear was there, for her the nag of doubt, infecting him in ways she did not know about. She walked on past the seats, past children with a nurse. A barge with barrels went by, painted roses on its prow.

A wasteland, it seemed like where she walked, made so not by itself but by her mood. She felt an anonymity, a solitude here where she did not belong, and something came with that which she could not identify. Oh, but it's over, she told herself, as if in answer to this mild bewilderment, bewildering herself further and asking herself how she knew what she seemed to know. Thought was no good: all this was feeling. So, walking on, she did not think.

She sensed, without a reason, the dispersal of restraint. And yes, of course, for all nine years there'd been restraint. There'd been no asking to be told, no asking for promises that the truth was what she heard. There'd been no asking about the girl, how she'd dressed, her voice, her face, and if she only sat there talking, no more than that. There'd been no asking if there had really been the usual misery on the Northern line, the waiting for a taxi in the rain. For all nine years, while work for both of them allowed restraint, there had been silence in their ordinary exchanges, in conversation, in making love, in weekend walks and summer trips abroad. For all nine years love had been there, and more than just a comforter, too intense for that. Was stealth an excitement still? That was not asked and Katherine, pausing to watch another barge approaching, knew it never would be now. The flat was entered and Sharon Ritchie lay suffocated on her sofa. Had she been the victim kind? That, too, was locked away.

Katherine turned to walk back the way she'd come. It wouldn't be a shock, or even a surprise. He expected no more of her than what she'd given him, and she would choose her moment to say that she must go. He would understand; she would not have to tell him. The best that love could do was not enough, and he would know that also.

Men of Ireland

The man came jauntily, the first of the foot passengers. Involuntarily he sniffed the air. My God! he said, not saying it aloud. My God, you can smell it all right. He hadn't been in Ireland for twenty-three years.

He went more cautiously when he reached the edge of the dock, being the first, not knowing where to go. 'On there,' an official looking after things said, gesturing over his shoulder with a raised thumb.

'OK,' the man said. 'OK.'

He went in this direction. The dock was different, not as he remembered it, and he wondered where the train came in. Not that he intended to take it, but it would give him his bearings. He could have asked the passengers who had come off the boat behind him but he was shy about that. He went more slowly and they began to pass him, some of them going in the same direction. Then he saw the train coming in. Dusty, it looked; beaten-up a bit, but as much of it as he could see was free of graffiti.

He was a shabbily dressed man, almost everything he wore having been abandoned by someone else. He had acquired the garments over a period, knowing he intended to make this journey – the trousers of what had been a suit, brown pin-striped, worn shiny in the seat and at the knees, a jacket that had been navy-blue and was nondescript now, the khaki shirt he wore an item once of military attire. His shoes were good; in one of his pockets was an Old Carthusian tie, although he had not himself attended Charterhouse. His name was Donal Prunty. Once big, heavily made, he seemed much less so now, the features of a face that had been florid at that time pinched within the sag of flesh. His dark hair was roughly cut. He was fifty-two years old.

The cars were coming off the boat now, beginning to wind their way around the new concrete buildings before passing through one of them – or so it seemed from where he stood. The road they were making for was what he wanted and he walked in that direction. Going over, the livestock lorry he'd been given a lift in had brought him nearly to the boat itself. Twenty-three years, he thought again, you'd never believe it.

He'd been on the road for seven days, across the breadth of England, through Wales. The clothes had held up well; he'd kept himself shaven as best he could, the blades saved up from what they allowed you in the hostels. You could use a blade thirty or so times if you wanted to, until it got jagged. You'd have to watch whatever you'd acquired for the feet; most of all you had to keep an eye on that department. His shoes were the pair he'd taken off the drunk who'd been lying on the street behind the Cavendish Hotel. Everything else you could take was gone from him – wallet, watch, studs and cufflinks, any loose change, a fountain pen if there'd been one, car keys in case the car would be around with things left in it. The tie had been taken off but thrown back and he had acquired it after he'd unlaced the shoes.

When he reached the road to Wexford the cars were on it already. Every minute or so another one would go past and the lorries were there, in more of a hurry. But neither car nor lorry stopped for him and he walked for a mile and then the greater part of another. Fewer passed him then, more travelling in the other direction, to catch the same boat going back to Fishguard. He caught up with a van parked in a lay-by, the driver eating crisps, a can of Pepsi-Cola on the dashboard in front of him, the window beside him wound down.

'Would you have a lift?' he asked him.

'Where're you heading?'

'Mullinavat.'

'I'm taking a rest.'

'I'm not in a hurry. God knows, I'm not.'

'I'd leave you to New Ross. Wait there till I'll have finished the grub.'

'D'you know beyond Mullinavat, over the Galloping Pass? A village by the name of Gleban?'

'I never heard of that.'

'There's a big white church out the road, nothing only petrol and a half-and-half in Gleban. A priests' seminary a half-mile the other way.'

'I don't know that place at all.'

'I used be there one time. I don't know would it be bigger now.'

'It would surely. Isn't everywhere these times? Get in and we'll make it to Ross.'

Prunty considered if he'd ask the van driver for money. He could leave it until they were getting near Ross in case the van would be pulled up as soon as money was mentioned and he'd be told to get out. Or maybe it'd be better if he'd leave it until the van was drawn up at the turn to Mullinavat, where there'd be the parting of the ways. He remembered Ross, he remembered where the Mullinavat road was. What harm could it do, when he was as far as he could be taken, that he'd ask for the price of a slice of bread, the way any traveller would?

Prunty thought about that while the van driver told him his mother

was in care in Tagoat. He went to Tagoat on a Sunday, he said, and Prunty
knew what the day was then, not that it made a difference. In a city you'd
always know that one day of the week when it came round, but travelling
you wouldn't be bothered cluttering yourself with that type of thing.

'She's with a woman who's on the level with her,' the van driver said.
'Not a home, nothing like that. I wouldn't touch a home.'

Prunty agreed that he was right. She'd been where she was a twelve-
month, the van driver said, undisturbed in a room, every meal cooked
while she'd wait for it. He wagged his head in wonder at these conditions.
'The Queen of Sheba,' he said.

Prunty's own mother was dead. She'd died eighteen months before he'd
gone into exile, a day he hated remembering. Word came in at Cahill's,
nineteen seventy-nine, a wet winter day, February he thought it was.

'You've only the one mother,' he said. 'I'm over for the same.'

Prunty made the connection in the hope that such shared ground would
assist in the matter of touching the van driver for a few coins.

'In England, are you?' the van driver enquired.

'Oh, I am. A long time there.'

'I was never there yet.'

'I'm after coming off the ferry.'

'You're travelling light.'

'I have other stuff at Gleban.'

'Is your mother in a home there?'

'I wouldn't touch one, like yourself. She's eighty-three years of age,
and still abiding in the same house eight children was born in. Not a
speck of dust in it, not an egg fried you wouldn't offer up thanks for, two
kinds of soda bread made every day.'

The van driver said he got the picture. They passed the turn to Adams-
town, the evening still fine, which Prunty was glad about. He had two
children, the van driver said, who'd be able to tell him if Kilkenny won.
Going down to Tagoat on a Sunday was the way of it when old age would
be in charge, he said; you made the sacrifice. He crossed himself when
they passed a church, and Prunty said to himself he'd nearly forgotten
that.

'You'd go through Wexford itself in the old days,' he said.

'You would all right.'

'The country's doing well.'

'The Europeans give us the roads. Ah, but sure she's doing well all the
same.'

'Were you always in Ross?'

'Oh, I was.'

'I cleared off when I had to. A while back.'

'A lot went then.'

Prunty said you'd never have believed it at the time. It would be happening all around you and you wouldn't know the scale of the emigration. He was listened to without much interest. The conversation flagged and the van drew up when there'd been silence for a few miles. They were in a quiet street, deserted on a Sunday evening. Prunty was reluctant to get out.

'You couldn't see your way to a few bob?'

The van driver leaned across to release the catch of the door. He pushed the door open.

'Maybe a fifty if you'd have it handy,' Prunty suggested, and the van driver said he never carried money with him in the van and Prunty knew it wasn't true. He shook his head. He said: 'Any loose change at all.'

'I have to be getting on now. Take that left by the lamppost with the bin on it. D'you see it? Take it and keep going.'

Prunty got out. He stood back while the door was banged shut from the inside. They said it because the mention of money made them think of being robbed. Even a young fellow like that, strong as a horse. Hold on to what you'd have: they were all like that.

He watched the van driving away, the orange indicator light flicking on and off, the turn made to the right. He set off in the direction he'd been given and no car passed him until he left the town behind. None stopped for him then, the evening sun dazzling him on the open road. That was the first time he had begged in Ireland, he said to himself, and the thought stayed with him for a few miles, until he lay down at the edge of a field. The night would be fine except for the bit of dew that might come later on. It wasn't difficult to tell.

The old man was asleep, head slumped into his chest, its white hair mussed, one arm hanging loose. The doorbell hadn't roused him, and Miss Brehany's decision was that she had no option but to wake him since she had knocked twice and still he hadn't heard. 'Father Meade,' she called softly, while the man who had come waited in the hall. She should have sent him away; she should have said come some time Father Meade would know to expect him; after his lunch when the day was warm he usually dropped off. 'Miss Brehany,' he said, sitting up.

She described the man who had come to the door. She said she had asked for a name but that her enquiry had been passed by as if it hadn't been heard. When she'd asked again she hadn't understood the response. She watched the priest pushing himself to his feet, the palms of his hands pressed hard on the surface of his desk.

'He's wearing a collar and tie,' she said.

'Would that be Johnny Healy?'

'It isn't, Father. It's a younger man than Johnny Healy.'

'Bring him in, Rose, bring him in. And bring me in a glass of water, would you?'

'I would of course.'

Father Meade didn't recognize the man who was brought to him, although he had known him once. He wasn't of the parish, he said to himself, unless he'd come into it in recent years. But his housekeeper was right about the collar and tie, an addition to a man's attire that in Father Meade's long experience of such matters placed a man. The rest of his clothing, Rose Brehany might have added, wasn't up to much.

'Would you remember me, Father? Would you remember Donal Prunty?'

Miss Brehany came in with the water and heard that asked and observed Father Meade's slow nod, after a pause. She was thanked for the glass of water.

'Are you Donal Prunty?' Father Meade asked.

'I served at the Mass for you, Father.'

'You did, Donal, you did.'

'It wasn't yourself who buried my mother.'

'Father Loughlin if it wasn't myself. You went away, Donal.'

'I did, all right. I was never back till now.'

He was begging. Father Meade knew, you always could tell; it was one of the senses that developed in a priest. Not that a lot came begging in a scattered parish, not like you'd get in the towns.

'Will we take a stroll in the garden, Donal?'

'Whatever would be right for you, Father. Whatever.'

Father Meade unlatched the french windows and went ahead of his visitor. 'I'm fond of the garden,' he said, not turning his head.

'I'm on the streets, Father.'

'In Dublin, is it?'

'I went over to England, Father.'

'I think I maybe heard.'

'What work was there here, all the same?'

'Oh, I know, I know. Nineteen-what would it have been?'

'Nineteen eighty-one I went across.'

'You had no luck there?'

'I never had luck, Father.'

The old man walked slowly, the arthritis he was afflicted with in the small bones of both his feet a nuisance today. The house in which he had lived since he'd left the presbytery was modest, but the garden was large, looked after by a man the parish paid for. House and garden were parish property, kept for purposes such as this, where old priests – more than one at the same time if that happened to be how things were – would have a home. Father Meade was fortunate in having it to himself, Miss Brehany coming every day.

'Isn't it grand, that creeper?' He gestured across a strip of recently cut grass at Virginia creeper turning red on a high stone wall with broken glass in the cement at the top. Prunty had got into trouble. The recollection was vague at first, before more of it came back: stealing from farms at harvest time or the potato planting, when everyone would be in the fields. Always the same, except the time he was caught with the cancer box. As soon as his mother was buried he went off, and was in trouble again before he left the district a year or so later.

'The Michaelmas daisy is a flower that's a favourite of mine.' Father Meade gestured again. 'The way it cheers up the autumn.'

'I know what you mean all right, Father.'

They walked in silence for a few minutes. Then Father Meade asked: 'Are you back home to stop, Donal?'

'I don't know am I. Is there much doing in Gleban?'

'Ah, there is, there is. Well, look at it now, compared with when you took off. Sure, it's a metropolis nearly.' Father Meade laughed, then more seriously added: 'We've the John Deere agency, and the estate on the Mullinavat road and another beyond the church. We have the Super-Valu and the Hardware Co-op and the bank sub-office two days in the week. We have Dolan's garage and Linehan's drapery and general goods, and changes made in Steacy's. You'd go to Mullinavat for a doctor in the old days, even if you'd get one there. We have a young fellow coming out to us on a Tuesday for the last year and longer.'

A couple of steps, contending with the slope of the garden, broke the path they were on. The chair Father Meade had rested on to catch the morning sun was still there, on a lawn more spacious than the strip of grass by the wall with the Virginia creeper.

'Still and all, it's a good thing to come back to a place when you were born in it. I remember your mother.'

'I'm wondering could you spare me something, Father.'

Father Meade turned and began the walk back to the house. He nodded an indication that he had heard and noted the request, the impression given to Prunty that he was considering it. But in the room where he had earlier fallen asleep he said there was employment to be had in Gleban and its neighbourhood.

'When you'll go down past Steacy's bar go into Kingston's yard and tell Mr Kingston I sent you. If Mr Kingston hasn't something himself he'll put you right for somewhere else.'

'What's Kingston's yard?'

'It's where they bottle the water from the springs up at the Pass.'

'It wasn't work I came for, Father.'

Prunty sat down. He took out a packet of cigarettes, and then stood up again to offer it to the priest. Father Meade was standing by the french windows. He came further into the room and stood behind his desk, not wanting to sit down himself because it might be taken as an encouragement by his visitor to prolong his stay. He waved the cigarettes away.

'I wouldn't want to say it,' Prunty said.

He was experiencing difficulty with his cigarette, failing to light it although he struck two matches, and Father Meade wondered if there was something the matter with his hands the way he couldn't keep them steady. But Prunty said the matches were damp. You spent a night sleeping out and you got damp all over even though it didn't rain on you.

'What is it you don't want to say, Mr Prunty?'

Prunty laughed. His teeth were discoloured, almost black. 'Why're you calling me Mr Prunty, Father?'

The priest managed a laugh too. Put it down to age, he said: he sometimes forgot a name and then it would come back.

'Donal it is,' Prunty said.

'Of course it is. What's it you want to say, Donal?'

A match flared, and at once there was a smell of tobacco smoke in a room where no one smoked any more.

'Things happened the time I was a server, Father.'

'It was a little later on you went astray, Donal.'

'Have you a drink, Father? Would you offer me a drink?'

'We'll get Rose to bring us in a cup of tea.'

Prunty shook his head, a slight motion, hardly a movement at all.

'I don't keep strong drink,' Father Meade said. 'I don't take it myself.'

'You used give me a drink.'

'Ah no, no. What's it you want, Donal?'

'I'd estimate it was money, Father. If there's a man left anywhere would see me right it's the Father. I used say that. We'd be down under the arches and you could hear the rain falling on the river. We'd have the brazier going until they'd come and quench it. All Ireland'd be there, Toomey'd say. Men from all over, and Nellie Bonzer, too, and Colleen from Tuam. The methylated doing the rounds and your fingers would be shivering

and you opening up the butts, and you'd hear the old stories then. Many's
the time I'd tell them how you'd hold your hand up when you were above
in the pulpit. 'Don't go till I'll give it to you in Irish,' you'd say, and you'd
begin again and the women would sit there obedient, not understanding
a word but it wouldn't matter because they'd have heard it already in the
foreign tongue. Wasn't there many a priest called it the foreign tongue,
Father?'

'I'm sorry you've fallen on hard times, Donal.'

'Eulala came over with a priest's infant inside her.'

'Donal —'

'Eulala has a leg taken off of her. She has the crutches the entire time,
seventy-one years of age. It was long ago she left Ireland behind her.'

'Donal —'

'Don't mind me saying that about a priest.'

'It's a bad thing to say, Donal.'

'You used give me a drink. D'you remember that though? We'd sit
down in the vestry when they'd all be gone. You'd look out the door to see
was it all right and you'd close it and come over to me. "Isn't it your birthday?" you'd say, and it wouldn't be at all. "Will we open the old bottle?"
you'd say. The time it was holy wine, you sat down beside me and said it
wasn't holy yet. No harm, you said.'

Father Meade shook his head. He blinked, and frowned, and for a
moment Miss Brehany seemed to be saying there was a man at the front
door, her voice coming to him while he was still asleep. But he wasn't
asleep, although he wanted to be.

'Many's the time there'd be giving out about the priests,' Prunty said.
'The hidden Ireland is Toomey's word for the way it was in the old days.
All that, Father. "Close your eyes," you used say in the vestry. "Close your
eyes, boy. Make your confession to me after."'

There was a silence in the room. Then Father Meade asked why he was
being told lies, since he of all people would know they were lies. 'I think
you should go away now,' he said.

'When I told my mother she said she'd have a whip taken to me.'

'You told your mother nothing. There was nothing to tell anyone.'

'Breda Flynn's who Eulala was, only a Romanian man called her that
and she took it on. Limerick she came from. She was going with the
Romanian. Toomey's a Carlow man.'

'What you're implying is sickening and terrible and disgraceful. I'm
telling you to go now.'

Father Meade knew he said that, but hardly heard it because he was
wondering if he was being confused with another priest: a brain addled

by recourse to methylated spirits would naturally be blurred by now. But the priests of the parish, going back for longer than the span of Prunty's lifetime, had been well known to Father Meade. Not one of them could he consider, even for a moment, in the role Prunty was hinting at. Not a word of what was coming out of this demented imagination had ever been heard in the parish, no finger ever pointed in the direction of any priest. He'd have known, he'd have been told: of that Father Meade was certain, as sure of it as he was of his faith. 'I have no money for you, Prunty.'

'Long ago I'd see the young priests from the seminary. Maybe there'd be three of them walking together, out on the road to the Pass. They'd always be talking and I'd hear them and think maybe I'd enter the seminary myself. But then again you'd be cooped up. Would I come back tomorrow morning after you'd have a chance to get hold of a few shillings?'

'I have no money for you,' Father Meade said again.

'There's talk no man would want to put about. You'd forget things, Father. Long ago things would happen and you'd forget them. Sure, no one's blaming you for that. Only one night I said to myself I'll go back to Gleban.'

'Do you know you're telling lies, Prunty? Are you aware of it? Evil's never forgotten, Prunty: of all people, a priest knows that. Little things fall away from an old man's mind but what you're trying to put into it would never have left it.'

'No harm's meant, Father.'

'Tell your tale in Steacy's bar, Prunty, and maybe you'll be believed.'

Father Meade stood up and took what coins there were from his trouser pockets and made a handful of them on the desk.

'Make your confession, Prunty. Do that at least.'

Prunty stared at the money, counting it with his eyes. Then he scooped it up. 'If we had a few notes to go with it,' he said, 'we'd have the sum done right.'

He spoke slowly, as if unhurried enunciation was easier for the elderly. It was all the talk, he said, the big money there'd be. No way you could miss the talk, no way it wouldn't affect you.

He knew he'd get more. Whatever was in the house he'd go away with, and he watched while a drawer was unlocked and opened, while money was taken from a cardboard box. None was left behind.

'Thanks, Father,' he said before he went.

*

Father Meade opened the french windows in the hope that the cigarette smoke would blow away. He'd been a smoker himself, a thirty-a-day man, but that was long ago.

'I'm off now, Father,' Miss Brehany said, coming in to say it, before she went home. She had cut cold meat for him, she said. She'd put the tea things out for him, beside the kettle.

'Thanks, Rose. Thanks.'

She said goodbye and he put the chain on the hall door. In the garden he pulled the chair he'd been sitting on earlier into the last of the sun, and felt it warm on his face. He didn't blame himself for being angry, for becoming upset because he'd been repelled by what was said to him. He didn't blame Donal Prunty because you couldn't blame a hopeless case. In a long life a priest had many visits, heard voices that ages ago he'd forgotten, failed to recognize faces that had been as familiar as his own. 'See can you reach him, Father,' Donal Prunty's mother had pleaded when her son was still a child, and he had tried to. But Prunty had lied to him then too, promising without meaning it that he'd reform himself. 'Ah sure, I needed a bit of money,' he said hardly a week later when he was caught with the cancer box broken open.

Was it because he clearly still needed it, Father Meade wondered, that he'd let him go away with every penny in the house? Was it because you couldn't but pity him? Or was there a desperation in the giving, as if it had been prompted by his own failure when he'd been asked, in greater desperation, to reach a boy who didn't know right from wrong?

While he rested in the sun, Father Meade was aware of a temptation to let his reflections settle for one of these conclusions. But he knew, even without further thought, that there was as little truth in them as there was in the crude pretences of his visitor: there'd been no generous intent in the giving of the money, no honourable guilt had inspired the gesture, no charitable motive. He had paid for silence.

Guiltless, he was guilty, his brave defiance as much of a subterfuge as any of his visitor's. He might have belittled the petty offence that had occurred, so slight it was when you put it beside the betrayal of a Church and the shaming of Ireland's priesthood. He might have managed to say something decent to a Gleban man who was down and out in case it would bring consolation to the man, in case it would calm his conscience if maybe one day his conscience would nag. Instead he had been fearful, diminished by the sins that so deeply stained his cloth, distrustful of his people.

Father Meade remained in his garden until the shadows that had lengthened on his grass and his flower-beds were no longer there. The air turned cold. But he sat a little longer before he went back to the house to seek redemption, and to pray for Donal Prunty.

Prunty walked through the town Gleban had become since he had lived in it. He didn't go to the church to make his confession, as he'd been advised. He didn't go into Steacy's bar, but passed both by, finding the way he had come in the early morning. He experienced no emotion, nor did it matter how the money had become his, only that it had. A single faint thought was that the town he left behind was again the place of his disgrace. He didn't care. He hadn't liked being in the town, he hadn't liked asking where the priest lived, or going there. He hadn't liked walking in the garden or making his demand, or even knowing that he would receive what he had come for in spite of twice being told he wouldn't. He would drink a bit of the money away tonight and reach the ferry tomorrow. He wouldn't hurry after that. Whatever pace he went at, the streets where he belonged would still be there.

Cheating at Canasta

It was a Sunday evening; but Sunday, Mallory remembered, had always been as any other day at Harry's Bar. In the upstairs restaurant the waiters hurried with their loaded plates, calling out to one another above the noisy chatter. Turbot, *scaloppa alla Milanese*, grilled chops, scrambled eggs with bacon or smoked salmon, peas or *spinaci al burro*, mash done in a particularly delicious way: all were specialities here, where the waiters' most remarkable skill was their changing of the tablecloths with a sleight of hand that was admired a hundred times a night, and even occasionally applauded. Downstairs, Americans and Italians stood three or four deep at the bar and no one heard much of what anyone else said.

Bulky without being corpulent, sunburnt, blue-eyed, with the look of a weary traveller, Mallory was an Englishman in the middle years of his life and was, tonight, alone. Four of those years had passed since he had last sat down to dinner with his wife in Harry's Bar. 'You promise me you'll go back for both of us,' Julia had pleaded when she knew she would not be returning to Venice herself, and he had promised; but more time than he'd intended had slipped by before he had done so. 'What was it called?' Julia had tried to remember, and he said Harry's Bar.

The kir he'd asked for came. He ordered turbot, a Caesar salad first. He pointed at a Gavi that had not been on the wine list before. '*Perfetto*!' the waiter approved.

There was a pretence that Julia could still play cards, and in a way she could. On his visits they would sit together on the sofa in the drawing-room of her confinement and challenge one another in another game of Canasta, which so often they had played on their travels or in the garden of the house they'd lived in since their marriage, where their children had been born. 'No matter what,' Julia had said, aware then of what was coming, 'let's always play cards.' And they did; for even with her memory gone, a little more of it each day – her children taken, her house, her flower-beds, belongings, clothes – their games in the communal drawing-room were a reality her affliction still allowed. Not that there was order in their games, not that they were games at all; but still her face lit up when she found a joker or a two among her cards, was pleased that she could do what her visitor was doing, even though she couldn't quite, even though once in a while she didn't know who he was. He picked up from the floor the Kings and Jacks, the eights and tens her fumbling fingers dropped. He put them to one side, it didn't matter where. He cheated at Canasta and she won.

The promise Julia had exacted from her husband had been her last insistence. Perturbation had already begun, a fringe of the greyness that was to claim her so early in her life. Because, tonight, he was alone where so often she had been with him, Mallory recalled with piercing rawness that request and his assent to it. He had not hesitated but had agreed immediately, wishing she had asked for something else. Would it have mattered much, he wondered in the crowded restaurant, if he had not at last made this journey, the first of the many she had wanted him to make? In the depths of her darkening twilight, if there still were places they belonged in a childhood he had not known, among shadows that were hers, not his, not theirs. In all that was forgotten how could it matter if a whim, forgotten too, was put aside, as the playing cards that fell from her hand were?

A table for six was lively in a corner, glasses raised; a birthday celebration it appeared to be. A couple who hadn't booked, or had come too early, were sent away. A tall, thin woman looked about her, searching for someone who wasn't there. The last time, Mallory remembered, their table had been by the door.

He went through the contents of his wallet: the familiar cards, the list of the telephone numbers he always brought abroad, some unused tickets for the Paris Métro, scraps of paper with nothing on them, coloured slips unnecessarily retained. Its *carte bancaire* stapled to it, the bill of his hotel in Paris was folded twice and was as bulky as his tidy wad of euro currency notes. *Lisa* someone had scribbled on the back of a fifty. His wine came.

He had travelled today from Monterosso, from the coast towns of the Cinque Terre, where often in September they had walked the mountain paths. The journey in the heat had been uncomfortable. He should have broken it, she would have said – a night in Milan, or Brescia to look again at the Foppas and the convent. Of course he should have arranged that, Mallory reflected, and felt foolish that he hadn't, and then foolish for being where he was, among people who were here for pleasure, or reasons more sensible than his. It was immediately a relief when a distraction came, his melancholy interrupted by a man's voice.

'Why are you crying?' an American somewhere asked.

This almost certainly came from the table closest to his own, but all Mallory could see when he slightly turned his head was a salt-cellar on the corner of a tablecloth. There was no response to the question that had been asked, or none that he heard, and the silence that gathered went on. He leaned back in his chair, as if wishing to glance more easily at a framed black-and-white photograph on the wall – a street scene dominated by a towering flat-iron block. From what this movement allowed, he established that the girl who had been asked why she was crying wasn't crying now. Nor was there a handkerchief clenched in the slender, fragile-seeming fingers on the tablecloth. A fork in her other hand played with the peas on her plate, pushing them about. She wasn't eating.

A dressed-up child too young even to be at the beginning of a marriage, but instinctively Mallory knew that she was already the wife of the man who sat across the table from her. A white band drew hair as smooth as ebony back from her forehead. Her dress, black too, was severe in the same way, unpatterned, its only decoration the loop of a necklace that matched the single pearl of each small earring. Her beauty startled Mallory – the delicacy of her features, her deep, unsmiling eyes – and he could tell that there was more of it, lost now in the empty gravity of her discontent.

'A better fellow than I am.' Her husband was ruddy, hair tidily brushed and parted, the knot of a red silk tie neither too small nor clumsily large in its crisp white collar, his linen suit uncreased. Laughing slightly when there was no response, either, to his statement about someone else being a better fellow, he added: 'I mean, the sort who gets up early.'

Mallory wondered if they were what he'd heard called Scott Fitzgerald people, and for a moment imagined he had wondered it aloud – as if, after all, Julia had again come to Venice with him. It was their stylishness, their deportment, the young wife's beauty, her silence going on, that suggested Scott Fitzgerald, a surface held in spite of an unhappiness. 'Oh but,' Julia said, 'he's careless of her feelings.'

'*Prego, signore.*' The arrival of Mallory's Caesar salad shattered this interference with the truth, more properly claiming his attention and causing him to abandon his pretence of an interest in something that wasn't there. It was a younger waiter who brought the salad, who might even be the boy – grown up a bit – whom Julia had called the *primo piatto* boy and had tried her Italian on. While Mallory heard himself wished *buon appetito*, while the oil and vinegar were placed more conveniently on the table, he considered that yes, there was a likeness, certainly of manner. It hadn't been understood by the boy at first when Julia asked him in Italian how long he'd been a waiter, but then he'd said he had begun at Harry's Bar only a few days ago and had been nowhere before. '*Subito, signore,*' he promised now when Mallory asked for pepper, and poured more wine before he went away.

'I didn't know Geoffrey got up early.' At the table that was out of sight her voice was soft, the quietness of its tone registering more clearly than what it conveyed. Her husband said he hadn't caught this. 'I didn't know he got up early,' she repeated.

'It's not important that he does. It doesn't matter what time the man gets up. I only said it to explain that he and I aren't in any way alike.'

'I know you're not like Geoffrey.'

'Why were you crying?'

Again there was no answer, no indistinct murmur, no lilt in which words were lost.

'You're tired.'

'Not really.'

'I keep not hearing what you're saying.'

'I said I wasn't tired.'

Mallory didn't believe she hadn't been heard: her husband was closer to her than he was and he'd heard the 'Not really' himself. The scratchy irritation nurtured malevolence unpredictably in both of them, making her not say why she had cried and causing him to lie. My God, Mallory thought, what they are wasting!

'No one's blaming you for being tired. No one can help being tired.'

She didn't take that up and there was silence while, again, the surface held and Mallory finished his Caesar salad. He was the only diner on his own in the upstairs restaurant, where for a moment on his arrival he had been faintly disappointed not to be recognized. He had recognized, himself, the features of the waiter who had led him to his table; there had later been that familiarity about the younger one; nor could he help remembering, from four years ago, the easy warmth of the welcome that had suggested stirrings of recognition then. But he hadn't been a man on his own four years ago, and naturally it was difficult for restaurant waiters when they were presented with only part of what there'd been before. And perhaps he was a little more crumpled than before; and four years was a longer lapse of time than there ever was in the past.

'My sister married Geoffrey,' the girl at the table behind him was saying.

'Yes, she did. And all I'm trying to say —'

'I know what you're saying.'

'It's just I wonder if you do.'

'You're saying I thought it would be like Geoffrey and Ellen. That I was looking forward to what isn't there.'

'It's hard to understand why anyone married Geoffrey.'

Tonight it didn't matter what they said. Dreary Geoffrey, who rose early to read his emails or scrutinize his bank statements, who liked to lead an ordered life, was enough tonight to nourish their need to punish one another. That her sister's marriage wasn't much was something to throw into their exchanges, to comment on tonight because it hadn't, perhaps, been touched upon before. 'Now, we don't know one single bit of that,' Julia in her occasionally stern way might have said, and seemed to say it now. 'Talk to me instead.'

He smiled. And across the restaurant a woman in the jolly birthday party waved at him – as if she thought he'd smiled at her, or imagined she must know him and couldn't place him, or just felt sorry for him, alone like that in such convivial surroundings. He nodded, not letting his smile go, then looked away. For all her moments of sternness, how often on their travels had Julia speculated as wildly as he ever had himself about people they didn't know! Lovers embracing in the Fauchon tea-rooms, the Japanese at the Uffizi, Germans in the Lido sun, or café-table chatterers anywhere. And they'd been listened to themselves, that stood to reason – he taken for a country doctor, Julia had maintained, and she an almoner or something like it. English both of them, of course, for anyone could tell, their voices confirmed as upper class when there'd been curiosity as to that.

'*Va bene?*' the waiter who'd been the *primo piatto* boy enquired, lifting away the Caesar-salad plate. 'Was fine?'

'*Va bene. Va bene.*'

'*Grazie, signore.*'

San Giovanni in Bragora was where the Cima *Baptism* they liked was: elusive on the train that morning and ever since, the name of the church came back. Sometimes when you looked it seemed that Christ was still in the shallow water, but looking again it wasn't so: the almost naked figure stood on dry land at the water's edge. The church of the Frari had Bellini's triptych; the saints he'd painted when he was over eighty were in San Giovanni Crisostomo. How could it make a difference, not going again, alone, to admire them? Or standing or not standing before the Vivarini *Annunciation* in San Giobbe and whatever there was in Madonna dell'Orto? She'd be asleep now. As early as five o'clock they were put to bed sometimes.

'I'm not,' the girl was saying. 'If we're telling the truth, I'm not.'

'No one can expect to be happy all the time.'

'You asked me. I'm telling you because you asked me.'

Their waiter brought them raspberries, with meringue and ice-cream. Mallory watched the confections going by and heard the murmurs of the husband.

'Why have we ordered this?' the girl complained when the waiter had gone.

'You wanted it.'

'Why did you say I should have married Geoffrey?'

'I didn't say –'

'Well, whatever.'

'Darling, you're tired.'

'Why did we come here?'

'Someone told us it was good.'

'Why did we come to Venice?'

It was his turn not to reply. Marriage was an uncalculated risk, Mallory remembered saying once. The trickiest of all undertakings, he might have called it, might even have suggested that knowing this was an insurance against the worst, a necessary awareness of what unwelcome surprises there might be. 'At least that's something,' Julia had agreed, and said she hoped it was enough. 'Love's cruel angels at play,' she called it when they upset one another.

The quiet at the other table went on. '*Grazie mille, signore,*' Mallory heard when eventually it was broken, the bill paid then. He heard the chairs pulled back and then the couple who had quarrelled passed close to where he sat and on an impulse he looked up and spoke to them. He wondered as he did so if he had already had too much to drink, for it wasn't like him to importune strangers. He raised a hand in a gesture of farewell, hoping they would go on. But they hesitated, and he sensed their realization that he, who so clearly was not American, was English. There was a moment of disbelief, and then acceptance. This registered in their features, and shame crept in before the stylishness that had dissipated in the course of their quarrel returned to come to their rescue. His polite goodwill in wishing them good evening as they went by was politely acknowledged, smiles and pleasantness the harmless lies in their denial of all he'd heard. 'Its reputation's not exaggerated,' the husband commented with easy charm. 'It's good, this place.' Her chops had been delicious, she said.

Falling in with this, Mallory asked them if it was their first time in Venice. Embarrassment was still there, but they somehow managed to make it seem like their reproval of themselves for inflicting their bickering on him.

'Oh, very much so,' they said together, each seeming instinctively to know how their answer should be given.

'Not yours, I guess?' the husband added, and Mallory shook his head. He'd been coming to Venice since first he'd been able to afford it, he said. And then he told them why he was here alone.

While he did so Mallory sensed in his voice an echo of his regret that foolishness had brought him here. He did not say it. He did not say that he was here to honour a whim that would have been forgotten as soon as it was expressed. He did not deplore a tiresome, futile journey. But he'd come close to doing so and felt ashamed in turn. His manner had dismissed the scratchiness he'd eavesdropped on as the unseemly stuff of marriage. It was more difficult to dismiss his own sly aberration, and shame still nagged.

'I'm sorry about your wife.' The girl's smile was gentle. 'I'm very sorry.'

'Ah, well.' Belittling melancholy, he shook his head.

Again the playing cards fall. Again he picks them up. She wins and then is happy, not knowing why.

The party at the corner table came to an end, its chatter louder, then subdued. A handbag left behind was rescued by a waiter. Other people came.

Tomorrow what has been lost in recollection's collapse will be restored as she has known it: the pink and gold of Sant Giobbe's *Annunciation*, its dove, its Virgin's features, its little trees, its God. Tomorrow the silenced music will play in the piazza of San Marco, and tourists shuffle in the *calles*, and the boats go out to the islands. Tomorrow the cats of Venice will be fed by ladies in the dried-out parks, and there'll be coffee on the Zattere.

'No, no,' he murmured when the husband said he was sorry too. 'No, no.'

He watched the couple go, and smiled across the crowded restaurant when they reached the door. Shame isn't bad, her voice from somewhere else insists. Nor the humility that is its gift.

Bravado

The leaves had begun to fall. All along Sunderland Avenue on the pavement beneath the beech trees there was a sprinkling, not yet the mushy inconvenience they would become when more fell and rain came, which inevitably would be soon. Not many people were about; it was after midnight, almost one o'clock, the widely spaced lampposts casting pools of misty yellow illumination. A man walked his dog in Blenning Road in the same blotchy lamplight, the first of autumn's leaves gathering there also. An upstairs window opened in Verdun Crescent, hands clapped to dismiss a cat rooting in a flowerbed. A car turned into Sunderland Avenue, its headlights dimmed and then extinguished, its alarm set for the night with a flurry of flashing orange and red. The traffic of the city was a hum that only faintly reached these leisurely streets, the occasional distant shriek of a police siren or an ambulance more urgently disturbing their peace.

Less than half a mile away, the night was different. Young people prowled about outside the Star nightclub, its band – Big City – taking a break. A late shop was still open, a watchful Indian at the door noting who came and went. A few cars drew away, but more remained. Then, with a thump of such suddenness that for a moment it might have been taken as a warning of emergency or disaster, music again burst from the Star nightclub.

By half past one this neighbourhood, too, had quietened. The bouncers at the Star drove off, couples made their way to the dark seclusion of the nearby canal bank. Others stood about, groups forming and dispersing. Locking up his shop, the Indian was argued with, and abused when demands for alcohol and potato crisps were refused. The last of the parked cars were driven off.

Two youths who were friends went together, undaunted by the prospect of an hour's walk to where they lived. One was in shirtsleeves although it was chilly, the arms of a red anorak tied around his shoulders; the other wore a black woollen jersey above ragged jeans. They talked about the girls they had come across on the dance-floor, one in particular, well known to them both, the others strangers. They talked about their intentions for the future: in the Merchant Navy and in car sales, an uncle's business. These were the changes that were soon to come about, when education ended, when so much they had known for so long was to be left behind for ever: the Brothers and the lay teachers, the cramped desks scratched with entwined initials and hearts and arrows, all they had learned of self-preservation and of survival's cunning. There was, in their conversation, an absence of regret.

They paused in their walk while the anorak was unknotted and put on, zipped up and buttoned. Their evening out had been a good one, they agreed while this was being done. 'Kicking,' one said. 'Big City can do it.' They walked on, talking about that band's touch of genius.

With his mobile telephone close to his mouth, the Indian loudly demanded the police: his usual ploy at this hour, speaking to no one. His tormentors swore at him, then tired of their invective and went away. Five there were, two of them girls, neither of whom had taken part in the abuse of the Indian; which had surprised him, for girls were often the worst. He kept an eye on the five when they moved off in a bunch, causing an oncoming car to slow down to a crawl as they crossed the street. Then he locked his shop, thankful that there hadn't been an incident.

'Howya doin'?' Manning shouted at the driver of the car. He drummed on the bonnet with his fists and, joining in, his companions – but not the girls – did the same. The car kept moving, then stopped and reversed. It went another way.

'Could you beat that?' Manning laughed, watching the car from the middle of the road. He was tallest of the bunch, his reddish hair falling over his forehead in a floppy shock that he was said to be proud of. An air of insouciance distinguished his manner, was there again in the lazy saunter of his walk, in his smile. Manning led when he was with Donovan and Kilroy, which he was most of the time, and was tonight. Aisling was his girl, fair-haired and pretty, with expressive blue eyes, younger than Manning by more than a year. The second girl wasn't known to the others; earlier she had asked which way they were going and then asked if she could go with them because she lived in that direction. Francie she was called.

Aisling clung to Manning as they walked. With his arm round Francie, Kilroy tried to slow her down, in the hope of setting up an opportunity for something when they had fallen far enough behind. But Francie, aware of his intention, kept up a steady pace. She was small, often called a little thing, but deliberate and determined in her manner. She, too, was pretty, but less dramatically so than Aisling, whom Manning liked to describe as drop-dead gorgeous. She denied that she was, but Manning's regular repetition of the compliment did not displease her.

She listened to him now, saying he didn't intend to set foot in the Star again, objecting to the way the shaven-headed bouncers had frisked him

for miniatures. They had taken one from him and afterwards said they
hadn't: they thought they owned you, louts like that. 'Did you ever do a
line, cowboy?' he called across Aisling to Donovan.

'Amn't I doing one with Emir Flynn?'

'You eejit!'

Laughing again, Manning sounded drunk. Not very, Aisling thought,
but a little. She'd been drunk once or twice herself but hadn't liked it,
everything slipping about, and the way you felt in the morning.

'Did you ever, though?' Manning pressed, offering Donovan a cigarette.

Donovan said he had of course, many a time, and Aisling knew all this
was for her and for the girl who'd tagged along, whose name she had forgotten. 'Fanbloodytastic,' Donovan said, he and Manning lighting their
cigarettes, sharing the match. No one else was a smoker.

They were going by the dyeworks now, where Manning had once
climbed over the high spiked railings. That had been for Aisling too, and
a girl called Maura Bannerman. The security lights had been triggered
and through the railings they had watched Manning roaming about, from
time to time peering in at the downstairs windows of the lumpy red-brick
building that was said to have been a lunatic asylum once.

Behind her Aisling heard Kilroy telling the girl he had monopolized
about that night. At the top of the railings, razor-wire was woven through
the spikes, adding to the hazards: none of them knew how Manning had
done it, but somehow he had, even though he was a bit drunk then too.

Kilroy had slit eyes that aptly suggested an untrustworthy nature.
Donovan was considered to be dense: almost as tall as Manning, he was
bulkier, clumsy in his movements, slow of speech. Kilroy had a stunted
appearance, accentuated by oiled black hair sleekly brushed straight
back, making the top of his head seem flat. Aisling didn't much like either
of them.

The first time she'd been in the Star – the first time she'd seen Manning,
no more than a face in the crowd – she had admired him. He'd noticed
her interest, he told her afterwards; he said she was his kind, and she
didn't hesitate when he asked her to go out with him. Mano he was called
in the Dublin manner, Martin John his given names. Martin was what his
family called him and Aisling thought of him as that when she was in her
convent classroom, and every night before she went to sleep. She and he
were an item, he said, which Aisling had never been with anyone before.

'I'd give a thousand bucks for a snort,' he was saying now, his voice
slightly raised, a laugh in it again. 'Where'd we get ourselves a snort,
cowboy?'

Donovan said maybe Dirty Doyle's, Kilroy suggested Capel Street. It was a kind of play; Martin Manning doing the big fellow, her father would have said. Aisling had become used to it ages ago.

They reached the quiet streets, St Stephen's Church at the corner of Goodchild Street, the shadowy sprawl of trees on either side of Sunderland Avenue ahead of them.

'Who're those geeks?' Donovan suddenly exclaimed and they all stopped, not knowing where to look at first. But when Francie pointed they saw the red anorak.

'It's bloody Dalgety,' Manning said.

The two parted in Sunderland Avenue, Dalgety turning into Blenning Road. On his own, he went a little faster, but paused when he noticed that one of the garden gates he was passing was invitingly open. He went through it and crossed a lawn to a corner near the house where he couldn't be seen from the windows. He urinated in the shadow of an eleagnus bush.

Once or twice, making their way from the nightclub, they had been aware of voices behind them but, engrossed in conversation themselves, they hadn't looked round to see whose they were. Dalgety couldn't hear the voices now and imagined that whoever they belonged to had gone in some other direction. A light hadn't come on in the house, which sometimes happened when you found a garden that was convenient for the purpose he had used it for. He unzipped his anorak because he'd noticed that the teeth of the zip hadn't been properly aligned. While he was zipping it up again he was struck, a blow on the right side of his head. He thought that someone had come out of the house, and was thinking he hadn't heard the front door opening when the next blow came. He stumbled and fell, and a foot smashed into his jaw when he was lying on the grass. He tried to stand up but couldn't.

Aisling had watched, not wanting to but she had. Francie had looked away when she saw what was happening. In the garden, standing back at first, not taking part, Donovan moved forward when the boy was lying on the grass. Kilroy stayed with the girl, calculating that he'd lose out with her if he joined in. Nobody spoke while the assault was taking place, not in the garden, not on the road. Nobody did when they all moved on, in a bunch again.

Aisling wondered what the boy had done, what insults had been exchanged in the Star or before that, how the boy had offended. Something of the headiness of the nightclub seemed to be there again, something of the music's energy, of the wildness that was often in a face as it went by on the dance-floor before it was sucked into the suffocating closeness of the crowd.

'Oh, leave me be!' Francie suddenly cried out. 'Just leave me, would you!'

'Behave yourself, cowboy.' Manning's rebuke came lightly, and for a moment Aisling saw the white gleam of his teeth.

Kilroy muttered, and desisted for a few minutes before he tried again and was again shaken off. In Charleston Road Francie parted from them, scuttling off, not saying goodnight. Kilroy hesitated, but didn't follow her.

'Dalgety's a tit,' Manning said when Aisling asked why Dalgety had been duffed up. 'Forget it,' he said.

'I never heard that name before,' Aisling said. 'Dalgety.'

'Yeah, a nerd's.'

Conversation lapsed then, but passing the entrance to the Greenbanks Hotel Donovan began on a story about his sister, how she was going to a shrink, and hated it so much she often didn't turn up for her weekly sessions.

'Some guy comes on heavy,' Donovan said. 'You end up with a shrink.'

Nobody commented. Donovan did not go on; the interrupted silence held. So that was it, Aisling thought, and felt relieved, aware of a relaxation in her body, as if her nerves had been strung up and no longer were. This Dalgety had upset Donovan's sister, going too far when she didn't want him to, whatever form his persistence took putting her in need of psychiatric care. And the anger Aisling had witnessed in the garden touched her, what had happened seeming different, less than it had been while she watched.

'See you, Mano,' Donovan said. 'Cheers, Aisling.'

She said goodnight. Donovan turned into Cambridge Road, and soon afterwards Kilroy turned off, too.

'All right, was he?' Aisling asked then.

'Who's this?'

'Dalgety.'

'Christ, of course he was.'

They went to Spire View Lane, where they always went when it was as late as this. 'You're a dazzler tonight,' Manning whispered, slipping his hands beneath her clothes.

She closed her eyes, kissing him back, his early-morning stubble harsh on her chin. The first time she had experienced that roughness it had excited her, and every time since it had. 'I'd best be getting back,' she said, not that she wanted to get back anywhere.

A dog came sniffing at them, some kind of small breed, black or grey, you couldn't tell in the dark. Someone whistled for it and it ran off.

'I'll walk you over,' Manning said, which he always did when she had to go. He lit a cigarette, as he always did too. The smoke would get into her clothes and she'd be asked about it if there was anyone still downstairs, although usually nobody was.

'I looked back,' Manning said. 'He was up on his feet.'

Bernadette rang, a note for her in the kitchen said, *and Sister Teresa about knowing your part for Thursday.*

No one was still up or there wouldn't be the note. Aisling made cocoa and had biscuits with it, sitting at the table with the *Evening Herald*, then pushing it away. She wished it hadn't happened, but thought about Hazel Donovan so badly affected that she had to be taken to a shrink and before she finished her cocoa she wondered if she really wished it. She might have stopped him but she hadn't, and she remembered now not wanting to. 'The hard man,' his friends said when they greeted him, knowing him well, knowing he took chances. 'Aw, come on,' he had urged, the time he gave her a lift on the bar of his bicycle, when they were caught by her father coming towards them on a bicycle too, his veterinary bag hanging on the handlebars. 'Don't ever let me see the like of that again,' her father stormed at her when she returned to the house. Being his favourite made being caught all the worse, her mother explained. Neither of them approved of Martin Manning. They didn't understand.

She washed the mug she'd drunk her cocoa from at the sink and put the lid on the biscuit tin. She picked up Sister Teresa's typed sheets and went upstairs. *Scenes from Hamlet* was Sister Teresa's title for the monologues she had put together, the first time she had attempted something that wasn't a conventional play. *That's fennel for you*, Aisling murmured, half asleep already, *and columbines . . .*

At Number 6 Blenning Road the elderly woman who had lived alone there since she was widowed seven months ago was roused from a dream in which she was a child again. She went to the top of her stairs, leaned over the banister, and shouted in the direction of the hall door, asking who was there. But all that happened was the ringing of the doorbell again. It would take more than that, she told herself, to get her to open her door at this hour.

When the bell ceased there was a banging and a rapping, and a voice coming from far away because she hadn't had time to put her deaf-aids in. Even when the letterbox rattled and the voice was louder she still couldn't hear a word of what was said. She went back to her bedroom for her deaf-aids and then trudged down to the hall.

'What d'you want?' she shouted at the letterbox.

Fingers appeared, pressing the flap open.

'Excuse me, missus. Excuse me, but there's someone lying down in your garden.'

'It's half past six in the morning.'

'Could you phone up the guards, missus?'

In the hall she shook her head, not answering that. She asked whereabouts in her garden the person was.

'Just lying there on the grass. I'd call them up myself only my mobile's run out.'

She telephoned. No point in not, she thought. She was glad to be leaving this house, which for so long had been too big for two and was now ridiculously big for one. She had been glad before this, but now was more certain than ever that she had made the right decision. She thought so again while she watched from her dining-room window a Garda car arriving, and an ambulance soon after that. She opened her hall door then, and saw a body taken away. A man came to speak to her, saying it was he who had talked to her through the letterbox. A guard told her the person they had found lying near her eleagnus was dead.

On the news the address was not revealed. A front garden, it was reported, and gave the district. A milkman going by on his way to the depot had noticed. No more than that.

When Aisling came down at five past eight they were talking about it in the kitchen. She knew at once.

'You all right?' her mother asked, and she said she was. She went back to her bedroom, saying she had forgotten something.

It was all there on the front page of the *Evening Herald*'s early-afternoon edition. No charges had been laid, but it was expected that they would be later in the day. The deceased had not been known to the householder in whose garden the body had been discovered, who was reported as saying she had not been roused by anything unusual in the night. The identity of the deceased had not yet been established, but a few details were given, little more than that a boy of about sixteen had met his death following an assault. Witnesses were asked to come forward.

Aisling didn't; the girl who had tagged along did. The victim's companion on the walk from the Star nightclub gave the time they left it, and the approximate time of their parting from one another. The nightclub bouncers were helpful but could add little to what was already known. The girl who had come forward was detained for several hours at the Garda station from which enquiries were being made. She was complimented on the clarity of her evidence and pressed to recall the names of the four people she had been with. But she had never known those names, only that the red-haired boy was called Mano and had himself addressed two of his companions as 'cowboy'. Arrests were made just before midnight.

Aisling read all that the next morning in the *Irish Independent*, which was the newspaper that came to the house. Later in the day she read an almost identical account in the *Irish Times*, which she bought in a news-agent's where she wasn't known. Both reports referred to her, describing her as 'the second girl', whom the gardaí were keen to locate. There was a photograph, a coat thrown over the head and shoulders of a figure being led away, a wrist handcuffed to that of a uniformed Garda. The second arrest, at a house in Ranelagh, told no more. No names were released at first.

When they were, Aisling made a statement, confessing that she was the second girl, and in doing so she became part of what had happened. People didn't attempt to talk to her about it, and at the convent it was forbid-den that they should do so; but it was sometimes difficult, even for strangers, to constrain the curiosity that too often was evident in their features. When more time passed there was the trial, and then the verdict: acquitted of murder, the two who had been apprehended were sent to gaol for eleven years, their previous good conduct taken into account, together with the consideration, undenied by the court, that there was an accidental element in what had befallen them: neither had known of their victim's frail, imperfect heart.

Aisling's father did not repeat his castigation of her for making a friendship he had never liked: what had happened was too terrible for petty blame. And her father, beneath an intolerant surface, could draw on gentleness, daily offering comfort to the animals he tended. 'We have to live with this,' he said, as if accepting that the violence of the incident reached out for him too, that guilt was indiscriminately scattered.

For Aisling, time passing was stranger than she had ever known days and nights to be before. Nothing was unaffected. In conveying the poetry of Shakespeare on the hastily assembled convent stage she perfectly knew her lines, and the audience was kind. But there was pity in that applause, because she had unfairly suffered in the aftermath of the tragedy she had witnessed. She knew there was, and in the depths of her consciousness it felt like mockery and she did not know why.

A letter came, long afterwards, flamboyant handwriting bringing back the excitement of surreptitious notes in the past. No claim was made on her, nor were there protestations of devotion, as once, so often, there had been. He would go away. He would bother no one. He was a different person now. A priest was being helpful.

The letter was long enough for contrition, but still was short. Missing from its single page was what had been missing, also, during the court hearing: that the victim had been a nuisance to Donovan's sister. In the newspaper photograph – the same one many times – Dalgety had been dark-haired, smiling only slightly, his features regular, almost nondescript except for a mole on his chin. And seeing it so often, Aisling had each time imagined his unwanted advances pressed on Hazel Donovan, and had read the innocence in those features as a lie. It was extraordinary that this, as the reason for the assault, had not been brought forward in the court; and more extraordinary that it wasn't touched upon in a letter where, with remorse and regret, it surely belonged. 'Some guy comes on heavy,' Donovan, that night, had said.

There had been a lingering silence and he broke it to mention this trouble in his family, as if he thought that someone should say something. The conversational tone of his voice seemed to indicate he would go on, but he didn't. Hungry for mercy, she too eagerly wove into his clumsy effort at distraction an identity he had not supplied, allowing it to be the truth, until time wore the deception out.

After the convent, Aisling acquired a qualification that led to a post in the general office of educational publishers. She had come to like being alone and often in the evenings went on her own to the cinema, and at weekends walked at Howth or by the sea at Dalkey. One afternoon she visited the grave, then went back often. A stone had been put there, its freshly incised words brief: the name, the dates. People came and went among the graves but did not come to this one, although flowers were left from time to time.

In a bleak cemetery Aisling begged forgiveness of the dead for the falsity she had embraced when what there was had been too ugly to accept. Silent, she had watched an act committed to impress her, to deserve her love, as other acts had been. And watching, there was pleasure. If only for a moment, but still there had been.

She might go away herself, and often thought she would: in the calm of another time and place to flee the shadows of bravado. Instead she stayed, a different person too, belonging where the thing had happened.

An Afternoon

Jasmin knew he was going to be different, no way he couldn't be, no way he'd be wearing a baseball cap backwards over a number-one cut, or be gawky like Lukie Giggs, or make the clucking noise that Darren Finn made when he was trying to get a word out. She couldn't have guessed; all she knew was he wouldn't be like them. Could be he'd put you in mind of the Rawdeal drummer, whatever his name was, or of Al in *Doc Martin*. But the boy at the bus station wasn't like either. And he wasn't a boy, not for a minute.

He was the only person waiting who was alone apart from herself, and he didn't seem interested in the announcements about which buses were arriving or about to go. He didn't look up when people came in. He hadn't glanced once in her direction.

In the end, if nothing happened, Jasmin knew she would have to be brazen. She called it that to herself because it was what it amounted to, because you didn't get anywhere if you weren't. All your life you'd be carrying teas to the lorrymen in the diner, wiping down the tables and clearing away plastic plates, doing yourself an injury because you were soaking up the lorrymen's cigarette smoke. 'Now, you don't be brazen, Angie,' her mother used to scold her when she was no more than five or six and used to reach up for the cooking dates or a chocolate bar in Pricerite, opening whatever it was before her mother saw.

'You carry that to a woman doing the shelves. You say a mistake, you tell her that. Brazen you are,' her mother always ended up. 'You just watch it, girl.' She kept quiet herself. She never approached a woman who was arranging the shelves, just put whatever she'd taken behind the cornflakes or the kitchen rolls.

Jasmin was her own choice of name, since she'd always detested Angie and considered it common when she was older. 'Oh, la-di-da!' her mother's riposte had been to this further evidence of brazenness. 'Listen to our madam!' she would urge Holby, trying to draw the husband she had now into it, but Holby had become fly about things like that, having learned a lesson when he'd been drawn into a no-go marriage. It wasn't even the way you spelled it, her mother witheringly commented, no 'e' at the end was your bloody Muslim way. But when her mother wasn't there Holby said all that was a load of rubbish. 'You spell your name like it suits you,' he advised. 'You stick to how you want it.' Her mother was a violent woman, Jasmin considered, and knew that Holby did too.

'Excuse me,' she said, crossing to where the man was waiting. 'I'm Jasmin.'

He smiled at her. He had a peaky face, his teeth crowded at the front, light-coloured hair left long. He was wearing flannel trousers and a jacket, and that surprised her. A kind of speckled navy-blue the jacket was, with a grey tie. And shoes, not trainers, all very tidy. What surprised her more than anything was that he could have been mid-thirties, maybe a few years older. From his voice on the chat line, she'd thought more like nineteen.

'You fancy a coffee, Jasmin?' he said.

She felt excited when he spoke. The first time, on the chat line, she'd felt it when he'd called her Jasmin. Then again yesterday, when he'd said why don't they meet up?

'Yeah, sure,' she said.

All the time he kept his smile going. He was the happy sort, he'd told her on the chat line, not the first time, maybe the third or fourth. He'd asked her if she was the happy sort herself and she'd said yes, even though she knew she wasn't. Droopy was what she was, she'd heard her mother saying when Holby first came to live in the house; and later on, when her mother wasn't there, Holby asked her what the trouble was and she said nothing. 'Missing your dad?' Holby suggested. Seven she'd been then.

'You like to go in here?' the man suggested when they came to a McDonald's. 'You all right with a McDonald's, Jasmin?'

Just coffee, she said when he offered her a burger, and he said he'd bring it to her. Her father had gone when he found out her mother was going with Holby. Her mother said she didn't care, but six months later she made Holby marry her, because she'd been caught, she maintained, having not been married to Jasmin's father.

'I like a McDonald's,' the man said, coming with the coffee.

He was smiling again, and she wondered if he had smiled all the time at the counter. She didn't know his name. Three weeks ago she first heard his voice on the chat line. 'I'm Jasmin,' she'd said, expecting him to say his name also, but he hadn't.

'I could nearly tell your age,' he said now. 'From talking to you I nearly could.'

'Sixteen.'

'I thought sixteen.'

They sat at the counter that ran along the window. People on the pavement outside were in a hurry, jostling one another, no cars or buses allowed in this street.

'You're pretty,' he said. 'You're pretty, Jasmin.'

She wasn't really. She couldn't be called pretty, but he said it anyway, and he wondered if there was a similar flattery he would particularly enjoy himself. While they watched the people on the street he thought about that, imagining the baby voice in which she gabbled her words saying something like he knew his way around, or saying he had an easy way with him.

'You think I'd be younger?' he asked her.

'Yeah, maybe.' She gave a little shrug, her thin shoulders jerking rapidly up and down. The blue anorak she wore wasn't grubby but had a faded, washed-out look. Other girls would have thrown it away.

'I like your charm,' he said, and pointed because she didn't know he meant the brooch that was pinned to the flimsy pink material of her dress. Her chest was flat and he could have said he liked that too because it was the truth. But the truth didn't always do, as he had long ago learned, and he smiled instead. Her bare, pale legs were like twigs stripped of their bark and he remembered how he used to do that, long ago too. Her shoes were pinkish, high-heeled.

'It's nothing,' she said, referring to her brooch. She shrugged in the same jerky way again, a spasm it seemed almost, although he knew it wasn't. 'A fish,' she said. 'It's meant to be a fish.'

'It's beautiful, Jasmin.'

'Holby gave it to me.'

'Who's Holby then?'

'My mother got married to him.'

'Your father, is this?'

'Bloody not.'

He smiled. In one of their conversations he'd asked her if she was pretty and she'd said maybe and he'd guessed she wasn't from the way she'd said it. They went in for fantasy, they put things on. Well, everyone did, of course.

'Same age as you, Jasmin – you think that when we talked? What age you think?'

'You didn't sound a kid,' she said.

She had a stud in one side of her nose and a little coil pierced into the edge of one ear. He wondered if she had something in her belly-button and wanted to ask her but knew not to. He wanted to close his eyes and think about a gleam of something nestling there, but he smiled instead. Her hair was lank, no frizziness left in it, brightened with a colouring.

'You take trouble,' he said. 'I thought you'd be the kind. I could tell you'd take trouble with yourself.'

Again there was the shrug. She held the paper coffee mug between her hands as if for warmth. She asked him if he was in work and he said yes, the law.

'The law? With the police?' She looked around, an agitated movement, her eyes alarmed. He could take her hand, he thought, a natural thing to do, but he resisted that too.

'The courts,' he said. 'If there's a dispute, if there's trouble I have to put a case. No, not the police, nothing to do with the police.'

She nodded, unease draining away.

'You going to be a nurse, Jasmin? Caring for people? I see you caring for people, Jasmin.'

When they asked, he always said the courts. And usually he said he could see them caring for people.

The Gold Mine was a place he knew and they went there to play the fruit machines. He always won, he said, but today he didn't. He didn't mind that. He didn't raise the roof like Giggs did when his money went for nothing. He didn't say the whole thing was fixed. Good days, bad days, was all he said.

'No, you take it,' he said when she had to explain she hadn't any money, and in the end she took the two-pound coin he gave to where they broke it down for her. He picked up a necklace for her with the grab, guiding the grab skilfully, knowing when to open the metal teeth and knowing not to be in a hurry to close them, to wait until he was certain. He'd cleared out everything there was on offer once, he said – sweets, jewellery, dice, three packs of cards, two penknives, the dancing doll, a Minnie Mouse, ornaments. He swivelled the crane about when he got the necklace for her, asking her what she wanted next, but this time the teeth closed an instant too soon and the bangle he'd gone after moved only slightly and then slipped back. They spent an hour in the Gold Mine.

'Go back to the bus station for a while?' he suggested, and Jasmin said she didn't mind. But on the way there were some seats, one on each side of a small concrete space with a concrete trough of shrubs in the middle. The shrubs were mostly dead, but one of the seats was empty and he asked her if she'd like to sit there.

'Yeah, it's nice,' Jasmin said.

An elderly man, asleep, was stretched out on the seat opposite the empty one. On another, a mother and her children were eating chips. On the third two women, in silence, stared at nothing.

'I come here when it's sunny,' the man Jasmin was with said. 'Nothing better to do, I come here.'

He'd made her wear the necklace, putting it on for her, the tips of his fingers cool on her neck as he fiddled with the clasp. He'd said it suited her. It suited her eyes, he'd said, and she wondered about that, the beads being yellowish. When they'd been going towards the machine that took you to the stars he'd said he was twenty-nine and she'd wanted to say she liked his being older, and almost did.

'The sun all right for you, Jasmin?'

The two women looked at them, one and then the other, still not speaking. The mother scolded her children when they asked for more chips. She bundled the empty cartons into a wastebin and they went away.

'There's vitamins in the sun. You know that, Jasmin?'

She nodded, although she hadn't been aware of this. She tried to look at her necklace but she couldn't see it properly when she pulled it taut and squinted down at the beads. If she'd been alone she would have taken it off, but she didn't like to do that now.

'Jasmin's a great name,' he said. On the chat line he had said that, complimenting her, although he didn't know she had given herself the name. She'd often thought he was affectionate when they had their conversations on the chat line, even though she'd been puzzled a few times when he described the telephone box he was in or read out what was written on a wall. The first time he'd read something out without saying he was doing it she'd wondered if he was all there in the head, but then he explained and it was all right. She imagined him in the courts, like you'd see on TV. She imagined him standing up with papers in one hand, putting a case. She imagined him looking to where she was watching, and his smile coming on, and wanting to wave at him but knowing she mustn't because he'd have told her that. The first time on the chat line he'd commented on her voice. 'You take it easy now,' he'd said, and she hung on because she didn't want him to go. 'Love that voice,' he said, and she realized he meant hers.

He was smiling at her now and they watched the sleeping man waking up. He had made a pillow of a plastic carrier-bag stuffed full of what might have been clothes. He had undone his shoelaces and he did them up again. He looked about him and then he went away.

'I thought you might say no, Jasmin, when I put it to you we'd meet up. Know what I mean, Jasmin? That you wouldn't want to take it further.'

She shook her head, denying that. She wanted her mother to go by, coming back from the betting shop, where the man Holby didn't know about worked. Holby was pathetic, her mother said, another mistake she'd made, same's the one with Jasmin's father. She had got into a relationship with the betting-shop man and the next thing would be he'd be a mistake too, no way he wouldn't.

'I'd never,' Jasmin heard herself protesting. 'I'd never have said no.'

She shook her head to make certain he was reassured. He'd lowered his voice when he'd said he had worried in case she'd say no. She didn't want anything spoiled; she wanted everything to go on being as good as on the chat line, as good as it was now.

'You at a loose end, Jasmin? You got the time today, come round to my place?'

Again there was the ripple of excitement. She could feel it all over her body, a fluttering of pins and needles it almost felt like but she knew it wasn't that. She loved being with him; she'd known she would. 'Yeah,' she said, not hesitating, not wanting him to think she had. 'Yeah, I got the time today.'

'Best to walk,' he said. 'All right with a walk, Jasmin?'

'Course I am.' And because it seemed to belong now, Jasmin added that she didn't know his name.

'Clive,' he said.

He liked that name and often gave it. Usually they asked, sometimes even on the chat line, before they got going. Rodney he liked too. Ken he liked. And Alistair.

'I never knew a Clive,' she said.

'You're living at home, Jasmin?'

'Oh, yes.'

'You said. A bit ago you said that. I only wondered if you'd moved out by now.'

'I wish I'd be able to.'

'Arm's length, are they?'

She didn't understand and he said her mother and whoever. On the chat line he remembered she'd said she was an only child. Her mother she'd mentioned then, the man she'd referred to in the bus station. He asked about him, wondering if he was West Indian, and she said yes. Light-coloured, she said. 'He passes.'

They had turned out of the busy streets, into Blenheim Row, leading to Sowell Street, where the lavatories were, the school at the end.

'A West Indian kid got killed here,' he said. 'White kids took their knives out. You ever see a thing like that, Jasmin?'

'No.' Vehemently, she shook her head, and he laughed and then she did.

'You ever think of moving out, Jasmin? Anything like that come into your thoughts? Get a place of your own?'

All the time, she said. The only thing was, she wasn't earning.

'First thing you said to me nearly, that you'd got nothing coming in.'

'You're easy to talk with, Clive.'

He took her hand; she didn't object. Her fingernails were silvery he'd noticed in the McDonald's, a couple of them jagged where they'd broken. No way she wasn't a child, no way she'd reached sixteen, more like twelve. Her hand was warm, lying there in his, dampish, fingers interlaced with his.

'There used to be a song,' he said. '"Putting on the agony" was how it went. "Putting on the style". Before your time, Jas. It could have been called something else, only those were the words. "That's what all the young folk are doin' all the while". Lovely song.'

'Maybe I heard it one time, I don't know.'

'What age really, Jas?'

'Seventeen.'

'No, really though?'

She said fifteen. Sixteen in October, she said.

When they were passing the Queen and Angel he asked her if she ever took a drink. It wouldn't do for him to bring her on to licensed premises, he explained, and she said she wasn't fussy for a drink, remembering the taste of beer, which she hadn't liked. He said to wait and he went to an off-licence across the street and came back with a plastic bag. He winked at her and she laughed. 'Mustn't be bad boys,' he said. 'No more than a few sips.'

They came to a bridge over the river. They didn't cross it, but went down steps to a towpath. He said it was a shortcut.

There wasn't anyone around, and they leaned against a brick wall that was part of the bridge. He unscrewed the cap of the bottle he'd bought and showed her how the plastic disc he took from one of his jacket pockets opened out to become a tumbler. Tonic wine, he said, but he had vodka too, miniatures he called the little bottles he had. What the Russians drank, he said, although she knew. He said he'd been in Moscow once.

They drank from the tumbler when he'd tasted the mixture he'd made and said it wasn't too strong. He'd never been responsible for making any girl drunk, he said. He had found the collapsible tumbler on the same seat where they'd been sitting in the sun. One day he'd seen it there and thought it was a powder compact. He carried it about with him in case he met a friend who'd like a drink.

'All right, Jas?'

'Yeah, great.'

'You like it, Jas?'

They passed the tumbler back and forth between them. She drank from where his lips had been; she wanted to do that. He saw her doing it and he smiled at her.

Nice in the sun, he said when they walked on, and he took her hand again. She thought he'd kiss her, but he didn't. She wanted him to. She wanted to sit on a patch of grass and watch the rowers going by, his arm round her shoulders, his free hand holding hers. There was some left in the bottles when he dropped them and the plastic bag into a wastebin.

'Sit down, will we?' she said, and they did, her head pressed into his chest. 'I love you, Clive,' she whispered, not able to stop herself.

'We belong,' he whispered back. 'No way we don't, Jas.'

She didn't break the silence when they walked on, knowing that it was special, and better than all the words there might have been. No words were necessary, no words could add a thing to what there was.

'I can see us in Moscow, Jas. I can see us walking the streets.'

She felt different, as if her plainness wasn't there. Her face felt different, her body too. In the diner she'd be a different person clearing up the plates, not minding the lorrymen's cigarette smoke, not minding what they said to her. Nothing she knew would be the same, her mother wouldn't be, and letting Lukie Giggs touch her where he wanted to wouldn't be. She wondered if she was drunk.

'You're never drunk, Jas.' He squeezed her hand, he said she was fantastic. Both of them were only tipsy, he said. Happy, he said. Soon's he heard her voice he knew she was fantastic. Soon's he saw her at the bus station. In the room they were going to there were the things he collected – little plastic tortoises, and racing cars, and books about places he wanted to go to, and pictures of castles on the walls. She imagined that when he told her, and saw a vase of summer flowers, curtains drawn against the sunlight. He played a disc for her, the Spice Girls because they were in the past and he liked all that.

They turned off the towpath into a lane with a row of garage doors running along it, and walled back gardens on the other side. They came out on to a suburban road, and crossed it to a crescent. He dropped her hand before they reached it and pulled down the back of his jacket where it had ridden up a bit. He buttoned all three buttons.

'Would you wait five minutes, Jas?'

It was as if she knew about that, as if she knew why she had to wait and why it should be five minutes, as if he'd told her something she'd forgotten. She knew he hadn't. It didn't matter.

'You be all right, Jas?'

'Course I will.'

She watched him walking off and when he reached a front gate painted blue. She watched him as she had when he crossed the street to the off-licence. She waited, as she had waited then too, seeing again the little tortoises and the racing cars, hearing the Spice Girls. Across the road a delivery van drew up. No one got out, and a minute or so later it drove off. A dog went by. A woman started a lawnmower in one of the front gardens.

She waited for longer than he'd said, for ages it felt like, but when he came back he was hurrying, as if he was making up for that. He almost ran, his flannel trousers flapping. He was out of breath when he reached her. He shook his head and said they'd best go back.

'Back?'

'Best to go back, Jas.'

He took her arm, but he was edgy and didn't take it as he had before. He didn't search for her hand. He pulled her anorak when it was difficult for her to keep up with him. Behind them somewhere a car door banged.

'Oh God,' he said.

A red car slowed down beside them as they were turning into the lane with the garage doors. When it stopped a woman with glasses on a string around her neck got out. She was wearing a brown skirt, and a cardigan that matched it over a pale silk blouse. Her dark hair was coiled round her head, her lipstick glistened, as if she hadn't had time to powder it over or had forgotten to. The glasses bobbed about on her blouse and then were still. Her voice was angry when she spoke but she kept it low, giving the impression that her teeth were clenched.

'I don't believe this,' she said.

She spoke as if Jasmin wasn't there. She didn't look at her, not even glancing in her direction.

'For God's sake!' she almost shouted, and slammed the door of the car shut, as if she had to do something, as if only noise could express what she felt. 'For God's sake, after all we've been through!'

Her face was quivering with rage, one hand made into a fist that struck the roof of the car once and then opened, to fall by her side. There was silence then.

'Who is she?' The woman spoke when the silence had gone on, at last recognizing Jasmin's presence. Her question came wearily, in a bleak, dull tone. 'You're on probation,' she said. 'Did you forget somehow that you were on probation?'

The man whom she abused had not attempted to speak, had made no protestation, but words were muttered now.

'She was looking for the towpath. She asked me where it was. I don't know who she is.'

The long, peaky features might never that afternoon, or any afternoon, have been other than they had become in the brief time that had passed: devoid of all expression, dead, a dribble of tears beginning.

Then Jasmin's companion of so many conversations, and whom she had begun to love, shambled off, and the woman said nothing until he reached the blue-painted ornamental gate and again disappeared around the side of the house.

'Was there anything?' she asked then. She stared at Jasmin. Slowly she looked her up and down. Jasmin didn't know what her question meant.

'Did he do anything to you?' the woman asked, and Jasmin understood and yet did not. What mattered more was that he had cried, his happiness taken from him, his smile too. He had cried for her. He had cried for both of them. All that she understood too well.

'Who are you?' the woman asked. Her clenched-back voice, deprived of the energy of its anger, was frightened, and fear clung to the tiredness in her face.

'Clive's my friend,' Jasmin said. 'There wasn't nothing wrong. We done nothing wrong.'

'That's not his name.'

'Clive, he said.'

'He says anything. Did he give you drink?'

Jasmin shook her head. Why should she say? Why should she get him into trouble?

'You reek of drink,' the woman said. 'Every time he gives them drink.'

'He done nothing.'

'His mother was my sister. He lives with us.'

If she'd asked him, Jasmin said, he would have explained about his name. But the woman just stared at her when she began to tell her that she, also, had given herself a name, that sometimes people wanted to.

'My sister died,' the woman said. 'He's been living with us since that. He thought the house would be empty this afternoon but it wasn't because I changed my mind about going out. You worry and you change your mind. Quite often you do. Well, naturally, I suppose. He's been on charges.'

'He was only going to show me, like, where it is he lived.'

'What's your name?'

'Jasmin.'

'If this is known they'll take him in again.'

Jasmin shook her head. There was a mistake, she said. The woman said there wasn't.

'We look after him, we lie for him, my husband and I. We've done our best since my sister died. A family thing, you do your best.'

'There wasn't anything.'

'My sister knew his chance would come. She knew there'd be a day that would be too terrible for her to bear. He was her child, after all, it was too much. She left a note.'

'Honestly, I promise you.'

'I know, I know.'

The woman got into her car and wound the window down as if she intended to say something else but she said nothing. She turned in the quiet road and drove back to her house.

Frying chops, Holby prodded them occasionally with a fork. He liked to blacken them, to see the smoke rising while still not turning down the gas. It got into her hair, Jasmin's mother maintained. Smoke like that was greasy, she insisted, but Holby said it couldn't be. He heard the door when Jasmin came into the kitchen and he called out to her, knowing it wasn't her mother who'd come in.

'How you doing, girl?'

All right, Jasmin said, and then her mother was there, back from her time with her betting-shop friend. Even through the smoke, her entrance brought a gush of the perfume she so lavishly applied when she met her men.

'What're you frying, Holby?' She shouted above the sizzling of the meat, and Jasmin knew there was going to be a quarrel.

In her room, even with the door closed she heard it beginning, her mother's noisy criticisms, Holby's measured drone of retaliation. She didn't listen. Probably he had guessed at last about the betting-shop man, as her father had once guessed about him. Probably it had come to that – the frying of the chops, the smoke, the grease no more than a provocation, a way of standing up for himself. And Holby – today or some other day – would walk out, saying no man could stand it, which Jasmin remembered her father saying too.

She pulled the curtains over and lay down on her bed. She liked the twilight she had induced; even on better days than this she did. Tired after the walk to the house with the man she had begun to love, and after that the walk alone to where she lived herself, she closed her eyes. 'You like to go in here?' he asked again. He carried her coffee to where she waited. She felt the touch of his fingers when he put the necklace on for her. 'The sun all right for you?' he said.

In the room she still had to imagine there were books on shelves, the vase of flowers, the pictures of castles. In a courtroom he put a case, his papers in one hand, gesturing with the other. They belonged, he said on the towpath, the rowers going by.

Downstairs something was thrown, and there was Holby's mumble, the clank of broken china when it was swept up, her mother's voice going on, her crossness exhausted as the woman's had been. He had been shamed by the woman getting things wrong and was the kind to mind. He didn't realize the woman didn't matter, that her talk and her fury didn't. He wasn't the kind to know that. He wasn't the knowing sort.

Her mother's voice was different now, caressing, lying. She sent Holby out for beer, which at this stage in the proceedings she always did; Jasmin heard him go. Her mother called up the stairs, calling her Angie, saying to come down. She didn't answer. She didn't say that Angie wasn't her name. She didn't say anything.

When she went there, he would not be on the seat in the sun. He would not be waiting in the bus station. Nor playing the machines. Nor in the McDonald's. But when Jasmin closed her eyes again his smile was there and it didn't go away. She touched with her lips the necklace that had been his gift. She promised she would always keep it by her.

At Olivehill

'Well, at least don't tell him,' their mother begged. 'At least do nothing until he's gone.'

But they were doubtful and said nothing. They did not promise, which she had hoped they would. Then, sensing her disappointment, they pacified her.

'We'd never want to distress him,' Tom said, and Eoghan shook his head.

She wasn't reassured, but didn't say. She knew what they were thinking: that being old you might be aware of death loitering near, but even so death wasn't always quick about its business. And she hated what had been said to her, out of the blue on such a lovely day.

She was younger by a year than their father, and who could say which would be taken first? Both of them suffered a raft of trivial ills, each had a single ailment that was more serious. In their later seventies, they lived from day to day.

'We'll say nothing so,' she said, still hoping they would promise what she wished for. 'Promise me,' she used to say when they were boys, and obediently they always had. But everything was different now. She knew they were doing all they could to keep things going. She knew it was a struggle at Olivehill.

'Don't be worrying yourself,' Eoghan said, his soft blue eyes guilty for a moment. He was given to guilt, she thought. More than Tom was, more than Angela.

'It's just we have to look ahead,' Tom said. 'We have to see where we're going.'

They were having tea outside for the first time that summer although the summer was well advanced. The grass of the big lawn had been cut that morning by Kealy, the garden chairs brushed down. What remained of tea, the tablecloth still spread, was on the white slatted table, beneath which two English setters dozed.

'It'll be cold. I'll make some fresh,' she said when her husband came.

'No. No such thing.' Still yards away and advancing slowly, James contradicted that. 'You'll rest yourself, lady.'

Having heard some of this, she nodded obligingly. Both of them disregarded a similar degree of deafness and in other ways, too, were a little alike: tall but less tall than they had been, stooped and spare. Their clothes were not new but retained a stylishness: her shades of dark maroon, her bright silk scarf, his greenish tweeds, his careful tie. Their creeper-covered house, their garden here and there neglected, reflected their coming down in the world, but they did not themselves.

'Thanks, Mollie,' the old man said when his wife uncovered his toast, folding away the napkin so that it could be used for the same teatime purpose again. His toast was cut into tidy rectangles, three to a slice, and buttered. No one else had toast at this time of day.

'You're turning the hay?' He addressed both sons at once, which was a habit with him. 'End of the week you'll bring it in, you think?'

Before Thursday, they said, when there might be a change in the weather. They were more casually turned out, in open-necked white shirts and flannel trousers, working farmers both of them. Tom and his family lived in a house on their land that once had been an employee's. When he could, which wasn't every day, he came to Olivehill at this time to be with the old couple for an hour or so. Once in a while his wife, Loretta, came too and brought the children. Eoghan wasn't married and still lived at Olivehill.

Spreading lemon curd on his toast, James wondered why both his sons were here at teatime; usually Eoghan wasn't when Tom came. He didn't ask, it would come out: what change they proposed, what it was that required the arguments of both to convince him. But in a moment Eoghan went away.

'You're looking spry,' Tom complimented his father.

'Oh, I'm feeling spry.'

'Fine weather's a tonic,' Mollie said.

And James asked after Loretta, which he always did, and asked about his granddaughters.

'They have the poor girl demented with their devilment.' Tom laughed, although it wasn't necessary, it being known that his demure daughters, twins of four, hadn't yet reached their mischievous years.

They were an Irish Catholic family, which once had occupied a modest place in an ascendancy that was not Catholic and now hardly existed any more. When Mollie first lived in this house the faith to which she and James belonged connected them with the nation that had newly come about. But faith's variations mattered less in Ireland all these years later, since faith itself mattered less and influenced less how people lived.

'Angela wrote,' Mollie said, finding the letter she'd brought to the garden to show Tom.

He read it and commented that Angela didn't change.

'Her men friends do rather,' James said.

Angela was the youngest of the children, a buyer for a chain of fashion shops. She lived in Dublin. The one that got away, Tom often said.

He and Eoghan hadn't wanted to. They still didn't, feeling they belonged here, content to let Angela bring a bit of life into things with her Dublin gossip and her flightiness.

Tom folded the letter into its envelope and handed it back. James slowly finished his tea. Mollie walked round the garden with her older son.

'You're good to indulge me, Tom,' she said, even though she had hoped to hear that what had been kept from their father would not come about at all. It made no sense to her that the greater part of Olivehill should be made into a golf-course in the hope that this would yield a more substantial profit than the land did. It was foolish, Mollie thought after Tom had gone, when she and James were alone again with the setters; yet her sons weren't fools. It was graceless, even a vulgarity, she thought as they sat there in the evening sun, for no other word was quite as suitable; yet they were not vulgar.

'Are we at one?' she heard James ask, and she apologized for being abstracted.

He loved to use that old expression. He loved to be reassured, was reassured now. How profoundly he would hate what she had protected him from, how chilling and loathsome it would seem to him, how disappointing.

'You're looking lovely,' he said, and she heard but pretended not to so that he'd say it again.

Eoghan drove carelessly to the hayfield. There never was other traffic on these byroads, never a lost cyclist or someone who had walked out from Mountmoy. A wandering sheep was always one of their own. But there wasn't a sheep today, only now and again a rabbit scuttling to safety.

You could sleep driving here, Eoghan used to say and once, in the heat of an afternoon, had dropped off at the turn to Ana Woods. He'd woken up before the old Austin he had then hit a tree. Not that it would have mattered much if he hadn't, he always added when he told the story: all the cars he had ever owned were past their best, purchased from Chappie Keogh, who had the wrecking yard at Maire. Easygoing, good-hearted, seeming to be slow but actually rather clever, Eoghan had grown from being a sensitive child into a big, red-haired man, different in appearance from the others of his family, all of whom were noticeably thin. He was

content to take second place to Tom. They had all their lives been friends,
their friendship knitted closer in each succeeding span of years.

He drove in to where earlier he'd been turning the hay. He finished it
within an hour, not hurrying because he never did. Then he went on, to
Brea Maguire's at the cross, where he drank and talked to the men who
came there every evening. It would be a bad mistake, disastrous even, to
go on doing nothing about Olivehill. They had wanted her to understand
that, and hoped she did.

Nine days later James woke up one morning feeling different, and had
difficulty on the stairs. His left leg was dragging a bit, a most uncomfortable business, and at breakfast he discovered that his left arm was shaky
too. Reaching out was limited; and he couldn't lift things as easily as he
used to. 'A little stroke,' Dr Gorevan said when he came.

'Should he be in his bed?' Mollie asked, and James said he'd no intention of taking to his bed so Dr Gorevan prescribed instead a walking-
stick. When she heard, Loretta came over with a sponge cake.

James died. Not then, but in the winter and of pneumonia. There had
not been another stroke and he was less incapacitated than he had been
at first from the one he'd had. A fire was kept going in his bedroom, and
the family came often, one by one, to talk to him. But he was tired and,
two days after his eightieth birthday, when the moment came he was glad
to go. It was a good death: he called it that himself.

In the house to which Mollie had come when she was a girl of nineteen,
where there'd been servants and where later her children were born, there
was only Kitty Broderick now, and Kealy was the last of the outside men.
In the bleak dining-room Mollie and Eoghan sat at either end of the long
mahogany table and Kitty Broderick brought them the meals she cooked.
Everywhere there was the quiet that comes after death, seeming to Mollie
to keep at bay what had been withheld from James. But one evening after
supper, when the days had already lengthened and there was an empty
hour or so, Eoghan said: 'Come and I'll show you.'

She went, not immediately knowing what for; had she known she
would have demurred. Well, anyone would, she thought, passing from
field to field.

'You can't do this, Eoghan,' she protested, having been silent, only listening.

'We wouldn't if there was another way.'

'But Ana Woods, Eoghan!'

They could go on selling timber piecemeal, as had been done in the past, another half-acre gone and replanted every so often, but that hadn't ever been a solution, and wasn't a way now in which the family could recover itself. It would tide the family over, but tiding-over wasn't what was needed. The woods were part of the whole and the whole had to be put right. Doing so on the scale that was necessary meant that the machinery for such an undertaking could be hired at more favourable rates. With more timber to offer it would fetch what it should, not dribs and drabs that added up to nothing much. And the well-cleared land could be put to profitable use. Eoghan explained all that.

'The Bluebell Walk, though, Eoghan! The beeches, the maples!'

'I know. I know.'

They went back through the yards and sat down in the kitchen. The setters, who had accompanied them in the fields and were not allowed in the kitchen regions, ambled off into another part of the house.

'For a long time,' Eoghan said, 'there's been waste. Papa knew that too.'

'He did his best.'

'He did.'

Parcels of land had been sold in much the same small way as timber had, a source of funds when need arose. Everything higgledy-piggledy, Eoghan said, the distant future forgotten about. It was an irony for Mollie that James, aware that he'd inherited a run-down estate, had struggled to put things right. The agricultural subsidies of the nineteen eighties and nineties were the saviour of many farms and were a help at Olivehill too, but they were not enough to reverse generations of erosion and mismanagement. 'It's maybe we're old stock ourselves,' James had said when he became resigned to defeat. 'It's maybe that that's too much for us.'

Often Mollie had heard this tale of woe repeated, although always privately, never said in front of the children. In his later life James's weariness marked him, as optimism had once. At least the furniture and the pictures were not sold, faith kept with better times.

'It's hard,' Eoghan said. 'I know all this is hard, Mamma.' He reached out for her hand, which Tom would have been shy of doing, which Angela might have in a daughterly way.

'It's only hard to imagine,' she said. 'So big a thing.'

They could keep going in a sort of way, Eoghan said. Tom and his family would come to live at Olivehill, the house they were in now offered to whoever replaced Kealy when the time for that arrived. A woman could come in a few mornings a week when Kitty Broderick went, economies made to offset any extra expense.

'But Tom's right,' Eoghan said, 'when he's for being more ambitious. And bolder while we're at it.'

She nodded, and said she understood, which she did not. The friendship of her sons, their respect for one another, their confidence in their
joint ventures had always been a pleasure for her. It was something, she
supposed, that all that was still there.

'And Angela?' she asked.

'Angela's aware of how things are.'

That night Mollie dreamed that James was in the drawing-room. 'No,
no, no,' he said, and laughed because it was ridiculous. And they went to
the Long Field and were going by the springs where men from the county
council had sheets of drawings spread out and were taking measurements. 'Our boys are pulling your leg,' James told them, but the men
didn't seem to hear and said to one another that Mountmoy wouldn't
know itself with an amenity golf-course.

Afterwards, lying awake, Mollie remembered James telling her that the
Olivehill land had been fought for, that during the penal years the family
had had to resort to chicanery in order to keep what was rightfully theirs.
His father had grown sugar beet and tomatoes at the personal request of de
Valera during the nineteen forties' war. And when she dreamed again James
was saying that in an age of such strict regulations no permission would be
granted for turning good arable land into a golf-course. History was locked
into Olivehill, he said, and history in Ireland was preciously protected. He
was angry that his sons had allowed the family to be held up to ridicule, and
said he knew for a fact that those county-council clerks had changed their
minds and were sniggering now at the preposterousness of a naïve request.

'We mustn't quarrel,' Eoghan said.

'No, we mustn't quarrel.'

She had been going to tell him her dream but she didn't. Nor did she
tell Tom when he came at teatime. He was the sharper of the two in argument and always had been; but he listened, and even put her side of things
for her when she became muddled and was at a loss. His eagerness for
what he'd been carried away by in his imagination was unaffected while
he helped her to order her objections, and she remembered him – fair-
haired and delicate, with that same enthusiasm – when he was eight.

'But surely, Tom,' she began again.

'It's unusual in a town the size of Mountmoy that there isn't a golf-
course.'

She didn't mention permission because during the day she had realized
that that side of things would already have been explored; and this present
conversation would be different if an insurmountable stumbling-block
had been encountered.

'In the penal years, Tom –'

'That past is a long way off, Mamma.'

'It's there, though.'

'So is the future there. And that is ours.'

She knew it was no good. They had wanted their father's blessing, which they would not have received, but still they had wanted to try for it and perhaps she'd been wrong to beg them not to. His anger might have stirred their shame and might have won what, alone, she could not. That day, for the first time, her protection of him felt like betrayal.

At the weekend Angela came down from Dublin, and wept a little when they walked in the woods. But Angela wasn't on her side.

The front avenue at Olivehill was a mile long. Its iron entrance gates, neglected for generations, had in the end been sold to a builder who was after something decorative for an estate he had completed, miles away, outside Limerick. The gates' two stone pillars were still in place at Olivehill, and the gate-lodge beside them was, though fallen into disrepair. Rebuilt, it would become the club-house; and gorse was to be cleared to make space for a car park. A man who had designed golf-courses in Spain and South Africa came from Sussex and stayed a week at Olivehill. A planning application for the change of use of the gate-lodge had been submitted; the widening of access to and from the car park was required. No other stipulations were laid down.

Mollie listened to the golf-course man telling her about the arrangements he had made for his children's education and about his wife's culinary successes, learning too that his own interest was water-wheels. She was told that the conversion of Olivehill into a golf-course was an imaginative stroke of genius.

'You understand what's happening, Kitty?' Mollie questioned her one-time parlourmaid, whose duties were of a general nature now.

'Oh, I have, ma'am. I heard it off Kealy a while back.'

'What's Kealy think of it then?'

'Kealy won't stay, ma'am.'

'He says that, does he?'

'When the earth-diggers come in he won't remain a day. I have it from himself.'

'You won't desert me yourself, Kitty?'

'I won't, ma'am.'

'They're not going to pull the house down.'

'I wondered would they.'

'No, no. Not at all.'

'Isn't it the way things are though? Wouldn't you have to move with the times?'

'Maybe. Anyway, there's nothing I can do, Kitty.'

'Sure, without the master to lay down the word, ma'am, what chance would there be for what anyone would do? You'd miss the master, ma'am.'

'Yes, you would.'

When February came Mollie took to walking more than she'd ever walked in the fields and in the woods. By March she thought a hiatus had set in because there was a quietness and nothing was happening. But then, before the middle of that month, the herd was sold, only a few cows kept back. The pigs went. The sheep were kept, with the hens and turkeys. There was no spring sowing. One morning Kealy didn't come.

Tom and Eoghan worked the diggers themselves. Mollie didn't see that because she didn't want to, but she knew where a start had been made. She knew it from what Eoghan had let drop and realized, too late, that she shouldn't have listened.

That day Mollie didn't go out of the house, not even as far as the garden or the yards. Had she been less deaf, she would have heard, from the far distance, rocks and stones clattering into the buckets of the diggers. She would have heard the oak coming down in the field they called the Oak Tree Field, the chain-saws in Ana Woods. A third digger had been hired, Eoghan told her, with a man taken on to operate it, since Kealy had let them down. She didn't listen.

It was noticed then that she often didn't listen these days and noticed that she didn't go out. She hid her joylessness, not wishing to impose it on her family. Why should she, after all, since she was herself to blame for what was happening? James would have had papers drawn up, he would have acted fast in the little time he'd had left, clear and determined in his wishes. And nobody went against last wishes.

'Come and I'll show you,' Eoghan offered. 'I'll take you down in the car.'

'Oh now, you're busy. I wouldn't dream of it.'

'The fresh air'd do you good, Mamma.'

She liked that form of address and was glad it hadn't been dropped, that 'master' and 'mistress' had lasted too. The indoor servants had always been given their full names at Olivehill, and Kitty Broderick still was; yard men and gardeners were known by their surnames only. Such were the details of a way of life, James had maintained – like wanting to be at one, which he himself had added to that list.

More and more as the days, and then weeks, of that time went by Mollie clung to the drawing-room. She read there, books she'd read ages ago; played patience there, and a form of whist that demanded neither a partner nor an opponent. Father Thomas came to her there.

When Kealy returned it was in the drawing-room he apologized. His small, flushed face, the smell of sweat and drink, his boots taken off so as not to soil the carpet, all told the story of his retreat from what was happening, so very different from Mollie's own retreat. He asked that she should put a word in for him with her sons and she said it wasn't necessary. She said to go and find them and tell them she wanted him to be given back the position he'd had as yard man for thirty-four years. In spite of his dishevelment he went with dignity, Mollie considered.

Every third weekend or so Angela came, and also offered a tour of what was being achieved, but Mollie continued to decline this, making it seem no more than a whim of old age that she did so. Tom came to the drawing-room after his day's work, to sit with her over a seven o'clock drink, and when his children asked if their grandmother had died too, they were brought to the drawing-room to see for themselves that this was not so.

The pictures that were crowded on the drawing-room walls were of family ancestors – not Mollie's own but often seeming now as if they were – and of horses and dogs, of the house itself before the creeper had grown, square and gaunt. Among the oil paintings there were a few watercolours: of the Bluebell Walk, the avenue in autumn, the garden. There were photographs too, of Angela and Tom and Eoghan, as babies and as children, of Mollie and James after their marriage, of similar occasions before this generation's time. The drawing-room was dark even at the height of summer; only at night, with all the lights on, did its record of places and people emerge from the shadowed walls. Rosewood and mahogany were identified then, bookcases yielded the titles of their books. Candlesticks in which candles were no longer lit, snuff-boxes that had become receptacles for pins were given back something of their due.

In this room Mollie had been in awe of James's father and of his mother, had thought they didn't take to her, had wondered if they considered the levity of her nature an unsuitable quality in a wife. The prie-dieu – still between the two long windows – had seemed too solemn and holy for a drawing-room, the reproduction of a Mantegna *Virgin and Child* on the wall above it too serious a subject. But since she had claimed the drawing-room as her sanctuary she often knelt at the prie-dieu to give thanks, for she had ceased, in the peace of not knowing, to feel torn between the living and the dead. Protecting James had not been a sin; nor was it a sin to choose a reality to live by that her mood preferred. There was no fantasy in her solace, no inclination to pretend – companionable and forgiving – the presence with her of her long-loved husband. Memory in its ordinary way summoned harvested fields, and haycocks and autumn hedges, the first of the fuchsia, the last of the wild sweet-pea. It brought the lowing of cattle, old donkeys resting, scampering dogs, and days and places.

In the drawing-room she closed imagination down, for it was treacherous and without her say-so would take her into the hostile territory. 'Oh, ma'am, you should see it!' Kitty Broderick came specially to tell her, and called all that there was to see a miracle. Ten years it would have taken once, Kealy said. Less than eighteen months it had taken now.

One day Mollie drew the curtains on the daylight and did not ever draw them back again. Her meals were brought to the drawing-room when she hinted that she would like that, and when she said that the stairs were getting a bit much her sons dismantled her bed and it was made up beside the prie-dieu. Father Thomas said Mass in the dimly lit room on Saturday evenings and sometimes the family came, Angela if she happened to be in the house, Loretta and the children. Kitty Broderick and Kealy came too, Mass at that time of day being convenient for them.

Tom was disconsolate about the turn of events, but Angela said their mother was as bright as a bee. She said allowances had to be made for ageing's weariness, for a widow's continuing sorrow, that being reclusive was really hardly strange.

Eoghan protested. 'What you're doing's not good, Mamma,' he chided.

'Ah now, Eoghan, ah now.'

'We don't want you to be against us.'

She shook her head. She said she was too old to be against people. And he apologized again.

'We had to, you know.'

'Of course you had to. Of course, Eoghan.'

The ersatz landscape took on a character of its own – of stumpy hillocks that broke the blank uniformity, long fairways, sandy bunkers, a marsh created to catch the unwary, flat green squares and little flags. *Olivehill Golf Links 1 Km*, a sign said, and later the golf-course's immediate presence was announced, the car park tarred, its spaces marked in white. Completion of the clubhouse dragged but then at last was finished. Niblicks flashed in the sun of another summer. Mountmoy boys learned how to be caddies.

*

In her meditative moments Mollie knew that James had been betrayed. His anger had not been allowed, nor had it become her own, for she could not have managed it. With good intentions, he had been deceived, and had he known he might have said the benevolence was as bitter as the treachery. He would have said – for she could hear him – that the awfulness which had come about was no more terrible, no less so either, than the impuissance of Catholic families in the past, when hunted priests were taken from their hiding-places at Olivehill and Mass was fearfully said in the house, when suspicion and distrust were everywhere. Yet through silence, with subterfuge, the family at Olivehill had survived, a blind eye turned to breaches of the law by the men who worked the fields, a deaf ear to murmurs of rebellion.

In the darkened drawing-room, as shielded as James was from the new necessities of survival, Mollie tentatively reflected what she believed he might have reflected himself. In that distant past, misfortune had surely brought confusion, as it had now – and disagreement about how to accept defeat, how best to banish pride and know humility, how best to live restricted lives. And it was surely true that there had been, then too, the anger of frustration; and guilt, and tired despair.

'I've brought your tea.' Kitty Broderick interrupted the flow of thought. Light from the door she'd left open allowed her to make her way safely into the room, to put the tray she carried down. She pulled the table it was on closer to where Mollie sat.

'You're good to me, Kitty.'

'Ach, not at all. Wouldn't I pull the curtains back a bit, though?'

'No. No, the curtains are grand the way they are. Didn't you bring a cup for yourself?'

'Oh, I forgot the cup!' She always did, was never at ease when the suggestion was made that she should sit down and share the mistress's tea.

'Kealy got drunk again,' she said.

'Is he all right?'

'I have him in the kitchen.'

'Kealy likes his glass.'

He wasn't as particular as Kitty Broderick, always accepting when he came to the drawing-room the whiskey she kept specially for him. When Tom came in the evenings it was for sherry.

'How silent it can be, Kitty, in the drawing-room. Nearly always silent.'

'It's a quiet room, all right. Sure, it always was. But wouldn't you take a little walk, though, after your tea?'

The bluebells had begun to grow again. They'd told her that. Kitty

Broderick knew she wouldn't go for a walk, that she wouldn't come out from where she belonged, and be a stranger on her own land. They'd wanted her to have the setters with her for company, but it wasn't fair to keep dogs closed up all day like that and she said no.

Nothing changed, she thought when the maid had gone; and after all why should it? Persecution had become an ugly twist of circumstances, more suited to the times. Merciless and unrelenting, what was visited on the family could be borne, as before it had been. In her artificial dark it could be borne.

A Perfect Relationship

'I'll tidy the room,' she said. 'The least I can do.'

Prosper watched her doing it. She had denied that there was anyone else, repeating this several times because he had several times insisted there must be.

The cushions of the armchairs and the sofa were plumped up, empty glasses gathered. The surface of the table where the bottles stood was wiped clean of sticky smears. She had run the Hoky over the carpet.

It was early morning, just before six. 'I love this flat,' she used to say and, knowing her so well, Prosper could feel her wanting to say it again now that she was leaving it. But she didn't say anything.

Once, before she came to live here, they had walked in the Chiltern hills. Hardly knowing one another, they had stayed in farmhouses, walking from one to the next for the two nights of the weekend. He had identified birds for her – stone curlews, wheatears – and wild flowers when he knew what they were himself. She was still attending the night school then and they often talked to one another in simple Italian, which was one of the two languages he taught her there. She spelled *giochetto* and *pizzico* for him; she used, correctly, the imperfect tense. He wondered if she remembered that or if she remembered her shyness of that time, and her humility, and how she never forgot to thank him for things. And how she'd said he knew so much.

'I love you, Chloë.'

Dark-haired and slim, not tall, Chloë dismissed her looks as ordinary. But in fact her prettiness was touched with beauty. It was in the deep blue of her eyes, her perfect mouth, her profile.

'I hate doing this,' she said. 'It's horrible. I know it is.'

He shook his head, not in denial of what she said, only to indicate bewilderment. She had chosen the time she had – the middle of the night, as it had been – because it was easier then, almost a *fait accompli* when he returned from the night school, easier to find the courage. He guessed that, but didn't say it because it mattered so much less than that she didn't want to be here any more.

The muted colours of the clothes she was wearing were suitable for a bleak occasion, as if she had specially chosen them: the grey skirt she disliked, the nondescript silk scarf that hadn't been a present from him as so many other scarves were, the plain cream blouse he'd never seen without a necklace before. She looked a little different and perhaps she thought she should because that was how she felt.

'Where are you going, Chloë?'

Her back was to him. She tried to shrug. She picked a glass up and turned to face him when she reached the door. No one else knew, she said. He was the first to know.

'I love you, Chloë,' he said again.

'Yes, I do know that.'

'We've been everything to one another.'

'Yes.'

The affection in their relationship had been the pleasure of both their lives: that had not been said before in this room, nor even very often that they were fortunate. The reticence they shared was natural to them, but they knew – each as certainly as the other – what was not put into words. Prosper might have contributed now some part of this, but sensing that it would seem like protesting too much he did not.

'Don't,' he begged instead, and she gazed emptily at him before she went away.

He heard her in the bedroom when she finished with the Hoky in the hall. The telephone rang and she answered it at once; a taxi-driver, he guessed, for Clement Gardens was sometimes difficult to find.

Exhausted, Prosper sat down. Middle-aged, greying a little, his thin face anxious, as it often was, he wondered if he looked as disturbed and haggard as he felt. 'Don't,' he whispered. 'For God's sake, don't, Chloë.'

No sound came from the bedroom, either of suitcases and bags being zipped or of footsteps. Then the doorbell rang and there were voices in the hall, hers light and easy, polite as always, the taxi-man's a mumble. The door of the flat banged.

He sat where she had left him, thinking he had never known her, for what else made sense? He imagined her in the taxi that was taking her somewhere she hadn't told him about, even telling the taxi-driver more – why she was going there, what the trouble was. There had been no goodbye. She hadn't wept. 'I'm sorry,' was what she'd said when he came in from the night school more or less at the usual time. His hours were eight until half past one and he almost always stayed longer with someone who had fallen behind. He had this morning, and then had walked because he felt the need for fresh air, stopping as he often did for a cup of tea at the stall in Covent Garden. It was twenty to three when he came in and she hadn't gone to bed. It had taken her most of the night to pack.

Prosper didn't go to bed himself, nor did he for all that day. There hadn't been a quarrel. They had never quarrelled, not once, not ever. She would always cherish that, she'd said.

He took paracetamol for a headache. He walked about the flat, expecting to find she had forgotten something because she usually did when she packed. But all trace of her was gone from the kitchen and the bathroom, from the bedroom they had shared for two and a half years. In the afternoon, at half past four, a private pupil came, a middle-aged Slovakian woman, whose English he was improving. He didn't charge her. It wasn't worth it since she could afford no more than a pittance.

All day Chloë's work had been a diversion. Now there was a television screen, high up in a corner, angled so that it could be seen without much effort from the bed. People she knew would have put her up for a while, but she hadn't wanted that. Breakfast was included in the daily rate at the Kylemore Hotel; and it was better, being on her own.

But the room she'd been shown when she came to make enquiries a week ago wasn't this one. The faded wallpaper was stained, the bedside table marked with cigarette burns. The room she'd been shown was clean at least and she'd hesitated when this morning she'd been led into a different one. But, feeling low, she hadn't been up to making a fuss.

From the window she watched the traffic, sluggish in congestion – taxis jammed, bus-drivers patient, their windows pulled open in the evening heat, cyclists skilfully manoeuvring. Still gazing down into the street, Chloë knew why she was here and reminded herself of that. But knowing, really, was no good. She had been happy.

It was the second time that Prosper had been left. The first time there had been a marriage, but the separation that followed the less formal relationship was no less painful; and in the days that now crawled by, anguish became an agony. He dreaded each return to the empty flat, especially in the small hours of the morning. He dreaded the night school, the chatter of voices between classes, the brooding presence of Hesse, who was its newly appointed principal, the hot-drinks machine that gave you what it had, not what you wanted, the classroom faces staring back at him. 'All right?' Hesse enquired, each guttural syllable articulated slowly and with care, his great blubber face simulating concern. In Prosper's dreams the contentment he had known for two and a half years held on and he reached out often to touch the companion who was not there. In the dark the truth came then, merciless, undeniable.

When that week ended he went to Winchelsea on the Sunday, a long slow journey by train and bus, made slower by weekend work on different stretches of the railway line.

'Well, this is nice,' her mother said, flustered when she opened the hall door.

She led him into the sitting-room he remembered from the only time he had been in this house before – the prints of country scenes on the walls, the ornaments, a bookcase packed with books that Chloë said had never been read. The fire was unlit because this morning the room was sunny. A black-and-white dog – reluctant when it was shooed out of the french windows – smelled as it had before, of damp or of itself. A Sunday that had been too.

'Oh yes, we've been well,' Chloë's mother said when she was asked. 'He has a new thing now.'

Metal-detecting this turned out to be, poking about with a gadget on Winchelsea beach, which was the best for this purpose for miles around. 'You'll have a cup of coffee? Or lunch? He'll be back for lunch.'

Prosper had always known she didn't like him, an older man and not a type she could take to: he could hear her saying it. And now he'd caught her with a curler in her wispy grey hair, forgotten, he supposed. He watched her realizing, a nervous gesture, fingers patting one side of her head. She left him on his own and came back saying she was sorry for deserting him. She offered sherry, the bottle almost empty.

'He said he'd get some more.' She poured out what there was, none for herself.

'I don't know where she is,' Prosper said. 'I thought she might be here.'

'Oh, Chloë's not here.'

'I wondered –'

'No, Chloë's not here.'

'I wondered if she said anything about where she is.'

'Well, no.'

He wondered what had been said, how it had been put, presumably on the telephone. He wondered if they'd been told more than he had himself, if they'd been glad, or at least relieved, both of them, not just she.

'He'll be back soon. He wouldn't like to miss you.'

Prosper believed that, seeing in his mind's eye the lanky figure prodding at the shingle of the beach with his detector. Her father had made a pet of Chloë and probably considered she could do no wrong; but even so it was he whom Prosper had come to see. It hadn't been the truth when he'd said he thought she might be here.

'It's difficult,' her mother said. 'In the light of everything, it's difficult.'

When she finished speaking she shook her head repeatedly. Prosper said he understood.

'He'd want to see you. He'd want me to invite you.'

'You're very kind.'

'He's never idle.'

'I remember that.'

'He made those ships in bottles all last winter. You see the ships, going through the hall?'

'Yes, I noticed the ships.'

'It's lamb I've got for today. A little leg, but it's enough.'

There was her husband's key in the front door while she spoke, then his voice called out to her, saying he was back.

Chloë left the Kylemore Hotel that same Sunday morning and took a taxi to Maida Vale, where she laid her things out in the room she'd been lent while the girl who lived there was on holiday in Provence. It would be better than the hotel, and three weeks might just be long enough to find somewhere permanent.

She filled the drawers that had been allocated to her and hung what clothes there was room for in a hanging space behind a curtain. A stroke of luck she'd called it when the girl – an office colleague whom she didn't otherwise know – had suggested this arrangement, quoting the rent and requesting that it should be paid in advance. Chloë had lived in a quite similar room before she'd moved into the flat at Clement Gardens.

He hadn't pressed her to do that; at no stage had he done so, at no stage in their relationship had he ever pressed her about anything. As soon as she saw the flat she had wanted to be there, enraptured by its spaciousness, and the grandeur – so she called it – of Clement Gardens. The gardens themselves, where you could sit out in summer, were for the use of the tenants only, the rules that kept them peaceful strictly enforced.

She went out in search of coffee and found a café with pavement tables in the sun. She told herself she wasn't lonely, knowing that she was. Would weekends always be the worst? she wondered. The worst because they'd meant so much, even before she'd come to Clement Gardens, or perhaps particularly so then? She made a list of things to buy and asked the waitress who brought her coffee if there was somewhere open near by. 'Yeah, sure,' the waitress said, and told her where.

People exercising their dogs went by, children in the company of fathers claiming their Sunday access, dawdling couples. A church bell had begun to ring; the elderly, with prayer books, hurried. Resentment grumbled in the children's features, the fathers struggled with conversation.

For a moment, feeling sleepy in the sun, for she'd been restless in the night, Chloë dozed; and waking, in memory saw the woman who had been his wife. 'Prosper!' this beautiful person had called out from the crowd at the Festival Hall, still possessing him, a little, with her smile. And Chloë had wondered as they returned to their seats for the second part of the concert if the man who was tonight the companion of this woman was the one she had run away to, and imagined that he was.

She made her list of what she needed. Mahler's Fifth Symphony it had been, a CD of which had been played for weeks before she was taken to the Festival Hall. One composer at a time had been his way of bringing music into her life.

Her father was shy, and made more so by what had happened. He was bent a little from the shoulders, which with his frailness made him seem older than he was, which was sixty-seven. 'I'm sorry,' he said when his wife was out of the room.

'I don't know why it happened.'

'Stay with us for lunch, Prosper.'

The invitation sounded almost compensatory, but Prosper knew he was imagining that, that nothing so ridiculous was intended.

'I don't know where she is.'

'I think she wants to be alone.'

'Could you –'

'No, we couldn't do that.'

They walked together to the Lord and Lady, which Prosper on that other Sunday had been taken to for a similar purpose: to bring back jugs of lunchtime beer.

'Have something now we're here?' the same offer came in the saloon bar and, remembering, her father ordered gin and tonic, and a Worthington for himself.

'We couldn't do something Chloë doesn't want us to,' he said while they waited for them.

There was a photograph of her framed on the sitting-room mantelpiece, a bare-footed child of nine or ten in a bathing dress, laughing among sand-castles that had been dotted around her in a ring. She hated that photograph, she used to say. She hated that sitting-room. They'd called her Chloë after a prim character in a film. She couldn't get to like the name.

'There's no one else,' Prosper said.

'Chloë told us there was nothing like that.'

The glass of beer was raised and Prosper did the same with his gin and tonic.

'There wasn't a quarrel,' he said.

'You did a lot for Chloë, Prosper. We know what you've done for her.'

'Less than it might seem.'

Teaching wasn't much, you passed on information. Anyone could have taken her to foreign films, anyone could have taken her to the National Gallery or told her who Apemantus was. She'd been the most perceptive and intelligent of all the girls he'd ever taught.

'I'll be honest with you, Prosper – at home here we haven't always seen eye to eye on the friendship. Not that we've ever come to fireworks. No, I don't mean that.'

'I'm an older man.'

'Yes, it's come up.'

'It hasn't made much of a difference. Not to Chloë. Not to either of us.'

A note of pleading kept creeping into Prosper's voice. He couldn't dispel it. He felt pathetic, a failure because he was unable to give a reason for what had happened. Why should they feel sorry for him? Why should they bother with a discarded man?

'Chloë's never been headstrong,' her father said. He sounded strained, as if the conversation was too much for him too.

'No,' Prosper said. 'No, she isn't that.'

Her father nodded, an indication of relief: a finality had been reached.

'You go there in the morning,' he said, 'you have the whole beach to yourself. Miles of it and you have it to yourself. It's surprising what you turn up. Well, there'll be nothing, you say. You're always wrong.'

'I shouldn't have come bothering you. I'm sorry.'

'No, no.'

'I've tried to find her. I've phoned round.'

'We'd best be getting back, you know.'

They said hardly anything on the walk to the house, and in the dining-room. Prosper couldn't eat the food that was placed before him. The silences that gathered lasted longer each time they were renewed and there was only silence in the end. He should have made her tell him where she was going, he said, and saw they were embarrassed, not commenting on that. When he left he apologized. They said they were sorry too, but he knew they weren't.

On the train he fell asleep. He woke up less than a minute later, telling himself the lunchtime beer on top of the gin and tonic had brought that about. It didn't mean there wasn't someone else just because she'd said it and had said it to them too, just because she never lied. Everyone lied. Lies were at everyone's disposal, waiting to be picked up when there was a use to put them to. That there was someone else made sense of every-thing, some younger man telling her what to do.

The train crept into Victoria and he sat there thinking about that until a West Indian cleaner told him he should be getting off now. He pressed his way through the crowds at the station, wondering about going to one of the bars but deciding not to. He changed his mind again on the way to the Underground, not wanting to be in the flat. It took an hour to walk to the Vine in Wystan Street, where they had often gone to on Sunday after-noons.

It was quiet, as he'd known it would be. Voices didn't carry in the Vine and weren't raised anyway; in couples or on their own, people were read-ing the Sunday papers. He'd brought her here when she was still at the night school, after a Sunday-afternoon class. 'You saved me,' she used to say, and he remembered her saying it here. At the night school, crouched like a schoolgirl at her desk, obedient, humble, her prettiness unnourished, her cleverness concealed, she'd been dismissive of herself. Trapped by her nature, he had thought, and less so when their friendship had begun, when they had walked away from the night school together through the empty, darkened streets, their conversation at first about the two languages she was learning, and later about everything. Sometimes they stopped at the Covent Garden coffee stall, each time knowing one another better. An only child, her growing up was stifled; net curtains genteelly kept out the world. There was, for him in marriage, the torment of not being wanted any more. She was ashamed of being ashamed, and he was left with jeal-ousy and broken pride. Their intimacy saved him too.

There was an empty table in the alcove of the wine bar, one they'd sat at. Hair newly hennaed, black silk clinging to her curves, Margo – who owned the place – waved friendlily from behind the bar.

'Chloë's not well,' he said when she came to take his order, her wrist chains rattling while she cleared away glasses and wiped the table's sur-face.

'Poor Chloë,' she murmured, and recommended the white Beaune, her whispery voice always a surprise, since her appearance suggested noisiness.

'She'll be all right.' He nodded, not knowing why he pretended. 'Just a half,' he said. 'Since I'm on my own.'

Someone else brought it, a girl who hadn't been in the bar before. Half-bottles of wine had a cheerless quality, he used to say, and he saw now what he had meant, the single glass, the stubby little bottle.

'Thanks,' he said, and the girl smiled back at him.

He sipped the chilled wine, glancing about at the men on their own.

Any one of them might be waiting for her. That wasn't impossible, although it would have been once. A young man of about her age, a silk scarf casually tucked into a blue shirt open at the neck, dark glasses pushed up on to his forehead, was reading a paperback with the same cover as the edition Prosper possessed himself, *The Diary of a Country Priest*.

He tried to remember if he had ever recommended that book to her. *The Secret Agent* he'd recommended, and Poe and Louis Auchincloss. She had never read Conrad before. She had never heard of Scott Fitzgerald, or Faulkner or Madox Ford.

The man had blond hair, quite long, but combed. A pullover, blue too, trailed over the back of his chair. His canvas shoes were blue.

He was the kind: Prosper hardly knew why he thought so, and yet the longer the thought was there the more natural it seemed that it should be. Had they noticed one another some other Sunday? Had he stared at her the way men sometimes do? When was it that a look had been exchanged?

He observed the man again, noted his glances in the direction of the door. A finger prodded the dark glasses further back, a bookmark was slipped between the pages of *The Diary of a Country Priest*, then taken out again. But no one came.

It was a green-and-black photograph on the book's cover, the young priest standing on a chair, the woman holding candles in a basket. Had the book been taken from the shelves in the flat, to lend a frisson of excitement, a certain piquancy, to deception? Again the dark glasses were pushed up, the bookmark laid on the table. People began to go, returning their newspapers to the racks by the door.

Suddenly she would be there. She would not notice that he was there too, and when she did would look away. The first time at the Covent Garden coffee stall she said that all her life she'd never talked to anyone before.

For a moment Prosper imagined that it had happened, that she came and that the man reached out for her, that his arms held her, that she held him. He told himself he mustn't look. He told himself he shouldn't have come here, and didn't look again. At the bar he paid for the wine he hadn't drunk and on the street he cried, and was ashamed, hiding his distress from people going by.

She watched while twilight went, and while the dark intensified and the lights came on in the windows of the flat that overlooked the gardens. 'Oh, a man gets over it.' Her mother had been sure of that. Her mother said he'd be all right, her father that they'd gone together for the lunch-time beer. She had telephoned because he would have been there; she'd guessed he would. 'Never your type, he wasn't,' her mother said. Her father said stick by what she'd done. 'Cut up he is, but you were fair and clear with him.' Her mother said he'd had his innings.

Eventually they would say he wasn't much. Often disagreeing, they would agree because it made things easier if that falsity seemed to be the truth. 'Oh, long ago,' her mother would say, 'long ago I remarked to Dad it wasn't right.'

A shadow smudged one of the lighted windows, then wasn't there. The warm day had turned cold, but in the gardens the air was fresh and still. She was alone there now, and she remembered when he'd led her about among the shrubs before she came to live in the flat. 'Hibiscus,' he said when she asked, and said another was hypericum, another potentilla, another mahonia. She remembered the names, and imagined she always would.

When she left the gardens she pulled the gate behind her and heard the lock clicking. She crossed the street and stood in front of the familiar door. All she had to do was to drop the key of the gate into the letterbox: she had come to do that, having taken it away by mistake. It would be discovered in the morning under the next day's letters and put with them on the shelf in the hall, a found object waiting for whoever might have mislaid it.

But with the key in her hand, Chloë stood there, not wanting to give it up like this. A car door banged somewhere; faint music came from far away. She stood there for minutes that seemed longer. Then she rang the bell of the flat.

He heard her footsteps on the stairs when he opened the door. When he closed it behind her she held out the key. She smiled and did not speak.

'It's good of you,' he said.

He had known it was she before she spoke on the intercom. As if telepathy came into this, he had thought, but did not quite believe it had.

'You went down to the Coast.'

She always called it that – was never more precise – as if the town where she had lived deserved no greater distinction, sharing, perhaps, what she disliked about the house.

They had been standing and now sat down. Without asking, he poured her a drink.

'I have a room for a few weeks,' she said. 'I'll look round for somewhere.'

'It was just there may be letters to forward. And awkward if people ring up. Awkward, not knowing what to say.'

'I'm sorry.'

'Well, there haven't been letters so far. And no one has rung up. I shouldn't have gone to Winchelsea.'

'I should have told you more.'

'Why have you gone away, Chloë?'

Chloë heard herself answering that, in hardly more than a whisper saying she had been silly. And having said it she knew she had to say more, yet it was difficult. The words were there, and she had tried before. In the long evening hours, alone in the flat while he was at the night school, she had tried to string them together so that, becoming sentences, they became her feelings. But always they were severe, too cruel, not what she wanted, ungrateful, cold. In telling him, she did not mean to hurt, or to convey impatience or to blame. Wearied by introspection, night after night, she had gone to bed and slept; and woken sometimes when he returned, and then was glad to be there with him.

'I didn't know it was a silliness,' she said.

Friendship had drawn them together. Giving and taking, they had discovered one another at a time when they were less than they became. She had always been aware of that and that it was enough, more than people often had. Still in search of somewhere to begin, she said so now. And added after a moment: 'I want to be here.'

He didn't speak. He wasn't looking at her, not that he had turned away, not that he resented her muddle, or considered that she should not have allowed it to come about: she knew this wasn't so, he had never been like that.

'I thought it would be easy,' she said.

There had been certainty. In her feelings she had been sure even when they were confused, even when she couldn't think because she'd thought too much and had exhausted reason. She had clung to her certainty, had sensed its truth: that she had lost, and was losing still, a little of herself. With kindness, and delighting her, her life had been arrested, while hungrily she accepted what was on offer. But her certainty was not there as soon as she was on her own.

'You make a mistake,' she said, 'and know it when you live with it.'

Prosper understood because he was quick to understand; and understanding nothing only moments ago, now understood too much. A calmness possessed him, the first time today there had been calmness, the first time since she had packed her things and gone away. He hadn't known there'd been misgivings.

He had been jealous in the wine bar: that was what happened when emotions rampaged out of control, what panic and distress could do. It was her fault, she said. No, it was no one's fault, he contradicted that.

She said he was forgiving. She said her mother's contempt was not meant, and that in time her father would be pleased. Mattering so much, he thought, that didn't matter now.

She made them scrambled eggs. They drank a little more, and the mood of relief being what it was for Chloë she celebrated their time together, recalling the Chilterns and their walks through the darkened streets in the early hours. And weekend visits to the cinema, her coming to the flat, their living there and never quarrelling, the gardens in summer.

Prosper didn't say much and nothing at all of what he might have, not wanting to, although he knew he must. The plates they'd eaten their scrambled eggs from remained on the coffee-table. Their glasses, not yet finished with, were there; her key to the gardens was. And they were shadows in the gloom, the room lit only by a single table-lamp.

Prosper didn't want the night to end. He loved her, she gave him back what she could: he had never not known that. Her voice, still reminiscing, was soft, and when it sounded tired he talked himself and, being with her, found the courage she had found and lost. His it was to order now what must be, to say what must be said. There had been no silliness, there wasn't a mistake.

The Children

'We must go now,' Connie's father said and Connie didn't say anything.

The two men stood with their shovels, hesitating. Everyone else, including Mr Crozier, who had conducted the funeral service, had gone from the graveside. Cars were being started or were already being eased out of where they were parked, close to the church wall on the narrow road.

'We have to go, Connie,' her father said.

Connie felt in the pocket of her coat for the scarf-ring and thought for a moment she had lost it, but then she felt the narrow silver band. She knew it wasn't silver but they had always pretended. She leaned forward to drop it on to the coffin and took the hand her father held out to her. By the churchyard gate they caught up with the last of the mourners, Mrs Archdale and the elderly brothers, Arthur and James Dobbs.

'You'll come to the house,' her father invited them in case an invitation hadn't already been passed on to them. But people knew: the cars that were slipping away were all going in the same direction, to the house three and a quarter miles away, still just within the townland of Fara.

Connie would have preferred this to be different. She would have liked the house to be quiet now and had imagined, this afternoon, her father and herself gathering up her mother's belongings, arranging them in whatever way the belongings of the dead usually were arranged, her father explaining how they should be as they went along. She had thought of them alone after the funeral, doing all this because it was the time for it, because that was something you felt.

Her mother's dying, and the death itself, had been orderly and anticipated. Connie had known for months that it would come, for weeks that she would throw her scarf-ring on to the coffin at the very last minute. 'Brown Thomas's,' her mother had said when she was asked where it had been bought, and had given it to Connie because she didn't want it herself any more. This afternoon, in the quiet bedroom, there would be other things: familiar brooches, familiar earrings, and clothes and shoes, of course; odds and ends in drawers. But she and her father were up to that.

'All right, Connie?' he asked, turning left instead of taking the Knocklofty road, which was the long way round.

There'd been no pain; that had been managed well. While she was at the hospice, and when she came home at the end because suddenly she wanted to, you could tell that there had been no pain. 'Because we prayed for that, I suppose,' Connie had said when everything was over, and her father said he supposed so too. More important than anything it was that there had been no pain.

'Oh, I'm OK,' she said.

'They have to come to the house. They won't stay long.'

'I know.'

'You've been a strength, Connie.'

He meant it. He himself had been the source of strength at first and had seen her through that time, before she began to give back what he had given her. She had adored her mother.

'She would want us to be hospitable,' he said, unnecessarily, saying too much.

'I know we have to be.'

Connie was eleven and had her mother's faded blue eyes, and hair the colour of corn-stalks, as her mother's had been too. The freckles on her forehead and on the bridge of her nose were a feature of her own.

'We can get down to it when they've gone,' she said as they drove on, past the two cottages where nobody lived, down the hill that suddenly became almost dark, beech foliage meeting overhead. Mrs Archdale had been given a lift by the Dobbs brothers, their red Ford Escort already turning in at the gates. On the uneven surface of the avenue other cars were progressing cautiously, watched by the fenced sheep on either side.

'Come in, come in,' Connie's father invited the mourners who had already left their cars and were conversing in quiet tones on the gravel in front of the house. He was a tall, thin man, dark hair beginning to go grey, a boniness distinguishing his features. Sombrely dressed today, he was quite notably handsome. He had known much longer than his child had that his wife was going to die, but always at first there had been hope of a kind. Connie had been told when there was none.

The hall door wasn't locked. He'd left it so, wanting people to go in as soon as they arrived, but no one had. He pushed it open and stood aside. All of them would know the way and Mrs O'Daly would be there, tea made.

When Teresa was left by her husband she'd felt humiliated by the desertion. 'You'll have them to yourself,' he'd said; with ersatz gentleness, she considered. 'I promise you I won't be a nuisance about that.' He spoke of their two children, whom she had always believed were fonder of him than they were of her. And it seemed wrong that they should be deprived of him: in her lowness at the time she had even said so, had felt she should be punished further for her failure to keep a marriage together, should lose them too. 'Oh no,' he had protested. 'No, I would never do that.'

Among the mourners in the drawing-room, she remembered that with poignancy, wondering if the pain of death so early in a marriage left behind the same cruel rawness that did not change and lingered for so long. 'I'm sorry,' she said when Connie's father put a hand on her arm and murmured that she was good to have come. 'I'm awfully sorry, Robert,' she said again, murmuring also.

She knew him as Connie's father, her own daughter, Melissa, being Connie's particular friend. She didn't know him well; more often than not he wasn't there when she brought Melissa to spend the day at the farm. She had liked Connie's mother but had never had much of a conversation with her, they being different kinds of people, and the house was a busy place. During all the years Teresa had known the house no one was employed to help in it, as no one was – except for odd days during the summer – on the farm itself. Teresa had guessed that the present bleak occasion would be in the hands of Mrs O'Daly, who in her capable countrywoman's way would have offered to see to things. She poured the tea now, cups and saucers laid out on a table that didn't belong in the drawing-room. O'Daly, a small, scuttling man who worked on the roads and took on anything else he could get, was handing round plates of biscuits and egg sandwiches.

'He did it very well,' someone remarked to Teresa. 'Your rector did.'

'Yes, he did.'

A couple she couldn't place, whose way of referring to Mr Crozier suggested they weren't of the locality, nodded a nervous confirmation of her agreement. Teresa thought she probably would even have known them if they'd come out from Clonmel. Yes, Mr Crozier did funerals well, she said.

'We're distant cousins,' the woman said. 'A generation back.'

'I live quite near.'

'It's lovely here.'

'Quiet,' the man said. 'You'd notice the quiet.'

'We didn't know until we picked up the *Irish Times*,' the woman said. 'Well, we'd lost touch.'

'Saddens us now, of course.' The man nodded that into place. 'To have lost touch.'

'Yes.'

Teresa was forty-one, still pretty, her round face brightened by a smile that came easily and lingered, as if it belonged to these features in a way as permanent as they were themselves. Her reddish hair was cut quite short; she had to watch her weight and adamantly did so. She shook her head when O'Daly pressed his plate of Bourbon creams on her.

'We drove over,' the woman she was in conversation with imparted. 'From Mitchelstown.'

'Good of you to come.'

They deprecated that, and Teresa looked around. When she woke that morning she'd found herself wondering if her husband would be here, if he'd drive down from Dublin, since the death would have shocked him. But among the mourners in the drawing-room she didn't see him. It seemed quite a sparse attendance in the large, ordinarily furnished room, for not everyone who'd been at the church had come. But Teresa knew her husband hadn't been in the church either. It was years now since they'd met; he'd ceased to bother with his children as soon as other children were born to him. As good as his word about not being a nuisance, Teresa supposed.

Afterwards, when everyone had gone, Connie helped the O'Dalys to clear up and when that was done the O'Dalys went too. She and her father did what her mother had requested then, taking her things from the wardrobe and the dressing-table drawers, disposing of them as she had wished, her charities remembered. It was late before all that was completed, before Connie and her father sat together in the kitchen. He poached their eggs when they'd decided to have eggs. He asked her to watch the toast. 'We'll manage,' he said.

The farm had come to Robert when he married, introducing him to a way of life he had not sought and which he did not imagine he would take to. In fact, he did, and over the years transformed the farm his wife had not long ago inherited as a sluggish, neglected enterprise into a fairly thriving one. It was a means of livelihood too; and, more than that, a source of personal satisfaction for Robert that he succeeded with crops and stock, about which he had once known nothing.

All this continued when he was widowed, when the house and land became entirely his. There were no changes on the farm, but in the house – to which Mrs O'Daly now came for three hours every weekday morning – Connie and her father, while slowly coming to terms with the loss they had suffered, shared the awareness of a ghost that fleetingly demanded no more than to be remembered. Life continuing could not fold away what had happened but it offered something, blurring the drama of death's immediacy. And then, when almost two years had passed since the funeral, Robert asked Teresa to marry him.

It was a natural thing. Having known one another through the friendship of their daughters, they had come to know one another better in the new circumstances, Teresa continuing to drive Melissa to the farm, with her much younger brother when he was made welcome there by Connie but was still too young to cycle. And Robert, doing his bit as often as he could, drove the two back to the bungalow at Fara Bridge, where their father in his day had attempted to get a pottery going.

The day he asked Teresa to marry him, Robert had looked up from the mangels he was weeding and seen her coming towards him, along the verge of the field. She brought him tea in a can, which she often did when she stayed all afternoon in order to save him the journey later to Fara Bridge. A year after the death she had begun to fall in love with him.

'I never knew,' he said in the mangel field when Teresa's response to his proposal was to tell him that. 'I thought you'd turn me down.'

She took the can of tea from his hand and lifted it to her lips, the first intimacy between them, before their first embrace, before they spoke of love. 'Oh, Robert, not in a million years would I turn you down,' she whispered.

There were difficulties, but they didn't matter as they would have once. In an Ireland they could both remember it would have been commented upon that she, born into a religious faith that was not Robert's, had attended a funeral service in his alien church. It would have been declared that marriage would not do; that the divorce which had brought Teresa's to an end could not be recognized. Questions would have been asked about children who might be born to them: to which belief were they promised, in which safe haven might they know only their own kind? Such difficulties still trailed, like husks caught in old cobwebs, but there were fewer interfering strictures now in how children were brought up, and havens were less often sought. Melissa, a year older than Connie, had received her early schooling from the nuns in Clonmel and had gone on to an undenominational boarding-school in Dublin. Her brother still attended the national school at Fara Bridge. Connie went to Miss Mortimer, whose tiny academy for Protestant children – her mother's choice because it was convenient – was conducted in an upstairs room at the rectory, ten minutes' away along the river path. But, in the end, all three would be together at Melissa's boarding-school, co-educational and of the present.

'How lovely all that is!' Teresa murmured.

There was a party at which the engagement was announced – wine in the afternoon, and Mrs O'Daly's egg sandwiches again, and Teresa's sponge cakes and her brandy-snaps and meringues. The sun came out after what had been a showery morning, allowing the celebration to take place in the garden. Overgrown and wild in places, the garden's neglect went back to the time of the death, although sometimes when she'd come to keep an eye on the children Teresa had done her best with the geranium beds, which had particularly been the task of Connie's mother.

She would do better now, Teresa promised herself, looking about among the guests as she had among the mourners, again half expecting to see the man who had left her, wanting him to be there, wanting him to know that she was loved again, that she had survived the indignity he had so casually subjected her to, that she was happy. But he wasn't there, as naturally he wouldn't be. All that was over, and the cousins from Mitchelstown with whom she had conversed on the afternoon of the funeral naturally weren't there either.

Robert was happy too – because Teresa was and because, all around him at the party, there were no signs of disapproval, only smiles of approbation.

Because the wedding was not to take place until later in the summer, after Melissa's return for the holidays, Connie and her father continued for a while to be alone together, managing, as he had said they would. Robert bought half a dozen Charollais calves, a breed he had never had on the farm before. He liked, every year, doing something new; and he liked the calves. Otherwise, his buying and selling were a pattern, his tasks a repetition. He repaired the fences, tightening the barbed wire where that was possible, renewing it when it wasn't. He looked out for the many ailments that beset sheep. He lifted the first potatoes and noted every day the ripening of his barley.

Teresa dragged clumps of scotch grass and treacherous little nettles out of the sanguineum and the sylvaticum, taking a trowel to the docks. She cut down the Johnson's Blue, wary of letting it spread too wildly, but wouldn't have known to leave the Kashmir Purple a little longer, or that *pratense*'s sturdy roots were a job to divide. A notebook left behind instructed her in all that.

Miss Mortimer closed her small school for the summer and Connie was at home all day then. Sometimes Melissa's brother was there, a small thin child called Nat, a name that according to Melissa couldn't be more suitable, since he so closely resembled an insect.

'You want to come with us?' Teresa invited Connie when Melissa's term had ended and Teresa was setting off to meet her at the railway station in Clonmel. Connie hesitated, then said she didn't.

That surprised Teresa. She had driven over specially from Fara Bridge, as she always did when Melissa came back for the holidays. It surprised her, but afterwards she realized she'd somehow sensed before she spoke that Connie was going to say no. She was puzzled, but didn't let it show.

'Come back here, shall we?' she suggested, since this, too, was what always happened on Melissa's first evening home.

'If that's what you'd like,' Connie said.

The train was twenty minutes late and when Teresa returned to the farm with Melissa and Nat, Connie wasn't in the house, and when her father came in later she wasn't with him either, as she sometimes was. 'Connie!' they all called in the yard, her father going into some of the sheds. Melissa and her brother went to the end of the avenue and a little way along the road in both directions. 'Connie!' they called out in the garden, although they could see she wasn't there. 'Connie!' they called, going from room to room in the house. Her father was worried. He didn't say he was but Melissa and her brother could tell. So could Teresa.

'She can't be far,' she said. 'Her bicycle's here.'

She drove Melissa to Fara Bridge to unpack her things, and Nat went with them. She telephoned the farm then. There wasn't any answer and she guessed that Robert was still looking for his child.

The telephone was ringing again when Connie came back. She came downstairs: she'd been on the roof, she said. You went up through the trapdoor at the top of the attic stairs. You could lie down on the warm lead and read a book. Her father shook his head, saying it wasn't safe to climb about on the roof. He made her promise not to again.

'What's the matter, Connie?' he asked her when he went to say goodnight. Connie said nothing was. Propped up in front of her was the book she'd been reading on the roof, *The Citadel* by A. J. Cronin.

'Surely you don't understand that, Connie?' her father said, and she said she wouldn't want to read a book she didn't understand.

Connie watched the furniture being unloaded. The men lifted it from the yellow removal van, each piece familiar to her from days spent in the bungalow at Fara Bridge. Space had been made, some of the existing furniture moved out, to be stored in one of the outhouses.

Melissa wasn't there. She was helping her mother to rearrange in the half-empty rooms at Fara Bridge the furniture that remained, which would have to be sold when the bungalow was because there wasn't room for it at the farm. There had been a notice up all summer announcing the sale of the bungalow, but no one had made an offer yet. 'Every penny'll go into the farm,' Connie had heard Teresa saying.

Nat, whom Teresa had driven over earlier, watched with Connie in the hall. He was silent this morning, as he often was, his thin arms wrapped tightly around his body in a way that suggested he suffered from the cold, although the day was warm. Now and again he glanced at Connie, as if expecting her to say something about what was happening, but Connie didn't.

All morning it took. Mrs O'Daly brought the men tea and later, when they finished, Connie's father gave them a drink in the kitchen: small glasses of whiskey, except for the man who was the driver, who was given what remained in the bottle to take away with him.

'That's a lovely piece of delft,' Mrs O'Daly commented in the hall, referring to a blue-and-white soup tureen that the men had placed on the shelf of the hallstand. Having finished her morning's work, she had gone from room to room, inspecting the furniture that had come, and the glass and china in the hall. 'Isn't that really lovely!' she exclaimed again about the soup tureen.

It was cracked, Connie saw, a long crack in the lid. It used to be on the sideboard of the dining-room in the bungalow. She'd never much noticed it then, but in the hall it seemed obtrusive.

Melissa was pretty, tall and slender, with long fair hair and greenish eyes. She liked jokes, and was clever although she didn't want to be and often pretended she wasn't.

'Time to measure the maggot,' she said later that same day. Her contention was that her brother had ceased to grow and would grow no more. She and Connie regularly made him stand against the door jamb of Connie's bedroom in the hope of finding an increase in his modest stature.

But Connie shook her head when this was again suggested. She was reading *London Belongs to Me* and went on doing so. Nat, on his way upstairs already, for he enjoyed this ceremonial attention, looked disappointed.

'Poor little maggot,' Melissa said. 'Poor little maggot, Connie. You've gone and upset it.'

'You shouldn't call your brother a maggot.'

'Hey!' Outraged, Melissa stared disbelievingly at Connie's calm features. 'Hey, come on!'

Connie turned down the corner of a page and began to walk away.

'It's only a blooming word,' Melissa ran after her to protest. 'He doesn't mind.'

'This isn't your house,' Connie said.

*

The day Connie's mother came back from the hospice Miss Mortimer had pinned up pictures of flowers. Miss Mortimer painted her pictures herself; before the flowers there'd been clowns. 'Foxglove,' Connie had said when Miss Mortimer asked.

Going home on the river path, she'd been thinking of that, of the four new pictures on the schoolroom wall, of Miss Mortimer saying that soon there wouldn't be a cowslip left anywhere. The schoolroom stayed on in her mind nearly always when she was going home, the writing on the blackboard, the tattered carpet, the boards showing all around it, the table they sat at, Miss Mortimer too. The rectory itself stayed in her mind, the two flights of stairs, the white hall door, three steps, the gravel.

Her father didn't wave when she saw him coming towards her. It was drizzling and she thought that was maybe why he was coming to meet her. But often in winter it rained and he didn't; it was her mother who used to. 'Hullo, Connie,' he said, and she knew then that her mother had come back from the hospice, as she had said she would.

He took her hand, not telling her because she knew. She didn't cry. She wanted to ask in case it was different from what she guessed, but she didn't because she didn't want to hear if it was. 'It's all right,' her father said. He went with her to the room that had become her mother's, overlooking the garden. She touched her mother's hand and he lifted her up so that she could kiss her cheek, as often he'd done before. Mr Crozier was standing by the windows in the drawing-room when they went downstairs again. She hadn't known he was there. Then the O'Dalys came.

'You stay here with me,' Mrs O'Daly said in the kitchen. 'I'll hear you your reading.' But it wasn't reading on a Tuesday, another verse to learn instead, and six sentences to write. 'You going to write them then?' Mrs O'Daly asked. 'You going to think them up?'

She didn't want to. She learned the verse and said it to her father when he came to sit beside her, but the next day she didn't have to go to Miss Mortimer's. People came in the morning. She could hear their footsteps in the hall and on the stairs; she couldn't hear voices. It was in the afternoon that her mother died.

'That's not like Connie,' Robert said.

'No, it isn't.'

When Teresa had been told by her children what Connie had said to them she had guessed, with sudden, bitter intuition, that everything going well was over. And she had wondered where she and Robert had gone wrong. Robert was simply bewildered.

The wedding – to be conducted by Mr Crozier as a purely family occasion

– was less than three weeks off. No going away afterwards, no honeymoon because the time of year on the farm wasn't right for that.

'What else does Connie say?'

Teresa shook her head. She didn't know but suspected nothing else, and was right.

'We want to be married,' Robert said. 'Nothing's going to stop that now.'

Teresa hesitated, but only for a moment. 'Nothing is,' she said.

'Children manage to get on. Even when they're strangers to one another.'

Teresa didn't say that being strangers might make things easier. She didn't say it because she didn't know why that should be. But Melissa, who never wept, wept often now, affected as a stranger would not have been.

The books Connie pretended to read were in the dining-room bookcases, on either side of the fireplace. They'd been her mother's books, picked up at country-house auctions, some thrown away when the shelves became full, all of them old, belonging to another time. '*The Man with Red Hair*,' her mother said, 'you'll love that.' And *Dr Bradley Remembers*, and *Random Harvest*. Only *Jamaica Inn* retained its paper jacket, yellow, without a picture. 'And *The Stars Look Down*,' her mother had said. 'You'll love *The Stars Look Down*.'

Connie took it to the roof, to the lead-covered gully she had found, wide enough to lie on between two slopes of slates. Every time she went there she wished she didn't have to disobey her father and always took care not to spend too long there in case she was discovered. Sometimes she stood up, protected from sight by the bulk of a chimney and, far away, saw her father in the fields or Teresa among the geraniums. Sometimes Melissa and Nat were on the avenue, Nat on the carrier of Melissa's bicycle, his small legs spread wide so that they wouldn't catch in the spokes.

Teresa felt she had never loved Robert more; and felt that she was loved, herself, more steadfastly even than before – as if, she thought, the trouble brought such closeness. Or was there panic? she wondered in other moments; was it in panic that the depths of trust were tapped? Was it in panic that the widowed and the rejected protected what they'd been unable to protect before? She did not know the answers to her questions. It only seemed all wrong that a child's obduracy should mock what was so fairly due.

'Connie.'

Robert found her in the outhouse where the furniture was. She had folded aside a dust-sheet and was sitting in an armchair of which the springs had gone, which should have been thrown out years ago.

'Connie,' he interrupted her, for she had not heard him. Her book was *Folly Bridge*.

She marked her place with a finger. She smiled at him. No one considered that recently she'd turned sulky; there was no sign of that. Even when she'd told Melissa and Nat that the house was not theirs, she had apparently simply said it.

'You're troubled because Teresa and I are to be married, Connie.'

'I'm all right.'

'You didn't seem to mind before.'

The armchair had a high back with wings, its faded red velvet badly worn in places, an embroidery of flowers stitched into where an antimacassar might be.

'It's very good,' Connie said, speaking about the book she held.

'Yes.'

'Will you read it?'

'If you would like me to.'

Connie nodded. And they could talk about it, she said. If he read it they could talk about it.

'Yes, we could. You've always liked Teresa, Connie. You've always liked Melissa and Nat. It isn't easy for us to understand.'

'Couldn't it stay here, the furniture you don't want? Couldn't we keep it here?'

'Out here it's a bit damp for furniture.'

'Couldn't we put it back then?'

'Is that what's worrying you, Connie? The furniture?'

'When the books are thrown away I'll know what every single one of them was about.'

'But, for heaven's sake, the books won't be thrown away!'

'I think they will be, really.'

Robert went away. He didn't look for Teresa to tell her about the conversation. Every year at this time he erected a corral where his ewes paddled through a trough of disinfectant. They crowded it now, while he remembered his half-hearted protestations and Connie's unsatisfactory responses. 'Oh, come on, come on! Get on with it!' Impatient with his sheep, as he had not been with his daughter, he wondered if Connie hated him. He had felt she did, although nothing like it had showed, or had echoed in her voice.

From the roof she saw a car she'd never seen before, and guessed why it had come. In one of the drawers of the rickety Welsh dresser she'd found a shopping list and thought she remembered its being lost. *Ironing starch. Baking powder*, she'd read.

The car that had come was parked in the yard when she came down from the roof. A man was standing beside it. He referred to the furniture that was to be sold, as Connie had thought he might.

'Anyone around?' he asked her.

He was a big red-faced man in shirtsleeves. He'd thought he'd never find the house, he said. He asked her if he was expected, if this was the right place, and she wanted to say it wasn't, but Teresa came out of the house then.

'Go and get your father,' she said, and Connie nodded and went to where she'd seen him from the roof.

'Don't sell the furniture,' she begged instead of saying the man had come.

One night, when the wedding was five days away, Teresa drove over to the farm. About to go to bed, she knew she wouldn't be able to sleep and wrote a note for Melissa, saying where she was going. It was after half past one and if there hadn't been a sign of life at the farm she would have driven away again. But the lights were on in the big drawing-room and Robert heard the car. He'd been drinking, he confessed as he let Teresa in.

'I don't know how to make sense to her,' he said when they'd embraced. Without asking, he poured her some whiskey. 'I don't know what to do, Teresa.'

'I know you don't.'

'When she came to stand beside me while I was milking this afternoon, when she didn't say anything but I could hear her pleading, I thought she was possessed. But later on we talked as if none of all this was happening. She laid the table. We ate the trout I'd fried. We washed the plates up. Dear Teresa, I can't destroy the childhood that is left to her.'

'I think you're perhaps a little drunk.'

'Yes.'

He did not insist that there must be a way; and knowing what frightened him, Teresa knew there wasn't. She was frightened herself while she was with him now, while wordlessly they shared the horrors of his alarm. Was some act, too terrible for a child, waiting in the desolation of despair to become a child's? They did not speak of what imagination made of it, how it might be, nurtured in anger's pain, in desperation and betrayal, the ways it might become unbearable.

They walked on the avenue, close to one another in the refreshing air.

The sky was lightening, dawn an hour away. The shadows of danger went with them, too treacherous to make chances with.

'Our love still matters,' Teresa whispered. 'It always will.'

A calf had been born and safely delivered. It had exhausted him: Connie could tell her father was tired. And rain that had begun a week ago had hardly ceased, washing his winter seeding into a mire.

'Oh, it'll be all right,' he said.

He knew what she was thinking, and he watched her being careful with the plates that were warming in the oven, careful with the coffee she made, letting it sit a moment. Coffee at suppertime was what he'd always liked. She heated milk and poured it from the saucepan.

The bread was sawn, slices waiting on the board, butter beside them. There were tomatoes, the first of the Blenheims, the last of the tayberries. Pork steak browned on the pan.

It was not all bleakness: Robert was aware of that. In moments like the moments that were passing now, and often too at other times, he discerned in what had been his daughter's obduracy a spirit, still there, that was not malicious. In the kitchen that was so familiar to both of them, and outside in the raw cold of autumn when she came to him in the fields, she was as events had made her, the recipient of a duty she could not repudiate. It had seemed to her that an artificial household would demand that she should, and perhaps it might have.

Robert had come to understand that; Teresa confessed that nothing was as tidy as she'd imagined. There were no rights that cancelled other rights, less comfort than she'd thought for the rejected and the widowed, no fairness either. They had been hasty, she dared to say, although two years might seem a long enough delay. They had been clumsy and had not known it. They had been careless, yet were not careless people. They were a little to blame, but only that.

And Robert knew that time in passing would settle how the summer had been left. Time would gather up the ends, and see to it that his daughter's honouring of a memory was love that mattered also, and even mattered more.

Old Flame

Grace died.

As Zoë replaces the lid of the electric kettle – having steamed the envelope open – her eye is caught by that stark statement. As she unfolds the plain white writing-paper, another random remark registers before she begins to read from the beginning. *We never quarrelled not once that I remember.*

The spidery scrawl, that economy with punctuation, were once drooled over by her husband, and to this day are not received in any ordinary manner, as a newspaper bill is, or a rates demand. Because of the sexual passion there has been, the scrawl connects with Charles's own neat script, two parts of a conjunction in which letters have played an emotional part. Being given to promptness in such matters, Charles will at once compose a reply, considerate of an old flame's due. Zoë feared this correspondence once, and hated it. *As ever my love, Audrey*: in all the years of the relationship the final words have been the same.

As always, she'll have to reseal the envelope because the adhesive on the flap has lost its efficacy. Much easier all that is nowadays, with convenient sticks of Pritt or Uhu. Once, at the height of the affair, she'd got glue all over the letter itself.

Zoë, now seventy-four, is a small, slender woman, only a little bent. Her straight hair, once jet-black, is almost white. What she herself thinks of as a letterbox mouth caused her, earlier in her life, to be designated attractive rather than beautiful. 'Wild' she was called as a girl, and 'unpredictable', both terms relating to her temperament. No one has ever called her pretty, and no one would call her wild or unpredictable now.

Because it's early in the day she is still in her dressinggown, a pattern of tulips in black-and-scarlet silk. It hugs her slight body, crossed over on itself in front, tied with a matching sash. When her husband appears he'll still be in his dressing-gown also, comfortably woollen, teddybear brown stitched with braid. *Dearest, dearest Charles*, the letter begins. Zoë reads all of it again.

This letter is special, of course, because of Grace's death. Others have been different. *Grace and I wondered how you are getting along these days . . . Grace and I have finally taken retirement . . . I'm to give you this*

address Grace says. Just in case you ever want to write ... A seaside
house. Grace always wanted that ... In 1985, in 1978 and '73 and '69,
Grace always had a kind of say. *A quick lunch some time?* each letter –
this one too – suggests before the *As ever my love* and the single cross
that's a reminder of their kissing. Somehow, Zoë has always believed, the
quick-lunch suggestion came from Grace. Did she, she wonders, make it
again on her deathbed?

The affair has developed in Zoë an extra sense. Without making an
effort she can visualize a tall woman she has never met, now the lone
occupant of a house she has never entered. She sees her smartly dressed
in shades of maroon, iron-grey hair fashionably arranged, the clarity of
her eyes a little clouded. Creases have multiplied on the skin of her face
and are a map of wrinkles now. Zoë imagines her entering her kitchen
and turning on the radio, to hear the same news she herself heard earlier:
football fans on the rampage in a German city, shop windows smashed, a
bus turned on its side. She imagines her standing with a cup of Nescafé
in the bow-window of her sitting-room: seen through drizzle on a pane,
the sea is a pattern of undulations, greyish green, scuffed with white. The
sky that meets it on the far horizon is too dull to contemplate. A single
mackerel-trawler slips into view.

If it's inconvenient or if you'd rather not well of course I understand.

The Alp Horn is where they lunch, have done so since first they loved
one another. Her inquisitiveness getting the better of her, Zoë went there
once. She actually went inside, giving a name she had made up, of someone she was to meet there. A musical instrument, presumably an alp horn,
stretched the length of a wall; Tyrolean landscape decorated two others.
There were checked tablecloths, blue and red; recorded music played; the
place was modest. 'I'm awfully sorry,' Zoë said to a waiter, half a lifetime
ago it seems like because in fact it is. 'Clearly there's been a muddle.'

She finds the Pritt where Charles keeps it, in the middle drawer of the
dresser, with his writing things and sealing-wax, Sellotape and scissors.
She boils the water in the kettle again, for coffee. She hears his footstep
above her, crossing the landing from their bedroom to the lavatory, crossing it again to the bathroom. Pipes rattle when he turns on the hot water
because he has never learned not to turn the tap all the way in order to
prevent it gushing so. All the years she has known him he has been impatient about things like that.

'It's time you saw Charles again,' Zoë knows Grace used to say in that
house, and guesses Audrey's reply: that Charles has his own life now, that
Charles has made his choice. Grace always pressed, gently, because she
loved Charles, too, but had to keep it to herself. 'My dear, I'm certain

Charles would welcome a sign.' Anything could have happened: they'd never know.

Thirty-nine years have passed since the first year of the great passion. Audrey and Grace were friends already, making their way in office life, both of them determined to use their secretarial posts as stepping-stones to something better. The day Charles appeared – the first time they laid eyes on him – he was being led around by the snooty, half-drunk Miss Maybury, both of them with glasses of *vin rosé*, which was what La Maybury – her office title – drank every afternoon, sometimes in the mornings also. 'Hullo,' Charles said, a lanky young man with floppy fair hair. It wasn't difficult for Zoë to imagine the shy smile he'd darted at Audrey and then at Grace. Afterwards he'd told her about La Maybury and the wine and the tour round the office.

'Poor Charles' he had become in after years. Poor Charles alone with his unloved, unloving wife. What was the point of any of it, now that his children were grown-up? In their seaside house they lived in hope – that one day he would sound less whispery on the telephone, passing on details of death by misadventure or disease. 'Given six months, a merciful release.' Or: 'Just slipped. A wretched plastic bag. In the rain, near the dustbins.'

Zoë places two slices of bread in the toaster but does not press the lever down because it isn't time to yet. Before the affair got going it had been a subject of fascination to him that two such apparently close friends should, in appearance at least, be so vastly different. 'Oh, that's often so,' Zoë said, citing examples from her schooldays, but he had never shown much interest in her schooldays and he didn't then. 'Grace the lumpy one's called,' he said. 'Back of a bus. Audrey's the stunner.' Old-fashioned names, she had thought, and imagined old-fashioned girls, frumpish in spite of Audrey's looks. Later, he'd always included Grace in his references to Audrey, clouding the surface because of the depths beneath.

She measures coffee into a blue Denby pot, the last piece of a set. There was a photograph she found once: Audrey as handsome as he'd claimed, a goddess-like creature with a cigarette; Grace blurred, as if she'd moved. They were sprawled on a rug beside a tablecloth from which a picnic had been eaten. You could see part of the back wheel of a car, and it wasn't difficult to sharpen into focus Grace's frizzy hair, two pink-rimmed eyes behind her spectacles. Where on earth had that picnic been? What opportunity had been seized – a slack afternoon in the office?

Zoë props the letter against his cup, doing so with deliberation. It will vex him that she has arranged it so, the gesture attaching a comment of her own; but then she has been vexed herself. She tore that photograph into little pieces and watched them burn. He never mentioned its loss, as naturally he wouldn't.

'Ah, good,' she greets him, and watches while he picks the letter up. She depresses the lever of the toaster. The milk saucepan rattles on the gas, a glass disc bouncing about in it to prevent the milk from boiling over. She pours their coffee. He returns the letter to its envelope. She halves each piece of toast diagonally, the way he likes it.

She hadn't guessed. It was a frightening, numbing shock when he said: 'Look, I have to tell you, Audrey and I have fallen in love.' Just for a moment she couldn't think who Audrey was. 'Audrey and I,' he repeated, thinking she hadn't properly heard. 'Audrey and I love one another.' For what remained of that year and for several years following it, Zoë felt physically sick every time that statement echoed, coming back to her from its own Sunday morning: 10th September 1968, eleven o'clock. He had chosen the time because they'd have all day to go into things, yet apart from practicalities there was nothing to go into. They couldn't much go into the fact that he wanted someone else more than he wanted her. After five years of marriage he was tired of her. He had spoken in order to be rid of her.

Finishing with the marmalade, she moves it closer to him. His face, less expert at disguise than once it was, hides nothing. She watches him thinking about the woman who has been left on her own, his sympathy reaching into a seaside house that's now too spacious for one. But Charles is not an imaginative man. He doesn't penetrate far. He doesn't see in the old flame's fridge a chicken joint for one, and fish for one tomorrow. Winter's a melancholy time to be bereaved, a mood reflected in the cold and wet, winds rattling and whining. Audrey'll miss her friend particularly when it comes to watching television, no one beside her to share a comment with.

'Oh yes, the Alp Horn's still there,' Zoë hears a little later that morning, having eased open a door he has carefully closed. 'Twelve forty-five, should we say? If your train's a little late, anything like that, please don't worry. I'll simply wait, my dear.'

He'd been saying something she hadn't managed to hear before that, his voice unnaturally low, a hand cupped round the mouthpiece. Then there'd been the hint of a reprimand because the old flame hadn't written sooner. Had he known he'd have gone to the funeral.

'I'm sorry to have hurt you so,' he said later that Sunday, but words by then made no sense whatsoever. Five years of a mistake, she thought, two children mistakenly born. Her tears dripped on to her clothes while he stood there crestfallen, his good looks distorted by distress. She did not blow her nose; she wanted to look as she felt. 'You would like me dead,' she sobbed, willing him to raise his fist in fury at her, to crash it down on her, obliterating in mercy all that remained of her. But he only stood there, seeming suddenly ill-fed. Had she not cooked properly for him? her thoughts half crazily ran on. Had she not given him what was nourishing? 'I thought we were happy,' she whispered. 'I thought we didn't need to question anything.'

'Nice to see the old Alp Horn again,' his murmur comes from the hall, and Zoë can tell that he's endeavouring to be cheerful. 'Tell you what, I'll bring a packet of Three Castles.'

There is the click of the receiver, the brief sounding of the bell. He says something to himself, something like 'Poor thing!' Zoë softly closes the door. Grace and Audrey had probably been friends for fifty years, might even have been schoolfriends. Was Audrey the one whom other girls had pashes on? Was Grace a little bullied? Zoë imagines her hunched sulkily into a desk, and Audrey standing up for her. In letters and telephone conversations there have been references to friends, to holidays in Normandy and Brittany, to bridge, to Grace's colonic irrigation, to Audrey's wisdom teeth removed in hospital. Zoë knows – she doesn't often call it guessing – that after Audrey's return from every visit to the Alp Horn Grace was greedy for the morsels passed on to her. Not by the blink of an eye could Grace reveal her secret; the only expression of her passion was her constancy in urging another letter. *We think of you with her in that coldness.* 'Quite frail he looked,' Audrey no doubt reported in recent years.

He did not stay with Zoë in 1967 because of love. He stayed because – quite suddenly, and unexpectedly – the emotions all around him seemed to have become too much: it was weariness that caused him to back off. Had he sensed, Zoë wondered years later, the shadow of Grace without entirely knowing that that was what it was? He stayed, he said, because Zoë and the two children who had then been born meant more than he had estimated. Beneath this statement there was the implication that for the sake of his own happiness it wasn't fair to impose hardship on the innocent. That, though unspoken, had a bitter ring for Zoë. 'Oh, go away!' she cried. 'Go to that unpleasant woman.' But she did not insist; she did not say there was nothing left, that the damage had been done for ever. To the woman, he quoted his economic circumstances as the reason for thinking again. Supporting two households – which in those days was what the prospect looked like – was more than daunting. *Grace says you wouldn't have to leave them penniless. What she and I earn could easily make up for that. Grace would love to help us out.* Had he gone, Grace would somehow have been there too.

*

Zoë knows when the day arrives. Glancing across their breakfast coffee at her, his eyes have a dull sparkle that's caused by an attempt to rekindle an obsolete excitement: he was always one to make an effort. In a letter once Audrey referred to his 'loose-limbed charm', stating that she doubted she could live without it and be herself. He still has that lanky look, which perhaps was what she meant; what remains of his floppy fair hair, mainly at the back and sides of his head, is ash-coloured now; his hands – which Zoë can well imagine either Grace or Audrey designating his most elegant feature – have a shrivelled look, the bones more pronounced than once they were, splotches of freckles on skin like old paper. His face is beakier than it was, the teeth for the most part false, his eyes given to watering when a room is warm. Two spots of pink come and go high up on his narrow cheeks, where the structure of the cheekbones tautens the skin. Otherwise, his face is pale.

'I have to go in today,' he casually announces.

'Not here for lunch?'

'I'll pick up a sandwich somewhere.'

She would like to be able to suggest he'd be wiser to go to a more expensive restaurant than the Alp Horn. Cheap food and house wine are a deadly combination at his time of life. A dreadful nuisance it is when his stomach goes wrong.

'Bit of shopping to do,' he says.

Once there was old so-and-so to meet but that doesn't work any more because, with age, such figures can't be counted upon not to give the game away. There was 'the man at Lloyd's' to see, or Hanson and Phillips, who were arranging an annuity. All that has been tapped too often: what's left is the feebleness of shopping. Before his retirement there was no need to mention anything at all.

'Shopping,' she says without an interrogative note. 'Shopping.'

'One or two things.'

Three Castles cigarettes are difficult to find. Audrey will smoke nothing else and it's half a joke that he goes in search of them, a fragment of affection in the kaleidoscope of the love affair. Another such fragment is their shared delight in sweetbreads, a food Zoë finds repellent. They share unpunctuality also. *Grace can't understand how we ever manage to meet!*

'Should keep fine,' he predicts.

'Take your umbrella all the same.'

'Yes, I'll take my umbrella.'

He asks about a particular shirt, his blue striped one. He wonders if it has been ironed. She tells him where it is. Their three children – the boys, and Cecilia, born later, all married now – know nothing about Audrey.

Sometimes it seems odd to Zoë that this should be so, that a person who has featured so profoundly in their father's life should be unknown to them. If that person had had her way Cecilia would not have been born at all.

'Anything you need?' he offers. 'Anything I can get you?'

She shakes her head. She wishes she could say: 'I open her letters. I listen when there's a phone conversation.' She wishes he could tell her that Grace has died, that his friend is now alone.

'Back about four, I expect?'

'Something like that.'

Had he gone off, she wouldn't still be in this house. She wouldn't be sitting in this kitchen in her black-and-scarlet dressing-gown, eyeing him in his woolly brown one. She'd be living with one of the children or in a flat somewhere. Years ago the house would have been sold; she'd not have grown old with a companion. It was most unlikely there would ever have been another man; she doubted she'd have wanted one.

'I dreamed we were on a ferry going to Denmark,' he unexpectedly says. 'There was a woman you got talking to, all in black.'

'Prettily in black?'

'Oh, yes. A pretty woman too. She used an odd expression. She said she was determined to have what she called a "corking child".'

'Ah.'

'You sat me down in front of her and made me comment on her dress. You made me make suggestions.'

'And did you, Charles?'

'I did. I suggested shades of green. Deep greens; not olive like my trousers. And rounded collar-ends on her shirt, not pointed like mine. I made her look at mine. She was a nice woman except that she said something a little rude about my shoes.'

'Scuffed?'

'Something like that.'

'Your shoes are never scuffed.'

'No.'

'Well, there you are.'

He nods. 'Yes, there you are.'

Soon after that he rises and goes upstairs again. Why did that conversation about a dream take place? It's true that just occasionally they tell one another their dreams; just occasionally, they have always done so. But significance appears to attach to the fact that he shared his with her this morning: that is a feeling she has.

'Why did you bother with me if I didn't matter?' Long after he'd decided to stay with her she asked him that. Long afterwards she questioned everything; she tore at the love that had united them in the first place; it was her right that he should listen to her. Six years went by before their daughter was born.

'Well, I'm off.'

Like a tall, thin child he looks, his eyes deep in their sockets, his dark, conventional suit well pressed, a Paisley tie in swirls of blue that matches the striped blue shirt. His brown shoes, the pair he keeps for special occasions, gleam as they did not in his eccentric dream.

'If I'd known I'd have come with you.' Zoë can't help saying that; she doesn't intend to, the words come out. But they don't alarm him, as once they would have. Once, a shadow of terror would have passed through his features, apprehension spreading lest she rush upstairs to put her coat on.

'We'll go in together next time,' he promises.

'Yes, that'll be nice.'

They kiss, as they always do when they part. The hall door bangs behind him. She'll open a tin of salmon for lunch and have it with tomatoes and a packet of crisps. A whole tin will be too much, of course, but between them they'll probably be able for whatever's left this evening.

In the sitting-room she turns the television on. Celeste Holm, lavishly fur-coated, is in a car, cross about something. Zoë doesn't want to watch and turns it off again. She imagines the old flame excited as the train approaches London. An hour ago the old flame made her face up, but now she does it all over again, difficult with the movement of the train. Audrey doesn't know that love came back into the marriage, that skin grew over the wound. She doesn't know, because no one told her, because he cannot bring himself to say that the brief occasion was an aberration. He honours – because he's made like that – whatever it is the affair still means to the woman whose life it has disrupted. He doesn't know that Audrey – in receipt of all that was on offer – would have recovered from the drama in a natural way if Grace – in receipt of nothing at all – hadn't been an influence. He doesn't wonder what will happen now, since death has altered the pattern of loose ends.

Opening the salmon tin, Zoë travels again to the Alp Horn rendezvous. She wonders if it has changed and considers it unlikely. The long horn still stretches over a single wall. The same Tyrolean landscape decorates two others. There are the blue-and-red tablecloths. He waits with a glass of sherry, and then she's there.

'My dear!'

She is the first to issue their familiar greeting, catching him unaware the way things sometimes do these days.

'My dear!' he says in turn.

Sherry is ordered for her, too, and when it comes the rims of their glasses touch for a moment, a toast to the past.

'Grace,' he says. 'I'm sorry.'

'Yes.'

'Is it awful?'

'I manage.'

The waiter briskly notes their order and enquires about the wine.

'Oh, the good old house red.'

Zoë's fingers, gripping and slicing a tomato, are arthritic, painful sometimes though not at present. In bed at night he's gentle when he reaches out for one hand or the other, cautious with affection, not tightening his grasp as once he did. Her fingers are ugly; she sometimes thinks she looks quite like a monkey now. She arranges the fish and the tomato on a plate and sprinkles pepper over both. Neither of them ever has salt.

'And you, Charles?'

'I'm all right.'

'I worry about you sometimes.'

'No, I'm all right.'

It was accordion music that was playing in the Alp Horn the day Zoë's inquisitiveness drove her into it. Young office people occupied the tables. Business was quite brisk.

'I do appreciate this,' Audrey says. 'When something's over, all these years – I do appreciate it, Charles.'

He passes across the table the packet of Three Castles cigarettes, and she smiles, placing it beside her because it's too soon yet to open it.

'You're fun, Charles.'

'I think La Maybury married, you know. I think someone told me that.'

'Grace could never stand her.'

'No.'

Is this the end? Zoë wonders. Is this the final fling, the final call on his integrity and honour? Can his guilt slip back into whatever recesses there are, safe at last from Grace's second-hand desire? No one told him that keeping faith could be as cruel as confessing faithlessness; only Grace might have appropriately done that, falsely playing a best friend's role. But it wasn't in Grace's interest to do so.

'Perhaps I'll sell the house.'

'I rather think you should.'

'Grace did suggest it once.'

Leaving them to it, Zoé eats her salmon and tomato. She watches the end of the old black-and-white film: years ago they saw it together, long before Grace and Audrey. They've seen it together since; as a boy he'd been in love with Bette Davis. Picking at the food she has prepared, Zoë is again amused by what has amused her before. But only part of her attention is absorbed. Conversations take place; she does not hear; what she sees are fingers undistorted by arthritis loosening the cellophane on the cigarette packet and twisting it into a butterfly. He orders coffee. The scent that came back on his clothes was lemony with a trace of lilac. In a letter there was a mention of the cellophane twisted into a butterfly.

'Well, there we are,' he says. 'It's been lovely to see you, Audrey.'

'Lovely for me too.'

When he has paid the bill they sit for just a moment longer. Then, in the ladies', she powders away the shine that heat and wine have induced, and tidies her tidy grey hair. The lemony scent refreshes, for a moment, the stale air of the cloakroom.

'Well, there we are, my dear,' he says again on the street. Has there ever, Zoë wonders, been snappishness between them? Is she the kind not to lose her temper, long-suffering and patient as well as being a favourite girl at school? After all, she never quarrelled with her friend.

'Yes, there we are, Charles.' She takes his arm. 'All this means the world to me, you know.'

They walk to the corner, looking for a taxi. Marriage is full of quarrels, Zoë reflects.

'Being upright never helps. You just lie there. Drink lots of water, Charles.'

The jug of water, filled before she'd slipped in beside him last night, is on his bedside table, one glass poured out. Once, though quite a while ago now, he not only insisted on getting up when he had a stomach upset but actually worked in the garden. All day she'd watched him, filling his incinerator with leaves and weeding the rockery. Several times she'd rapped on the kitchen window, but he'd taken no notice. As a result he was laid up for a fortnight.

'I'm sorry to be a nuisance,' he says.

She smoothes the bedclothes on her side of the bed, giving the bed up to him, making it pleasant for him in the hope that he'll remain in it. The newspaper is there for him when he feels like it. So is *Little Dorrit*, which he always reads when he's unwell.

'Perhaps consommé later on,' she says. 'And a cream cracker.'

'You're very good to me.'

'Oh, now.'

Downstairs Zoë lights the gas-fire in the sitting-room and looks to see if there's a morning film. *Barefoot in the Park* it is, about to begin. Quite suddenly then, without warning, she sees how the loose ends are. Everything is different, but nothing of course will ever be said. *So good the little restaurant's still there*, the old flame writes. *Just a line to thank you.* So good it was to talk. So good to see him. So good of him to remember the Three Castles. Yet none of it is any good at all because Grace is not there to say, 'Now tell me every single thing.' Not there to say when there's a nagging doubt, 'My dear, what perfect nonsense!' On her own in the seaside house she'll not find an excuse again to suggest a quick lunch if he'd like to. He'll not do so himself, since he never has. He'll gladly feel his duty done at last.

The old flame bores him now, with her scent and her cigarettes and her cellophane butterflies. In her seaside house she knows her thank-you letter is the last, and the sea is grey and again it rains. One day, on her own, she'll guess her friend was false. One day she'll guess a sense of honour kept pretence alive.

Grace died. That's all that happened, Zoë tells herself, so why should she forgive? 'Why should I?' she murmurs. 'Why should I?' Yet for a moment before she turns on *Barefoot in the Park* tears sting her eyelids. A trick of old age, she tells herself, and orders them away.

Faith

She was a difficult woman, had been a wilful child, a moody, recalcitrant girl given to flashes of temper; severity and suspicion came later. People didn't always know what they were doing, Hester liked to point out, readily speaking her mind, which she did most often to her brother, Bartholomew. She was forty-two now, he three years younger. She hadn't married, had never wanted to.

There was a history here: of Hester's influence while the two grew up together in crowded accommodation above a breadshop in a respectable Dublin neighbourhood. Their father was a clerk in Yarruth's timber yards, their mother took in sewing and crocheting. They were poor Protestants, modest behind trim net curtains in Maunder Street, pride taken in their religion, in being themselves. Her bounden duty, Hester called it, looking after Bartholomew.

When the time came, Bartholomew didn't marry either. An intense, serious young man, newly ordained into the Church of Ireland, he loved Sally Carbery and was accepted when he proposed. Necessarily a lengthy one, the engagement weathered the delay, but on the eve of the wedding it fell apart, which was a disappointment Bartholomew did not recover from. Sally Carbery – spirited and humorous, a source of strength during their friendship, beautiful in her way – married a man in Jacob's Biscuits.

Hester worked for the Gas Board, and gave that up to look after her father when he became a widower, suffering from Parkinson's disease for the last nine years of his life. That was her way; it was her nature, people said, compensation for her brusque manner; her sacrifice was applauded. 'We've always got on,' Hester said on the evening of their father's funeral. 'You and I have, Bartholomew.'

He didn't disagree, but knew that there was something missing in how his sister put this. They got on because, dutiful in turn, he saw to it that they did. Bartholomew's delicate good looks – fair hair, blue eyes – made the most of a family likeness that was less pleasing in Hester, his lithe ranginess cumbersome in a woman. All in all, it seemed only right that there should be adjustment, that any efforts made in the question of getting on should be his, and without acknowledgement.

Bartholomew didn't have a parish of his own. He assisted in one on the north side of the city, where Maunder Street was too: visiting the elderly, concerned with Youth Reach and Youth Action and the running of the Youth Centre, on Saturdays taking parties of children to ramble in the Dublin mountains or to swim in one of the northside's swimming-pools. He and Hester shared the family possessions when it was clearly no longer practical to retain the rented accommodation above the breadshop; Bartholomew found a room in the parish where he worked; Hester looked about for one. She made enquiries at the Gas Board about returning to a position similar to the one she had filled in the past, but for the moment there was nothing. Then she discovered Oscarey.

It was a townland in the Wicklow mountains, remote and bleak, once distinguished by the thriving presence of Oscarey House, of which no trace now remained. But the church that late in the house's existence had been built on the back avenue, for the convenience of the family and its followers, was still standing; and the estate's scattering of dwellings – the houndsman's and its yard and kennels, the gamekeeper's, the estate agent's pebble-dashed house – had undergone renovation and were all occupied. There was a Spar foodstore at Oscarey crossroads, an Esso petrol pump; letters could be posted a few miles away.

Bartholomew drove his sister to Oscarey when she asked him to. They went on a Monday, which was his free day, leaving early in the morning to avoid the Dublin traffic. He didn't know the purpose of their journey, hadn't yet been told, but Hester quite often didn't reveal her intentions, and he knew that eventually she would. It didn't occur to him to make the connection he might have.

'There's a man called Flewett,' Hester said in the car, reading the name from her own handwriting on a scrap of paper. 'He'll tell us.'

'What, though, Hester?'

She said then – a little, not much, not everything. The small church at Oscarey that had served a purpose in the past was being talked about again. A deprived Church of Ireland community, among it the descendants of indoor servants, gardeners and estate workers, was without a convenient means of worship. A consecrated building was mouldering through disuse.

They drove through Blessington, Bartholomew's very old A-30 van – used mainly for his Saturday trips to the mountains – making a tinny sound he hadn't noticed before. He didn't mention it but went on, hoping it was nothing much.

'It came to me,' Hester said.

'Who's Flewett, though?'

'One of the people around.'

She didn't say how she had heard about this man or offer further information about him.

'We'll see what Mr Flewett has to say,' she said.

Conversation with Hester was often like that; Bartholomew was used to it. Details withheld or frugally proffered made the most of what was imparted, as if to imbue communication with greater interest. Strangers sometimes assumed this to be so, only to realize a little later that Hester was not in the least concerned with such pandering: it was simply a quirk – without a purpose – that caused her to complicate conversation in this manner. She didn't know where it came from and did not ever wonder.

'What d'you think?' Bartholomew asked the man at the garage where he stopped for petrol, and the man said the tinny noise could be anything.

'Would you rev the engine for me?' he suggested, opening the bonnet when he'd finished at the petrol pump. 'Give her the full throttle, sir,' he instructed, and then, 'D'you know what I'm going to tell you, sir? The old carburettor in this one's a bit shook. Ease her down now, sir, till we'll take a look.'

Bartholomew did so, then turned the engine off. As he understood it, the carburettor had loosened on its fixing. Adjusting a monkey wrench, the man said it would take two seconds to put right, and when it was done he wouldn't charge for it, although Bartholomew pressed him to.

'There was a line or two about Oscarey in the *Gazette*,' Hester said as they drove off again, referring to the magazine that was a source of Church of Ireland news. 'They're managing with a recorded service.'

It was as it always had been, she was thinking, Bartholomew offering the man money when it hadn't been asked for. The soft touch of the family, their father had called him, and used that same expression, laughing a bit, when Bartholomew first wanted to become a clergyman. But even so he hadn't been displeased; nor had their mother, nor Hester herself. Bartholomew's vocation suited him; it completed him, and protected him, as Hester tried to do in other ways.

'Lucky I called in there,' he was saying, and Hester sensed that he had guessed by now why they were driving to Oscarey. He had put it all together, which was why he referred again to the stop at the garage, for often he didn't want to talk about what had to be talked about, hoping that whatever it was would go away of its own accord. But this was something that shouldn't be allowed to go away, no matter how awkward and difficult it was.

'Good of him to want to help,' he said, and Hester watched a flight of rooks swirling out of a tree as they passed it.

'It's interesting, how things are,' she said. 'At Oscarey.'

It was still early when they arrived there, ten to eleven when Bartholomew drew up outside the Spar shop at the crossroads. 'A Mr Flewett?' he enquired at the single check-out, and was given directions.

He left the main road, drove slowly in a maze of lanes. Here and there there was a signpost. They found the church almost immediately after they turned into what had been the back avenue of Oscarey House, grown over now. There were graves but hardly what could be called a churchyard, no more than a narrow strip of land beside a path close to the church itself, running all the way round it. One of the graves, without a headstone, was more recent than the others. The church was tiny, built of dark, almost black stone that gave it a forbidding air.

'A chapel of ease it might have been,' Bartholomew said.

'Mr Flewett'll know all about that.'

Inside, the church was musty, though with signs of use. The vases on the altar were empty, but there were hymn numbers – 8, 196, 516 – on the hymn board. The brass of the lectern was tarnished, and the brass of the memorial plates; the altarcloth was tattered and dingy. The slightly tinted glass of the windows – a bluish grey – did not have biblical scenes. You couldn't call it much of a church, Bartholomew considered, but didn't say.

'It could be lovely,' his sister said.

Mr Flewett was elderly, which Hester had predicted he would be. He was on his own these days, he said, bringing tea on a tray, with biscuits in a tin. He had been welcoming at the hall door, although he had examined his visitors closely before he invited them into his house.

'We have the recording of the service, of course,' he said. 'I'm in charge of that myself. Morning prayer only.'

Oscarey Church was one of several in a combined benefice, the most distant being seventeen miles away. 'Too far for Canon Furney and there are a few who can't take to the recording so they make the journey to the canon at Clonbyre or Nead. On the other hand, of course, there's Mrs Wharton's kindness.'

That took some time to explain. The small scattered community of Oscarey was a mixture now of poor and better-off: besides the remnants of the estate families, there were newcomers. Mrs Wharton – no longer alive – had been one of the latter. Her will left her house and a considerable legacy to Oscarey Church, this money to provide a stipend for a suitable incumbent, the house to become Oscarey Rectory.

'That's what this is about,' Mr Flewett went on, pouring more tea.

Hester nodded. 'I heard something like it,' she said. 'That perhaps a younger man . . .'

'Indeed.'

Bartholomew felt uneasy. Hester often became carried away. In the sad, grimy little church he had understood how her imagination had been excited and still was; but the poverty of the place had a finality about it; even the attempts to disguise its neglect had. There was no obvious way in which the impossible could be reversed.

'The Church of Ireland moves slowly,' Mr Flewett said. 'I think we can agree about that. And of course Mrs Wharton died only five months ago. But time eats away at good intentions. Her wishes must be honoured. She is buried in our little graveyard.'

'I think we might have noticed,' Bartholomew said.

'Canon Furney is seventy-one. He'll not retire and there's no reason why he should. He's a good, dear man and no one would want him to. What we fear, though, is that when he goes, Clonbyre and Nead will be taken in with Oscarey again and Oscarey possibly abandoned, so far away we are. But Mrs Wharton's house would be a better rectory than the one there is now at Clonbyre, and her generosity otherwise is what the benefice is crying out for.'

'You've been very kind, Mr Flewett,' Bartholomew said. 'It's been interesting. But we've taken up your time and we mustn't do that.'

'Indeed you haven't. No, not at all.'

'I hope it all works out for you.'

'All of us at Oscarey hope that.'

Bartholomew stood up. He held out his hand, and then Mr Flewett shook Hester's hand too.

'I meant it in my letter,' he said. 'Come any time. I'm always here. People will be pleased you came.'

Hester nodded. She had a way sometimes of not smiling and she didn't now. But she nodded again as if to make up for that.

In the car Bartholomew said: 'What letter?'

Hester didn't answer. Preoccupied, she stared ahead. It was February, too soon for spring, but fine.

'Did you write to him, Hester?'

'The little piece in the *Gazette* was about that woman leaving money and the house. It gave his name.'

Bartholomew said nothing. His sister did things for the best: he'd always known that. It sometimes didn't seem so, but he knew it was.

'Will we have another look at the church?' she said.

He drew in when they came to it. The hump of earth they'd noticed, the newest of the graves, was just beginning to green over and had been tended, the grass clipped in a rectangle round it.

'I hope they know what they're doing,' Hester said, pushing open the heavy west door. 'I'd keep it locked myself.'

The missionary leaflets by the collection box were smeared and dog-eared, and Bartholomew noticed now that there was bird-lime on curtains that were there instead of a door to the vestry.

'I'd get rid of that coconut matting,' Hester said.

They didn't stop on the way back to Dublin. Hester was quiet, as often she was, not saying anything until they were in Maunder Street. 'I have eggs I could scramble,' she said then, and Bartholomew followed her through the empty rooms.

'How long have you left here?' he asked, and his sister said until the end of next week. There'd been a place near Fairview Park and he asked about it. No good, she said, Drumcondra the same.

'I'm sorry you're having difficulties. I've kept an eye out.'

'The Gas Board'll have me back. Someone they weren't expecting to left.'

'Well, there's that at least.'

Hester was not enthusiastic. She didn't say, but Bartholomew knew. In the denuded kitchen he watched while she broke the yolks of the eggs with a fork, beating them up, adding milk and butter, then sprinkling on pepper. Since their childhood he had resented, without saying it, her interference, her indignation on his behalf, her possessiveness. He had forgiven what she couldn't help, doing so as natural in him as scorn and prickliness were in her. She had never noticed, had never been aware of how he felt.

'You'd take to Oscarey,' Hester said.

Before Bartholomew and his sister made their lives at Oscarey, there was an inevitability about the course of events. In private, Bartholomew did not think about what was happening in terms of Hester, considering rather that this was what had been ordained for him, that Hester's ordering of the circumstances was part of that. Fifteen years ago, when Sally Carbery had decided against marriage at the last minute it was because she feared Hester. She had been vague when suddenly she was doubtful, and was less truthful than she might have been. Unaware of that at the time, Bartholomew was bewildered; later he came to believe that in influencing Sally Carbery's second thoughts Hester had, then too, been assigned a role in the pattern conceived by a greater wisdom. 'Silly', Hester's word for Sally Carbery had been, even before Sally Carbery and Bartholomew loved one another.

The Church approved the rescuing of Oscarey; and it was anticipated, as Mr Flewett had surmised, that when old Canon Furney died the benefice of Clonbyre, Nead and Oscarey would become one again, that the unnecessarily spacious, draughty rectory in poor repair at Clonbyre would be abandoned in favour of a smaller, more comfortable one at Oscarey. This came about, and the manner in which human existence – seeming to be shaped by the vagaries of time and chance but in fact obedient to a will – became the subject of more than one of Bartholomew's sermons. Verses of the scriptures were called upon to lend credence to his conclusions, which more than anything else claimed that the mysterious would never be less than mysterious, would always be there, at the heart of spiritual life. That the physical presence of things, and of words and people, amounted to very little made perfect sense to Bartholomew.

It did to Hester too. Belief was part of Hester, taken for granted, a sturdy certainty that brought her confidence and allowed her to insist she must be taken as she was, allowed her to condemn as a dishonesty any concealment of personal traits. When her brother's fourteen parishioners at Oscarey, and the twenty-seven at Clonbyre and the eleven at Nead, came to know her there was agreement – as elsewhere there had often been before – that she and Bartholomew were far from alike. None among the parishioners feared Hester as Sally Carbery had, since none possessed a fiancée's intuition, only strangers' perspicacity. Sally Carbery's fear – to do with the prospect of the future, of being more closely involved with Hester – was understandable. At Oscarey, and Clonbyre and Nead, there was only Hester as she was, a talking-point because of it.

As the two aged, the understanding between them that had survived the cramped conditions of Maunder Street was supported by reminiscence – the smell of fresh bread every early morning, the unexpected death of their mother, their father's mercilessly slow, the two cremations at Glasnevin. Seaside photographs taken at Rush and Bettystown were in an album, visits to both grandmothers and to aunts were remembered; and hearing other generations talked about were. The present was kept a little at bay: that congregations everywhere continued to dwindle, that no ground had been regained by the Church or seemed likely to be, was not often mentioned. Hester was indifferent to this. Bartholomew was increasingly a prey to melancholy, but did not let it show, to Hester or to anyone.

For her part, Hester had given herself the task of restoring Oscarey Church, scraping the tiled floor, washing the altarcloths, polishing the neglected pews and brass. The church was hers, she considered, for she had found it and brought life to it, making more of it than a mere outward

and visible sign. It was not her way to say that all was well, that because of
her work everything was good: there was a presumption in that she didn't
care for, and such sentiments cloyed. But as she knelt before her brother at
the altar-rails, while he raised the cup or again wiped clean its rim, she
knew that all this was meant to be: he was here, where he should be, and
so should she, where her unyielding spirit had brought them. 'The peace
of God,' he ended each occasion of worship, and gave his blessing. The
words were special. And her brother saying them in the hush while Hester
still knelt among the few who came to Oscarey Church, before the shuffling and the whispering began, was special too.

Except at weddings and the christenings that sometimes followed them
there were no young among the congregations of the three churches, and
with nostalgia Bartholomew now and again remembered Youth Reach
and Youth Action and the Saturday rambles to Kilmashogue and Two
Rock. On Sundays when he looked down from the pulpit at aged faces, at
tired eyes, heads turned to hear him better, and when his hand was afterwards shaken at the door, he sensed the hope that had flickered into life
during the service: in all that was promised, in psalm and gospel, in his
own interpretations, the end was not an end.

Then – as it happened, on a Sunday night – Bartholomew, with cruel
suddenness, was aware of a realization that made him feel as if he had
been struck a blow so powerful it left him, though not in pain, without
the normality of his faculties. This happened in his bedroom before he
had begun to undress. The bedside light was on; he had closed the door,
pulled down the two blinds, and was standing beside his bed, having just
untied the laces of his shoes. For a moment he thought he had fallen
down, but he had not. He thought he could not see, but he could see. A
shoe was in one hand, which brought something of reality back, and sitting down on the edge of the bed did too. The clatter of the shoe on the
linoleum when it slipped from his grasp brought more. Sensations of
confusion lingered while he sat there, then were gone.

'*Thy Kingdom come, Thy will be done on earth, As it is in heaven . . .*'

His own voice made no sense, and yet went on.

Afterwards, Bartholomew told himself that what had occurred must
surely be no more than a mood of petulance, an eruption from his half-
stifled impatience with the embroidery and frills that dressed the simplicity of truth with invasive, sentimental stories that somehow made faith
easier, the hymns he hated. For Bartholomew, the mystery that was the
source of all spiritual belief, present through catastrophe and plague and
evil, was a strength now too, and more than it had ever been. Yet there was

disquiet, a stirring in his vocation he had brought upon himself and wished he had not. Seeking guidance, he dwelt on his memories of the euphoria he had been aware of when his profession had first seemed to be chosen for him. There were no reservations then, and he searched for what it was, in himself, that had allowed his unquestioning credence. But no help came from that far-off time, and Bartholomew – not knowing what he should otherwise do – continued to visit the lonely and the sick, to repeat the *Te Deum*, the Creed, the Litany. He felt he should not and yet he did.

Hester noticed no change in her brother, and he had told her nothing. Her own fulfilment, through him, continued, her belief undiminished, her certainties unchallenged. In her daily life all she distrusted she still distrusted. Her eye was cold, her scorn a nourishment; and then, for Hester too when more time passed, there was adversity. She did not complain. 'Oh, we all must die,' she said when she learned that she was to herself, sooner than she had ever expected. A doctor whom she had hardly bothered since coming to Oscarey confirmed his first suspicions, gently taking from her the small hope he had permitted to remain since her previous visit. He told her what she had to know, and she said nothing. Afterwards, alone, she did not weep; nor did she prepare her brother for what awaited both of them. But one morning, when the remains of spring and all of summer had gone, when they were sitting in warm September sunshine in their small garden, she told him. Hester was not yet sixty then.

Bartholomew listened with incredulous dismay. Yet Hester spoke so fearlessly, accepting as her due a simple fact, that a display of emotion on his part seemed out of place. Her tone was casual, her clasped hands still, her eyes unflinching. She did not ask for pity, she never had. The next remark she made was about their Indian summer.

'I'm sorry,' Bartholomew said.

He didn't know her: that thought came, which never had before. Her severity, the outspokenness that was natural to her, told too little. She had saved him from Sally Carbery, she would have said, believing that was the honest way to put it. He'd known in childhood that she wasn't liked. He had tried to make it up to her, and was glad now that he had.

But shadowing these reflections, and belittling them, was what Hester bore so stoically. It stalked the past, and was in charge of all the time that now was left. And yet, for Bartholomew, his own trouble was the greater agony; he could not help it that this was so and in a familiar manner guilt began. That day he did more in the house, taking on his sister's tasks.

*

'What courage you have!' Bartholomew said when autumn had passed, and winter too.

Hester shook her head. Courage came with misfortune; she took no credit for it. She asked for primroses and watched while Bartholomew picked them from the bank where they grew. That night they were on her bedside table, in a glass there'd been at Maunder Street.

'Why did they give me that awful name?' she asked when Bartholomew came to her later, to say goodnight. The name had come from somewhere outside the family; she wondered where. When Bartholomew was born they said it was the day the Huguenots had been slaughtered in France.

'I've brought you Ovaltine,' he said.

It made her sleep, or was supposed to, but when he came with tea in the mornings he didn't ask if she had lain awake. The nights were long. He brought the tea as early as he could.

On Sundays she could no longer manage the journey to church; but messages came from the Oscarey parishioners, prayers were said for her. 'O, Lord,' she imagined Bartholomew pleading on her behalf, 'look down from heaven, and relieve Thy servant . . . Look down upon her with the eyes of Thy mercy . . . give her comfort and sure confidence in Thee . . .'

This was the form she preferred; and she knew as she lay in her bed in the stillness of the rectory that these were the words said.

Bartholomew wondered if, afterwards, he would want to go away; if, without her, his own misfortune would be a desolation he could not bear. Back to the northside, he thought, which he knew better than the rest of Dublin. There would be employment of some kind; of any kind, he didn't much mind what, provided only that he was capable of whatever it was. He wondered about helping in one of the shops or a bed-and-breakfast house. Middleaged now, the youths he had worked among might be able at least to find him something, if not to employ him. And yet it seemed ridiculous that he should even consider such a dramatic move. He knew he would remain, and be silent.

'How tidy it is!' Hester murmured. 'Living for your while, then not being there any more. How well arranged!'

There was contentment in how she put it, and in her tone. Bartholomew sensed that and, concerned with her again, rather than with himself, he was pleased. His deception of her and of his scanty congregations would one day assault his conscience, would one day make continuing impossible, but at least she would not have to know.

*

When the time came, Hester knew that she would die that night.

Bartholomew was with her. There was no sentiment, she didn't speak, and Bartholomew sensed that there suddenly was only pain. God's will, he knew, was what she repeated to herself, as she had since she'd realized her illness was a visitation that would only end as it was ending now. The intensity of her faith, the sureness of her trust, was unaffected by the pain she suffered, and he prayed that she would close her eyes and die. Yet she did not, and Bartholomew telephoned to request that more morphine should be brought.

'No, I can manage,' she whispered, hearing this plea, although he had made it in another room. No doctor was available; a message had had to be left. 'Soon,' Hester said, her voice just audible, no more. 'It will be soon.' She asked for Communion then.

Outside, a frost had stayed all that day and, icing over now, still whitened the small garden, the patch of grass, the fields beyond. Bartholomew stood by the window, watching another dusk becoming dark, wishing there was not now, unknown to her, a gulf between them. Her courage was her belief, a dignity in her need, her eternal life already lit, its stately angels waiting to take her to the mansions of their paradise, and choral voices singing.

When Bartholomew returned to the bedside she was quiet. Then she spoke incomprehensibly. She winced, her closed eyes tightening, her head jerking on the pillow; and he went again to the telephone. 'Please,' he begged. 'Please.' But there was still a message. He said a little more, whispering now, the desperation in his voice concealed. Outside, a blackbird, tame in the garden, scratched at the frost.

'Hester,' he said, again beside her, and there was no response; he had not expected one. She would die and still be here and nowhere else: in his dissent he could not escape that. 'There will be nothing,' he might have said, and wanted to share with her his anguish, as she shared the ordeal of death with him.

'Hester,' he murmured.

She turned away, shuddering off a convulsion as best she could, but another came and she was restless. Confused, she tried to sit up and he eased her back to the pillows. For a moment then her eyes were clear, her contorted features loosened and were calm. Bartholomew knew that pain was taken from her and that she shed, in this first moment of her eternity, her too-long, gnawing discontent; that peace, elusive for a lifetime, had come at last.

He reached out for her hand and felt it warm in his. 'Thank you,' he thought she said, but knew she had not. He gazed for a little longer at the dead features before he drew the sheet up.

He made the telephone calls that were necessary, cancelling the message that requested morphine, informing an undertaker. He tidied the room, clearing away medicine, a cup and saucer.

He sat downstairs, close to the fire, for it was colder now. He remembered days there had been, and Maunder Street, the games they played in the backyard, the afternoon Hester took him into the Botanic Gardens, another time to see a band going by in the streets.

Bartholomew watched the fire become embers, not taking anything to eat, disturbed by no one. That night he slept fitfully and woke often, his sister's death entangled in his dreams with his own deprivation. He woke often, and soon after dawn he went to Hester's room.

When he drew down the sheet the moment of calm was still caught in her features. He stayed with her, the mercy of her tranquillity seeming to be a miracle that was real, as it had been in the instant of death. Heaven enough, and more than angels.

Folie à Deux

Aware of a presence close to him, Wilby glances up from the book he has just begun to read. The man standing there says nothing. He doesn't smile. A dishcloth hangs from where it's tucked into grubby apron-strings knotted at the front, and Wilby assumes that the man is an envoy sent from the kitchen to apologize for the delay in the cooking of the fish he has ordered.

The place is modest, in rue Piques off rue de Sèvres: Wilby didn't notice what it is called. A café as much as a brasserie, it is poorly illuminated except for the bar, at which a couple are hunched over their glasses, conversing softly. One of the few tables belonging to the café is occupied by four elderly women playing cards and there are a few people at tables in the brasserie.

Still without communicating, the man who has come from the kitchen turns and goes away, leaving Wilby with the impression that he has been mistaken for someone else. He pours himself more wine and reads again. Wilby reads a lot, and drinks a lot.

He is a spare, sharp-faced man in his forties, cleanshaven, in a grey suit, with a striped blue-and-red tie almost but not quite striking a stylish note. He visits Paris once in a while to make the rounds of salerooms specializing in rare postage stamps, usually spinning out his time when he is there, since he can afford to. Three years ago he inherited his family's wine business in County Westmeath, which he sold eighteen months later, planning to live on the proceeds while he indulged his interest in philately. He occupies, alone now, the house he inherited at that time also, creeper-clad, just outside the Westmeath town where he was born. Marriage failed him there, or he it, and he doubts that he will make another attempt in that direction.

His food is brought to him by a small, old waiter, a more presentable figure than the man who came and went. He is attentive, addressing Wilby in conventional waiter's terms and supplying, when they are asked for, salt and pepper from another table. 'Voilà, monsieur,' he murmurs, his tone apologetic.

Wilby eats his fish, wondering what fish it is. He knew when he ordered it but has since forgotten, and the taste doesn't tell him much. The bread is the best part of his meal and he catches the waiter's attention to ask for more. His book is a paperback he has read before, *The Hand of Ethelberta*.

He reads another page, orders more wine, finishes the *pommes frites* but not the fish. He likes quiet places, and doesn't hurry. He orders coffee and – though not intending to – a calvados. He drinks too much, he tells himself, and restrains the inclination to have another when the coffee comes. He reads again, indulging the pleasure of being in Paris, in a brasserie where Muzak isn't playing, at a small corner table, engrossed in a story that's familiar yet has receded sufficiently to be blurred in places, like something good remembered. He never minds it when the food isn't up to much; wine matters more, and peace. He'll walk back to the Hôtel Merneuil; with luck he'll be successful in the salerooms tomorrow.

He gestures for his bill, and pays. The old waiter has his overcoat ready for him at the door, and Wilby tips him a little for that. Outside, being late November, the night is chilly.

The man who came to look at him is there on the street, dressed as he was then. He stands still, not speaking. He might have come outside to have a cigarette, as waiters sometimes do. But there is no cigarette.

'*Bonsoir*,' Wilby says.

'*Bonsoir.*'

Saying that, quite suddenly the man is someone else. A resemblance flickers: the smooth black hair, the head like the rounded end of a bullet, the fringe that is not as once it was but is still a fringe, the dark eyes. There is a way of standing, without unease or agitation and yet awkward, hands lank, open.

'What is all this?' Even as he puts the question, Wilby's choice of words sounds absurd to him. 'Anthony?' he says.

There is a movement, a hand's half gesture, meaningless, hardly a response. Then the man turns away, entering the brasserie by another door.

'Anthony,' Wilby mutters again, but only to himself.

People have said that Anthony is dead.

The streets are emptier than they were, the bustle of the pavements gone. Obedient to pedestrian lights at rue de Babylone where there is fast-moving traffic again, Wilby waits with a woman in a pale waterproof coat, her legs slim beneath it, blonde hair brushed up. Not wanting to think about Anthony, he wonders if she's a tart, since she has that look, and for a moment sees her pale coat thrown down in some small room, the glow of an electric fire, money placed on a dressing-table: now and again when he travels he has a woman. But this one doesn't glance at him, and the red light changes to green.

It couldn't possibly have been Anthony, of course it couldn't. Even assuming that Anthony is alive, why would he be employed as a kitchen worker in Paris? 'Yes, I'm afraid we fear the worst,' his father said on the telephone, years ago now. 'He sent a few belongings here, but that's a good while back. A note to you, unfinished, was caught up in the pages of a book. Nothing in it, really. Your name, no more.'

In rue du Bac there is a window Wilby likes, with prints of the Revolution. The display has hardly changed since he was here last: the death of Marie Antoinette, the Girondists on their way to the guillotine, the storming of the Bastille, Danton's death, Robespierre triumphant, Robespierre fallen from grace. Details aren't easy to make out in the dim street-light. Prints he hasn't seen before are indistinguishable at the back.

At a bar he has another calvados. He said himself when people asked him – a few had once – that he, too, imagined Anthony was dead. A disappearance so prolonged, with no reports of even a glimpse as the years advanced, did appear to confirm a conclusion that became less tentative, and in the end wasn't tentative at all.

In rue Montalembert a couple ask for directions to the Métro. Wilby points it out, walking back a little way with them to do so, as grateful for this interruption as he was when the woman at the traffic crossing caught his interest.

'*Bonne nuit, monsieur.*' In the hall of the Hôtel Merneuil the night porter holds open the lift doors. He closes them and the lift begins its smooth ascent. 'The will to go on can fall away, you know,' Anthony's father said on the telephone again, in touch to find out if there was anything to report.

Monsieur Jothy shakes his head over the pay packet that hasn't been picked up. It's on the windowsill above the sinks, where others have been ignored too. He writes a message on it and props it against an empty bottle.

At this late hour Monsieur Jothy has the kitchen to himself, a time for assessing what needs to be ordered, for satisfying himself that, in general, the kitchen is managing. He picks up Jean-André's note of what he particularly requires for tomorrow, and checks the shelves where the cleaning materials are kept. He has recently become suspicious of Jean-André, suspecting short-cuts. His risotto, once an attraction on the menu, is scarcely ever ordered now; and with reason in Monsieur Jothy's opinion, since it has lost the intensity of flavour that made it popular, and is often dry. But the kitchen at least is clean, and Monsieur Jothy, examining cutlery and plates, fails to find food clinging anywhere, or a rim left on a cup. Once he employed two dish-washers at the sinks, but now one does it on his own, and half the time forgets his wages. Anxious to keep him, Monsieur

Jothy has wondered about finding somewhere for him to sleep on the premises instead of having the long journey to and from his room. But there isn't even a corner of a pantry, and when he asked in the neighbourhood about accommodation near rue Piques he was also unsuccessful.

The dishcloths, washed and rinsed, are draped on the radiators and will be dry by the morning, the soup bowls are stacked; the glasses, in their rows, gleam on the side table. '*Très bon, très bon*,' Monsieur Jothy murmurs before he turns the lights out and locks up.

Wilby does not sleep and cannot read, although he tries to.

'A marvel, isn't it?' Miss Davally said, the memory vivid, as if she'd said it yesterday. You wouldn't think apricots would so easily ripen in such a climate. Even on a wall lined with brick you wouldn't think it. She pointed at the branches sprawled out along their wires, and you could see the fruit in little clusters. 'Delphiniums,' she said, pointing again, and one after another named the flowers they passed on their way through the garden. 'And this is Anthony,' she said in the house.

The boy looked up from the playing cards he had spread out on the floor. 'What's his name?' he asked, and Miss Davally said he knew because she had told him already. But even so she did so again. 'Why's he called that?' Anthony asked. 'Why're you called that?'

'It's my name.'

'Shall we play in the garden?'

That first day, and every day afterwards, there were gingersnap biscuits in the middle of the morning. 'Am I older than you?' Anthony asked. 'Is six older?' He had a house, he said, in the bushes at the end of the garden, and they pretended there was a house. 'Jericho he's called,' Anthony said of the dog that followed them about, a black Labrador with an injured leg that hung limply, thirteen years old. 'Miss Davally is an orphan,' Anthony said. 'That's why she lives with us. Do you know what an orphan is?'

In the yard the horses looked out over the half-doors of their stables; the hounds were in a smaller yard. Anthony's mother was never at lunch because her horse and the hounds were exercised then. But his father always was, each time wearing a different tweed jacket, his grey moustache clipped short, the olives he liked to see on the lunch table always there, the whiskey he took for his health. 'Well, young chap, how are you?' he always asked.

On wet days they played marbles in the kitchen passages, the dog stretched out beside them. 'You come to the sea in summer,' Anthony said. 'They told me.' Every July: the long journey from Westmeath to the same holiday cottage on the cliffs above the bay that didn't have a name. It was Miss Davally who had told Anthony all that, and in time – so that hospitality might be returned – she often drove Anthony there and back. An outing for her too, she used to say, and sometimes she brought a cake she'd made, being in the way of bringing a present when she went to people's houses. She liked it at the sea as much as Anthony did; she liked to turn the wheel of the bellows in the kitchen of the cottage and watch the sparks flying up; and Anthony liked the hard sand of the shore, and collecting flintstones, and netting shrimps. The dog prowled about the rocks, sniffing the seaweed, clawing at the sea-anemones. 'Our house,' Anthony called the cave they found when they crawled through an opening in the rocks, a cave no one knew was there.

Air from the window Wilby slightly opens at the top is refreshing and brings with it, for a moment, the chiming of two o'clock. His book is open, face downward to keep his place, his bedside light still on. But the dark is better, and he extinguishes it.

There was a blue vase in the recess of the staircase wall, nothing else there; and paperweights crowded the shallow landing shelves, all touching one another; forty-six, Anthony said. His mother played the piano in the drawing-room. 'Hullo,' she said, holding out her hand and smiling. She wasn't much like someone who exercised foxhounds: slim and small and wearing scent, she was also beautiful. 'Look!' Anthony said, pointing at the lady in the painting above the mantelpiece in the hall.

Miss Davally was a distant relative as well as being an orphan, and when she sat on the sands after her bathe she often talked about her own childhood in the house where she'd been given a home: how a particularly unpleasant boy used to creep up on her and pull a cracker in her ear, how she hated her ribboned pigtails and persuaded a simple-minded maid to cut them off, how she taught the kitchen cat to dance and how people said they'd never seen the like.

Every lunchtime Anthony's father kept going a conversation about a world that was not yet known to his listeners. He spoke affectionately of the playboy pugilist Jack Doyle, demonstrating the subtlety of his right punch and recalling the wonders of his hell-raising before poverty claimed him. He told of the exploits of an ingenious escapologist, Major Pat Reid. He condemned the first Earl of Inchiquin as the most disgraceful man ever to step out of Ireland.

Much other information was passed on at the lunch table: why aeroplanes flew, how clocks kept time, why spiders spun their webs and how they did it. Information was everything, Anthony's father maintained, and its lunchtime dissemination, with Miss Davally's reminiscences, nurtured curiosity: the unknown became a fascination. 'What would happen if you didn't eat?' Anthony wondered; and there were attempts to see if it was possible to create a rainbow with a water hose when the sun was bright, and the discovery made that, in fact, it was. A jellyfish was scooped into a shrimp net to see if it would perish or survive when it was tipped out on to the sand. Miss Davally said to put it back, and warned that jellyfish could sting as terribly as wasps.

A friendship developed between Miss Davally and Wilby's mother – a formal association, first names not called upon, neither in conversation nor in the letters that came to be exchanged from one summer to the next. *Anthony is said to be clever*, Miss Davally's spidery handwriting told. And then, as if that perhaps required watering down, *Well, so they say*. It was reported also that when each July drew near Anthony began to count the days. *He values the friendship so!* Miss Davally commented. *How fortunate for two only children such a friendship is!*

Fortunate indeed it seemed to be. There was no quarrelling, no vying for authority, no competing. When, one summer, a yellow Lilo was washed up, still inflated, it was taken to the cave that no one else knew about, neither claiming that it was his because he'd seen it first. 'Someone lost that thing,' Anthony said, but no one came looking for it. They didn't know what it was, only that it floated. They floated it themselves, the dog limping behind them when they carried it to the sea, his tail wagging madly, head cocked to one side. In the cave it became a bed for him, to clamber on to when he was tired.

The Lilo was another of the friendship's precious secrets, as the cave itself was. No other purpose was found for it, but its possession was enough to make it the highlight of that particular summer and on the last day of July it was again carried to the edge of the sea. 'Now, now,' the dog was calmed when he became excited. The waves that morning were hardly waves at all.

In the dark there is a pinprick glow of red somewhere on the television set. The air that comes into the room is colder and Wilby closes the window he has opened a crack, suppressing the murmur of a distant plane. Memory won't let him go now; he knows it won't and makes no effort to resist it.

Nothing was said when they watched the drowning of the dog. Old Jericho was clever, never at a loss when there was fun. Not moving, he was obedient, as he always was. He played his part, going with the Lilo when it floated out, a deep black shadow, sharp against the garish yellow. They watched as they had watched the hosepipe rainbow gathering colour, as Miss Davally said she'd watched the shaky steps of the dancing cat. Far away already, the yellow of the Lilo became a blur on the water, was lost, was there again and lost again, and the barking began, and became a wail. Nothing was said then either. Nor when they clambered over the shingle and the rocks, and climbed up to the short-cut and passed through the gorse field. From the cliff they looked again, for the last time, far out to the horizon. The sea was undisturbed, glittering in the sunlight. 'So what have you two been up to this morning?' Miss Davally asked. The next day, somewhere else, the dog was washed in.

Miss Davally blamed herself, for that was in her nature. But she could not be blamed. It was agreed that she could not be. Unaware of his limitations – more than a little blind, with only three active legs – old Jericho had had a way of going into the sea when he sensed a piece of driftwood bobbing about. Once too often he had done that. His grave was in the garden, a small slate plaque let into the turf, his name and dates.

They did not ever speak to one another about the drowning of the dog. They did not ever say they had not meant it to occur. There was no blame, no accusing. They had not called it a game, only said they wondered what would happen, what the dog would do. The silence had begun before they pushed the Lilo out.

Other summers brought other incidents, other experiences, but there was no such occurrence again. There were adjustments in the friendship, since passing time demanded that, and different games were played, and there were different conversations, and new discoveries.

Then, one winter, a letter from Miss Davally was less cheerful than her letters usually were. *Withdrawn*, she wrote, *and they are concerned*. What she declared, in detail after that, was confirmed when summer came: Anthony was different, and more different still in later summers, quieter, timid, seeming sometimes to be lost. It was a mystery when the dog's gravestone disappeared from the garden.

In the dark, the bright red dot of the television light still piercingly there, Wilby wonders, as so often he has, what influence there was when without incitement or persuasion, without words, they did what had been done. They were nine years old then, when secrets became deception.

It was snowing the evening he and Anthony met again, both of them waiting in the chapel cloisters for their names, as new boys, to be called out. It was not a surprise that Anthony was there, passing on from the school that years ago had declared him clever; nor was it by chance that they were to be together for what remained of their education. 'Nice for Anthony to have someone he knows,' his father said on the telephone, and confirmed that Anthony was still as he had become.

In the dim evening light the snow blew softly into the cloisters, and when the roll-call ended and a noisy dispersal began, the solitary figure remained, the same smooth black hair, a way of standing that hadn't changed. 'How are you?' Wilby asked. His friend's smile, once so readily there, came as a shadow and then was lost in awkwardness.

Peculiar, Anthony was called at school, but wasn't bullied, as though it had been realized that bullying would yield no satisfaction. He lacked skill at games, avoided all pursuits that were not compulsory, displayed immediate evidence of his cleverness, science and mathematical subjects his forte. Religious boys attempted to befriend him, believing that to be a duty; kindly masters sought to draw him out. 'Well, yes, I knew him,' Wilby admitted, lamely explaining his association with someone who was so very much not like the friends he made now. 'A long time ago,' he nearly always added.

Passing by the windows of empty classrooms, he several times noticed Anthony, the only figure among the unoccupied desks. And often – on the drive that ended at the school gates, or often anywhere – there was the same lone figure in the distance. On the golf-course where senior boys were allowed to play, Anthony sometimes sat on a seat against a wall, watching the golfers as they approached, watching them as they walked on. He shied away when conversation threatened, creeping back into his shadowlands.

One day he wasn't there, his books left tidily in his desk, clothes hanging in his dormitory locker, his pyjamas under his pillow. He would be on his way home, since boys who kept themselves to themselves were often homesick. But he had not attempted to go home and was found still within the school grounds, having broken no rules except that he had ignored for a day the summoning of bells.

Dawn comes darkly, and Wilby sleeps. But his sleep is brief, his dreams forgotten when he wakes. The burden of guilt that came when in silence they clambered over the shingle and the rocks, when they passed through the gorse field, was muddled by bewilderment, a child's tormenting panic not yet constrained by suppression as later it would be. Long afterwards, when first he heard that Anthony was dead – and when he said it himself – the remnants of the shame guilt had become fell away.

He shaves and washes, dresses slowly. In the hall the reception clerks have just come on duty. They nod at him, wish him good-day. No call this morning for an umbrella, one says.

Outside it is not entirely day, or even day at all. The cleaning lorries are on the streets, water pouring in the gutters, but there's no one about in rue du Bac, refuse sacks still waiting to be collected. A bar is open further on, men standing at the counter, disinclined for conversation with one another. A sleeping figure in a doorway has not been roused. What hovel, Wilby wonders as he passes, does a kitchen worker occupy?

In rue Piques the brasserie is shuttered, no lights showing anywhere. Cardboard boxes are stacked close to the glass of three upstairs windows, others are uncurtained; none suggests the domesticity of a dwelling. Le Père Jothy the place is called.

Wilby roams the nearby streets. A few more cafés are opening and in one coffee is brought to him. He sips it, breaking a croissant. There's no one else, except the barman.

He knows he should go away. He should take the train to Passy, to the salerooms he has planned to visit there; he should not ever return to rue Piques. He has lived easily with an aberration, then shaken it off: what happened was almost nothing.

Other men come in, a woman on her own, her face bruised on one side, no effort made to conceal the darkening weals. Her voice is low when she explains this injury to the barman, her fingers now and again touching it. Soundlessly, she weeps when she has taken her cognac to a table.

Oh, this is silly! his unspoken comment was when Miss Davally's letter came, its implications apparent only to him. For heaven's sake! he crossly muttered, the words kept to himself when he greeted Anthony in the cloisters, and again every time he caught sight of him on the golf-course. The old dog's life had been all but over. And Wilby remembers now – as harshly as he has in the night – the bitterness of his resentment when a friendship he delighted in was destroyed, when Anthony's world – the garden, the house, his mother, his father, Miss Davally – was no longer there.

'He has no use for us,' his father said. 'No use for anyone, we think.'

Turning into rue Piques, Anthony notices at once the figure waiting outside the ribbon shop. It is November the twenty-fourth, the last Thursday of the month. This day won't come again.

'*Bonjour*,' he says.

'How are you, Anthony?'

And Anthony says that Monday is the closed day. Not that Sunday isn't too. If someone waited outside the ribbon shop on a Monday or a Sunday it wouldn't be much good. Not that many people wait there.

Wind blows a scrap of paper about, close to where they stand. In the window of the ribbon shop coils of ribbon are in all widths and colours, and there are swatches of trimming for other purposes, lace and velvet, and plain white edging, and a display of button cards. Anthony often looks to see if there has been a change, but there never has been.

'How are you, Anthony?'

It is a fragment of a white paper bag that is blown about and Anthony identifies it from the remains of the red script that advertises the *boulangerie* in rue Dupin. When it is blown closer to him he catches it under his shoe.

'People have wondered where you are, Anthony.'

'I went away from Ireland.'

Anthony bends and picks up the litter he has trapped. He says he has the ovens to do today. A Thursday, and he works in the morning.

'Miss Davally still writes, wondering if there is news of you.'

Half past eight is his time on Thursdays. Anthony says that, and adds that there's never a complaint in the kitchen. One speck on the prong of a fork could lead to a complaint, a shred of fish skin could, a cabbage leaf. But there's never a complaint.

'People thought you were dead, Anthony.'

Wilby says he sold the wineshop. He described it once, when they were children: the shelves of bottles, the different shapes, their contents red or white, pink if people wanted that. He tasted wine a few times, he remembers saying.

'Your father has died himself, Anthony. Your mother has. Miss Davally was left the house because there was no one else. She lives there now.'

No response comes; Wilby has not expected one. He has become a philatelist, he says.

Anthony nods, waiting to cross the street. He knows his father died, his mother too. He has guessed Miss Davally inherited the house. The deaths were in the *Irish Times*, which he always read, cover to cover, all the years he was the night porter at the Cliff Castle Hotel in Dalkey.

He doesn't mention the Cliff Castle Hotel. He doesn't say he misses the *Irish Times*, the familiar names, the political news, the photographs of places, the change there is in Ireland now. *Le Monde* is more staid, more circumspect, more serious. Anthony doesn't say that either because he doubts that it's of interest to a visitor to Paris.

A gap comes in the stream of cars that has begun to go by; but not trusting this opportunity, Anthony still waits. He is careful on the streets, even though he knows them well.

'I haven't died,' he says.

Perfectly together, they shared an act that was too shameful to commit alone, taking a chance on a sunny morning in order to discover if an old dog's cleverness would see to his survival.

For a moment, while Anthony loses another opportunity to cross the street, Wilby gathers into sentences how he might attempt a denial that this was how it was, how best to put it differently. An accident, a misfortune beyond anticipation, the unexpected: with gentleness, for gentleness is due, he is about to plead. But Anthony crosses the street then, and opens with a key the side door of the brasserie. He makes no gesture of farewell, he does not look back.

Walking by the river on his way to the salerooms at Passy, Wilby wishes he'd said he was glad his friend was not dead. It is his only thought. The pleasure-boats slip by on the water beside him, hardly anyone on them. A child waves. Raised too late in response, Wilby's own hand drops to his side. The wind that blew the litter about in rue Piques has freshened. It snatches at the remaining leaves on the black-trunked trees that are an orderly line, following the river's course.

The salerooms are on the other bank, near the radio building and the apartment block that change the river's character. Several times he has visited this vast display in which the world's stamps are exhibited behind glass if they are notably valuable, on the tables, country by country, when they are not. That busy image has always excited Wilby's imagination and as he climbs the steps to the bridge he is near he attempts to anticipate it now, but does not entirely succeed.

It is not in punishment that the ovens are cleaned on another Thursday morning. It is not in expiation that soon the first leavings of the day will be scraped from the lunchtime plates. There is no bothering with redemption. Looking down from the bridge at the sluggish flow of water, Wilby confidently asserts that. A morning murkiness, like dusk, has brought some lights on in the apartment block. Traffic crawls on distant streets.

For Anthony, the betrayal matters, the folly, the carelessness that would have been forgiven, the cruelty. It mattered in the silence – while they watched, while they clambered over the shingle and the rocks, while they passed through the gorse field. It matters now. The haunted sea is all the truth there is for Anthony, what he honours because it matters still.

The buyers move among the tables and Wilby knows that for him, in this safe, second-hand world of postage stamps, tranquillity will return. He knows where he is with all this; he knows what he's about, as he does in other aspects of his tidy life. And yet this morning he likes himself less than he likes his friend.